A Wicked Way to Burn

A Wicked Way to Burn

MARGARET MILES

Margaret Miles

BANTAM BOOKS

New York   Toronto   London
Sydney   Auckland

Bantam Books are published by Bantam Books, a division of Bantam
Doubleday Dell Publishing Group, Inc. Its trademark, consisting of the
words "Bantam Books" and the portrayal of a rooster, is Registered in U.S.
Patent and Trademark Office and in other countries. Marca Registrada.
Bantam Books, 1540 Broadway, New York, New York 10036.

PRINTED IN THE UNITED STATES OF AMERICA

For Richard, with love.

Search me, O God, and know my heart:
Try me, and know my thoughts:
And see if there be any wicked way in me,
and lead me in the way everlasting.

PSALMS 139: 23–24

A Wicked Way to Burn

Chapter 1

⎯☙ *Monday*

"**D**AMN THEM ALL!" cackled the merchant, not for the first time. Then his smile broadened as he glimpsed, through autumn leaves, the upper arm of Narragansett Bay.

Duncan Middleton had ridden out from Boston early, taking the post road whose windings had carried him inland for many wearisome hours. Far from streets full of people and fine carriages, he had lately seen only villages, tedious stretches of woodland, and empty stubble fields left to the crows that cawed from the treetops, well above the rustling, slithering, hopping life that foraged below.

Carefully, he uncurled gnarled fingers and reached beneath the scarlet cloak that covered his bent and withered form. It should be said that his curious shape was due to a gouty disposition of the joints: the merchant was barely fifty. But he had already acquired the face of an old man who cultivated a wintry soul. Certain acquaintances had been heard to comment, in private, that both face and twisted skeleton served to warn men of the merchant's undernourished and corrupt spirit . . . as Jehovah had probably intended when he made him that way.

But now, on this mild October evening, the wizened rider felt almost kindly as he gently stroked something held against his chest. Satisfied, he breathed deeply of the brisk salt air. Was it a love of the sea that made Middleton's small, sunken eyes lift and sparkle briefly? Unhappily, no—the merchant's pleased expression was born of his belief that what he smelled on the air was profit. He already had a hoard of money—enough to buy courtesies from others whose manners and breeding were far better than his own. But, as he often said, more money never hurt . . . and everyone knew that a shipping fortune was never entirely safe. With a few fierce storms, or an unseen reef or two, one could be ruined. And who would shed a tear?

Well, at the next milestone, he would see. The next milestone . . . one of those set up by order of the Great Man, Middleton sneered to his mount in lieu of anyone else to complain to. He'd always said the stones were a waste of money, erected only to mark Franklin's own advancement on Fortune's road. But on this evening, in a rare burst of good humor, the merchant decided to excuse "Poor Richard." At the next milestone, Middleton intended to do a quiet bit of business himself.

The thin, tired nag that carried him stumbled over the deeply rutted soil, occasionally lifting its head to the whine of gulls above. Ill-fed and rarely rested, the horse had again grown used to shivering under the cut of its owner's whip. Now, although it had no way of knowing, its troubles were nearly over.

Middleton continued to strain his eyes across the glinting waters ahead. He entertained mixed feelings about what he saw. Like many others who took their living from the ocean, he rarely allowed his own body to brave her rolling green waves. In fact, the death of his last brother by shipwreck three years before had hardened his suspicion of the sea, however much that event had pleased him. Oh, young Lionel had been a worthless relation—shunned by a family who disapproved of his gambling and lusting after things he was unable to pay for—forced to become a sailor. When he eventually sank to his final reward, Lionel followed the lead of the merchant's pious brother Chester, a truly tedious soul, and was followed in turn by a spinster sister, Veracity, who had been "as chaste" (and as cold) "as unsunn'd snow."

Middleton didn't miss any of his siblings at all. With the pack of them gone, none were left to try to steal from his corpse, with the help of their lawyers, what he'd managed to pull together into a considerable fortune even by Boston standards. His own death would simply be the end of the line. And the ornate tombstone he planned would be a fitting memorial to the last and best fruit of a dead branch of the family tree. Where the *rest* of the money would go would be Duncan Middleton's final surprise for the good people of Boston.

Curiously, there were still several gentlemen living in that city, entirely unrelated to him, who believed they might receive a piece of his fortune when Middleton went to meet his Maker. These birds of prey (who nested in law firms and merchandise warehouses) had lately given him far more entertainment, as he watched and baited them, than Lionel, Chester, and Veracity together had ever managed to do. The crooked man looked forward to keeping the vultures guessing. He would continue to enjoy seeing them squabble among themselves, making flattering, unctuous bids for his favor. Just let them try to gain from his death—it was years away, at any rate. Recently, he even thought some of them had secretly followed him about Boston . . . probably trying to glean details of his holdings, or to find something in his activities that might be held over his head.

Damn them all!

The purpose of this particular trip might have surprised even those who thought they knew the worst about the merchant's ways. Middleton had started out after receiving an answer to a letter of his own on the previous evening. The missive had made his lips curl with its promises.

"I foresee no trouble in transporting the commodities you require, and selling same, regardless of their eventual use. . . ."

The merchant had wisely burned that letter to keep it from Mrs. Bledsoe's notice. The old biddy only knew that he would be gone for at least two days. She would be free to gossip and pry where she might, as she went about her housekeeping duties. Still, she would never guess what he was up to, nor see the end of the lucrative plan he was about to set in motion.

Abruptly, the traveler's thoughts of home were interrupted by the hurrying approach of another horse and rider. After a few moments, they overtook him and passed by, probably making for shelter before night fell. Duncan Middleton averted his face, giving the passing stranger only the back of his wig and an edge of his tricornered hat, until the other had gone.

If all went well, he thought as he rode on, it would be a simple matter, this buying up of cheap turpentine and black powder (but quietly, through an agent) before mixing them with a bit of rum from his stores. Once the doctored item had been recasked, it would be sent inland by someone who had nothing to do with the coast trade.

The deadly new product would be difficult to trace back to him. On the frontier, it would be as welcome as any other intoxicant, and would be bought up by enough willing customers to make him a quick and satisfying profit. If a few delicate guts were poisoned by the drinking of it—why, they might have known better, and couldn't they follow their noses to save their lives? Most who bought would be heathens and savages anyway, and good riddance.

His knobby hand continued to fondle the bag of Dutch gold kept snug and warm beneath the red wool cloak. If all went well, he could soon laugh at the backs of the blasted customs men who peered out to sea. Not that he generally disliked these men; most of them were quite sympathetic, and took pity on a hard-pressed merchant—took bribes, really, for overlooking the outrageous duty of sixpence a gallon on non-British molasses brought up from the Caribbean.

(The commodity was, after all, one of the mainstays of colonial shipping. Everyone knew that much of the coast lived by sending fish, lumber, and livestock to the British, French, and Dutch sugar islands, in exchange for their dark syrup. Brought back to Massachusetts, it then went into dozens of distilleries, and came back out as rum that could be easily moved, and sold for a large profit at home or abroad. Some went as far as Africa, where it was traded for slaves, who were shipped to the sugar islands, where they were sold for more molasses, which would again be brought back to the colonial distilleries. It was a system that worked and would continue to work, because everyone concerned could share in the profits. Well, nearly everyone.)

Lately, however, rumors from London suggested that special interests might soon prevail, and that far stiffer controls could be expected within the coming year, now that Grenville had hold of a depleted royal purse . . . as well as the young George's ear. The coffeehouses had been full of it for weeks.

Thirty years before, old George's infernal Molasses Act had threatened to stop the Triangular Trade with its tariff on the foreign syrup that now satisfied more than two-thirds of the distilleries' demand—had even with the war going on! Thankfully, war or no, the Act's provisions had never been much enforced. But what if that were to change?

There was even an absurd new idea of requiring customs officials to actually *live* in the colonies—instead of staying safely at home in England, leaving their responsibilities to colonial men who were paid nearly nothing.

It was almost unnecessary to pay such men anything at all. Everyone knew where to find their pockets, and had long stuffed them with a little something extra, to feed their families. If the Crown started paying them a decent wage, their eyesight might improve dramatically. Next, they'd be expecting shipping manifests to actually agree with goods carried! Then, where would everyone be?

Long an avowed Tory, Duncan Middleton had lately become interested in Whiggish ideas of liberty, and British abuse of the colonies—which he often read about in the newspapers—although he also felt it was a shame they gave encouragement to the rabble. Still, noisy mobs might keep the long arms of the king and his advisors busy, and away from things that didn't concern them, like warehouses, and cargo holds.

Suddenly the sea wind hit him fully, and he had a clear view of a nearly spherical moon rising through the trees. Pulling wool closer for warmth, Middleton gave a harsh laugh.

In Rhode Island, away from the old Commonwealth, Britain saw far less, and a man of business could do far more. Of course a great many of Providence's men of business were pirates plain and simple—if few went to the trouble of stealing on the high seas. Not unlike himself, smiled the sly old merchant. Let Sam Adams and the rest in Boston earn His Majesty's displeasure: the Crown would soon make it hot enough for the City on the Hill. Meanwhile, *he* would build a second home to the southwestern, while he fleeced the frontier.

And so, thoughts of death and taxes, pain and profits winged peacefully about the merchant's head on this quiet evening, complimenting each other pleasantly. The fading light had left the sky a soft rose, and the sea sent up moonlit reflections of lilac and silver.

That must be the final milestone up ahead, and there was a figure waiting just off the road, standing in the shadow of a leaning pine. Next to it stood two oxen and a loaded wagon, as promised. Soon, Middleton thought, he would go on alone to Providence. He looked forward to a very large bowl of crab bisque, and a dozen or two of oysters, for he was keenly hungry. But business first.

Once more, capriciously, he whipped the shuddering animal beneath him, and hurried on his way.

It might be mentioned that the gold the merchant carried was of an interesting and unusual stamp. Several pieces of it would soon leave a glittering trail as they lay about the countryside like autumn crocuses. And watching them from the shadows would be an old reaper. He, too, would appreciate their bright, ageless bloom, while he held a scythe to the ready in his grasping, bony hands.

Chapter 2

_ᴏ Tuesday

Tʜᴇ ꜱᴜᴍᴍᴇʀ ᴏꜰ 1763 had sent a good harvest to the village of Bracebridge, just west of Boston. Now, with Nature's work nearly done, the countryside caught its breath. A well-earned calm, buzzing like a gentle spell, settled over all.

All, that is, except the kitchens, for truly, woman's work is never done. This was the season of preserving and laying away for the long New England winter. And in more than one house, the steamy air was full of apples—small, striped apples bubbling into applesauce and apple butter in black pots suspended above steady fires, while sliced apples dried slowly on threads among the rafters.

Inside one such kitchen at the edge of the village, close by cupboard shelves lined with crockery, pewter, and china, a young woman stood in a warm ray of amber light. She sighed as she passed a sticky wrist over a wisp of hair that had fallen from its pins. It was the color of clear, sweet cider, glinting richly with red and gold. Today, Charlotte Willett would not have been pleased with the comparison. She longed to be out walking, waiting for a cool twilight. Thoroughly tired of bending, carrying, peeling, and coring, she tossed down a paring knife with a defiant glance at her stout companion.

"Any more outside?" Hannah Sloan inquired without looking up. She paused to catch at a billowing linen sleeve.

"Three more bushels. And that's the end. Thank heaven."

Hannah kept peeling and slicing on the boards that stood between them, her broad back to the fire. The monotonous routine of several days had taken its toll. Words were currently few and far between.

Charlotte leaned back to squint through one of the open windows, adjusting the light muslin bodice that stuck to her skin. Above the house, the barn, and the farmyard between, a huge white oak dropped acorns and leaves around chickens scratching and muttering below.

In the same shade, an old dog lay stretched and dozing, his brown, curling fur dappled with sun and flecked with gray. Once a herder of sheep, Orpheus was now reduced to lifting an eyelid occasionally when a hen came to close. But he *would* stay within earshot, his mistress thought fondly.

Charlotte turned again to watch Hannah reach deep into a basket. On most days, the older woman walked up from her home by the river bridge to work with Mrs. Willett for several hours, leaving her own household to the care of daughters who were in no hurry to see their mother return. Now, her face below her mobcap was colored like an Indian's—red from the fire on one side, blue from the cooler reflections of a late October sky on the other.

"Hannah, will you still go at four?"

"I'll stay until we're done."

Another hour—maybe two!

Abruptly, knowing there would be eyebrows raised behind her, Charlotte spun around in the heat, and lunged through the open door to freedom.

THE SUGARED STEAM of the kettles was no match for the whispering breeze outside.

As Charlotte, led by Orpheus, rounded a corner of the house, she was humming an appropriate hymn to the world's blessings, her plain skirts swinging gently over the cropped grass. Before long, she took stock of all she saw, each thing hers to care for.

The little cherry's summer leaves were curled and faded, nearly ready to fall. She and Aaron had planted it together. Six years ago they had set the tree in, the same week Reverend Rowe had joined them together. Now, almost three years had gone by since another Sunday— when ropes in loving hands had lowered Aaron into nearby ground. That unbearable winter, Reverend Rowe had counseled Mrs. Willett to listen to the Lord and her elders, and to avoid examining her own inclinations, at least until she married again. The memory of this advice caused Charlotte to lower her round chin thoughtfully and kick a little at the grass.

The first time Aaron had come up from Philadelphia, he had only planned to visit the Quaker community near Boston. A young gentleman of some means, he'd also hoped to take home one of his own for a bride. Instead, he had been taken with Charlotte Howard, and finally chose to stay in Bracebridge. Her family were not Friends. Still, she shared her husband's trust in an inner light, in the truths revealed by Nature, and in the virtues of simplicity. They both knew that they were fortunate, and blessed, in each other. But even as they started their life together, they also knew that what comes to a young couple can as easily go.

Well, life *had* moved on, even without Aaron Willett, although it had taken a while for her to accept the idea. Now, it looked as if the country entered a great new era. There was a new king, tall, boyish George III, who promised to take good care of his subjects while he tended his own fields. (Farmer George, they had begun to call him.) The Great War that had unsettled much of the world, fought in North America against the French and their Indian allies, was over. And the peace treaty signed in Paris the past February had given Great Britain uncontested right to Canada, as well as most of the country east of the Mississippi. People were flooding back to abandoned settlements, and pushing the frontier farther west.

For her part, Charlotte Willett had for three years been the sole manager of a farm that had once held a whole family. Still held them, she thought with a familiar stab, in the high, fenced plot that overlooked the river, above the hillside orchard. Not so long ago, her parents had been carried there to join three infants who'd never grown to childhood. Then, suddenly, her sister Eleanor had been taken on the eve of her own marriage. And Aaron had died of the same choking fever within a few weeks, leaving the sharpest ache of all. Why, she wondered, should it be that some families increased, while others declined? For she had no children. Neither had two young cousins, buried where they fell— one with Braddock in '57 near Fort Duquesne, the other in Quebec with Wolfe, in '59. Already, their faces were a blur in her memory. Now, of her own generation, only she and her younger brother remained.

But the family farm continued to thrive under her hand, allowing Jeremy to go on with his studies across the Atlantic, in Edinburgh. They had agreed that the land, while left to him, was hers to care for, as long as she chose to live there. And he meant to visit as often as he could. These two thoughts gave her frequent pleasure, as well as a life-sustaining sense of purpose.

Fingering a twig of cherry leaves, Charlotte walked on toward the front lawn and its broad view, admiring the flaming golds and reds of the maples that ran down the road from Boston, and into Bracebridge. The town itself was spread out below.

Just down the hill was the property of her closest neighbor, gentleman farmer and scientist Richard Longfellow. Although some considered him peculiar, she thoroughly enjoyed Longfellow's company. In the fields yesterday, he'd worn a broad-brimmed straw hat he'd recently brought back from Italy, and wielded an iron sickle with the strength of one possessed, next to his hired men. She knew he sometimes toiled extravagantly for hours, until his strength, or his mood, played out. Then, he would go inside to brood or to plan, and eventually set his hand to something new. This afternoon, however, the cleared field was empty, and Richard was nowhere to be seen.

Almost across the road from Longfellow's front lawn stood the Bracebridge Inn, with stables and a yard behind. Farther on, placed among bright trees and hedges and lanes, Charlotte looked over a few dozen houses, some she knew with shops in their lower rooms, one with a schoolroom run by old Dame Williams. The Common with its rectangle of tall elms lay just before the wide-arched stone bridge that spanned the Musketaquid River. On its grassy southern edge stood the white meeting house, next to Reverend Rowe's somber house of hewn granite.

Through more distant trees, she could just see the top of the gristmill on the opposite side of the river's span. There was the crossroads, and the old Blue Boar, a country tavern for the rough-and-tumble. It got much of its trade from local farmers, and those traveling the north-south road that went with the river current to the town of Concord. The same road's southern aspect was quickly lost to the eye as it climbed past the mill and up into abrupt hills, on its way to Framingham. On the north, though, one could study several miles of a plain filled with plowed fields that were set apart by stone walls, as well as squares of fruit orchards bordering thicker wood lots. Bisecting all of this was a green strip of flowing river marshland, where wild ducks and geese fed and chattered among the reeds.

Charlotte continued to watch through the afternoon haze for occasional signs of distant movement. The playful air had finally taken the smell of cooked fruit from her substantial nose; in its place, it left more subtle scents from the drying fields and water meadows, and the woods across the road where birds called.

The weight of her memories began to lift. Happy to be free, she tilted her head back to admire the greens and golds, crimsons and oranges of the rustling leaves above her, and the deep blue of the sky beyond. And then, at a hint of a whimper from Orpheus, she looked to see a scarlet movement nearer to the earth.

A lone figure came walking down from the road's crest, leading a tired old horse. Both were odd enough to make her stare. The old man was especially startling. Crabbed and shrunken, he was draped with a long, full cloak of brilliant red. His head was covered with a heavy wig and a spreading, tricornered hat. Had he been younger, she thought, the full town costume on his buckled frame would have been unbearably hot for the sunny afternoon. But he appeared not to mind as he and his horse stepped cautiously, leading their shadows westward, down the dusty road.

The odd gentleman at first appeared to turn away when she took notice of him, but then he stopped and faced her squarely, with a curiosity that seemed to match her own. Without thinking, she reached down to smooth her skirts, and it was only then that Charlotte realized she still held an apple in her hand. When the old man bobbed his head in silent greeting, she instinctively held the apple out to him, coloring as his eyes met hers: met, and held them, and widened. Perhaps he was surprised at her forwardness. Or it could have been that he simply admired her face and figure. This was something that happened frequently enough. As a young widow, she knew she was sometimes referred to as "fair game."

"An apple, sir?" she asked, determined not to mind whatever the cause of his piercing stare.

"Many thanks!"

His voice was high-pitched and thin. But she was to have only the two words to judge by when considering it later.

A gloved hand reached out and accepted her gift without further comment. Then, he gave a stiff, old-fashioned bow that made Charlotte smile in return.

The stranger's jaws parted. He took a large bite, and she heard the crisp apple crunch. His smile grew and the white wig nodded gently. As he chewed, her quick eyes took in more about his person.

He might have been near sixty, or even older, she thought. And what she saw of his shaded face looked oddly white. Probably the pallor of a recent invalid, she imagined, or one who generally kept to his letters and ledgers—a man of business? His was certainly not the face of someone used to walking in the sun, as he was doing now, unless he always protected his features well whenever he went into the open air.

As for his clothing, she noticed a pea green velvet

coat beneath the bright cloak; below this were striking rich green velvet breeches, and white silk hose. His cloak, too, was lined with the best quality silk—once again, in scarlet. She also observed a frilled shirt of cambric, and soft leather shoes with bright silver clasps, hardly made for riding. Overall, she concluded, he was certainly a colorful old gentleman, but one out of his element in the country.

In another moment, she might have asked herself (or even him, since she wasn't particularly shy) where he had come from, and why he went on foot. But before she had the chance, the old man tossed the apple core into the roadside cornflowers and turned to pull himself with great effort onto his horse, while Charlotte held her breath for him. Finally in his seat, he touched his hat and started off toward the town.

At that instant, Charlotte felt the gentle touch of her conscience as she remembered Hannah toiling all alone, surrounded by apples. And so, taking one last look at the odd, retreating figure, young Mrs. Willett walked with renewed purpose back toward her kitchen door, leaving all other thoughts behind her.

Chapter 3

"WELCOME TO THE Blue Boar!" called the tavern's proprietor, standing in the doorway beneath a bristling azure monster with yellow eyes and a sharp red tongue. He gestured broadly to the open door that awaited all comers, including the stranger in a scarlet cloak who approached on foot at sunset.

Inside the tavern's smoky main room, a dusty twilight had already fallen. A few tallow ends glowed on rough tables flanked with benches, where country men sat talking over cider and ale. Nearby, a blazing fireplace had drawn a brace of elderly patrons who hunched like two fat quail, smoking long clay pipes and toasting themselves. To their backs, winding stairs led up to three dark sleeping rooms that offered accommodation to those who made no demands in the way of luxury, and had few expectations of comfort. To see to customers' stomachs, a

small scullery below produced a more or less regular serving of game stews, pickled pork, and bought bread.

The whole of this adequate establishment was presided over by a former Salem man called Phineas Wise.
The landlord now walked to a mounted barrel and drew
off a pitcher with a practiced eye, magically extending its
head of froth. Wise was a thrifty individual of lean face
and thin nose, with a keen, calculating expression and a
stubble of beard; in brief, he was a man who would be
recognized as a Yankee up and down the coast.

When the cloaked stranger appeared, everyone
stopped what they were doing to examine him carefully,
and to speculate briefly about the brown cloth bundle he
carried under one arm. He had evidently interrupted a
vigorous discussion; he had heard several words of it as
he approached the door. Soon, it began again. The
stranger sat down and listened.

"Well, some of these bastards think they have as
much right as anyone else to be here, but I say to that,
think again!" This sentiment came from a giant of a man
with curling red hair and a freckled skin.

"That's right—they better think twice about it,"
echoed a man with bloodshot eyes who sat next to the
first speaker.

"Let them go back to France, and take their heathen
friends with 'em!" came from near the west windows.

"But I say," said the first voice, "they'll take *no more*
from us here!"

General enthusiasm rose from around the room.

It was with some uneasiness that the landlord finally
drew himself away from the loud talk to ask the stranger's pleasure, which was a small tankard of local ale.
Clearly, the heated discussion was being led by the massive man dressed in a loose homespun shirt and stained
buckskin breeches. During a lull, this confident speaker
picked his teeth with a bench splinter, while he leaned

on his elbows over a pewter plate that held the remains of a greasy dinner. Two lesser companions sat beside and in front of him. The one who had recently spoken up displayed the rubbery features and rolling eyes of a man well into his cups, while the other seemed to wear a more permanent look of befuddlement on his up-turned face.

"Maybe we thought we knew the enemy before, when we mustered at Worcester six years back," the bullying voice boomed out again, "fighting men, from all over Middlesex County . . . men who'd heard what the savages, and the Frenchmen who paid them, had been up to along the Hudson. But by God, we knew far more after the bloody massacre at Fort William Henry! A dirty coward's trick that was, killing soldiers under a white flag!"

A loud chorus again agreed with the smooth speaker; most of them knew Peter Lynch, the local miller, well. He continued when the flood of voices ebbed away.

"They were damned fools ever to trust Montcalm. They might have guessed he'd let his redskins get at our soldiers, with or without a truce, and rob them of everything they had—right down to the shirts on their backs! We all know those who survived saw a good many scalps taken that day, too. Saw women stripped, and worse— watched infants' heads break open against the stockade walls! Saw more killed as they lay in their beds, burning with fever. And after that, the ones left were marched two hundred miles, all the way up to Montreal, to be sold for slaves! Well, we learned from that, all right. The whole world has learned of it by now, to their eternal disgust, so I don't want to hear any more damned lies about how a Frenchman can *ever* be trusted!"

"Cowards, every one of 'em!" cried the drunken man beside the miller, who went by the name of Dick Craft.

"Well, Peter, some of the things you're saying," began another, "weren't exactly as you say. . . ."

Peter Lynch lowered his voice and looked around with a meaningful squint. "But there's worse than those who fight in plain sight, as I just described. Spies, I'm thinking of now. Some of them are still in these parts, looking for mischief, and mayhem! Aye, they're waiting . . . watching for ways to get back at decent folk who let 'em be, more's the pity. Ready to go after 'em, even though hostilities be over."

"It's a terrible truth," Dick Craft shouted, shaking his wooden tankard in the air. "And I hope to God none of us forgets it in *this* lifetime!"

Several listeners fervently agreed, while a few others belched. Thus encouraged, the drunkard continued.

"If they plan to hang around, stealing what's ours, then maybe we'll help 'em up into the treetops with a rope or two! Or—or maybe we'll be having ourselves a feather party—what do you say to that, Jack Pennywort? We'll bring along our own f-feathers, and some nice, warm tar, we will! What do you say to that, now?"

The daft-looking man sitting next to him took a sharp nudge in the ribs, and nodded with a simple smile. "Might there be," he ventured, "some ale, Peter, for after?"

Interrupted from wiping his nose on his sleeve, the miller leaned over and cuffed the man with an enormous hand, as a laughing Dick Craft jerked back out of the way, almost upsetting himself. Once righted, Dick managed to fling a challenging glance over his shoulder into a corner, where a younger man sat near the red-cloaked stranger, glowering at what was being said.

Although he might have been taken by his dress for a local farmer, several details about this guest who sat in shadow marked him as something more unusual. For one thing, long black hair fell in waves down the sides of his face, without the constraint of a ribbon. For another, his smooth skin had a deep olive glow. And his dark eyes were startling in their intensity. Set almost flush with high cheekbones, they shone out in the limited light, like a cat's. Taken all together, one might have guessed that this was a Frenchman, with perhaps some Iroquois blood flowing in his veins. Though several men had glanced his way as the miller kept on, the young man's full lips remained together, and he held himself remarkably still.

Phineas Wise scratched his beard and frowned at the miller and his friends. Lynch had a few years and inches, and a good many pounds, over the youth he seemed to be tormenting. Although Peter had admittedly gone to fat lately . . . probably the result of a growing appetite for all sorts of things. As he gathered up some empty vessels, the taverner spoke cautiously.

"Wartime's one thing, boys. But now, thank the Lord, that's all over. And there's no law against being brought up to speak French, even around here! Besides, Peter, the Frenchmen you mean aren't exactly strangers. The Neutrals have lived next to us for nearly eight years now, and they've given no trouble to speak of, have they? I know the ones in Worcester as well as you. And from everything else I hear, they're decent, honest folk."

"Whether they live here or anywhere else, I say they're still Frenchmen! You can tell by their *smell*." Peter Lynch caught the eyes of several of the others; one by one, his leer either convinced, or sickened, those who took it in with their drink.

"I don't know, though," said a man over by the now dark west windows, "if the French can be called worse than any others in the war. If you'll read your city papers, you'll see it's the Europeans all together who forced war on the rest of us—not only France, but England, too, as well as Prussia, Russia, Austria, and Sweden, and even—"

"Oh, give it a rest, Eli," called someone from across the room.

"That may be," said another by the cider kegs. "And you might even say, now, that there's honor in fighting for your own country, whatever it may be—and whatever the reason. I suspect it's some of our *own* men who ought to be ashamed, for doing business with the enemy just to get hold of their blessed sugar, and fa-la's to sell to city folk, even while the fighting was going on! Your own brother, Dick, for one. So I wouldn't be so quick to call the kettle—"

"Oh, if we're naming names, then, what about your three Falmouth cousins, Henry?" cried out a disgruntled neighbor. "Don't we all know they were sending their grain and cattle up to Cannadee, across the blockade?"

"Supplying the very ones who planned to come and lift my scalp in the night," chimed in a farmer finishing a plate of heavy stew, "just waiting to run down and burn our houses soon as we marched off to fight! Though they never did manage to get here—"

"At any road, we did *our* part," boasted another. "And with precious little help from the bloody-backed lobsters, and their prissy lords sent to teach us how to fight!"

"*That's* for certain!" came a quick reply. "They must've sent over some of their worst dunderheads, judging by what I saw with my own two eyes. Yet we *still* managed to snatch their bacon from the fire, didn't we, lads?"

Between vigorous assent and rolling laughter, several heads and chests rose and swelled.

"And took many a fort for them, too! Beausejour, Frontenac, and Duquesne, Niagara, Fort Ti, and Crown Point, then Quebec—"

"Oh, well, you'll have to admit that Wolfe was an awfully good tactician—"

"Now *that* was enough for young Montcalm—"

"And finally, Montreal!"

"Well I remember when we took Louisbourg, in '45," broke in one of the old birds roasting by the fire, who puffed with animation. "With old Pepperrell, bless him. Sailed up to Cape Breton, took it single-handed!"

"The British Navy may deserve some small thanks," observed a younger man rather dryly, causing the other quail to come alive with a sputter.

"You can thank the British all you want for giving it *back* to the froggies, too, soon as peace was signed. If you'll remember, that's why the lobsters had to go up and do it all over again, and blow it to bits this time. And now, I wonder, just how long our *latest* peace will last?"

It was a sobering question. The war just concluded had often seemed won. Yet hostilities had flared up again and again, like flames from a burning seam of coal. But tonight, many seated in the Blue Boar only laughed at this lesson. And all the while, the young Frenchman continued to sit, listening silently in his dark corner, waiting for a further goad. The miller soon supplied it.

"What about your own pet frog, Phineas? When did he hop in this time? And why is it that you let him stay, when his kind is bound to give offense to all your decent customers?"

Those seated by Peter Lynch eyed the Frenchman in the shadows expectantly, while the speech drew groans from some at the back tables.

"You know, you're the very first to complain, Peter, since Mr. Fortier joined us yesterday evening."

"Maybe you can explain what brought him to Bracebridge, where he's got no proper business that I know of. And then he can tell us if he imagines he's going to spend another quiet night in a bed upstairs."

"He's very likely staying here," the landlord responded patiently, "because it's cheap, as you all know . . . unlike

Mr. Pratt's fine lodgings up the hill. Show me he's a bit of trouble to anyone, and I'll have him out. Meanwhile, my guests may come and go as they please. It's still a free country. As to his business—" Phineas Wise regarded the miller with a gleam in his eye.

"—as to his business, well, I think many of us know what that might be, don't we, gentlemen? And I say good luck to him, as I would to any man trying to coax a young lady—or any other kind of female, for that matter."

"Especially a young colt like Mary!" someone called, and several of the men joined in with loud good humor.

"You know what else the ladies say about French-men, don't you, Peter?" called an older man, before hooting with laughter.

For a moment, it looked as though the red-faced miller might leap over his seat. But instead, a determined look crept across Peter Lynch's broad features, while his great voice softened to a syrupy growl.

"Oh, he's not afraid to walk in here, bold as brass, and sniff around—as long as I'm off trying to get custom for my mill. I suppose he saw me riding into Worcester on Monday, and came running here to try his luck. But I'm back now; and I'm only saying God's truth when I tell him he'd be better off keeping to his own kind. I'll just add what we all feel—that any of his kind that hope to get half-breeds by our women will soon be escorted *straight to hell!*"

At this, the silent young man jumped lithely to his feet, throwing out a curse and nearly overturning the ta-ble in front of the red-cloaked stranger. The miller, too, rose up and spit on his hands in preparation, followed by a wobbling Dick Craft. While others braced themselves, the two old men silhouetted against the leaping firelight spun their chairs around eagerly, hoping for a new tale to add to their threadbare stock. And Phineas Wise hurried to the back of the bar to pick up a stout ash stick he'd often found handy in a brawl.

It was in this final moment of relative calm, when calculations of positions and odds were swiftly being made, that a sound—not a very loud sound, but one that is frequently found to be commanding—gained the attention of each and every one of the Blue Boar's inhabitants, calling an immediate truce.

Its cause was simple. The old stranger, who had been in the process of rising when the excitement began, had taken a purse from an inner pocket of the scarlet cloak he wore. In the confusion, he'd tipped the open bag until its contents fell in a glittering stream onto the table before him. There, more than two dozen pieces of gold sang out loudly as they danced and reeled against each other, and finally settled down before an audience that was as fascinated as a swaying cobra hearing a snake charmer's horn.

The stranger bent his head quickly. He picked up the coins from the table, then dropped them back into the leather pouch, one by one. Around him, eyes narrowed in speculation.

Phineas Wise quietly set his club against the wall. He bent to retrieve a few more pieces that had skipped to the floor. While he held them, he was surprised to see that they were Dutch gold—guldens, from God knew where. He stood and gave them up a little wistfully. Then he retreated a few paces, to be well away from the circle of staring faces.

Slowly, the men sat down to their tables again. But they continued to watch the stranger as he produced a dull coin from another pocket, and put it by his empty tankard. After that he gave a nod to the landlord, snugged the brown bundle up under his arm again, and made his way carefully toward the open door.

Gabriel Fortier was in the doorway ahead of him.

The young Frenchman stopped to look back with a frown, then drew his foot over the frame and disappeared into the evening.

The old stranger seemed to hesitate, but soon followed, and the tavern let out its breath.

Candles again flickered quietly, and conversation, when it resumed, was subdued. Several times, one man or another looked deeply into the dark recess that now held only a table and two empty chairs.

Who was the old man in the scarlet cloak, they asked themselves and each other, and how had he come by all of that money? Everybody knew that gold and silver coins were scarce throughout the colonies. Spanish silver dollars—"pieces of eight"—were sometimes seen, as well as British sterling. But most silver received was sent straight back to England, to help pay for the flood of goods the colonies required—or else it was melted for plate, or other items. So it was with gold. And the odds of seeing Dutch coins? They were very, very slim.

Where had the stranger come by it? And more to the point, where was the frail old man going with his gold, out on the dark road at night, and all alone?

The two quails by the fire (whose names were Tyndall and Flint) relit their pipes, and issued the first of several dire predictions involving footpads, demons, and wolves. Meanwhile, Phineas Wise shook his head as he went to stand on the doorstep and jingle pockets full of copper. He peered out and saw that the chilly night was less complete than it had appeared from inside the lighted tavern. A bit of bloodred twilight still clung to the western horizon, while the sky overhead was a deep blue dotted with small, pale clouds, and several points of twinkling stars.

A breath of cold flowed down the hillside that the stranger had just begun to climb. Eventually, the road the old man followed disappeared near the crest in dense forest, with a wide stretch of old burned-over meadow coming before. As he continued to watch, the land-lord heard the lonely voice of a whippoorwill calling out from nearby woods. It cried, it was said, for lost souls who wandered in the night. The practical man listened, and half believed. Someone would die soon. The cry of a nearby owl joined that of the other bird, echo-ing Phineas Wise's own unasked question in an eerie staccato.

Whoo-who-whooo?

Where was the old man going, Wise wondered, watching him climb slowly past dark fingers of a bending hemlock that overhung the road. There was no other tavern to stop in for a good five miles. Ahead, there were only a few isolated farms nestled in a hilly stretch of for-est, and unprosperous ones at that. Was there something wrong with him? Didn't he know how to tell direction? Beyond that, did the old man feel no fear? It was a puzzle, but in the end Wise turned back to his own hearth and business, and shut the tavern door firmly behind him.

Inside, it was as if his customers could still hear the happy ring of the falling gold coins, while they called for more of the same. Now the miller, too, seemed con-cerned for the old man's safety.

"I only say," maintained Peter Lynch, "that he'd be far better off investing it, than carrying it around."

"Investing it with you?" Dick Craft asked with a wink. The miller did not return his amusement.

"Better than to lose it somewhere in the night," Lynch intoned ominously.

"Myself," Dick continued, "I've lost more money in broad daylight than in the dark. But that's rarely called stealing, is it? Not when there's signed notes, and all, to make it right—"

The miller's glowering face soon made Dick bite his

tongue, and remember that he spoke to a man quite used to doing business.

The third of their party, Jack Pennywort, had less to say on the matter. His own concern was that he should be getting home, and that his wife would scold him properly if he came in late—or do even worse. This led to the usual comments from his heartier friends who feigned surprise that Jack should care. Undoubtedly, they joked, he had become accustomed to his punishment. What of it, if he should be locked outside his own door to sleep where he might? There could be unexpected pleasures in such a system, if a man knew where to look, and what to do about it. So then, why not stay a little longer?

But Jack got up, found a copper or two for the landlord, and made his way somewhat unsteadily to the door. It should be added that this clumsiness was not entirely the result of drink. Jack had been dragging a clubfoot behind him all of his life. It was generally considered by his friends and neighbors to be quite a humorous appendage.

Eventually, followed by loud laughter, the shuffling little man gained the door. His departure allowed the tavern to concentrate on an entering party of thirsty new arrivals, who jostled Jack rudely as they passed him on the sill.

Chapter 4

At tuesday's twilight, Richard Longfellow, the eccentric neighbor of Charlotte Willett, sat alone in his paneled study. As the light faded, he contemplated an object on one of the walls. The object was a portrait. Its subject was Eleanor Howard, a young woman with direct eyes, and hair that fell in dark ringlets.

Longfellow continued to gaze, but he no longer saw the portrait. Instead, memory had taken over, giving him the only other images he would ever have of her striking beauty—for the original had been tragically lost.

From time to time, he still imagined her sitting there beside him, sometimes rocking a cradle. But Eleanor Howard had been taken when an illness settled in her throat and choked the breath and life from her, as it had done to others nearby. His own grief at the loss of his fiancée had been shared by her sister Charlotte, who soon endured more sorrows of her own. Unlike Eleanor,

Aaron Willett had refused to be bled, but in the end it had made no difference.

Longfellow turned to the window, to find most of the sky's color gone. It was lucky, he told himself, that he had learned long ago to enjoy a bachelor's life. At least, he still had Charlotte. He had admired her from the first. Her features were nothing as special as Eleanor's; he was reminded of the fact as he turned back to stare at the portrait once more, through the gloom. But Eleanor's older sister had her own quiet charms, with an intelligent spark grown strong in a soul that had always been loved, and kindly treated. Charlotte, too, was capable of thinking eternal thoughts, possibly almost as capable as he was himself.

Uncurling his legs, which had a habit of becoming entwined, Longfellow sprang to his feet, determined to buoy his mood by lighting a candle. Eleanor had frequently experienced bouts of feverish imagination and activity, coupled with an exciting lack of restraint. Charlotte's mind was quieter, more even, but still quite curious . . . although it did sometimes seem to him that she tended to plod.

Curiosity about the larger realities of the universe, things outside one's personal life—that was the secret of lasting contentment! But when Longfellow felt the urge to philosophize, he imagined the scheme of things to be chaotic, and nearly unsolvable. He certainly held little hope for any rational system of order that tried to alter the petty obsessions of most of humanity, who did their best to ruin the world for each other. Wryly, he watched Charlotte perceive a natural harmony all around her, while she noticed human discord as a force of only minor importance. It was a rare turn of mind, he thought—possibly even one to be envied.

Whatever the truths of the cosmos, her bright moods invariably spilled over onto his darker ones when the two sat and talked. She sometimes made him laugh out loud. Besides that, she listened well. And his neighbor had often helped him weather his frequent melancholia. She made him feel necessary . . . as her steadfast supporter, and as a good companion. He knew this to be a rare thing for a man whose quick, passionate nature had lost him nearly as many friends as he had ever claimed.

Not that he minded having few friends. He was, after all, respected. And as long as there were new ideas to explore, experiments to be conducted and studied, seeds to plant and stars to ponder, who could be bothered with courting admiration? Let others fear loneliness. The cup offered up by the physical world was filled to overflowing.

Energized by a new idea, Longfellow picked up the candlestick in front of him, and strode away from the fire toward a gold-framed mirror that graced one side of the simply appointed room. As he did so, he felt the pleasant flap of the long linen trousers he'd recently affected (taking the style of certain Italian peasants), which he wore outside his boots to further confound custom. The trousers were cool and comfortable, and they didn't constrain him at the joints like common knee breeches, with buttons that bit into you when you sat. They also concealed lower legs he found quite adequate for the most part, if they did not bulge enough to meet fashionable standards.

Lighting two more wax tapers that stood in brass-backed sconces on either side of the Venetian mirror, he peered at his own image. It was less beautiful than the one he had been contemplating on the wall, but it had the advantage of being alive. By the light of candles and fire, the mirror revealed a pliant, if solemn, face. It could have been a trifle underfed, but it had full lips, and now it experimented with a pleasant smile—nothing like the pinched, aristocratic sneer so popular in his former home by the Bay. Longfellow saw that false token all around him when he rode in to Boston to visit. It was enough to make a parson growl.

Further study brought to light the presence of new gray hairs among the dark mass that fell down his back—tied, but neither pomaded nor powdered. Still thick, by God, for a man who could no longer call himself young. And the eyes were certainly distinctive—the rich color of hazelnut shells. It was fortunate, he told himself, he was not a vain man by nature.

Moving away, Longfellow tapped the glass barometer that hung on the wall. For the moment, it held steady . . . steadier, he thought ruefully, than he felt himself. Would the evening *never* end?

He knew he had become dangerously mercurial again. Right now, he had the urge to argue about something—anything. Perhaps Locke, or Rousseau, or some other misleading and overblown fool. Cicero would take whatever side was left in an argument, and keep it up until they were both worn out with it, run down like clocks and ready for sleep. But Cicero was late returning home.

Longfellow sat at the pianoforte for a while, picking out a tune on the cool ivory keys, considering fate's rude manners. In his father's time, in Boston, Cicero had been far more than an adequate servant—in fact, he had nearly run his father's city house . . . especially after Richard's mother had died. He had also assisted the members of the family he'd "adopted" in delicate matters, often requiring a certain amount of finesse. At Jason Longfellow's death, his will had ended the black man's bondage, providing him with the legally required funds to remain free. But Cicero had agreed to stay in service to Richard Longfellow (who else, he asked, would have the job?) and had moved with him when the aging young man, in love, purchased the house next to the Howards four years before.

Tonight, Cicero was down at the taproom of the Bracebridge Inn, imbibing news with his wine. Like his Roman namesake, he enjoyed society even while he frequently objected to it, and it to him. Since he was no longer a slave, he had a right to sit with the others. But for several reasons he preferred a warm, hidden nook around the chimney corner. Jonathan Pratt served him Madeira there, often bringing him stories as well. And as the evening progressed and the wine and rum flowed, Cicero frequently chuckled at what was meant for very few ears (and certainly not his own), coming from patrons warming themselves beside the fire.

Bored again with his train of thought, Longfellow shifted, and started a new tune. "Maybe I'll have to get a cat to talk to," he muttered to himself, sulking while he cocked an ear at something in the distance.

Abruptly, the front door opened and shut, and quick feet sounded in the hall. In another instant, Cicero stood before him, bent almost in two.

"I came . . ." he gasped, "because I supposed . . . even in your mood . . . that you'd be interested in what I've heard . . ."

Overcome, he again lowered a head that appeared to be topped by a gray, tailless, fashionably short-curled periwig, although it wasn't.

"Difficult for me to say," Longfellow replied, waiting for more. It was not forthcoming. Cicero still fought for breath and equilibrium. Longfellow tapped his fingers on the piano lid impatiently. "And difficult for you, it seems. Another secret?"

"No. Better hurry, though . . . the rest of the town's . . . probably there already."

"Really."

"It seems Jack Pennywort . . . over at the Blue Boar . . .

started walking up the Worcester road, following an old man who's a stranger in these parts—aaaahhh! . . . and the old man . . . it seems that the old man . . . well, he caught fire! Ignited all by himself . . . nobody knows how."

There was quite a long pause, and the ormolu mantle clock chimed the hour.

"He *what?*" Longfellow inquired, squinting with impatience.

"They say . . . he . . . went up in flames."

Catching his breath, Cicero studied the effect his news had produced. He had been aware of his employer's black humor since suppertime. He believed this new event would be able to change it, and perhaps provide them both with amusement for several days.

"What—on the road? And who, if you don't mind my asking, are *they?*" Longfellow queried, taking several steps to peer out of a window into the darkness. There were lights on the opposite hillside, where none should have been.

"Over the bridge, up past the tavern. Jack Pennywort was the only one to see it. Some already say it's the Devil's work. Or witchcraft, at least. Jack claims there's nothing left of the fellow at all!"

"Ah, Pennywort. There's an opinion to value," Longfellow retorted. "And witchcraft, too," he ventured with slightly more interest. "What won't the undisciplined mind get up to, on a dull evening."

"An interesting story, though, especially for Jack to make up by himself."

"True. Especially for Jack. Although he might have remembered—"

"The reason I ran was because I thought you'd like to go over and take a look for yourself, while the thing was still hot."

"A look at what? I wouldn't imagine there'd be anything left to see. Not if the Devil made a real job of it."

A jumble of voices could be heard coming from the direction of the inn. But Longfellow had a stubborn streak, and would not be easily moved from a mood.

"Well, you might want to observe everybody *else* going out for a look!" Cicero cried, falling into a chair. "It would be a shame to have to listen to it all tomorrow, secondhand."

Finally unable to resist the urge to go, Longfellow bolted toward the hallway. "Are you coming?" he threw back behind him.

"Not just yet I'm not," Cicero said with a sigh, bending closer to the fire.

"Then I suppose it's up to me to watch the curtain rise, and take in the show . . ."

The declaration had barely stopped ringing through the hallway when Longfellow, still wrestling with his coat sleeves, slammed the heavy door behind him, leaving the lion's head knocker to pound out a final farewell.

ONCE THROUGH HIS front gate, Richard Longfellow paused, faced with a dilemma. If he "forgot" to go and ask Mrs. Willett to view with him the scene of whatever had occurred, she might think the oversight was intentional. She would also ask him endless questions, probably well into the next week.

But if he turned and went to find her, while all Bracebridge was tramping across the river (she might even have gone ahead of him already!) then he would miss the beginnings of what promised to be a ridiculous entertainment—the sort of thing that pleased Longfellow more than most social events. Undecided, he stood with his feet pointed downhill.

When he finally did turn, he saw Charlotte's cloaked figure coming out of her yard with a lantern, walking so that she was unable to see an enormous yellow face with a toothless grin coming up behind her. Longfellow waited and watched the timeless spectacle of a rising autumn moon, noting how the eastern blackness had turned blue again around the luminous disk with its heavily pocked surface.

"You'd make a fine Diogenes," he offered pleasantly as she approached.

"It's less an honest man I'm after than an answer to what's causing all this noise! Did someone ring the fire bell?"

Longfellow shook his head as she took his arm. Soon, they hurried through inky shadows that lay across the road.

"No . . . but flames of a kind were involved." He smiled to see her face, lit from below by the horn box she carried, take on the look of a jack-o'-lantern.

"According to Cicero," he went on, "there seems to have been a case of what's been called *spontaneous human combustion* here. Not unheard of, although I believe it is the first time it's been managed in this part of the world. At least, it's the first I've heard of it."

"But can you tell me what it all means?"

"There was a strange story from New York in the papers last year, which was widely repeated. It seems a very respectable and well-liked Long Island farmer, sitting in his chair on a Sabbath morning, smoking a small pipe, was seen to be quickly and thoroughly consumed by a mass of flames that came from within him. At the same time, the chair in which he sat was scarcely charred."

"Oh!"

"His wife was in church, but the event was witnessed by a young female servant. She became hysterical, of course, and finally called for help. It was said she was so unnerved that she fled from the place the same day."

"Poor girl!"

"Later, the man's wife unhappily admitted that the

husband had been fond of blasphemy, and that she had recently heard him repudiate a solemn oath he had made to the Almighty—on what issue, I don't recall. That satisfied the local magistrates as to both the agency and motive."

"It was called an Act of God?" Charlotte's eyes widened with surprise.

"Apparently. A blow for the Deists and their mechanical universe. But then, who knows? Who actually saw it happen? One simple child—a pretty thing who lost her wits, they say—and, of course, the Lord himself. While I'd accept in perfect faith anything He cared to tell me directly, I'm not sure the ravings of the only other human there guarantee us an accurate account."

"So what *do* you believe took place?"

Longfellow took a moment to form his answer. Ahead of them, through the darkness, a string of bouncing lights ended in an undulating circle.

"A hearty Sunday breakfast, most likely with plenty of fermented cider. Then a seizure of the brain or heart . . . a quick death, one would hope . . . a hot coal dropped onto the waistcoat . . . and finally, a great deal of exaggeration by the press." Longfellow shrugged eloquently. "One more martyr to tobacco! Or . . ."

"Or . . . ?"

"On the other hand, the natural world is full of surprises, and no one yet knows the cause of many events we call unnatural phenomena. If, in truth, he did burn down to nothing, it would be very interesting to know exactly how, and why. It's a shame there wasn't a reliable witness."

"But you said the girl saw what happened."

He waved the idea away.

"It's one thing to *see* something—another to *observe* and discover the actual truth of a matter. Observation, of course, requires a proper perspective. It can't be done hastily, or with the emotions. The first part involves using your eyes—the second, using your brain. Rational men will tell you there's no place in Science for feelings of the heart. And Science is the place to look for explanations that will stand the light of day."

Charlotte seemed to consider all of this quietly as they increased their pace. At the time, it was unclear to her companion how much of what he'd said she had truly taken in.

SOON AFTER CROSSING the bridge, they neared the torch-lit group of milling people. Here, Charlotte considered, the road went uphill through brown, grassy fields with knots of dark firs and pines, and a few clusters of ghostly white birches. The roadbed at this stretch had been raised a few feet by the local citizens years before, to stand above the spring torrents that melted down on either side from the woods above. Once, these floods had brought rocks and pine cones to the track, which then eroded until it was full of small, winding gullies. Now only occasional wheel ruts impeded one's progress through much of the year; tonight, these were filled with a fine, dry dust that muffled every step. There wasn't much else to see.

"Do you suppose," Charlotte asked her neighbor as he eyed the crowd, "that he was a pleasing man?"

"Who?"

"The husband in your story. You said he was well liked."

"Pleasing? A farmer? He was hardly a strict church-man, from what his wife tells us. And he probably had good land to farm, living on Long Island. So yes, I'd imagine he was pleasing enough."

"And his wife . . . was she very young, or of the same age as her husband?"

"Hmmm. If she had been young and comely, the New York papers would have remarked on it, as I recall they did in describing the girl."

Charlotte looked off across the sloping moonlit field.

"And you say a similar thing might have happened here? On this road?"

"I only know what Cicero overheard and told me, and that it's close to Allhallows Eve. When the dead walk," he whispered, opening his eyes in pretended horror.

"Well, I wonder," said Charlotte as they began to make out words from the crowd in front of them.

"What do you wonder?"

Longfellow gave her only his nearest ear now, using the other to decipher some of the noise that rose up into the night air.

"I wonder," said Charlotte, who knew something about human nature, if not a great deal about Science, "whether the widow on Long Island really was a widow, after all."

Chapter 5

"T HEN," LITTLE JACK Pennywort went on, working sweeping gestures into the retelling of the amazing story, "as I followed along, there was a pale sort of flickering just up around his shoulders. Just before I saw the yellow gleam . . . and then I tripped over a stone, and fell down in the road."

"Not an unusual event in itself," Richard Long-fellow said in a low voice to Charlotte, as he began to weigh the elements of Jack's story.

"That's only the beginning," an old hand assured new-comers who had missed the first telling at the Blue Boar.

"But as I looked again, the flames came right up out of him—all around! They rose with a *roar*, they did—rose up and danced like Satan himself, all around the old man right where he stood, waving his arms up in the air before he disappeared! Black smoke, first, black as night . . . and when the wind took it off, all I saw was a white mist rise up, and a spot of blue fire, *damme* if I didn't! There was heat enough to water my eyes, and the Devil's stink of hellfire and brimstone!"

"Sulphur, most likely," Longfellow commented quietly.

"There was an old woman burned up once," began one of the two quails who had come with the rest of the tavern men, "down in Baltimore, I believe it was—"

"And after that he was gone," Jack continued, raising his voice to be heard by all, "*disappeared*, from what I could see! Though to make sure, I turned myself complete around, and round again." He demonstrated by hopping about on his good foot, holding out both arms for balance.

"He might have run off into the trees," mused a skeptical new arrival.

"Ain't any, as far as you can throw a rock," Jack retorted, pointing.

There was murmured agreement. That much of what Jack said was true. It was at least sixty paces to the woods near the crest, with no other growth between high enough to hide in—not even a large boulder to stand behind. Back along the road to the last clump of firs was another hundred paces. Jack had already assured them that this, too, was out of the question, and most seemed to believe him. Which created a logical puzzle, unless a man *could* simply catch fire on a rare October evening. Or unless, of course, Jack Pennywort was telling a tall tale.

"—until only a kneecap and a foot were left of her," concluded the story from Baltimore, during the lull. "Nobody ever knew why."

"So I stood and looked as far as I could see," Jack insisted, "but there was nothing at all—naught of his red cloak, no body, nothing so much as a shoe buckle. This is all that's left right here!"

Looking like a curiously diminished Mark Antony on a stage, in Longfellow's opinion, Jack extended an open hand dramatically toward the dark patch on the ground before him. A lantern was lowered so that all could see for themselves a thin, gummy mass about the size of a cartwheel, under the pool of light. It was the only sign of anything unusual on the road.

On the face of it, Jack Pennywort wholly believed his own story. Among his audience, gooseflesh rose on the limbs of more than one.

"Say, Jack—would you know what happened to all that gold?" called out drunken Dick Craft.

This time, only an owl in the woods replied.

Charlotte didn't understand the question, but the mention of a red cloak gave her a start. She thought back to her own afternoon walk, to the bent old man, the offered and accepted apple. She looked up at Longfellow, but found him wholly engrossed in examining the reactions of the crowd.

A chorus of voices rose up again, repeating not only the last query, but also asking who the old man was, where he came from, and what he had been doing out alone, on foot, in the road at night.

"He's stopping over at the inn—I know that much," broke in a deep voice. "Came today. Saw him there before supper." Charlotte recognized the large head of Nathan, the inn's blacksmith, towering over those around him.

"Maybe he's there now, then," reasoned another. "Maybe somebody should—"

"If he went up in smoke, I say it must be *witchcraft!*" cried a voice that exploded into a screech. This new idea was met by a rustle of misgiving from some of the listeners, while others responded with clucks and whistles of disapproval.

"In that case, ask Phineas Wise," somebody else yelled.

"He was born up the coast, where they know all about such things."

Phineas ignored the barb that had been old even in his grandfather's day. Amidst more laughter, his sharp eyes continued to measure the strength of the gathering, looking for the first sign of any plan to turn back to his tavern for a warm mug of new cider, or something stronger.

Meanwhile, the beginnings of scattered arguments showed that some conclusions had already been drawn, and sides taken—a natural thing among men and women raised on political talk and sermons, and quite used to examining and judging their fellows.

Charlotte recognized several of her neighbors, lit strangely by their lanterns, or more broadly from above by pitch torches that flickered in the rapidly cooling night breeze. There was Peter Lynch, the miller, next to Nathan, who himself stood solid and quiet, with folded arms as strong as barrel bands. Near the center of the wide circle she saw Tinder and Flint, as they were sometimes called, the two old fixtures of the Common bench and the Blue Boar's fireside. And crowding in next to them were three boys—young men, really. She could name one member of the trio: Sam Dudley, who lived along the Concord road.

She was surprised to note that the Reverend Rowe was absent, then remembered that Hannah had said he'd gone to Boston for a day or two. (Hannah was probably already asleep, along with her husband and oldest son who had lately been wearing themselves out with haying the Willett farm, and helping at others.) If the preacher *had* shown up, Charlotte thought, something dogmatic would surely have been heard by now.

As it was, she did hear some of Reverend Rowe's flock whispering uncharitable things in the darkness— ideas they would have been ashamed to repeat in church, or in the light of day. The sound of it made her heart beat faster. But it was a question of economics that was being discussed in the most lively tones.

"Even if the gold's melted down, shouldn't it still be here somewhere?"

"There's nothing like it in this muck," said a man with a stick.

"Maybe it flew away," joked another. "That's often happened to me!"

"Or ran, with a little help," another replied ominously.

"Well, Jack was only gone for a couple of minutes."

"Could've taken the gold—I'm not saying you did, Jack—but he *couldn't* have hid a body anywhere near here, could he? Or carried it away himself, either."

Several men again looked around carefully, while Jack began to squirm. Finally, he voluntarily turned out pockets which contained nothing unusual.

"What about the Frenchman? Didn't he lead the old man out the door?" Peter Lynch called out harshly, casting his eyes about for support.

But before anyone could say more, an edge of the crowd swung open to make way for the hurrying figure of a short, portly man.

Everybody knew Constable Bowers. Hiram and his wife kept a notions shop in their home near the bridge, besides farming some land west of the millpond. Constable Bowers had few duties to perform beyond collecting and recording taxes levied by the Bracebridge selectmen, the ones who had picked him the past January for the twelve-month job. For nearly a year he had attended their meetings, where he generally dozed until they adjourned to a nearby house for refreshment.

Although the crowd made way for Constable Bowers tonight, it expected little of Hiram's brain, and only a bit more from his ear. He had dressed in a great hurry; the cuffs of his shirt were caught up inside his coat, his bulging waistcoat was buttoned one off the mark, and his neck cloth was entirely missing.

Several spoke, or shouted out the few facts known at the moment, for the constable's benefit. Meanwhile, Charlotte again surveyed the faces around her. Most were masculine—of course, at this hour—and weather-stained to a warm mahogany. But she was surprised to see, bobbing behind the others, a lighter one that really shouldn't have been there at all.

What was Mary Frye doing here, apparently all alone? The girl sometimes came to Charlotte's door to fetch extra butter or cream. Originally from Worcester, Mary had been bound over by her father for three years to Jonathan Pratt and his wife Lydia. For two years more, until she was seventeen, she was expected to do whatever was asked of her at the Bracebridge Inn. Tonight, by torchlight, her wild eyes and tangle of black hair showed she had escaped Lydia's influence for the moment. And she was clearly in search of something, or someone. Charlotte wondered who, and waited to see.

The wattles under the constable's chin shook as he held up his hands for a chance to speak. Tomorrow, he told them, he would take down testimony at the inn from anyone who had something to say. To that end, he would remain there for most of the afternoon. After that, he would report to the selectmen to see if anything more should be done.

If, by that time, joked a wit hidden by darkness, Hiram was capable of seeing anything at all. Others immediately insisted that the Reverend Rowe be consulted as soon as he returned. From his vast reading and experience the preacher would know if a man could be kindled by human design, or by craft with witches or devils. Some already guessed the stranger had been lifted up and set down elsewhere on earth . . . they'd heard older folk speak of such things. Then again, he might have been removed to some far more unpleasant part of the cosmology.

"But what," shouted Peter Lynch with determination, "has become of the Frenchman? Find *him* and ask what happened! He left the Blue Boar right before this stranger, didn't he? He's the one we should go after!"

Dick Craft opened his mouth, as was to be expected. But whatever he had to say was stopped by a piercing scream. Mary Frye's terrified cry shocked the air; before it died, the girl swooned and fell back lifeless. As luck would have it, her limp body was caught up by an extremely strong arm, extended at the nick of time. The crowd gasped, then let out its breath in relief. All, that is, but one man.

"Take your dirty hands off her!" the miller spat fiercely. Peter Lynch's face was red as a roasted beet, and his eyes bulged with fury. Several men who stood between Lynch and the smith, who held young Mary, stiffened. Charlotte saw Nathan look to Richard Longfellow, and watched Longfellow ease his way around the circle.

"Of course you realize, Peter," Longfellow began as he approached the miller, "that Nathan would be the best one to take Mary safely home. I believe Mr. Pratt would expect it of him . . . to return a maid who probably has no leave to be out in the first place. By the way, I'm glad I found you here tonight. I've been meaning to talk a little business, when you have a moment. My men tell me I have some hay acres I might sow next year with grain, but much depends on both the yield and the price of the milling, so I wanted to consult with you first, to ask you about a possible contract for grinding that I might pay for *now*, which would entitle me in future to a set price of, oh, say . . ."

When Charlotte looked around again, Nathan was already escorting a recovered but trembling Mary back along the road toward the bridge. And in a few more moments, Jack Pennywort and the rest were returning to the Blue Boar, where they might find means to counter the evening's growing chill.

"The miller was anxious enough to earn a dollar," Longfellow remarked when he returned to Charlotte's side. "It seems Peter Lynch is a man with two loves."

"Love, you call it?" she returned with a grimace.

"I'm afraid it passes for that, with some. I suppose 'lust' would be a more precise term."

Charlotte turned her flushed face into a cold wind, away from the moving crowd. Several questions leaped and fought for place in her anxious mind. What had happened here? And what was likely to happen next? It was possible that an old man had disappeared from the road. According to Jack, he had quickly burned to a blackened mess, in a way some explained as a freak of Nature. Others were already calling it the Devil's work. According to the miller, the stranger might have been murdered for some gold he carried, perhaps by a Frenchman who had also disappeared. From the laughter around her, it was clear that at least some of the townspeople were unconcerned, believing that the whole thing was a Halloween prank.

One thing seemed to be agreed—nobody knew where the old man with the red cloak was now. Hiram Bowers couldn't be expected to reach the heart of the matter any time soon. And until someone did . . . someone else might be in for trouble. Crippled, henpecked Jack Pennywort would certainly be teased, hounded, and accused. Of what, though? Possibly, only of telling a good story. But if it were proved that something had really happened tonight, a few among them might decide Jack was responsible.

And this Frenchman . . . She was well aware that feeling against the French was still running high. If Peter Lynch insisted that one of the old enemy had something to do with stealing, and possibly murder, she knew of several who wouldn't rest until more than one person had paid. It was a disturbing thought.

But broader horror hid in the first feeble cries of "Witch!"

People could smile, now, when they talked of the withered belief. Charlotte had reason to suspect that *the Devil's work* might still become a terrible rallying cry in New England, especially at a time when fear and anger divided neighbors. Oh, town folk might quickly assure you that things had changed since the days when suspicion had led to tragedy up and down the coast. But she herself remembered recent talk, when Aaron had been called worse than "Quaker" by men and women who were suspicious of anyone from beyond the village they were born in. One or two of them were on the road tonight. Were her neighbors all so different from their ancestors of seventy years ago?

If the village concluded the stranger's disappearance was due to a quirk of Nature, there would be interest in discovering how it had happened. But if witchcraft was suspected by more than a few, the *how* would become unimportant. Then the only question likely to be asked was *who?* Who knew enough to call down fire and brimstone; who would be held responsible? While other possible explanations of what had happened tonight could result in some kind of justice, this last one, if it were believed in Bracebridge, promised nothing of the sort. Charlotte shivered at the idea.

Still, one could hope that the old man would turn up again soon, with an explanation of his own. And certainly, Jack Pennywort—like the young girl on Long Island—might not be the most reliable of witnesses. It was an odd time of night to take the air, but it *was* possible that that was all the man in the red cloak had in mind. Jack could have made up the rest, especially after an evening at the Blue Boar. And yet . . .

Had anyone walked to the hill's crest to see if the stranger had gone down the other side? Or perhaps he'd doubled back, and was settled in his bed at the inn even now. She could think of several other questions Hiram Bowers might ask, if and when he thought of them.

Coming out of her own world, Charlotte was relieved to see a dark, familiar face beside Richard Longfellow's.

"You might ask Cicero," she quickly proposed to her escort, "to walk me home, after he's seen enough here. Then, Richard, you could go on to the tavern and hear what's being discussed. You know I'll look forward to hearing your opinion of the whole matter in the morning," she said sincerely.

It was a speech designed to flatter as well as encourage him, but it hadn't been necessary. Longfellow, too, had read the crowd and was uneasy. As a selectman, he felt it his duty to watch the mood of those he represented, and to see what might develop. He was also anxious to see if anything in the tale Jack told might stand up to the scrutiny of a logical mind.

"But you'll have to wait a little longer for my opinion," he added, after he'd agreed to go on without her. "I'm off early for Boston. Diana has decreed one of her country retreats should take place. I'll go in with the chaise and bring her back . . . followed, no doubt, by a wagon full of necessities."

"Dinner, then? I'll make a fricassee. And we'll drink syllabubs," she added with a ghost of a smile.

On that expectant note, they parted.

A few minutes later, Cicero ushered Charlotte Willett homeward among the last of the observers. In the forest behind them, the horned owl continued to laugh at the curious ways of mankind, and the pines sighed in soft surprise at the rising of the autumn wind.

Over the broad valley, the moon shone down on the black reaches of the Musketaquid, turning the river to winding strips of silver. And walking just ahead, the three boys Charlotte had noticed earlier playfully pushed and challenged one another. From the talk that drifted back to her, it was clear they were alive to the possibilities of the night: elves and goblins that could be expected to move through the electric air, and strange lights that might dance in woods and bogs.

One by one, each dared the others to stay and find out what kinds of things lurked in the deepest shadows. But before long, the boys branched off onto different paths through the fields, headed home, while Charlotte and Cicero kept to the Boston road.

Despite his protests, Charlotte left Cicero at Longfellow's gate, and walked the last of the way by herself. While the lantern cast its warm light on the ground in front of her, a colder light frosted the trees that had begun to writhe in a boreal wind, under brightly twinkling stars.

By the time she reached her front yard, the ground seemed to dance under moaning branches. Remembering that she'd bolted the main door early in the evening, she continued around the house to the barnyard, and entered through the kitchen. Inside, banked coals gave out a welcoming warmth, and Orpheus thumped his tail in greeting.

Charlotte went to the pantry, brought out some bread and cheese, and sat by the hearth to share it with her companion.

As the room retreated to a familiar, spice-scented background, she went over what she'd heard and seen. But she made little progress, and finally decided, with a yawn, to go to bed. Before leaving the kitchen, she went to the door. The old dog slowly rose, shook himself, then padded up to the open portal. And there he stood perfectly still.

Charlotte saw the hair between his shoulders rise before she heard the low, uncertain growl. Orpheus took a step forward, sniffing, and one step back again, careful to stay between his mistress and the night. Outside, the rushing sea-sounds of the leaves and the tortured creaking of bough on bough left her own ears unable to distinguish anything closer. But the old dog, whose nose was even better than her own, suspected something was in his path. He finally ventured through the doorway and went on for a few feet, as if carrying out a duty. Within a minute, he had retreated back inside, still growling softly to himself as he watched the dark.

Charlotte closed the door quickly, deciding that tonight she would set the heavy crossboard inside its iron brackets. Surely, it was only the wind. But an evening like this might frighten a Berkshire bear!

Taking up a candle, she went out of the kitchen through one of two doors that flanked the fire, into the main room of the house. She walked toward the tall clock at the bottom of a flight of steps. Pausing as she had done on most nights of her life, she patted its burled sidewood, before ascending the narrow stairs.

In the upper hall, her candle guttered beside a partially open sash, to which she reached out and brought down with an unexpected bang. As her heart pounded, she gasped at something that lurched against her skirts. But it was only the furry body of Orpheus, who had followed her silently on her way to bed.

The old dog jumped away when she whirled. He, too, looked around, wondering what was wrong. It was enough to make Charlotte laugh at the state of her nerves, but at the same time, it brought home to her how Jack Pennywort's curious story might be affecting her own mood—as well as encouraging fear in others. Apparently, even she was anxious to believe the worst on this windy, moonlit night.

When she was in her nightgown, she pushed back the covers, sat on the edge of the large feather bed, leaned to pat Orpheus's head, and slid her feet between the cool smoothness of trousseau linens.

It was then that she recognized a familiar scent—a sweet, medicinal aroma that came to her at odd times, and for no earthly reason. She felt the hairs on her arms rising. But this time, instead of knowing fear, she felt a sense of wonder and relief.

Horehound had been Aaron's favorite candy. Every autumn, she had made the lozenges he enjoyed whenever he had a cough, or when he worried about his throat after a day outside. Although she no longer made them, their scent was as vivid tonight as if Aaron stood by, clattering the candy against his teeth.

She knew it was impossible. But it wasn't the first time she'd noticed the penetrating aroma in this room.

She hoped it wouldn't be the last.

Blanketed by a feeling of protection and love, Charlotte settled back, closed her eyes, and slept.

Chapter 6

—◦ Wednesday

THE YOUNG MAN finished his breakfast at a brisk pace, slowing only to pour more heavy cream over the remainder of his porridge.

"You didn't hear anything before you went to bed?" Charlotte quizzed Lemuel Wainwright from a low stool, as she toasted two more pieces of bread by the fire. He thought, then shook his head. Lifting his spoon again, he remembered one thing.

"A ton of acorns fell on the roof, when the wind rose."

Charlotte handed him a piece of the hot bread to butter. "Nothing woke you later? Did you hear me coming home?"

The boy shook his head. As the sun crept into the yard, he watched the blue bolt of a diving jay, and heard it squawk. They'd already finished milking Mrs. Willett's cows. Before long, he would walk them out to pasture, through the crisp morning air that was just starting to warm.

The two had made their bargain when Lem still attended the village school run by Dame Williams, where he'd learned to read the Bible and to cast accounts as all boys were expected to do. His large family lived only a few miles away, but a brood of hungry mouths had made their oldest look around for another place to board, as soon as he could. All the noise at home had shown him the joys of solitude, so he had slept happily in Charlotte's barn for more than a year, coming inside only during spells of bitter cold.

Lem was still learning. But at fourteen his duties were nearly those of a man. On most days, he left the cows where he'd led them, and walked back across the meadow to see to the poultry, haul water, and take care of odd jobs, and to make sure the firewood was piled high. At day's end he gathered the herd back in, helped milk them once more, and then returned to the kitchen for supper and a look at a borrowed book—often with Charlotte nearby . . . always after a disapproving Hannah had gone home. Her own sons had better things to do than read, as she'd told him herself more than once.

"You didn't happen to see the old man on the road yesterday afternoon, wearing a scarlet cloak and leading a horse?" Mrs. Willett now asked gently.

Finished with his breakfast, Lem continued to cast dreamy eyes at the window while he shook his head. Soon, Charlotte told him what he'd missed by going to bed at sundown, as usual. She waited for his comments. He offered only a question.

"Should I take them to the river today, or back behind the orchard hill?"

"The hill, I think," she answered.

In another minute the boy disappeared, and soon

Charlotte heard the bell of the lead cow as it swung away into the fields.

Strange, how events that left one person unmoved could act like a burr on the mind of another. But then, people rarely asked Lem what he thought of anything. Maybe one needed practice, to answer. She would have to think about that.

Today, Charlotte took morning coffee to her south facing study, where sunlight and shadow from the maples outside leaped over polished wood, and along walls painted the blue of a robin's egg. Looking around the place she'd made into a sort of private nest, she ticked off her latest tasks on her fingers, listing them out loud.

The apples were finished; most of the herbs were gathered in and drying; the root cellar was well stocked with potatoes, turnips, and parsnips from the garden; the bees and their hives had been seen to, although they might need to be fed a little sugar water again, before the hard frosts. And the hay had provided more than enough winter fodder for the dairy herd—she was relieved at that.

No other areas seemed to need her immediate attention, so she turned her mind eagerly to what her neighbor had called the second part of observation. As she did, the miniature portrait of Aaron on her desk, the one painted before he left Philadelphia, seemed to stare directly into her eyes. Whether he would have liked it or not, she knew what he would have expected her to do. Charlotte leaned on the brocade-covered arm of her chair, and thought.

The old man had been there, and now the old man was gone. But was he really gone from the earth, or only the Boston road? Maybe the whole occurrence was nothing more than an involved jest—though it certainly seemed a poor one. This, she thought, had been Longfellow's first opinion. She wondered if he still stuck to it.

A further possibility was that Jack Pennywort, never

the most sober of men, had "decorated" (knowingly or not) whatever it was he really saw. But what *had* Jack seen, and *why*?

The stranger might, understandably, have taken fright at being followed up the road from the tavern. Perhaps somehow, cleverly, he had diverted Jack's attention before slipping away. But how? Unless . . .

Charlotte's next idea seemed even more fantastic, at least at first. The old gentleman might have *planned* to give a dumb show. What if he wanted people to believe he'd gone up in smoke and flames? What if he'd chosen to leave his past behind, to start a new life? Hadn't that been her conclusion as soon as she'd heard the story of the Long Island farmer and his servant? (She would have guessed that the figure she'd seen herself was well beyond affairs of the heart—but one never knew for sure.) Still, how fast could the bent old man have trotted off? And exactly *how* had he fooled the wary Jack Pennywort?

On the other hand . . . Jack wouldn't have had to be fooled at all . . . *if he had been a paid accomplice*. Or it could even be that Jack, perhaps with someone else, had actually done away with the stranger.

Steeling herself to the last unlikely possibility, Charlotte thought on. While Jack returned to the tavern to tell a story that might have been carefully planned, a larger man (perhaps this Frenchman they talked of?) could have taken the body, and the gold, and hidden them somewhere. But this really didn't seem plausible, either, considering what she knew of Jack's character. After all, here was a man who rarely did *much* wrong, and who lived in fear even of his wife! Nor could Charlotte imagine anyone else trusting Jack to share that kind of awful secret for long. But for a coin or two, Jack Pennywort *might* have gone along with something *less* than murder. . . .

Another possibility remained. There could have actually been an extraordinary occurrence of some kind, a phenomenon that had caused the stranger to be entirely consumed by internal flames. Some believed it possible, at least on Long Island. Spontaneous human combustion, Richard had called it. Was it credible? She knew that numerous forces in Nature were still largely unexplained. And some of them *were* deadly. For instance, even though Dr. Franklin had recently coaxed lightning down from the clouds, it still had a mind of its own, and might take a life in an instant.

Thinking hard, Charlotte recalled having once heard from Aaron's brother, Captain Noah Willett, about something called Saint Elmo's fire. Reportedly, this could turn a ship's entire rigging blue with an eerie, dancing flame that sometimes played on seamen. That sounded more like Jack's story. But this phenomenon rarely caused harm to those it touched . . . and she'd not heard that it made anybody disappear.

The bright morning sunshine had turned a tray of cut-crystal glasses on a sideboard into several miniature suns. For a few seconds, Charlotte stared into their brilliance. Then, realizing her thoughts had run away with her reason, she looked down to open a drawer and search for paper and ink. At first, because her eyes were dazzled, she saw nothing within. Just like the night before, in the kitchen doorway, when she'd been unable to see anything outside—

Light? Could that be the answer? Coming from the lighted tavern into the darkness would have made it difficult for Jack to see clearly. Further, blinding flash could have kept him from seeing the stranger in the scarlet cloak jump off the road and run away. Thinking again of lightning, she recalled there had been nothing like it in the sky the night before—just steady moonlight, which should have shown Jack what he expected to see . . . an old man running away. Still, if the stranger carried a source of light *with* him . . . it might be part of a reasonable explanation. The thing simply called for more thought, and more questions. At least, it was something.

Now, what about the other show, the one put on by Mary Frye? Could her fainting have had anything to do with the evening's first act? At any rate, it was probably fortunate for Mary that Nathan had been there to lead her out of harm's way. She wondered what excuses Mary had made, while the girl and the smith walked back to the inn. Well, she could soon find the answer to that easily enough.

Finishing her cup of coffee, Charlotte decided on a course of action. She wrote out a list of tasks for Hannah, who would arrive before long.

After that, she embarked on a journey of her own, not knowing that it would raise far more questions than it would easily, or safely, answer.

THE FRAGRANT HALLWAYS of the Bracebridge Inn were quiet when Charlotte Willett entered softly through a side door. No one, she was glad to see, was about.

Unlike the Blue Boar, the Bracebridge Inn was a refined establishment that frequently housed distinguished guests . . . patrons who would appreciate a good wine, a meal of several courses, and a bed without bugs. Its landlord was both tolerant and pleasant. He was also insightful, well informed on regional gossip, and more than a little fat. Together with his wife, Lydia, he was quite able to maintain the atmosphere of safety and comfort demanded by his clients.

Jonathan Pratt took a pocket watch from his protruding vest when Charlotte knocked on the door of the tiny room where he kept his accounts. At his urging, she came in and sat delicately.

"You're very early this morning, Mrs. Willett. Especially considering the hours I hear you've been keeping.

"I came to see if you could spare me a sack of coal," she began innocently.

"A sack of coal," Jonathan repeated slowly, pinching his nose.

"I ordered some to be delivered next month," she replied, "but the nights are already so chilly—"

"That you need some coal today. Certainly. We wouldn't want you to freeze. Would you care to go and make the arrangements with our smith, or shall I speak to him for you?" The innkeeper already knew the answer. He also knew that it could be extremely tiresome for a single woman in a small village to follow convention, but that it was often necessary if she wanted any peace. This was especially true when one entered the home of a stickler for propriety in others—like Lydia Pratt.

"I think," said Charlotte, after considering, "that it would be just as well if I spoke to Nathan myself."

"It would be a great deal simpler," the innkeeper agreed with a nod. He had met this grown and respectable woman as a forthright girl of ten, when he was the inn's new owner. In those days, Charlotte Howard came and went as she pleased, bringing pails of cream, butter, and honey, and taking home sugar, tea, or coffee beans for her family. Sometimes, she walked over just for news and conversation. Often enough, their talks supplied Jonathan with more information than he had to give. Over the years, he had watched his pretty young friend train her ears and eyes well, although not everyone was aware of her skills ... probably because she refrained from using what she learned to her own advantage, unlike so many others.

"I hear you and Longfellow were taking the evening

air across the river last night, along with half the town,"
Jonathan offered now in the way of conversation.

Charlotte watched the large stomach in front of her
rise and fall more quickly, while the landlord began to
wheeze rapidly, in the manner of a concertina.

"What you say is quite true. I wonder, though,
which of your many friends happened to pass this information on?"

"Nathan . . . coincidentally."

The landlord shifted his round figure, and settled
back into his chair. "You wouldn't be after Hiram's job,
would you? We all know he isn't much good at it, what
with the thread and button trade to look after. And you
know he only has a few months left."

"It's charming, Jonathan, that you'd consider a
woman as your next constable. And surprising."

"I don't know why. This isn't the first time a
woman's extra measure of curiosity—and your snooping
specifically—has captured my attention. And that's perhaps the foremost requirement for the job, wouldn't you
say? What surprises *me* is how someone can think her
fishing expeditions appear innocent, when her intentions can be read as easily as the *Boston Gazette*. I believe
I can be trusted. Is there anything you would like to ask
me, before you go? Perhaps about one of my guests?"

"Did he come back in last night?" she responded immediately, perching on the edge of her chair. Jonathan
was forced to smile, a little proud that with him Charlotte would still expose the exuberant nature she'd been
born with.

"If you mean Mr. Middleton, who took a room with
us yesterday, he doesn't seem to have spent the night. I
believe he rode in around three or four, bringing only a
small valise. His full name, by the way, is—or was, depending on which story you believe—Duncan Middleton. Of Boston."

"What about his horse?"

"Still here."

"Did you have any kind of feeling about him?"

"He seemed nothing special to me. Actually, we hardly spoke. I'm afraid I paid very little attention to the man."

"Then you probably wouldn't know why he was here."

"It isn't something I generally ask, being none of my business. Let's say I assumed he was taking a break in a short journey, since he made no inquiries about anyone in town, that I know of, and brought very little with him."

"I see. Do you suppose he may be dead?"

Jonathan sighed and regarded her more seriously.

"This morning, I sent word to his house in the city, letting them know that something might have happened to him. I expect to have a reply this afternoon. That's all I can tell you."

"Did he take any meals here?" Charlotte asked after some further thought.

"He arrived too late for breakfast, of course; no, I don't believe he took any dinner, either. And he certainly wasn't here in the evening."

"Jonathan—where do *you* think he is now?"

"On that, my dear, I will not comment. I have enough troubles, so I leave it to you and the other ladies to supply the most likely answer. You might ask Reverend Rowe for his help; he seems to enjoy that sort of thing. All I know is that I have everything that's left of Mr. Middleton, locally at least, and I wish that I did not."

"Oh! Jonathan, show me what you have!"

Having fallen into a hole of his own digging, the innkeeper groaned, then scuttled behind a familiar breastwork.

"Unfortunately, I don't believe my wife would approve."

"No, I suppose not. I wonder where Lydia is now? I would guess she's in your kitchen, making life difficult for your excellent cook. I only hope it doesn't affect the pudding, or the pie, or whatever you were planning to enjoy for your dinner this afternoon."

"That's probably what she is doing," admitted Pratt, after sucking in his breath. Then, he began to work his lips with annoyance at the thought.

Ponderously, he lifted himself from his squeaking chair, reflecting uneasily that here was a woman who enjoyed dangerous entertainment. From such a person, no one was safe—not even an innkeeper with the best of intentions.

Chapter 7

FURTIVELY, JONATHAN PRATT led Charlotte over a path of polished boards and dark Turkish runners, up the whitewashed back stairway and along the hall to a highly lacquered door.

"The Jamaica Room," the innkeeper whispered, while he turned the brass knob.

A glow of reflected light, along with a scent of beeswax and lemon polish, seeped out of the room as they entered. Pratt quickly closed the door. The morning sun that had warmed the air inside played on a multi-colored quilt spread between the bed's four turned maple posts.

The overall effect of the room was soothing. Late roses stood in a blown glass vase, sprigs of lavender peeped from beneath the pillows, and a watercolor of a bright Caribbean scene hung on one wall. There were several things that might have told someone something about the inn's owners and its staff. But there was very little of a personal nature to help explain the room's most recent occupant.

A traveling valise made of the best quality leather stood on a painted chest across from the bed. Charlotte at once crossed a figured carpet, and paused over the bag for only an instant before reaching down and undoing its clasp. Little inside surprised her. As Jonathan cleared his throat and modestly looked away, she lifted out a shirt, a pair of white silk hose and some undergarments, equipment for shaving, a box of peppermints, and a shoehorn. Duncan Middleton had apparently been a man careful of his things. Not many took the trouble to travel with a shoehorn.

"That's all," Pratt concluded nervously, "that, and his horse. By the way, one of my other guests told me the man is a merchant and a shipowner. This same guest took my message to Middleton's household this morning. Now, as I believe that's all that could interest you . . ." But before she could take his offered arm, Jonathan flinched at a footstep in the hall, though it soon passed away harmlessly.

In that brief moment Charlotte, too, was shocked by something unexpected—a bright flash of light from a place she thought odd. It had come from behind a small cabinet that stood between the chest and a corner. The cabinet held a large china wash set on its marble top. She moved closer, and pulled one edge away from the wall.

The innkeeper moaned softly when he saw the broken mirror. A few splinters reflected the daylight, while its thin wood backing showed through in spots where the glass was missing. More lay on the floor.

Charlotte bent and picked up a large shard with an edge of her skirt. An accident, hidden quietly away? She straightened as the innkeeper continued to voice his dismay.

"I've *told* her not to cover mistakes, but to just come and tell me when something goes wrong, so that it can be fixed! You'd think I made a practice of beating my household daily, when you see the lengths some of them go to. Some day, I pray she learns to trust someone, somewhere."

"Mary?" guessed Charlotte, setting down the jagged fragment.

"She's had difficulties learning her duties here, coming from a house where everything ends up on the floor. It's certainly not the first thing she's broken. And that's not all. What, in your opinion, is to be done with young women who are in love?"

Knowing no good answer, Charlotte simply smiled, and changed the subject.

"Jonathan, did Middleton give you anything on account?"

The innkeeper looked slightly embarrassed. "Now that you mention it, he did leave a piece of gold. A Dutch gulden, actually. I plan to give it to Reverend Rowe for his fund, as soon as I see him. In return, I'll ask him to send up a prayer, for a poor soul beleaguered by women."

Another show of gold! It seemed to Charlotte that Middleton might have taken more pains to hide his wealth in a small place like Bracebridge, where he was a stranger. In fact, the man seemed to have enjoyed displaying it. It was something to consider.

THEY HAD NEARLY made the top of the stairs when another door, next to the one they'd passed through, abruptly swung open, and a bespectacled man with a body like a sapling backed into the hall. He had a canvas pack slung over one shoulder and was dressed in a jacket and breeches of faded tweed. Looking up, he gave them a casual salute.

"Mr. Pratt!" The rich, full voice made the landlord wince and look about. "I've just come back for my spyglass. I was glad to have it with me last night—training it on the full moon. Quiet a performance!"

Pratt bowed silently, as if he'd had something to do with the lunar display, and seemed more than ready to move on. But Charlotte held him back. Sighing, the landlord did his duty.

"Mrs. Willett, might I present Mr. Adolphus Lee, of Cambridge. Mr. Lee calls himself a naturalist. He is writing a volume, so he tells us, on animal life in our region."

That, Charlotte observed with an inclination of her head, explained his robust complexion, the collapsing telescope he was securing, and two thick books that stuck out from between the laces of his knapsack. His eyes also told her he had a knavish nature. Here was a man who might enjoy spending some of his time peering into the lives of his own species as well as others, she decided with an interest of her own. And she especially wondered what news of Bracebridge Lee's telescope might have brought him lately.

"I'm always very pleased to meet a man of Science," she began with only partial honesty, for she had in fact met a good many with widely varying results.

"I'm honored, Mrs. Willett. Have you an interest in these things, too?" asked Mr. Lee. His spectacles sparkled, but he seemed to stare above them as he regarded her freely; quite carefully, he looked his new acquaintance up and down in a most methodical way which, scientific or not, made her ears feel warm.

"In some things. I was fascinated to hear what happened last night, across the river. Did you happen to see the mysterious fire yourself, sir?"

"Alas, no," replied Mr. Lee with a look of genuine

sorrow. "I went out walking, it's true, but toward the east . . . well over the next hill. They tell me now that I only returned after the thing was over. At the moment," he explained, "much of my work involves observing creatures who are most active at night. I got up early to go across the river this morning, though, to see what I can see; they say it isn't much after all. Frankly, I don't know what to make of the story."

"You're not alone there," remarked the innkeeper. "Your room, you know, is next to the one Mr. Middleton occupied."

Mr. Lee gaped with delight at the door to the Jamaica Room, as if it might still hold a potential conflagration.

"Did you . . ." Charlotte asked with polite hesitation, "speak with old Mr. Middleton yourself?"

"Oh, no—no. In fact, I hadn't realized! I did notice him when he arrived yesterday. Well, with that red cape, it would have been difficult not to. I'd come in for my lunch and was examining some of my findings, before taking a nap. That's when I saw him, through the window. I heard him, too, now that I think of it, when I awoke later. I believe he was speaking to our landlady, probably about the room—the sheets, I think, or something of that nature. As I remember, he had a rather reedy voice, and seemed a bit out of sorts."

"Lydia never mentioned it to me," Jonathan murmured.

"Well. If you'll permit me?"

Charlotte was taken by surprise when Mr. Lee picked up her hand and bent to kiss it soundly.

"Mr. Pratt," he continued after releasing her, "Mr. Pratt, I believe I will be staying for the remainder of the week, after all; I've found rather more of interest than I'd hoped for. If you'd be so good as to keep my room for me?"

He tipped his hat, twisted his lean body down the

narrow back stairs, and was soon out the side door below them.

"We get all kinds here, and I try to make everyone feel at home. But there's something I don't care for in that one," Jonathan said uneasily. "He's too sleek . . . like a weasel."

Charlotte laughed at the rotund landlord's unflattering observation.

"Something very supple, I agree," she replied, picturing for herself a high-swinging monkey in the wilds of South America. "How long has he been here?"

"Since Sunday night, this time. He's popped up before—stays a while, and then he's off again, with a few more butterflies in his bottles, or pickled voles, or whatever it is he's after at the moment. I can't say he doesn't pay me, and he certainly eats well enough, which adds a great deal to my profit. But I feel as if he might bring trouble with him, too, which is something I have very little desire for—especially now, with this other nonsense."

And with a pace far more subdued than the one used by Mr. Lee, Jonathan Pratt squeezed his way down the narrow stairway, while Charlotte stepped lightly behind.

IT WAS ONLY a few more yards to the second reason for her visit to the inn. Charlotte walked briskly back along the front of the red-painted coach house, past the stables, and on to the old log smithy.

A hammer rang rhythmically near the open doorway, as it bounced on a crescent of glowing iron. Upon seeing her, Nathan plunged the horseshoe into a pail of water where it hissed and steamed, and emerged a midnight blue. The smith set the shoe and tongs aside, and wiped his gritty brow.

Outside, Charlotte waited under a tall beech, near a thin horse grazing in the shade.

"Is this," she called, "Middleton's mount?"

"It is. And it would certainly be a piece of luck for the poor animal if Middleton never returned. Looks like he's been mistreated as a rule, even whipped to bleeding a day or two ago. Brought in tired and hungry, besides. But he's better now . . . the cuts are healing quite well. Keeping him out in the air helps."

Nathan flicked away a flake of metal from the curling hairs on his broad arm, and stood watching her run a hand over cruel ridges on the animal's side. There did seem, thought Charlotte, to be a large number of old wounds there.

"Maybe he was a bad horseman, more used to a carriage."

"Whatever his excuse, I consider it a sin to harm a good servant."

Charlotte agreed. Nathan, she thought, was a fair man, and not afraid to tell the world what he thought of it.

"Speaking of servants, have you any idea what caused Mary Frye to faint on the road last night?" she asked.

"Mary wouldn't tell me anything, but I expect it has to do with a long string of troubles. You must have heard the talk," he answered, walking out and squinting up at the clouds.

"Some. Nathan, you didn't take Mary out there last night yourself?"

The smith let out a groan.

"No, she went out alone. Probably to meet her young Leander—a lad called Gabriel Fortier."

"In that case, wouldn't she have been afraid of being seen by the miller?"

"They probably planned to walk on the east side of the bridge, down along the river path. Very private after dark, if you overlook others there with the same idea. As I imagine you might recall." He grinned suddenly, but a new idea soon sobered him. "I'd guess he wasn't waiting for her where he promised, because of the trouble over at the Blue Boar."

Nathan told her the story of the near-brawl he'd already heard twice that morning, from early customers. So that, she thought, explained the Frenchman of Jack's tale!

"I knew Peter Lynch was an admirer of Mary's," she admitted, unable to suppress a shudder, "but then, when I saw her fall into *your* arms, I imagined . . . something else."

Nathan's face grew grave again, and she asked herself if she'd touched a sore spot, or only a tender one. In his position at the inn, he'd seen Mary every day for a year now. He might view himself as her protector, from Lydia and from the occasional traveler who made overtures. Might it also have occurred to Nathan to hope for something more?

Charlotte remembered back to when the smith first made his appearance in Bracebridge, shortly after her own world had turned upside down. At the time, each of them enjoyed a new acquaintance who could talk about something besides the past. On her almost daily visits to the inn, they had frequent opportunity to discuss the town and its habits, as well as its visitors.

But all of this was before Jonathan married, late in '61. Since then, cold words from Lydia, and piercing looks when he transgressed, kept Nathan close to his forge, and away from the inn's halls and taproom. No one quite knew why Lydia Pratt treated those who helped her as badly as she did; it had simply become an unquestioned habit for them to avoid her, whenever possible.

Naturally, Mary Frye would have looked for ways to

get around Lydia, and she, too, would have enjoyed speaking with a man who had a sympathetic heart. She might even have encouraged him as a likely provider for her future. Until she met Gabriel Fortier.

Nathan was still thinking about the Frenchman, as well.

"Mary told me she met him in Worcester over Christmas, when she went home for a few days. You've seem him around since then, I expect, though you probably weren't introduced. He's a Neutral, you know."

So that was it. Fortier was one of the Acadians, some six thousand French-speaking British subjects who'd been transported from Nova Scotia. They had settled that island themselves, long before the British took over, and had remained there peacefully under British rule for fifty years. But in '55 it was feared they might turn against their rulers, especially if French troops were to arrive and give them aid. So the Acadians were offered a loyalty oath to sign. Those who refused had been sent south. Charlotte had seen one or two of a handful of families who'd settled near Worcester. They'd lived up to their name, and caused no trouble during the late war. But some of their neighbors still distrusted them because they kept to themselves, and held on to their own language and customs.

Nathan brushed at a horsefly that attempted to land on his sweat-beaded forehead.

"Once the miller got wind of it, he made quite a fuss. You know Mary's father promised her to Peter Lynch, once her indenture's over. That'll be in two more years."

"She's so young . . ."

"Lynch wanted to marry her last year, when she was only fourteen! But old Elias Frye balked. I suppose he saw more money to be made by sending her out first. Now, he's said he'll promise the next of her sisters to another of his friends, unless Mary's willing to accept the miller in the end. At least she's not beaten here," he added with a black scowl.

"Do you suppose her father hoped she'd find some-one better to marry while she worked here at the inn?"

"I think Elias did hope she'd find a man who'd offer her more. With or without marriage," Nathan added, averting his eyes. "But Jonathan, and Lydia too, I sup-pose, have kept her from that. So there's no reason for Mary to feel sorry yet."

"Except that she wants something that's forbidden to her. Is Gabriel Fortier a decent man?"

"That's hard for me to say. What I do know is there's a good chance that if Mary runs away with the French-man, Lynch will try to get her back, if only for appear-ances. There's no telling how far he'd go if he's made to look a fool before his friends—especially the ones in Worcester. A raw lot, from what I've seen."

"Then what's Mary to do?"

Nathan shrugged. He unmatted his damp, curling hair with thick fingers.

"They'll still need her father's consent to marry, or the law will be against them. But she has time—and who knows what might happen? Even though Lynch has of-fered more than was paid for her bond, Jonathan won't let her go."

The blacksmith grasped a branch over his head, and shook it until a few blazing leaves fell down.

"If there's one thing I hate to see," he continued, "it's a man who gets his way by frightening people . . . es-pecially young girls. But Peter Lynch isn't the only man who's been given a strong arm in this world." The smith looked up at his clenched fist thoughtfully. "And two years," he concluded, "is a long time."

"It might even seem like an eternity," said Char-lotte. In her heart, she felt another small bundle of trouble store itself in an empty spot, without waiting to be invited.

When she left Nathan a short while later (after arranging for the delivery of some coal she didn't need) her thoughts rushed and tumbled like water in a mountain stream. And behind her, the red iron the blacksmith returned to was again forced to conform to his will—this time, under even fiercer blows.

Chapter 8

ER WAIST WAS held straight by the whalebone under the tight top of her silk gown, but Diana Longfellow managed to lean back in her chair as she yawned with contentment. It was a thing Diana wouldn't have allowed herself to do in Boston, thought her hostess with a drowsy smile.

"They say life in the country flows like cold molasses," Charlotte's guest continued. "I must admit, I do feel unusually sweet today."

After a twenty-mile ride, Richard and his considerably younger half-sister had arrived with good appetites. Foreseeing this, Charlotte had asked Hannah Sloan to kill and pluck a large hen. Later, she had done the rest. The fowl had been pan-fried, and then simmered into a golden fricassee that included onion, carrots, and woodland mushrooms. Finally, it had been graced with a gravy of stock, egg yolks, and cream. This was offered up with a dish of potatoes and parsnips, mashed together and laced with butter and parsley. There was a small plate of boiled autumn spinach, as well. Everything on the table but the service and the salt, Charlotte thought with pride, came from her own farm.

They sat in the front room, across from a cold hearth. However, its chimney-mate in the kitchen crackled audibly, and Hannah perspired freely while she served them. The rich air that moved between the two rooms was further warmed by bright sunlight that had passed through a filigree of waving leaves outside. And a small current of Canadian air, delightfully fresh, was democratically allowed in under one of the sashes to mingle with the more fashionable variety inside.

Entertainment during the ample meal had come mostly from Diana, who now seemed in danger of becoming overheated. The young woman fanned herself while she continued to relate anecdotes of city life and its hardships, most of them imaginary. Once again, her brother was reminded of countless English fops, as well as certain home-grown ones, who were in her thrall, men who dressed in enough satins and ribbons to delight the heart of a child: perfumed men with embroidered speech, and too little sense to cultivate any interests besides the ladies, or food, or fashion, or possibly the regiment to which they belonged. They saw Diana, approaching twenty, as an heiress more than old enough to marry. But she remained undecided, while her suitors multiplied. Her brother imagined she enjoyed the single state too well to choose for quite a while. After all, it gave her an opportunity to hear a great deal of good about the charms of her person, as well as a chance to tweak the noses of those around her, both male and female. Not that he blamed her for that, he thought charitably, laughing at an anecdote she told. Still, he would have been happier to have her settled and out of his hands . . . if indeed she ever thought of herself as in them, which he rather doubted.

Charlotte watched and held her own thoughts, while brother and sister continued to banter and exchange tidbits about people and places. It was said that Diana Longfellow had the cool, proud nature one expected in a beauty, and she *did* often hold herself aloof from the world. But in several years of visits to Bracebridge, the elegant young woman's facade had developed a succession of small doors that she sometimes left ajar, to give brief views into well decorated, if rather disorganized, rooms.

This afternoon, her eyes, at the moment almost an emerald green, danced to the varying tunes of lively conversation, exposing a quick spirit much like her brother's. Until, of course, she wanted to be certain of having her own way. Then, Diana's dark lashes fell while she turned up a pretty ear under her elaborate auburn curls, exposing a long, downy neck. It was a pose that invariably led gentlemen, if not always ladies, to see things from Diana's point of view. Surprisingly, it often worked on her brother, as well.

Hannah brought in the last course—syllabubs made of whipped cream, sherry, sugar, and lemon mixed together, and floated in wine glasses on top of hard cider. While they sipped, the talk revolved again to the disappearance of Duncan Middleton. The subject had barely caused Diana's fine eyebrows to rise when it had first been mentioned earlier. It was not, she had implied then, the kind of thing one took much notice of, in her society. But now, she had apparently changed her mind.

"So," sighed Diana, watching her rings catch the sunlight, "our country cousins seem to become more imaginative every day. What phantasmal news! I suppose bursting into flame will become a new rustic style."

"If it does," her brother replied, "remember that it was invented by one of your own. Duncan Middleton is, or was, a wealthy Bostonian, as I believe Charlotte already mentioned."

"Oh, I've heard of Middleton—though I've never received him," Diana added, settling the matter of the merchant's standing. "But what on earth was he doing here?"

"That," answered Longfellow, "is something no one seems to know. Hardly anyone spoke to the man before he vanished."

Charlotte dipped a spoon into her glass. Stirring some of the cream into the cider below, she ventured into the stream.

"*I did* . . . as he was walking down the road, at about three o'clock—"

"You didn't tell me that last evening, Carlotta," interrupted Longfellow, "when you asked me to be your eyes."

"A lady need not tell a man everything she knows, Richard," Diana countered briskly, a trace of the new radical spirit in her manner.

"Although in Boston, many ladies do try," her brother retorted waspishly.

As this was not one of her few acknowledged faults, Diana maintained a haughty silence, but her eyes flashed at his irritating comment.

Charlotte attempted to smooth the waters.

"You didn't seem to be particularly interested in him, Richard, at the time."

"I see. Well, I'll admit that Pennywort's tale did strike me as being thin; in fact, it seems to have very little meat on it now. One might even conclude, '. . . it is a tale told by an idiot, full of sound and fury, signifying nothing.' "

" 'Out, out, brief candle!' " his sister warbled with a pleased look, for Diana had her own collection of the Bard. She continued to play the Thane's part.

> " *'Life's but a walking shadow, a poor player,*
> *That struts and frets his hour upon the stage,*
> *And then is heard no more.'*

"It sounds as if Middleton made quite a colorful candle, too," she concluded. "I believe I'd like to see where it happened. Would anyone care to go with me for an after-dinner promenade?"

"Perhaps, when I'm through," Longfellow replied moodily. He played with his glass and said no more.

"You said this all happened at twilight, did you not?" asked Diana. "It's usually a good time for imagining things. In fact, I've led a number of gentlemen to imagine things myself, after sunset. Now, this Jack person . . ."

"Pennywort," supplied Charlotte.

"Jack Pennywort. Is that *really* his name? Jack Pennywort may have also had a wee bit to drink last night, if I know my country ways."

"There's a thought," Longfellow exclaimed, and tossed back the last of his syllabub.

"And I am able to reason," Diana went on, pushing back her chair, "that he knew the old Bostonian had money. Well, you said he dropped a good deal of it on the floor, didn't you? In that case, I should be watching, if it were up to me, to see if Jack Pennywort has an unexpected windfall anytime soon. Although I suppose it might be natural for someone like that to squirrel it away for a good while, too. . . . Your provincials can be very secretive. And they normally spend so little, after all. I mean, one has only to *look* at them!"

Hannah, who had come in to tidy the table, held up her nose at Diana Longfellow's manners, and gave Charlotte a moment's fear for some of her best china. Meanwhile, Longfellow rose to his feet.

"It's your opinion, then, that Jack went out, dispatched Duncan Middleton, secured the gold, and put a sticky mess down on the road to support his ridiculous story. After that, he ran back—all within the space of five minutes—to alert the tavern. Oh, and at the same time he dragged off the body, as well. Tell me, what do you suppose has become of the corpse?"

"I wouldn't know. But if you can't find it, perhaps no one has looked for it in the right place. That often happens to me. Not with bodies, of course. I usually lose track of smaller items; but then I've been led to believe I don't have your larger talents in all things."

"*Has* anyone been looking?" asked Charlotte.

"Several men went out with Bowers this morning— we met some of them just over the hill, on our way back. Apparently, no one has seen any sign of him."

"As you'll remember, you said you would tell me your conclusions. Have you come to any?"

"I don't know," Longfellow admitted, tapping his fingers against the back of Charlotte's chair after he helped her to rise. He chose to ignore Diana, who had to help herself.

"But I would suspect," he went on, "that this merchant will show up somewhere, someday, when the time is right."

"Yes—and he'll be dead," Diana added darkly.

"What's the village view?" Charlotte asked. "Did you hear anything new last evening in the tavern?"

"The more pious believe whatever happened to him is God's will, and several agree it's probably a rich man's due. But, there was very little to go on last night.

Most suspected that Jack had imagined the whole thing, but that if he *hadn't*, it must have been some clever trick of the Frenchman's. Young Ned Bigelow, who reads, thinks Middleton is, most likely, a Rosicrucian alchemist in disguise."

"Who, and where, is this French influence you mentioned?" Diana interrupted.

"A man called Fortier—a Neutral."

"Oh, I see . . ."

"Fortier hasn't been spotted since he left the tavern after sunset, just before the merchant went out."

"Alchemy," Charlotte repeated uneasily, reaching for her shawl. "Do you think anyone might actually believe he used magic to make the coins?"

"Why not? Lead to gold is a very old idea based on wishful thinking, which is powerful stuff. And except for Jonathan, not many around here have a prayer of touching much gold *except* by magic. Curiously, still others at the Blue Boar were much more impressed by the scarlet cloak. There was some idea that Middleton was an Italian prelate on a secret mission, and that his hobble suggested cloven hooves under his shoes. By the time I left, when several rounds of rum had warmed them up a bit further, they were so carried away that even Pennywort looked worried, bobbing around on his poor foot. I thought they just might throw him into the millpond to see if he would sink or float! And they say we live in the Age of Enlightenment," Longfellow finished morosely, shaking his head.

"It seems to me that your villagers will never change," laughed Diana. She had by now collected her wrap, long gloves, fan, and a small umbrella to protect her face. Placing her veiled hat carefully onto hair that was puffed and rolled, she sent out a further appeal.

"Now, Richard, take me to the scene of this great

Happening, and I will at least be able to say that I saw the sights, when I was in the country."

It was a request delivered with admirable Boston spirit. With no more coaxing, her brother guided both of the ladies through Mrs. Willett's front door.

Chapter 9

UNDER A RIVER of dust running through the afternoon haze, a good amount of traffic moved along the Boston-Worcester road. Charlotte Willett, Richard, and Diana Longfellow were met and overtaken on their way down to the river by farmers driving wagons full of hay, sacks of nuts, and pumpkins. They also saw men on horseback and one or two in carriages, as well as a strong country girl riding pillion behind a young man, the sun giving an additional coat of bronze to her round, carefree face.

Diana watched the parade at a distance, but appeared not to notice as individuals came closer and examined her own defenses against dust, light, and air. A few politely lifted their hats. Others, dressed in homespun linsey-woolsey, simply stared at her dress. It made no difference to Diana, who had often remarked that she loathed everything about the country. But, she found it

increasingly difficult to appear uninterested when Charlotte and Richard went on with their discussion of Duncan Middleton, each discovering what the other had
learned about him, or hadn't.

"He seems to have been dressed as garishly as young
Hancock in town," was Longfellow's comment after Charlotte described her chance encounter with the merchant
more fully. "And you're sure he said nothing more?"

"Only two words."

"Not much like John there! Very pale, you say . . ."

"I guessed he wasn't used to being out. In fact, he
was so pale, he looked almost ill." Charlotte glanced
over at Diana's rice-powdered face, and again considered
the odd requirements of fashion.

"Curious," mused Longfellow. "Still, he did ride here
on a horse, which would indicate reasonable health."

"Incidentally, I met another one of Jonathan's guests
this morning, who said he heard Middleton speaking
with Lydia in the room next to his. The man's name is
Adolphus Lee."

"Interested in Nature, hair like a bird's nest, step
with a curious spring to it?"

"That sounds like the same man."

"I met him in Cambridge, last year. He'd come up to
study from somewhere . . . Connecticut, I think, and
seemed moderately interesting. He was studying botany
at the time," Longfellow added.

"Now it's animals."

"A Jack-of-all trades. I'll have to talk with him
again."

"He has a rather pretty brass telescope with him."

"Does he? Hmmm. Now, here's something you may
not know. It seems Middleton also carried a brown bundle of cloth with him on his last outing, wrapped with
string."

"That is interesting—"

"And the gold mentioned last night was not only gold, but *Dutch guldens*, according to Phineas, who got a fair look at a few of them."

"The old man gave one to Jonathan, too."

"Did he? Then he certainly wasn't trying to be inconspicuous."

"That was a great mistake, I'd say," Diana offered. "One shouldn't flaunt money even in Boston, at least without being in good company. Not even then, if someone might produce a pack of playing cards."

"Still," Charlotte ventured, "in the country, it's usually a good deal safer—" She stopped, remembering her own fears of the night before.

"I wouldn't be too sure of that," Longfellow warned. "I will say that Jack Pennywort, at least, seems an unlikely murderer. From what I've seen, he has the mind of a child."

"But you don't believe he's honest?"

"Should I, because he's childlike? You amaze me, Carlotta. I only say he doesn't seem capable of a great deal of criminal planning. Children know what's right and wrong, and should be held accountable. But a child might also be unable to keep itself from telling fanciful stories. Let's just say I believe Jack when he says he saw *something*. His story's too involved for him to have manufactured the thing entirely on his own."

"How do you propose to separate the grain from the chaff?"

"By scientific methods, for a start. Last night, I gathered up a specimen of the burned material from the road, which I'll attempt to analyze after supper. I've already sent to Boston for the necessary chemicals. They should be here by evening."

"For the love of *heaven!* Must you always find something horrible to do, every single time I visit?" came a plaintive wail.

In the midst of further argument on the subject between sister and brother, they reached their destination.

The spot was still marked by a dark, ominous ring,
for few had summoned the courage to touch it—though
more than one had bent with that idea in mind. Diana
glanced at it briefly with a handkerchief to her nose, and
then began to readjust her apparel. Meanwhile, Longfellow embarked on a vivid description of the previous
night for her edification.

During his monologue, Charlotte had some time for
uninterrupted thought. She carefully observed the lay
of the land around them. A running figure in a red
cloak would have had a hard time escaping someone's
eyes, unless they had been blinded by sudden bright
light, as she'd already surmised—and, as Jack stead-
fastly maintained. Jack had mentioned smoke that
had drifted off to his left. This seemed probable: the
wind had come from the northwest for most of the last
two days. He'd also mentioned that he'd stumbled on a
stone. Where was it? The road beneath her feet was
trampled smooth, and seemed free of anything larger
than a pebble.

She walked to the road's left edge, and looked off in
a line with the scorched patch. The elevated grade
sloped off a little more than two feet before it met the
level of the surrounding field. For quite a distance,
several kinds of wild grasses mingled with goldenrod and
Queen Anne's lace, and an occasional clump of weaver's
weed. She leaned down to examine the nearest clump of
barbed teasel heads on straight, prickly stalks, and gently
pulled something away.

Several wool fibers remained between her fingers.
They appeared to be bits of a coarse yarn, dyed a dull
brown. Charlotte tucked the strands into a handkerchief, which she slid back into her pocket. Then, she

looked more closely at the immediate landscape and its inevitable roadside clutter.

She soon identified some cheap glazed crockery, perhaps from a traveler's jug . . . a fragment of greasy newspaper long exposed to the sun, the wrapper of a sandwich, probably . . . a bit of discarded leather. But nothing more revealed itself in the vegetation.

She was about to stand, when a glimmer from something (a chip of quartz?) made her reach into the field grass, where her fingers recoiled from something sharp. She tried again. This time, to her satisfaction, Charlotte lifted up a piece of silver-backed mirror.

Unfortunately, further examination of her curious find was halted by a sound of warning that caused all three of the walkers to turn as a horse cantered up the road.

The approaching dark stallion, decided Richard Longfellow, was bred for racing. It occurred to his sister that the rider, too, was well-bred, although to what purpose would have been more difficult to say. The man appeared to be a few years younger than himself, Longfellow observed further, and under his tricornered hat he sported a finely made powdered wig, which set off his high complexion nicely, and made him look a very proper fool. Diana Longfellow thought the newcomer extremely well proportioned, particularly noticing a nicely formed thigh resting on an expensive leather saddle, and the masterful, gloved hand that guided the bit of his spirited mount.

To Charlotte Willett, the man before them appeared to be riding on a very high horse. She realized that this was a difficult position to maintain, especially should one have the misfortune to be galloping toward a fall. Or, she thought, observing him more closely . . . or, he might be a man of authority, who yet harbored a desire to dismount and walk among his fellows.

He was certainly dressed in style, in a deep blue coat with gold buttons, and silk smallclothes of canary yellow. His handsome black felt hat with a white plume completed the picture. As the rider reined in, the group on foot could see in his boots dark reflections of their own faces, while his horse pranced, snorting and foaming.

Longfellow—realizing what a dangerous thing it was to bring this nervous animal so close to the two women—stepped forward to protect them. The ladies, nevertheless, stood their ground.

The gentleman dismounted with surprising speed, to bow before the disapproval of at least two of the party below. He took the measure of the silent trio before speaking to Longfellow.

"From your interest in that mark on the road, I'd guess that this is the location of last night's curious incident."

His accent and manner confirmed that he was an Englishman, probably lately arrived in Boston. It also informed his audience that he came from the aristocratic world, especially noted, in the colonies, for its corruptions and prejudices. But there was also something more about him to hold one's interest—something that hinted at intelligence, and a character accustomed to measuring its surroundings.

"It is the place where *something* happened," Longfellow agreed. "I suppose you've come to gawk?"

"To gawk—and to find out what's become of Duncan Middleton. My name," he finally decided to tell them, "is Montagu. Captain Montagu. The Crown has appointed me to assist those who keep order in this colony and judge its wrongdoers: namely, the Superior Court of Massachusetts. For that reason, I have come out to investigate, and to discover whether this" (here he gestured to the road) "was some kind of country farce, meant to amuse your farmers . . . or whether it was some-thing else."

"We're not particularly fond of tomfoolery in the country," said Longfellow slowly, eyeing the other's feather, "especially when there's work to be done."

"You believe, then, that this was no more than a harmless annoyance?"

"That's not exactly what I said."

"What if some say it was murder?" the captain asked boldly.

"I, for one, say nothing of the sort. If you've come to investigate, Captain, then by all means, investigate—if you can find someone who has the time to stop and talk. As I say, most of us are quite busy at the moment."

The anger in Montagu's eyes warned Longfellow that here was a man who was not only proud, but per-haps even dangerous.

"As I can see," the captain replied with a grand sneer that made Longfellow grind his teeth. "However," Montagu went on, "I have spoken to Governor Bernard, and have his instructions. You and your countrymen are required . . . *requested* . . . to be of assistance, if indeed you can be of any help at all. Perhaps, as you say, that's beyond you. Still, someone here must know *something*, if only a very little."

Diana laughed at this, and favored Montagu with a look of her own, which she was glad to see had some effect.

"I presume," said Longfellow, "that you'll be leaving us shortly?"

Montagu shook his head with a twist of a smile.

"In that case, I imagine you'll be staying at the inn."

"I have arranged for accommodations there."

"Then I suppose our further meeting is inevitable. I'm Richard Longfellow, one of the local selectmen. My house is across from what you'll undoubtedly call your 'headquarters.' Captain Montagu, this is my neighbor, Mrs. Willett—and my sister, Diana, on a brief visit from Boston."

"Captain Edmund Montagu, at your service, ladies."

Longfellow grimaced at what he considered archaic and overlong formalities, as more bows were exchanged. His sister, on the other hand, used the chance to expose herself to better advantage, while she plied her lashes.

To Charlotte, who alone had no particular ax to sharpen, it seemed that something interesting and un-usual had occurred, beyond all of the verbal fencing she had just witnessed. Somehow, the attention of the gov-ernment in Boston had been directed toward tiny Brace-bridge. And although it was no great distance away, she had found that the people of that city were generally un-interested in the concerns of outlying places. So why should Montagu be here?

Middleton, of course, had come from Boston, and was a wealthy man. But why should the Crown send out one of its own to question them, and so soon? This cap-tain had even mentioned murder—with no body to indi-cate foul play.

Montagu's eyes had now come to rest on Charlotte Willett.

"I've been to see Middleton's room at the inn, and I've looked through his possessions there. I can tell you that these do, in fact, belong to the man. Also, the re-port of the clothes he wore here tallies with what his housekeeper saw when he left, two days ago. But none of this leads me to where he is now."

"*Two* days ago?" Charlotte asked with some surprise.

"He left his home on Monday morning."

This, Charlotte considered—and then she won-dered how much Montagu had learned from Jonathan, and if her own interest in Middleton's valise had figured in their conversation. Looking into his composed face,

Charlotte knew only that she would never be sure what Captain Montagu knew.

"Curious, isn't it?" Montagu continued. "Oh, by the way, his horse is also the genuine article—the one that's housed in Pratt's stables. I've seen it before, as well."

"I, myself, have seen Duncan Middleton before," said Diana, "and cannot explain why anyone would particularly care if he arrived late for dinner, or disappeared entirely. I can only imagine that you have some special reason for your interest. Something rather devious, I suspect. Am I right, Captain?"

"I have my reasons," he admitted. "But, unfortunately, they are reasons I am not at liberty to share."

"Not even in confidence?"

"Not even with you, my dear."

Diana's unclouded gaze turned stormy in an instant at this familiarity, coming from a man she had obviously failed to captivate. At the same time, Charlotte felt her natural sympathy for Captain Montagu growing.

"I fear the sun is beginning to tire me," Diana declared, "and I've developed a most *obnoxious* headache."

She turned to link Charlotte's arm in her own, and marched her friend away.

Longfellow watched Montagu remount his dark horse. He stood defiantly, his hands behind his back, while the nervous animal and rider turned in circles, prancing first clockwise, and then the other way around.

"After I've spoken to this fellow Pennywort," Montagu called down, "and the others who saw Middleton last evening, I would like to have your opinion. So, may I invite you and your party to supper?"

"I'm afraid we've been well filled for today."

"Then dinner, tomorrow."

Something in Montagu's tone made Longfellow agree, although he did it with a sigh.

"All right, then, tomorrow. I rarely refuse an invitation

to dine at the expense of the Superior Court of Massachusetts. I accept for the three of us—provided, of course, that
Mrs. Willett doesn't object. As to my sister, no one ever
knows what will capture and hold her interest next; but I
believe she, too, will come."

"Tomorrow then," said Montagu, touching his hat.
The horse tried to wheel once more, but its rider turned
it furiously, digging his heels into the animal's flanks until it leapt away through spurts of flying dust.

"WELL, 'MY DEAR,'" Richard teased his sister when he finally caught up with the two ladies, "what do you think
of our fine friend from Boston, and beyond?"

"I wish he were tied down to a plank in his chemise,
and then I would have some amusement with that silly
feather of his."

Longfellow's shock wasn't entirely pretended. After
some thought, he relayed Montagu's invitation to Charlotte, who accepted with pleasure. Eventually, so did
Diana.

"I presume Montagu won't get much help from anyone else, if he treats others in the style he's just
displayed," Longfellow added, to be soothing. Diana
appeared to relent slightly.

"At least it *was* a sort of style. And he appears to
have enough wit to be amusing. Maybe we'll be able to
play fox and hounds with him. What do you think,
Charlotte? Will Captain Edmund Montagu be good
sport for us?"

"What I'm wondering," replied Mrs. Willett, who
had watched Montagu clatter over the bridge and past
the village green, "is whether any fox could run far and
fast enough to escape, with a man like that on its trail."

Chapter 10

RICHARD AND DIANA Longfellow spent Wednesday evening at home with Cicero, where they supped on broth and bread. The young woman offered a further torrent of Boston observations, which the two men followed with keen, if irreverent, interest.

Much later, Longfellow retired alone to his kitchen, from which came curious noises and a variety of unique odors, until well into the night.

Across Longfellow's flower garden and up the hill, past Mrs. Willett's beds of herbs, Charlotte and Lem shared a simple meal of corn cooked into a hasty pudding, thinned with cream, and sweetened with syrup, full of apples and walnuts. When they had finished, the boy took a book from a collection that shared a shelf with some crockery, and lay down with Orpheus to read beside the fire.

Charlotte sat at a small table by the north windows,

prepared to use what light remained to answer letters from her relatives in Philadelphia. But while trying to put recent events into words, her thoughts raced faster than her pen. Finally, she put down her quill to light a candle, and let her mind play as it would.

In all probability, the whole thing *had* only been a kind of farce—or a sleight of hand intended to inspire awe and fear, to hide some unknown purpose. She was nearly sure of it. Maybe it was the old man's own business, as long as no law was broken. But a nagging sense of injury made her reconsider. Should Duncan Middleton be allowed to come into Bracebridge and arouse suspicion and anger . . . and possibly even create blame for a crime that had never really occurred? And what kind of man was he, to expose others to danger, for his own ends?

The piece of mirror and the strands of wool she'd found by the road were now in a cupboard drawer. Edmund Montagu might find them interesting. She considered getting them out again, and half turned in her chair.

For an instant, through a pane of glass, she saw a face—a white, featureless face that pulled back and disappeared in the near dark as she focused on the spot where it had been. Quickly, she looked toward the hearth where Lem read slowly and Orpheus slept forepaws and whiskers twitching.

Charlotte blew out the candle, then leaned across wax-scented smoke to peer into the night. Long black shadows in the yard ran from the newly risen moon, which had just begun to illuminate huge sunflower heads hung to dry on the barn. Could *that* have been what she had seen, without really seeing?

She turned back toward the fire. This time, she saw Lem and Orpheus watching her. The old dog rose and padded to the door. When it was opened, he loped off into the darkness, curious but still unconcerned.

She could let her imagination run wild, Charlotte told herself, as well as anyone in the village. Maybe she'd seen her first moonlit ghost, or a goblin! More probably, it was just another trick of smoke and mirrors, this time staged by Nature. She pulled a handkerchief from her sleeve and wiped her twitching nose. The night was getting colder. She felt herself shiver. Suddenly, the powerful surge of an idea, almost a premonition, threatened to overwhelm her.

She had good reason to believe that love sometimes found ways to reach back from the grave. What, then, about pain—or even a blazing hatred? Somehow, she felt sure that the old man she had seen on Tuesday afternoon was not dead. But her intuition also told her that something sinister had entered Bracebridge. What that something was, though, she couldn't say.

Tomorrow, she, too, would have a talk with Jack Pennywort. And then she would tell Edmund Montagu what she suspected about the old merchant, the mirror, and the brown fibers. After that, the captain could continue to search for Middleton for his own mysterious reasons. She would be quite happy to return to thinking about her farm, and her neighbors, and her own quiet business.

IN THE TAPROOM of the Bracebridge Inn, Edmund Montagu sat over a superior bottle of Madeira, after a surprisingly good supper.

No matter what lack of manners might be shown by the rural clods one had to deal with, he thought, their comforts here were substantial. At least the innkeeper was bearable. Even if he did have the misfortune to possess a bitter-faced, sharp-tongued wife.

Montagu still smarted from a mistake of his own, that had started things off entirely on the wrong foot that afternoon. But it had *not* been entirely his fault. Unfortunate that the horse had shied when he rode up the road toward Mrs. Willett, Longfellow, and his startling sister. He hadn't intended to alienate them from the very beginning—but that's apparently what he had done. Regrets mixed with shame had made him more formal, more officious, more galling, perhaps, than he ever meant to be.

If he hadn't borrowed Peabody's damned horse when he left Boston—did the thing never tire? Had he been a better rider himself, more than appearance suggested, it might not have seemed . . . he might not have needed to pretend . . .

Later, he'd been unsuccessful with the others, as well. Three of the village selectmen had called on him, but each had been busy on his own farm on the previous day, just as Longfellow had predicted. Although they wished him well, they had been very little help. The constable, a buffoon named Bowers, had scratched out a written statement, but beyond this he seemed unlikely to venture. He and two others had even asked Montagu to lead their local investigations. This he had agreed to do, temporarily, to avoid more questions about why he was there, as well as to keep these bumpkins from accidentally intruding into his own plans.

After they'd left him, Montagu had reviewed the notes in his personal journal. There, accumulated bits of information from the records of Boston and other places gave him a surprisingly long and detailed account of the elusive Duncan Middleton's past. No, it really wouldn't do, Montagu thought again, for his fellow inquisitors to follow him too closely, or too far.

As for Pennywort, the little man had obviously told his story so many times that anything he said now was bound to be out of proportion. Jack had no real explanation of his own for what he'd seen. Montagu had also

sent for and spoken to several others who had been at
the nearby tavern on the night in question. An uncouth
flourmonger had disclosed some interesting things about
a visiting Frenchman. A few had quietly mentioned
witches, speaking behind their hands. In fact, one had
insisted that his cow had been made dry by the evil do-
ings, and asked quite seriously who would repay him for
his loss.

But Montagu had drawn no nearer to discovering if
anyone might have learned where Middleton had actually gone, or if the merchant had employed any help in
going. And that was the heart of the matter.

Someone, he thought, must know more than he,
or she, had already told. Others might unwittingly
have seen something that would be of use to him. So far,
the only sensible people he had met in the town were
the three he'd offended, but he hoped to do better on the
morrow.

Montagu stuck to his conviction as he slowly sipped
from a long-stemmed glass. Someone knew something.
Eventually, someone would talk. In the morning, with
that in mind, he would start again.

Chapter 11

꙰ Thursday

THE YOUNG BOY who tramped the river marsh was buffeted and chilled by the night winds. But an object over his heart warmed him as he sloshed through the dark. The sun was an hour from the eastern horizon; no color yet showed in that quarter of the sky. To the west, through racing clouds, the boy glimpsed a dying moon. Its pale light was reflected on thin ice along the edges of the Musketaquid's leaden passage.

As the river mud pulled at his boots, Sam Dudley balanced his long fowling piece in one hand, and wiped his running eyes with the other. He made for a small lean-to made of stones and brush, used by village men when they were after waterfowl. It was a place where they could wait out of the wind for the light of day, and for the flights of ducks and geese that settled onto the marsh at sunrise.

This morning, Sam's thoughts were far from ducks

and geese. He had taken his gun in case anyone should be up to see him leave the house. And he had announced he'd be off early to go hunting. But it was not exactly the truth he'd told his mother the night before, while his father was still out drinking. He *had* gone hunting for something, but not for birds.

Once he was seated cross-legged in the rough hut, Sam's mittened hand reached up to the small deerskin pouch he wore around his neck, the one his mother had sewn and embellished with shell beads and given him at Christmas. If he played his cards right, what was inside held the answer to his future. It would be the first of many, he devoutly hoped. And he thought that if the Lord did help those who helped themselves, as his father and Reverend Rowe so often told him, then he was as close to heavenly assistance now as he was ever likely to get. Because it was for what he had seen and confronted on his own that he'd been paid his shiny gold piece two nights before—as well as for what he'd sworn he wouldn't tell.

Sam thought again of the way he'd doubled back and waited alone on Tuesday night, in the clump of firs just off the road, to see if goblins and witches might appear after all. He had seen someone come down from the woods, enter one of the village habitations, and converse with its owner. He had seen someone leave. Then, there had been the red gleam of the large bundle going down into the black water, weighted by a stone.

It was really all a joke, and only a matter of business . . . not life and death at all, as people had been led to believe. And *business*, he'd been instructed, was a thing that a man had to learn about firsthand . . . something he had to be on the lookout for, unless he wanted advantage to pass him by. Well, the sooner he learned how business worked, the sooner his friends would have to follow his example. He would lead all of them in building up profit, if things went well.

It was a little like a game, he decided, when you were not quite sure of the rules. It wasn't anything like education in the dame school, where an old woman taught you letters and sums. It wasn't like hunting or farming, either. There, what your parents or grandparents or uncles taught you would usually be right, and would help you do a job properly. No—this was a final initiation, he reckoned, into the real world of manhood, where you had to take things as they came and make the best of them . . . even without being sure if they were really *right*.

He frowned, but realized it was too late to reconsider. From the sweeping clouds above he heard the uncertain winnowing of a snipe, like the lament of a lost child. Maybe he would take the money he was about to make and go West, to start a new life. He'd heard—

Sam turned at a crackle of ice. Walking toward him on the river path came the one he had expected to meet. Gun in hand, the boy rose with a greeting.

The two spoke for a few moments, and then Sam was asked to turn and estimate the time from the slowly spreading glow in the eastern sky. He looked and considered, appreciating the long thin line of scarlet under a blanket of dark cloud. It wasn't yet dawn, but it was the closest thing to one the boy would ever see again.

An arm reached up behind him and came down swiftly over his face. Sam dropped the flintlock, as another arm tightened around his throat. He clutched frantically through heavy mittens. But with wool-covered fingers, he was unable to find a grip.

Then it was too late.

After the boy had lost consciousness, the other dragged his limp form to the river's edge. Sam began to revive when the cold water touched his face. But he was pushed down hard into a pool of icy mud and held there, until his body ceased to move.

Before leaving, the murderer tore off the deerskin pouch that hung around the boy's neck, opened it, and dropped the contents into one hand. There was a packet of powder, some extra shot . . . and a gold coin. Pocketing the latter, Sam's instructor in life tossed away the rest, and walked off briskly into the moonset whistling a tune—having no idea that what had befallen Sam Dudley had been witnessed by other eyes.

THURSDAY BEGAN FOR Charlotte Willett when she rolled over and patted Orpheus, who sat beside the bed. Thick clouds through her window promised a morning of bleak gray.

When she made her way outside just before sunrise, she found the yard had been transformed. Bushes and trees had been stripped of their leaves. The tall oak over the barn shuddered and wailed in protest under a renewed high wind, while in front of the house, the tops of the younger maples swayed and bent in supplication. Clutching the hood of her cloak against the fierce gusts, she bent forward and hurried on.

When Charlotte opened the small side door to the dairy, it was wrenched from her hand and flung against the low building's clapboard side before she quickly claimed it back. Once she had pulled it shut from the inside, she stood gulping the sweet aroma that surrounded her.

Her eyes soon adjusted to the subdued light that came in through a line of small windows. Facing her was a long row of dark, empty milking stalls. Hay had already been put into the continuous manger, at the edge of the flagstone aisle where pails were cleaned and stored. Lem had taken care to fork the manger full the evening before, working from a pile of loose hay near the double door. That door was still barred on the inside. She removed its crosspiece from large metal supports. In a few more minutes, her young helper would lead the herd in from the barn. Then they would both begin to fill the wooden pails with warm milk for her buyers—and for their own breakfast.

This morning, Charlotte felt oddly uneasy in the darkness, despite the quiet, and the familiar animal smells of the barn. She picked up one of the empty pails, removed its lid, and examined it for cleanliness. Then, a small sound that seemed to come from the middle of the dairy made her look up. Whatever it was, it stopped almost before she could be sure she'd heard it; turning her head, she could hear nothing more. It might have come, she guessed, from the trench against the wall where the cows soon would be driven in. (Occasionally, a rat from the fields decided to move in as well, until Orpheus changed its mind.) Even though the hay inside tended to absorb noise, she could still hear the wind's sharp play. Perhaps something had fallen onto the roof. She tilted another bucket and began to examine its depths, sniffing.

And so it was a complete surprise when the door she had recently entered blew open again and banged repeatedly. Shock caused Charlotte to lose her balance and fall back. Happily, her descent was cushioned by her heavy skirts, as well as the pile of hay behind her. She had just begun to laugh, when she quickly stopped. It had taken only a moment for her hands to feel the hay she had fallen into, truly feel its texture, its depth, and above all its unexpected warmth.

Charlotte stood up with a movement almost as sudden as the one that had seated her. Quickly, she turned around to stare at the dim depression. Very recently, someone else had been on that same hay, out of the wind, hidden in quiet sanctuary.

The door banged again. She remembered the careful way she had latched it against the wind when she came inside. Then she heard a cowbell, and in another second a tall figure opened one of the double doors behind her, fastening it back so that the black and white animals he escorted could amble slowly to their stalls.

A look of surprise grew on Lem's face as he took in her dazed expression. And then, once more and with a *whoosh*, Charlotte Willett sat down.

"IT STILL MAKES me fidget," said Hannah Sloan later in the morning, "to hear of that Frenchman around here somewhere, up to no good." She pulled a pile of bread dough into another large fold, and pushed it down again into the low wooden bin in front of her. Charlotte looked over from the table where she tallied her accounts.

"But you never felt that way about any of the Neutrals before."

"We never before had such strange things going on! An old man disappears ... and Emily Bowers says Hiram's had reports of all sorts of trouble—from a child with fits, to a horse with the staggers. Though I suppose such things aren't unheard of during the best of times. But as to this Frenchman, why, what if he *was* to lurk around, waiting to prey on a woman alone? Worse yet, what if one of the local men was to find him here?" Hannah added with a darting look.

Charlotte was glad she hadn't mentioned the unknown guest in the diary that morning. But had Hannah seen him go?

"Mary Frye seems to think Fortier is an honest man,"

she finally answered. "Good enough to marry, according to what Nathan tells me."

"When does a girl who's lost her heart have any control over her head? Oh, I don't blame Mary—she's all right. But *he's* an angry one, from what I've heard. And I'm not sure but he's got cause to be. The way they were all treated, sent off from their homes like blackamoors, by His Majesty's fine governor! If you ask me, it'll be a long time before the Acadians forgive our king. Who's to say war won't break out all over again? What if the French should decide to come back? I say I'd rather know where the Neutrals in this country *are*, and keep my eye on them."

"It's my guess that Gabriel Fortier isn't here. He probably went home to Worcester," said Charlotte, skirting complete honesty.

"He might have . . . but with Peter Lynch pressing Mary for an answer, I doubt if the Frenchman's in any mood to go far. No, he only left the Blue Boar to avoid the miller. He's still around, somewhere."

"But do you really think he's guilty of any crime, Hannah?"

"Well, he was the first to leave, just in front of the merchant that night . . . though probably all of them had the same idea of lining their pockets," Hannah said with a sniff as she thumped the stiff dough. "Still, I don't see how anybody could have robbed the old man and then made him disappear that way, without being seen. But *somebody* must be guilty of something! I hear from my boys," she continued, "the talk at the tavern, and the apple press, and the mill; and they tell me stories have come back from Concord and Worcester. Some are saying crime goes unpunished in Bracebridge, that ungodly things have been happening, and that it's not safe here anymore. Well, the way our own men are starting to talk about taking the law into their own hands, it may be all too true!"

MEANWHILE, OUT IN the barnyard, Lem drove a maul deep into a section of pine. While the report of his hammer still rang, he stooped with a practiced, easy movement to throw the split pieces onto a small mountain of winter firewood. As soon as he saw Charlotte approaching, he greeted her with a broad, lopsided grin.

Admiring his work and enjoying the scent of the fresh slabs, she returned his silent greeting. More than the countryside had grown during the summer, she realized. Nearly to full height now, Lem seemed to have found a new grace, after a year or two of tripping over his feet. There was a promise of strength in his broadening shoulders, too. It was a fair trade for the sweat he put into his work.

"Autumn's the busiest time for most of us," Mrs. Willett began cautiously.

Lem agreed with a nod, wiping his face with a sleeve.

"So many jobs to take care of all at once. Do you think you could use some help this afternoon?"

He gave her a curious look through a lock of hair, and rubbed his hands over his upper arms, making no guesses.

"I only thought," Charlotte added, "that we might share some of the work, and a little food, with someone less fortunate."

He had to agree with that—and to admire again her kindly way of thinking.

"Like Jack Pennywort," she added.

Now he looked at her with plain astonishment. He shifted from one foot to another, waiting to hear more.

"I have an idea he'll be sitting in the Blue Boar, still

telling his story. I'd like you to go and ask him to come here in about an hour. And Lem . . ."

He brushed some wood chips from his sunburned arms, still listening.

". . . if you should happen to see, or hear, anything that might be interesting . . . you might tell me about it when you come back. If you'd like to talk. Over a cup of tea."

He gazed at her with new concern. Maybe he should think about asking Mr. Longfellow to drop in and speak with his mistress more often. Mrs. Willett must be desperate for someone to talk to . . . however impossible that seemed. Though it *was* pleasant to know she considered him a source of conversation. But he was apparently on a par with Jack Pennywort there. Lem wished he knew what he should say.

"I know what I'm asking may seem strange," she went on, after trying to read his look, "but you see, I'm going out to dine later, at the inn. And I was hoping to learn more of the truth from Jack about what's been going on. More than he's thought to tell—or has been willing to! I need your help to get him here," she finished in a rush.

Ducking his head, Lem shoved long arms into his coat. He was glad she couldn't see the expression of pride on his face. Pride was a thing that looked silly enough, he often felt, on an older man's face, let alone on a younger one's, who should know better. That his mistress might consider him a man now, too—that she had even asked him to join her in a conspiracy of sorts—was something he'd have to think about.

I'll do my best, his final nod signified. Then he walked out quickly to the main road, to be further tousled by the gusty afternoon.

Chapter 12

WHEN LEM WAS gone, Charlotte continued through the yard, looking forward to a visit with Richard Longfellow, reasonably confident he'd be hard at work on matters of interest to them both. Under bright autumn clouds she forced her way against the wind, across the fading gardens.

She eventually found him in his greenhouse, built against a rock wall that formed the south side of his barn. Cicero sat in its small vestibule, surrounded by late roses on trellises set against the costly glass walls. He appeared to be engaged in pleasant contemplation, with his eyes closed. Through the inner door, Charlotte could see Longfellow bending over a workbench.

"His experiments with the love apples?" she asked the old man, stopping for a moment to share his limestone seat.

"He'll kill us all, before he's through," Cicero growled after a yawn.

"And Diana? Where is she?"

"*Miss* Longfellow is out this morning. She let it be known she didn't care much for the smell last night, and that she was going to the inn to recover herself."

"Ah," said Charlotte. Diana's current visit was proceeding along the lines of most previous ones.

The glasshouse was a breath of July in late October, due to the rich soils and growing things within its humid warmth. Southern honeysuckle twined next to pots of Appalachian rhododendrons and bare stalks of South American orchids. This year, a raised bed of West Indian pineapples grew below a permanent and fantastic palm, next to an orange tree in a Spanish jar. Several other beds were generally used for starting annual vegetables, or for growing strawberries.

Near the back, a multi-flued Baltic stove sat ready to protect the tenderest plants on the coldest nights, though the stone wall behind it stored sufficient heat from sunlight to keep the frost away during much of the spring and fall. Each morning, after late September, large felt shades which were attached to the rafters were rolled up, while at sunset, they were unrolled again and overlapped for more thermal protection.

Longfellow frequently explained the workings of the place to Mrs. Willett, and to anyone else willing to listen. And many did. The building and its contents, the result of years of research and experimentation, were the wonder of the neighborhood. This was especially true during the snowy months. Then, favored guests might be asked in for a meal taken *almost alfresco*. Others had to make do with peering in from outside.

"How are the *lycopersicon*?" Longfellow's neighbor inquired with interest, joining him as he bent over clusters of dark green leaves that partly hid several glossy red fruits.

"These inside are still doing nicely," he remarked, picking back some errant stems with his long fingers, "but I don't believe *pomodori* will ever be seriously grown for food here, the way they're being cultivated in Italy— even though they're one of our own natives. I've found they make an interesting condiment, with some spice added. But I predict it will never take the place of oyster sauce."

"I seem to remember you telling me that all of the solanaceae, including these, can be deadly."

"Some parts of them . . . and the nightshades, in particular. Although even they can have their uses. I'm sure you're aware that Italian women often court love, and death, by widening their eyes with *belladonna*. Insanity is another frequent effect. In my opinion, however, it's tobacco that's the worst of the family. A wretched, dangerous thing to foist onto society. Our plantation friends are happily leading the rest of us to perdition, solely to line their pockets."

" 'It's good for nothing but to choke a man, and fill him full of smoke and embers.' "

"Hmmm! Old Ben Jonson was perfectly right. Though he neglected to mention snuff! However," Longfellow went on more cheerfully, "the potato of the same genus seems to be a more healthful success." He dropped the tomato shoots he held into a basket of clippings meant for the compost heap outside, and sniffed at his fingers.

"And so, we conclude that this family is both dangerous and beneficial, like so many others. Which reminds me . . . is Diana enjoying her stay?" Charlotte asked politely.

"About as much as she ever does. If my sister can find something to gossip about, or someone to admire her silks and scents, she's reasonably happy. If she's forced to live simply like the rest of us, however, she dies a thousand deaths—and few of them are quiet ones. Still," he added, reconsidering, "she's certainly good at creating amusements."

"As we'll no doubt discover tonight. Do you think she'll bite Captain Montagu, or will she be content simply to mumble him?"

"We'll have to wait and see. But let me tell you what else I've discovered, through my scientific inquires. I've been reviewing what's known of combustion, to help you with your interest in this absurd affair out on the highway."

"And?"

"Not an easy task! No one knows the exact components of combustion. The theory of phlogiston maintains that this element, and another called calx, must be present in all combustible matter—the one escaping in the burning process, the other remaining as a residue. Although personally, I agree with the ideas expressed in the work of the Englishman Boyle, and his pupils Hooke and Mazori. They believed that the mixture of air and the volatile sulphurous parts of combustible bodies causes them to act one upon the other—and, that parts of both ascend during combustion, generally accompanied by smoke and flame, leaving a final, unburnable residue behind."

"Oh, yes?" Charlotte commented, frowning.

"It's also known that a volume of air in a sealed chamber is diminished by the process of combustion— and that once diminished, this air will no longer support burning, if one should attempt to ignite *another* object within the unopened chamber. It's curious that the same effects may be obtained by enclosing an animal in the space, and allowing it to breathe until some necessary part of the air is removed."

"But that's—"

"This leads many to assume that *combustion* and *respiration* are actually the same thing. Although during respiration, of course, combustion is not observed. Still, if the process were to be altered by yet another cause, then the effect of actual fire might conceivably result from respiration in an animal, or even in a man—perhaps even in our Mr. Middleton. No one yet comprehends such a cause, if one does exist. The original research was done nearly a century ago, and it's high time for some additional progress to be made. Once we know exactly what this substance in the air necessary to combustion *is*—

Longfellow threw his arms apart and breathed deeply of an unknown source of inspiration.

"But as yet," countered Charlotte, "we have no good reason to suppose that the man just *burst* into flames—"

"There are precedents, as well as similar things in Nature. For instance, we all know that spontaneous combustion of certain things can occur when they're carelessly stored, especially when damp—and that they will sometimes explode into flames after smoldering for a while. Hay, coal, logs—it's not uncommon. A farmer considers this to be a naturally occurring process, without truly understanding the cause. That is why he dries his hay before storing it in his barn."

"I think we can assume, though, that Mr. Middleton was neither damp, nor confined in any particular way."

"But *something* might have altered his original state, in a way that could be repeated in a similar situation, at another time—something *perhaps* linked with his natural respiration."

"Then you do believe it's likely Duncan Middleton was consumed in some kind of fire?" asked Charlotte cautiously, fingering a stalk of rusty chrysanthemum tied to a stake of cane. Longfellow smiled his sweetest smile, and let his true conclusion out.

"I believe nothing of the kind," he said firmly.

"None of this is actually relevant to the matter we're looking into. I find it much more likely that substances far simpler than the bodily tissues of Duncan Middleton were burned on Tuesday night."

"I've wondered myself if it might not have been something like Greek fire."

Longfellow stared at her blankly. He had planned to explain the rest of his idea after Charlotte had been suitably impressed with its beginning. Instead, he was forced to pause and admire the fact that she'd reached his own conclusion without him.

"My library isn't a very new one," she reminded him gently, "but it's well stocked with the classical authors, and I do find some time to read."

"Come with me."

"I've read of its historical use, of course," she managed as he towed her by the arm past a startled Cicero, and then on toward the house. "The Byzantines created Greek fire for warfare, didn't they? And it was later taken up by the Crusaders, I think who used it against the Saracen. But whatever the secret formula was, I seem to remember it was activated by contact with *water*, so I don't quite—"

"Sometimes it was," Longfellow shouted back over the wind. "But with the substitution of phosphorus, which burns when exposed to *air*—"

"—a kind of land bomb could be made! Oh! But what exactly is phosphorus?"

"A highly unstable element, isolated in Hamburg in the 1660s, derived from . . . well, at any rate, isolated. It burns first with quantities of white smoke—very useful for camouflage, by the way—and then with a clear blue flame."

He slowed for breath, and looked up. The faint cries of Canada geese filtered down from the sky, as a flock passed overhead like hounds running after prey.

"Phosphorus may be kept," Longfellow continued, "in a vial of turpentine, or even water. If the vial is broken and pieces of phosphorus exposed to air, they should burn very nicely. If you add to this a bit of charcoal for a base, some pitch, sulphur, and a dash of saltpeter, then you have a fine, portable package full of fire, smoke, and the smell of Satan at your disposal, waiting to be tossed down. The intense heat would of course cause the glass to melt while the rest burned, making the entire thing *appear* to have occurred without a natural source!" Reaching the house, he opened the kitchen door.

"I tried it last night with the materials I had delivered. And here you see the results. Nearly identical with what I removed from the road."

Charlotte stared at kitchen surfaces scattered with glass dishes and tubes, and at a large, flat rock covered with black material, on the floor in front of her feet.

"So that's how the effect was created," she finally managed, while her nose wrinkled at the lingering stink of combustion. "I certainly hope *your* information, with what I have to tell you, will bring us close to a solution."

"Then Captain Montagu will be forced to conclude that there are more than roots and vegetables inhabiting the country! But, I'm still in the dark, Carlotta, when it comes to explaining how Middleton managed the *rest* of his trick. How do you think he kept Pennywort from seeing him, as he ran away?"

"I do have a few ideas—"

At that moment there was a banging of the door, and the sound of silk brushing along the hall. Diana Longfellow flounced into the room, the fashionable hoops at her hips causing her skirts to swing barely within the bounds of safety. It was eminently clear that the morning had seen another triumph, and that it, too, was soon to be related.

• • •

"YOU SHOULD BOTH be glad," Diana began vigorously, "that *someone* cares for the safety of your little village. I've just come from expressing my thoughts on recent matters to Captain Montagu."

"Captain Montagu?" her listeners asked together. Diana paused to examine a fingernail.

"Could it be," inquired Longfellow, "that you've re-judged the man, and found him human after all?"

"As I say, Captain Montagu—who, by the way, was particularly glad to speak with someone respectable, and intelligible. I've been making myself very useful . . . un-like, he informs me, certain others in the neighborhood."

Charlotte and Longfellow waited for more.

"He's apparently having trouble discovering the facts from the local rabble, so I related to him what I had heard of this monster Pennywort, stalking innocent trav-elers and then covering his crimes by spreading tales so *absurd* that your rustics were bound to believe them. I convinced the captain that this blackguard Pennywort should be arrested immediately, and locked up some-where until he can be tried."

"Diana," her brother asked at last, smoothing back his hair from his forehead, "have you ever seen this char-acter you describe so vividly?"

"No," she had to admit. But she kept her chin high, inviting a challenge to her powers of intuition.

"Well, Jack Pennywort is shorter than you, he has a deformed foot, his mind is about as active as that of a possum that's been hanging at a cider bung—and to lock him up would deprive a wife and four small children of the rather dubious livelihood they now enjoy. While it may be fashionable for some in your world to ridicule and torture Nature's unfortunates, following perhaps the great courts of Europe, it will hardly do to taunt such vic-tims of misfortune *here*. We should all, I think, have a lit-tle more compassion than that."

Much of what Longfellow said was, of course, a lie; laughing at Pennywort had been a sport enjoyed by a good portion of the village for much of their lives, although it was not especially popular among the more enlightened. But Diana's eyes lost some of their snap as she listened, and considered.

"Besides," her brother added, "Charlotte and I have already concluded it's very likely Middleton isn't dead at all, but only gone away. It seems he himself was the inventor behind his rather theatrical demise."

"What! But how? And *why*?"

"Why? How should I know? But the fact is that you are out to hang an innocent man. My experiments, which you objected to so heartily last night, prove that the merchant *planned* to disappear. And so he did."

"Yet doesn't it seem strange," Diana asked very slowly, savoring each word, "that Middleton, a prominent, wealthy merchant, would leave everything behind—even his ready funds?"

"Do you happen to be acquainted with the man's lawyers? Or have you acquired a crystal ball?"

"No, I heard it from Edmund— from Captain Montagu," she corrected herself, smiling at the memory of his confidence. "The captain informs me that his own inquiry leads him to suspect foul play, as none of the man's wealth has been touched. He's clearly dead, Richard."

"Middleton probably arranged to have his property sold by an accomplice. Or else he plans to claim it himself, when he's good and ready."

"Then we'll see," was all he could get in reply.

Charlotte, though surprised by Diana's information, also remembered suddenly that she had something else to attend to.

"Shall I call for you around four?" Longfellow asked as she lingered for a moment at the door.

"No . . . you go on. I'll join you at the inn. Right now, there's someone—well, I'll tell you about it later."

Leaving her neighbors to continue their family fray, Mrs. Willett made her way back across to her own safe and ordered kitchen. She felt greatly in need of a strong cup of tea, as well as a few moments for quiet thought.

Chapter 13

HANNAH SLOAN WAS peacefully shredding cabbage for pickling when the kitchen door burst open and Charlotte bustled in, with Lem trailing close behind.

At first, the young man only stood, and gulped. Then, quite abruptly and to the amazement of both women, he began to pour forth a description of his visit to the Blue Boar. While she listened, Charlotte filled a green glass goblet with buttermilk, from the jug on the cellar steps. It was as if, she thought, a lava cone had been lifted up, and a new Vesuvius born.

"Right away, I found Jack Pennywort sitting there, the way you said he'd be. When I told him you'd offered to give him work for a day, and food, he called for another pint of ale. I doubt," Lem added, pausing in his narration for a moment, "if we'll get much work out of him when he comes, or if he'll have much money left from what you pay him, after Mr. Wise collects what he's owed."

"Why on earth do you want Jack Pennywort coming *here?*" Hannah cried out, her cap shaking. "The man's liable to make off with anything that isn't pegged in or nailed down! The last time he worked for Julia Bowers, and her husband the constable, no less—"

"Don't you think offering a kindness to someone in need is worth our taking a chance?" Charlotte interrupted softly, a quiver of unclear origin in her voice. Hannah swallowed a further protest for the moment. But her expression showed that she was far from convinced.

"Then," Lem leaped on, apparently enjoying the new exercise, "there was a noise at the door, and Peter Lynch came in with several others, who could barely keep still while the miller spoke. He told Mr. Wise that he'd been harboring a thief in Mary's friend, the Frenchman, and then Peter and the rest demanded to see the Frenchman's room."

At this, Hannah stopped her muttering to listen.

"And did Phineas agree?" Charlotte asked quickly.

"They pushed Mr. Wise aside before he could even answer, and started climbing the stairs. I went up behind, and when I got to the door, the farthest one, I saw Peter Lynch rise up from behind the bed. And he was holding a gold coin! It was a Dutch one, too, he said, a gulden; then he passed it around for all to see."

"No!" Hannah breathed softly.

"He made Mr. Wise admit it was exactly like the ones he'd picked up from the floor on Tuesday night, when the old man dropped his purse."

Abruptly, Charlotte felt her neck begin to tingle. Jonathan Pratt had been given one coin. She'd already guessed there was a second one about, and would soon see if her theory was right. Yet here was a third! And this coin promised to do far more harm than the others.

"After that, the miller shouted here was proof Gabriel Fortier killed the old man for his money. He said when the Frenchman came back to get his clothes, Providence made him drop a piece of the treasure he'd stolen. Some of the men talked about finding the Frenchman and giving him a taste of the whip, before they gave him over to the law. But since nobody knew where to look for him, they finally settled on going to hand the coin over to Mr. Bowers."

"It's clear what Peter Lynch thinks to gain by it," Hannah interjected, her face livid with indignation. "It's the girl Lynch wants, and he's out to get her, no matter what he has to do!"

Charlotte felt the color drain from her own cheeks, and put her hands to her face to warm them again. Neither she nor Hannah believed the miller's accusation to be true. But how had Peter Lynch come by the coin? Could it be that her recent conclusions were wrong? What if the merchant really *had* died after all—been killed, or at least abducted? If his gold had been taken from him by force—but in that case, where could the body have gone? And why would a man like Peter Lynch risk suspicion by producing such a coin, *if he had actually killed Middleton for it?* No; it was all too ridiculous. Especially when she herself could offer an even simpler explanation for the appearance of the second coin—and show there *was* no third.

"The main thing holding the others back is that no one's found what's left of the merchant," Lem finished, gingerly setting down his empty goblet. "But as soon as someone does, several of the miller's friends promised to help him turn Bracebridge upside down to find the Frenchman, and then hang him from a tree!"

It was a terrible thought. Yet it was something at least a few of the local folk, whose families had recently suffered at the hands of the French, might easily do.

"I only hope they don't become tired of waiting," Charlotte said bleakly, as she slowly brought a canister of black tea down from its shelf, and took the kettle from the hob.

THE TEA WAS half consumed when Lem insisted on going back to his hammer and maul. Shortly after that, Jack Pennywort knocked lightly at the back door. Looking somewhat the worse for wear after his few days of fame, the little man sat and took a cup with plenty of sugar, along with a heavy slice of nut loaf spread with butter.

Between mouthfuls, Jack attempted to explain again, in language suitable for his new audience, what he'd seen and done on Tuesday evening. Outsized and outnumbered by the two women, he also fidgeted, and kept a close watch on the door, even as he accepted a second piece of buttered bread. And yet, thought Charlotte, Jack managed to answer the questions she put to him with at least the appearance of honesty.

"Then you actually saw the gentleman's figure moving for a few moments through the flames. But you didn't see him again afterward?" she asked as she leaned forward on the table, while Hannah kept her eyes on Jack from across the room. Pennywort had obviously tired of telling a story he no longer dared (or cared) to embellish. By now, it was far from fresh, and had begun to shrink a little, which seemed to have caused it to lose some of its flavor. Still, as long as the ladies were interested. . . .

"That's right," he agreed, staring blankly at a pair of candlesticks that gleamed on the window ledge. "As I say, I saw a pale flash, and another gleam, like, after that. Then came the flames and smoke. After the smoke had gone off and the *blue* fire rose, I looked far and wide, but I saw no sign of anybody there at all."

"And at your feet?" Charlotte asked, watching him intently. "Did you think of looking there?"

Jack said nothing, but regarded her with a wary expression.

"You say the road was brightly lit by the flames?"

"There was light, and shadow, of course," he answered finally. " 'Twas too bright to look at the fire for long."

"And then you saw the man waving through the flames—now I can't seem to remember, did you say these flames looked to be red?"

"First regular, then blue, I said, mistress. And no one can tell me different, because I know what I saw!" he added hotly, sensing that she might be trying, as others had, to confuse him.

"I'm sure that's so," she answered with another offer of the bread plate, which Jack again accepted. "Earlier," she went on calmly, "I heard—well, they say you left the tavern on the heels of the old man, and went off in the same direction. But I never heard anyone say why you decided to follow him—"

Jack winced suddenly. Clearly, a piece of nut had affected a rotten tooth. As Charlotte watched with sympathy, he readjusted the morsel with his tongue and thumb, and then went on.

"Because I expected he might get into trouble, as the Frenchman had gone off before him, and we'd all seen that gold."

"Extremely sensible. And thoughtful of you, too." Her kind words were rewarded with a crooked, gaping smile. "But you didn't actually see the Frenchman outside, did you?"

"He could've been waiting behind some trees. Soon

as I saw the old man slip down from the road, that's the first thing I thought—"

"Down from the road?"

"He went off toward a clump of fir trees. It was the ale, and the cold—that's what I figured. Not worth mentioning. When he came back, I followed him a little longer, until I saw the rest."

"So, it's not very likely that Gabriel Fortier was in the trees, or somehow made Mr. Middleton disappear a moment later."

"Could've had a charm—maybe put a spell on him, some say. I don't know about that myself."

"More tea, Jack? I'm sure you'll wait for another cup, with more sugar? Now, I wonder if I can recall what it was I heard about a brown bundle the merchant carried. . . ." she added to herself, getting up to spoon more leaves into the warm pot.

Jack had by now begun to massage his jaw. When Charlotte poured the hot water, she saw him reach into his breeches pocket for something, probably an oil-soaked clove, which he expertly nestled into the source of his pain.

"What *about* his bundle?" Jack asked after a bit more thought.

"Well, did he have a bundle when he came back to the road?"

"I never said he had a bundle."

"But he had, before. I'm sure Mr. Longfellow told me he was seen with one earlier. Did you go back to look for it in the trees? Perhaps some time later?"

Pennywort gazed around, consulted with his crooked foot, and finally replied: "Next morning, I did. No harm in that, is there?"

"None at all. A man has a perfect right to be curious, I'd say. Even a woman. What did you find? Something mysterious?"

"All I found was string."

"String?"

"Aye, string. Only a piece of string. Not worth mentioning, you see."

Jack had ceased to see the point of retelling the
story, especially its pointless details. He began to stretch
on his chair, looking toward the backyard, his tongue
working its way around his mouth to catch the last of his
small meal.

"Do you know, Jack," said Charlotte, almost done
with him, "you tell your story so well that I can practically see it happening. You first saw two glimmers of
light. The first was just a pale flash. And then, a gleam.
Now, I can almost see that gleam, and it looks to me like
a coin catching the moonlight—maybe a piece of gold
dropped carelessly onto the road? One you might naturally bend down to pick up, when you reached the place
where it fell?"

"What if I did?" Jack answered, puffing himself up
with sudden fright. "I'd be an honest man still, though
there'd be them as would say I stole it *all*, if I said I
pocketed the one! Why, I only come *here* to do an honest day's work for you. But some might say it looks like
you be trying to trap me—"

"I do believe you only picked up what had been
dropped . . . but dropped for a very good reason. Of
course, you know the main reason I called for you is that
our woodpile needs another splitter, and that's certainly
warm work I'm sure you'll enjoy this cool afternoon.
Only tell me one thing more—aren't you a close friend
of our miller, Peter Lynch? Could it be he took the coin
you'd found away from you, afterward, for reasons of his
own?"

The little man had gone as white as fresh bleached
linen. Whether it was the pain of his tooth again, or a
fear of something greater, she couldn't be sure. But he

held so strongly to his story that Charlotte was finally forced to let him go, after he'd repeated it all once more, at top speed.

"I got nothing out of it, God help me!" Jack concluded shrilly. "Naught from the miller, naught from the old stranger! Naught but *string*! I'll give you no more talk now, and no work, either! Not this day, I won't."

With that, Jack Pennywort hurled himself lopsidedly into the yard, leaving his gentle inquisitor to tap her chin thoughtfully, while Hannah Sloan put down her broom.

Chapter 14

IT WAS NEARLY four o'clock when Charlotte Willett put the final touches to her costume, and slipped a few small objects into a pocket that hung beneath her petticoat. Then, taking up her skirts, she left her bedroom and moved carefully down the narrow stairs.

Before slipping wool over silk, she stood for a moment by a long glass at the door to take stock of her appearance. The clear blue of the dress she'd chosen certainly complimented her eyes. The pinned-in square of wide lace that lay over her bosom covered it modestly, but not entirely, which was the expected effect. And although there were no preparations on her lips or cheeks, her natural high color (and steady exercise) kept her looking healthy, capable, and consequently interesting, without attracting overdue attention. It was a pleasing thought.

She gave the small stays at her waist a final, chastening

tug. Then, she swept her cloak over all, and fastened it with an ivory scrimshaw clasp Aaron had obtained for her from Captain Noah Willett. At last, she felt ready.

Pulling up her hood, Charlotte opened the door and gave a final thought to the supper she'd laid out in the kitchen for Lem. After that, she pointed the toes of her Morocco shoes (the ones Longfellow had bought on his travels) toward the inn, and braced herself as she felt a waiting hand of autumn wind come up to accompany her.

AT THE SAME time, Lydia Pratt looked into another mirror, adjusted a loop of black hair, then touched the beauty mark she had recently applied to her cheek— quite possibly to confound her husband, for Lydia rarely adorned herself at all.

"But you told me you *hadn't* spoken to him," Jonathan Pratt reminded his wife. They stood alone under the large chandelier in the front hall, watchful for interruption from without, or within.

"I told you I didn't see him arrive; *that's* what I said. As for being in his room, I'd simply forgotten about it. Don't you think I have enough to worry about? After all, it's Mary's job to see to their needs once they're settled. But she was nowhere to be seen when he called, and I remember now that I had to go up instead. Of course I had strong words for the girl, as soon as I found her!"

"But you did say—"

"It wasn't anything of the least importance—only something about the sheets—now where *is* that girl? I suppose she's gone off again, with dinner to serve to the captain!" Lydia Pratt's looks were always sharp. But when she frowned, the tightness of her mouth made her jaw stand out even farther, and her black eyes glinted under what sometimes looked like one thin eyebrow set atop her narrow face.

"Lydia . . . dear . . . Captain Montagu was naturally anxious to hear the details of your conversation, when I mentioned Lee told me one had occurred. Naturally, I was somewhat embarrassed that *you* hadn't mentioned it when the captain questioned you. I told him you'd probably overlooked the whole thing . . . but you might have been the last one ever to speak to Middleton, if you don't count his ordering a tankard of ale. If Lee hadn't said anything—"

"Which is another thing!" His wife seemed about to go on in the same vein, but abruptly decided to hold her tongue. "If and when I get a chance," she began again with better composure, "I'll speak to the captain. Wasn't it enough today that you brought that great green *thing* into my kitchen, to scratch up the floor and the walls with its horrible claws? On top of that, you actually seemed to expect me to dispatch it!"

"Sweetheart, it was quite chilled and slow when I left it there. Besides, you wouldn't have wanted it brought dead all the way from Boston? It might have given us all the flux!"

The sea turtle had been a bargain, Jonathan went on. It also kept him from asking more about his wife's whereabouts on the day of Duncan Middleton's disappearance, for which *she* was grateful—to the turtle, at least. If anyone should ever find out what she'd done . . .

Nervously, Lydia stepped back as Jonathan moved past her to open the door for a guest he'd seen through a tall window, hurrying up the walk.

Charlotte Willett entered with an entourage of swirling leaves. When she'd lifted her hood and unfastened the clasp of her cloak, the landlord took it from her shoulders with a flourish.

"Your two gentlemen are already in the taproom," he told her, gesturing to the familiar passageway.

"Good evening," Charlotte said formally as she made a small bob to Lydia, expecting a similar courtesy in return. Her greeting was answered only by a stiff nod as the landlady turned and walked away. Jonathan shrugged his apologies to an old friend. He was about to offer her his arm when they saw, through the multipaned window, something else that made them both stand still.

Now Diana Longfellow approached the inn. She was accompanied for the sake of convention by Cicero—who could barely keep up with the young woman's flying figure as it moved precariously across the road and up the stone walk, buffeted by sharp gusts that caught her widespread skirts as if they were sails.

Once the door was safely closed behind her, Diana's wave indicated to Cicero that he might go along. He gave Diana a withering glance as he headed toward his usual spot in the taproom, but smiled to Charlotte, approving of her quiet air and her sensible lack of hoops.

"I really don't know how I manage," Diana began huskily after the landlord, too, had retreated. She sat and bent down with a small gasp and several jingles to replace her leather shoes with silk ones, taken from a banded box she carried. There were tiny bells, Charlotte noticed with astonishment, on the upper part of Diana's costume, bells which could be flounced casually to call attention to one's bosom. She wondered if fashion (if that was what it was) had taken a backward look to the Elizabethans, or if it had simply gone mad once again while trying to change the future.

"I told Richard I'd be ready in just a few more minutes, but he insisted on coming ahead by himself, and left only Cicero to help me here. What if I'd been blown down in the road, or run over by a dung cart? I really don't believe he would have cared."

"I'm fairly sure his appetite would have suffered."

"Are you? Lord! I must catch my breath before I move." Sliding the shoe box under her chair, Diana straightened and took a small bottle from an embroidered bag. She removed its tiny cork stopper, and Charlotte leaned closer, drawn by a wonderful aroma.

"*Parfum parisien,*" said Diana, dabbing a bit from finger to neck before offering the bottle to her friend. "I'm afraid the first application has been blown away."

"It's a wonderful scent," Charlotte responded truthfully. And the little container was a thing of beauty, she noted, turning it to catch the light. Made of black enameled porcelain, the bottle had the design of a red-and-blue dragon winding its way around the surface in a highly effective manner. It was one of the best of Diana's frequently presented discoveries.

"It's new, of course—Captain Harper lately brought a few in to Providence. He maintains there are only a half dozen in existence! The scent's the product of a French firm, but the bottles come from Canton, according to Lettie Hitchbourn. She brought two of them back with her to Boston a few days ago, and sold one to me. Sold, mind you. Lettie would have made a wonderful merchant. That woman has a heart of gold. *Minted* gold. Most of us have more interesting things to do, though, than to think of money all day long."

Charlotte's smile came easily. She knew that Diana played to whatever audience she had—but also that she had a great deal more knowledge, and perception, than one might think. It was a secret that by now the two women shared comfortably with one another. Unfortunately, her elegant looks and withering babble were greatly admired by many town acquaintances, and were what Diana generally enjoyed displaying. It was something that caused Mrs. Willett to be thankful for her own lot in life.

"Well, I think I can manage now," Diana said at last. The two began to walk toward the smell of pipes and wood smoke, and other comforts.

The room they entered was hardly full, but Charlotte recognized several faces that turned to watch their entrance. She smiled toward Adolphus Lee next to the fire, who dipped his shining spectacles with an energetic bow (although his eyes were clearly on the lady he had yet to meet). Apparently, it was too rough tonight even for naturalists to be abroad, Charlotte decided as she inhaled the heady aroma of spirits and foods. Two slightly rumpled and bewigged gentlemen sat beside Mr. Lee; they, too, paused in their discussion, and bowed in tribute to the ladies, causing Diana to look with some pleasure in the opposite direction.

Charlotte soon spotted Longfellow and Edmund Montagu, perched, she thought, like owls in a nest. In fact, they sat in a small area at the top of a few steps, set off by a wooden divider—much like the officers' deck of a ship. They, too, rose from their chairs as the women approached, and helped them to glasses of Madeira from a silver tray as soon as they were comfortably arranged.

It was obvious that the gentlemen had been engaged in a heated discussion. Even Diana's charms failed to divert them for long.

"As I say," Longfellow rejoined, "leaving ten thousand troops here after the end of hostilities was sheer folly. Today, most sit in New York—but where will they turn up tomorrow? You'll keep these men on short pay, and what's more important to your own interests, they'll be kept from looking for employment back in England. But the war is over. I don't see why anyone thinks we'll be happy to pay your soldiers to retire with *us*."

"They may be kept busy enough. Pontiac and his

Ottawas are setting fire to much of the West as we speak. In Virginia, Pennsylvania, New York—you must know that every one of our forts, except for Detroit, has fallen to Indian—"

"—not a great surprise, considering the quality of the officers you've been sending—"

"—predation, which leads me to suspect that even here, near the coast, you may one day be glad you help pay for British troops. And I say *help* pay, sir . . . no one expects you to assume the entire cost of their upkeep. But England has already been saddled with tremendous debt, paying for your last defense—"

"So in return, you arrange to have redcoats prowling our waterfronts."

"*And* your frontiers! We may not have seen the end of French intrigue. Your merchants might also be glad of someone with money to spend, ready to consume your truly amazing surplus of foodstuffs."

"While your customs men begin taking away our sea trade! We read lately in our pamphlets and papers that the Crown plans—"

"You would do better with a few less of those! From what I've read they're all filled with lies—"

"—to go along with this idea of Grenville's to raise further revenues with an enforcement of the molasses tax, and several new ones. Yet we have always sympathized with the king's needs, and raised and delivered our own revenues. When we are asked with some consideration—"

"Asked?" Montagu appeared to hardly know whether to smile or frown.

"Well, then, is this new way supposed to please us more? Let us levy taxes in our own assemblies, just as you do. After all, it's the right of every British subject to be *requested*, rather than forced, to supply the Crown with funds. *And* to be represented directly in Parliament, most of us will maintain."

"Do you *really* think you and your colonists here are on equal footing with the people of England—those by whom Parliament is chosen?"

"Certainly; we're English, and men too, and yet you treat us like children!"

"The analogy has some justice, surely, when you look at—"

"Do I look like a child to you?"

Charlotte had heard much of this before, on otherwise enjoyable evenings spent in her neighbor's study with a decanter of canary wine, or perhaps some old French brandy that had slipped through the blockade. Now, she looked down with more interest at the hand-lettered bill of fare lying next to Longfellow's tapping fingers. Diana, too, read it over when Charlotte placed the card telling what was to come between them.

To start, a green turtle soup—something Elizabeth, the inn's cook, born and bred in Marblehead, would know how to do to perfection. Then, roast goose with oranges and oyster sauce. (The goose would be one of Lydia's ill-natured pirates who hissed and grumbled around her kitchen door. It would not be long lamented.)

Goose was to be followed by a wood pigeon pie made with celery and walnuts—an excellent idea, Charlotte decided, for her own purse as well as Jonathan's. The cook would use not only a great deal of cream from her dairy, but a large quantity of butter as well. And a 'made' dish like this one of game birds would be, for Jonathan, mostly a matter of a little shot and powder, some seasonings, and a simple, flaky flour-and-lard crust.

With the birds would come a dish of greens and gravy, as well as one of fresh roasted beets, peeled and buttered hot from the coals. And finally, rum-baked spiced apples, and a cranberry custard. Edmund Montagu had arranged to give them a good dinner, although it was something less than a feast. Still, it was a fine offering to occupy an odd afternoon, even without the further amusements Charlotte saw ahead.

"—and this Dutch gold piece that Bowers tells me was found by the miller ..." Montagu went on, "of course, you realize it indicates the West Indies, or Surinam. Either way, it means smuggling."

"That wouldn't be surprising, since we can't get enough molasses from Britain's islands to keep our distilleries going. And just how do you expect us to keep buying goods from you without hard currency?"

"Distilleries which in turn supply rum to trade for slaves. A very nice business," Montagu added haughtily.

Here, Charlotte managed to interrupt. She had never seen a slave in Bracebridge, but she had heard about Dutch gold very recently.

"Were you speaking just now about the coin from Gabriel Fortier's bedroom at the Blue Boar?"

"We were, ma'am," Montagu replied.

"By the way, Captain," Longfellow interjected, "are you conducting a search for Fortier now?"

"Not at the moment. But with the insistence of half the town, someone may soon have to organize one."

"I believe Mrs. Willett is about to try to convince you to clear Fortier's name. Indeed, we talked about a mutually discovered theory this afternoon, which sheds some light on your mysterious merchant. But I won't stand in her way. I'm sure she'll tell it beautifully."

Seeing the eyes of all the rest upon her, Charlotte gathered her courage, took a deep breath, and began.

"I propose a succession of events. I think they might help to explain Jack Pennywort's adventure, and the part played, I believe, by Duncan Middleton in his own disappearance."

Montagu tilted his head briefly, and again raised piercing eyes to hers.

But Charlotte's beginning was delayed as Jonathan Pratt came to inform them their first course was ready. They all rose and soon climbed the main stairs, before they were ushered into a small private dining room with its own fire, several candles, and a large linen-covered table. Here, Lydia Pratt met them as well, coming from the kitchen end of an interior passage, and carrying a heavy tray.

The party sat as a bread basket and a large tureen were transferred to the table. Then, as they broke open crisp rolls, a thick green soup was ladled into bowls. It was tasted and pronounced delectable, having just a hint of amontillado to set off its richness.

Finally, when they were settled in comfortably, Charlotte recommenced the story she and Richard Longfellow had pieced together, recapping what was already known, and adding even more.

AT TWILIGHT (SHE recounted), following the tavern's usual talk and a threatened brawl, complete attention was drawn by the spilling of a bag full of gold coins. Shortly afterward, Fortier got up to leave; soon after that, the merchant followed. Jack went out as well, driven by habit, curiosity, and very possibly a touch of greed. He would provide the necessary audience for what was to come.

When Middleton saw that he was being followed, he quickened his steps, drawing away from the crossroads and the tavern as he climbed the lonely road to Worcester. It was a quiet night, and a suitably mysterious and auspicious one. Jack Pennywort must have wondered where the stranger could be heading as he left the safety of the village—wondered, too, if he himself would be seen following. Unexpectedly, Middleton left the road and made his way to a cluster of nearby fir trees, presumably to answer a call of Nature. This left Jack with more time to think, and to grow afraid.

When Middleton returned to the road, the brown bundle he had been carrying had vanished . . . because it was now worn under his cloak! The brown "bundle" had actually been a second long garment which he had planned to put under the first, covering that garment's bright red lining. The merchant again hobbled uphill, followed by a limping Jack, who vowed to himself to return later to examine those trees. (When he did, he found only a piece of string.)

"Excellent! Something I hadn't thought of," Longfellow interjected.

Before long (Charlotte continued carefully), Middleton approached a clear spot he'd already chosen in the elevated road, where nothing obstructed his view for a hundred yards to the sides, and nearly as far ahead and behind. Next, he took a small piece of mirror from his pocket, which came from the one broken in his room at the inn. (Although he himself broke the mirror to obtain the useful fragment, he knew it was almost certain that a servant would be blamed.) Now, he used this fragment of mirror to look back, and saw Jack still there. It was the reflection of the rising moon in this glass that Jack saw as a first faint flickering, up near the old man's shoulders.

Now, Middleton held something else in his hand—a gold coin. This he dropped into the road; then he took several more steps. In his mirror, he saw Jack stoop to pick up the shiny object. It was time to bring the performance to its conclusion.

Here, Charlotte paused for breath and took a sip of

wine, while her audience waited in silence with anticipation. Thus fortified, she continued.

"Perhaps pretending to stumble on a stone, in case
anyone was watching, Jack bent to pick up the coin.
This gave Middleton a chance to twirl his cloak so that
the dull brown inside was on the outside. Then, he threw
a small bomb, previously concealed in his bundle, onto
the road. It was filled with specially prepared ingredients;
Richard can tell you how it was made. As it burst into
flames, Middleton waved his arms and leaped about behind the fire. When enough smoke came to hide him
completely, he jumped down onto the south slope of the
road. He lay flat in the weeds with the dull cloak over
him, knowing Jack would be partially blinded by the
smoke, the light, and by the tears that heat, and fear,
brought to his eyes.

"After he recovered from the first shock, Jack looked
far and wide, but could find no one. He was still unable
to see what was under his own feet! Then even the blue
fire that followed the first began to die away, and before
long, darkness returned. This time, it brought even more
than its usual terrors. So Jack turned and ran down the
hill to alert the tavern, and to find safety again among
his friends. After a few more moments, Middleton got up
and went about his business, probably making for the
woods to watch the further proceedings—apparently no
longer under the constraints of an earthly body, and yet
not quite ready for heaven, either!"

In hindsight, it was a simple and effective plot.
Charlotte was pleased to hear her explanation immediately declared quite likely, even before she took from her
pocket fibers from the brown cloak, and the piece of mirror, which she'd found beside the road. She also took
pains to point out that if Lynch had wanted to get his
hands on a gulden with which to incriminate Gabriel
Fortier that afternoon, he had only to look to his smaller

friend, for Jack Pennywort would likely have told him he had "found" such a coin.

Longfellow next gave them a recipe for the making of something like Greek fire, which Edmund Montagu followed closely. Against all expectation, the British captain felt a growing respect for these new country acquaintances. Not only did he appreciate the methods of Mrs. Willet and her neighbor, but he had to agree with Longfellow that in one or two ways, at least some Americans *were* something more than children—even though their political opinions might still be those of innocents.

He had information of his own to add to their story, which he knew would surprise them. He also saw a rare chance to join in an amusement with a fair amount of safety, without risk to his own mission. Perhaps it was the combination of the quantities of sharp cider he'd taken earlier, as well as the wine, and the warmth, and even the company, that led him to feel an unaccustomed glow in this cozy place. He would have to remember to be careful.

At this juncture, the soup was removed while a crisp-skinned goose was brought in, along with the dishes of vegetables.

"All of which probably means," sighed Diana as she helped herself, "that I was wrong about Pennywort. And that you, Captain Montagu," she added with obvious satisfaction, "were misled by the merchant into believing him dead, when he's not dead at all! But *why* did Duncan Middleton go to all of this trouble, simply to disappear? And more to the point, where on earth is the irritating old man *now*?"

Chapter 15

THAT'S WHERE I begin my tale," Montagu started, laying down his knife while the others gave him most of their attention.

"If I may," he continued, "I'll tell you the story of a young man intended for the army, who found that company not entirely to his liking, once he'd bought his way into it. While there, he met too many other 'second sons' who were at loose ends, engaging the enemy rarely, gaming, drinking and fighting each other far too often. Understandably, many of these fine young men got themselves into trouble. A few others, like myself, pulled them out when we were able—smoothed over the rough spots . . . hid what sins we could with appropriate compensation—and were rarely seen or thanked directly.

"It has for some time been my way to follow those who find themselves in trouble. More recently, I have watched those who may be *creating* it . . . against the Crown's interests. Which is why I came to Boston."

"Then you are a spy," Diana breathed softly, with a dazzling smile.

"If you like, although if I were, I'd scarcely tell you so. At any rate, I assume that we are all on the same side! Let us say that I'm the tax collector's helper, at least temporarily."

"That should make you a popular fellow," Longfellow commented, after barking out a dry laugh. "Why *do* you want to tell us about your business?" he asked point-blank, staring hard at Montagu's unreadable features.

"Largely because you seem to know a great deal about one part of it already. I'm sure I needn't ask you not to broadcast what I've said, or am about to say. Why make my life more difficult than it is?" the captain asked rhetorically. "But I believe this affair will soon be over. Until it is, I can tell you something about Middleton that could help you settle things in your own little community, when I am gone away tomorrow."

Pausing, Montagu glanced at Diana, but she only picked delicately at a wing joint with her teeth. He went on, addressing her brother.

"I've been watching Duncan Middleton for six months. He is a shipowner, as well as a merchant who deals heavily in cargo taken to and from the West Indies. And I, too, believe that he is very much alive!"

"But you told me . . ." Diana began to object. Then she saw Montagu's smile, and knew that he had toyed with her. With a cold calm, she settled back to listen to the rest.

"Middleton recently met with one of his captains who had returned from Curaçao, which explains the pocketful of Dutch guldens he was seen carrying about," Montagu continued. "Our merchant is a notorious smuggler—like a great many others who avoid payment of duties on certain listed goods which they import—and who buy and sell foreign commodities directly, thus bypassing His Majesty's home ports, and pockets. None of this is what one might call news; enough people know it to fill a prison. Let's just say that these things may not go on quite so freely, in a short while.

"Happily, at least for us, Middleton has recently devised a novel and even odious scheme to cheat his fellow man. By diluting the rum he ships with other substances . . . mostly cheaper turpentine, as well as a bit of black powder . . . he is hoping to make money on the frontier. Mysterious death at the edge of civilization is still rather commonplace, and he believes his poisonous brew will be overlooked as its occasional cause. But as soon as it can be proved that his drink is deadly, we will be able to stop him."

"I should hope so," said Longfellow thickly, wiping goose fat from his chin with his napkin. "But what was it that got you to focus your attention on the old reprobate in the first place?"

"In most criminal affairs, local officers know a great deal before they have proof . . . or before they're allowed to use what proof they have, against those who break the law. It's simply a matter of asking them what they know. And, with the new interest in colonial controls, some of them will soon be authorized to take to court what they, and I, have learned. At the moment, Middleton seems a prime candidate for prosecution. In fact, your merchant has already been tried for holding improper manifests, but this was done by a judge and jury of his own peers— which, oddly enough, didn't seem to do much good. This time, though, it will be the Admiralty Court. Without a jury of his fellows, and especially with his new sins exposed, I believe Duncan Middleton will have very little

hope of remaining a free man. He'll find he has an enormous fine to pay, as well. He should be an invaluable
cautionary example to others who might have similar
plans in mind. This will be doubly true when government begins to confiscate the goods of all those who
benefit from cheating it out of its due."

"So—taxes are one thing, but tainted spirits quite
another," Longfellow concluded at the end of Montagu's
rather long speech. "A man indeed goes too far, when he
becomes a threat to civilization."

"I'm glad you agree. I had hoped I would be able to
appear to believe in his death here, so that Middleton
would feel safe in taking further chances. Toward that
end, I encouraged your sister to carry misinformation back
to Boston," the captain admitted, still addressing Longfellow, "but I see I can no longer use that strategy."

"But you feel sure he's gone on from *here*?"

"What would keep him in a backwater like this? No,
I'm fairly certain he's off to take care of other affairs—
although the fact that he's left so much in Boston for us
to seize does indeed surprise me. He must have had much
more hidden abroad than we ever imagined . . . perhaps
in Curaçao, or Aruba. At any rate, a close watch is being
kept for a wagonload of his rum we have reason to suspect was sent west from Providence on Monday night.
An officer who had . . . delayed, shall we say, the post
from there to Boston on an earlier day was waiting for
him, though he somehow missed meeting Middleton on
the road."

"Lost him, did he?" asked Longfellow with a trace of
scorn. "Until we found him in this little backwater. Too
bad you didn't have one of our local lads with your man
in Providence, to help you track the fellow. Most are
quite good at it—apparently, better even than some from
England. Do you hunt, Captain?" He was gratified to see
Montagu stiffen slightly.

"As most gentlemen do."

"I'm sure you've followed many beasts in your time, and dispatched them. Although it's always seemed to me there's generally so little harm in those poor old foxes, it's a puzzle why you'd want to dress up in a red coat and run after them, when you could be doing far more helpful things about the countryside."

"I still don't understand," interjected Charlotte, hoping to at least delay the squall that blackened the Captain's brow, "why Middleton came here to stage his disappearance in the first place. I imagine it's likely he thought we were 'bumpkins,' as the Dutch say. Or possibly, small potatoes," she added, smiling. "I know the world thinks life is slow and backward here, which is a thing that can sometimes put our people's noses out of joint. But why Bracebridge, in particular?"

Montagu approved of the lady's modesty and tact, as much as he felt her neighbor's attitude rub against his nature and breeding. For Mrs. Willet, at least, he found it necessary to add a warning.

"It's probable that Duncan Middleton came to Bracebridge because he has an accomplice here. He hasn't taken his own horse away, nor have I heard of him buying another. And it's a long walk from here to Boston, especially for a man crippled with gout. So, someone must have obtained one for him. As I've said, I'll go after him tomorrow, and I'll send word when we have him in custody. But until we've had a chance to question the man thoroughly, it might be wise to keep watch for any other unusual activities here. Middleton plays a dangerous game, and so might anyone he's chosen to help him."

"You think, then," Longfellow said gravely, his barbs forgotten, "that someone among us might be planning to do more harm."

"I really can't say," Montagu admitted. "But I think it would be prudent to assume that could be the case."

CONVERSATION WAS ABRUPTLY arrested by the arrival of the pigeon pastry. This time, the new dish was brought in by Mary Frye.

The girl's tense features reminded Mrs. Willett of other matters at hand. As Richard Longfellow cut open the steaming, egg-glazed crust, and Mary gathered the previous course onto her tray, Charlotte decided it was high time to clear the name of Gabriel Fortier.

"Captain Montagu," she began with a look of hope, "I believe we can assume the coin Peter Lynch found this morning is likely to have come from Jack Pennywort, who picked it up on the road—"

"I'll enjoy roasting Pennywort later this evening for lying to me, after I've had him plucked," Montagu assured her.

"Yes, well, then don't you think you might tell the village that you've laid to rest any reason for suspecting Mr. Fortier of committing a crime? I believe he has friends who would be relieved to hear he's no longer being sought."

A grateful look from the serving girl was quick in coming.

"Everyone certainly seems upset when they talk about him," Diana agreed. "In fact, I wonder if it might not *still* be a good idea to find him, and watch him for his own good."

"Why, exactly, do you say that, Miss Longfellow?" Montagu asked gently, perhaps hoping to mend a fence or two.

"From what I hear, it's more than stealing or murder that they accuse the Frenchman of now. He's being talked about as some sort of hellish magician."

"Where have you heard this?" her brother asked.

"From Cicero, of course. For instance, they say it's because of Fortier that one of the local men injured his arm at the cider press this morning. It seems they were all standing around as usual, and one man's eyes suddenly grew as big as saucers, like the dog in the children's tale. Then he began to speak in tongues to the owner's cat, which of course instantly became a witch's familiar in the opinion of everyone there. After that, he knocked down several of the men like ninepins, before he fell against the gears and did himself harm."

"I've heard something else quite recently, about a boy who may have disappeared . . ." Charlotte added quietly, as Diana continued to laugh at her own story, and Mary left by the passage door.

"They get together and drink themselves silly," Longfellow muttered through his napkin, as he worked a stray piece of shot out of a mouthful of bird. "Then they blame anything but themselves when the inevitable happens. One would hardly think they needed magic for that."

"What's this about a missing boy?" Montagu asked Charlotte.

"Two men were discussing it by the gate outside . . . they greeted me as I came in. I didn't think very much about it, knowing how some young men have a way of getting lost, from time to time. Now, I wonder . . . They asked me if I'd seen him, thinking, I suppose, that he might be with Lem Wainwright, who lives with me. Oh—the missing boy's name is Sam Dudley."

"Sam?" Longfellow responded, alerted as much by her tone as her words. "Where was he last seen, and when?"

"They said he went out to hunt some time before dawn. No one remembers where he planned to go, but as of four o'clock, he hadn't returned. His family, or at least his mother, is quite worried."

They followed Montagu's gaze as he stared toward the steamy window. The faintly illuminated branches beyond showed that the wind was still very active, while the darkness had fallen completely. As they watched, beads of rain appeared on the glass, then flew against it as if thrown in handfuls, before racing down in gathering streams. Behind them, the fire beneath the wide chimney hissed a warning.

"It's hardly an afternoon to stay outside, is it?" Diana ventured, a little uncertain.

"How old is this boy?" Montagu asked abruptly.

"Fifteen, or sixteen," Charlotte answered.

While his sister returned to her portion of the pigeon pie, Longfellow leaned back with a blank look. "He's probably found someone to visit—possibly a young lady," he suggested at last.

"And the Frenchman's still missing, too," Montagu mused, pushing a piece of carrot across his plate. "If he weren't, I'd have his hide or the truth," he added, plainly worried about the possibilities before him.

Quite suddenly, a gust of wind blew every flame on the table sideways.

Then, as if by some form of magic, a silent form appeared in the dark mouth of the kitchen passage.

"THE FRENCHMAN WAS missing, *Capitaine*. Now, he is here."

The new voice that broke the silence caused heads to swirl, and in an instant, all eyes took in the man who stood before them.

On closer inspection, there were two figures standing there, one behind the other; Gabriel Fortier stood to the front, while over the Frenchman's shoulder, Mary

Frye's pale face could just be seen. Clearly, she had known where he was all along, and had brought him in from nearby.

"I hide no more," Gabriel stated flatly, looking around the room at all of them, but letting his glance rest on Diana longer than on any other. He seemed to see something to address in her eyes, while she returned his look with unconcealed interest. Her evident approval, thought Charlotte, could not have been lost on anyone present.

"I have come, also," he continued boldly, "to claim my Marie. We are in love. We would run away together, but she is bound here. I respect this ... I respect Jonathan Pratt for giving her his protection. It is for this reason only that we wait—not for any fear of a *tyranneau*," he said bravely, barely refraining from spitting on the floor to drive home his point in the time-honored way.

Edmund Montagu put down his fork and knife, and dabbed his lips with a damask napkin.

"I hope several questions will be answered before *either* of you leaves this inn tonight," he said. But Montagu made no attempt to rise; he had seen Gabriel's hand go toward his belt, half hidden beneath a billowing shirt. It was not unlikely that Fortier, clearly a woodsman, carried a weapon of some sort, concealed but within easy reach.

"I may answer questions for you, *Captaine,* but I am protected by the rights of an Englishman. I know that you are unable to hold me without just cause. And I remind you that you have no legal body behind you, as well."

"Is everyone here mad?" Montagu asked the company at large. "The rights of an Englishman? Who'll claim them next—Louis Quinze?"

But Fortier went on in language that was well chosen, if delivered with a distinct accent.

"There are witnesses, you know, who will say that I was not there when the old man in the red cloak disappeared. Jack Pennywort saw no one else, as he tells everyone. On that night, I was by the river, regarding the moon. Mary and I were to meet, but I saw all the people, so I waited. Later I heard them return, calling out my name. Many of them were angry. I saw the smith, Nathan, give Mary his arm, and take her home. I only returned to the Blue Boar at midnight, through a loose window. No one saw me but for Phineas Wise. He warned me to go very early in the morning, and I followed his advice."

Gabriel Fortier paused and glanced back at Mary, who again seemed about to faint. Silently, he took her hand and helped her to sink gently into a chair that stood against the wall. The girl looked up into the Frenchman's passionate face. Charlotte saw with interest that Mary was still unused to such tenderness.

"There is really no need for an alibi now, Fortier—" Longfellow began.

"Did you see anyone else by the river?" Montagu interrupted.

"No—no one."

"What did you do with yourself after that?"

"Most of the time, I watched from the woods. The next night, I slept in Mme. Willett's *laiterie*—her dairy. This morning, she nearly found me. I hope she was not afraid."

Charlotte only smiled in reply. That explained, she quickly reasoned, why Orpheus hadn't growled last night, when she thought she saw a face at the window. The two had probably been introduced by Mary some time before.

"The Devil, you say! And no one told *me*?" Now it was Longfellow who interrupted, realizing that Charlotte might have been injured—at the very least, by sharp tongues of the village.

"But why do you stay, away from your family and your work, when you believe Mary is protected at the inn?" Montagu demanded.

"If Peter Lynch were to force Marie to—" Fortier swallowed hard before he summoned enough calm to continue. "If he can get her into his bed, then she will be made to marry him, even against her will. That must not happen. So, I spend my time watching him, or her. What else can I do?"

It was an answer that affected them all, and made Mary lower her eyes to hide tears that filled them. Was it love, wondered Charlotte, or shame? Or perhaps hatred, for Peter Lynch?

"It is difficult to hide, when you are poor—though the fault is not your own," Gabriel went on practically, possibly to draw their attention away from Mary. "Even when you begin to know a place. Much of the time, one can only live like an animal in the woods. It is very difficult, with men and boys coming to hunt, or looking at the birds in the trees; even little girls arrive, picking up nuts and nearly finding you. It is not a position for anyone to admire. And it is cold at this time of year, and very wet. So I have decided to come inside again."

"Where will you stay tonight?" asked Jonathan Pratt behind him. Gabriel turned.

"I am a free man. I do not need to answer," the young man finally replied, reminding Charlotte of the rooster who ruled the roost of her hen house.

"I suppose not," the innkeeper said. "I was about to offer you a place here. I had an idea that I might need some heavy chores done before winter sets in. Since my help is mostly female, I thought I could make use of another man's hands."

While Gabriel considered, Pratt brushed by him

with the tray holding the party's baked apples and a red custard, which he set down.

"Stay in the stable then, for now," Jonathan continued. "It's dry, and reasonably warm. Later, we'll arrange for something better."

First Gabriel, and then Mary, seemed ready to speak. But the landlord looked severely at them both.

"If you're finished, this is a private dining room. I'll finish serving the guests myself."

"Two lost, one found," Charlotte sighed softly as the relieved couple left the room, and the desserts were set upon the table. But the peaceful finale that Jonathan Pratt expected for his guests was not to be. Only moments after they had started on the fruit and the pudding, an explosion of sound came from the direction of the kitchen. It was quickly followed by Elizabeth the cook, who burst into the room with her plump arms flying.

"It's the miller—full of rum, and come to take our Mary!" she cried.

Then, she turned around and rushed back out through the open doorway, and down the reverberating hall.

Chapter 16

B Y GEORGE!" SHOUTED Jonathan Pratt, following at
the large woman's heels.

Chairs immediately scraped as all four diners rose
to pursue the cook and the innkeeper down the dark
passage. Because Charlotte and Longfellow knew the
miller's ways, as well as his strength, they hurried on
with trepidation. Diana was only glad for some exercise
to counteract the dulling effects of a large dinner. And
Edmund Montagu thought, as he followed Miss Longfellow's swinging skirts, of Tom Jones's preposterous inn
at Upton—though he suspected this situation might prove
to be far more dangerous. The scene they found in the
kitchen did little to allay his fears.

Elizabeth stood facing the scowling Peter Lynch
with a butter churn paddle, while several feet away, Mary
wielded a wickedly sharp boning knife—not, Montagu
noted with interest, in the usual way of women, but low

and underhand, as one who had witnessed this sort of fight before. Trapped against a table near the far wall, Fortier could only watch. So far, he alone had been unable to find a weapon. The whole scene was lit by the glow from the long fire, where meat continued to roast on an unturned spit while its attendant, the cook's young daughter, cowered in the warming nook.

"I need no one else to tell me my business," Peter Lynch roared, shifting away from the two women and making for the Frenchman. Gabriel picked up a bench and held it like a shield before him. He had not been carrying a gun or a knife after all, thought Montagu, while he watched Longfellow walk bravely between the miller and his intended victim.

"Since you're careful of your own affairs, Peter," Longfellow soon suggested in a remarkably dry tone (considering the circumstances), "you might want to consider this: Captain Montagu represents the law; in fact, he has been sent on the king's business by Governor Bernard. Perhaps you know that the governor takes a dim view of the murder of his subjects, be they court or country . . . or even Frenchmen. He's also fond of taking their persecutors to court, because it gives him a chance to make someone's possessions his own. Or, let us say, the Commonwealth's. This sort of thing also helps keep many lawyers busy and well exercised, which in turn keeps them out of trouble—at least as much as can be expected.

"After considering the evidence, Captain Montagu sees no reason to charge Fortier with any crime. So you can see, Peter, that it would be in your interest to stop now, turn around . . . and leave."

"Leave her to lie with *this*?" the miller snarled, flinging an arm at the corner. "Why, for all I know he's already—"

Abruptly, a new thought struck Peter Lynch, causing

first a grimace, and then a grin. Slowly, he lowered his clenched fist, and soon a heavy chuckle could be heard coming from his straining, casklike chest.

As Lynch relaxed, Gabriel took the chance he'd been waiting for. With the scream of a panther, the smaller man raised the bench he held up into the air, rushed forward, and brought it down hard against the miller's head. The whole thing was done with such force that the two soon found themselves lying on the plank floor, in a tangle of limbs and boards.

At the same time, Mary bent and crawled closer, as if to better see what damaged had been done. But as she began to rise, Montagu came up behind her and clapped a hand onto her wrist. Then he took away the deadly knife. Her face in her hands, Mary fell forward and wept. Gabriel saw, and his face reflected her anguish. Peter Lynch looked, and grew a cruel, lopsided smile. Thrusting himself up and back onto bulging haunches, the miller rose to totter unsteadily on his thick boots, and finally broke into an ugly laugh.

"She's promised to me, innkeeper, as soon as you're done with her. And no brat of a boy is going to stand in my way! Let him follow me like a pup, and starve if he wants to. It won't change the way things are with you or me, or with Elias Frye, either. Her father's given me his word, and I intend to see he keeps it! Sooner or later, the girl will be mine."

Finished with his speech, he turned to go, but Charlotte Willett's clear voice surprised him into stopping. In fact, the ringing tones startled even her own ears.

"Remember, Peter Lynch, there's still a matter of bearing false witness against your neighbor."

"Why should any of us listen to a woman who hides criminals . . . especially one who's being sought by the whole village?" countered Peter. "We know you sheltered the Frenchman, and it won't soon be forgotten, I can promise you that! They burned his kind for witches, in years gone by. Remember, mistress, they hanged Quakers, too, in the town of Boston—and not so very long ago!"

"Friends," Charlotte corrected him without rancor, while Gabriel Fortier defended her in more bitter tones.

"She knew nothing! If you do more against this lady, or mine, I swear that I will come for you, Lynch, and then I will *kill* you!"

The hush that fell was brought to an end by the miller's drunken laugh.

"It could be that one of you, or all, might disappear first, one fine night. Poof!" Lynch exclaimed, exploding his bunched fingers in a startling gesture. And with another gale of scornful laughter, he slammed out of the kitchen and into the rainy night.

Mary rushed to shut and bolt the door. Then she flew to Gabriel's arms, while Elizabeth pulled her child from the hearthside and hugged her tight, for the little girl had begun to cry. Montagu laid down the narrow, horn-handled knife he'd taken from Mary. Everything was again moving toward harmony . . . at least for the moment.

The four guests had barely agreed to go back and finish their dinner, when they found their retreat blocked by a scurrying Lydia Pratt. Her eyes were bright, and her breath was short. Lydia looked all around; then, her glance rested questioningly on her husband. Jonathan calmly played down the recently concluded drama, as he thought how to approach a delicate subject.

"Lydia, my dear . . . I have offered to give Mr. Fortier a chance to do some work for us, in exchange for his keep and a little something more. It strikes me we could use another man about the place, for a while."

His wife seemed ready to argue. But quite suddenly

she drew up short. It appeared to some of the others that as she looked at Mary, she eyed the girl with something beyond her usual disdain. Lydia had never had any true cause to dislike her servant, as far as anyone knew. Still, her refusal to favor Mary in any way had been marked— until now. To her husband's pleasure, Lydia only nodded at his latest suggestion, keeping her lips tightly together. It was an unexpected triumph.

"I thank you," Gabriel said quite simply.

"Prove yourself useful then," Lydia finally responded grimly, leading Charlotte to wonder again at the woman's motives.

"I think I'll retire to make some small repairs," Diana decided, walking around the landlady. "Mary might be of help. Shall we withdraw upstairs, Mrs. Willett, while the gentlemen start their coffee and brandy?"

Charlotte agreed at once, and Mary followed them up to a small pair of rooms set aside for the immediate comforts of the inn's female guests. While Diana sat at a table and removed several items, including her new perfume, from her bag, Charlotte watched Mary pour water from pitcher to basin, then arrange two embroidered towels.

"It looks as though you, too, have triumphed over a dragon, like St. George," Charlotte suggested to the girl, once she decided they would not be overheard. But Mary's face looked back from the mirror with its usual solemn expression.

"I won't believe it. No matter how willing she seems."

"If Lydia really means to help you and Gabriel—"

Mary laughed briefly, and dabbed at her face with a dampened corner of her apron to remove the remains of her tears.

"You *must* know better!" she replied bleakly, looking away from the mirror. "She's only agreeing now because . . . because of something I know, although she's not sure I know it. Something best left unsaid, as long as I still have to live under the roof of a witch! It may be that something will come out, when I leave—or it may not," she considered, offering both women a smile that was at once mysterious, and a little sad.

"Well," said Diana, resetting a curl, "this is one of the most dramatic evenings I've had for months! I'd no idea life in the country could be so full of passion, and danger! What do you suppose will happen next?"

With one little finger, she rouged her lips from a tiny pot on the table in front of her, and then reapplied a dab of scent from the Oriental bottle.

"If it were up to me," she continued, "I'd choose something comic to end the evening, and send everyone home in high spirits. Although I'm not entirely disposed to laugh after such a large dinner, with these stays!" She stood and twisted her torso in several different directions, causing her hoops to brush against the vanity table. It teetered alarmingly, until she stepped away.

"Let's go back before the gentlemen forget we exist. I'm sure they've already begun to bore each other with their political views again," she concluded, waiting for Charlotte to finish a brief appraisal in the small mirror. After she had cleared the tabletop, Diana's rustling skirts led Mrs. Willett down the hall, while Mary stayed behind to tidy up the room.

Only when she was sure the two women had gone did Mary take a small enameled bottle from her pocket. For a moment, she looked at it with great curiosity, watching the way the dragon caught the candle's light, as she turned it round and round in her work-rough hands.

Chapter 17

I THOUGHT THE Court of St. James's less impressive than it might be," Longfellow said languidly to his new acquaintance, as they both sipped well deserved brandy, after their bold encounter. "One could wish it had more brain and culture attached to it, and a little less pomp and powder. It might be wise for the gentlemen of the upper classes to try breeding not for wealth, as they do now, but for brighter children—*that* would be progress."

They saw the ladies returning, and Longfellow rose to pour for them, as well. But the conversation continued much as it had gone on during their absence. Richard now waited for Captain Montagu to take the next shot.

"One can hardly disagree with your . . ." Montagu cleared his throat, wondering if a word existed to describe them. ". . . your *antic* observations. Of course, from your own dress and habits, sir, I'd already guessed that you might prefer the company of, how shall I put it? People who work with their hands? But then, you Americans have many origins, which allows you to choose your fashion from a very great diversity of tinkers and farmers."

"Ah, yes, we do enjoy the styles of many countries here, and many occupations."

Apparently, thought Charlotte, noting an absence of ill humor, their exertions together in the kitchen had begun to form a bond.

"That, to my mind," continued Longfellow, "is preferable to relying on the tastes and foibles of a crumbling elite in a moribund capital—although your Old World does have notable *architectural* remains. But as you've said, Captain, we have admirably simple tastes here. And our colonies are even more widely admired for having men of inventive minds, like Dr. Franklin, whom I imagine you've heard of by now. I expect that's also true of most countries of the Old World, however—in their *general* populations. I've been impressed by a great many things I've seen throughout Europe, both in science and the arts," he finished, pleased with himself for the fairness of his argument.

"Then perhaps you've also seen the way the Continental peasants struggle to survive outside the gilded capitals your wealthy young men tour and overpraise. Have you visited the less lovely sections of Paris? At least we English rarely starve *en masse*, the way they do now throughout France. Englishmen all enjoy certain rights, as Monsieur Fortier pointed out. Rights developed, I might add, solely by your English ancestors, and upheld by the government they alone created!"

"A greater pity, then, since you're so proud of them, that you don't extend all of these rights to Americans!

But we 'children,' I assure you, must soon grow larger and stronger than you or your ancestors . . . as children will, when given a superior diet. As the proprietor of a dairy, I'm sure Mrs. Willett agrees."

"Well, I—"

"I hope, at least, that we can *all* agree on the benefits of the British parlimentary system?" Montagu asked the table.

"Of course," Longfellow assented, "despite the fact that the body *you* elect is filled with men who would pre-fer neither to see nor to hear us, and who rarely do any-thing in our interest at all . . ."

"It's allowed you to enjoy what you call your 'liberty' this long! But it may be that you Americans should start a united Parliament of your own. Then you would know *real* trouble. And don't forget to include the ladies among your revolutionary representatives!"

Both men, along with the women, soon found them-selves laughing together at the idea—although the Ameri-cans laughed less than their host, and for different reasons.

"Have you seen conditions across the Channel your-self?" asked Charlotte of the captain. Montagu became serious again.

"It's an increasingly hard life in France. While most struggle just to exist, a very few enjoy everything money can buy. I suspect that in a dozen years, the French will have problems at home which will keep them from fight-ing with us, or with you."

"I have read in the *Gazette*," said Diana with new energy, "that children in London can still be put into prison for debts, and hanged for stealing a loaf of bread—while royalty continues to think up new fashions and diversions."

"Ah yes, the *Gazette*," Montagu replied. He picked up the bill of fare and slowly fanned himself, rather than saying exactly what he thought of that newspaper, or any other touted as an honest, unbiased source.

"Yet here," he continued, gazing at Diana's clothing as he spoke, "many of your ordinary citizens choose to wear silk and lace, rather than less costly attire, even though they live far from any court. Wouldn't you agree with my earlier argument, Miss Longfellow, that people like these, able to pay more than a poor weaver or a plowman in England, should at least pay the Crown for *some* of the cost of their own protection, or be thought ungrateful . . . perhaps even disloyal? No one here is truly poor, after all."

That point, too, would soon have been debated, but for the reappearance of Jonathan Pratt.

"I'm sorry to interrupt—"

"'Jonathan, what's happened?" From the landlord's somber face, Mrs. Willett feared she already knew.

"What, indeed," he answered hesitantly. "Sam Dudley's been found. He seems to have drowned in the river, just to the north of the footbridge."

"The boy drowned?" Montagu inquired sharply. "How?"

"No one knows for certain. It could be that he slipped in the early darkness. Startled by a deer, perhaps—or simply lost his balance. It's likely he was stunned, he fell, and drowned in the shallows. At any rate, he was found in the marshland, and was taken home to his mother."

"Most unfortunate—I'm sorry for her. I presume a physician has been called to examine him," Montagu added, somewhat to Pratt's surprise.

"Oh, he's been dead for some hours, by all appearances. No need for a doctor. Anyway, there's none here in Bracebridge. When we have a serious need of one, we send word to Cambridge. If there's time."

"I'll go and have a look at the lad tomorrow, then, before I leave. Where is his house?"

Still somewhat mystified, the innkeeper gave him directions. Jonathan hadn't heard, Charlotte realized, all that they'd been discussing before, nor did he know of Montagu's warning of possible danger to come. She felt her emotions welling as her throat tightened, and she imagined the quiet body stretched and tended by his mother for the last time. Sam Dudley! She'd seen the boy for years, hurrying here and there. Sam Dudley, one of the youths she had seen, and heard as well, walking home on Tuesday night—

This final thought decided her. She would pay a visit to the Dudley farm in the morning. It would be a call of sympathy, and something more. But she would be sure to go early, before Captain Montagu arrived. At the moment, she had no desire to encounter any more of his disconcerting stares.

Richard Longfellow had risen while Mrs. Willett considered. Silently, he left the room after the innkeeper. In the hall he caught Jonathan's arm.

"Have you still got Timothy about the place?"

Timothy helped the hostler look after the horses, and sometimes did other jobs. Often, the boy ran errands, or took assignments from the inn's guests when they needed messages delivered. Tim was a devil in the saddle, especially for the right price.

"He's around somewhere," Pratt replied, trying to think where he had seen the young fellow last.

"Well, if he's not otherwise engaged, I'd like you to give him a letter."

Saying this, Longfellow took the landlord's candle, forcing Jonathan to follow him as he made his way to an alcove desk where he knew paper, ink, and quills were to be found. While Jonathan watched, Longfellow sat and quickly wrote out a note, folded the paper twice, put a name and a Boston address on the outside, and sealed it with a drip of wax.

"Where, by the way, is Nathan? He'd have been interested in what went on in the kitchen earlier."

"If he were here, I'm sure we would have heard from him."

"Out of town?"

"No, at the Blue Boar, I imagine. He's been there quite often lately."

"Has he?" Longfellow returned the candle, and leaned back while the landlord went in search of the boy.

Soon, at the approach of the alert Tim, Longfellow rose and gave him the letter and some copper coins, shook his hand solemnly, and then went back to rejoin the party with at least one new question in mind.

"I propose," said Edmund Montagu as Longfellow re-entered, "that each of us escort a lady home through the storm—for the wind is strong enough to blow either off to Providence. Rhode Island, of course," he added, winning at least one smile with the ancient joke that was still new to the Englishman. "Mrs. Willett," he concluded, "may I offer my arm?"

Charlotte was quick to catch the look in Diana's eye. She replied gracefully, but firmly. While she appreciated his offer, there were tiresome proprieties in village life, she told him, that had to be considered. Perhaps it would be better if Mr. Longfellow, a family friend and neighbor, were to escort her. As he and Diana were both residents of Boston, she continued, rather than Bracebridge, and thus probably considered to be odd already, they would have little to lose by going together. The captain might even escort Miss Longfellow home in an official capacity, while her brother was otherwise occupied.

Montagu smiled at the transparent refusal, but readily agreed. Before long, the four left the inn and passed through its outer gates with wavering lanterns, then turned to go their separate ways into the driving dark.

• • • •

"I'M CERTAINLY GLAD," said Diana, once they were safe inside her brother's house, "that Richard keeps a good cellar, although he has a strange prejudice against tobacco. But I suspect you take no snuff. May I offer you a glass of something?"

Montagu watched her toss her cloak onto a stand in the large entry hall, and again heard the small bells over her chest rustle.

"Thank you, no. I believe I've already had enough tonight to unsettle my brain."

"Then a cup of Dutch chocolate, as only I can make it. Please, take off your cape. You won't leave me all alone? My brother is sure to be away for an hour or two. And an empty house is so dreary. Besides, there is something about which I'd like to ask a man's advice. I have been struggling to understand a poem," she continued, walking through a doorway.

This came as quite a surprise to Edmund Montagu. He'd hardly thought the colonials the sort of people likely to appreciate Milton, Pope, or even Gray. It was especially odd, he thought, to be asked for such advice by Diana Longfellow. Here was a lovely woman indeed—yet he wouldn't have guessed this particular female concerned herself with inner beauty, or spirit in general.

He followed her through a passage and into the kitchen where he stood, watching and recalling. When they had been together before, the talk had been of fashion, then intrigue, secrecy, and others things she appeared to find increasingly exciting. Since then, he had used her rather shamefully . . . even admitted it over dinner. Not that she hadn't deserved it, in return for subjecting him to her own flirtatious fictions. Now, she wanted to talk to him of poetry. Was it simply a ruse to get him to speak to her of love, for her own amusement—or even, possibly, for revenge? For all he knew, that brother of hers might be waiting for a chance to challenge him to a duel—probably with pitchforks, or even manure shovels.

Montagu had no way of knowing that Diana had taken care to ask Mary Frye earlier if the captain had brought any books with him. Had she noticed, while arranging his towels and tidying his room? A book of collected poems had been Mary's answer. No—Montagu only knew, as he followed Diana into the kitchen (and saw the enchanting way she looked about for materials and means to prepare him a cup of cocoa, leaning and reaching) that his own reserve was beginning to thaw beneath a shower of smiles, to the music of those maddening bells.

"Please, sit there in that comfortable chair by the hearth, while I just—"

He sat. Now that her curls and clothing had become disheveled by the wind, she had a look quite unlike that of the lady he had met only yesterday on the Boston road. This new unbending, even an unraveling, might lead to further surprises. Herrick had put it well, back when men and women were keenly aware of the truths of life under its various costumes.

> A *sweet disorder in the dress*
> *Kindles in clothes a wantonness.*
> A *winning wave, deserving note,*
> *In the tempestuous petticoat,*

He drew a breath as Diana, climbing a short kitchen ladder, kicked one foot into the air, and steadied herself—

> A *careless shoestring, in whose tie*
> *I see a wild civility,*

Hoops that hid a figure, he now realized, might lead to other possibilities as well. He averted his eyes as her skirts lifted, but soon looked back again.

Do more bewitch me than when art
Is too precise in every part.

Gad! Had the strange mood of the little town transformed *him* now, as well? When in London, or Boston,
for that matter, he found it easy to maintain his sense
of place and order. Under the eyes of men and women
besotted with themselves and their positions he, too,
could appear stylish and self-absorbed, and would be accepted. But in this place, he seemed to be held suspect
for the very manners that had earned him entry to the
best houses in Boston. And now, he was teased with
their opposite, by a lady of that town! Could she have
realized his secret—that he longed to enjoy life without
its many artifices—life that was good, simple, even po-
etic, thanks to the rural influence? How he would have
enjoyed seeing the lady before him in simple country attire! Yet even with this strong urge, he knew from experience that life was never *really* simple, not even in the
country . . . not even here.

Montagu wiped his brow carefully with a handkerchief, pretending that all he wiped away was a lingering
drop of rain. Thank heaven, he thought, he would be
leaving in the morning. He seemed to be under some
kind of spell—but was the bewitching agent Diana
Longfellow, or his own frustrated hopes? This might
prove to be, he warned himself, a very dangerous cup of
cocoa. He would have to be on guard.

"Fie, fie, fie, Captain Montagu," his companion gently chastened, turning around on a step with a tin of
dried fruits in her hand, "only watching me move about
this chilly room, when you might be down on your
knees, coaxing the embers of our fire. A warm country
kitchen, in rain and storm, is an appealing place to be—
even a desirable one on a night like this, don't you
think? Now, if you will rise and hand me down . . ."

• • •

LATER, SITTING IN his room at the inn, Edmund Montagu suspected he would have gone a great deal further, had not Cicero chosen that moment to enter through the kitchen door. Odd, he thought at the time, that the expression on the rain-slick face of this country servant should remind him of quite a different face—one he'd stared at somewhere else quite recently. Where had it been? Well, at least it had diverted his attention from Diana Longfellow!

Finally, as he lay in bed, he had it. Curiously, the unusual smile he remembered had been on a woman's face, in a small, dark oil he'd seen hanging in an enormous palace in Paris. It was a painting that had some indefinable magic about it. It had been painted by the old Italian . . . what was his name? Oh yes, he thought as he drifted off. Leonardo. Vaguely, he wondered if the man had known anything about poetry.

EARLIER, A LAMP across the way had moved from house to barn, as Lem left Charlotte's kitchen for the sweetness of his bed of new straw, next to warm and quiet bovine companions.

On their own, Charlotte and Richard Longfellow sat for another hour, watching the dying embers with Orpheus between them. The dog sighed while Longfellow curled and spread his fingers into the old fellow's silky coat, working out a cocklebur.

Longfellow, too, had been offered refreshment, and had settled on a cup of mint tea, hoping it would help his digestion. He'd watched carefully as his neighbor prepared it for him, admiring her straight form, her country woman's quickness, her efficiency of motion as she performed a familiar task. If only Diana had some of Mrs.

Willett's natural desire to please, framed in a domestic setting of her own, he thought with little hope.

"I wish we could think of something between us to improve Mary Frye's future," said Charlotte after she had poured out the tea. "I know it would be difficult to go against her father directly. But Richard, you're a well-respected man; if you could find something to tell him against Peter Lynch as a husband—"

"Would recent threats against another woman's life do?"

"I don't suppose we need to take much notice of that. After all, he hardly knew what he was saying."

"He knew well enough, since the same threat had just been made to him! Whatever way he has in mind to carry it out, *that* was a warning."

"But why? Lynch must know I have little influence with Mary. As for bringing up the coin—"

"Yes, now about that coin. As you so kindly pointed out, he could be blamed, even sued, for making false statements against Fortier, since he knew they *were* false. With lawyers as thick as hickory in the woods, our miller may yet find himself in a trap of his own making. Lynch has valuable property to lose, too, which seems to be a major attraction for the legal mind."

"And Mary? Do you believe she'll be safe now?"

"My guess would be she's safer than the miller. The Frenchman seems to have a grand passion, and a short fuse. It's a triangle of the oldest kind, and one that no one else should try to alter," he added, waggling a finger in her direction.

"Am I to take two warnings in one night?"

"You are. I know gossip is not your worst vice, but the desire to find things out for your own satisfaction is a thing I've seen you carry to extremes. In this case, it might be unsafe, as well as unwise."

Charlotte spread her fingers on her skirt, then

looked up with a toss of her hair which, Longfellow thought, looked surprisingly like honey in the firelight.

"Do you want to know what really piques my curiosity at the moment?" she asked him abruptly. "I'd like to know what's come over Lydia Pratt. Mary said that Lydia *had* to go along with Jonathan tonight, because of something the girl could tell us, if she chose to. Which she did not. I'd like to know what Mary uses to keep Lydia at bay. The girl sounded as if she might consider blackmail as a weapon—although the word is probably too strong."

"Blackmail, and Lydia Pratt the victim? That would be a satisfying twist. For someone who calls the tune as often as she does, a little enforced behavior is a delightful thing to contemplate. Ha! But what do you think this charge against Lydia could be? Is she keeping the profits of her geese from Jonathan? Great Heaven, she might be the leader of a local coven! She does have the face for it. She could even be the chief thinker of a criminal band ... highwaymen who hide their plunder in her linen chests. Which will it be?" he asked, rubbing his chin with enjoyment.

"Did you know," asked Charlotte solemnly, "that Lydia Pratt was the last person to speak with Duncan Middleton, and that she failed to mention it to anyone? She happened to have been overheard by your old friend Mr. Lee. At least, Diana overheard Jonathan telling Captain Montagu about it, and told me. So tonight, when the captain mentioned an accomplice—"

"You don't think that *Lydia*—?"

"What if Lydia knew Middleton before, and drew him here? After all, we've known her here in Bracebridge for barely three years."

Longfellow couldn't be sure what lay behind Charlotte's look, but he allowed himself a chortle, nonetheless.

"You take none of this too seriously either, I see," she finished with a small laugh.

"Some of it I do. And so should you," he warned again, getting slowly to his feet. "When I go, I'll check to make sure you've bolted the door behind me. And you might go to your study and watch my lantern—or Jonathan's, at any rate, which I'll take with me—until I'm safely through my own back door."

He gazed out at the thrashing rain. His eyes became vague, even grave, filling Charlotte with new apprehension.

"The miller made no threats toward you, Richard," she said, puzzled by the sudden change.

"No, he didn't. But then, it's not only the miller I'm worried about," he replied, just before he gave her a quick brotherly kiss, and disappeared into the swirling night.

Chapter 18

                                                   Friday

"G OD'S WILL," SIGHED Rachel Dudley, indicating the body of her son. A mother came to accept that the Lord worked in mysterious ways, her early visitor concluded, and that heaven answered few questions. But exactly how the young man had got to heaven was a question that might still be answered on earth, Charlotte Willett reminded herself as she stood in the doorway.

Sam Dudley lay on his own bed in a room he had shared with his younger brother, Winthrop. Now, Winthrop could be seen through small glass panes, sitting by the woodpile and holding on to a fowling piece that had come into his possession only the day before. What had become of Sam's father, Charlotte could only guess— though John Dudley's jug today might be a welcome consolation, she thought with some sympathy.

Charlotte stepped forward to examined the motionless figure. Sam's chestnut hair had been carefully combed.

He was fully dressed, except that he wore no shoes. But his mother had covered most of the body with one of her quilts. A quilt in progress, on the stretching rack in the main room, was made of finer remnants; probably, it would be sold to pay for necessities, while Mrs. Dudley's own family made do with rougher work. Sam's loss would surely be felt as they continued the struggle to "get by."

"He was so stiff with cold, it took me till this morning to lay him out proper."

Somehow, she'd managed. Charlotte had half expected to see signs of a fight for life. But Sam looked as if his last day on earth had ended in peaceful sleep. The only odd thing to be seen was a scrape on his forehead. Had it been, after all, a simple misadventure, a misreading on the boy's part of some known danger? Or had it been something far less common, and far more horrible?

Charlotte reached to touch a beardless cheek. Then her fingers took the quilt away from the long neck. Now, she saw a small bruise at the front of the boy's throat. And the throat, she speculated uneasily, seemed not quite as round as it should have been.

Meanwhile, Rachel Dudley had taken up a beaded deerskin bag from the bedside table, to explore it with fingers tired from clutching. She spoke proudly, through trembling lips.

"This was a gift I made for him last Christmas, right after his father gave him the musket to hunt with. He told me he needed something to hold powder and shot. I made it as pretty as I could, and he always wore it under his shirt, right next to his heart."

Her voice caught, and she stopped to whisk away a new tear almost angrily. With a determined motion, she sat and took up the cold hand lying next to her. Then she pushed the bag into its limp, curled fingers. Only now did Charlotte notice that the little bag's knotted leather thong had been broken partway up its rawhide length. "I guess it caught on something when he fell . . ." the woman went on, seeing the question in Mrs. Willett's eyes. "I don't know if he tangled himself in some bushes in the dark, or just exactly . . . what. They found it lying not far away, next to his gun. Winthrop's got that now. I hope he'll be more careful. . . ."

Rachel Dudley suddenly shuddered, and she gave in to harsh, dry sobs. Charlotte's own thoughts were far from calm, but she hid them for the sake of the grieving woman whose arms she held, until they stopped shaking.

In a little while, Rachel took up the cold hand once again. Then, as the mother became absorbed in memories, Charlotte offered soft condolence, and left the room.

A little girl with pigtails like braided corn silk stood just outside the doorway. She politely escorted her guest through the large room that served as kitchen, storehouse, and living area. There was a small cot next to the fire. It must belong to her tiny guide, Charlotte decided.

"Would you take some cider?" the child asked, as she'd certainly heard her mother do. Charlotte sank onto a low stool by the hearth. She shook her head as she adjusted the young girl's homespun dress, which had lost one of its wooden buttons.

"Your name is Anne, isn't it?"

"Yes—"

"Have you had your breakfast?"

"I had some with Win. We had porridge and syrup. Are those your combs?"

Charlotte's eyebrows rose as she saw Anne looking at the top of her head.

"Yes, they are." She stopped, recalling the warm spring day when Aaron had brought them home.

"I guess they're made of real shell."

"From a very large tortoise, I should imagine," Charlotte agreed.

Anne drew in her breath to think of it. "My brother

Sam was going to get me a comb, when he went to Boston. That's what he told me."

There wasn't much to say in reply. Sympathy would mean only unwanted pity to a serious girl of six or seven. The child had simply stated a fact. But now, the full sadness of the lost promise seemed to strike Anne, as she looked wistfully past Charlotte to her brother's room.

"He told me he would, just like when he brought me back my ribbon." Reaching up, Anne fingered the ends of a grease-spotted grosgrain band she'd tied around her neck.

"A very pretty ribbon. Golden, like your hair," Charlotte said gently.

"Yes, but not as golden as *real* gold. A gold coin—"

The child suddenly gasped and dropped her eyes. In her open palm, she traced a circle the size of a small coin with the nail of a stubby finger, frowning. Then she sighed, and her eyes closed briefly with the effects of a night of fitful sleep, taken while others were weeping.

"Gold is pretty, isn't it?" Charlotte agreed quietly. "Have you seen very much of it?"

"The only time I *ever* saw it," said Anne, leaning closer, and lowering her already small voice, "was the gold Sam showed me. But he said I shouldn't tell. I've seen silver before. After the harvest last year we had some, for a while. I got to hold it. It shined, by the fire, and there were crowns on it, too. The gold was prettier, but Sam wouldn't let me hold it as long. He said it was a secret, after I spied on him and saw him pull it out," she confided.

"From his neck pouch?"

The girl nodded.

"Did Sam tell you where he got the coin?"

Anne shook her head and pulled on a braid. "But he said if I didn't tell, he would bring me a comb, the very next time he went to Boston. Like those." She let go of her hair to point again, then let her hand fall back to her side.

The combs—one of Aaron's gifts. One of many. Slowly, Charlotte reached up and pulled them from her hair, hoping that several pins would continue to hold most of it where it sat. She looked at the combs seriously for a moment, and then handed them to young Anne, whose fingers were already outstretched near eyes wide with disbelief.

"I think these are just like the ones Sam would have brought you from Boston. But promise, if you take them, that the gold coin you saw will still be a secret, until I tell you otherwise. Will you promise?"

Anne bobbed her head vigorously.

"Good. Now I have to go . . . but you'll have more visitors before very long—"

"Thank you!"

"You're welcome . . . and you're to tell Mr. Long-fellow, when you see him, that you're very fond of crowns, especially on silver. He'll enjoy speaking with a little girl about coins, I think—and then you might have a piece of Spanish money to look at, at least for a little while. But you mustn't tell *anyone* about the other coin—remember!"

"Sam says a lady wouldn't want to talk about money, anyway. Sam says I'll be a lady someday, too." The child watched with a look of hope, lost in a world of imagining.

"With combs to spare," Charlotte soon answered from the doorway, as she sent a farewell glance past the happy little girl, to the boy and his silent mother in the room beyond.

ALTHOUGH RAINDROPS STILL wept from the black limbs of the trees, gusts no longer rattled the thinned woodland borders as Charlotte walked home. The storm appeared to be over. She paused along the way to admire rainbow prisms within a thinning tangle of blackberry vines, while the gray clouds above made way for patches of blue, high and to the west. It was a day, as well as a season, for abrupt changes.

She left the Concord road and followed a path to a narrow wooden footbridge, crossed the river, and walked through field grass toward her own pasture. She was glad to have escaped meeting anyone when she hurried away. It was only when the path began to climb that she turned and saw three figures walking north along the main road she had just come from, making their way toward the Dudley home.

Charlotte squinted into the distance, trying to assist her imperfect eyes. One of the men she knew by height and gait to be Richard Longfellow. A second, with wig and winking gold buttons, was Edmund Montagu. The last, pumping behind the others, was Constable Bowers. It would be his duty to go along and examine the facts surrounding any surprising death. Not that she believed he would be likely to actually look for any problems—unless someone forced him to.

After the three men disappeared through the door that opened for them, Charlotte turned and resumed her lonely walk. In another moment, she had to brush back her hair as it began to fall down in front of her eyes in wisps and strands, then locks—and finally, in something like a cascade. She was taken aback to be so far from comb and mirror, but was amply compensated by the memory of Anne Dudley's delighted face, and her small, open hands.

But this was no time for pleasant thoughts. Instead, she forced herself to concentrate on questions of a darker nature—of exactly what was so, and why. It had first seemed possible that Sam Dudley, out alone in that dark morning of cold and wind, had stumbled and fallen. Had his brain been stunned by a quick meeting with a rock, death could have come even in those shallow waters. Charlotte wondered if she should have examined the scalp under the thick hair more closely. But it hadn't seemed necessary, especially after she had seen the throat. Most would have said it was not her place to pry any further. After all, others would soon see what she had noticed. But the mention of gold again—that was a question almost heaven-sent, for her alone to consider.

Small Anne had described a highly unusual object, something rarely seen at the Dudleys', or in any other house in Bracebridge. Assuming it was another Dutch gulden, wouldn't logic dictate that it most likely came from the same source? Jonathan had received one coin, and was waiting to give it to Reverend Rowe. Bowers now had another, the one she supposed Jack Pennywort picked up on the Boston-Worcester road, and later gave to Peter Lynch—the same coin Lynch had pretended to pick up in Fortier's room at the Blue Boar. Lynch turned the coin over to Bowers yesterday afternoon—but it was yesterday *morning* that Sam Dudley had apparently died.

She felt as if a chill tide were rising around her. Couldn't the coin she believed came from Jack—the one Peter Lynch claimed was dropped by Gabriel Fortier—as easily have been taken from Sam's body? But if that was true, how had Sam come by it originally? Had it been given to him by Duncan Middleton? If Sam had come upon the merchant sometime after he had "gone up in flames"—

It was barely possible. But—what if the miller had taken the coin from the boy, knowing Sam had it because *he* had given it to him, some time after he'd received it himself from Middleton, who then left the village? Her mind swiftly made a further leap. Could Peter Lynch have been the reason Duncan Middleton came to Bracebridge in the first place? Edmund Montagu had already explained Middleton's scheme to sell tainted rum. Wouldn't the miller, who made frequent trips to Worcester and beyond, make a useful accomplice? Maybe the old man carried his gold to Bracebridge to pay for stores, as well as the miller's future service. If so, Peter would have been the one who found the merchant a horse on which he might quietly leave the village. But why would Middleton want to make such a spectacle of himself, and disappear so *obviously* in the first place? That was still a question she couldn't answer.

And just how far would Peter Lynch have gone to keep up the pretense of the merchant's death, if Sam had stumbled onto the truth? Worse yet, the miller could have *truly* killed Middleton, to remove the merchant from the scheme Peter planned to carry on himself. What if *that* was what Sam had realized? Peter Lynch might have given one of the coins to Sam for his silence . . . knowing he could reclaim it soon—and end the boy's life in the process!

She fought against the whirl of her thoughts, determined to calm her mind and methodically examine its quick conclusions. So far, these were all mere suspicions, without solid foundation. And surely, not all the gold in the world belonged to Duncan Middleton! What if Sam had gotten the coin somewhere else, and been envied by a friend who clumsily tried to take it from him? Or, he might actually have stumbled and fallen by accident, as his mother believed.

One never knew what fate held in store. That's why, thought Charlotte as she continued on her way, all days had to be cherished, like precious jewels. Or gold coins—Dutch guldens that could mesmerize and enthrall even a small girl, let alone a hardened, twisted soul full of jealousy and greed, and capable of the worst crime imaginable!

It was an awful thing to ponder. To accuse the miller would be a most difficult thing. Yet her conscience told her that men and women were not put on earth only to enjoy goodness and innocence, nor should they refuse to see or hear the evil around them. And so she continued to screw her eyes into a fierce squint. But they were focused on the muddy ground now, rather than on higher things. And they saw very little that was uplifting along the winding trail that guided her feet.

SO DEEP WERE her thoughts that Charlotte barely heard the first quick calls of a familiar voice, as it began to peal through the open air. Her concentration was finally shattered when she recognized it as the sound of the brass bell that hung over the meetinghouse. On the Sabbath, it rang out in a joyful manner. Occasionally, as on the evening before, it tolled more ponderously to announce the death of one who had belonged to the community. But now it rang with a clamoring that was nearer to its third purpose, that of summoning folk to a fire. Yet she could see no smoke coming from the village houses. Certainly no flames threatened from the wet forest, or the thoroughly dampened fields.

Still, someone rang the church bell with a great deal of determined energy. From both sides of the river, she saw people hurrying toward the meetinghouse at the edge of the Common, some arriving with buckets and tools in hand, others with their skirts and aprons and petticoats lifted out of the new mud as they looked around in puzzlement and alarm. Charlotte, too, hurried over the hillside's slippery grass and down onto the Boston road. But before she could reach the meetinghouse, she saw several of the same people who had just gone in come back out again. Leading them was the unmistakable figure of Reverend Christian Rowe. So he was back! Apparently, the preacher had summoned them all with the now-silent bell to his (and God's) house.

And then the reverend began to run, leading his flock with an animated face framed by flashing white collar ends. His black coattails flew out behind him like witches' weeds, while his white-stockinged legs twisted and bent like a spider's, as he attempted to look around and move ahead at the same time. Where could they all be going? Charlotte saw the crowd cross the stone bridge over the river. There wasn't much of anything on the other side, except for the tavern . . . and the grist mill!

Sure enough, they turned south on the road to Framingham. But instead of heading for the mill's wide doors, her neighbors turned off and went around to one side, back to the millpond. And there they stopped, flapping and buzzing like a disturbed hive with something decidedly ominous in mind.

Chapter 19

EVERYONE IN THE village knew the still reaches of the millpond that took its water from the river. Overhanging branches were reflected on its black face, ringed with pickerelweed, arrowhead, and water lilies. It was a fine spot to spend an hour in meditation, or to walk with a valued companion, or even to throw stones at the flat surface of the water in the hopes of rousing a frog. It was a sheltered, peaceful place loved by many—even by the Reverend Rowe, who might be seen following its encircling path while he searched for inspiration.

Perhaps that was what he'd been doing this morning, thought Charlotte as she caught up with the rest near the water's edge. He might have been trying to shed the taint of Boston in this quiet haven. Had the reverend received a startling message from above, or been given divine commands, like Moses?

What the Reverend Rowe had to show for his early

morning walk was something far more down-to-earth, Mrs. Willett realized when she joined the gasping crowd. At its head, deep voices and weed-draped arms had joined to negotiate the removal of a sagging, dripping body.

There was little question how the miller had met his death. Peter Lynch's face and forehead were horribly cleft in a gaping line that ran for nearly five inches, light pink and clean, its edges resembling the flesh of a large pike ready for the pan. Behind this peeped something else that would also be familiar to a frugal cook—something convoluted and gray.

All in all, it was a terrible sight. If the wound had not been so fascinating, thought Charlotte, who was by now encircled and supported by the crowd as it swayed collectively—if it had looked less awful, it would have been impossible not to gaze first and overlong at Peter Lynch's eyes. For they, too, were ghastly—open, staring, bulging from white sockets. The eyes were surrounded by puffy folds of skin, some of which showed what looked like a reddish rash. Other parts had already helped to sustain the pond fish.

There was nothing to be done for Peter Lynch, except to lift him. As the corpse came up, a rush of dark water dropped onto the shoulders of several men, who turned their faces away. Then, getting firmer grips, they began to convey Peter toward the meetinghouse, where he would be lowered directly onto the coffin boards, to wait until a box could be made. These boards had held many other corpses in their day, in a dim alcove just off the unheated building's entrance. But the miller would no longer care about the cold.

Clutching her cloak for warmth, Mrs. Willett was very glad to have more air and room as the throng spread out and moved away, following the body. Up to this point, most talk had been in the form of short and sharp reactions, or brief, necessary orders. There had been only

one or two simple questions. (What there had been none
of, she noticed, were tears for the miller.)

But by now, numbed minds were beginning to function again. Charlotte watched with quiet concentration,
reflecting on many of her own recent thoughts, while
voices rose up around her. It seemed to her that the
crowd had begun to steam and swell, like a pie without
a vent.

"How could it happen?" one of the village women
asked her husband, who gave no immediately answer.
"How could a man as big as a tree be hit in the head like
that? There's no one *here* large enough to do it—not that
I can see!"

"I'll bet he was robbed, too," threw in Phineas Wise,
speaking his own worst fears.

Dick Craft, too, found his voice, which showed less
sympathy than one might have imagined. Yet he, too,
seemed puzzled.

"The miller was no ordinary man to be fooled, as we
all know. He'd fight, by God—unless whatever came after him had more than mortal strength . . ."

"Oh, come," began another, soon stopped by a chorus
demanding that he and all the rest let the man speak.

"First, a rich old buzzard disappears," Dick went on.
"Then a young boy dies, and now a man in his prime is
clearly *murdered*. I say, it looks like someone trying out
his powers, until he's sure of 'em. Someone who doesn't
belong here, and doesn't care *what* in hell happens to the
rest of us! It looks to me as though the Frenchman came
to Bracebridge to practice his evil arts, until he got good
enough to overcome his rival, Peter Lynch, face to face!"

"With black magic!" and "Witchcraft!" joined in
several voices at once, to a furious wagging of heads.

"The French themselves are extremely nervous on
that subject," began Tinder from the Blue Boar, and Flint

immediately began to reflect on witchcraft in the Pyre-
nees, which he had visited in his youth.

"Done with his own hatchet," called a voice panting
behind them a minute later. "The one Peter kept buried
in a post, inside by the big stone. It isn't there now. But
there's blood there! Dripped onto the floor!"

"Most likely the hatchet's in the pond," someone
else ventured, to more nods and shouts.

The Reverend Christian Rowe watched the growth
of discontent and fear with lofty pleasure, holding high
his head with its astounding halo of flaxen hair, waiting for the right moment to take command. Before long,
it came.

"I tell you," began the Reverend Rowe severely, causing some to stop dead in their tracks. Unfortunately, the
preacher continued to walk, and so they had to hurry
after him again.

"I tell you something foul has been happening here
in my absence, but now I mean to get to the bottom of
it! Certain members of our church came to me late last
night to talk of these matters, and to ask me to set things
right. And that is what I intend to do! I have also heard
there are those from Boston who've come to our village
to give us their opinions—with no good result. I tell
you it is time for the people of Bracebridge to take their
own business in hand, and root out the cause of their
own trouble!"

Strong approval from every side greeted this idea,
but again the reverend held up his hand, and this time
he *did* stop walking. The few behind him who thought
they had learned their lesson kept on until they bumped
into the men carrying the miller's corpse, which added a
few new snarls to the general confusion.

"What news is there of the whereabouts of this
Frenchman?" Rowe called out. "Who is sheltering him?"

Several voices spoke up at once, but one rang above the rest.

"He's gone over to the inn! Peter came and told us so, back at the Blue Boar last night. Jonathan Pratt offered Fortier work—and this even after the Frenchman threatened to kill the miller!"

"Threatened to *kill* him?" Rowe repeated, glaring from left to right.

"He's not the only one who's made threats against him, either!" came a rejoinder.

"That's right! Peter told Mistress Willett he knew she'd hidden the Frenchman on her farm, when we were looking for him—"

"He did! And she accused him of terrible things—"

"Mrs. Willett!" Rowe's voice thundered. Then it turned to honey, as he spied her in the crowd. "Mrs. Willett . . . *why* have you given refuge to this unwelcome stranger in our midst?"

"It's true he told me he'd slept in my dairy," Charlotte began, speaking loudly enough to be heard by the reverend across several heads. "But I know him to be innocent of anything to do with the first—"

"Innocent! And how is that for *you* to say? I would have thought you would have plenty to do just now, madam, without the help of a man on your large farm, without even a man to protect and instruct you, and with harvest time upon us. And yet, you come here and tell us that a fugitive whom we all seek is *innocent?*"

"Reverend Rowe, there are things known only to Captain Montagu which—"

"Ah, Captain Montagu! The man sent here to assure our safety. The man whose presence has done nothing to prevent one certain murder, and possibly even two!"

A worried rumble rose around the preacher as the others considered his bold statement. An official from

Boston was, after all, a voice of authority, and one to be heeded rather than annoyed, if such a thing were possible. But could the death of the miller, and that of Sam Dudley, now somehow fit together? And *would* Montagu do anything about either of them?

"Mrs. Willett," Rowe added, his voice softly menacing again, "how is it that your hair has fallen down in a most unusual manner? Could it be that you've had no time to put it up after some recent . . . *rendezvous*? It would be well for you to remember that what's often overlooked in Philadelphia, or in Boston, will not be tolerated here! Go home, and look to your own person, and to your own business!"

This barb met with derisive laughter that caused Charlotte's cheeks to flame—though little enough of it was meant for her. More than a few of the men and women present thought Rowe had gone too far in his personal attack on a neighbor. Phineas Wise, for one, disagreed with Rowe. After all, he asked several of those around him, weren't the Quakers plainer folk than most of those now living in Massachuetts? And didn't Charlotte Willett take pains to follow many of their ways? Hardly a brazen woman, she—though certainly comely, one might admit. Even so, he couldn't remember there being any scandalous talk about Mrs. Willett's virtue before. (At least, nothing that she could be blamed for.) And as for adequately running her brother's farm, well, what was wrong with that?

"An interfering woman has hidden the source of our contamination, and led to murder," shouted Dick Craft, using a biblical turn of phrase that astounded more than one person in the crowd. "Let's go and search her farm, to see what else someone might have hidden there. Maybe that's where the gold is!"

For a moment, the crowd held its breath, and considered.

"First," Reverend Rowe jumped in, "we'll go to the inn and find this Frenchman." It seemed to Charlotte now that even Rowe wondered if he had overstepped his bounds, at least in the case of her appearance.

"I doubt if he'd dare to stay there if he did kill Peter Lynch," spoke up Mrs. Hiram Bowers. A few other women agreed that this was only sensible, including Esther Penny-wort, who still scanned the crowd from time to time, looking for her husband.

"We will divide ourselves, for speed," instructed Rowe, "into two groups. I will lead the first to the inn, where we will inquire of this Captain Montagu what he knows, and where the Frenchman might be. The second group will escort Mrs. Willett to her farm—for her own safety—will look for the same Frenchman, and do whatever else must be done. Let us be quick and let us be quiet, lest the guilty be warned."

By this time, they had reached the meetinghouse doors. Those who carried Peter Lynch made their way inside, where the unwieldy body of the miller was deposited with little ceremony into the alcove, and the damp men who'd carried him tromped out again into the chilly morning air.

"What about Bowers?" one of them inquired, and the rest hesitated, although many were on their toes to go.

"Where is the constable now?" Rowe asked, looking around.

"Gone off somewhere this morning," his wife announced. "With Mr. Longfellow, he told me."

"I believe Mr. Longfellow—" began Charlotte, until one of the surly men clasped his hand firmly onto her arm.

"Yes, Mrs. Willett?" asked the reverend, as he would have asked a tiresome child what it wanted.

"Nothing," she replied, and left it to them to find out for themselves.

"We may not have had a body before, but we've got

a body now, by God—and a murderer to catch," thundered a tall man in the back, who beckoned to the rest. "Let's go and find him!"

At that, the crowd started out, scuttling on its way like a centipede, one undulating segment carrying along a captive woman with flying, cider-colored hair.

HANNAH SLOAN LOOKED up as she heard shouting. Before she could rid her hands of laundry water and cover a wooden tub with its lid, two men who held Mrs. Willett between them entered the low kitchen—only to find that the odds were now about even. Hannah's stern countenance, and her firm-footed stance, told them that they should advance no farther—at least for the moment.

"We've come to find Fortier," one of them said, causing Hannah to look at him closely.

"Here? There's no one here! And what do you mean, holding onto Mrs. Willett that way?"

"We've escorted her home, where she ought to be."

"I happen to know she's been out this morning offering her assistance to Mrs. Dudley. I doubt you can say as much good for yourself, Ephram Dawes. What was the bell for? And why are these men—" Hannah stared in disbelief out the window. ". . . stealing Mrs. Willett's chickens?"

"They're searching the farm, although I guess it's not going to do much good. I came here, Hannah, to keep this lady from harm. There are some who think she deserves a lesson, after what they heard in the Blue Boar last night from Peter Lynch—"

"Who is dead," Charlotte interrupted, staring hard at Hannah.

"Murdered, you mean," the large woman answered sharply.

"And just how would you know that?" Ephram

asked, suddenly suspicious. "We only found him a few minutes ago!"

"A lucky guess. Now, run upstairs, open all the doors, look where a man might hide, and then leave this house, or I swear I'll carry you both out myself. It's a child's game you're playing, and no mistake."

Shaking her head grimly, Hannah set about starting a pot of tea, while Charlotte gazed at Ephram, seeming to ask if he needed any further instruction. He did not.

The two men went into the next room and through the house quickly, then left by the kitchen door with something like an apology offered in passing.

"I think," said Charlotte, removing the last of her pins, "that they may have difficulty finding what they're looking for."

"Was Peter Lynch really killed?" asked Hannah Sloan, sitting down. Charlotte nodded thoughtfully, holding on to a twist of her hair.

"And I don't believe he's the first, either. What I have to wonder now," she added, staring at her friend, "is whether he'll be the last."

Chapter 20

THE THREE MEN visiting the Dudley farm had also heard the ringing of the bell, but had continued their examination until they were satisfied. Leaving young Sam's corpse and returning to the open air, they glimpsed a crowd in the distance. It seemed to be gathered around the meetinghouse. As the trio hurried forward, they saw it move off, heading up the hill on the Boston road.

Soon, the main body turned toward the inn, while others continued on to Mrs. Willett's gate. Longfellow felt a familiar disquiet. Taking long strides across the bridge, he wondered what Charlotte had done this time. First, she had married a Quaker. Now, she lived without a husband, or a relative of any kind. And recently, she had pulled the miller's beard. The woman didn't exactly encourage trouble, but it seemed to court her—as he wished a man of substance might do, and soon. Had the miller now come for his revenge, leading a mob?

Longfellow looked back at the thickset public servant who rolled along like a galleon behind him, fully aware of the man's limitations, as well as those of his temporary position. He knew well it was not a constable who kept order and peace, but the will of the people. And this was a will Richard Longfellow trusted only so far.

Beside him, Captain Edmund Montagu thought once more of what he had seen of Sam Dudley. Without a physician, there was no way to be absolutely sure. But Longfellow had said he'd already sent for one of the best, and that he should be arriving soon. The man would confirm what they both suspected. The bruising had been slight, but the coincidence was great—far too great to ignore. It was more than likely, thought Montagu, that the boy's death had not been an innocent one. And he decided to postpone his departure for one more day.

The sluggish mind of Hiram Bowers was also mulling over the possibilities suggested by the body, the alarm, and the crowd that had just turned toward the inn—but why were some of them advancing to Jeremy Howard's property, up and across the way? The townspeople were on edge—the constable knew that only too well! Many of them even expected *him* to set their minds at ease. If only they would learn to settle their own fears, as he so often had to do with his own. Now, something seemed to have irritated them again. Hiram thought that he would be glad when the end of the year rolled around, and he could go back to selling buttons. Now, what was it someone had said the other day about Mrs. Willett? Ah, yes. It seemed Jack Pennywort—the last one to see the merchant Middleton alive—had paid a visit to Mrs. Willett yesterday, supposedly to do some work, which he avoided in the end. Phineas Wise said he'd come back for another pint, just half an hour after he'd left in the first place. But Jack would not discuss his visit with the lady, and that in itself was very strange . . . not even after he'd been brought two free tankards. Jack had even gone home early. Very queer indeed! Well looking on the bright side, maybe the crowd that now entered the inn had found something to celebrate. It was possible. Any- thing could happen, and often did. Maybe the others had gone to invite Mrs. Willett to join them. In his usual fog, Hiram Bowers marched on, looking forward to enjoying a pint with the rest.

When they reached the inn's gate, Montagu and the constable plunged into the crowd, while Longfellow continued on. He soon found the search of Charlotte's outbuildings nearly concluded, and the two women in- side idly drinking tea. As long as they were safe, they urged him, might he not do better to see what else was going to happen? After taking a moment to catch his breath and have a swallow of hot tea, Longfellow, too, made for the Bracebridge Inn.

Sadly, he was too late to witness the lengthy initial confrontation between the Reverend Rowe and Edmund Montagu—one an acknowledged pillar of godliness, the other a jealous protector of the Crown's prerogatives. But the latter was only one official protector, in the face of many curious souls. And so, Montagu followed a flus- tered Jonathan Pratt through a search of the inn's first floor, while the landlord, in turn, trailed a group led by the reverend. Finding nothing, they next prepared to ex- plore the rooms above.

It was now suggested that the inn also housed one other stranger who had been in Bracebridge for several days, and for no good reason—unless one believed the absurd idea that he observed the ways of animals, and was paid to reveal them. This man was also known to have been out of doors at all hours, able to see, and hear, and possibly do evil. This stranger was Adolphus Lee. By the time the reverend and his followers mounted the

stairs to the second floor, they were buoyed by the remainder of the crowd that had returned from Charlotte's
farm, and those who had completed an unsuccessful
search of Jonathan Pratt's outbuildings. Still notably absent were three members of the inn's own family. There
was no sign, Montagu realized as he looked around, of
the servant girl Mary Frye. Nathan, the smith, was missing as well—so, too, was the landlord's wife.

Jonathan Pratt also wondered why his wife had not
come forward at the beginning of the commotion. It was
unlike Lydia to let anything take its natural course, if she
could hope to direct it and perhaps even hand out blame.
Climbing the steps, he heard those ahead corner a bewil-
dered Tim (who had gone up for a better view of what was
coming), and demand to know Adolphus Lee's whereabouts. The boy pointed to a door that stood next to the
Jamaica Room, behind which the man usually slept for
much of the day. A knock produced no result. A path was
cleared for the landlord, who by right might open.

But . . . something stood in the way. Apparently, a
chest of drawers had been pulled across to slow, perhaps,
an unwanted entrance. But enter the stout landlord did,
with a push and a shove, until light flooded out to the
dark hallway, forcing the visitors to blink—against their
will, for none of them wanted to miss a thing.

Inside, as expected, was Adolphus Lee. He sat upon a
rumpled bed, wearing only his breeches, his face con-
torted in a look of fascinated horror. At the same time,
through the crack at the door's hinges, frills of a shift
could be seen. And although the woman who wore it
could not be observed in her entirety, those who noticed
suspected they saw a portion of Lydia Pratt within. *Whoever* the woman was, there was no doubt that, as Jonathan
Pratt's searching eyes peered around the door, she emitted
a squeak.

Meanwhile, caught in a trap with no easy exit, Mr.

Lee looked longingly through the window, as if hoping for some assistance from the natural world.

The hushed crowd shifted its feet uncertainly. Finally, Jonathan Pratt cleared his throat to address his neighbors.

"Seeing that you have not found what it is you are searching for, I hope you will finish with the empty rooms, and then leave my house. It would appear that my guest and I have certain matters to look into." With this, he gently closed the door on the room's occupants.

Even the Reverend Rowe, hearing whispers around him, believed that some things were sacred to marriage— at least, in the first round. He had hardly been prepared for what he'd discovered. Pratt, after all, was one of the largest and most regular contributors to the church, a man who saw to many of its needs; in fact, he'd just sent over that rare and valuable coin the night before. The reverend quickly decided that he had an entire flock to consider first, however much one erring member might have earned his, and the Lord's, wrath. Besides, he had always greatly admired Lydia Pratt himself, feeling that she was something of a kindred spirit. Later, they would talk, and he would show her a better way.

Already envisioning the encounter, Reverend Christian Rowe licked his lips, as he silently led the others in a quick peek at the remaining rooms. Then, they went down the steps and out through the inn's side door.

Watching them go, Jonathan Pratt stood whistling quietly, his cheeks playing with the beginnings of a satisfied smile.

"LIKE SOME BUFFOONERY from a recent novel," was the way Longfellow described the scene later in the afternoon to Charlotte and Hannah Sloan, after he had knocked some of the season's first snow from his coat and planted himself by the fire. Next to him, Lem (who had hurried in the cows earlier) grinned at what he heard, and decided in future to ask Mr. Longfellow for suggested reading material.

"Finding Lee with . . . a lady . . . restored part of the town's good humor, and certainly gave them something to talk about—as well as yet another excuse to adjourn to the Blue Boar."

"Let's hope they stay there for a while," said Hannah, vowing to herself to find more for her own menfolk to do.

Charlotte remained silent as a further revelation came to her. So *that* was what Mary Frye had meant! The maid had probably caught Lydia before, hearing her say she had been one place, when Mary knew the landlady had really been in another. At a small inn, secrets of that sort could only be kept for so long.

"'Diana will be pleased when I tell her," Longfellow added, "though it will make her wish she hadn't slept so late. My sister has wished Lydia gone more than once. And now I suppose she'll have her way. As usual."

"She won't be the only one who's pleased," agreed Hannah.

"They tell me," Longfellow went on, "that Lee's moved over to the Blue Boar until he can finish his work."

"He's staying?" Charlotte asked with surprise.

"Since he's already produced letters from respected men at Cambridge, the village can't very well throw him out for this—at least not without Jonathan's help, which he doesn't seem anxious to give. So, since Jonathan is one of our own selectmen, and I happen to be another, there's not much anyone can do about Adolphus Lee. The situation certainly shows us how times have changed. I doubt if we could have kept poor Lydia out of the stocks several years ago. If anyone had wanted to."

"How is Jonathan?"

"Quite happy, I should say. When the rest left without speaking—general embarrassment was quite plain, and after all, Jonathan hadn't said the first word against her—then I wondered if he might not enjoy having the upper hand, for once. As for Lee, he's a sort of hero now, having deprived the local dragon of her fire!"

At least, thought Charlotte, some steam had escaped from the pie before any further harm had been done.

"But they didn't find . . . anyone else they were looking for?" she asked.

"Who, Lynch's murderer? They didn't find Gabriel Fortier, if that's who you mean. At first, they thought at the inn that Mary had run off with him. But she came back a while later, with her apron full of butternuts she'd been off gathering before the snow started. She says she only saw Fortier in the morning—said Nathan woke him up early, and set him to work mending an ax in the back. Where the Frenchman is now, I couldn't say."

Charlotte again saw the long, bloodless wound in the miller's forehead.

"An ax?" she whispered.

"Many hours *after* the work you're thinking of, from what you've described to me of the body, which, incidentally, I greatly look forward to seeing. I might even try an experiment or two . . . but I believe the miller must have been floating for most of the night—probably since late last evening, I would guess."

"Then—"

"It would seem Gabriel Fortier escaped today from what must have looked to him like a mob coming for his blood. Whether he's guilty of anything or not, he had reason enough to run."

"Then you don't think—"

"I think Mary Frye is far better off today than she

was last night. Beyond that, I have several *other* things to think about, at the moment."

"Richard, I only know a little about anatomy . . . some of medicines, I'll admit, but very little about the rest. It did strike me when I saw Sam Dudley this morning that a physician—"

"—might tell us how, exactly, he died. An excellent idea! Given the circumstances, I thought as much last night, so I sent for a fellow named Warren I met in town a few months ago. I've been meaning to invite him here. I think you'll like Joseph. He speaks his mind, and he listens, too, from time to time. One of the most promising of the recent graduates of Harvard College."

"Oh! I look forward to meeting him."

"You might do a little more, Carlotta, since he's coming all the way from Boston, and he'll be here this morning. As you know, the inn's kitchen is upside down at the moment."

"And yours hasn't held much appeal for anyone lately."

"Well—yes. I'd hoped you'd allow us to share a little something at your generous fireside. Nothing fancy."

"If I'm ever at a loss for funds, I might make ends meet by opening a public house. I imagine you'd steer quite a healthy business my way."

"A privilege I would offer *only* to those who meet your high standards of behavior and taste."

"You're lucky I've heard, too, that Dr. Warren is a handsome man who has a delightful beside manner. Have you heard that as well?"

"Not from any Tories, certainly; he's most noted in town for his republican manner, above anything else."

"Are you trying to frighten me?"

"Would it be possible?"

"Quite! Still, none of us should cast the first stone, I suppose. I've heard we are all by nature political animals;

although I'm not sure the man who said so meant to include females."

"Would that be a quotation from Dr. Franklin?"
asked Lem, who had been following only some of the
conversation.

"Aristotle," replied Longfellow. "An older gentleman, and not quite as popular. Although he had his
day. Look in Mrs. Willett's library, and we'll discuss him
later."

A new noise at the front door made Charlotte rise
with a hand to her cheek. But it was only Cicero, who
brought in Joseph Warren before retiring across the
garden.

LONGFELLOW ROSE FROM the table, and immediately
went to clasp Warren's hand and shoulder, aware that
Charlotte had already begun to examine the visitor for
herself.

"I also have it on good authority that most of his
teeth are his own," her neighbor offered with a grin.

Warren quickly caught his meaning, and turned to
scrutinize his hostess boldly, causing her to look away
from his sky-blue eyes.

The physician was, she had already decided, a very
pleasing man, exceptionally fair but with a kind of glow.
His face could probably hide little. She could imagine
that he was as she'd heard—a man who would fly to action whenever the call came, wherever he felt he was in
the right. It was said he had an argumentative nature.
Still, he would probably prove a rewarding friend.

"I believe our hostess is satisfied," said Longfellow.
"But now, we have to go. We'll be back shortly. Bodies,
if you'll excuse my mentioning it, may not be preferable to dinner, but they claim precedence—and now we
have two."

"Two?" asked Warren, turning. "Your note said only that a young man—"

"Oh, that was last night! This morning, we found another. However, let me show you, before I spoil the surprise. By the way, Mrs. Willett has invited us back here to dine."

"I'll see what can be done," Charlotte answered, looking to Hannah.

"Our thanks, Carlotta. Say, Warren," asked Longfellow, in the highest of spirits, "could we use more company, do you think?"

"From what I hear of these parts lately, we would be wise to seek a crowd."

"You may change your mind about that, when I tell you the rest," rejoined Longfellow, "but one more man wouldn't hurt. *Avanti!*" he cried, stalking out of the kitchen door after Warren. At the same time, he beckoned to a startled Lem, who followed in a rush.

Chapter 21

SOME TIME BEFORE, Mary Frye had been given an order to see to things downstairs—just before Lydia Pratt went up to the second floor, leaving the girl to guess at her quiet business. Then, the others had rushed in from the meetinghouse, bringing the news of the death of Peter Lynch—news that made Mary's heart leap, and race with fear. Hurrying out to Gabriel, she sent him off to a secret place known to them both. After that, she kept back from the crowd, while she strained to hear what it planned to do next.

Now, as the villagers headed homeward and the occupants of the inn watched them go, Mary returned to the empty kitchen and acted quickly. First, she snatched up some bread and meat, which she tied in her apron. Then she ran out the back door, pulling her cloak around her. Under her arm, wrapped in a cloth, she clutched a thin blade with a handle of deer horn—the same knife she'd wanted to bury in the miller on the previous evening.

Soon, Mary began to climb toward tree-covered knolls. As she crossed a tilted pasture, the air chilled her through her woolen garments. She saw that the sky to the north over the river plain had filled with layered clouds the color of pewter, while the heights away in New Hampshire brooded in smoky purples and blues.

In a few minutes she reached the trees, and began to thread her way between the trunks without a backward glance. Once inside the light wood, the girl felt entirely alone; she could hear only her own footsteps treading on the thick bed of leaves, and the distant cawing of a single crow. A sudden volley made her whirl with fear; but it was only icy snow beginning to fall around her. It brushed past high twigs, drummed through upstretched branches as its pellets multiplied, and finally skated across the frost-dried leaves that littered the forest floor.

Climbing on, Mary heard a ground wind rise and cry in the branches. A hiss like rising water came from everywhere, as more pellets began to slide in tiny drifts along ledges of exposed rocks. A deeper sound came suddenly on a downsweep—a roar from the churning sky. As bits of snow were blown against her body like spent shot, she imagined in quick terror the presence of an angry God she'd heard about so often.

Stilling her fears, she chose to challenge this freezing world. Though the inn's warmth was only minutes away, she plunged instead into a realm without duty or privilege, into a primitive land filled with a spirit that spoke loudly, whatever its message . . . and with enough power to cool even her own burning. But she had no intention of letting her passion die easily. Soon, she would see Gabriel. Again Mary felt a familiar thrill, shuffling her feet through the leaves to better smell the sweetness that mingled with the bitter scent of snow.

Looking down at her feet, she missed seeing the Frenchman as he watched her approach from behind a tree; nor did she have time to do anything more than let out a small scream when he leapt out after she'd passed. In an instant, Fortier threw his arms around Mary's slender waist. Before she could do anything at all his mouth covered hers; then hot breath warmed her frozen cheek while tears of pleasure spilled through her eyelashes, and trickled back onto her ears. Suddenly, he pulled away. Twining his cold fingers between her own, he pulled her up and over the granite boulders that guarded his hiding place. When he finally stopped, he took the food she offered, and laid it under a projecting ledge.

"Never leave me," he demanded, rather than asked, and her eyes widened.

"Never," she gasped as he clutched her to him. She could feel the strength of his arms beneath heavy woolen clothing.

"No matter what they tell you?"

Mary watched him lovingly, through a mist of tears.

"What do they say of you," she finally asked, "that couldn't as easily be said of me? We both had reason to hate him. I'll fight too, if I have to! We'll make our plans, and then we'll leave this place behind!"

There was a trace of wildness in her voice, as well as a new strength that Gabriel had not heard before.

"There's more to do first," he reminded her. "For now, I'll wait here. And you will go back to safety."

"But you'll freeze!"

"I'll build a fire when it's too dark for anyone to see the smoke from below."

"Gabriel, I think I know where you can hide inside, where it's warm—somewhere they won't look for you."

"Where?"

"I'll tell you tomorrow. I'll come for you as soon as I'm sure."

"Why do you love me, *chère* Marie?" Gabriel asked, pulling her close again.

"Because you're handsome, which you know is true," she answered, managing a smile. He brushed back her hair, wondering at its new perfume. Again, the space between them closed and words became unnecessary. For a while longer, they huddled together for warmth, then sought something more. The wind continued to howl, and a fresh, clean snow fell like a blanket all around.

"THE KILLER MUST have been an unusually strong man." Joseph Warren settled the quilt over Sam Dudley's throat, softened now that *rigor mortis* had gone from the young body.

Longfellow had watched closely as the doctor made his examination, guessing Warren's conclusions before they were spoken. Now, he looked to Lem, who still stood uncertainly by the door, staring at the neighbor he had long known.

"Impossible," the physician said finally, "to be certain of all the damage done. The crushed area I showed you would have been enough to make the boy lose consciousness; then, his face could have been immersed while he was unable to struggle. If he died from the throttling, there would be no water in the lungs . . . but I don't think there's any reason to look for it. Either way, we know someone was responsible for his death."

"So there's no longer a chance that it was an accident," Richard Longfellow concluded. He watched Lem's face harden. Then, he turned back to observe Warren's expression in the fading light.

"I'd say none at all. No more than with the miller."

"Which is what I thought."

"Although," Warren continued, "how the Devil that leviathan you showed me at the church was overcome in the open is another question I'd like to hear the answer to."

All three were silent for a moment before Warren had an inspiration.

"It could be that whatever struck him was thrown."

"A tomahawk?" Lem asked suddenly.

"I suppose that's unlikely, isn't it? It's probably a special talent."

"Not particularly special, around here," Longfellow allowed.

"I did notice that the blow was a little off center," Warren went on, "if that's any help to you. If it was caused by someone holding on to a shaft, then it was probably held by a person who generally uses his right hand."

"Which would be most of us," said Longfellow, wondering again at the extent of the doctor's dedication to Science.

"And I could be wrong. As you know, this sort of thing isn't usual in Boston, either—for all the wild Indians said to live there."

"If someone did manage to strike at him from an *ambuscade*," mused Longfellow, "say, from somewhere inside his mill where a hatchet was handy—then why, and *how*, did he take the miller outside? He's nearly the size of a side of beef."

"He is that," Warren agreed. "Another difficulty, and again one requiring a powerful individual. As for the *why*, I imagine the killer might have wanted to get the body out of the mill to hide it—although the corpse naturally rose to the surface later, in spite of sinking initially. Most might not realize that it would. But—if he was dragged to the pond after being killed . . . as we believe Sam here was put into the water after he was throttled . . . that could be a further indication, could it not? Showing a similarity of habit."

"Then you feel we are looking for one large, cold-hearted, somewhat tidy double murderer."

"Or, two smaller—who both did the deed, and the dragging?" Warren countered, one eyebrow climbing. "What, Richard, do you say to that?"

For once, Longfellow only scowled, and said nothing at all.

OUTSIDE, THE SKY had stopped dropping snow, at least for a while, and there was a welcome lull in the wind for their walk back. As the three figures started away from the house, a smaller shot around the corner from the back, trying to catch them before they went far. Anne Dudley had been unable to reach the ear of her tall visitor earlier in the day, when he'd been with the constable, and the man from Boston with the lovely buttons. Now, she had another chance.

"Mr. Longfellow, please?" her tiny voice asked.

Longfellow looked down after feeling a tug on his sleeve. He saw again a short blond creature, and noticed familiar tortoiseshell combs inexpertly nestled above her braids.

"Yes, madam?" he asked, bending. "What is it you require?"

"I was told you're very fond of crowns," the child said boldly. Joseph Warren laughed long enough to bring a smile even to the face of the solemn little girl.

"A secret monarchist after all, Richard?" the doctor chided. "This will be quite a story for our club. Sam Adams will be particularly thrilled."

"Friend Adams can . . ." Longfellow hesitated, then addressed the little girl with curiosity. "What kind of crowns?"

"Silver ones—" Anne held her two first fingers apart at the proper distance, to give him a better idea.

"Silver ... on Spanish dollars, do you mean?" She beamed her approval, and he thrust a hand deep into a pocket to see what he could find, while he asked a further question—though he was certain he knew the answer.

"May I know who told you so?"

"Mrs. Willett. Charlotte's a queen's name, too, my mother says, just like mine. Mine's Anne."

"A very good name." He brought out a coin, examined it for a moment, and then gave it over to a remarkably quick hand, while Lem watched with disapproval.

"Mrs. Willett's quite right. I am fond of them, which is why I occasionally give them to my friends," said Longfellow, straightening. He was rewarded with a low curtsy before the little girl rushed away.

"Not a very honest way to make a profit," Lem threw after her. Dr. Warren seemed interested, and answered the boy's accusation himself.

"So you think talk and flattery are poor things to be paid for?"

Longfellow took the girl's side. "It was well done, and well coached, if you ask me. Young Anne might make a fine actress on the stage some day, if they ever allow a decent one in Boston."

"She has lost something this day, as well as gained," Warren reminded Lem. "Mrs. Willett, I take it, has been here before us," he added to Longfellow.

"A woman of unusual curiosity, Warren, so beware. Though she's an admirable neighbor, and a good example to follow, in most things. You might ask this young man about her; he's apparently begun to formulate opinions on women."

Longfellow leaned over and ruffled Lem's wayward hair, before they began the walk back.

"Do you suppose Mrs. Willett noticed what those

who found him apparently missed?" Warren eventually asked.

"I believe she did. She thought to call a medical man earlier today, before I'd mentioned you were coming."

"One more thing . . . should we report to your village constable before we enjoy our dinner, or after?"

"After. But then, I think we'd do better to go and tell Edmund Montagu instead—"

"Montagu!" Dr. Warren stopped in his tracks. "Is he here?"

"He's staying at the inn."

"Is he?" Warren's pale eyes flashed. "Then there must be even more here than I've seen so far."

"You know him?"

"Of course. As someone who takes a particular interest in what the governor and his quiet men are up to, I would."

"Would you, indeed?" Longfellow asked as he regarded the other, wondering how far his new friend would be willing to explain. Warren, meanwhile, attempted to hide his curiosity from man and boy by scanning the clouds above them, as all three crunched along the snowy road.

Longfellow noticed that Lem, too, usually so dull with company, had seemed quite interested in the doctor's remarks. That, and other things, made him decide it might be time to begin to study this boy more carefully, to see exactly what he was made of—and to guess, from that, what he might become.

IN THE SMALL parlor attached to his bedroom at the Bracebridge Inn, Edmund Montagu sat and stared at a length of steaming wool. He had spread the scarlet cloak over the back of a tall chair, where it continued to drip in front of the fire. Other clothes had been found tied up in the cape, along with a large stone. These were stretched over a nearby table. They, too, matched what had reportedly been worn by Duncan Middleton on the day the merchant disappeared. But why were they here?

Montagu had already looked each article over carefully. The only thing of interest seemed to be that it had all been hidden in the same pond where they'd found the body of Peter Lynch a few hours before. The searchers had hoped to find the missing ax, and find it they did on a later pass with their hooked poles, although the weapon's recovery had been unable to excite the waiting crowd as highly as the first unexpected find. To them, the bundle of clothing was certain proof that someone had wanted to hide what was left of Middleton.

Montagu was still convinced that the merchant was alive. But he couldn't help wondering why the man hadn't simply taken his cloak away ... or at least the smallclothes that had been pitched into the water. Perhaps the cloak was too bulky, too conspicuous to risk leaving with. But all the rest? Montagu smiled to think of the old rascal itching now in some farmer's Sabbath attire.

At any rate, he hoped there would be no more nonsense from the villagers about a mysterious fire lit by witches. He pulled his hands from his pockets and rubbed them together briskly. His work here was nearly over. But there was something else he needed to reconsider. Someone had very likely helped Middleton in his "disappearance" and his flight. Time had pointed a finger at Peter Lynch, whose mill stood conveniently near the scene of the merchant's fiery show. If the odd pair *had* met before, was Lynch also the agent who was planning to take the tainted rum off Middleton's hands? If so, it was no surprise that Lynch had a gold coin to spare, to give proof to his tale about the Frenchman. Middleton could have arranged for the miller to supply him with a horse and a place to wait until he might leave Brace-bridge unnoticed. But now, Peter Lynch was dead. *Why?*

Had Middleton come back later, surprised the miller, and killed him to protect the fiction of his demise? Un-likely, if Lynch was part of his future plans. And it wouldn't have been an easy job for an old man. The cap-tain thought again of the *scenario* Charlotte Willett had followed, when she described Middleton jumping down to hide under his cloak at the side of the road. It had sounded plausible at the time; but now, he wondered.

Another thing—if Middleton had murdered the miller, it meant the merchant had hidden somewhere in the vicinity for at least forty-eight hours. Why had he waited? And where? Someone would certainly have no-ticed the old devil skulking around, white and crabbed. Who in Bracebridge would not see him and tell others, when everyone was aware of what they thought was the man's spectacular demise? No, Montagu still believed Middleton was long gone, and that there must be a better answer to the question of who had killed Peter Lynch.

The Frenchman, of course, was the most likely can-didate. Gabriel Fortier had a very good reason to want the miller dead, and soon. He had youth and agility, even if he wasn't especially large. And further, if Lynch had encountered him in the dark, and Gabriel Fortier already had the hatchet in his hand, surprise or even a quick woodsman's toss could explain how he had avoided the miller's steely arms. Montagu happened to know from experience that a man carrying a candle at night made a superb target. And afterward? For Gabriel to have carried the miller outside by himself was just possi-ble. Montagu also knew, from witnessing events of the battlefield, that a fatal head wound might take minutes or even hours to kill. Often, the most ghastly wounds did not to stop a man from speaking, or babbling at least; an injured man might even get up and run a while before he collapsed and died. The brain was still a mystery to medical men, however much they peered and prodded when they got the chance.

So—the wounded miller could have stumbled out of his mill, dislodged and thrown away the ax in his death throes, fallen, and landed in the water. Or, the hatchet might have been thrown far into the pond by the Frenchman, who would undoubtedly have been following to see a proper end to his work. If things had gone as he had just imagined, thought Montagu, one thing was clear. It would be difficult for Gabriel Fortier to claim self-defense if ever he came to trial.

At any rate, the sodden cape hung before him; it would be something to show to Longfellow and his lovely sister. A fascinating creature, but on the whole, he wasn't sure if he wouldn't be happier spending a quiet evening with Charlotte Willett. There was a woman who came from a different mold. And she was fair in more than the usual ways. Her conclusions concerning the disappearance of old Middleton had been brilliantly simple, and quite possibly correct—although her theory now seemed to him a little skewed. Maybe Mrs. Willett hadn't been *entirely* right, after all. Still, she had certainly led the pack at the start.

It would be interesting to hear her views on the murder of the miller, as well as thoughts she might have on Mary and the Frenchman, and on Fortier's current whereabouts. He even longed to know what she thought about the trials of Pratt the landlord, and the devious wife with her simian lover. One thing was certain. These people he'd met here were hardly the Puritans he had imagined still populated Massachusetts. This place was a good deal like England, after all!

Almost as an afterthought, he added the death of

the boy to this bubbling stew. What had Dr. Warren concluded about young Dudley? Montagu would know before long. But very soon, he would have to let someone
else take over the problem of finding Fortier, and bringing the boy's killer, whoever he was, to justice. His own
problem was still to discover the whereabouts of Duncan
Middleton. And it was barely possible, he had to admit,
that the old man himself was in no way connected to
these two deaths at all.

Still, coincidence could be pushed only so far. And
yet—

Was it also possible that something else was going
on here, something he hadn't even begun to understand?
Reaching for his glass of wine, Edmund Montagu lifted
both feet onto the low table in front of him, settled into
his cushioned chair, and stared intently into the dancing fire.

Chapter 22

AFTER DINNER, WHILE logs crackled in the grate over a bed of squeaking, popping coal, Charlotte offered coffee to Longfellow and Dr. Warren.

Before returning for their promised fare, the doctor had agreed to stay the night in one of Longfellow's extra bedrooms. Now, in no hurry to go, both men took their ease, while outside the window a drier, colder snow fell gently, drifting over garden, lawn, and fields.

It was a shame Diana had chosen to stay at her brother's with Cicero, thought Charlotte, but she had found it necessary—she said—to wash and curl her hair. Possibly, she waited for a visit from a certain captain. And probably, she realized that death must be dinner's main subject—as it had been.

Warren had repeated for his hostess his reasons for believing that Sam Dudley's death had not been accidental. For her part, Charlotte took the story of the

Dutch gold one step further; she told them how, according to the boy's young sister, a piece of gold had been
given to Sam. And she explained her notion that the
coin had been taken away after his death by whoever
killed him. She also offered her earlier thoughts on Peter
Lynch's connection to both Middleton and the boy. The
next problem was to come up with a way to explain the
miller's murder. They had each stopped talking, and
spent several moments in thought.

"The miller," Warren began again, "from what I've
heard, probably knew several men who might have
wished him dead."

"An accurate epitaph," Longfellow interjected with
a bleak smile, "if not a very happy one."

"So there probably weren't many he would have
welcomed," Warren continued, "on hearing someone in
his mill after his usual hour for closing. And untrusting,
he would seem to have been a very hard man to undo.
An interesting paradox."

"Lynch had at least a few friends, for all his lack of
charm. Jack Pennywort, for instance, listened to his
boasts and stories, and Wise, the tavern keeper, fed him
on a fairly regular basis. There might have been one or
two more."

"But not this Frenchman of yours. Surely, though,
he couldn't have approached Lynch, at least in a threatening manner, unless it was from behind—which is not
the way he was killed. Upon reflection, I don't really
believe the ax was thrown after all. I've been thinking,
and I believe that if it had been, the gash would have
been deeper. I have seen what that kind of an edge can
do, when you fellows practice on trees. Yet you tell me
that Fortier isn't large. One very big individual, or two
smaller—it comes to that again. Now, if one of a *pair* had
provided a distraction, then the other might have come

up close behind. At the last moment, Lynch might have turned, and—"

Warren brought the side of a surprisingly delicate hand up like an ax against his forehead. Longfellow's lips twisted, while he looked to their hostess, hoping to see her shudder. He only saw that Charlotte seemed far away. Following her eyes, he, too, watched the snow fall into the shivering maples beyond the curtains.

"Or it might still be one person," she murmured, "if the helper happened to be some kind of unseen agent."

"Agent?" asked Warren alertly.

"If you mean whiskey," ventured Longfellow, "don't forget that Lynch was a man who could hold his liquor. He'd had a good deal of practice."

"What if he'd been lulled half asleep," Charlotte said, still apparently trying the idea on herself, "befuddled, or even frightened by something else he didn't know was affecting him? What if he'd been given some sort of concoction—a medicine, or even a poison? I know several things to quiet an illness that are easy enough to come by; so do most women who nurse their families. If I wanted to attack the miller myself, I'd first try to make him as helpless as possible."

"A good idea," Longfellow responded uneasily. He was alarmed by the avenue of thought this opened up to him, but the doctor seemed encouraged.

"Would you, Dr. Warren," Charlotte asked hesitantly, "think to look for signs of anything of the kind, while you were examining a corpse?"

"With an obvious injury to blame, no. I probably wouldn't."

"I remember that the miller had a slight rash."

"Yes—a recent brush with nettles, I'd thought. But you're right! Such a rash could have been caused by a reaction to some kind of plant, or even a poison. Unfortunately, my knowledge of botany isn't great," he added.

"I can help you there," Longfellow threw in. "Lynch might have been affected by a great many things. I know of several plants that plague our farms by causing harm to animals . . . although I've not seen detailed descriptions of how they affect man. At any rate, there's Jamestownweed, for one—what Linnaeus calls *Datura stramonium*. Bad for sheep and cattle, though it's sometimes smoked to relieve constriction of the chest. Then there are the banes. The Mediterranean henbane has unfortunately been introduced, and now grows wild here, dropping seeds that sometimes kill chickens; hence, the name." He paused, and Charlotte took a breath to speak.

"But—"

"Wolfbane, or monkshood—aconite," he continued, "is particularly deadly, though it's sometimes used in small amounts as a sedative. Its blue flower is attractive, so it is frequently found in pleasure gardens. There's also the wild arum, or wakerobin; cowbane, or water hemlock, very deadly; garden foxglove—to name but a few."

"I'm aware of problems with yew," Warren added thoughtfully. "Especially when its red berries interest our children."

"In short, we have a plethora of plants that might be used to sicken or kill a man, woman or child, growing right outside our doors."

"But," Charlotte tried again, to no avail.

"And yet some, as you say, Richard, are used for medicines as well. Poison or medicine might be only a matter of degree. What holds off the gout in one man may kill a patient unused to it outright."

"You speak from experience?"

"Well, I've only begun to practice, so I've not yet been in a position to kill off *many* on my own," Warren retorted dryly.

"You'll get to it, if you're like the rest. I'll tell you,

though, that if you're looking for a killer, certain poison-ous metals seem to be the preferred thing today."

"You're referring, of course, to the therapeutic use of mercury, arsenic, antimony—"

"But what," asked Charlotte quite loudly, "about the *miller*? Could you discover now, Dr. Warren, if anything had been introduced into his system before he died, that might alter his abilities, or his perceptions?"

"Tests of that kind are difficult enough when the victim is alive," Warren admitted. "I need to observe symptoms while a patient is able to tell me how he feels, to be reasonably sure of the cause. I believe it's circum-stance that catches most poisoners—where they ob-tained the poison, who saw them applying it, that sort of thing. That, and their natural desire to talk about what they've done. It's something we read about in the news-papers, time and again."

Longfellow nodded. "Just the other week, there was a story in the *Mercury* about a man in Newport—"

"Yes, I saw that!"

"Many times, too, it's a woman who does the deed, remember."

"Yes, well, I'll grant you poison is known as a woman's weapon. Certainly, a man might be wary of a sex that would use deadly nightshade drops, simply for beauty's sake. He might wonder—would they shrink from experi-menting on him, especially if their minds had already been affected by the action of the plant?"

"It does make one think."

"Not that females neglect the metals, either. You'll remember Captain Codman, no doubt—fed arsenic by two slaves for weeks, until he finally died of it. Although he probably deserved his fate." Dr. Warren went on to mull over the details, as well as the ghastly fate of a co-conspirator, whose mummified body still hung in chains on Charlestown Common, across the river from Boston.

Charlotte had given up trying to speak, and scarcely listened. Instead, she rose quietly and went out to look through the library shelves in the blue room. After that, she laid out a sheet of paper, opened some ink, took up a quill, and paused to consider. If she belonged to the circulating library in Boston . . . but at £1.8 per year! If only she were allowed to use the one at Harvard College, like her brother Jeremy. But that was unthinkable. No woman would ever be welcome in that place. Poisoning, Warren had said, was generally a woman's work. Slightly peeved, Charlotte took small pleasure in their apparent concern at how easy it might be. But in several more minutes, when she returned to the table, she discovered that her guests had moved on to another topic altogether.

"I must apologize for beginning to talk shop, Mrs. Willett, but I've just remembered meeting your merchant once, at the house of a surgeon who gave me instruction in dentistry. I've begun to tell Richard about the man's work," Warren explained, well aware of a social duty to win back his hostess's approval. She nodded for him to go on, for teeth were a subject of painful interest to most people, sooner or later, even if they cleaned and cared for them as well as—

What was it in the passing thought that made her jump in her chair? She had nearly remembered something important. She was sure of it . . . something that was trying to join itself to a statement the animated doctor had made but a moment before.

"They can be wired directly onto your own, and fill in a gap or two quite well. There are, of course, now whole plates made of gold, and set in front with ivory teeth from all kinds of tusks; these make quite a good show if your own are completely gone. Not that they would be of any actual use in eating, but they do improve the appearance."

"Did you say," Charlotte interrupted abruptly, "that Duncan Middleton had his teeth cared for by this man?"

"Not his teeth, exactly. Prescott usually works in construction now. Although he still looks at live teeth, too. Which is fortunate, for you'd be surprised how many do nothing but pull and staunch the blood, when with a little planning, some could be saved. But since Middleton had none—"

"Are you saying Duncan Middleton has *false* teeth?"

"Oh, yes. He came to see if Prescott could adjust them. Middleton is as toothless as a turtle. Mrs. Willett, are you feeling well?"

Quite well, thought Charlotte, if amazingly dull-witted. She remembered how Duncan Middleton had looked at her, with the eyes of a man who had something familiar on his mind. She recalled his pale complexion . . . almost as pale as Diana's had been the next afternoon. She thought of the valise she had examined in Middleton's room at the Inn, with its absence of toothbrush or cleansing powder, both of which a Boston man of wealth, certainly one who took the trouble to carry a shoehorn, would more than likely carry with him. Unless, of course, he had no use for them at all!

Again, in her mind's eye, she clearly saw the old man take a large bite of the new apple she'd given him. And she remembered how she had heard it crunch between what were obviously several sound teeth.

"The simplest things," she replied to both Longfellow and Warren, who were watching her face with some alarm, "are sometimes the least obvious. But I think—I really think that the 'old man' I saw on the road on Tuesday afternoon wasn't old at all. And he most certainly *wasn't Duncan Middleton!*"

Chapter 23

THE MAN I saw," Charlotte Willett hurried on, "wore the merchant's scarlet cloak. And rode his horse. But he had to be an imposter." She want on to explain about the teeth, causing Longfellow, who was speechless for a time, to slap his thigh.

"Montagu was so sure!" he exploded.

"Sure that the merchant is missing from his home, and that we have his horse and clothes and traveling bag here. Beyond that, the captain had only our vague descriptions to go on, and I'm afraid they might have been misleading. Now that I stop to think, the figure I described was nearly covered by a hat and wig, a full cloak, probably face powder and possibly even some other kind of theatrical disguise, as well. The high voice that I heard speak very briefly, and that Mr. Lee also remembers, proves nothing, since we'd never heard it before—and remember that he took care to *say* almost nothing, except to Lydia. For all we know, the man might even have been an actor hired to play a part."

Longfellow threw down his napkin and leapt up, to begin pacing the floor. "It would explain why Middleton's business and assets are intact. The real man only wanted to throw Montagu off his scent for a time! Drawing him here, the merchant would have had a few days clear. I wonder what else he has up his sleeve?"

"And the horse!" Charlotte exclaimed.

"Of course! Something did bother me when I heard Nathan's description, so I had a look myself. Then, I managed to forget all about it."

"How do you mean?" asked Warren.

"It's too absurd. No—let me tell you. The horse had been habitually and *recently* flogged, a thing I always find irritating, and a damning indication of a rider's poor sense and temper. Yet Nathan mentioned that its sides had already begun to heal when it got here. It was as though it had carried an altogether different rider on the day it came. And so it had."

On an impulse, Charlotte rose and closed the curtains. Then she moved away from the windows, closer to the fire. She remembered the tired animal that she, too, had seen. At least, she considered, the impostor who rode him into town was kinder to horses than the real Duncan Middleton had been. But what if . . . ?

"There is," she said quietly, "another possibility."

"Which is?" Longfellow inquired, watching her sink back into imagination.

"It could be someone knows that Middleton has died, and wants to hide the real cause and place—by making us think he came to Bracebridge. Don't forget that Captain Montagu said Middleton left home on Monday. The man we saw didn't arrive here until Tuesday, almost at evening."

"In that case," said Longfellow, "our imposter might also be . . ."

"A murderer."

"And where to you suppose that man is now?" Warren's quiet words continued in a placid way that made the others remember he was a trained physician, after all. "If I were you, Mrs. Willett, I would take great care. You've just told us something that might also have occurred to the imposter as well. You, alone, saw this man in an unguarded moment, in an attitude outside his pose. He may feel that you, of all people, are able to identify him—by this, or even by some other little slip he could have made. Or might make."

"There's still a good chance he left the area after performing his fireworks," Longfellow ventured cautiously.

"And you believe the two other deaths that occurred here were unrelated? In that case, I'll be glad to get back to the safety of the city! Everyday village life appears to be very bad for one's health."

"Warren, I think it's time for us to visit Edmund Montagu. And time for you, neighbor, to bolt your doors and windows again." Longfellow took Charlotte's hands and rubbed some warmth back into them. "Inside," he added with a grimace, turning for his hat and cloak, "it's *possible* that you might manage to stay out of further trouble, Carlotta."

The physician, too, rose. "Walk me over to your study, Longfellow, and I'll write out a quick report of my examinations of the miller and the boy. It might come in handy. Thank you again, Mrs. Willett, for your generosity. You will take care of yourself? And if there's ever anything I am able to do for you—"

Charlotte pressed a folded piece of paper into Warren's hand. "I did wonder earlier if you would look something up for me, and send me word of what you find. I know you're welcome to use our best scientific library."

"At Harvard College, you mean? Certainly. In fact, the place is on my way."

"It's a list of complaints—or what you'd call symptoms. They've been the talk of Bracebridge lately. Witchcraft has been whispered as their cause. But I believe something natural might produce many of them. I suspect it's an herb. I visited John Bartram's botanical garden in Philadelphia a few years ago, and we spoke at length about the healing properties of some of his specimens, but I'm afraid this is something quite different. While you and Richard were talking, I leafed through my father's copy of Josselyn's herbal, but it only contains New England species, and I don't think it's a native plant we're looking for. I know Richard has a great deal of knowledge about these things, but I'd hoped that as a physician you might also be interested."

Concentrating, Warren studied the list, and then returned her earnest look.

"There really should be some universal reference for poisons, or plants that might induce illness rather than health, but I don't believe one exists. I'll see what I can do. Though I *have* heard of a treatise on wounds and the appearance of various causes of death, written by a man in Leipzig. What an interesting new science to pursue— medicine, as it affects criminal behavior. A fascinating thought. Well, if you can spare your young man, he could ride in with me to Cambridge; I'll send him back with whatever I can find. Since I know the librarian, I don't think I'll have much trouble in borrowing a few volumes for a week or so. And Lem might like to see the sights of Harvard for himself."

"He could be needed here, especially now—" Longfellow began to object, but Charlotte stopped him.

"I think he'd like that," she said, giving the doctor her hand. She also promised to have Lem ready to ride, when Warren called early in the morning.

• • •

CHARLOTTE'S FRONT DOOR had barely been opened to the cold when Diana Longfellow mysteriously appeared, nearly hidden under a forest cape whose shoulders were dusted with snow.

"I've come to keep you company, Mrs. Willett. I'm afraid there's very little hope of society at the house where *I'm* staying. But I see that you have some of your own! Good evening, Dr. Warren," she finished with a brisk curtsy, after moving inside so that the door could be shut again.

A few moments more and the men were off, leaving only their regrets behind. For consolation, the ladies sat to drink a pot of tea by the replenished fire.

"Now there's a curious man. Still, he's not unattractive, and he's unattached." Diana gave her neighbor a meaningful glance. "By the way, did you see what I did with the small bottle of perfume I showed you at the inn yesterday afternoon?" she queried, slipping off a pair of her brother's jockey boots that had previously hidden under her skirts.

"The dragon bottle? No, I don't think so."

"How maddening! It's irreplaceable," Diana said with a sigh, settling herself into a chair in her stockinged feet, "and I hadn't even grown tired of it yet. Oh, well—perhaps it will turn up somewhere. I'm forever misplacing things, especially when I come here. At home I have much more to lose, but Patty always keeps an eye out. I've just come from the inn, where I had my own small dinner party with Captain Montagu, who still thinks he's the most exciting man in town—which, unfortunately, he is. I wonder, though, how other women deal with his smugness. Deep inside, you know, I'm convinced he's a passionate man. That doesn't surprise you? You know how I love to find what's underneath others' pretenses, when there's anything worth finding. In his case," she added, poising a fingernail delicately in the air and dimpling at the thought, "I think there is. If I can get under his skin just a little further . . ."

Charlotte had seen Diana's pursuits before, and didn't doubt that it would be an interesting time for both parties, whenever Miss Longfellow and Montagu might meet again.

"You'd better watch your step," she warned her coquettish friend. "The captain seems to be a clever man who usually gets what he wants. And I'm not sure he would approve of some of your friends."

"Well, neither do I, when it comes to that. Especially the ones who *will* dwell on business and politics. Hurrah for Captain Montagu, if he can keep them quiet on those subjects when he's around! Incidentally," Diana continued in a different tone, "you might like to know they've found the red cloak and other things in the millpond. Oh, and I should tell you before I go on—Mary stopped me as I was leaving, and asked me to thank you for all you've done. Now—have I told you about the patterns from Paris that Lucy Devens brought back last month? She swears it's the new fashion to dress like a shepherdess and picnic in the woods! Can you imagine?"

As dusk turned to dark, the ladies talked of many things, each cleverly managing to keep the other (or so she thought) from worry.

EDMUND MONTAGU REACHED out and accepted Dr. Warren's report from Longfellow's hand. Before examining it in front of the fire, he provided his guests with claret.

While he read, the others examined the cloak and smallclothes, which still hung from the furniture.

"This has more to do with your problems than mine," said the captain when he had finished, handing the paper back. He recrossed his silk-clad legs and cleared his throat before continuing. "I had planned to help with your investigations only as far as they advanced mine. Now, I find I have to leave them to you. Only a moment ago, I received word from friends in Boston who tell me that a body, naked and as yet officially unclaimed, was washed up along the coast near Providence. On Tuesday."

"Duncan Middleton," Longfellow returned quickly.

"A guess, of course."

"Hardly that. A scientific deduction, based on fact."

"How?" asked Montagu. And how were they always a jump ahead of where he imagined them to be? He watched Longfellow set the tips of his fingers together carefully, and draw them apart again.

"Actually, I had it from Mrs. Willett. The man she saw here, she now tells me, was an impostor. As to the how, she notices little things. And little things with her often lead to larger ones. For instance, there was the time when one of her hens disappeared, and she eventually discovered— but I digress, Captain, when you have more serious things to consider. I take it you still plan to return to Boston, in order to watch what happens to Middleton's estate?"

"Indeed," Montagu replied, further annoyed. He would have to guess about the hen, and would miss learning more about Mrs. Willett's methods. Whatever they were, they succeeded. For an instant, he imagined he saw the shorebird of the same name. Rather unspectacular, until she decided to fly; then, the willet displayed an arresting wing pattern, white and black bands that could hardly fail to catch the eye and raise the spirit. Another instant decided him.

"But please," he insisted, reaching for the decanter of claret. "Go on. I would like to hear Mrs. Willett's reasoning."

"It has to do with teeth," Longfellow went on, as his

glass was refilled. He related all that Charlotte had concluded after dinner. At the end, Montagu had to admit that the affair was far from finished.

"Do you have," he queried, "further plans of your own?"

"I had meant to ride to Worcester tomorrow, to see Mary Frye's father. Now, that seems unnecessary, strictly speaking. But I believe I'll still go and talk to him, and ask a few others if anyone has seen a man of means who might have arrived there on Wednesday, possibly carrying Dutch gold. I may have some luck. And I'll inquire about the miller's stay earlier in the week—if in fact Lynch went that way. He might have dropped hints about this imposter he was in league with."

"You will save me the trouble. And I'm sure someone of your experiences can speak with a frontier person better than I. Send me word if you discover anything of interest."

The three men rose, but Montagu had not quite finished.

"Please give Mrs. Willett my regards, and my regrets at not having more time to spend with her. You might also take my respects to your most unusual sister. I suppose our paths will cross again, in town. Dr. Warren, I look forward to seeing you as well."

"The question is, will I be seeing you, Captain?" Warren asked knowingly.

Montagu nodded slightly, acknowledging the hit. "That's a question I wouldn't wager on, either way," he finally smiled, putting down his glass and walking them to the door.

THE NIGHT HAD begun to clear by the time Charlotte retired to her feather bed. She curled her toes around a squat stoppered jug full of kettle water, while she watched the stars that crept westward behind racing clouds, winking like distant eyes. Drifting toward sleep, she began to imagine others in their beds throughout the village.

Diana, of course, would be in her scented boudoir, draped in satin, kept warm by who knew what secrets and desires. Always a late riser, she was probably still at a book, or writing in her diary.

Then there were those at the inn. Charlotte wished she had managed to speak with Edmund Montagu again—Diana had told her he planned to leave in the morning. Together, they might have discovered why certain things, like the coins, connected the three confirmed murders. (She had been only partly relieved to hear from Richard, when he returned for his sister, that the merchant's body had, in fact, been found far away.) Willing herself to forget about serious matters, she pictured Captain Montagu readying himself for bed, his wig beside him on a chair looking like a small, sleeping dog; she smiled to think what he might look like without it.

Resting near Edmund Montagu would be Mary, and Jonathan, and Lydia. Where would Lydia be sleeping now, she wondered? In a room usually kept for guests? It would be a cruel wound to Lydia's pride, though a source of amusement (and a warning) for most of the village. She wondered what Nathan would have to say on the subject in days to come.

Mr. Lee would probably be in an upstairs room at the Blue Boar, if he was in bed yet; more than likely, he was still in the noisy room downstairs. He would certainly be the victim of many jokes in poor taste. But he would probably be the receiver of more than one free pint as well. Would he be telling further stories for his supper? Surely, he would be urged by the rest of the men to "spill the beans." She wondered if she might find a way to talk with him again, without setting tongues wagging. As a naturalist with a knowledge of plants, he might be able to instruct her. Beyond that, Lee could have learned more from Lydia when they were, well, together ... about what exactly Lydia had discussed with Middleton or, more accurately, with the imposter, on the day he disappeared.

As sleep began to overtake her, a darker image of Gabriel Fortier loomed in her thoughts. Somewhere out there, in the wind, she seemed to see—no, not Fortier, but a short, dark figure with its back to her, coming closer—a back bent over and unaccountably moving along like a crab, sideways, but growing larger, and larger, until it flapped its dripping red cape, and turned to show a face that had been eaten away—a sight which woke her abruptly, and left glistening sweat on her lips and forehead.

In a move as familiar as childhood, she patted the side of her blankets and whispered softly. Orpheus, thus invited, rose stiffly to his feet and climbed up beside his mistress, where he settled with a happy groan.

For a long time after, comforted by the soft breathing beside her, Charlotte continued to look up at the flickering stars.

Chapter 24

_ᴄ Saturday

Fᴿɪᴅᴀʏ'ꜱ ꜱɴᴏᴡꜰᴀʟʟ ᴡᴀꜱ followed by a day of clear sun and brisk wind, with the sky a deep blue. As usual on Saturday, people hurried about, trying to complete the week's chores before sundown when the Sabbath began. In homes along the road, birch brooms swept at the open doors, beans simmered in pots, and linen fluttered on lines and trees.

Two horses clopped and snorted through the early morning air, over a landscape covered with shining, melting snow. As they left Bracebridge behind, Warren amused Lem with stories of life in Boston, sensing unborn ambition in the boy. In fact, he might well benefit from encouragement, Warren thought, and become a force for change, or at least resistance to all that was threatening the future of Boston. Most people who were given purpose, the doctor believed, could do amazing things. He himself had left Harvard in '59 to enter not only into medical studies, during his indenture to Dr. Lloyd, but into political life as well. A member of what was softly called the Long Room Club, he met others at unannounced meetings above the office of the printers Edes and Gill, who put out the *Boston Gazette*. Here, men worked to develop friendships, public spirit . . . and treason, according to some.

Warren believed young men should be helped to knowledge that might allow them to lead their countrymen, especially when they showed a talent for leading. He had recognized something he liked in Lem Wainwright on the previous afternoon. If someone—say, Longfellow— were to sponsor the boy at Harvard, anything might happen—as long as the lad held onto his native reserve and pride, and kept a natural suspicion of both the British and easy money.

Eventually, through the fields, they saw the spires and rooftops of Cambridge ahead. The town of about fifteen hundred souls was no larger than Worcester, but its atmosphere was vastly different. Here, the bells of Boston could often be heard coming across the water, and that city was a nourishing presence which provided a good deal of money, as well as a constant flow of new thought and information.

They soon passed a large Congregational church, whose yard held many of the Commonwealth's founders, Warren observed. Then, on the left, they saw an open quadrangle of buildings neatly fenced off from the ordinary world.

There was Massachusetts Hall, four stories with a large clock that faced the road, Harvard Hall with its bell towers and unbelievable library of 3,500 volumes, and Stroughton Hall—all three constructed of redbrick around a large, bare courtyard, where students crossing and recrossing between meetings continually wore out the grass.

Warren had already told his youthful companion about Professor Edward Wigglesworth, the scholarly old man who still prepared most of the future theologians of Massachusetts, while he also taught the students Greek and Latin, rhetoric, logic, and ethics. Now, the doctor told several amusing stories about the far less ancient John Winthrop, who was responsible for teaching mathematics and natural philosophy, as well as calculus, astronomy, and geography. It was Winthrop who had created and still presided over the experimental laboratory on the second floor of Harvard Hall. There, a twenty-foot telescope had enabled him to learn more of the nature of sunspots, and comets. Winthrop also had an orrery in his apparatus chamber; this showed, by means of hanging brass bells moved by a wheelwork, the paths of the principal bodies in the solar system.

But when they entered Harvard Hall and looked in at the laboratory on their way to the library, it was a hanging skeleton that stopped Lem and held him dumb. Warren took the opportunity to show his new friend just how Sam Dudley had been approached and strangled, to the considerable interest of several students occupying the room.

Somewhat later, Lem sat under the eye of a watchful librarian, looking through a book he'd found on a huge oak table before him. As his eyes flitted over the pages he let the smell, the sight, and the sounds of the place work on his agitated mind. Poring over a single volume by the fire had once been a thrill. But now, that prospect gave him only a brief glow. Here, an entire world of books surrounded him, all of them waiting to be tasted, acting on the boy like a bonfire—even if, as Dr. Warren had warned him, three-quarters dealt with divinity.

Lem's own questions had more to do with the stars and their names, details of inventions, places mentioned in the newspapers, and the curious habits of weather and atmospherics described in the Almanac. *How,* and *why,* figured largely in Lem's unspoken thoughts, along with an occasional and sometimes even heretical *why not?*

One question that didn't trouble his mind at the moment (although he was later to wonder why about that, too) was this: What was going on at home, in the house of Charlotte Willett, which he had left unprotected? And why, he might have wondered (had he been looking down from his favorite hillside perch at that moment)—why was a crouched figure creeping up to Mrs. Willett's kitchen window, looking around to make sure Hannah Sloan continued on her way down the hill on a quick errand, then stealing like a shadow to the unbolted door?

EDMUND MONTAGU, TOO, had passed Harvard College as he came through Cambridge very early, on his way back to Boston. But Montagu had no thought of stopping. Continuing on, he reached Roxbury and crossed over the Neck.

Nothing much, he decided with satisfaction, looked to have changed. Boston claimed a population these days of well above fifteen thousand, and its business kept on growing, in spite of the latest conflagration in 1760 which he'd often heard mentioned, and a currently rumored depression. He could see the masts of ships that had hurried to cross the Atlantic before the worst of the winter storms, clamorously unloading now on the wharves at the ends of east-running streets. As he rode on, he passed farm carts from the western mainland towns rumbling along the Common, bringing produce to markets and warehouses, as well as the cargo holds of the tall ships.

Commerce would always take care of itself, he

thought—unlike one particular participant of the Boston trade, whose business was finished. Soon, Montagu would mount granite steps he'd only watched before. A constable had already made inquiries there, when word of Middleton's disappearance first arrived from Bracebridge. Later, he'd received word that Constable Burns had what nearly amounted to a wrestling match with the merchant's housekeeper, a Mrs. Elizabeth Bledsoe. It appeared to have been a draw.

This time, the captain would try himself. All through his journey, a homily had rarely left his head: Where there's a will, there's a way. And a will was just what Montagu wanted to find, now that Duncan Middleton was known to be really and truly dead.

Leaving his horse at a nearby stable, he stopped briefly at his rented quarters in a house in Pond Street. After that, he strode the half mile down to the big house off Water Street, near Long Wharf. Eventually, he lifted the heavy knocker on the large carved door.

After he had knocked several times more, the door was opened by a kitchen maid with greasy hands and a crooked cap, and coal dust around her nose. Montagu was about to ask to speak to someone else, when a bleating sound behind him announced the timely return of the housekeeper.

"Good afternoon, sir." She slid by him, shooing away the unpresentable maid. Mrs. Betty Bledsoe was, as reported, a very ruddy and cheerful woman. She was also very round, and despite the cool weather, her face was covered with perspiration from her morning's marketing. There was no doubt that she could use a good washing. The image of Mrs. Bledsoe in a bathtub helped considerably as the captain struggled to maintain a pleasant smile, while both caught their breath, for quite different reasons.

"Good day, madam," he finally responded, and bowed.

Mrs. Bledsoe had already admired the fashionable young gentleman from behind; now, she enjoyed admiring him face to face, while trying to decide if his visit promised fair weather or foul.

"I'm afraid the master's not in at the moment. Might I be of some service?"

"Certainly, for it's you that I came to see, Mrs. Bledsoe."

"Oh! Then you'd better come into the parlor. Unless—you might like to follow me into my kitchen? Nice and warm there, sir, and I could offer you a pot of tea, and some fresh buns, too."

Having won a small victory, Mrs. Bledsoe led the way, taking just a moment to send the maid upstairs to polish a distant pair of andirons.

When the kettle was on the fire, the housekeeper lowered herself into a chair. Montagu watched her feet rise into the air, before hearing them meet the floor again with a plop. Curls like yellow sausages hung beside her flaming cheeks, and bobbed vigorously as she began uttering pleasantries, which soon moved toward the colony's many faults. Montagu had quickly discerned that she was an Englishwoman. As it turned out, Mrs. Bledsoe had been born in Portsmouth, and proudly considered herself more loyal to the king than most of those around her. Had she, he asked, suspected that some of Middleton's dealings had been less than aboveboard, when it came to their monarch's interests?

Oh, they all stretched the laws a bit, didn't they, businessmen? Especially these colonials. And didn't the government generally overlook these things, for its own good reasons? Not that she could ever condone what sometimes went on. . . .

"Anyways," she concluded, "wherever was I to find an honest man to work for? My own Mr. Bledsoe always believed America to be the land of opportunity, but when he left . . . when he *died*," she stressed, "I had very little. I really had no choice but to take a post here in Boston. Unfortunately, my upbringing was not *quite* fine enough to get me a position in the house of a real English gentleman."

"Of course," said Montagu, bringing the conversation grandly back to his own design, "one doesn't always have a choice. But I give you one now, as a personal representative of His Majesty." He almost expected the woman to raise a hand in salute, considering her new expression. "I can only tell you so much, you understand . . . but I can say that you might assist your king and country greatly—and perhaps yourself—by answering a few questions."

He now dropped a Dutch gulden on the table, causing Mrs. Bledsoe's pale eyes to widen. "Certainly," she replied, moistening her lips, "I'd like to accommodate a gentleman like yourself, especially if, as you say . . ."

"Mrs. Bledsoe. Betty . . . have you seen many of these before?"

"Didn't they come in with the *Jenny Dean*! One of our ships, that was, back from Curaçao just this August. I remember quite well, as I saw Mr. Middleton counting them out before he hid them away in his strongbox."

"And where is this strongbox, Mrs. Bledsoe?"

"Oh, sir—" A sudden coldness in his expression decided her. "Well . . . it's in the master's study."

Montagu again smiled affably. "Show me," he said firmly, sweeping the gold to one side of the table, without taking his gaze from her.

Mrs. Bledsoe licked her lips again and swallowed. Then, seeing that the coin was not about to disappear by itself, she led the way down a hall. Rising to follow, Montagu quickly pulled a small flask of rum from his coat pocket, and poured a dollop into her teacup.

She stood waiting at the door of a dark, shuttered room with a fireplace full of ashes, and a dusty feel about the rest of it. After walking to a pine highboy with soiled knobs, she opened a low drawer. She removed a painted tin box with an iron device over its clasp.

"It's locked, I'm afraid, sir."

"Please don't trouble yourself any further, Mrs. Bledsoe."

"Would you be needing anything else, just at this moment?" she inquired with an air of innocence that would have been out of place, he thought, in a child of four.

"Perhaps you need to attend to something in the kitchen? I'll do quite well alone," he assured her. "You go and have another sip of tea." And he set to work with a pocket knife and a small metal pick, as soon as the door had shut behind her whispering skirts.

The contents of the flat box were, at first, a disappointment. On top were some signed papers promising payment of money borrowed against eventual delivery of goods, at an exorbitant rate of interest; a few hopeful letters from other firms, and one or two that less politely requested payment; lists of cargo; lists of captains and crew members.

Under these, he found two pieces of newspaper, both from the *Boston Gazette*.

The first was a brief homage to Veracity Middleton, who left no one, and was probably missed by few. A second yellowing page was an account of the wreck of a cargo ship, the *Gloria Jones*. Out of Providence, she had gone down with all hands on the harbor rocks of a small port in the Canary Islands. It had happened during a hurricane that had savaged the area, and must have meant something to the old man. Then Montagu remembered that under similar circumstances the last remaining brother, Lionel, had perished as a sailor three years before. According to Montagu's informants, who had taken a look at the city's tax lists, Lionel's name had, in fact, been removed.

And then he found the packet containing a series of old wills, most of them made when Duncan Middleton's brothers and sister were still alive.

Presumably, the first slim document had been made at the urgings of his elder brother Chester, to whom it left most of a very little nest egg; small bequests went to a sister and two former servants. Next came a will leaving out the elder brother, presumably dead by now, and recognizing a younger one named Lionel, who had come of age. He was set to share a somewhat larger fortune with Veracity. A third will specifically excluded a disfavored Lionel, and left the sister all. The fourth and final document, made shortly after Veracity's death in 1761, named only one person as the recipient of a smallish sum, to be given after the man carried out Duncan Middleton's last wish. It seemed that the bulk of the now weighty estate, with all other claimants gone, went to—and here Montagu heard himself laugh out loud—a home for drunken sailors, to be established in Marblehead on Duncan Middleton's death. As the merchant made very clear in a stinging paragraph, sailors were welcome to their vices, which he believed were far less wicked than those of most of his Boston acquaintances.

When Montagu returned to the kitchen, Betty Bledsoe again sat at her table. The gold coin had disappeared, as had several sugary buns from the previously offered plate. Standing, and giving a sly look toward his coat pockets, the housekeeper offered to pour another cup of tea.

"When your master left on Monday last, where did he tell you he would be going, my dear?"

"He didn't tell me. But not to where he ended up, I'm sure ... this place called Brainbridge—or Bracebridge. If that *is* where he ended up."

"You doubt it?" he asked with a look that led the woman on.

"I really don't know. It sounds like one of his tricks

to me! I'm not a superstitious person myself, so I don't see him burning up, like they say. And I can't see him going off and leaving all this behind. As it is, no one's told me *what's* to become of his fortune—although I can tell you he promised me my living, for the great many things I've done for him over the years. At any rate, no one has told me to leave or to stay, so I'm sure I don't know what's to become of Betty Bledsoe!"

Neither did Montagu, but he suspected that fate would soon arrange a new life of small pleasures, and considerable future pain, for some unwary son of England.

LATER, CAPTAIN MONTAGU paid a visit to his benefactors at Town-house, who gave him little reason to go further in any particular direction. They did, however, alert him to the curious fact that the wagonload of tainted rum was still nowhere to be found.

Duncan Middleton's final will had told him very little. On the other hand, what it didn't tell him brought new questions to Montagu's active mind.

First, he decided, he would have a well-earned dinner. Then he would view Middleton's body, and talk with the man who had brought it home. After that, he planned to change his clothing and spend some time prowling the lower parts of town, where he hoped to find a few among the living who could tell him what he now wanted to know.

They said all roads in these parts led to Boston. Let's hope so, the captain said to himself as he walked to the door of a welcoming tavern. With any luck at all, he might be able to avoid a long ride to Providence.

Chapter 25

EVERAL HOURS EARLIER, Richard Longfellow had mounted the dappled gray in his stable yard and had spoken severely from his high seat to the small collection of humanity that stood below.

"Stay close to home, the two of you! Tell Cicero if there's anything you need. He's seen you through difficulties before," Longfellow reminded his sister especially, "and I expect you to rely on him."

At this, Cicero watched the weather vane on the roof of the barn, neither acknowledging the compliment, nor admitting to Longfellow that, in his opinion, the battle to restrict these two ladies' behavior had been lost long ago.

More than ready to ride, Longfellow leaned down to take up a small package from his neighbor.

"It's a meat pie, and a flask of perry," Charlotte informed him.

"I'll probably be back for a late supper." The horse jerked his head up into the bright morning air and snapped it down and up again, wheeling while his rider paused to hold on.

"Do try to stay calm," urged Diana, knowing her brother's distrust of what he considered to be irrational animals. "They can sense it when you're not. You really should take the chaise, you know."

"Too slow. Besides, the ride will do both of us good."

"Godspeed, then," his sister sighed. "But I can't stand this cold any longer!" With that, she turned and went back inside.

"Will you be stopping at the Three Crows?" Charlotte called.

"I will. The horse will need rest, and I have in mind a few questions I might ask Thankful Marlowe."

"Be sure you measure out the oats yourself. They have a new stable boy every week. You'll give the lady my regards?" she added, allowing a small smile to have its way.

"If I see her," he replied vaguely. Longfellow chucked and nudged his horse with his heels, while he loosened the reins. And before any further leave taking could begin, he was flying off to Worcester.

Left all alone in the snowy yard, Charlotte knew Diana would expect her to hurry back inside for another bite of breakfast, at least. She could easily have done so, and revealed her own plan for the rest of the morning, before taking her leave.

But that, thought Charlotte, might be unwise.

Instead, she turned and went her own way. She prayed the weather of the night before would have kept Adolphus Lee inside like everyone else, so that he would now be rested, rather than asleep. But would he be willing to speak to an unlikely (and an inquisitive) visitor? Probably, he would. She even suspected he might be eager to listen to her questions and to answer them, if only for the pleasure of her company. It was a thought that made her less than happy, but it was based on good evidence and sound reasoning.

After a brisk walk of fifteen minutes, Charlotte arrived at her destination. She entered the Blue Boar by the front door, where she was relieved to discover few guests inside. In fact, there were only two travelers resting at a table near the ale barrels, engaged in their own business. While her eyes adjusted—and her nose became a little used to the strong smell—she saw Phineas Wise approach, his hands busy at his apron.

"Mrs. Willett! A surprise this morning! How might I help?"

"I would like to have a word with one of your guests."

Wise scratched his stubble, speculating before he replied.

"You mean my only guest, at present. Seeing you, I half supposed we'd made a date to barter again, as I'm reminded of the lovely cheeses."

"You drove a hard bargain for the cider, I thought, but a fair one," she replied, knowing it was the sort of thing Phineas would enjoy hearing. "I can bring you another, tomorrow, but . . . would you think it out of place for me to see Mr. Lee alone this morning? Only for a moment or two," she added, seeing the other's eyes dim. (As a man reliant on the selectmen for the renewal of his tavern's license, she knew he would be unlikely to allow anything that might influence the town against him. Of course, what its wives, in particular, didn't know . . .)

"I would of course be pleased to see you any morning, Mrs. Willett, whenever you might care to drop by. And I believe Mr. Lee *is* upstairs. I gave him the large room, the one with the windows. But let me call him down," he offered, still hoping to have his own way.

"I think that I'd rather ask him my question up-stairs, instead of down . . . so the others wouldn't be bothered . . . if you see what I mean."

"Well, better upstairs than outside, since you are no doubt cold from your walk here. It would be unwise to stand too long out of doors—or anywhere else without a fire. A few minutes, of course, might do you no harm. But *questions*, you say? Is it something to do with Lee's re-cent behavior? You haven't been sent—"

"No! It's only curiosity, on my part. About the old man on the road. Duncan Middleton."

"Him, again!" Phineas growled. "First, he's dead, and now they say he's alive after all. Which is it to be?"

Charlotte said nothing, but her eyes were grave. Waiting to hear no more, Phineas Wise threw up his hands and led the way up a flight of winding stairs.

"Stomp your foot when you're ready to leave, if you want me to help you down again. But the kitchen door at the back will be open. They say, you know, that curi-osity killed the cat. That is what they say," he repeated, reaching the middle of three doors and knocking.

A series of small noises came to their ears before footsteps approached, and Charlotte felt her heart race faster. But the sight she saw when the door opened did much to dispel her uneasiness, while it encouraged her lively imagination.

Inside was a cramped room quite unlike the large and tidy one Adolphus Lee had undoubtedly enjoyed at the Bracebridge Inn. Here, instead, were jammed to-gether boxes and bottles, books, and what appeared to be several small wooden presses, all residing on or under a long plank table that stood between the door and a nar-row, rumpled bed. In addition, several cases suitable for carting stood around the walls. It had become more of a work room than a bedroom, and might even be heading in the direction of becoming a sort of museum, she thought after a brief look around.

Mr. Lee, Charlotte was glad to observe, was fully dressed and quite alert, as she has suspected he would be. After a moment of amazement he flung himself backward while he opened the door more widely, sweeping a hand inward at the same time with a gallant bow.

"Mr. Wise and Mrs. Willett! What a surprise . . . and a pleasure, to be sure. Have you come on an errand of mercy? For I've surely been wondering what to do with myself this morning. I would be most happy if you would both come in, although . . ." (he added with a grimace) "I would not be surprised if you thought it . . . unwise."

Taking a breath and lowering her head, Charlotte did plunge inside. Even as she heard the grumbling proprietor shut the door, she saw an expression of real pleasure play across the malleable face before her.

"I'm quite delighted! And I promise, you have no cause to fear anything at all while you're here, at least from me. I believe I've learned a lesson, of sorts."

Hardly knowing what to reply, Charlotte walked to the long table. It was stained and burned with use, and probably came as a temporary loan from the barn outside. Her eye was next caught by a particular box with a glass front, partially covered by a cloth. She thought for a moment to lift it, but decided to send a question with her eyes, instead.

"Ah—now I remember that you are interested in Science. Could this be your reason . . . ? Well, no matter. If there is anything you would like explained, I'll be happy to try. What you are wondering about at the moment is an example of one of your local fliers, which, of course, are beginning their winter's sleep, so I had little difficulty in capturing it. I would guess many of your sex would be put off by this sort of thing. But if you'd like to see it more closely . . ."

Watching her eyes widen, Lee gently lifted the cloth, causing the bat beneath, hanging upside down from a stick, to twitch slightly. However, it kept its eyes tightly closed. Its skin, thought Charlotte, was beautiful—much like a dull satin, worn perhaps for mourning. The thought reminded her of the purpose of her visit, and she resolved to get on with it.

"Have you other . . . live things?" she asked after a second thought, with an eye to her own safety.

"One or two," Lee replied. "But perhaps it would be best not to wake them."

"Actually, I'm more interested today in plant life."

"Somehow more fitting, I think, for a lady. Or, possibly, a healer?" he asked shrewdly.

"Most of us do live some distance from more educated hands."

"I see. Well, I've pressed several things here, which I'm preserving until I can take them back to a water colorist in Connecticut. You probably know most of them yourself. We're attempting to catalog some of the marsh plants, which I suspect have more uses than we realize. It may do some good."

"I'm sure you're right," Charlotte agreed quickly, glad to speak with a man who gave a thought to the future in something other than terms of his crops and his land, or his business. While Lee probably had little in the way of wealth, he must have enough for his simple needs. He certainly seemed far removed from the worries of most farmers she knew (who generally found it difficult to support the land they'd been left, even while they scraped and saved to acquire more).

"I'm interested, just now," she said finally, "in plants that might do harm, rather than good."

"Oh? And what," Lee asked, absently picking up several pages of notes revised with smaller scribbles in their margins, ". . . what exactly is it you look for?"

"Something that might produce visions, and could make someone subject to unusual fears. Something that might also impair the workings of the limbs, as well as the mind."

"Many things might fall into the category you sketch," Lee said thoughtfully. "Can you tell me anything else?"

"A rash—something to cause a small, red rash about the face. And, something that might be found growing locally."

"I'm afraid I can think of no one thing, at least not immediately." Lee took a few steps, and turned. "Combinations of two or more might also be worth thinking about. But I'm scarcely a physician. I, myself, am more interested in the rare specimen no one else has yet seen. Or very few," he added, smiling. "You see, I have no wife, no children. But if I were to make a discovery or two, and if they were to be called after me, it would keep the name of my line alive just as well, to my mind. And, perhaps, some day, some might even thank me for my trouble. It would not be much, but to another scientist, surely, it would seem worthwhile."

"I know one or two who would agree with you," Charlotte returned kindly.

"Mrs. Willett. I must ask you one thing. You are not planning . . . that is, you wouldn't think of using this plant on someone else? No—I'm sorry to even think such a thing. Certainly, you must have quite another reason for your concern."

"As for that," Charlotte said, "I do." Deciding that the man might be trusted with what she'd found, she went on to explain that the supposed Duncan Middleton seen by Bracebridge, and heard by Adolphus Lee himself, was not the actual Boston merchant at all. "What I wonder," she added as she finished, "is if you have seen anyone here, Mr. Lee, whose voice you might recognize as the one you heard speaking to Lydia—or Mrs. Pratt . . . but of course, you know . . ." Her voice trailed off awkwardly.

After thinking for a few moments with his eyes closed, Lee responded. "I did see several gentlemen come and go while I stayed at the inn, and I spoke to most of them downstairs, over a glass of one thing or another. There was the man from Boston who came to visit a niece, he said, who lives somewhere nearby—but his voice was so hoarse you might have taken him for a bull-frog, and I doubt if he could have disguised it, even if he'd wanted to. Then there was Purdy, from Gloucester. But he left the day before Middleton, or whoever it was, arrived. Wait—what about . . . no . . . no. Mr. May-hew, from the Vineyard, of course, could not be the man, for he stayed until the day *after* the merchant disap-peared. There were several others, but they all were far too old to be the gentleman with the good set of teeth you've just described to me. Is there anything else about him you can recall? Anything in the least?"

"I'm afraid not," said Charlotte, turning to go. It had been a wasted trip, after all, for she knew no more than when she'd come in. Now, if she could only manage to leave without being found out . . .

"You know, Mrs. Willett," said Lee, moving as well, "the few afternoons I spent with Lydia Pratt were not only for my own pleasure. Please—do listen. I sensed some-thing in the lady immediately, when I first saw her last year . . . something I recognized, that spoke to me of a loneliness . . . and a need. I don't know why I tell you this, and I hope it will not offend you. But as a woman, and a friend of Science, you must agree that some things are only natural. Not that I believe I was right—far from it! But there are certain habits, learned in youth, I'm afraid, which are very hard to break. That, too, for a man at least, and a traveler, is only natural. And I am a naturalist my-self." He grinned, leaping around her to the door, an eager and almost childlike fellow, she finally had to admit.

Lee held the door open, then looked at Charlotte for a moment in all seriousness. "It is important for me to know the world will not despise me for my past sins, which I deeply regret. Is it possible that you, as a representative of this fine village I've grown to admire, can forgive me? I would, I assure you, never in the world hurt one of the female sex. On my honor."

Just what that might be worth, Charlotte was not quite sure as she heard the door close behind her. And yet, somehow, she did believe Adolphus Lee. She had favored him with a slight nod, and a small smile. But again, she thought as she crept down the stairs, she had learned nothing new or especially useful from this unusual man. Except, perhaps, that it might be only fair to think somewhat differently of Lydia Pratt. Lonely? She supposed it was possible. And certainly, she herself knew well enough what loneliness could mean. Should she try to comfort the woman, when few others were in a mood to do so? So far, she had avoided seeing Lydia and posing the few questions she would have liked to ask. The landlady might indeed be able to add something to the description of Middleton, having spoken to him at some length, as Lee had just mentioned again. Of course, there was another possibility concerning Lydia—one that had already been suggested, which she might also explore. . . .

Avoiding Phineas Wise, Charlotte walked out into the cold air and shivered suddenly. Somehow, in answer to her last question, she didn't think it a very good idea. And besides, Saturday chores were still to be done, before anything else could be accomplished. Tomorrow, possibly, she would ask herself once more.

VERY MUCH LATER, toward the end of the afternoon, Mrs. Willett walked in a corner of her kitchen garden, still considering loneliness. Only this time, after thinking deeply of Lydia Pratt's situation, she thought of her own. Longfellow had gone off to Worcester, Lem and Warren were in Cambridge, even Edmund Montagu had by this time arrived in Boston. At the moment, Mrs. Willett wished she could rise and sail like winged Pegasus, to see beyond the horizon.

She stooped to pluck the last blossoms of some meadow saffron, gathering them into a bunch. As she sniffed her nosegay, she even began to feel a little like the unfortunate girl in Monsieur Perrault's fairy tale. *She* had been cruelly kept from a ball, while her sisters put on all their finery and went to enjoy the social world.

But—was a horseback ride to Boston, or Worcester, worth the saddle aches, and possibly even frostbite for her trouble? Not really, Charlotte decided. There was a great deal to be said for taking journeys beside one's fire, with an improving book . . . or even one that wasn't very improving. She would have to ask Richard to pick out something amusing for her from the bookstore on King Street, when he went to take Diana home.

Curiously, Diana had earlier mentioned something about cooking. That in itself was amazing; given the circumstances, it also seemed highly unlikely. But Charlotte hadn't been summoned to join Diana this afternoon, which left both of them free to get on with their own business.

Maybe she was still hoping a crystal slipper would come into her life again, she thought with some regret. Her eyes settled on the clump of horehound holding onto its pale, woolly leaves, growing in the shelter of an old rock wall. Perhaps this year she could bring herself to boil down the hard candy again. She stiffened, and walked on. It was almost as if her mind, now refreshed and cleansed by the astringency of bittersweet thought, could finally turn to the problem she had come outside to ponder.

Just like the characters in the fairy tale, she knew that real people often spent time dreaming of change, and especially of gain. Maybe it was wealth, or maybe it was position that they hoped for. Maybe it was love. But who, exactly, she wondered, stood to gain *in some material way* from the deaths of the last several days? In her own experience, death had added to her stock in life more than once. It wasn't something one liked to think about, but it was something one *did* think about, after—and sometimes even before—someone died. It was, after all, only human.

What about Peter Lynch, then? Had the miller left an heir? Had he possessed the foresight to contemplate the certainty of his own death? Surprisingly, many people didn't. But he certainly had enough property to consider making out a will. He had no family in Bracebridge. She had no idea if he had relations away from the village, or if he was alone in the world. Peter Lynch hadn't been a man many would have cared to ask about his personal history. She only knew he hadn't always lived there. Then again, he might not have cared to leave his goods to a family he had forgotten long ago. He might have preferred to leave them to a family he'd planned to have in the future. Could he have promised money to Elias Frye, or even to Mary directly? Her rejection of him had seemed total, but that hadn't made a difference to Peter Lynch! If he planned to use his wealth as a bargaining point, Mary might at least have heard where he planned it to go at his death.

No one had yet come forward, and so it was something the selectmen would probably need to look into. She would ask Richard Longfellow, as soon as he came home.

The cries of a pair of hawks circling above echoed strangely through the newly empty trees. She drew her shawl tighter, chilled in spite of the thin yellow sunshine that fell at a slant onto her shoulders.

As for the other two deaths: she had no idea who might benefit from Middleton's removal, nor did she particularly care. Anyway, Edmund Montagu would no doubt see to that end of things. And it was, of course, sadly unnecessary to ask the question of young Sam, who had owned next to nothing—only a well-worn musket, and one gold coin. In fact, at the end, not even that.

The walk hadn't given her much insight after all. But an earlier suspicion, while it hadn't blossomed, had gained another inch of fresh growth in her mind. It involved someone she had hoped wouldn't suffer from the week's evil events. Suspicion was not proof, she reminded herself. Nor was it a reason for withdrawing one's support from a fellow creature—especially one in need.

She snapped off some last stems of purple asters for the table, adding them to the crocus blooms. Then, Mrs. Willett wound her way to the kitchen door, intending to set some wool-dying herbs to boil. But first, she would make herself a strong, welcome, comforting pot of tea.

Chapter 26

THE DAPPLED HORSE traveled over snow patches, puddles, and mud, through a wooded countryside spotted with ponds and open meadow. At first, Richard Longfellow enjoyed watching the sunlit silver trunks moving by, while he listened to the voices of migrating waterfowl. Tiring of that, he began to listen to himself.

While much of Bracebridge looked to the East for news and ideas, Longfellow knew that most of Worcester—when it looked beyond its limits—looked to the West. New land was still to be had past the mountains, if one could take it. Dynasties continued to be carved out of the distant forests and marshes; Indian trails and war roads led the way. Worcester saw itself as part of the future, allied with Springfield and Albany, and all the other towns just starting to expand on the web of great and lesser inland waterways.

Had it really been nine years since representatives

from all the colonies made their way up the Hudson to Albany, to consider Dr. Franklin's plan against the French and Indian threat? That these men were not able to agree to its sensible provisions for joining together struck Longfellow as a perfect illustration of the divisive and selfish ways of mankind in general, and those of the men who sat in the various colonial legislatures in particular. But it was all water over the dam now, with European peace upon them again.

Eventually, he was sorry that his ride was almost over, when he trotted past Lake Quinsigamond and reached the town of Worcester. He saw the courthouse and the Congregational church, the bowing elms of the Common, the large, painted clapboard houses of the wealthy, and the shops and businesses that had grown up around the county seat. But he didn't stop until he'd reached a comfortable inn on the other side of town.

There, he pulled his horse up and dismounted at the thick plank steps of the Three Crows, where, sure enough, an unfamiliar boy ran out to take the reins and lead the gray to the stable for its dinner. At the door, Longfellow was greeted warmly by the proprietor, who sent him in to her sitting room fire while she went for some refreshment.

"It's a brisk day," Thankful Marlowe commented moments later as she swept in to see Longfellow's cold-reddened fingers come from under his gloves. Her look told him she approved of his unusually high color. She herself was anything but pale, in either appearance or personality. Everyone knew that Mistress Marlowe had already enjoyed a pair of husbands (both of whom she'd outlived). And it was presumed that, at the age of twenty-seven, she might consider one or two more. The sole owner of a well-known inn and tavern, the widow could afford to pick and choose, which was something Longfellow had been aware of for a little over a year—

since, in fact, Asa Marlowe took his leave. For this reason, he now never failed to consider his possible peril
when he stopped during trips to and from the western
villages. (That Thankful might doubt he would do for
her was something Longfellow hadn't considered, and so
he worried while he relished her robust presence. In this,
it might be said, he had considerable company.)

"What are the chances," he asked, sipping the toddy
she'd brought, "that this impostor of ours came through here
on Wednesday, possibly carrying some Dutch guldens?" He
had already gone over the news, detailing the latest observations and conclusions of those in Bracebridge.

"To the Three Crows? I'm sure he didn't. Most of my
stopping customers I know, or I soon get to know . . . although not quite as well as Lydia Pratt, apparently,"
Thankful couldn't help adding with a wicked laugh. "I'll
ask Angus if he's noticed anyone spending guldens in the
taproom, but I think he would have mentioned it to me.
We're all well aware of what the man was said to look
like. I tell you, we've been watching our shadows since
this whole business started!"

She stood by the mantel, and soon leaned down to
prod the logs with a brass poker until she was satisfied.

"It's certain he looks nothing like what he did, without his disguise," Longfellow cautioned. "We really have
nothing to go on there, other than the fact that he's not
overlarge . . . or oversmall."

"What about this fiery display of his?" Thankful
asked with curiosity.

"That? Just a parlor trick. I could do it myself. In
fact, I think I might attempt it for the effect it would
have on the town. They need someone to teach them a
thing or two about believing in black magic."

"You had better pray they don't go after you next! Of
course," she continued, sitting and picking up a bowl of
nuts, "lately there's been the usual talk of spirits here,

too. We generally hear it more during the autumn. I suppose it's mostly done for amusement. But it's not only between the young and the simple, you know. For every girl who casts a ball of yarn through the window to see her future husband pick it up—oh yes, they still do it—there's a sensible man wondering who might have made his pig sick, or a calf die."

She twisted a wooden screw into a walnut shell, and gave her guest the results with a handsome smile.

"So you were already looking out for something unusual," Longfellow commented, looking along his outstretched legs to the riding boots he wore today over woolen knee breeches. In the heat of the room, both had become somewhat uncomfortable.

"Oh, yes. But we've always got new people coming through, and many of them are noticeably odd, especially those going to the West. A good half of Worcester moves that direction every year, as well. Lately, though, some of them have come back with stories that are *truly* frightening."

"Pontiac?" He sat up, and set his glass on a table to look at her more carefully.

"It seems the war's not over yet, after all. Not his war, at least, and not for the Ottawas. It's farther away this time, but it's led to even more fear and hatred than there was before. No one here knows them any more— the Indians, I mean. So they don't look on them as warriors worthy of respect—and that's no way to go to war, if you want to keep your scalp! But our young men see only the few who stayed around here—most nothing like they once were. In fact, it's tragic to see what they've become."

"What about the French Neutrals in the area?"

"That's another charming story. I'd say they're worried, and with good cause."

"About the frontier?"

She shook her head, frowning. "They don't have much to gain there any more. No, mostly they fear some of the good people of Worcester, and what they're likely to do to them, now that Gabriel Fortier is gone missing. They say he's being hunted for your unpleasant miller's death. Is it true?"

"Mmm, although I think it's unlikely they'll find Fortier now, unless he's a very simple fellow. Which I doubt."

"I've had him here—this summer. He helped clear stones from some of the old fields around the place, the ones Asa couldn't be bothered with. Gabriel should have stayed a farmer; it's apparently what he wanted. But his family had him learn a trade. They bound him to a cooper. He served his time, and then was let go. It seems he wasn't the most pleasant soul to have around, even in a barrel shop—being very sensitive to things that were said of him. You know how men are always going on, especially about politics and the war. Now, I suppose Gabriel is at loose ends, with no tools and no custom of his own."

"You know about the girl?"

"Frye's daughter? Yes, I've heard. Poor thing."

"That's why I've come. I plan to see him, if you'll give me directions."

"Oh-ho! Would you like to take along one or two of the dogs? He's been known to hide from certain visitors, and to turn on others with a cudgel."

"I think he'll talk to me. In fact, I think he'll be expecting a visit."

Thankful Marlowe gave her guest directions to the Frye farm, and walked him to the front door.

"Good luck, then. Will you be back tonight? No? Come by again when you can stay longer. There's always a bed for you here, no matter how full up we are. And be sure to give my regards to the very patient Mrs. Willett."

"Of course," Longfellow replied uncertainly. Only after he had ridden away did Mistress Marlowe let out a peal of laughter—which rang so loudly that one of her lodgers stuck his head out of his window, wondering what he'd missed.

ELIAS FRYE SAT on the porch of his house in the woods, sipping at intervals from a cup he replenished from a stone jar by his knee. As Longfellow rode into the cabin clearing, the gray's nostrils flared at a dozen different smells and sights that confronted them. Ahead, a wolf's pelt was nailed to the logs of the house to cure; to one side, the thick red fur of a fox hung beside several lesser skins from the limb of a dead tree. Assorted gnawed bones lay strewn about the snow-spotted yard, between the ribs of broken casks and old wheels, and a few rusting beaver traps. It was a scene Richard Longfellow was prepared for. But it was still enough to disgust him.

Drawing himself up, he squinted at the unpleasant old person under the mossy roof, who gave him back a false smile. Longfellow dismounted, kicking away a pack of curious dogs who turned out to be more sniff than bite, and tied the horse's reins to a branch of a tree.

It soon became evident that Elias Frye had no qualms about discussing his old acquaintance.

"I did hear tell of Peter being dead—killed by that boy, I imagine," said Frye, taking another sip and watching Longfellow prod a clump of wood fungus on a stump with his boot.

"No one knows," he finally replied, "though as a selectman, I can tell you we're not making any accusations just yet. But we have a few questions for you, concerning the miller."

Elias Frye lowered his eyes; he seemed to be trying hard to recall something.

"Peter Lynch was here on business," he finally began, looking up again. "On Monday, it was, he stopped to see me, like the good friend that he is. Or was," he said with a frown. "Asked me how my family were, and he give me a few jugs of cider, too, as a present. He's spoken for my oldest girl, you know."

Frye fastidiously picked a bit of food from the sleeve of his filthy jacket, and flicked it off onto the ground.

"Did you *actually* want to marry your daughter to Lynch?" asked Longfellow, pinning the man with his eyes.

"Course I did! Why not? Hadn't he money, and property? That's a fine mill to run, too. And didn't he ask me proper, paying me for the honor?"

"Oh, I'm certain he did that. Just as Jonathan Pratt paid you to have your daughter work for him for three years, rather than see her go from childhood into the miller's arms. You relied on Pratt's sympathy, didn't you? It was worth money in your pocket. And there was always later for the miller, although he would have preferred sooner. At any rate, you'd have been glad to do another favor for Lynch if he asked you—isn't that right?"

"What kind of favor?"

"Oh, you might say that he was somewhere, when he wasn't."

"I told you he was right here, on Monday."

"Yes, even before I'd asked you."

"Well, I knew *somebody* ought to come and ask me about him, because he's dead, ain't he! And we both know who did it," Elias Frye whined.

"Yes, he's dead. That's why you can tell me the truth now, and not just what Lynch told you to say. I believe he was nowhere near here on Monday. I think—I *know*—he had another errand to do. Perhaps on the coast?"

At this, Elias Frye paled; even his dogs seemed to sense the fear that had shaken through his narrow body. They slunk quietly in a row around the corner of the house, with hardly a backward glance.

"What do you want from me?" Frye eventually managed, his throat tight and bobbing.

"The truth. And a promise that you'll leave Mary alone, so she might make up her own mind about what to do next."

"Well, the Frenchman can have her, and welcome—if he keeps his neck free of a noose! I've got more. I doubt anyone *else* would have her, now. I only tried to get her something better for herself, and for us all! Though there's some say I ain't done as well as a father might for his motherless children, I done what I could, all alone, with what I got," he wheezed, pulling a horrible handkerchief from his pocket and dabbing at an eye, then mopping his forehead.

Longfellow looked slowly around, sensing that there were others hiding nearby. One young girl in particular was in his thoughts . . . Mary's likely successor in Frye's plans.

"Let me warn you about something," Longfellow began again. "If you don't tell the truth, you could very well anger whoever it was that murdered the miller. In any event, I'll see that the courts and the lawyers tear apart this story of yours. And they may do far worse! This thing is far from over. Very possibly, it's about much more than Lynch's murder. So there *will* be more questions, until we learn the truth."

Frye said nothing. But a girl of twelve or thirteen, wearing a ragged homespun dress, now walked out of the door behind him and stood facing Longfellow defiantly. At first, he thought she meant to join her father, but such was not the case.

"The miller never came here on Monday, sir. He

never came at all last month. Old Man barely knows what truth is, so you'd be foolish to trust him!"

"Your father had no contact with the miller at all?" Longfellow asked with some surprise.

"He went to see Peter Lynch last week in Bracebridge, and stayed the night," the girl replied. "We don't know what they did, but if it was wrong, it's not the first time he's shamed us. Might be the last, though." She gave a sour little smile to the back of her father's head. "One day soon we'll leave, and then *he* can drink himself to death . . . if he can find the money."

"Has Mary been here recently?" Longfellow pressed her. He watched the young girl's expression change abruptly.

"Mary hasn't been able to come since winter, but she writes us, and I can make most of it out," her sister replied anxiously. "Did she send you?"

"No, but I've seen her, and she's well. My name is Longfellow. I live next to the inn where Mary stays. If you have information about your father and Peter Lynch, you might be asked to testify in court. Then again, you might not. You could prefer to keep what you know in reserve . . . in case someone should try to make you do something you don't care to—as Mary was nearly forced into doing. If anything like that should happen, go to the Three Crows, and ask Mistress Marlowe to send for me."

The young girl nodded sharply, though he thought he saw a question in her gaze. At the same time, the old man seemed to deflate. He again applied his handkerchief in a gesture that asked for pity. A sudden wail from a child sent the girl flying back inside. Longfellow's eyes followed her in silent admiration.

What the girl had said probably proved some kind of collusion, he thought when she'd gone. As he had supposed. Satisfied for the moment, he started for his horse.

"She'll do what she likes, that one will," Elias Frye

rambled on to himself, after taking another long pull from the jug. "She's smart, she is, there's no doubt of it. Go away and leave her old father alone. Ah, let her go! Let her try to find a man herself. *She's* no beauty— not like my Mary. My very own, very nice Mary," he snickered drunkenly to himself, apparently thinking of happier days.

Was *that* the real reason the father had kept Peter Lynch on a string—fear of his anger at learning, on his wedding night, the vilest of family secrets? By sending his daughter to work at the inn, had Frye hoped to put the blame for a sin of his own on someone else, if and when time revealed it? Suddenly, the stench of the place became unbearable.

It was enough, thought Longfellow as he rode away, to sicken a man. Surely it was enough to make a child do whatever it could to be free of the abuse, the squalor, and the ugly lies that life at home had always held. A young woman would naturally dread the continuation of such a life, in the arms of another man equally cruel, or quite possibly worse. That kind of fear, Longfellow realized, might have driven a person like himself to go beyond the law, beyond the rules of sense and decency. Might it even, he thought morosely, in a like situation, have driven him to murder?

Chapter 27

"I f there's one thing I know, it's human nature," Diana Longfellow confided. Seated in a chair to one side of the kitchen hearth, she smoothed her skirts, while Cicero shook his head at the old Dutch oven whose three feet straddled a mound of glowing coals.

"How *could* he have done what they say?" she went on airily. "There's certainly no real proof against the Frenchman, and I don't intend to help your village ruffians tear him to pieces, before they find the real culprit. He's far too handsome for that! Which is why I'm allowing him to hide in Richard's greenhouse."

Cicero's gasp did nothing to alter her serene smile; it rarely bothered Diana when she shocked others.

"He's already out there?" the old servant finally asked unhappily, knowing trouble when he saw it. And right now he saw it sitting next to the kitchen fire.

"Well, you didn't think I'd be making this pot of

stew and the kettle cake all for us? I'm sure the poor man hasn't eaten decently for days. That's why we're going to feed him. After it's dark, when he can come inside. Mary told me he almost froze, out alone in the woods last night."

Women who are forever petted and praised, thought her temporary guardian, often display as much sense as the little dogs they keep on their laps. At least this time Diana hadn't brought along Bon-Bon; not a good traveler, the ratlike thing preferred to stay at home where Diana's maid Patty stuffed it with sweetmeats. Cicero longed for a chance to try his own hand at stuffing the animal; he had seen a well-mounted skunk in a shop window once, in Boston.

He poured the yellow batter he'd mixed into the greased pot, covered it, and turned to attempt to reason with his charge.

"What," he asked somewhat severely, "will we do if someone looks in and sees him? Have you thought of that?"

"Well then, of course, we . . . well, we say we have no idea how he got here. But most of the town will be inside by sunset, because it's the Sabbath. Besides, it's quite cold out, and I doubt if anyone *really* wants to interfere with this house; there's talk Richard is clever enough to raise the very Devil whenever he wants to. Besides, as we all know, one must occasionally make sacrifices for others."

Cicero looked at her sharply. It was not the kind of thing he was accustomed to hearing from the rosy lips of this particular young lady. His own lips moved slightly.

"Pardon?" she challenged.

"I only wonder if there's a new young minister in Boston," he muttered, leaning forward to look into the stew pot that hung over the fire.

"I grant you that good works are not my usual occupation, for I generally have enough trouble trying to make sure *I'm* happy. But today, everyone *else* has something to do, and here I sit, twiddling my thumbs!"

"Go home, then," the old man suggested, seeing a glimmer of hope.

"To Boston? Back to more of the same? Balls, and dances, and whist parties, and dinners where everyone chatters on and on, like a flock of parrots? I suppose I shall have to, soon enough. But I propose to have some excitement first."

"This wouldn't be something you want to do to bedevil your brother, would it? And what if the town finds out, with him in a position of responsibility?"

"Richard can take care of himself," Diana countered saucily. "He always has; he always will. It's a trait of the Longfellows."

"And if Captain Montagu discovers what you've been up to?"

At that, her eyes twinkled along with her rings in the firelight. "It *would* be amusing to find out what he would do with me," she answered with a graceful smile. "You, of course, he'd probably hang. But he's not here, is he? We'll tell him all about it some other time—after the whole thing's over. Now, we will cut up five or six large potatoes, as soon as we bring them up from the cellar, and then we'll add them to the pot. Don't be long," she called after him, wiggling with anticipation on her cushioned chair, while a sighing Cicero took himself down the creaking wooden stairs.

ACROSS TWO GARDENS, Charlotte entered her own kitchen. A rushed Hannah Sloan had just hurried in with some items for the pantry. Anxious to return home before sunset, she was soon through the back door and gone.

Alone again, Charlotte warmed the teapot and filled

it. Several ideas crowded into her mind, one on top of another. First came thoughts of supper. With Lem gone, fried hasty pudding with maple sugar would do, with dried blueberries soaked in cream for after. She was in no hurry. The kitchen was warm, and the fire right for making up a batch of dye.

She let Orpheus out when he whined softly at the door. She was surprised that the garden walk hadn't been enough for him. She supposed that the dog, too, felt restless, probably sensing her own state of mind. Putting dried goldenrod from a corner rafter into a pot of water with a bit of indigo, Charlotte stirred and hoped for a green as good as the one she'd made the year before. She had enough alum for fixing several pounds of wool and a smaller amount of flax for napkins. There would soon be plenty of time to put it to the loom, when the snow drifts began to grow up the sides of the house and barn. Time, and time to spare.

On Monday, bayberries could be set to boil. Hannah's youngest had already collected gallons for her from the marshes and rocky wastes—enough to melt off a film to skim and add to beeswax for a few dozen special candles. And she would have books from the Harvard library to explore, if Dr. Warren kept his word. It would be another full week.

Slowly sipping the tea that seemed bitter as dregs today—it was, in fact, the last of the August-bought tin, and full of powder—Charlotte began to imagine the road to Boston once more, a road as full of memories as any she knew.

Outside the kitchen windows, the sun hit the limbs of a beech behind the barn, and played among the final leaves of the darker oak branches nearby. As day turned to evening, the world seemed to crackle with electricity. While the frost prepared to fall again like a lace coverlet, the eastern sky turned the color of lapis lazuli, complete with faint gold stars. And the setting sun lit up the barn's windows, until they appeared to be turned into Indian rubies! She had seen it all many times before, but tonight it was particularly vivid and clear. So were the huge flocks of geese flying through the upper light in long, trailing forks—hundreds, thousands of spots of darkness covering up the sky . . .

Charlotte suddenly realized she had been staring blindly into the night through the dark window, seeing nothing, only imagining. Her eyes were wide. Her breath came in swift shudders. And her mouth was dry. Mechanically, she finished the cup of tea, wondering what was wrong with her surroundings. An unlit candle stood beside her. Without thinking, she got up and went to the fire. Fumbling with a splinter, she produced a flame on one end—touched flame to wick—then blew the source away. The resulting smoke coiled up into the air in a thick rope like a monstrous, twisting cobra, hissing and dancing hypnotically. She stared in amazement, then looked away with growing fear.

And yet the hearth fire still sparked and crackled softly. The pot had begun to steam, the tea was still before her.

The tea! It was something to do with the tea. Bitter, and musty; she could still taste it on her dry tongue. And the books, what was it about the books she'd been thinking of? Her head echoed with sounds she knew came from her own imagination. With great effort, she concentrated on the few things that still seemed real.

Of course—this must be what it was like to feel first-hand something that had afflicted others around the village during the week. Curious signs that marked their victims as being . . . what was the word? Oh, yes, *possessed*. She had been possessed once; as a wife, she thought dizzily, possessed and cherished. Till death do us part. No, that was over. This was her own kitchen, though a new world. Yet not unlike the old . . .

Scratching her fingers against the back of her hand, she looked down to see a red rash. She had seen the same rosy dots before, when she looked down into the miller's horrible face—

She saw that dead face again, growing out of the table in front of her. It was a thing too terrifying to look at for long. But at the same time, the words of someone, she couldn't quite tell who, sounded in her ears. It was a man of Science. Something he had told her. Emotion. No place for emotion in science. She heard herself laughing merrily, and wondered why.

Clinging onto the back of her chair, Charlotte twisted and rose to her feet, then took the candle to a small mirror by the door. On her face were more blotches, and she could hardly believe that the eyes she gazed at were her own. All black, their pupils completely covered the blue. These were the eyes of paintings, eyes of the beauties of Italy, and Spain. Black eyes, like round chips of shiny, hard coal—eyes as big as saucers, *belladonna* eyes. Wasn't that a serious problem? Didn't people sometimes die of it? The thought was frightening—or might have been, except for other thoughts that overrode her fears.

"In the midst of life, we are in death." She knew that to be true, always. Though Death was hardly a friend, he was not entirely a stranger. She decided to sit and watch for him to come, if he would, while she strove to calm the pounding of her heart.

Had the fire grown brighter? The room was hot, stifling. It was smaller, too, and the china winked with eyes, like cats sitting on the cupboard shelves, waiting to leap down and begin to fiddle in the firelight. There was altogether too much going on in the little room, she told herself, beginning to admire her own control. Perhaps a solution to all of her problems lay outside the bolted door.

It was difficult at first to raise the latch. But once opened, the door swung inward on its hinges, and Charlotte stumbled out. Suddenly, she felt much cooler, though she soon ceased to notice. The night sky, filled with stars, seemed boundless. As she turned, she saw the constellations twirling, some of them caught in the ensnaring arms of trees, some pulling free. And then, at both sides of the sky, they began to disappear.

Near panic, she forced herself to be still, and to look down to earth again. What little she saw around her feet was vague and blurred. Something pulled at her; she felt her feet responding. When she next looked up, nearby shapes grew menacing, and her heart leaped to her throat as they seemed to lunge forward, only to subside again into surrounding calm. For a moment, the acrid smell of wood smoke clawed at her throat and made her sneeze. When she again opened her eyes, the ground churned and rolled under her, and seemed to groan. Suddenly, her empty stomach rebelled; with a rush, she felt herself turning inside out.

Finally, the spasms ceased.

She realized that it must have been her own voice she had heard groaning, and noticed that she had fallen to her knees. Once more, her breathing quickened as she sensed an unknown presence drawing closer, and closer still.

Abruptly, her arms were filled with fur. Orpheus had found her on his return from the fields. He whimpered as he searched her face and hair with his nose, wondering what was wrong.

Her own wild giggles brought momentary comfort, and a partial return of reason. But that was soon lost in a further blur of motion and sound. Again, the wet nose bent over her, and a large tongue licked her forehead.

Once more, Charlotte lifted her head and stretched out her arms to encircle the dog's neck—and then slid back and out of the world entirely.

Seeing his mistress lying silent, Orpheus lifted his head to the cold stars, and howled.

WHEN SHE AWOKE, Mrs. Willett was puzzled by the change in the air around her. Now delightfully moist and warm, it was filled with a strong, flowery scent. She opened her eyes, half expecting to find the Heavenly City around her. But instead of ethereal light, there was almost total darkness, and a snaking dragon coiling itself in front of her face. Was this place Hell, then?

The dragon moved away and, she saw light come through the slits in a small copper lantern, on a stone beside her. It was a hard slate floor she lay on, but hardly Hades. Rolling her head to look up, she saw the long fingers of a palm frond against the starry sky, and suddenly knew exactly where it was that her body had somehow landed. How it had arrived there, she couldn't recall. And why her head, when she tilted it to one side, caused her such agony was another mystery; she'd felt no pain before.

Focusing her eyes, she saw the dragon approach once more. But this time, she recognized its painted face. It was the same creature she had seen on the little bottle that Diana had shown her at the inn. It seemed like weeks before; was it only two days ago? But now, the bottle was in the hands of Mary Frye.

Gabriel Fortier also knelt to one side, his face full of concern. The Frenchman bent forward to help when Charlotte struggled to raise her head, and she noticed that Mary's little bottle went swiftly back into the pocket beneath her skirt. Fortier helped her to slide back against the warm brick wall, and then smiled ruefully.

"I am unlucky for you," he began, but Mary wouldn't let him go on with the thought.

"It would have been far worse if Mrs. Willett had frozen to death in her own garden, with no one there to find her! It's a good thing that you heard the dog, and went to look."

Mary stood to remove a canvas drapery from its pegs, which she then drew around Charlotte's shoulders. "But she can't stay here, and neither can we. We'll take you in to Miss Longfellow. You haven't even worn a shawl," she chided, shaking her head with disapproval, as if at a child. "And then to faint in a lonely spot like that!"

It was too much to explain, Charlotte realized; and so she didn't try.

Mary and Gabriel had begun to help her to her feet, when the outer glass house door made a sound, and moved. All three turned as one, expecting the worst. Instead, they saw Cicero, whose soft cry at seeing Charlotte on the ground was answered by sighs of relief.

Mrs. Willett, the old man saw immediately, had somehow managed to get herself into the middle of more trouble. He stooped to look deeply into her eyes.

Soon, they were on the path to the house, with Orpheus leading the way.

"What on earth. . . !" Diana boggled, when the kitchen door opened and she saw the procession enter. In an instant, she had gone for a heavy quilt to wrap around her friend.

When everyone was settled, with a fresh pot of tea brewing and smells of a simple dinner rising from the table, the story was slowly pieced together.

"Then someone must have gone into your house," Diana concluded when Charlotte had finished, "and left something in the tea while you were in your garden. It

was certainly a coward; who else would choose such a
way to silence a woman?"

"Would you have preferred a duel?" her neighbor
asked with a laugh that was still not quite her own.

"I would have preferred for you to stay indoors, as
Richard suggested. Oh! I'm starting to sound like my
brother. But never mind; it wouldn't have helped much
if you'd done that, anyway. The poisoner might simply
have found a faster, surer way." She hesitated, shocked by
the picture this brought to her mind, before she continued. "I suppose it's uncertain whether he wanted to actually kill you or not. But with you wandering outside, out
of your senses, the cold certainly could have done the
job. As it is, it's a good thing I'm here to watch you. I
doubt if you'll be able to think clearly for quite some
time."

"Otherwise, she would have been wondering by now
why you're hiding a fugitive in your brother's greenhouse," Cicero said pointedly.

"Yes, I *was* going to ask you that, Diana. Especially
since Richard said—"

"What he always says? Oh, well. He's not here to
think for us, so I suppose it's up to me to say they *can't*
stay here now. Whoever was after you might have been
watching all of us tonight, and seen all of *you* come inside. I suppose it was the impostor—the one Richard
tells me everyone thought was Duncan Middleton?"

"He was not?" asked the Frenchman, unacquainted
with the newest developments. Charlotte related the
story of the old man's teeth, or lack of them, and her
own slight connection with the red-cloaked stranger—as
well as the warning given to her by Dr. Warren.

"If he is still alive then, at least no one has reason
to blame me for being a sorcerer," Gabriel proclaimed
with relief. But they soon realized that the news did little
to change his position as someone who might well have

sought the death of Peter Lynch. To the village, at least, he was still outside the law. And it was likely that Mary's part in helping him would soon be discovered.

"Go back to the inn," he begged, his fingers gently touching Mary's hair. "For now, there is no future with me. Soon, I can be far away, in a place where I will work for money. When I have earned enough, then I will send for you."

"Unless . . ." Charlotte ventured, raising a hand to her aching head, and thinking as clearly, and as quickly, as she could.

"Unless I go with you now," Mary finished, holding her own head proudly, staring in the face of trouble that was likely to come.

". . . unless you stay until tomorrow, or the next day at the latest," Charlotte suggested quietly. "I know it's a risk, but when I can put two and two together again, and we have a few more facts, I think we will be able to clear Gabriel's name for good. Although there's a chance that would bring other dangers," she finished, looking squarely at Mary, her blue eyes grave.

"I think," Mary responded, bravely, "that I know one more place where no one will find you. And if the worst should happen, I swear by God that you won't die alone!"

It was an extremely foolish oath, Charlotte knew immediately. Foolish, and deadly serious—and very likely to be carried out, if things should go against Gabriel Fortier.

Charlotte reached to stroke Orpheus's silky fur, and thought for a moment about the selflessness of love. She knew it was something that might hold two people together even in the face of death—sometimes, even after death itself. Looking at the lovers before her, she hoped that the strength of their passion might not also prove to be their undoing.

Chapter 28

_⌐ Sunday

"'H<small>E DISCOVERETH DEEP</small> things out of darkness, and bringeth out to light the shadow of death,'" boomed the Reverend Christian Rowe, reading from the Book of Job, while his congregation fittingly huddled in the unheated meetinghouse. Some probably shivered, too, while taking the sobering words to heart.

Did it mean, wondered Charlotte Willett, that it was only the Lord's business to make known these deep things—the depths of human iniquity and frailty? Or was it for man (or woman) to help matters along? Am I my brother's keeper? If so, am I to be his executioner as well? She wished she knew.

Charlotte was herself a great deal fonder of earlier words in the same chapter, those exhorting man to listen to the beasts, and the fowls of the air, and to learn from the earth as well as the fishes of the sea. Certainly there was much to be learned by using one's senses and examining Nature, in the manner of Mr. Lee, among others. On the other hand, Reverend Rowe clearly relished the somber passages that came later; his eyes flashed with pleasure as he went on.

" 'Man that is born of a woman is of few days, and full of trouble. He cometh forth like a flower, and is cut down; he fleeth also as a shadow, and continueth not. And dost thou open thine eyes upon such an one, and bringest me into judgment with thee?' "

God, we're told, Charlotte continued on her own, helps those who help themselves—and He requires that we help each other. But what she now considered telling meant something more than help for the living, or even a quiet rest for the dead. It might also bring dreadful harm. Was it her business to interfere, by pointing a finger? She was certain now that at least a single murderer was still in their midst. But just how did one decide what to reveal about one's fellows, and what to leave to others, or to God?

Three men had died . . . although one of them had really been only a boy. Peter Lynch had been a menacing, grasping man; but the taking of his life, too, was surely of some importance, if even a sparrow counted. Every death had meaning; each meant loss. " 'And therefore never send to know for whom the bell tolls,' " she remembered Aaron saying. " 'It tolls for thee.' " Once more, Donne's lines provoked many thoughts within her. But soon they whirled with all the rest of the morning's words in a glittering mass inside Charlotte's head, which still ached from the previous evening's adventure.

And what about preserving one's own life, if it were threatened? It was true she could have died in her garden—might well have died of the cold, at least, if it had not been for a combination of lucky circumstances, or perhaps divine help. That, too, was a thought. Before leaving home this morning, she had taken several cups of strong coffee to fight off a fatigue that sleep hadn't cured. Now, its effects caused her body to tremble. The rash had gone, but an irritating itch remained.

Still, she'd taken a little time this morning to study the books Lem had brought back for her from Boston. But on the face of it, she'd decided it might be impossible to prove anything, even if she *had* found a likely herb. After all, knowledge of what had been used still didn't say who had left it, even though she felt she knew.

Looking for distraction, she studied Richard Longfellow and Diana in their front pew. It was a position her neighbor had paid well for, as was expected, although she knew he would have preferred a less conspicuous place.

At the same moment, Diana, too, was feeling constrained by her highly visible position, but at least she didn't feel the cold, wrapped in a thick, fur-lined cloak, with her feet on a warmer full of coals. What a bore the preacher was, she thought, and had been for two hours and fifty minutes, according to a small gold watch she glanced at from time to time. She was used to sermons dealing with urban life, with politics and personalities chastised or supported from the pulpit. Sundays *could* be very exciting, especially if one knew the individuals referred to, and could turn to look at them. And sermons in Boston were generally shorter. She wondered if Edmund Montagu went to meeting today in the city, or if he had found some official excuse.

Once again, Diana reached into a large satchel that held several comforts, to get a scented handkerchief and perhaps a lemon drop. It was then she saw a gleam from within, indicating something which, on further fishing, turned out to be the lost enameled dragon vial with its delightful perfume. She had been wrong; she'd never lost it at all.

Only now, she remembered dropping the bottle into

a small pocket in the larger bag, for safekeeping. Well, that was fortunate. She would have to tell Charlotte not to keep looking for it, when the sermon ended. The thought of Mrs. Willett made Diana sigh again, as it recalled her mind to more serious matters.

Seated beside his sister, an attentive Richard Longfellow continued to frown at Christian Rowe, trying to decide if the minister's hairline receded as quickly as his own. Longfellow had already gone over his conversation with Elias Frye several times in his head, until he had run out of new conclusions. It was now very likely that the miller had not been in Worcester when he said he was; wherever Lynch *had* been, it was also very likely that he'd been up to no good. It might have been Providence . . . but there was no proof. Still, he couldn't have been the one to attempt to poison Charlotte. Tea from the same canister had been drunk since Lynch's death with no ill effects, by both Charlotte and Hannah. And there had been no other guests in the Willett house since then. So, someone *must* have crept into Charlotte's kitchen when no one else was there on Saturday afternoon, and left a nasty calling card. As a selectman, Longfellow felt especially unhappy about the way the thing had been carried out. Had it really come to this— had people to lock all of their doors when leaving now, if only for half an hour? It was undoubtedly a sign of the growing lawlessness of the times.

On Longfellow's left, Cicero sat gazing at the preacher with what appeared to be admirable piety. But his thoughts, too, were wandering. It had been another interesting night, and a neat trick to get Gabriel and Mary out the back door, while Longfellow came in through the front. Later, he would enjoy hearing Diana's explanation of the brief use she'd made of Longfellow's glass house. Last night there had been enough to say about the attempt on their neighbor's life. All three had resolved to do everything they could to keep such a thing from happening again. They had also agreed that no one else should be told. It was enough that Charlotte had been singled out twice in one week—first, by Peter Lynch, then by the preacher, in front of his mob. Cicero knew it would do little good for even Longfellow to challenge a man like Reverend Rowe, if he should get it into his head to stir up more trouble. But, there were other ways to persuade the fellow, should the need arise.

" 'For thy mouth uttereth thine iniquity, and thou choosest the tongue of the crafty. Thine own mouth condemneth thee, and not I: yea, thine own lips testify against thee,' " intoned the reverend.

That's why certain pious people really should be more careful, thought Cicero, of what they wish for, even to themselves, after a few toddies on a cold night at the tap-room of a village inn. Especially when they're standing near a corner nook that hides an old man with excellent ears. Cicero's smile grew until it nearly connected those two prominent features, and he raised his kindly face as if exalting in the Word. If some of the ladies present only knew!

Two pews away, but in another world, young Lem sat among his large family, remembering the novel things he'd seen and done at Harvard College. If he worked hard, Dr. Warren had told him, he might become a student, although an extremely low ranking one to start. Still, with sponsorship—and if he learned his Greek and Latin—Warren had also said he might earn a degree with the best. Odder things had happened. In fact, it seemed to Lem that odd things lately made up the bulk of his limited experience.

Nathan Browne, the inn's smith, sat in the middle of the room, thinking how curious it was that both Jonathan and Lydia Pratt sat next to him in church today, as though nothing had happened. Well, no one *could* say, for sure . . . and given another chance, Lydia might change her spots, he supposed, but it was not a thing he'd be willing to wager on. Still, in the last two days she had spoken surprisingly kind words to them all. At the same time, Mary was in such a nervous state that those around her had begun to fear for her health. One moment the girl would be flushed; another she was as pale as a snow bank. Something else had happened to make Nathan hide whatever feelings he'd once had for her. So far he'd told no one, and wondered if Mary knew herself. The way things were, it might be dangerous to say too much . . . but he'd made new plans. . . .

Toward the back of the meetinghouse, others filled less polished pews. Phineas Wise sat with glazed eyes, next to Jack and Esther Pennywort, who actually appeared to be listening. Across the aisle, the four remaining Dudleys, their eyes cast down, privately mourned one of their own, speaking through their hearts to their Creator. On a corner bench, Hannah Sloan, her husband, sons, and daughters had begun to imagine their afternoon meal together, while in front of them Constable Bowers and his large fidgeting family held onto their prayer books and each other, and prayed that Mr. Bowers would not be the next one murdered for his official part in the ongoing investigations.

And then, abruptly, Christian Rowe ended his reading on the woeful ways of man, to the relief of the entire congregation. No doubt he'd worked up a thirst. He may also have sensed that after three hours he'd lost most of his listeners. At any rate, the preacher released his flock for their dinner, prior to a second service in an hour and a half. Some noisily bustled out on their way home. More made their way to common pastures to wait— heading for the Bracebridge Inn, and the tavern at the crossroads.

· · ·

"I KNOW IT'S cruel to keep him out," declared Esther Pennywort, who sat in her faded cloak, sipping a cup of warm cider by the Blue Boar's fire. "Though what's a woman to do but treat a husband like a child, when he acts that way? Not that I'd keep a child of mine out in the cold," she corrected herself, "if it had no place else to go. But Jack always has his ways, and he can shift for himself if need be."

Charlotte raised a glass of sherry that Phineas had brought her against the new season's chill, quite glad to be out of the drafts of the meetinghouse. Earlier, she had excused herself from Longfellow and Diana, saying she needed to have a brief word with a friend. Now, at her suggestion, she and Esther Pennywort cast their minds back to the evening of the old man's burning.

"Do you know just where he weathered the night?" Charlotte asked with a certain amount of hope. She watched as the small, fussy woman's eyes narrowed in thought, while worn hands rubbed one another.

"Well, when Jack's had enough, he usually goes to sleep in a barn or a shed, next to wherever he's found whatever it is he's been drinking. If he's been here at the Blue Boar, I'm told he goes across to the mill to sleep under some flour sacks. I know drunkenness is common enough in country and town alike, but I won't put up with it in my house! So when he came home carrying that strange tale, and with the fumes of a whiskey barrel about him, it made my blood boil! We have little for what we need, with the children growing. And for him to spend it on drink is too much!"

"It is hard," Charlotte sympathized. "But did he tell you where he went on that *particular* night?"

Again, Esther paused to think, her upper lip puckered into soft, vertical waves.

"Now, that's funny. He didn't say, but I thought he might not have gone to bed at all—he was so tired when he came in next morning. He slept for most of the next day and night, and after that he was up and gone again early."

"The morning Sam Dudley died."

"Yes," Esther replied hesitantly, "that would be the day. My Jack isn't a bad man, when he's sober," she insisted, worried more than a little at what Mrs. Willett might be thinking. "Although most believe him to be dim-witted. Oh, I know they do. Still, he's good enough for me."

"Times haven't gotten any easier for you lately, have they? No extra money has come in to make a difference?"

"Extra money! No, I'm afraid not. But as you mention it, lately he *has* taken to carrying on just like he's 'somebody'—even carrying snuff about. Imagine! A habit for his betters, if indeed it's for anyone at all! Quite nasty, I call it, sniffing tobacco up your nose, even if a lord cares to do it—even if it's soaked with something sweet."

"Where do you suppose he came by it? Perhaps someone gave it to him?"

Mrs. Pennywort looked around her, then lowered her voice. "I doubt that. I'm afraid to say it, but Jack has been known, occasionally, to be a bit—well, light-fingered. It's not all his fault, and I'm not sure but it's fair play, really. You see, his *friends*, as he calls them—these friends of his think he's simple, and encourage him to drink for the joy of watching his antics. It's never been all because of drink, either. It's his medicine, you know. For his teeth."

"Ah," said Charlotte, letting her breath escape in a sigh of enlightenment.

"They're none too good, nor are most of ours at this age, I suppose. But his are something dreadful, what's left of them in back especially. And he's too afraid to have them pulled! But he went to Boston one day, and in a tavern by the docks, he met a fellow—"

"Who gave him something for the pain?"

"That's right!" smiled Mrs. Pennywort. "They use it in eastern lands, he told Jack. Little seeds he was to chew on. Something like clove—he used to put a clove on a tooth for the pain, like most of us do. Well, these did him far more good, but they do make him quite queer. Sometimes, he can't tell what's what after he chews them. Still, they help him over the worst. He got a dreadful rash at first, but he's over that now. They call it henbane—funny name, isn't it? Anyway, that's why so many think of him as childlike. So do I, sometimes, I'll admit. But it isn't good for grown men to be teased and laughed at, or treated like children, is it? Nor for women, either, although men treat us the same as Jack often enough, and for less reason. It's a shame, really."

Charlotte sat very still, while Esther Pennywort sighed at the world's folly, took another sip of cider, and sat back with a small frown. Then she began to examine the company around them, unaware of the great secret she'd just betrayed.

So Jack Pennywort had left her henbane, thought Charlotte with a tiny smile . . . probably for fear of what she might suspect about his dealings with the miller. She'd already guessed that Jack knew more than he'd told. Had he feared, after their interview, that she might soon guess more?

She had given him tea on Thursday; that might have planted the idea in his mind. And perhaps he had only tried to discredit her, by causing her to act as he often did himself. After that, in the same way that others had always laughed at him, they would laugh at her, whatever she told them. Surely, her death hadn't been part of his plan. After all, he chewed the seeds himself. And she believed for Jack Pennywort that one murder would have been enough. As for Peter Lynch—how easy it would have been for Jack to offer his powerful "friend" one pinch of tainted snuff . . . then, another. And in a while, if the miller had begun to worry, or if he had rushed toward the smaller man, threatening—

She thought it likely Jack had only resorted to murder after he'd witnessed the miller commit one of his own. Poor young Sam must have seen the miller getting rid of the evidence of "Duncan Middleton" in his pond on Tuesday night; the boy had probably agreed to meet Lynch at a later time, when things had calmed down. If Jack had already gone to rest in the dark mill on Tuesday night, and overheard Sam talking with Lynch—and if he had followed later, to see the miller choke the life out of the boy—he might well have thought his own life was in danger. As it probably had been.

It all fit. So did the many reports of "the Devil's work" heard during the week. No doubt Jack had enjoyed offering others some of his own medicine in an innocent pinch of snuff. After all, he had been chosen to tell a shocking story to an admiring world, only to discover that it had all been a hoax. The whole thing, his whole life, had been a peculiar sort of amusement for others. Perhaps, thought Charlotte, there were more than a few people in Bracebridge to blame for Jack's recent sins.

She drew her mind back to the buzzing room full of farmers. The smells of ripe stew, lunch baskets, tobacco and wood smoke, wet linen and wool, and the pungency of several infants all swirled together over the subtler fumes from mugs and glasses.

Right now, Jack would be out behind the tavern with a few other men, enjoying tall stories and the cheap comfort of jug liquor, out of view of their women and children who preferred the crowded warmth inside. If he should enter now, what would be his reaction at seeing her sitting beside his wife?

And what about the man who had started the whole thing by coming to Bracebridge with the red cloak and the gold coins belonging to a dead man—an impostor whose own location no one, as yet, seemed to know? Had the stranger truly been responsible for the real Duncan Middleton's murder, with perhaps some help from Peter Lynch? Whoever he was, he was probably far away. Or then again, it was possible that he could be about to walk in through the tavern door at any moment.

Thinking it all over, Charlotte came to one final conclusion. She had very little idea of what would happen next.

Chapter 29

ODDLY ENOUGH, THE next person to actually sweep through the front door of the tavern turned out to be Diana Longfellow, who had never been known to visit the Blue Boar, but who seemed to find it worth a brief look now.

"You'll wonder," she said to Charlotte Willett with feigned ennui, "what draws me here, and all alone. It's a question with two answers, really. First, Richard and Cicero are quite busy on the bridge, debating whether the flow of water would be increased if the millpond were reduced, and whether that would alter the pleasures of some kind of fish. For my part, I wanted to tell you I've found my dragon vial. It was just where I'd left it, I'm afraid. But why don't we all go for our dinner now, if you're through with your business?"

"Then it wasn't Mary—" Charlotte began. Immediately, she thought better of denying what she'd been forced to suspect earlier . . . that the young woman might be a thief, and worse. It *had* seemed odd that Mary would be interested in taking such a thing, while her lover's life was at stake. Diana's news, then, meant that there must be *two* identical bottles in Bracebridge. But why had Mary been so quick to hide one of them the night before?

"Didn't you tell me that bottle was one of only half a dozen just arrived?" she asked Diana instead.

"Yes, brought in by Will Harper. If I'd been in Providence to ask him directly, I'm certain I could have gotten it at a much better price. For a song, really," Diana concluded, her eyes taking on a dreamy expression. "Did I tell you that I met the captain once before, while I was in London?"

"But then, Mary's bottle must have been brought from Providence, as well," Charlotte labored to explain. "So that means Peter Lynch was in *Providence*, not Worcester, on Monday . . . and that's where he intercepted Duncan Middleton! As he may have been *told* to do—by someone far smaller, who would be able to impersonate the merchant here. Then, both came back to Bracebridge on Tuesday, with the clothes, the horse, and the money. The impostor took the money, put on the clothes, and rode the horse to the inn. I saw him; so did Jonathan, and Lydia . . . although she tried to hide the fact—unsuccessfully, for the two of them were overheard by Mr. Lee. And then later at the Blue Boar, Gabriel went out first, and Jack followed them both onto the road, just as they knew he would—"

And at that instant the end of the story came to her, along with the knowledge of where her reasoning had gone wrong before. Stunned by her conclusion, she barely heard the faint clatter of horses' hooves outside. Then, realizing that delay might be dangerous, Charlotte turned and started to explain to Diana exactly who it was they should be extremely careful to avoid, and why. She had time to utter a name which put a look of astonishment on Diana's features. But before Mrs. Willett could go further, a commotion rose above the room's babble. One by one, heads turned to see five horsemen dismounting under the bare trees in front of the tavern.

Those outside quickly gathered around the newcomers, obscuring the view through the windows. But Charlotte and Diana had seen the vivid finery of Edmund Montagu, surrounded by the lesser uniforms of four others. Two, in loose blue and white, were sailors, while two more in scarlet coats and white breeches were clearly members of the king's regiments. It was an unusual spectacle this far inland, in time of peace, and more than a little grumbling punctuated the immediate excitement of the men outside.

Curiously, the sailors followed Montagu into the tavern while the redcoats kept watch over the horses, in the face of an increasingly agitated and demanding crowd.

Montagu at once spoke in low tones to Phineas Wise, who had seen his arrival and hurried forward. As he spoke, the captain's eyes caught those of a worried Charlotte Willett. He stared at her with concern of his own, before he was captured by a look from Diana Longfellow. The conference with the tavern's owner lasted only a moment more. Then, while Wise continued to shake his head, Montagu approached the two ladies whom he'd so often thought about lately, for different reasons.

"Captain Montagu!" Charlotte exclaimed softly. "I think we have proof our miller killed your merchant in Rhode Island."

"Yes, but how the devil—"

Rapidly, Charlotte began to explain.

"There was a perfume bottle, given to Mary Frye by Peter Lynch, while he pressed her to marry him. She took the bottle because she was forced to, but was ashamed to show it to anyone. Diana has its twin, one of

a very few lately arrived on a ship now at anchor near
Providence—" Montagu held up a hand in supplication,
and she let her sentence trail off.

"Peter Lynch was seen along the waterfront, boasting
and spending Dutch gold, as you say, Mrs. Willett. But of
far more importance now is the man I've come for, the imposter in the red cloak you saw on Tuesday afternoon—"

Now, Edmund Montagu was forced to halt, when a
group of boys burst into the Blue Boar. They soon set the
place whirling like a hurricane.

"We've found the Frenchman! The murderer's in the
mill!" They chanted it eagerly, over and over, forcing all
other conversation to stop short. "We've *found* him, and
he's gone into the room above!" their leader screeched.
Behind him, someone climbed onto a table to shout,
"Let's get the beggar, and finish it!" A rasp of voices
sounded an angry chorus.

"Throw him in the millpond, and see what he says!"

"Don't wait to send him to Cambridge, or Worcester, where his friends be! Let's do it now, and have it
done—"

"Come on!"

A flurry erupted all around the room, as some tried to
get to the door so as not to miss the excitement, while
others attempted to pull themselves and their children out
of harm's way, out of view of what promised to be a grisly
scene. Charlotte watched Esther Pennywort jump up and
join the rest, no doubt going to find Jack—just as Richard
Longfellow pushed into the room against the tide.

"Edmund," he began as he reached the captain,
"what's to be gained by bringing—"

"Do your duty," Montagu quietly ordered his two
sailors, who turned and disappeared into the crowd. "You
two stay here," he added to Charlotte and Diana, while
he grasped Longfellow's shoulder. But they weren't able
to leave quite yet.

"Save him!" Diana implored, pulling on Montagu's hand with strength enough to turn him back to her. It was a tense look he gave her—one that she would long remember with a thrill, and a certain pride.

Then the captain and her brother were gone, following the crowd that headed for the mill.

THE PLACE HAD already been thoroughly searched. A few concerned with trespass had lately avoided it, as did many more who believed rumors that the mill now had its own ghost. All of these ideas made it a likely spot for Gabriel Fortier to hide.

Somewhat earlier, Mary had imagined herself unobserved as she crept around behind the millpond on the small path. But several boys playing a game of settlers and Indians had seen her going by. They, in turn, had eagerly and carefully crept after, and proved her undoing.

Like King Philip a century before, leading the Nipmucks, the Narragansetts, and his Wampanoag brothers against the settlers, the boys had been careful to keep out of sight until the moment called for action. They imagined that they, too, wielded guns and tomahawks, and that these tomahawks were much like the hatchet the Frenchman had recently used to destroy the miller, as most of their fathers maintained. And so it was with a mixture of terror and delight that they came to see a young woman in the arms of that very same murderer.

When they screamed, hoping to make him let go of her, they expected the woman to run behind them to safety. Instead, both had stood with looks of disbelief frozen on their faces. And then she had turned and run *up* the stairs to the mill's second floor, where the large post of the grinding stone was held in place; next, the boys had seen the Frenchman go running after her, calling out her name.

Now, their shouts had created an extremely satisfactory chaos outside the mill, where fifty men debated what to do. Some wanted to smoke the Frenchman out; others urged someone should wait with a rifle, until he showed his face. Most simply wanted to storm the building.

All of their plans were short-lived. Edmund Montagu, back on his horse now and followed on foot by Richard Longfellow, cleared a way for the two redcoats who carried muskets set with bayonets. At the water's edge the captain turned to address the enflamed crowd.

"There is *no reason*," he shouted over a barrage of threats and suggestions, "to go in after Gabriel Fortier, *or* to endanger the life of the young woman with him. But there is *every reason* for all of you to listen to me! The man who was said to catch fire last Tuesday evening was *not*, as you must know, the merchant, Duncan Middleton. But he *was* someone who arranged for that man to be killed! Middleton's body was found washed ashore on Tuesday morning, near Providence. Yet on Tuesday afternoon, *after* the discovery of that body, someone else walked through Bracebridge wearing Middleton's clothes, carrying a supply of Dutch coins obtained by the merchant in a recent exchange. *That* man then caused himself to disappear, to cover up the real murder of Middleton, which he himself could not have committed—but which he had *caused to happen* by promising payment to your own Peter Lynch!"

Now a different sort of cry rose from the crowd—one of outrage mingled with disbelief.

"Who was it killed the miller, then?" one man shouted. Others quickly turned to ask each other the same. In the new commotion, Montagu's horse tripped and turned with a discomfort that matched its rider's, while those next to it warily moved back.

"That is of only secondary importance at the moment," Montagu argued with consternation.

"What about my boy?" came a sharp cry from Rachel Dudley, who had followed the crowd hoping to learn more of her son's death. She finished with a sob that did much to still the violence in those around her, at least for the moment.

"They're saying it was no accident that killed Sam," the bereaved woman continued. "Well, no one cared about this man Middleton—no one knew *him*! All they really cared about was his gold. No one even minds what happened to Peter Lynch, who surely deserved what he got. But Sam was only an innocent boy! So you tell me, who would want to murder *my son*?"

"It's nearly certain that he, too, was killed by the miller, for something he saw," Montagu called down to her, "and for that, I'm truly sorry. I believe your boy frightened Lynch, though he might not have known it. But there's one here who's responsible for *all* of this! A man who arranged to have his own brother killed—a man assumed dead by all those who insist on believing *what they read in the newspapers*—a man thought to be drowned in a shipwreck three years ago! I have brought two of his former shipmates from Boston; they can rely on their own eyes to tell them the truth, and will say if *Lionel* Middleton is still here, maintaining his masquerade!"

Montagu pointed, and the crowd turned to see the two sailors in an upper window of the Blue Boar, waving their arms, then shaking their heads violently—while from another window Diana, and Charlotte behind her, leaned out and pointed back. Taking the hint, many turned around again, to see a stream of smoke rising from the base of the mill; it was immediately followed by a sheet of flames that began to climb the outer walls of the old wooden building with a roar, racing into its upper story.

Suddenly, the crowd was electrified by the knowledge that two innocent young people were trapped inside, and would soon burn before their eyes. Immediately, water pails and a ladder were rushed from the tavern; others ran to nearby homes to bring more buckets. Few noticed a lone figure leading a horse from the stable be- hind the Blue Boar; few heard the approaching clatter of iron shoes on the road.

There was a scream from the crowd as Mary and Gabriel appeared in an upper window. Together, they stood on the brink, in the midst of a flow of black smoke that was already filled with bright sparks. Both were choking, trying desperately to fill their lungs with air. Then, still together, hand in hand, the pair leaped out into the air, and fell down into the millpond.

In a few moments, Mary Frye was pulled out of the pool by several men, to be bundled into a blanket and rushed off by a group of solicitous women. Gabriel still clutched at water weeds and struggled to get his footing on the millpond's muddy bottom, until the strong arm of Nathan Browne reached out to him, hesitated briefly, then slowly pulled him to the bank and safety.

By this time, two lines passed to and from the fire; these were manned by most of the able-bodied, while the two old quails, Tinder and Flint, stood back and shouted lustily at the flames, as if together they might somehow blow them out.

"But where," cried an elderly farm wife, who had been trying to think of something to do, "is this *other* man the captain accused? The one who's responsible for all that's happened? Is he going to get away?"

As it happened, her question was answered almost immediately. Six redcoats and a third sailor now rode down toward the town bridge from the direction of Boston. Between them, his hands bound and his head low, rode the finally defeated naturalist, Adolphus Lee.

Chapter 30

Within the hour, the Blue Boar and the Brace-bridge Inn were filled with sooty, happy patrons who gave thanks for an end to the fire, and to their fears of the past week. Warmed by their own efforts, they raised their glasses to the saved mill and to each other, and there were some who said a prayer for their reprieve from any further preaching that day.

Meanwhile, in Charlotte Willett's kitchen, Longfellow and Diana, Charlotte and Edmund Montagu feasted on toasted bread dipped into heated cheese, a few bottles of French wine, and a heaping plate of apples. Much had been discussed, but more remained unclear.

"So Lionel Middleton," Diana tried again, "arranged for the miller to kill his brother, which each of them did for money . . . and then the miller, already a murderer, killed the boy when he thought Sam had seen too much . . . and when Jack saw Lynch kill the boy, he decided to kill the miller?"

"Actually," Montagu corrected her, "when I spoke with Pennywort half an hour ago, he assured me he only meant to find out if Lynch had any further plans for *him*. Then, when he suspected he had, Jack thought he might make the fellow less dangerous with some of his doctored snuff. He hoped it would give him his chance to get clear, and planned to alert the rest of the town so that Lynch would be taken into custody. But when the miller threatened to kill him then and there, Pennywort swears he only did what he had to, as soon as he got the chance. Luckily, the ax was handy. After that, he watched the miller reel into his pond, wrench the thing from his head, and drown."

"And now Jack will look something of a hero," Longfellow added, smiling at the irony of the situation.

"Maybe it won't be such a bad thing," Charlotte told him gently, remembering again what Esther Pennywort had told her.

"Even though he tried to kill you, too, Carlotta?"

"But I don't think he did, Richard. Remember, he'd already put ground seeds into the snuff he carried. If that same mixture was what he put into my tea canister, he meant no real harm. My illness might have been as much from drinking an infusion of the *tobacco*, as the other. I doubt if he would have realized that."

"But how on earth did you know enough this morning to warn me about Adolphus Lee?" Diana asked her, a slice of red apple in her hand. "I can understand why Captain Montagu suspected Lionel Middleton was here. But even he didn't know for sure who Lionel *was*, until his former shipmates identified him. You concluded it was Lee from the other way around." She shook her head. "I don't see how."

"Mr. Lee gave himself away twice, really. I finally realized that he must have lied, when he said he'd heard Lydia Pratt talking to Middleton in the room next to his—remember? Because Lydia, with her love of meddling, never mentioned it to Captain Montagu when he questioned her. She couldn't have, since it never happened. She went along with Lee's story because she thought he'd invented it for *her,* to make it seem they hadn't been together on Tuesday afternoon. The truth, of course, was that they'd been very much together. And Lee had no real *reason* to make up that lie; he certainly hadn't been challenged. The discovery of their . . . activities together only came on Friday. But he knew Lydia wouldn't refute the story, and must have decided that it added a little sauce to his claim that he and Middleton had been inside the inn at the same time. When she knows the rest, Lydia Pratt will be more than a little ashamed of not having told the truth before . . . especially when she sees that Lee—or rather Lionel—only used her. I don't suppose Lydia has had many offers of that kind before . . . certainly not from a man so attentively energetic, which made Lee, or Lionel, all the more difficult to resist."

"But still, you only *suspected*—"

"But when I did, and I saw his eyes again, I remembered the way the old man had looked at me on the road. It's possible to disguise quite a few of one's features and intentions, but the eyes generally give the game away. Don't you think?" Charlotte queried, looking from Diana to Edmund Montagu.

For the moment, Diana said nothing. Then Montagu took the lead.

"Lee, or I should say Middleton, will go back to Boston tonight under close guard. I have little doubt that his trial will be a brief one. By the way, what was left of the gold that he paid to Lynch has been found in the mill. It seems it had been under floorboards that were warped by the fire."

"What will happen to Jack now, do you think?" Charlotte asked Montagu, feeling a pang for the man's family.

"I imagine he'll be tried for attempting to poison you. If you'll accuse him."

"Do *you* think I should accuse a local hero, Captain Montagu? I would guess it might do me more harm than good."

"It's possible you're right, Mrs. Willett, and I've no desire to meddle in village affairs. At any rate, Pennywort is now in the inn's cellar. Perhaps it *would* be best for his wife to have him back, after his day in court for the way he stopped Lynch."

"You had some opportunity to speak with Lionel Middleton as well, I suppose." Longfellow had just burned a finger on good English cheddar, and examined the digit as he spoke. "What, exactly, is *his* story?"

"Apparently," Montagu continued, dipping a piece of apple more cautiously into the pot, "when Lionel survived the wreck of his ship, and found he was listed as dead in the Canaries, it was a simple matter to adopt a slight disguise, sign onto another ship, and return to Providence, where he'd sailed from originally. His brother had disinherited him long before, after a family quarrel. But Lionel realized that if his brother made *another* will, and left him out of it entirely, then Lionel might still claim his share as an overlooked legal heir, after Duncan's death. Keeping his ears open, he learned that there *was* talk of a new will, made after his sister Veracity's passing. He knew that with clever counsel, he might stand to gain a fortune."

"And yet," mused Charlotte, "he made himself a good life during the time he waited. Richard said he'd become at least a convincing scientist more than a year ago, and he seems to have pursued his work happily since then."

"He had a knack for it," Montagu agreed, "and his years of travel gave him a great deal of experience. But he was also a man with an obsession—a burning desire, if you'd like. Strangely, if the Crown's trial against his brother had proceeded, there's little chance there would have been much left to inherit, after the government took its share. If Lionel had learned of the possibility, he might have reconsidered. Then again, it might only have made him hurry, I suppose."

"But how did Duncan Middleton happen to make the acquaintance of Peter Lynch?" asked Longfellow.

"It was hardly chance. After following his brother for several weeks, Lionel suspected what Duncan was up to with his adulterated rum. Duncan had already made some profit trying the scheme on his ships going to South America. Now, Lionel thought his brother would jump at an inland contact who could help him transport some of his poisonous drink to the frontier. And it happened that on earlier collecting trips, Lionel had met Peter Lynch. Thinking him a likely candidate for a murderer, as well as a smuggler, Lionel approached the miller. Lynch agreed to help him. Lionel told Lynch that Duncan was about to make one of his trips to Providence, and would stay at a particular inn he was known to frequent. Lynch went there and gained Duncan's trust; after that, it was only a matter of choosing a time and place for the old man's removal. A letter was written, and Duncan Middleton rode to Providence with a sackful of gold on Monday night—gold meant to pay for stores and transportation, which ended up instead financing his own murder. And I suspect we never will find a wagonload of poisonous spirits, because the miller never actually intended to deliver or transport anything at all!"

"Yet getting entirely rid of Middleton turned out to be more difficult than it seemed," Longfellow commented, cutting himself another cube of bread.

"Neither Lionel nor Lynch thought anyone would connect a body that eventually turned up on a beach in Rhode Island—if in fact it ever did—with a man's disappearance by most mysterious circumstances in a place like Bracebridge. Nor would there be much chance of identifying someone who had been floating in the water for a while, especially one so far from home. And they were nearly right. But Lynch knew little of tides or currents, being neither a sailor nor a coastal man; when he threw Middleton into the water, he didn't realize he would come back so quickly, and in such good shape. Of course, neither of them knew of *my* continuing interest in the merchant's whereabouts, or my man watching in Providence."

Charlotte had gazed long into the fire. Now, she spoke again.

"So they were all entangled in nets of their own making. Soon, the last of them will pay the price. It seems a sad defeat for a man who might so easily have continued to prosper on his own."

"A defeat for vengeance, a victory for love—and for a certain handsome Frenchman and his bride," Diana reminded her, lifting a glass of claret from Bordeaux. "And who would have thought that Paris scent would ever undo a man in such an *unusual* way? I must say I adore it now even more than before. To all things French!"

"Are you ready to switch your allegiance, then," asked Montagu in a particularly offhand manner, "to France, from England?"

"Oh, my *dear* Captain Montagu—you know we Americans are of independent mind. Most especially the ladies! I think you'll find it extremely difficult to pin us, like butterflies, to any flag—or alliance."

"My employers," Montagu hurried on, addressing her brother, "will have more for me to do as soon as I return. I'll be leaving very early tomorrow morning—"

"In that case," Diana interrupted, "perhaps you'd let me come along? I happen to have a riding dress with me, and if you don't mind going a little slowly . . . You know, these roads aren't entirely safe for a lady without an escort. Really, if I were to go back alone, my honor might even be at stake."

Charlotte reddened to a shade resembling one of her apples, as she tried to hide her amusement.

At the same time, a snatch of poetry floated unbidden through the captain's thoughts.

> Full many a flower's born to blush unseen,
> And waste its sweetness on the desert air.

Looking at the two women in front of him, Montagu was quite positive that Gray's verse hadn't been brought to mind by Diana. But perhaps it didn't really describe Charlotte Willett, or this place, either. He found himself wondering just how often Mrs. Willett might make the trip to Boston. And he thought that he would like to have a look at the next husband she chose for herself—just to see what kind of man he would be.

BY MONDAY MORNING, most of Saturday's snow had melted in air that was again almost warm. After Lem returned from leading out the cows, Charlotte Willett walked alone through the same clover, and climbed the orchard hill until she reached the low fence on top.

Perhaps, she thought, she was drawn to the family graves in sympathy with those who had suffered in recent days. It was also the end of another harvest season; time to give thanks for all that had been gathered in, as well as for things held only in memory, but held dear nonetheless.

When she arrived, Charlotte placed a sprig of rosemary on Aaron's stone. Reflecting, she looked off down the hill, where she saw her cows ... and Richard Longfellow. As she continued to watch, her neighbor turned from his own track through his field and began to climb the other side of the hill, long before he could have known that she was there among the low ring of hawthorns, now bereft of nearly all of their bright leaves.

When he did see her, he raised his felt hat, and his expression turned from pensiveness to one of pleasure.

"I was just thinking about love," he confessed. "My sister maintains that love often turns men into little more than beasts. But I have been concluding that so does the need of it, the *lack* of it, sometimes—as does a lack of simple respect from one's fellows."

"As I recall, love or the lack of it is rumored to have caused a great deal of trouble in the past," Charlotte agreed.

" 'Look to the future' is my motto. Speaking of that, have you heard what young Fortier and Mary have decided?"

"Let me imagine. They're to go ahead and marry now, with Jonathan's blessing?"

"The real news is that they'll soon be going to Nova Scotia, and that they plan to take the children from Worcester with them, leaving the father on his own— which will be smaller punishment than the wretch deserves! I hear a great many of the Neutrals are returning, probably hoping that no one will ever call them by that pitiful name again. I suspect they'd much rather be known for who they are, than what they were. Fortier says he is thoroughly tired of running about, and of living in the woods. I suppose they'll be quite happy plowing their own fields."

"We all need to tend our own gardens," replied Charlotte, gazing across her farm. "Do you know what's going to happen to Peter Lynch's property?"

"It's quite likely to wind up in the colony's treasury, like Middleton's, although we will be able to keep the mill for the village, since it's on common land. We haven't learned of any other relatives, and he did die a suspected felon. All this should do wonders for the governor's morale. Although I suspect at least *some* of the gold Lynch got his hands on won't find its way to Boston, after all," Longfellow added, with a look that went off toward New Hampshire, or possibly as far as Acadia.

"I've heard some news myself," Charlotte said with spirit, "about another impending marriage. It seems Nathan has been courting a woman in Concord, and he's planning to bring her here to live. Knowing Nathan, I imagine she'll be well worth having as a neighbor."

"I hope she's a match for Lydia Pratt . . . although our Lydia seems to be a changed woman. She actually manages to speak with respect and affection to her husband, which is certainly a very good thing . . . though it's one most of us never thought we'd live to see."

"Some help themselves by helping others," Charlotte replied, glad to have her long-standing opinion of Jonathan's good sense confirmed once again. Had he chosen, he could have seen to it that Lydia paid a steep price for her dalliance—but it would have cost him a valuable asset. "And have *you* any plans for the future, Richard?" she queried, quite interested in his answer.

"As a matter of fact, I'm thinking of putting on a little show tonight, around dusk, not far from the Blue Boar. Perhaps you'd like to attend. It seems there are still a few who persist in believing that witches were responsible for an unholy fire on Tuesday night. So I thought I'd treat them to a scientific demonstration. However, I have it in mind to change the formula a bit. For the turpentine, this time, I'll try substituting rum. And I plan to make a few other adjustments, as well."

"That," said Charlotte, with a smile, "should be most instructive. But if you don't mind, this time I'll stay at home."

THAT EVENING, CICERO sat under the portrait of Eleanor Howard in Longfellow's warm, quiet study. Things were nearly back to normal, and he was glad of it. Diana had gone back to Boston with Captain Montagu—God help the man to keep his wits about him, with no one to intervene for him the next time. And Longfellow had gone out to have a little fun with his chemicals, in a bright mood. Now, Cicero looked forward to enjoying a little peace, at least until the next crisis came.

He took a bite of cake and a sip of tea from a tray on his lap, and looked deeply and contentedly into the fire. Excitement was well enough for some. But after a certain age, he had decided, philosophy was better. He lifted a small volume from the table beside him, and again began to savor its classic phrases as he ran them softly over his tongue.

The dark face he suddenly glimpsed out of the corner of his eye, as someone tall strode past the window, startled him into dropping his book. There had been something very familiar about the figure, and its apparel.

It was when the man entered the study itself, and Cicero smelled the acrid scents of burning wool, and hair, and pitch, that the story came to him in a flash. His face dissolved into a beatific smile. Things *were* back to normal.

AND FINALLY, ACROSS the gardens, Charlotte, Lem, and Orpheus sat in front of their own fire; this time, it was one that burned in the hearth of the blue room. Lem waded through elements of Latin grammar from a book once used by Jeremy Howard and his sisters. As the old dog watched him sounding out new words, its eyebrows rose and fell to match the reader's own.

Meanwhile, Charlotte concentrated on a letter she knew should have been written days before. She would send it to her brother in Europe, and duplicate its information in one to the Willetts in Philadelphia. Even in the City of Brotherly Love, she had found a taste for shocking events, no matter if they sometimes came at the expense of one's neighbors. That was the way the world went, she reminded herself, dipping her quill into the inkpot again. Life went on.

Then she heard a rhythmic bumping, as a long tail began to thump against the bare wood floor. She looked down, and followed Orpheus's gaze to a spot in the middle of the room. Nothing seemed to be happening there at all. It was at that moment that she smelled the familiar scent of horehound, although she also noticed that it was fainter than usual. In another moment, she saw Lem raise his head and curiously test the air. After that, Charlotte watched him yawn and return to his work, and kept on watching with quiet pleasure, while the old dog before her settled with a sigh.

About the Author

MARGARET MILES currently lives in Washington, D.C., with her husband Richard Blakeslee, and a black cat named Rocket. After writing and coproducing short films and videos for nearly twenty years, she now enjoys spending most days in the eighteenth century.

Like Everyone Else . . . But Different

Like Everyone Else . . .
But Different

The Paradoxical Success of Canadian Jews

Morton Weinfeld

M&S

National Library of Canada Cataloguing in Publication Data

Weinfeld, Morton
Like everyone else ... but different : the paradoxical success of
Canadian Jews

Includes bibliographical references and index.
ISBN 0-7710-8912-0

1. Jews – Canada. I. Title.

FC106.J5W43 2001   305.892'4071   C2001-901103-2
F1035.J5W43 2001

We acknowledge the financial support of the Government of Canada through the Book Publishing Industry Development Program for our publishing activities. We further acknowledge the support of the Canada Council for the Arts and the Ontario Arts Council for our publishing program.

Designed by Ingrid Paulson
Typesetting in Minion by M&S, Toronto

Printed and bound in Canada

McClelland & Stewart Ltd.
The Canadian Publishers
481 University Ave.
Toronto, Ontario
M5G 2E9
www.mcclelland.com

1 2 3 4 5   05 04 03 02 01

CONTENTS

Writing this book has been a true labour of love. I wrote it over more than four years, but its gestation period has been much longer, dating back at least to the late 1970s, when I began teaching a course on the Sociology of North American Jewry at McGill. I am deeply involved, personally and professionally, in the subject.

The book grapples with all the major themes of modern Jewish life in Canada. Jews have always been interested in their own saga, and, as I shall argue, with very good reason. Canadian Jews are no different. Regardless of how involved or well-versed they are in Canadian Jewish life, they should find much in this book that is informative, engaging, and provocative. But this book is also written for those who are not Jewish. I have found a sincere fascination among Canadian non-Jews concerning this strange people. This has been my happy experience for many years with my eclectic band of (mainly non-Jewish) lunchtime regulars at the McGill Faculty Club. In subtle ways they, too, have contributed to this book. No subject has been off limits. Often a Jewish topic would arise, not from my own prompting. Whatever the issue – the latest turn in Israeli politics, a movie with a Jewish theme, free speech and Holocaust denial, the mysterious behaviours of Hasidic Jews, the latest Jewish joke – I would find collegial interest and fresh perspectives. This general curiosity is growing with increasing contact between Jews and non-Jews, not least through the rising rates of inter-marriage. I hope this book helps.

I base my assertions, at least most of them, on evidence. But I have also cut down on the jargon of social science, provided basic infor-mation, and explained Jewish and technical terms. The book is for anyone interested in the modern Jewish experience, in Canada, in the challenges of cultural diversity, and in the intersection of all three. I offer my own interpretations, and some of these are controversial. In the face of a Jewish community which feeds on crises and pessimism,

I argue for a different vision of the Jewish future. In my own view, to be a Jew is to be an optimist.

I owe many people a debt of gratitude. Mordechai Ben-Dat, Desmond Morton, Harold Troper, and Gerald Tulchinsky read the manuscript and offered valuable comments, suggestions, criticisms, and facts. I spoke to many people, most in person, but others by phone or e-mail. They helped me as formal interview subjects and as sources for specific bits of information or assistance. Several students helped as researchers. To (without titles and honorifics) Ron Aigen, Murray Baron, Tzila Baum, Ian Beitel, Franklin Bialystok, Cathie Best, Myer Bick, Irv Binik, Jay Brodbar, Shari Brotman, Robert Brym, Mervin Butovsky, Warren Clark, Harvey Cohen, Sergio DellaPergola, Paula Draper, Honey Dresher, Celia Economides, Daniel Elazar, Baruch Frydman-Kohl, Ronald Finegold, Tzipie Freedman, Robert Fulford, Linda Glustein, Yechiel Glustein, Hy Goldman, Michael Goldman, Allan Gotlieb, Sid Gotfrid, Howard Goldstein, Charles Gradinger, Frank Guttman, Gershon Hundert, Howard Joseph, Norma Joseph, Joe Kislowicz, Linda Kislowicz, Bobby Kleinman, Penny Krowitz, Jean-Claude Lasry, Susan Le Pan, Malcolm Lester, Ho Hon Leung, Bob Luck, Peyton Lyon, Sheldon Maerov, Herbert Marx, Norman May, Joel Miller, Richard Menkis, Lionel Moses, Doug Norris, Gunther Plaut, Carol Polter, Reuben Poupko, Manuel Prutschi, Anita Rappaport, Janice Rosen, Anna Rubalsky, Jonathan Sarna, Diane Sasson, Randal Schnoor, Stuart Schoenfeld, William Shaffir, Charles Shahar, Moshe Shulman, Rob Singer, Stephen Speisman, Ted Sokolsky, Norman Spector, Heidi Stober, David Taras, Harriet Tobman, Marion Van Horn, Joel Wardinger, Bryna Wasserman, Martine Whitaker, and to several others who wished to remain anonymous, my sincere thanks. I apologize to any whom I have omitted. Many others not listed here have shaped my understanding of Canadian Jewry through countless informal encounters and conversations over the years. This is certainly true of many academic colleagues in the fields of ethnic relations and modern Jewish Studies.

I would like to thank several people at McClelland & Stewart: Doug Gibson for recognizing the need to tell this story, Alex Schultz for helping to shape the manuscript and guide it home, and Adam Levin for his careful copy-editing and attention to detail. I thank my agent, Beverley

Slopen, for her continuing support. Special thanks to all the office staff at McGill, both in the McGill Institute for the Study of Canada and in the Department of Sociology, who helped in so many ways. Lynne Darroch and Natalie Zenga were there to help me with computer challenges as they arose. Several sources contributed financially. I would like to thank the Multiculturalism Branch of the Department of Canadian Heritage, the Department of Citizenship and Immigration and the Social Sciences and Humanities Research Council through their funding of the Metropolis Project and the Montreal consortium Immigration et Métropoles, and McGill University through its support for the Chair in Canadian Ethnic Studies and its sabbatic leave policy.

Most important of all, I thank my family. Much of this book has been shaped by my experiences first with my wife, Phyllis, and later with my three wonderful children, Rebecca, David, and Joanna. They were an inspiration, a source of encouragement, and tolerated absences and long nights at the computer. But family also means generations past, specifically my parents and my wife's parents, now all deceased, who came to Canada. To all of them, I dedicate this book.

A PARADOXICAL
PEOPLE

DIVERSITY AND SUCCESS

Can they all be Canadian Jews? A Hasid with a black hat and coat and *payess* (sidelocks) who prays three times a day; a Modern Orthodox Jew with a knitted *yarmulka* (skullcap) worn at home and at work; a Conservative Jew who drives to synagogue every Sabbath; a Reform Jew in a mixed marriage who celebrates both Hanukkah and Christmas; a European Ashkenazi; a North African Sephardi; a recent immigrant from Russia, Israel, South Africa, or Ethiopia; a fourth-generation Canadian; an atheist; a left-wing Zionist supporting Peace Now; a right-wing Zionist who supports Likud; a dentist, stockbroker, business executive, teacher, psychotherapist, cab driver, or secretary; a knee-jerk liberal or a neo-conservative; a native speaker of English, French, Polish, Russian, Spanish, German, Yiddish, or Hebrew? Yes, they are all Canadian Jews. This book tells their story. Their diversity provides the context and an explanation for the paradoxical successes of Canadian Jewish life.

Jewish life in Canada today is as good as it has been anywhere since the Golden Age of Spain. In an atmosphere of relative security, Jews are able to fulfil the twin promises of Canadian multiculturalism: They participate fully in the life of their surrounding society, and at the same time maintain a vibrant Jewish culture. Jews have stumbled onto a magical equilibrium. For most minority groups, these two objectives stand in sharp opposition. Usually the more the members of a minority group participate in the majority society and culture, the less they succeed at preserving their own. They will join a different church and set of organizations, harmonize their social and political values with those of the majority, lose interest in their ancestral language and culture, and socialize and marry outside the group. Jews do this as well, but far less than non-Jews. The Jewish success at combining both objectives is remarkable. For Jews, the trade-off is not nearly as severe; they can have their honey cake and eat it, too.

Jews are a paradoxical people, full of contradiction, diversity, conflict, irony, and, yes, mystery. In this, Jews are not unique; paradox is a feature of the human condition. But what is special is the extent and the outcome of paradox in the modern Jewish experience. Jews – as much by luck as by design – have created a workable synthesis of opposites. This success has at times proved elusive or fleeting. But nowhere does its prospect shine brighter than in Canada today. Jews are at once Biblical and postmodern, religious and ethnic, devout and secular, admired and reviled, conservative and liberal, prosperous and insecure. Jewish communal and cultural institutions are thriving, yet evidence of assimilation appears to mount. Jews are affluent and increasingly accepted everywhere, yet insecure about the potential revival of anti-Semitism. By their social class, Jews are among the haves, but by their politics they are among the have-nots.

In many ways Jews are a precursor of modernity, and epitomize the avant-garde, the cutting edge. In the past hundred years, Jews have been overrepresented on the liberal end of the political spectrum. They have passionately embraced civil liberties and support for the welfare state. They have achieved the highest levels of educational and occupational success, often in the most modern fields. Some Jews have gained fame as scientific or artistic geniuses. Others have earned great wealth. They have been the first group to achieve zero population growth in the United States, and have low fertility rates in Canada. All these are hallmarks of modernity.

Yet at the same time, Jews retain strong ties to their ancient history and traditions. They express this attachment in countless practices and preoccupations. They adhere to the same religious principles, revere the same ancient land, and use essentially the same language as King David did. They study the same texts as did the commentators in and the commentators on the Talmud. They practise rituals going back centuries and millennia. The traditional Jewish family remains a powerful ideal. The Holocaust has confirmed the Jewish status as an archetypal victim and pariah, continuing a tradition going back for centuries. Orthodox and ultra-Orthodox Judaism have managed to survive and thrive in North America, defying earlier scholarly predictions that Orthodoxy would remain the weakest of all branches of Judaism. Even non-religious Jews cling to ancient religious rituals and holidays with a perplexing tenacity. All of these contradictions, the intermingling of the old and the new, are played out among Canadian Jews.

Canadian Jews differ by region across the country, by religious denomination, by social class, by lifestyle, by ethnic and national origin, even by ideology. The old joke "*For every two Jews, there are three organizations*" captures this profusion. For some analysts these differences, and the fractious conflicts that arise, are a source of weakness, or of danger. My own view is that these differences and the paradoxes that spring from them are a source of strength. This diversity is a key to Jewish success. There are Jewish eggs in many baskets. There is no one formula that applies to each Jew. Not every group of Jews needs to maximize both multicultural goals, of external participation and internal solidarity. Different groups will work out their own balance between the two.

The central theme of this book is the story of how this balance operates in the day-to-day lives of modern Canadian Jews and the Jewish community. We explore the particular way Canadian Jews confront the paradoxes of modern Jewish life. Some chapters will focus on participation in the broader society: how Jews earn a living; their relations with non-Jews; their encounters with the many forms of anti-Semitism; their involvement in Canadian politics. Others will focus on issues of internal Jewish concern: the nature of Jewish marriages, families, and sexual relations; how and why Jews pray; the many varieties of Jewish culture; how Jews educate their children and participate in

Jewish organizations. Every part of the story is revealing; together they help us understand the enigma of Jewish survival.

American authors have written many books pondering the present and future of American Jewry. Their recent mood has been pessimistic, but it was not always so. As recently as 1985, Charles Silberman's *A Certain People* hailed the American Jewish experience as an unmitigated success story.[1] American Jews, like Canadian Jews today, were achieving the impossible: they enjoyed full participation and acceptance in American society while retaining a seemingly strong Jewish cultural life and identity. In 1986 Calvin Goldscheider's *Jewish Continuity and Change* argued boldly that American Jewish life would continue despite transformations and declines in religious observance.[2] Then, with the publication of the results of the National Jewish Population Survey of 1990, the roof fell in. The NJPS offered American Jews the first statistical portrait of their community in twenty years. While experts debated whether the recent mixed-marriage rate was 52 per cent or 41 per cent, the dangerous trend seemed clear. Through cultural assimilation or by marrying out, American Jews were disappearing. And those who remained were becoming an increasingly fractious group, torn apart by a growing religious *Kulturkampf* over the issue of "who is a Jew?" Panic set in among communal leaders. Jews needed a religious or cultural revival, as well as a new unity, to prevent the unthinkable. The titles of some recent books capture the pessimism: Alan Dershowitz's *The Vanishing American Jew*, Elliott Abrams's *Faith or Fear*, Jack Wertheimer's *A People Divided*, Samuel Freedman's *Jew Versus Jew*.[3]

The debate between the optimists and pessimists continues, in Canada as well as in the United States. The organized Jewish community has now embraced the pessimistic view. Some Jews love to worry, and after all, they know their history. Recall that the Golden Age of Spain was followed by the Inquisition and the Expulsion in 1492. The varied and vibrant Jewish culture which emerged later in Eastern and Central Europe was destroyed during the Holocaust. And today, the "Golden Age of Canada" presents new challenges and contradictions. The security of North American Jewry is not immediately threatened by anti-Semitism. But many see even greater dangers in assimilation, intermarriage, and divisions within the Jewish fold. As the old lament reminds us: "If everything is so good, why are things so bad?" If Jews want to feel good, they should read anti-Semitic hate literature: "Jews are powerful, Jews are in control." If they want to feel bad, they should read the Jewish press: "Jews are divided, Jews are assimilating, anti-Semitism is rising, Israel is in danger."

I do not share the prevailing pessimism, though I recognize there are real challenges ahead. Historian Simon Rawidowicz has rejected the image of Jews as "an ever-dying people," arguing that almost every generation in Jewish history has felt that it was the last link in the chain. The current generation is no different.[4] But the problems of continuity and unity, which dominate the collective Jewish agenda, are neither new nor daunting. Innovative responses to these challenges are already underway, as part of the new "continuity agenda." In addition, no one should assume that present trends establish the blueprint for the future; the only guarantee about the Jewish future is that the unpredictable will happen. And I am even less pessimistic about the future of Jews in Canada, where the toll taken by assimilation is not as severe.

But my optimism is sustained by another, more intuitive feeling. Given the broad sweep of Jewish history, I see no reason why the current conjuncture in North America, with evidence of erosion mixed with signs of innovation and vitality, must sound the death knell of (non-Orthodox) Jewish life. Things are not so bad. If Auschwitz was not the end of the line, neither will be Madonna dabbling in Kabbalah. Jewish survival has resulted from an unintended but fortuitous blend of diverse, indeed contradictory, demographic and cultural strategies that can adapt to changing circumstances. Jews, as we shall see, maintain an uneasy equilibrium of opposing forces pulling them outward and inward. This has been the case throughout the modern period. They struggle – like a fiddler on the roof – to maintain their balance. Certainly, compared to most other immigrant and minority groups, Jews are doing something right.

THE CANADIAN DIMENSION

The story of Canadian Jews today has its own particular interest and importance. There are striking similarities between Jews and Canada. Jews are chronically insecure, like Canadians, or Québécois, and love to take their collective pulse. No one should be surprised. It is only two generations since the death camps, and now the new threats of cultural extinction and demographic attrition have appeared. Given English-Canadian insecurity *vis-à-vis* the Americans, and Québécois insecurity *vis-à-vis* English Canada (and Western Canadian insecurity in relation to the East), Jews with their legendary insecurities are the ideal Canadians. Even the staunchest Jewish federalist has a visceral empathy with the French efforts at *la survivance*. I know I do. The discourse of survival, so common to both English- and French-speaking Canadians, also describes the Jewish experience for two thousand years.

At any rate, the contemporary Canadian Jewish story remains to be told. Despite the increased visibility of Jews in Canadian life, there are few current books which analyze their daily lives. The exceptions are edited collections of academic articles, memoirs, or research monographs focused on specific topics. (See the Bibliographic Essay.) These books add to Canadian Jewish scholarship, but there is very little for any reader – Jew or non-Jew, generalist or specialist – who wants to see the big picture, to understand the subtleties and complexities of Canadian Jewish life.

Understanding Canadian Jews is important for two reasons. First, the Jewish community in Canada has become an increasingly significant player in the Jewish Diaspora. Many other Diaspora communities are in trouble. The demographic future of Jewish life in Western and Central Europe is bleak.[5] In Eastern Europe and specifically the former Soviet Union, the exodus to Israel and to the West has led to a demographic and cultural depletion. Despite heroic attempts at communal revival, ongoing economic, political, and social instability makes it unlikely that Eastern Europe will reproduce strong Jewish communities. The communities in Latin America and South Africa continue to atrophy. Even the American Jewish population is stagnant. In the entire Diaspora, only Canadian Jewry continues to grow. Canada, with over 350,000 Jews, has the sixth-largest Jewish population after the United States at about 5.6 million, Israel at 4.3 million, France at 700,000, Russia at 550,000, Ukraine at 400,000, and is ahead of the United Kingdom at 300,000 and Argentina at 220,000.[6]

The second reason is the assumption that the experience of Canadian Jews can teach us something about the limits and possibilities of diversity, and in particular about multiculturalism in Canada. While many Canadians take a possessive pride in multiculturalism, it did not emerge out of nowhere in the 1970s. American Jewish writer Horace Kallen popularized the formal idea of "cultural pluralism" early in the twentieth century to symbolize what he saw as the impact of mass migration on American life. Kallen later described the term in his famous metaphor of an orchestra: "The American way is the way of orchestration. As in an orchestra the different instruments, each with its own characteristic timbre and theme, contribute distinct and recognizable parts to the composition, so is the life and culture of a nation, the different regional, ethnic, occupational, religious and other communities compound their different activities make up the national spirit. The national spirit is constituted by this union of the different."[7]

Cultural pluralism of course fits the Canadian reality perfectly. Canada was settled by the First Nations, then the French and the English, and waves of later immigrant groups. For many people, a tolerance for and appreciation of diversity is the essence of being Canadian. Well before Kallen's writing, Prime Minister Wilfrid Laurier, at the dawn of the twentieth century, anticipated future multicultural sentiments in his famous comparison of Canada to a cathedral: "The cathedral is made of marble, oak and granite. It is the image of the nation I would like to see Canada become. For here I want the marble to remain the marble; the granite to remain the granite; the oak to remain the oak; and out of all these elements I would build a nation great among the nations of the world."[8]

For Jews who had for generations been living within yet apart from host communities throughout the Diaspora, this was music to their ears. Jews were, and are, are a Canadian multicultural community par excellence. Many minority communities see the Jews as a model for what they can accomplish. In some ways they are. But in others they are not. If there are lessons in the Jewish experience, they apply only selectively to other minority groups. In many ways, as I shall illustrate, Jews and their experience are unique. The fact that Canadian Jews are

doing well is due not to the official policy of Canadian multiculturalism so much as to previously established features of Canadian law and
society which reflect the values of liberal democracy. Neither is it due
to any intrinsic merit or talent on the part of Canadian Jews. Rather,
it derives from their inherited cultural characteristics and their long
history as a product of diverse Diaspora communities. The many facets
of Jewish identity enhance the odds of some form of communal survival. The Jewish experience as a minority struggling in many different
Diasporic settings for close to two thousand years helped Jews develop
resourceful strategies and flexible institutions. Jews were well placed
to take advantage of what multiculturalism had to offer.

The contemporary Canadian Jewish story is also fascinating on its
own terms for what it tells us about Jews and diversity in Canada. That
story was first told in *Canada's Jews*, a book by the pioneer Canadian
Jewish demographer Louis Rosenberg, which was the last attempt to
provide a comprehensive "contemporary" overview.[9] First published
in 1939, that classic volume was statistical and relied largely on analysis of the 1931 census data. Nothing like it has been done since. Although
this book is partly inspired by Rosenberg's work, it is not a compendium of demographic statistics. Rather, it seeks to capture the
textures of daily life of Jews and their communities.

Jews remain a source of curiosity, admiration, and fear among
many in the non-Jewish world, and this is also true for Canada. For
the most part, the general curiosity that many non-Jews have about
Jews is well meaning. I have found it in casual conversation with a range
of non-Jews, from blue-collar workers to sophisticated academics.
Scholars have tried to pinpoint exactly what makes Jews so unusual.
Non-Jewish writer Ernest van den Haag accepts common, generally
flattering, stereotypes held about Jews.[10] He implies that Jews are
smarter than other people, have a distinctive Jewish character, even
make better doctors and more aggressive lawyers. Anthropologist
Raphael Patai argues that Jews are indeed a unique people, not because
they have remained separate, but because they have over the centuries
absorbed significant cultural influences from the outside world.[11]
Combining these two perspectives, we conclude that Jews are the same
as everyone else, but they are also very different.

PERSONAL BIASES

No writer comes to a topic with a clean slate. And no analysis of a topic is based on a neutral set of facts and a self-evident interpretation of their meaning. There is always selectivity at work, based either on the writer's biography or on an intellectual predisposition.

> *Some years ago, the Bata Shoe Company sent two sales representatives to Africa to check out the potential market. The pessimist returned and said, "It's terrible! No one is wearing shoes! There's no market at all." The optimist returned and said, "It's terrific! No one is wearing shoes! The market is enormous."*

In the interests of full disclosure, it is now common for writers to reveal personal background and biases. So where am I coming from? I am a committed Jew who is optimistic about the future of Canadian Jewry. I was born in 1949 in Montreal to Polish Jewish Holocaust survivors. My parents sent me to Jewish day school until the end of high school, and for ten summers to a Hebrew-speaking camp in the Laurentian Mountains. I am married to a Jewish woman, and my three children have attended a mix of Jewish schools and camps. We belong to a Reconstructionist synagogue. My father lived in Israel from 1975 until his death in 1990, and I have visited many times. I love Israel, warts and all. I value the full spectrum of Jewish life, from ultra-Orthodox to Jewish secularist, from Likud to Labour. Not for one second do I think that my brand of Jewishness has a monopoly on virtue. It just happens to suit me.

My Jewishness also embodies all sorts of inconsistencies. Take my approach to keeping kosher. Jews are forbidden to eat certain foods, like pork and seafood, and to mix dairy products with meat. So what do I do? Our home is kosher, sort of. We cook only kosher products and have separate meat and dairy dishes. But we also keep paper plates and plastic cutlery so we can eat Chinese food at home. Our dishes are kosher, but not our stomachs. We eat at any sort of restaurant. I eat cheeseburgers, as well as bacon and pork spareribs, but refuse to eat ham, shrimp, and lobster, and gag at the thought of a glass of milk with a salami sandwich. On Passover, we use a separate set of dairy and meat Passover dishes, empty out the kitchen cupboards, and eat only special kosher-for-Passover products. I will even schlep a box of matzo to the university Faculty Club so I can have it during Passover along with the unkosher lunch I buy there. Of course all this makes no sense and is thoroughly illogical. But I am not alone. Many Jews have their own idiosyncratic kosher habits. Modern Jewish life is one big cafeteria, where Jews pick and choose.

As an academic, I have been teaching about contemporary Jewish life for a quarter of a century. I began as a teaching assistant at Harvard, working for the eminent sociologist – and my advisor – Nathan Glazer, who taught a course on American Judaism. Since 1977, I have been teaching a course on the Sociology of North American Jews at McGill, which was the first of its kind in Canada. My reflections and interpretations have been shaped by my teaching and research over the years. Let me borrow a rabbinical dictum: I have learned much from my teachers, more from my colleagues, but most of all from my students.

As a sociologist, I have a behaviourist bias. When evaluating phenomena I prefer to know what people actually do, and not only what they say or think or believe. While it is interesting to know about people's attitudes, talk is cheap. Academic readers who are seeking the latest esoteric theoretical fads will also be disappointed. My sociological work and this book are resolutely empirical; wherever possible, I deal in facts.

An old Jew wants to join the navy. The recruiter asks him if he can swim. He replies, "Don't worry, I know the theory."

Lastly, I am favourably "biased" towards Canada.[12] When it comes to the treatment of minorities, it is an imperfect country (which country is not?), yet the amount of overt bigotry which exists is far less than in the past. United Nations surveys in the 1990s have ranked Canada as the best country in the world. Perhaps those studies overstate the case. But on balance Canada is a good place, a very good place, for Jews to live.

COMPARATIVE METHODS

There are a number of comparative themes in this book. To determine whether there is anything distinctive about Canadian Jews, I will compare them regularly to Jews in the United States. How could I not? As Canadians, we are used to looking over our shoulder to the south. Most of the challenges of Jewish life exist on both sides of the border. For Jews already deeply committed to certain forms of Jewish life, the religious and cultural opportunities in places like New York are unmatched by anything Canada has to offer. But that is a poor basis for comparing the two countries. On most measures ranging from knowledge of Hebrew or Yiddish to ritual observance, Canadian Jews are on average "more Jewish" than their American cousins. The differences, as we shall see, are remarkable.

Jewish scholars and communal leaders on both sides of the border recognize the greater Jewishness of Canadian over American Jews but disagree as to the reasons. Some claim the greater Canadian Jewishness is due mainly to circumstances of Jewish immigration and demography. Jews in large numbers came earlier to the United States, so they have had more time to assimilate. Recently, Canada has had relatively far more Jewish immigrants, who presumably have stronger ties to Jewish tradition. As of 1990, only 10 per cent of American Jews were immigrants, compared to 30 per cent for Canadian Jews. In this view, it is immigration, not Canadian multiculturalism, that gives Canadian Jews their edge. Others feel that the greater Canadian Jewishness is due to the much-vaunted Canadian multicultural "mosaic" versus the American "melting pot." This suggests that Canada was and is more nurturing of minority groups than the United States, regardless of the proportions of immigrants.[13] Such tolerance could retard Jewish assimilation. I suppose I tilt more to the position that highlights Jewish immigration patterns rather than specific features of the Canadian environment. According to this view, eventually American and Canadian Jewish life will converge – but as a proud Canadian, of course I hope I am wrong.

In this book I will also compare Jews to other minority groups. (Think of the many jokes that start, "A rabbi, priest, and minister were. . . .") Recent research in the fields of modern Jewish studies and Canadian ethnic studies has consisted largely of in-depth case studies. Detailed comparisons are sadly lacking.[14] In a sense this volume, too, is a singular case study, since it is essentially about Canadian Jews. But I have long agreed with sociologist Seymour Martin Lipset that one of the best ways to study Jews is to study Gentiles.[15] Any statement describing Jewish behaviour – for example, "Jews look after their own" – relies on an explicit or implicit comparative framework. So I began this book espousing the value of comparing Jews to other groups. If I will end with the same view is another question. I will also compare groups of Jews with each other. (Think of jokes that start, "An Orthodox, Conservative, and Reform rabbi were. . . .") This is a natural outgrowth of the emphasis on diversity as a cornerstone of the Jewish paradox and as an asset that sustains Jewish life.

Since regional variations loom large in Canadian life, I will also compare one Canadian Jewish community to another. Many of the vignettes and interviews I use are taken from Montreal, where I grew up and have worked and raised my family. Many others come from Toronto, a city I know well. Montreal and Toronto are different from each other, and both differ from Calgary and Halifax. And small-town Canadian Jewish life differs from that of the majority who live in large cities. A comprehensive treatment of the regional variations in all the issues discussed here would require several additional books. But unless specified otherwise, I will assume that events or experiences drawn from one setting are generic, and apply to all others. My stress is on commonalities. The meaning of denominational boundaries, relevance of religious rituals, dilemmas facing Jewish gays or Jews in mixed marriages, encounters with anti-Semitism, foibles of Jewish schools and organizations are familiar to Jews throughout Canada.

Where we find differences between Jews and non-Jews, or among groups of Jews, I will try to suggest which of two broad reasons apply. The first is *cultural*. Accordingly, Canadian Jews differ from non-Jews because elements of traditional Jewish or Judaic culture shape their behaviour. These factors can include religious laws and precepts rooted in the Torah and Talmud. This line of argument dates back to the work of German social theorist Max Weber. In his classic work *The Protestant*

Ethic and the Spirit of Capitalism, Weber raised the possibility that religious doctrines, like other ideas, could have an influence on seemingly non-spiritual things like economic behaviour.[16] Extending this approach means that many mundane aspects of Jewish life – how Jews earn a living, or their political positions – are rooted in the Judaic religious tradition.

The second explanation for differences in Jewish and non-Jewish behaviour relates to *social structure*. This argument owes much to the thought of Karl Marx and to more liberal social theorists. In this view people's social position, specifically their economic class or the discrimination they face, determines their behaviour and thoughts in many non-economic areas. Socio-demographic characteristics also play a role. The urban history of Jews, their concentration in middle-class and lately upper-middle-class occupations, their historical and ongoing confrontation with anti-Semitism, and features of their immigrant experience, are examples of social structural reasons that could account for such differences. I happen to be agnostic about the relative importance of cultural or social structural explanations. It depends on the issue at hand. But I am confident that both play a role.

Before turning our attention to the specifics of Canadian Jewry, we begin with two introductory chapters. The first reviews the full spectrum of Jewish diversity and Jewish identity. The second outlines contrasting qualitative and quantitative approaches to the challenge of Jewish survival.

1 WHO ARE THE JEWS?

The Elements of Jewish Diversity

"So the people of Israel did everything the Lord had commanded Moses. They camped, each under his own banner, each with his own ancestral house."

— Numbers 2:34

"A Jew is a Jew and finished."

— David Ben Gurion

THE ORIGINS OF JEWISH DIVERSITY

The story of Canadian Jews, like all Jews, begins in the ancient Middle East. The Bible tells us the Israelites who left Egypt and settled in the Holy Land were a people composed of twelve tribes. The word "Jew," or *yehudi* in Hebrew, comes from the tribe of Judah, and later their kingdom of Judea, but was used popularly only after the end of the first Babylonian Exile. An independent sovereign Jewish existence as one or more kingdoms in the area ceased with the Roman conquest of Palestine in 70 A.D. and the subsequent exile of most of the Jewish population. While Diaspora Jews today are an urbanized, cosmopolitan lot, the foundations of Judaic religious thought were laid in that early period when Jews were an agricultural people living on their own territory. The holidays of Sukkoth, Pesach, and Shavuot are all tied to the agricultural cycle, and much of the Talmud – that great compendium of rabbinical debates and decisions on matters of Jewish law – concerns issues revolving around rural, agricultural life. Part of the secret of Jewish success has been the ability to reconstruct their origins and adapt them to the exigencies of the modern world.

While a continuous if fragile Jewish presence remained in Israel after the Exile, from then on the major centres of Jewish life and culture developed in the Diaspora. It is only in the past one hundred years, and particularly after the Holocaust, that North America replaced Europe as a major centre of Jewish life. Early in this century, the Jewish population in Israel will likely surpass that in the United States to become the largest Jewish community in the world. The tension – in my view a creative tension – between the Israeli core and the Diasporic periphery is a major feature of Jewish diversity.

Jews have never – ever – been a unified people. Internal conflict is a dominant theme of the Bible, beginning with the non-Jewish Cain and Abel. Even wandering in the desert, and after settling in the land of Israel, the Hebrews maintained their identities and loyalties to the twelve tribes. While no minority group is truly homogeneous, Jews have been spread far and wide with a recorded history which has spanned four millennia and five continents. The diversity described below has been instrumental in Jewish survival. The Canadian Jewish community of the twenty-first century, while an important part of the Jewish Diaspora, is itself a microcosm of the Jewish world. Most Canadian Jews are of Eastern European origin. But we also find Jews from other European origins, from the Middle East, North Africa and Ethiopia, from Latin America, South Africa, and Israel. To this geographic, racial, and cultural mix must be added a wide spectrum of religious and cultural diversity, from ultra-Orthodox Hasidic sects to liberal Reform and secular Jews.

This diversity is nothing new. In the Canada of 1900 or 1950, there were also great distinctions between *Litvaks* (Lithuanians) and *Galicianers* (eastern Polish) and Hungarians and Romanians and *Yekkes*

(German Jews) and Anglo-Saxons; between uptowners and down-towners; between old-timers and greeners; between left-wing Zionists and right-wing Zionists and non-Zionists and anti-Zionists; between communists and socialists and capitalists; between Hebraists and Yiddishists; between workers and bosses. The political and social tensions at the time were probably greater than today, and it was more misleading back then to speak of one Jewish community. It simply did not exist.[1]

Today, there is a new element of Jewish diversity: the increasing proportions who see themselves as "partly" Jewish, whether a result of intermarriage or simply an embrace of multiple identities. Many eagerly say they are "Jewish Canadians" or "Canadian Jews." A growing number are part Jewish and part Christian. Some Jews blend their Jewish identity with one based on gender, or sexual orientation, or a profession. Some may tilt more to the Jewish and others to the non-Jewish pole. For others their identity is an ever-changing postmodern mish-mash. In this chapter I present three core elements – ethnicity, race, and Israel – in some detail. I then briefly outline several others, to which I will return in more detail in later chapters.

ETHNICITY: DIFFERENCES WITHIN DIFFERENCES

Jews are a people, *am Yisrael* ("the nation of Israel"), an ethnic group defined by a common descent, a sense of history, and other cultural attributes. The expulsion of 70 A.D. sent Jews into the Roman Empire's European territory, north through the Italian Peninsula, westward to the Iberian Peninsula, and then into Northern, Central, and eventually Eastern Europe. In addition, Jewish communities developed throughout the Middle East and North Africa. By the eve of the Spanish Expulsion in 1492, there were three major population and cultural concentrations of Jews.[2]

Oriental Jews came from long-standing Jewish communities throughout the Middle East and North Africa, which preceded the rise of Sephardi Jewry and the Inquisition. For example, the Jewish communities in Iraq date back over 2500 years.

Sephardi Jews (the word *Sepharad* means "Spain" in Hebrew) were those originally from Spain and Portugal. After the expulsions from both these countries at the end of the fifteenth century, many moved elsewhere in Europe as well as into the Middle East, North Africa, and the Americas. The European-centred Sephardi tradition moved to countries like Holland, Greece, Turkey, and Bulgaria. At times, in popular discussion, Sephardi and Oriental Jews are collapsed into one category, as the overlap has become more noticeable recently, and particularly in the Israeli context. Thus, many Oriental Jews could loosely be considered Sephardi.

The third group are Ashkenazi Jews (*Ashkenaz* is the older Hebrew word for Germany). This group refers to the Jews whose origins are in Central and Eastern Europe dating back to the Middle Ages, associated with Yiddish language and culture, and influenced by Christianity and European civilization.

Until the destruction of European Jewry during the Second World War, Ashkenazi Jews comprised perhaps nine-tenths of the Jewish world. In 1931, the world Jewish population was estimated at 15.5 million, of which 30 per cent were in America, 60 per cent in Europe, and the remainder in Asia, Africa, and Australasia.[3] Roughly six million European Jews were lost during the Holocaust. After the war, fertility rates declined and intermarriage rates increased among westernized Ashkenazi Jews compared to Sephardi Jews newly concentrated in Israel. As a result, the world demographic balance shifted somewhat, though Ashkenazi Jews remain in the majority. In Israel, about half of the Jewish population is Sephardi; that proportion was even higher before the massive migration of Jews from the former Soviet Union in the 1990s. If intermarriage rates increase between Ashkenazim and Sephardim in Israel, the distinction and social relevance of these categories may well decline, even as they continue to be used to rally political parties.

Ashkenazi Jews today comprise about three-quarters of the world Jewish population. They were shaped first by an environment of European Christianity, and later by the various ideological currents of liberalism, secularism, political Zionism, socialism, and communism. Yiddish was the language of Ashkenazi Jews. It emerged as a form of Judeo-German, which borrowed extensively from Hebrew, German, and other European languages. From its beginnings in Germany, it spread to Poland and Russia. Ashkenazi Jews today tend to be lighter skinned; Sephardim are in general darker. Canadian Jews are 90 per cent Ashkenazi in origin and most Canadians reflexively identify Jews with Europe. In its publications of census results, Statistics Canada lists the figures for Jews under the heading "Other European." Ashkenazi Jews developed a pluralistic, institutionalized form of Judaism, from ultra-Orthodox to Orthodox to Conservative and to Reform.

Sephardi Jews and Oriental Jews, particularly the larger communities in North Africa and the Middle East, were shaped by Arab cultures and Islam, and were relatively less influenced by modernizing trends and secular ideologies of Europe. Ladino, a form of Judeo-Spanish, was the classical language of the Sephardi Jews of Europe. Sephardi Judaism was highly traditional, albeit less rigid than Ashkenazi Orthodoxy, and the Sephardi love of Zion was more likely to flow from religious passion than political ideology. Sephardi religious Judaism tends to be more traditional, and Orthodoxy is the benchmark even for those who are in practice less observant. There is no Sephardi Reform Judaism. A Sephardi religious service will have distinctive liturgical melodies and minor differences in some prayers. Prayer books are in Hebrew only, and little English or French is likely to be part of the actual service.

While both Ashkenazi and Sephardi traditions in Canada are now diluted, their cultural legacy should not be ignored. The culture of Eastern European Jewry, particularly Yiddish language, literature, and music epitomized by the klezmer revival, exerts a powerful nostalgic appeal. Hundreds of Jews participate in a klezmer camp retreat in the Laurentian Mountains outside Montreal. And thousands of Jews attend the biennial "Ashkenaz: A Festival of New Yiddish Culture" in Toronto, which features literature, music, dance, theatre, and films reflecting Yiddish culture. In Montreal, Sephardi identity is strong. The major communal organization is Communauté Sépharade du Québec, and the primary langauge is French. The Centre Communautaire Juif sponsors a "Quinzaine Sépharade," which celebrates the many facets of Sephardi culture.

Historically, there were not only differences between Ashkenazi and Sephardi Jews, but among Ashkenazim themselves. The major division was that between Jews of Germany and those of Eastern Europe. The former were more likely to be westernized, speak German, and embrace Reform Judaism, which itself was founded in Germany. Arriving earlier in the New World, they became wealthier and more established. Eastern European Ashkenazi Jews were more traditional, more devout, and committed to Yiddish language and culture. At the same time, they were more likely to be skilled workers, union members, and sympathetic to socialist and other left-wing ideologies. More stereotypically, German Jews were seen as excessively formal, timid, stiff, snobbish, prone to assimilation, and wealthy. The term *Yekke* for German Jew comes from the German word for "jacket," which the supposedly stuffy and strait-laced German Jews reputedly never took off.

> *A Yekke comes home with a headache, complaining that on the train he had to sit facing the rear. His wife asks, "Why didn't you ask the person sitting across from you if he would mind changing seats?" He replies, "I wanted to ask someone, but I couldn't; there was no one there!"*

Eastern European Jews were seen as uncouth, less civilized, and potentially embarrassing to the more established "uptown" Jews. But even among Eastern European Jews, there were group differences. Jewish origins in Lithuania, Russia, Galicia, or Romania were associated with stereotypes and character traits – usually negative – which helped set social boundaries among these immigrant subgroups.[4] And among religious Eastern European Jews, there were historic differences, and clashes, between Hasidim and Mitnagdim. The Hasidim were Jewish sects led by a *rebbe*, and emphasized spirituality and joy. By contrast the Mitnagdim – mainly from Lithuania – emphasized learning and strict piety. And there were even conflicts among the competing Hasidic *rebbes* and their followers. In contemporary Montreal, where Hasidic communities are relatively strong, one can still find tensions, or at least isolation, among Hasidic groups such as the Belz, Lubavitch, Satmar, and Tash. As yet, these have not degenerated into the street brawls seen several years ago in New York. In addition, there are today clear demarcations between Hasidim as a whole and the "yeshiva" crowd, legatees of the Mitnagdim, who look to a *rosh yeshiva*, a leader of the yeshiva, rather than a charismatic *rebbe* as their leader. But despite all these internal and seemingly microscopic variations, the major distinction today is that between the Orthodox and the non-Orthodox.

How important are these ethnic differences? Those between Germans and Russians, and between *Litvaks* (from Lithuania) and *Galicianers* (from eastern Poland) have disappeared. But not long ago, marriages across these boundaries were rare, and greeted by parents with dismay. The Sephardi–Ashkenazi distinction, with its racist baggage, continues to sour Israeli social and political life. In Montreal, Sephardi–Ashkenazi relations are interlaced with French–English tensions. A study in the late 1960s found high intermarriage rates between Sephardim and French Québécois, reflecting in part the hostility of anglophone Ashkenazi Jews toward the newly arrived francophone Sephardim. Some of these prejudices persist.[5] The term "Moroccans" is at times used pejoratively in Canada, just as it is in Israel.

These ethnic communal differences have cultural dimensions in language, music, ritual, and cuisine. But these differences should not be overstated. All Ashkenazi and Sephardi Jews share basic religious elements: the centrality of the Torah and Talmud, and the observance of the Sabbath, dietary laws, and major holidays such as Rosh Hashanah, Yom Kippur, and Passover. Most key prayers are identical. Both groups share a strong attachment to the goal of Jewish survival and the security and well-being of the State of Israel. Jews are not a unified, homogeneous community (neither are most ethnic groups), but the common religious core and early history sustain the idea of a Jewish people.

GENETICS: RACE AND BIOLOGY

Many people think of Jews as a race, or at least in racial categories. But Jews are not a race. In general, anthropologists think the concept of a genetically pure race, or any type of race, is bogus. And even if there were "pure" races, it is unlikely that Jews would qualify. The Bible reminds us of the very diverse ancestral origins of the Israelites. The house of David, for example, is descended from a Moabite woman, Ruth. And the prophet Ezekiel describes his fellow Judeans as follows: "Your mother was a Hittite and your father an Amorite." (Ezekiel 16:45) This "racial" diversity is obvious to anyone who has visited Israel, since among Jews there is a wide array of skin colours and physical characteristics.

Two Ethiopian Jews are airlifted to Israel, and as they walk off the plane they see a Yemenite. Says one: "Look, a Swedish Jew!"

It is not only among Ethiopians that we find authentically black Jews. They also exist in the United States, tracing their origins in part from Jewish slaveholders.[6] Up to the early twentieth century – by which time their descendants had been thoroughly assimilated – there were even Chinese Jews who looked just like non-Jewish Chinese. In general, Jews throughout the Diaspora approximated some of the physical characteristics of the host populations including not only skin colour but variations in fingerprint patterns and other traits.[7] Despite what Jewish parents preach to their children, historically it is clear that sexual contact took place between Jews and non-Jews.[8]

Yet in their genes, as in much else, Jews are like everyone else, but different. If Jews are not a pure race, they do represent a distinctive group within our conception of population genetics. What this means is that while Jews, over the generations, certainly did absorb genes from other peoples, their experience of forced or voluntary segregation also reproduced distinctive genetic patterns. One result is that many Jews share certain physical and character traits which set them apart. These reflect environmental factors, but as we shall see, recent research also suggests a role for genetic/biological sources. Ashley Montagu, a Jewish anthropologist who played a key role in attacking the concept of race, particularly as it was used to demean non-whites, nevertheless wrote:

> There undoubtedly exists a certain quality of looking Jewish, but this quality is not due so much to any inherited characters of the person in question, as to certain culturally acquired habits of expression, facial, vocal, muscular, and mental. Such habits do to a very impressive extent influence the appearance of the individual and determine the impression which he makes on others. . . . It is possible to distinguish many

Jews from members of other cultural groups for the same reason that it is possible to distinguish Englishmen from such groups, or Americans, Frenchmen, Italians, and Germans. . . . Members of one cultural group do not readily fit into the pattern of another.[9]

Jews – like me – who claim they can recognize some Jews by looks, gesture, or accent probably can. For the longest period, Jewish in-marriage patterns have produced identifiable results. There is an Ashkenazi Jewish look – though not every Ashkenazi Jew has it – that others could identify. Combined with cultural clues like names, speech patterns, body language, and mannerisms, it helps Jews pick out other Jews at social gatherings. But with increasing intermarriage, people will have to be more careful at cocktail parties. There are more and more non-Jews with thoroughly Jewish-sounding names, Jews who look and act like stereotypical non-Jews, and vice versa.

Despite this growing physical diversity, Jews can still be traced back to a common ancestral gene pool originating in the Middle East and eastern Mediterranean, which has spread even farther. The Lemba, an African Bantu-speaking tribe from northern South Africa, claims to be descended from Jews and maintains some practices like circumcision and abstention from pork. A recent scientific study of the Y chromosome profiles of male Jewish and non-Jewish populations found greater genetic correlations among, say, Russian and Moroccan Jews than between those Jews and their immediate non-Jewish countrymen. Even the Lemba pattern matched the Jewish one more closely than other sub-Saharan groups. The fact that Jewish patterns correlated closely with non-Jewish Palestinian and Syrian populations also confirms the Middle Eastern origin of world Jewry. Jewish genetic ancestry is a blend of distinctive Jewish traits and infusions from surrounding populations. Fingerprint patterns are one indicator that has shown both local variations among Jews throughout the world and core similarities to other eastern Mediterranean groups, indicating a possible common genetic origin. Jews also have distinctive patterns of blood types. The biological basis of Jewish identity may even extend to smaller subgroups of Jews. Cohanim, those male Jews who claim descent from Moses' brother Aaron and the Biblical priestly caste, show a higher transmission of certain genetic markers or variations in the Y chromosome than do other Jews. This suggests a multi-generational pattern of father-son inheritance and the possibility of a common genetic ancestor – presumably Aaron![10]

Any group with a history of geographic isolation or separation with relatively low rates of intermarriage will demonstrate distinctive patterns of disease, some genetically based. There are many conditions or illnesses peculiar to Ashkenazi Jews, the most famous being Tay-Sachs, a fatal disease of the central nervous system, and others specific to Oriental and Sephardi Jews. Some, like lactose intolerance, are found in all groups of Jews.[11] More recently, evidence has emerged about increased genetic mutations among Ashkenazi Jews that pre-dispose them to higher rates of breast, ovarian, colon, and prostate cancer. The American Jewish newspaper *The Forward* publishes an annual supplement devoted to "Jewish Genetic Diseases." This supplement includes updates on the current status of about twenty "Ashkenazi" diseases, as well as reviews of other potentially upsetting topics. A recent article discussed Jews and mental illness. While the experts cited claimed that Jews were no more likely than any other group to suffer from mental illness in general, Jews were more likely than others to suffer from some specific conditions.[12]

But Jews should not panic. Their common ancestral gene pool has not condemned them to ill health. Far from it. Jews enjoy on average better health than non-Jews despite these genetically based diseases. This was true even early in the twentieth century. Looking at the years 1926 to 1936, demographer Louis Rosenberg found that the crude death rate for Jews was half that of the Canadian rates, and their infant mortality rate was less than half.[13] This was also true for the immigrant Jews in the United States.[14] Those advantages did not likely result from any common genetic heritage. Most researchers emphasize cultural attitudes toward health, ranging from cleanliness, to greater readiness to consult physicians, to worry – perhaps excessive – about the health of children.[15] In other words, Jewish health advantages flow from non-genetic factors associated with Jewishness, such as higher income and educational levels, while any health disadvantage has a genetic basis.

Nevertheless, the attention given to the increased risk of some diseases with a genetic/hereditary component has raised Jewish anxieties and made genetic screening a hot button issue in the Jewish community.[16]

Intelligence levels for Jews, like health, have also been analyzed in terms of possible genetic or environmental causes. Historically, Jewish intelligence or "cleverness" was seen as an innate Jewish racial or biological characteristic, certainly among anti-Semites. Even the philo-Semite Ernest van den Haag speculated that Jews gained intellectual benefits from their tradition of marrying the brightest Jewish males to the daughters of the wealthiest Jewish families. This quasi-Darwinian process guaranteed two things. First, the genes of the brightest males would be passed on to succeeding generations, which did not happen in the Catholic tradition of priestly celibacy. Second, the children of these arranged Jewish unions would be more likely to survive because of better nutrition, sanitation, housing, medical care, financed by the wealthy parents of the daughter. This marriage pattern, along with the positive health effects of urbanization on Jews, could explain high levels of Jewish intelligence.[17]

The social and cultural environment of Jews has also played a role. Writing at the end of the First World War, the American social critic Thorstein Veblen argued against the Zionist idea because the process of "normalizing" the Jews would rob them of a creative spark that benefited all humanity.[18] Veblen was afraid of losing the Jewish scientists, writers, musicians, and artists who flourished a century ago. In his view, "renegade Jews" rebelling against the strictures of Orthodoxy and conventional morality were the source of Jewish genius and creativity, not any advantageous genetic endowment. Tilling the soil and fighting the British or the Arabs in Palestine would deprive Jews of that creative tension. European nations would enjoy fewer scientific and artistic breakthroughs.

The link between Jews and intelligence or creativity predates the modern period. Any image of Jews in earlier periods as being devout and insular is misleading. One study identified 626 "outstanding" scientists alive between 1150 and 1300 A.D., and found that ninety-five were Jewish. This was an estimated thirty times greater than their population proportion in countries which practised science. Those tendencies anticipated the achievements in the modern period. Between 1901 and 1975, Jews won an estimated 15 per cent of Nobel Prizes, proportionately more in the sciences and fewer in literature and peace. This reflects the more objective, meritocratic, and non-discriminatory world of science – a discovery is a discovery. In the world of "high culture," Jews could be subjectively judged as unwelcome interlopers. In countries where residents won ten or more prizes, Jews won 19 per cent. Again, a high degree of overrepresentation.[19] Another study noted that of the fifteen world chess champions from 1851 into the 1980s, seven – Steinitz, Botvinnik, Smyslov, Tal, Spassky, Fischer, and Kasparov – could claim Jewish ancestry.[20]

More important than counts of Jewish geniuses are above-average Jewish scores on IQ and other intelligence tests. (There is an ongoing debate as to what IQ tests actually measure. They do not exhaust the possible measures or types of intelligence, but they do measure something probably worth having.) It was not always so. American studies of standardized intelligence measures in the early 1900s found that Jews – usually the children of Yiddish-speaking Russian immigrants – did poorly. One of those early studies labelled Jews, along with other immigrant children, as "feeble-minded." A 1921 study showed that Jews had more certificates of mental defect than any other immigrant group. Another test of American soldiers drafted in the First World War found that only 19 per cent of those of "Russian" origin – mostly Jews – exceeded American national norms, compared to 49 per cent of soldiers of German origin and 67 per cent of soldiers of English origin. The conclusion was that Russian-Jewish immigrants were of inferior racial stock.[21] In fact, many of the Jewish children taking the tests likely had poor English language skills. Moreover, the test content at the time was likely far more culturally biased than such tests today. There was no biological or genetic basis for their lower scores.

Following the Second World War, Jewish scores began to improve. One nationwide study of American high-school students in the 1960s found that Jewish boys and girls outperformed their non-Jewish counterparts in math and verbal tests. On the other hand, there were no differences in tests of visual-motor co-ordination, and Jewish students did worse on tests of spatial reasoning.[22] Some of the findings about higher Jewish scores in intelligence tests, or greater levels of education, flow from the fact that the Jews involved in these comparisons are more urban and more likely to come from middle-class homes with educated parents. Still, noted American sociologist Christopher Jencks concluded bluntly that "Jewish children . . . do better on IQ tests than Christians at the same socio-economic level."[23] These advantages were not only concentrated among those Jews who were more secular, and more focused on secular educational achievement. Orthodox children in the United States have also shown similar high IQ scores.[24]

These patterns of Jewish intelligence do not stop at the American–Canadian border. A Canadian study compared over one hundred eleven-year-old Jewish boys to boys from four other Canadian groups. That study also found Jewish advantages in the area of verbal and mathematical reasoning, but not in perceptual, motor, and spatial skill abilities. Perhaps it is not surprising that Jews are overrepresented in law, medicine, math, and science, compared to architecture, engineering, and design. A Darwinian hypothesis might suggest that generations of Talmudic study might favour certain verbal and cognitive traits over perceptual ones. In any event, there is no one convincing explanation – genetic, social structural, or cultural – for this particular pattern of Jewish intellectual ability.[25]

It is far easier to describe than to account for the greater Jewish performance on intelligence tests. If it is "nature," Jews somehow have acquired over the years more of the genetic endowment needed for intelligence. If it is "nurture," something in Jewish culture or in the surrounding environment – maybe even the threat of persecution – enhances Jewish intelligence. While we cannot know precisely, there are solid grounds for caution in overstating the case for a biological or genetic basis. First, the relatively high degree of Jewish in-marriage and inbreeding – though far from complete – poses genetic risks regarding intelligence. Moreover, the studies cited above involved Ashkenazi rather than Sephardi Jews. Studies in Israel have found gaps in intelligence test scores between Ashkenazi and Sephardi students, and both are Jews with similar genetic profiles. The poorer socio-economic environment of many of the Sephardi immigrants in Israel – reflecting conditions in their countries of origin as well as discrimination in

Israel – is clearly decisive. Moreover, for several centuries the dominant centres of Judaic learning and civilization were found among Sephardi Jewry in Spain and North Africa. Had intelligence tests been taken back then, gaps would surely have favoured Sephardi over Ashkenazi Jews. As historical currents shifted in favour of Christian Europe, Jews in those European countries, despite significant episodes of persecution, reaped the benefits compared to Jewish communities within the declining orbit of Islam. We should not make too much, therefore, of any possible genetic or biological explanation for Jewish–Gentile differences, as we should not for black–white differences.

A number of esoteric non-genetic arguments have been made for the strong intellectual performance of Jewish children. These include the benefits of the type of infant swaddling found among eastern European Jews, of styles of "hyper-verbal" communication between Jewish parents and children, and of early literacy instruction for Jewish children.[26] What is important for the purpose here is to note Jews in North America have performed very well in verbal and mathematical intelligence tests through most of the twentieth century. For Jews and non-Jews alike, intelligence is an essential trait associated with Jewishness.

But the intellectual future for Jews may not be as bright as the present. My impression – there are no definitive studies – is that Jewish students are no longer so concentrated among the highest ranks of younger educational, professional, and scientific achievers in North America. They are being supplanted – as are whites generally – by Asians. This is certainly true in math and the sciences, where Jews once dominated. The drive and intellectual curiosity found in many children of Jewish immigrants led them to dominate in academic honour rolls, and among prizewinners. No longer. Affluence and conformity have dulled the Jewish edge, as Asians, poor or wealthy, foreign or Canadian-born, take their place. Again, environment over heredity.

The discussion of Jews, race, and genetics has sometimes been used for more twisted reasons than the explanation of commonalities of health/disease or intelligence. In one case, it was employed to challenge the link between European Jews and Israel. In the mid-1970s, the Hungarian-Jewish intellectual Arthur Koestler recycled theories published in Hebrew decades earlier regarding a non-Semitic racial origin of the Jews. In his controversial *The Thirteenth Tribe*, he challenged the conventional view that lighter-skinned and lighter-haired Ashkenazi Jews were the result of generations of sexual encounters between European Gentiles and the Jews exiled from Israel after the destruction of the second temple.[27] Instead, he focused on the wholesale conversion of the Khazars – a tribe of Turkish or Finnish origin which flourished in the lower Volga region of Russia – to Judaism in the ninth century A.D. That event introduced an entirely new population into the gene pool of European Jewry. For reasons which are not clear, the Khazars adopted Judaism as their state religion, and several thousand nobles converted. (One theory is that adoption of Judaism offered a tactical escape from the more dangerous choice of either Islam or Christianity, the two dominant and contending faiths in the region.)

Koestler argued that the numbers and impact of Jewish Khazars were far greater than previously thought. As this tribe moved west, and as Jews from Central Europe moved east, a fusion occurred which produced the non-Semitic features, including a good deal of fair skin and light hair that we have come to associate with most Ashkenazi Jews. This argument not only solved the genetic puzzle of the source of the fair-skinned Jews; it also posed a political challenge to Zionist theory. It suggested that most European Jews were not descended from the original inhabitants of Jewish Palestine. This weakened the Zionist claim of a "return" to their Biblical, ancestral homeland, and the Koestler argument was used in anti-Zionist and anti-Israel polemics, where it occasionally reappears.

Most historians do not accept Koestler's maverick theory as to the biological origins of modern European Jewry. The accuracy of the entire Khazar episode is not firmly established, while the eastward migration of Jews from Central Europe, notably Germany, is well documented. The genetic mixing that has undoubtedly taken place could just as easily have occurred over the centuries as Jews, following the Exile, were dispersed up through the Italian peninsula and throughout the Roman Empire, into Central and later Eastern Europe. The findings of genetic commonalities in both Ashkenazi and Sephardi Jews, and between Jews and other Middle Eastern peoples, also refute Koestler's contention that Jews experienced a sharp racial break with their Semitic ancestors. It is therefore clear that Jews trace their genetic ancestry to the Middle East. They are descendants, like Arabs, of a mythic Abraham. Still, there are plenty of non-Semitic-looking European Jews around. Genetic mixing with European peoples through illicit sexual encounters may explain it only in part. It is also possible that there was a greater variation in the physical appearance, or pheno-types, among Middle Eastern peoples thousands of years ago than generally assumed. The ancient Israelites may have had less tradition-ally Semitic features even then.

The racial theme has been prominent in the history of anti-Semitism, even in its theological form. Beginning in the late 1300s, Jews in Spain and Portugal began to convert to Christianity in order to escape heightened waves of persecution which marked the Inquisition and culminated in the expulsions of 1492 and 1497. These Jewish con-verts to Christianity, or "*Marranos*," perplexed Christian authorities. Despite being exposed to the teachings of the Church, they and their descendants often continued to practise Judaism in secret. In other words, something prevented them from truly embracing Christianity. Only some non-human force could explain this stubborn trait of Jews (which was found in the early Christian period, when Jews likewise refused to embrace Jesus). Jews, the anti-Semites reasoned, must not be fully human, they must be a biologically distinct species, linked to the Devil, and replete with horns and a tail.[28] The foundations of modern racial anti-Semitism can thus be found in the Middle Ages, and have theological roots.

In later periods, racial stereotypes of Jews as Semites with dark skin, curly black hair, and aquiline noses were common in anti-Semitic car-toons and publications throughout Europe, regardless of the wide range of actual Jewish facial and physical characteristics. The Nazis pushed this to an extreme in the cartoons of their newspaper, *Der Sturmer*. They also warned of the infectious power of Jewish blood, arguing that even those with one Jewish grandparent were to be con-sidered Jews, requiring extermination. The image found in Hitler's *Mein Kampf* of the Jew as non-human, as a parasite or a bacillus, builds on the earlier foundations of racial anti-Semitism. But racial thinking about Jews did not always lead to genocide. The racializing of religious or national groups was a common discourse through the first half of the twentieth century, and at times benign. The term "race" was used loosely throughout the West to denote national or ethnic groups. Jews, along with Poles, Italians, English, French, and other ethnic groups were designated as races in the Canadian census up to and including that of 1941. After the horrors of the Second World War, racial classification was discredited, and the census terminology was changed to "ethnic origin" in 1951.

The issue of race, Jewishness, and the census may yet re-emerge in the new context of affirmative action or employment equity programs. Many Sephardi Jews are from the Middle East, and some are certainly dark-skinned. Ethiopian Jews even more so. The 1991 Canadian Census, which contains information on both the religion and ethnicity of respondents, enables us to get a sense of racial diversity within Canadian Jewry. Looking at those who are Jewish by religion, we find some Jewish individuals, roughly 2.5 per cent, are classified by the census as "visible minorities" – likely Black, Asian, or Hispanic. But Jews as a group – rightly – are not, at least not by Statistics Canada and other government agencies active in designing employment equity programs. Preferences to individuals based on visible minority status are not yet as extensive in Canada as they are in the United States; in Canada the classifications are used mainly for record-keeping. One assumes Ethiopian Jews or other darker-skinned Jews would be eligible for preferential treatment if and when such programs arrive in full force in Canada.

Regardless of census classifications, the perceptions and misperceptions about Jewish looks and physical traits reinforce racial images of Jews. Any discussion of "typical' Jewish looks suffers from the historic legacy of racist, anti-Semitic caricature. There is a grain of truth here. Much of Woody Allen's humour draws on his playing off his physical appearance and personality traits as a "New York Jew." Historically, Judaism, as well as the Jewish powerlessness in the Diaspora, has created an image of Jews as weak and uncomfortable with male aggression and physicality, quite the opposite of the Hellenistic tradition. Only in the modern period do counter-images appear, in which Jewish athletes, soldiers, and even criminals emerge to a sort of contentious hero-worship in some Jewish circles.[29] I cherish my dog-eared copy of *Great Jews in Sports* – alas, not the world's thickest book and with too much fencing and table tennis for my liking – but still a Jewish pantheon.[30] I confess that I get a charge out of the fading photos of muscular Jewish wrestlers, boxers, basketball players, and gymnasts that adorn the walls of the YM-YWHA. Despite the image of the brainy Jew, sports played an important role in the socialization of the children of Jewish immigrants.[31]

Zionism and the Israeli army also helped develop the newer "macho" images of tough Jews in North America. Today Jews have become obsessed with their bodies. They are not only the people of the book; they are now equally the people of the health club. Jews are not limited to Albert Einstein or Jonas Salk when choosing role models; they also have the enigmatic Sandy Koufax or the wrestling sensation Goldberg. Many Canadian Jews sweating on their treadmills may not know of the track and field star Fanny ("Bobbie") Rosenfeld, chosen by sportswriters in 1950 as Canada's female athlete of the first half-century.

Biological definitions of Jewishness raise ethical problems. Many Jews feel that Jews are born, and not made. But does this mean converts must remain permanently second-class? Despite increases in intermarriages and conversions to Judaism, some Canadian Jews – primarily older immigrants – still feel suspicious about converts. They don't trust them. They perpetuate old-country prejudices that both Jews and Gentiles are fundamentally, biologically, different – once a Gentile always a Gentile, with anti-Semitism lurking just below the surface. Conversely, Jewish folklore has it that every Jew, no matter how estranged from the tradition, still retains a spark or Jewish essence which cannot be extinguished. In the Jewish case, this ascribed quasi-biological origin is reinforced by "*halacha*" (the term means "way" in Hebrew, and denotes the rules and regulations of Jewish conduct accepted by Orthodox rabbinic Judaism). Accordingly, a Jew is anyone born to a Jewish mother, or converted to Judaism by an Orthodox rabbi.

This emphasis on matrilineal descent dates back to Biblical days. It makes sense; it is easier to identify a child's mother than its father. This definition affirms the biological basis of Jewish ethnic and even most religious identification (the exception being formal Orthodox conversion). The Orthodox rabbinate has championed this biological and legalistic basis of Jewish identification. This contrasts with more voluntaristic and non-biological approaches, in which a Jew is anyone who identifies as a Jew. Someone born of a Jewish mother and Gentile father, and who does not embrace another faith officially, remains Jewish no matter how secular or irreligious their conduct, according to Orthodox law. However, someone born of a Gentile mother and Jewish father remains a non-Jew from the Orthodox perspective, no matter how involved or committed to Jewish life that person may be. And a non-Orthodox conversion will not help. These people, and their descendants, are not to be counted as Jews, unless they undergo a conversion supervised by an Orthodox rabbi. There are tens of thousands of Jews in Canada today who are not considered Jewish according to Orthodox Jewish law. They include people converted to Judaism with non-Orthodox rabbis, people who embrace Judaism voluntarily without any formal conversion procedure, and their children.

A final irony is that while the vast majority of Jews are white, this offers scant protection from Canadian racists. After all, Jews were the twentieth century's major victims of racist genocide. Even now, Jews rank with blacks, aboriginal Canadians, and other visible minorities as potential victims of active hate groups, who usually target Jews and non-whites together in their propaganda.[32] In this, Jews differ from other European ethnic groups, who today face far milder forms of prejudice, and very little that we might classify as hate speech.

ISRAEL: THE JEWISH HOMELAND

For many Canadian Jews, Israel is an indispensable element of their identity. For some this results from a formal Zionist ideology. For others, it flows from a reaction to the Holocaust or admiration of Israel's achievements or simply because it is a place where many Jews live. Emotions range from blind love to critical support, with the exception of fringe anti-Zionists among left-wingers and the ultra-Orthodox. Canadian Jews are not unique in having a special tie to a piece of land. Think of Hutterite farm colonies in the West, First Nations reserves and territories, and the Québécois attachment to Quebec. As for most other Canadian immigrant groups, the role of land is that of a homeland, the place from which they or parents emigrated, the fondly remembered "old country" where generations of ancestors lived and struggled, and the place which continues to nurture ethnic culture and traditions.

But for other immigrant groups there is a different sense of Diaspora, one associated with a homeland that remains unfree. I recall once chatting with a young Armenian-Canadian student many years ago who kept arguing that Armenia might one day be free and invoking the example of Zionism. I sagely pointed out to him the differences between Israel, which had to oppose the ostensibly civilized British empire, and poor Armenia, which had to defeat the Soviet Union's "Evil Empire." I am happy to say that I failed to convince him to give up hope ... and history ultimately proved him right. Palestinians, Kurds, Tibetans, as well as the many captive nations of the Eastern Bloc, all have had a similar sense of loyalty to an idealized homeland.

None of these examples fully captures the role of Israel, as state and as territory, in defining Canadian Jewish identity. Identification with Israel at times competes with and at times blends into religious, ethnic, and cultural themes. The Jewish Diaspora is older than that of most other groups. If Jews can be thought of as a people or a nation, then Israel is the territory where that people first emerged as a historical entity. Israel has both a symbolic and real meaning for Canadian Jews. Accordingly, Israel is a holy land – *the* Holy Land – promised by God to the Jewish people. It is not by coincidence that one of the key moments of the Passover Seder is the call "Next Year in Jerusalem!" The Torah, the central text of Judaism, as well as the word meaning "knowledge," is described in a key prayer as "going forth from Zion" (*key mi'tzion tey'tzey torah*). The theme of exile, or *galut*, is also at the core of traditional Judaic thought. Accordingly, the Jews were exiled from the Promised Land two thousand years ago because of their sins. Redemption in the Messianic Age will also include the return to Zion and the re-establishment of the Kingdom of Israel, and the process of the "ingathering of the exiles," or *kibbutz galuyot*. The Zionist pioneers have hastened this day, to the dismay of some ultra-Orthodox traditionalists who prefer to wait for the Messiah.

In the second half of the twentieth century, Israel assumed mythic, quasi-religious proportions for other reasons. The Israeli experiment has been, and remains, a source of pride for most Jews. In the aftermath of the Holocaust, the success of Israel, whether in pioneering, farming, fighting, immigrant absorption, or basic economic development, has helped reshape the general image of bookish, nerdy Jews. Despite these successes, most Jews still worry about Israel's security and welfare, which in turn strengthens the identification. A terrorist bomb in Jerusalem is like a bomb on their street. When Israelis are killed in terrorist attacks, many Canadian Jews feel bereaved in a way they do not for innocent victims in other countries. This tie should not be confused with unwavering support for policies of any particular government. But neither should criticism of a specific Israeli policy by Canadian supporters of Labour or Likud be misconstrued as a lack of basic support. Many Jews also worry about the quality of Israeli democracy or Israeli Jewishness and all these worries reinforce the tie to Israel.

Christians and Moslems also have an attachment to the Holy Land. Christians make pilgrimages to visit the holy places. But in practice Israel, and certainly Jerusalem, is simply not as central in the theology of the other monotheistic faiths as it is in Judaism. Indeed, some religious Jews seek to be buried there, to make permanent their attachment to Zion. Christians have nothing like this degree of intensity, though some Protestant fundamentalists are strong supporters of Israel. Catholics can invest as much centrality in the Vatican as in the Holy Land. Moslems have their prior religious attachment to Mecca and Medina. Israel is the only religious homeland of the Jews.

Jews' connection to Israel as their homeland differs from the connection other Canadian immigrant groups have to their country of origin. Whatever the tie Italian or Chinese Canadians may have with Italy or China – an open question – Jews in Canada do not have the same attachments to their "old country," be it Poland, Germany, or Iraq. For Jews, the old country is not their homeland. In most of these places of emigration, the Jewish experience was at best bittersweet, with the accent on the bitter. For Jews, the homeland – in the abstract as well as in reality – is Israel. This is the place where most relatives are found. And not only do Canadian Jews visit Israel, but Israelis more and more frequently visit Canada, reinforcing these people-to-people ties. Israel is the place to visit or to send children to reinforce their identity; indeed, two-thirds of adult Canadian Jews have visited Israel. An estimated sixteen hundred Jewish teens and young adults from Canada visit Israel annually on various tours and programs.[33] More are now going as a result of the new Birthright Israel project, which sends thousands of North American youth to Israel on free ten-day trips. To the extent that Jews pray for the welfare of ancestral homelands in Europe, it is mainly because they worry about the welfare of the few Jews still living there.

In recent years it has become fashionable for Jews to visit cities or towns – de facto shrines – in Eastern Europe. They seek to explore the places where their parents or grandparents were raised or buried. In some cases, these visits become macabre rites, focusing on death camps. The popular March of the Living program aimed at Jewish teenagers combines one-week visits to Eastern Europe, including death camps, with one week in Israel, to coincide with Israel's Independence Day. It is an orchestrated, draining, yet exhilarating encapsulation of the transition from the despair of the Holocaust to the triumph represented by the rebirth of Israel. Several hundred teens from Canada attend the event. In short, Jews do not visit the "homelands" of Eastern Europe to visit relatives. They visit graves, if they can find them.

Apart from the minimal Jewish attachments to the old countries as political entities are the cultural bonds, which may well linger. The klezmer and Yiddish revivals, as well as the Sephardi celebrations mentioned earlier, represent a continuing attachment to the cultures which flourished in those source countries, as well as among the immigrant generations in the New World. Indeed, recent immigrants from Russia and North Africa have brought with them a number of (non-Jewish) cultural characteristics. Many of the recent Russian Jewish immigrants seem more Russian than Jewish and remain quite attached to many elements of Russian culture, from ballet to chess. And Moroccan Jewish immigrants retained a surprising affection for King Hassan until his death in 1999. But none of these cultural affinities overshadow the tie to Israel. Some liberal Jews express growing political and cultural estrangement – at times with a nasty edge – from Israel and the religious hegemony of the Orthodox there. Diaspora Jews rightly or wrongly no longer reflexively see Israel as morally impeccable, militarily weak, or economically dependent. But when Israel comes under physical or political attack, these differences are muted, at least temporarily.

OTHER BASES OF JEWISH IDENTITY

Religion: For many people, Jews and non-Jews alike, religion is the core element of Jewish identity. Jews are a religious group and Judaism is their religion. Jews can be religious through a belief in God and basic Judaic tenets or through observance of Jewish rituals and commandments. There are, however, many Judaisms. Sephardi religious Judaism is Orthodox in spirit and tradition, if more flexible than many forms of Ashkenazi Orthodoxy. The Judaism of Canadian Ashkenazi Jews can be divided into four formal denominations: Orthodoxy, Conservatism, Reform, and Reconstructionism. The progressive, avant-garde Jewish Renewal Movement could become a fifth. Secular Judaism, or secular humanist Judaism, enjoying a bit of a revival, could almost be considered a sixth. This ordering supposedly reflects the degrees of religiosity; the Orthodox are more likely to observe more of the precepts of traditional religious Judaism, followed by the other denominations in descending order. Yet each of these denominations is in turn diverse, none more so than the Orthodox. And none is static. Many groups of Jews are uncomfortable within denominational boundaries and define their own brand of Judaism. The growing diversity, the constant change, all are signs of vitality.

The Jewish religion interacts with all other bases of Jewish identity. The very notion of a Jewish people – an amalgam of ethno-racial, national, and biological concepts – is paradoxically rooted in a sense of religious obligation. Jews are a "chosen people," chosen by God, as well as by themselves and by others, to fulfil a religious destiny. Not chosen as superior, but different; chosen to bear the burden, the yoke, of Jewish religious observance.

Immigration: The immigrant saga is an indelible part of the identity of North American Jews, even though a minority are in fact immigrants. No matter. The image of the "wandering Jew" is ingrained in

Jewish history and folklore and in the Canadian Jewish reality, where immigrants are far more present than in the United States. And many Canadian-born adult Jews have parents, grandparents, or other relatives who were immigrants, and who in one way or another brought to life the struggles of the epic immigrant generation. The legacy of this immigration experience is that many Jews – and this is true, albeit to lesser degrees, for other migrant groups – feel like eternal strangers, newcomers still hoping for full acceptance. All the civic equality and economic success in the world does not eradicate the feeling. Nor does the fact that Jews love and appreciate the Canada of today.

This identification with the stranger is reinforced by the continuing influx of Jews to Canada in significant numbers. Advocating for Jewish immigrants and integrating them into the Jewish community are major preoccupations of the established community. At the same time, the new groups of immigrant Jews add to the diversity – and tensions – within Canadian Jewry, even as they reshape and reinvigorate the community.

Culture: Jews are also a cultural group, and many Jews prefer to construct their identity in cultural terms. For every Jewish subgroup, there is a high culture of elite artistic creation, a popular or folkloric culture, and a culture of everyday life. Jewish culture is expressed in every type of artistry, and conveyed in virtually all entertainment media. A perennial question is whether Jewish art is any artistic expression done by someone who happens to be Jewish. The Yiddish theatre is Jewish art; is Wayne and Shuster? And if yes, in what way? Whether there are distinctive Jewish artistic styles, or more precisely Canadian Jewish styles, is a difficult question to resolve.

A specific language is crucial to most cultures. The central linguistic element of Jewish identity comprises classical ethnic languages, such as Yiddish, Ladino, Aramaic (the language of the Talmud), other minor dialects, and of course Hebrew, which has a dual role for Canadian Jews. On one hand, Hebrew is the ancient language of prayer and the Bible, of the Mishnah and other commentaries. It is practically impossible to be a religious Jew of any kind without knowing some minimal amount of Hebrew. But the religious culture of Christianity makes do without. Methodists or Episcopalians do not have a specific language. Catholics used to have the Latin Mass in all its awe and majesty but – for reasons this sympathetic outsider still fails to grasp – dropped it.

On the other hand, Hebrew is the language of modern Israel and Israeli culture, a living language. In this sense, Hebrew and Yiddish are somewhat like Italian or Chinese for Italian or Chinese Canadians. Very few among the Canadian-born are fluent, but Hebrew is useful for singing Israeli songs, or visits to Israel. And even as Yiddish shrinks as a language of daily use, it persists as a language that functions as a kind of Jewish code. Many Yiddish words have infiltrated into normal use in English. While Gentiles may well use them, for Jews they often serve as a signal of recognition. Moreover, Jews, like many other ethnic groups – Italians come to mind – are a kind of "audible minority" whose blended languages combining English and the mother tongue are called "ethnolects."[34] Even apart from use of Yiddish or Hebrew words in speech, there are specific cadences, rhythms, accents, and speech habits which are common and intelligible among Jews, particularly if they are immigrants or second-generation. For instance: "*Why do Jews always answer a question with a question?*" "*Why not?*" Or: "*How are you?*" "*How should I be?*" Most Canadian Jews can understand this type of "Yinglish." Other examples: "This weekend I have a wedding" means I have to go to a wedding; "Give me a dozen bagel" needs no plural. And Montreal Jews were notorious for their "I have to make an order," which meant they had to go to the supermarket.

Culture is more than art or language. Jewish culture can also include distinctive Jewish values, or lifestyle habits, though we can debate whether they are specifically Jewish or simply common among educated, middle-class North Americans. I had a Jewish student who assured me in the late 1970s that a key cultural difference between Jewish and Gentile teens was that the former were into cocaine and the latter were into beer or pot. Jewish food, whether kosher or kosher style, is central to modern Jewish culture, though some Jews criticize "bagels and lox" Judaism. My students disagree with my emphasis on the importance of ethnic foods, thinking that ethnic cultures should be dealing with loftier concerns. They will learn. Even more slippery than food are middle- and upper-class lifestyle traits, mannerisms, and consumption patterns. I know Jews who feel that a Sweet Sixteen is a particularly Jewish life-cycle ritual, and that some cars or hobbies or vacation spots are more Jewish than others. Jewish culture, and identity, become equated with an easy affluence.

Family: For some Jews, the Jewish family is the source of their identity. Most of our life is lived in families, where we were raised or where we now raise our own children. Relations with parents, spouses or partners, and children, or our gender and sexual orientation, are fundamental determinants of who we are. There is a strong tradition which sees Jewish family life as distinctive. Stereotypes and myths about Jewish families and patterns of Jewish intimacy abound, from Jewish American Princess jokes to the images of the devoted *Yiddishe mameh*, or Jewish mother.

The Community: Jewish identities are acquired not only through a family. For some Jews, their identity is constructed through belonging to a tightly knit community. The Jewish community has every type of organization, for every type of need, and then some. Jews are probably the most institutionally complete minority group in the country.[35] For Jews, the network of such institutions spans cradle to grave (Jewish daycare centres and schools to old-age homes and cemeteries) and all manner of cultural, social, fraternal, recreational, and political interests. Nothing is left to chance.

Jews have had lots of practice at forming these networks. They can draw upon 2,000 years of experience as a Diaspora community faced with the task of surviving as best it could within an often hostile environment. Diaspora communities were embryonic forms of self-government, and the Jewish polity, like any polity, required organizations to accomplish its tasks. Absence of ingrained anti-Semitism, prosperity, and a general tolerance made all this easier in North America. Large cultural groups like the Italians or Ukrainians have a far briefer historical experience as immigrant minorities needing to set up their own communal organizations. It is only a century since the major migrations at the end of the nineteenth century funnelled masses of these European immigrants to the New World. They are still learning the ropes.

Liberalism: For many cosmopolitan Jews, the essence of their Jewish identity is social and political liberalism. Give them a progressive cause, an injustice, a social movement, often one not centred on the Jewish community but linked to another oppressed group, and they come alive. Some Jews embrace conservative or neo-conservative politics, and since the 1970s many analysts have predicted or urged a large Jewish shift to the right. But the main Jewish political tradition remains left-of-centre. Historical and current reasons are offered for this persisting leftward tilt; some make more sense, and others make less. For some activist Jews, their politics are a deliberate expression of their understanding of either Jewish tradition or Jewish issues. For others, their Jewishness is coincidental. But there is no escaping the role that political expression plays in their lives.

Anti-Semitism: Finally, there are many Canadian Jews who see their Jewishness in their role as eternal victim. The persisting pressure of anti-Semitism – real, perceived, or anticipated – paradoxically reinforces their Jewish identification and the organizations that defend Jewish interests and rights. A swastika daubed on a Jewish building, an anti-Semitic slur by a public official, can work wonders for even the most assimilated Jews. This is an argument that Jean-Paul Sartre made in extreme, reductionist form in his book *Anti-Semite and Jew*. Sartre went too far; obviously, Jews are far more than just the people anti-Semites love to hate. But an old Jewish saying echoes Sartre's point, comparing the Jews to eggs: the longer you boil them, the harder they get. By seeing themselves as victims, many Jews identify with visible-minority Canadians as a part of a righteous brotherhood of the oppressed. But others go further. Drawing from the legacy of the Holocaust, they can try to claim special status as super-victim, in a kind of Olympic Games of suffering. The terrible uniqueness of the Holocaust stands at the core of their being. They feel that regardless of how well things are going in Canada, they can always turn sour.

There are obviously many dimensions of Jewish identity. There is no one answer to the question of who is a Jew. Jews are not an easy people to understand, and challenge many of the accepted truths about how minority groups can and do function. Each of the elements of Jewish identity listed above contributes to the unique, paradoxical blend of inward- and outward-looking forces that defines Jewish success in Canada. Later, I will review them in detail. But first, in the next chapter, I offer a brief discussion of two competing approaches to Jewish survival.

2

QUALITY, QUANTITY, AND CONFLICT

The Social and Demographic Context of Jewish Survival

"Who has counted the dust of Jacob or numbered the stock of Israel?"

– Numbers 23:10

"What is happening in the Western world may be termed a 'self-inflicted Holocaust.'"

– Rabbi Adin Steinsaltz, in *The Jerusalem Post*, International edition, November 6, 1993

DEMOGRAPHIC FOUNDATIONS

Any discussion of Diaspora Jewish life at the beginning of the twenty-first century is part of an ongoing Jewish conversation about survival.[1] On the table are the twin challenges of continuity and unity, with the Jewish future hanging in the balance. In the 1990s, a double consensus emerged. First, American Jews (with Canadian Jews not far behind) were facing a demographic disaster because of rising rates of mixed marriage and low fertility, fuelled by a general assimilation. Second, those Jews who remained were locked in an increasingly fratricidal conflict, fought mainly along religious lines. The bleak prognosis was of a shrinking Jewish population, increasingly at war with itself.

The two issues were linked. The Orthodox Jews were the ones having more babies and fewer mixed marriages than the non-Orthodox. The religious polarization was not based simply on doctrinal differences, but on which Jews were helping and which hindering the cause of Jewish continuity.

I reject both elements of this gloomy consensus. What some people see as demographic threats or as dysfunctional divisions is part of a successful balancing act, an equilibrium that actually maximizes current and future possibilities. It is why I am optimistic about the Canadian Jewish future. My key argument is that there are both quantitative and qualitative demographic approaches to minority group survival. Most people, especially Jews, assume that they operate at cross-purposes. But they do not. As I shall illustrate, different Jewish groups use both approaches successfully.

But most Jews just do not see it that way. Differences in demographic patterns and their corresponding cultural contexts have led to polarized feelings. An angry letter to *The Jerusalem Report* illustrates this conflict:

> Why is it that the defenders of the ultra-Orthodox life style invariably quote their higher birth rate as being one of their major achievements?
>
> Humankind as a whole derives little, if any, benefit from yet more yeshiva students whose undoubted intellectual energy might better be applied to seeking solutions for some of the world's problems.
>
> Perhaps the ultra-Orthodox should ponder the suggestion that, in human terms, one Jonas Salk has done more good and brought more "light to the nations" than all the rabbis in their yeshivot.[2]

The letter is a pure sample of the undercurrent of hostility between the Orthodox and non-Orthodox. It interweaves cultural and demographic themes. It also assumes there can be no possible link between

Jonas Salk's polio vaccine and ultra-Orthodox rabbis. To the writer, the religious and secular dimensions of Jewish life exist in a clear zero-sum relation. Of course, many Orthodox and ultra-Orthodox Jews share that view, but from the opposite starting point. I argue that such views are historically and practically wrongheaded.

The fact is, numbers alone cannot be a decisive barometer of Jewish survival. Much of the alarm about the Jewish future is based on dire demographic projections. I am skeptical about these despairing forecasts: there is an important distinction between prediction and projection. The basic strength of demography, the science of human population, is *projection*. It is the ability to describe a current population, make some assumptions about trends in fertility, mortality, and net migration, and then project population size and composition into the future. To estimate future Jewish populations, demographers also make assumptions about future mixed-marriage rates. The most common assumption is to extrapolate current trends. These assumptions yield a range of projections, some higher and some lower, in a mechanical fashion.

Even projection is not problem-free. We assume demographers know what they are counting. This is easy for national population counts, or subgroups clearly defined by gender or age. There is generally no confusion about what we mean by "male," or "people aged sixty-five and over," or "years of education." It is much less clear when dealing with ethnic, racial, or religious groups. Different ways of defining Jews – or Latinos, Chinese, or Italians – will yield different counts and population projections. Estimates of any Jewish population will vary depending on whether we are counting Jews by religious conviction, Jews by full or partial ethnic origin, or variations in between. But if we can solve the problem of definition, and choose various sets of assumptions, we can easily compute a range of projections.

Prediction is a different story, and it represents the major limitation of demography. Making a prediction is making an educated guess, not applying an arithmetic formula. Usually a prediction is the most likely of a set of projections. But many unforeseen or unknowable factors can intervene to upset any assumptions. The future is unknowable. It is difficult – happily – to predict changes in human behaviour, such as the propensity for divorce or the impact of birth control on child-bearing, as well as major events such as changes in retirement legislation, or wars, or new diseases, or new vaccines. Few people want to live in a world in which every aspect of the future, our own or that of our society, is known. I know I would not. Projections assume that all variables outside the stated assumptions remain constant. But they never do. Demographers, and indeed all social scientists, have a uniquely dismal record in predicting major changes in social and political life, and new cultural trends. Demographers did not predict the post–Second World War baby boom nor the movement towards zero population growth in the past two decades in North America and Western Europe. They did not predict the dramatic changes and demographic consequences brought on by the women's movement, the sexual revolution, the increased use of birth control, or the rise in divorce rates and out-of-wedlock births.

Jewish history in the twentieth century is an extreme example of unpredictability. In the early 1900s, who would have predicted the genocide of the Holocaust and the role that Germany – as opposed to France (remember Dreyfus) or Russia – would play as its engine? (Recall that Germany at the time was the centre of Western civilization and culture.) Who except for a handful of Zionist writers would have predicted the emergence of a strong modern Israel as a centre of world Jewry? Or the total eclipse of Europe, North Africa, Iraq, and Iran as centres of Judaic culture? Or the collapse of Yiddish secular culture, or the rise of modern Jewish Studies in the academy, both in North America? And no one predicted the resilience of Orthodoxy in North America – certainly not pioneer American Jewish sociologists like Louis Wirth or Marshall Sklare – and the surprising strength of ultra-Orthodoxy in particular in both Israel and North America.

Pessimistic forecasts about the Jewish demographic future are not new. In 1964 *Look* magazine featured its now famous cover story on "The Vanishing American Jew." By the new century, American Jews were still around but *Look* magazine had vanished. In the late 1970s, I co-authored one of my first articles in the American Jewish magazine *Midstream*.[3] It was a response to a pessimistic projection made by a demographer who looked at some data from the first 1970 National

Jewish Population Survey (NJPS) in 1970 and projected that in one hundred years all or most of American Jews would have disappeared. He may yet be right, we still haven't reached 2070, but I was not apprehensive. I offered a perhaps overly optimistic interpretation of the trends, including those on intermarriage, and was taken to task by at least one critic for seeming to advocate intermarriage. He was partially right; while I do not advocate it, I do feel Jews have no choice but to live with it.[4] Still, to date Jews have not disappeared in the United States. Those dire predictions were wrong.

And what of the most recent apprehensions? Despite the general pessimism, it is possible to take a more positive view of the evidence. The much discussed 52 per cent mixed-marriage rate for American Jews marrying between 1985 and 1990, derived from the 1990 NJPS, may be too high. As those most at risk for intermarriage leave the group, the rate of intermarriage will level off for the more committed Jews who remain. Demographers also argue over issues of sampling and definition. Consider that infamous figure of 52 per cent. It was computed for an American sample that included large numbers of respondents who had "some" Jewish ancestry but who did not necessarily identify as Jewish. Obviously, a mixed-marriage rate computed for such a group would be a high one. Many respondents were not really Jews to start with and would have had no problem marrying a non-Jew. Focusing only on those Jews who actually identified themselves as Jews yielded a lower intermarriage rate of 41 per cent. Still high, but less ominous.[5] The short-term trend for the American Jewish population is likely to be stability, rather than sharp decline. But then again, even this prediction is risky.

TWO DEMOGRAPHIC APPROACHES

Groups concerned with survival and continuity can develop two demographic strategies – quantitative and qualitative – to achieve those goals.[6] A quantitative strategy fostered by high rates of fertility and no intermarriage is not the only option. Jewish history, dating back to the Bible, contains examples of massive demographic loss and assimilation. The Jews in the desert embraced the golden calf en masse. As further evidence, recall that of the twelve tribes of Israel, ten were lost.

Yet Jews overcame that blow, that "assimilation" of 83 per cent of the total group, and survived.

What is a quantitative strategy? The more, the better. Think of the Hutterites, the Amish, or, if you will, Hasidim. Demographers are often fascinated by the Hutterites of Western Canada because of their demographic uniqueness and their geographic isolation on agricultural colonies.[7] The Hutterites have almost no intermarriage and extremely high rates of fertility, even if the average is below the twelve children per family found in some families. This is a quantitative, survivalist demographic strategy, and Hutterite culture meshes well with it. There is no partial or plural or varied mode of Hutterite identity. You are either 100 per cent Hutterite, living on a Hutterite colony, faithful to basic Hutterite values and way of life, or you cease being a Hutterite. There are no urban Hutterites, no secular Hutterites, no Hutterite physicians or philosophers or Nobel Prize winners.

But the pattern of Jewish demographic behaviour is puzzling. Jews are considered a survivalist group par excellence, a model for other minorities. Yet Jewish intermarriage rates have risen and Jewish fertility rates have fallen. The finding of lower rates of fertility for Jews compared to other groups is not new. In the modern period in the United States, Jews were the first to attain zero population growth. Of course, Jewish family size among the early waves of immigrant East European Jews to North America was much larger than at present. But it was still not as large as that of other (mainly Catholic) European groups. Data from the 1931 Canadian Census confirm that pattern among the still largely immigrant Jews. Both the fertility rate and the birth rate for married Jewish women aged fifteen to forty-four were about one-half the national rates.[8]

What, then, is a qualitative demographic approach? It is one which maximizes the attributes of each individual member of the minority group so as to compete successfully within the wider society. Small is beautiful. Children in smaller families tend to do better in school, which may help explain the relative educational success of the children of Jewish immigrants. This successful competition goes along with high levels of participation, and may involve forging contacts with the majority group that can further the interests of the minority. Jews as a whole have much lower fertility and higher intermarriage rates than do Hutterites. Could we therefore say that Hutterites are committed to survival and Jews are not? Of course not. Both groups are committed to survival but have different demographic behaviours because of different cultural features. It is not possible to maximize both the qualitative and the quantitative for an entire group. There are trade-offs between the two approaches as some sort of equilibrium emerges. For Jews, different subgroups display identifiably different demographic patterns, some quantitative, some qualitative. The blend of strategies is linked indelibly to the culture, and indeed the collective agenda of North American Jews, a whole which is indeed the sum of different parts. Some Jews discover vaccines, others master the Talmud.

For most committed Jews, low fertility rates and mixed marriage are dangerous, sapping the quantitative base of Jewish life. But aspects of these specific demographic patterns can be understood paradoxically as contributing to collective group needs. Anthropologists have long argued that intermarriage can help to cement alliances between tribes, as a sign of friendship and acceptance. Clearly, very high rates of outmarriage can threaten the group. If all Jews married out and retained no ties to Judaism, Jews would disappear.

There is no doubt that at the individual level, intermarriage is a cause and an effect of assimilation. Yet the relation is more nuanced at the group level, where demographic patterns shape and reflect the varied cultural characteristics of Jews. Increasing rates of Jewish intermarriage are more than simply a flight of Jews from their heritage and an attack on Jewish interests. There are actually benefits. The more Jewish–non-Jewish friendships, the greater the sympathetic understanding of Jewish concerns by non-Jews.[9] Jews who engage with the non-Jewish world, particularly at the level of social relations and close friendships, take risks which other Jews avoid, and so for other, less outward-looking Jews they serve as scouts or pioneers at the frontier of the external world. They risk their own Jewish identity (which some may not value that highly anyway) to promote broader Jewish interests of the group.[10] As long as Jews wish to win Nobel Prizes or send effective lobbyists to defend Jewish interests before government, there will be a risk of intermarriage.

HUTTERITES, QUÉBÉCOIS, AND JEWS

Consider again the demographic behaviour of Hutterites. We can make sense of that behaviour only within the context of a specific culture and its corresponding agenda. Hutterites live a devout, agricultural life. Work, worship, and Bible study are the major preoccupations, and for older Hutterites their Germanic dialect serves a protective function. Hutterites minimize all contact with the outside world. There is no political agenda relating to a homeland that requires political lobbying or effective advocacy. No Hutterites have won, or wish to win, a Nobel Prize. As a result, the Hutterite model of no intermarriage, a traditional status of women within the family, and a large number of children makes a great deal of sense.

To illustrate again the link between demographic patterns, collective group survival, and cultural characteristics, consider the Québécois. After the Second World War their fertility rates plummeted. Would we therefore conclude that the French in Quebec had given up on *la survivance* and that they were less able to meet the challenges of survival? Certainly, some Québécois leaders think so, bemoaning the quantitative threat posed by the drop in fertility, sounding much like Jewish leaders condemning intermarriage and small family size. Quebec policy-makers periodically tried to encourage Quebeckers (basically women) to increase their fertility behaviour through baby bonus programs, much to the consternation of feminist critics. But they were misguided. The post-war Quebec drop in family size did not indicate a rush to collective suicide. The political and cultural context was changing, as Quebec society modernized rapidly, invested in education, and abandoned the high degree of church control over many social institutions. The flight from rural life, which had begun before the war, continued. The commitment to survival remained as intense, but it was pursued with a qualitative rather than quantitative approach, to match an evolving cultural and political agenda. This was a move to embrace modernity, including higher education and science, which even included a proactive immigration policy to make up for the demographic shortfall. There is a correspondence between demographic behaviour and the social, political, and cultural agenda of the Québécois. And the same logic applies to Jews.

Jewish demographic behaviour has reflected the cultural and political agenda of the Jewish community, sub-communities, and of individuals. In the Jewish case, smaller families have had positive impacts on long-term qualitative characteristics of the Jewish community. Smaller family size leads to more nurturing per child, greater educational attainment, and later occupational success. Smaller family size provides more opportunities for Jewish women to make contributions to Jewish communal life and to the general society, given the still prevailing unequal division of household duties between men and women. Women can fulfil their own career aspirations while also raising children.

Jews do not all adhere to the same demographic patterns. While the majority demonstrates a qualitative approach of low fertility and increasing intermarriage, a growing religious minority embraces a quantitative strategy. It is important to recognize that the use of the term "quantitative" is not meant to denote any inferiority – or lack of quality – among those Jews who have larger families and little intermarriage. And certainly pious Jews are found today studying at top universities, working as scientists, lawyers, or business executives, or running for American vice president. The term simply denotes a socio-demographic situation in which fewer children lead to the possibility of greater familial and communal investments per child. This in turn leads to greater contributions from each member towards material or secular objectives, as well as successful competition with the non-Jewish world. The training, strategy, and tactics of the outnumbered Israeli army over the past fifty years have emphasized qualitative approaches – out of necessity – and have been rather successful.

If all North American Jews were Hasidim, with high fertility rates and almost no mixed marriage, of course the Jewish population would grow. And rapidly. The quantitative future would be secured. Each (male) Jew would have an in-depth knowledge of Torah. But at the same time the nature of Jewish life as we know it would be dramatically different. There would be no academic conferences held to discuss the nature of Jewish life in the future. There would be no Jews like me. There would be no Jewish Studies curricula on any campus, no art exhibits or symposia. There would be no non-Orthodox Jewish cultural life as we understand it. The capacity to organize effective lobbying or public relations efforts, whether against the former Soviet Union or domestic anti-Semites or recalcitrant Swiss banks or European governments, would be highly constrained. Of course this is one extreme.

Now suppose all Jews were secular. They could still identify as Jews. They could be interested in Jewish literature, Jewish philosophy, the security of Israel, Jewish communal institutions, Jewish culture. They could in theory speak Hebrew and Yiddish. (In fact, the American evidence suggests they would score less favourably on all these sorts of measures than religious Jews.) They could talk the language of bureaucrats. But chances are they would never darken the door of any synagogue, never fulfil a religious ritual of any kind. They would intermarry in droves. In those conditions I think there would be no more Jews left in two or three generations. They would in fact suffer the declines which have befallen Jewish secularism in this century. That is the other stark extreme.

What Jews have evolved more than any other comparable group is an equilibrium that harmonizes both extremes. Some Jews have larger families, do not intermarry, and live very traditional, relatively insular Jewish lives. Others lie at the other end of the spectrum, with multiple contacts with the non-Jewish world. And others fall in the middle. They all contribute, directly and through their interactions, to the organic whole we call modern Jewish life.

PLURALISM AND CONFLICT

And what is the result? We have a Jewish community that is highly pluralistic. But many fear that this pluralism has gone too far, leading to conflict and disunity – which it often does. In the modern era, we have seen sharp ideological and group differences mark Jewish life. Let's review the current list: Orthodoxy, Conservatism, Reform, Reconstructionism, New Age Judaism; religious and secular; Hasidic and other ultra-Orthodox; Hebraist and Yiddishist; Zionist and non-Zionist; left-wing or right-wing Zionist; traditional and avant-garde. These groups have different cultures and agendas. In fact, modern Jewish pluralism has been very fractious indeed; Jewish disunity has been the rule. A remarkable exception was the brief period after the

Holocaust and the creation of Israel, when Jews fashioned a communal consensus that lasted perhaps into the late 1970s. But that idyll is over. Jews remain a "stiffnecked," cantankerous people.

In the wake of Yitzhak Rabin's murder in 1995, and again after the new intifada beginning in the fall of 2000, there have been understandable calls for Jewish unity. But unity can lead to sameness and stifle creativity. A respectful pluralism is far preferable to an inflexible, suffocating homogeneity. But what if the pluralism is not respectful? Jews must not confuse difference with treason. There are some who claim that now of all times Jews cannot afford too much difference, too much disunity. Perhaps. But let us recall that in the ghettos and even in the concentration camps, Jewish rivalries persisted. Difference, dissent, debate are an unchangeable part of Jewish identity today as in the past.

But there is more. This fractious pluralism is not simply a cross (pardon me) which Jews must bear. It is a source of Jewish strength. There are so many ways to be a Jew. Some decades ago a leading sociologist, Lewis Coser, published a major work with the paradoxical title *The Functions of Social Conflict*.[11] In his study, Coser outlined a variety of scenarios in which conflict can benefit both the competing groups and the society as a whole; in the Jewish case, this would mean both Jewish sub-groups and Jewry writ large. Conflict among the denominations has the unanticipated benefit of forcing each to sharpen and deepen their commitments and self-understanding.

Moreover, the actual intra-group conflicts in the daily lives of Canadian Jews are minimal. This is because so much of Jewish life is organized on a pattern of voluntary self-segregation. For most matters, Jews associate with similar Jews, in neighbourhoods, their synagogues, their children's Jewish schools or summer camps, in Jewish organizations, and in their private socializing. The conflict that people worry about is found mainly in public pronouncements, and has a nasty edge. Some fear it could grow into a complete schism between, say, the Orthodox and the non-Orthodox. In the short run that would be agonizing and for most Jews simply unthinkable. As for the long term, there are no evident parallels, and prediction is always risky. But let us take a deep breath in the face of such a worst-case scenario. Consider whether Christianity is stronger or weaker today because of the split into Catholicism and Protestantism several centuries ago. I think that is a tough question, with no clear answer.

So conflict within the Jewish world is not a problem that Jews have to solve with the creation of a unified mode of Jewish life, replete with a single demographic pattern and a single dominant cultural orientation. Conflict is a permanent, intrinsic feature of Jewish life, part of a vital diversity. In fact, the various poles of Jewish life today complement each other rather well. The sub-groups within the Jewish world perform different strategic and collective functions, which together help achieve the diverse goals of the communal Jewish agenda. Jewish survival owes much today to this blend of quantitative and qualitative demographic strategies. There are no villains.

COUNTING JEWS

These complexities underlie the simple task of asking how many Jews there are in Canada. The answer depends on whom we decide to count. As we have seen, Judaism is a faith, but Jews are also a people with common ancestry. The Canadian census addresses this dualism head on. For many people, the census is a dry, uninteresting set of numbers. Not true for Canada, and not true for anyone interested in Canadian Jews. In the United States, estimating the number of Jews has been a challenge, since their census collects no data on religion – the U.S. constitution forbids it. Questions on nationality in the American census leave Jews out as a category. That is why for a long time analysts trying to say something quantitative about American Jews were forced to use the census numbers for "Russians" as a proxy for Jews, or rely on cumbersome and expensive special national surveys. Canadians are more fortunate. The census is a wonderful if still imperfect tool for understanding an enigmatic group like the Jews. (See Table 1, page 357, for a demographic comparison of the Canadian and American Jewish populations.)

The Census of 1991 lists 318,070 Canadians who identify themselves as Jewish by religion, and 369,565 as Jewish by ethnic origin. (Of the ethnic Jews, 281,680 are also Jews by religion, 38,245 have no religion, and 49,640 have another religion.) Some of these ethnic Jews are no longer Jews. The question for religion asks simply "What is your religion?" The question on ethnic origin asks "To which ethnic or cultural group(s) did this person's ancestors belong?" While you can choose more than one ethnic origin, only one religion is recorded. That may well have to change, as interfaith marriages increase.

For Jews there is clearly no one-to-one correspondence between these two definitions. For example, the 1991 Census finds that there are 36,390 Jews by religion who do not claim to be Jews by ethnic origin. This is the "good" news. Known as "Jews by choice," they could be formal converts into Judaism or technical non-Jews who call themselves Jewish. They can also be Jews who for some reason picked another ethnic origin as their census answer, such as Polish, or English. On the other hand, there are 49,640 Jews by ethnic origin who claim another, non-Jewish faith. This is the "bad" news. Either they themselves, or some ancestors, converted out of Judaism. They are truly lost to the Jewish community.

But even these non-Jews can have a tough time escaping fully from their Jewish background, as former American Secretary of State Madeleine Albright can confirm. Once the media found out that her parents were Czech Jews who had escaped the Holocaust and converted to Christianity, she was forced, with apparent reluctance, to acknowledge her background in public. Many Jews – including me – found it hard to believe that she had not known about her Jewish ancestry. In Canada there are comparable examples of "Christian" Canadians of European background who, deliberately or not, have kept their Jewish ancestry hidden in their closet. A rich vein of Jewish humour reinforces the difficulty Jews face in escaping their Jewishness by conversion; it manages to bubble to the surface.

A Jew converts in order to join an exclusive country club. On his first day as a member he accidentally falls into the swimming pool fully clothed. Climbing out soaking wet and embarrassed, he groans, "Oy gevalt . . . whatever that means!"

Finally, there are 38,245 Canadians who select "Jewish" as an ethnic origin – but claim to have no religion. In terms of Jewish identity, this group of secular Jews or Jewish atheists or agnostics is a mixed bag. A non-Jew with a Jewish grandparent or great-grandparent may decide, depending on their mood during a particular census-taking, to claim a Jewish ethnic origin. Others in this group might be thoroughly assimilated, with no ties to or feelings for Jewish life, and could barely distinguish an *aleph* from a *bet*. Still others could have a strong Jewish cultural sense and identity, perhaps anchored in the local Jewish community, in Yiddish, or in a bond with Israel. They might even attend the odd synagogue service and be able to follow the prayers. Here, too, Jewish humour has long stereotyped the difficulty of being a real Jewish atheist or agnostic.

Two Jewish atheists in the shtetl are arguing over who is the greater non-believer. One is a devotee of Spinoza, the other of Marx. In the midst of their heated argument one suddenly stops and says, "Moishe, it's getting late, we have to hurry to the synagogue in time for the evening prayers!"

Many Canadian Jews wrestle with the distinction between being "ethnically" and "religiously" Jewish. The gap in census counts is proportionally greatest in Vancouver, part of the new western "frontier" for Canadian Jewry, with only 14,360 Jews by religion but 21,275 by ethnic origin. Vancouver is full of Jews of mixed Jewish ancestry who no longer identify their religion as Jewish, as well as secular Jews. This leads to mixed or very fluid conceptions of Jewish identity, as seen in the following quotations from a Vancouver study.[12]

"I was born Jewish and will pass on the traditions as I know them, e.g. Pesach, Hanukkah, etc. However being an agnostic, to go further than that would be impractical. I did not circumcise my son because I felt it to be hypocritical and also since the latest medical literature says it is barbaric and unnecessary."

"Up to college I only had Jewish friends. In college I started meeting non-Jewish people and found a whole different lifestyle in them. Two of my best friends are Christian and I celebrate Christmas. I consider myself Canadian first, then Jewish. I found the Jewish community in Montreal too close, too stifling. I understand how important it is for the Jewish people here in Vancouver to get close and get a better sense of identity, but it's not important to me. However my heritage is Jewish and ethnically I will always be a Jew."

"As a convert or Jew by choice, I feel strongly that I converted to a religion. There is an ethnic component but the religion is the centre of Judaism."

To get the best estimate of the number of Jews in Canada in 1991, we add the secular Jews to those who are Jewish by religion, for a total of 356,315 or 1.3 per cent.[13] This compares to the 1990 estimate from the NJPS of 5,515,000 American Jews or 2.2 per cent of the American population. Between 1981 and 1991, the Canadian Jewish population actually increased by 14.2 per cent, slightly greater than the increase of 13.4 percent for Canada as a whole. This differs sharply from the American case where the Jewish population is at best static and is becoming a smaller proportion of the American population.[14] As of 1991 there were few clear demographic signs of the "vanishing Canadian Jew." Those seeking a more extensive demographic discussion can find it in Appendix II: Demographic Predictions and Comparisons. Much of this Canadian advantage in identity and population growth – which is not guaranteed in perpetuity – comes from the greater proportion of foreign born-Jews. We therefore turn to a discussion of the growth of the Canadian Jewish community through waves of immigration, and its distribution throughout the country.

BUILDING A COMMUNITY

Migration and Regional Settlement

"Get thee out of thy country . . ."

– Genesis 12:1

"Love ye therefore the stranger for ye were strangers in the land of Egypt."

– Deuteronomy 10:19

FOUNDATIONS

From the time of Abraham, Jews have been on the move. Many people think of Jewish immigration to Canada as a topic best studied by historians. After all, the days of the great mass migrations at the end of the nineteenth century are over. But Jews are still moving. The immigrant saga occupies a mythic place in the identity of Canadian Jewry, as it does in the United States. It combines elements of economic struggle and sacrifice for children with a warm, idyllic sense of culture and community. Never mind the occasional exaggerations. And never mind that Jewish immigrants, from the early Eastern Europeans to the recent Holocaust survivors, North Africans, Russians, and Israelis, were often met with ambivalent receptions by the established Jewish organizations as well as Canadian-born Jews. The immigrant is a heroic benchmark for all Jews. And they continue to come.

The profile of Canadian Jews mirrors that of Canada itself. As immigration and regionalism are two defining characteristics of the Canadian reality, so, too, do they mark the life of Canadian Jews. Part of the vaunted uniqueness of Canada's mosaic compared to the American assimilationist melting pot stems from the higher general levels of immigration to Canada. In the 1990s about 8 to 10 per cent of the American population was foreign-born, compared to over 17 per cent in Canada. Immigrants help all minority communities, including Jews, retain their culture. Thus the far greater level of contemporary Jewish immigration in Canada helps explain the differences between the two Jewish communities. This chapter tells the story of Jewish immigration to Canada, and the spreading out of Canadian Jews throughout the country. Immigration continues to add to the diversity, and tensions, within the Canadian Jewish community. Yet paradoxically it adds to its strength and vitality.

Jewish migration to Canada, like that of other groups, is the story of different waves of immigrants, from different backgrounds, and motivated by different concerns. The very first Jews in Canada arrived as individuals, their stories the stuff of high drama. Joseph de la Penha was a Jewish trader from Rotterdam who in the 1670s was driven by a storm onto the coast of Labrador. While King William III of Orange and England granted de la Penha title over Labrador some twenty years later, the family never acted on the offer.[1] In 1738 a teenage French Jewess named Esther Brandeau arrived disguised as a young man; she was sent back after one year.

The first organized migration was that of merchant families originally from Germany and Great Britain, who settled first in Halifax and later in Montreal, Trois-Rivières, and Quebec City following the British conquest. This population of traders and merchants grew slowly, reaching 154 souls by 1841. All were of British or Central European origin, some having arrived via the United States.[2] These Jews were mainly Sephardi, and founded the oldest continuing synagogue in Canada, the Spanish and Portuguese Congregation of Montreal, in 1768. The legacy of that first Sephardi immigration to Montreal largely disappeared, as did that of the first Sephardi immigrants to the United States.[3] But the post-Second World War North African Sephardi immigration to Montreal has revitalized the Sephardi influence in a way not felt in most American cities.

The first large wave of Jewish migration to Canada was from Central Europe, arriving between 1840 and the 1880s. This wave included some Eastern European Jews who migrated to Germany, and later to the New World, for a variety of economic and political motives. Some were tradesmen and artisans whose livelihood was threatened by large-scale industrialization. The failure of the European Revolution of 1848 added to Jewish insecurities. While tens of thousands of Jews emigrated from Central Europe at that time, the large majority went to the United States. By 1877 there were an estimated 280,000 Jews in the United States, the vast majority the product of a German migration.[4] In Canada, the total Jewish population as of 1881 numbered only 2,456.[5]

Perhaps because these early numbers were so small, a Germanic/Reform stamp on the nascent Canadian Jewish community was far weaker than in the United States. Reform Judaism never achieved the dominance in Canada that it established early in the United States.[6] Stephen Birmingham's *Our Crowd*, a chronicle of the nineteenth- and early twentieth-century German Jewish "aristocracy" in America, could not have been written about Canada.[7] The German Jewish migration to the United States established niches in banking (Loeb, Kuhn, Goldmann), journalism (Sulzberger, Pulitzer), and retail trade (Saks, Niemann-Marcus, Bloomingdale, Sears) in a way that did not take place in Canada. By 1871, Jews represented a minuscule .03 per cent of the Canadian population. But slowly and surely Jews began to spread throughout British North America.[8]

The second large wave of Jewish migration was from Eastern Europe: Russia, Poland, Lithuania, Ukraine, and Romania. This phase began in the late 1870s, and was given added impetus by the Russian pogroms of 1881. As a result of the partitions of Poland and the Napoleonic Wars, Polish Jews came largely under Russian control. Jews were confined to an area along the western borders of Russia, known as the Pale of Settlement, set up by Catherine the Great in

1791.[9] Conditions for the Jews in the Pale worsened in the second half of the nineteenth century. Following the emancipation of the serfs in the 1860s, Jews faced increased competition from non-Jewish artisans, workers, and traders. Mobility restrictions and other laws and regulations limited Jewish opportunities. In addition, climbing fertility and declining mortality rates increased the Jewish population faster than the growth of economic opportunities. Russia underwent a period of political and ideological foment at the turn of the century, which saw increases in anti-Semitism as well. Migration was the solution. Millions of Eastern European Jews left for North America between the 1880s and 1920s.

Precise records of the ethnic origin of immigrants to Canada prior to 1900 are unavailable. In addition, we have no numbers about immigrants to Canada via the United States.[10] During the years 1900 to 1920, government statistics report a total of 3,246,051 immigrants who came to Canada, of whom an estimated 138,467 or 4.3 per cent were Jews.[11] The total Canadian Jewish population increased from 2,456 in 1881 to 126,201 in 1921, much of that by immigration. By comparison, in the United States the Jewish population increased from 280,000 in 1877 to an estimated 4.5 million in 1925.[12] The peak year of migration to Canada was in 1913–14, with 18,000 Jews out of a total influx of 400,000. The migration of Eastern European Jews also coincided with the expansion of the Canadian population westward. While Jewish life was indeed centred in the cities of Montreal, Toronto, and Winnipeg, there were also many Jews living in rural areas and smaller cities and towns.

The story of Jewish immigration is one of travail, and eventual triumph. The forces that propelled Jews to come to Canada were economic deprivation and persecution. The early Central and Western European immigrants to Canada, as in the United States, laid the foundations for many welfare institutions that served later waves of immigrants. This included Montreal's Young Men's Hebrew Benevolent Society, founded in 1863, and the Baron de Hirsch Institute, founded in 1902. In Toronto, welfare in the late nineteenth century was concentrated in the (male) Toronto Hebrew Benevolent Association, in the (female) Ladies Montefiore, associated with the Holy Blossom Synagogue, and in the Toronto chapter of the Anglo-Jewish Association.[13]

The occupational structure of the Eastern European Jews differed from that of the earlier Jewish migrants, where merchants, traders, and professionals had predominated. Between 1870 and 1900, the majority of them were artisans, unskilled labourers, small-scale merchants, clerical workers, and people in unspecified occupations. By 1920, over 70 per cent were skilled labourers and artisans, a much higher proportion than found among the general immigration to the United States and Canada.[14] Relatively few Jews were farmers and unskilled labourers. Efforts to set up Jewish agricultural colonies in the Prairie Provinces in the 1930s under the patronage of the Baron de Hirsch eventually came to naught. But those agricultural efforts grew to assume a mythic status in the history of Canadian Jews.[15] The descendants of Jewish farmers in Western Canada enjoy a kind of *yichus*, or respect for their lineage, normally reserved for bluebloods.

Compared to the migration of other European groups to Canada or the United States, Jewish migration was more likely to be a one-way move. While some Jews returned to Europe, this was less common than among other European immigrants who would return to the homeland after they saved enough money to buy some land. Anti-Semitism made a return less attractive for Jews, and as a result Jews immigrated as families. Men were more likely to send home for a spouse than to return to re-establish ties in the old country. This and the presence of children encouraged the immigrant Jews to build communities and work hard. Jews knew they were in Canada to stay, and had to plan for the economic future of their children. This meant acting responsibly and energetically in their own jobs, and encouraging their children to do well in school.

We should neither understate nor overstate the extent of early Jewish economic success. The streets of Canada, like those in the United States, were not paved with gold – at least not for the immigrants. The Eastern European Jewish migrants and most of their children were overwhelmingly working-class, a condition which lasted well into the 1930s. Mordecai Richler's hustling Duddy Kravitz is a typical character of the 1940s, a Canadian-born Jew trying to move up. Nevertheless, compared to other urban immigrant groups, the Jewish climb up the occupational ladder was rapid. This was also true for New York in the early twentieth century.[16] But it was not until the post-war period that large and stable Jewish middle class began to emerge.

Jewish migration to Canada persisted in substantial numbers up to 1931, when immigration was drastically curtailed. Compared to the United States, the Canadian government's motives were more economic than racist. The United States effectively restricted immigration in 1924 as a result of anti-immigrant pressures, typified by the newly remobilized Ku Klux Klan. The American economy was still strong. In Canada, the onset of the Depression was the catalyst. The timing could not have been worse for Jews. Economic insecurities fed into existing anti-Semitic prejudice to help close the doors even to desperate Jewish refugees from Nazi Germany.[17] While Jewish immigration throughout the 1920s averaged several thousand per year, for the dangerous 1930s the number was only several hundred. General anti-Semitism, a poor economy, and racist government officials played their part in lowering Canadian pre-war immigration levels. Jewish immigration to Canada resumed, albeit slowly, only after the end of the war.

The next Jewish immigrants to arrive were the Holocaust survivors. The first group arrived from 1947 to 1952. A total of about 34,000 came to Canada, of whom some 11,000 were official Jewish DPs, or displaced persons. Of a total of about 98,000 DPs of all origins coming to Canada, Jews ranked third, after non-Jewish Poles and Ukrainians.[18] The survivors strengthened the ties of Canadian Jewry to Eastern European Jewish life. While many, probably most, were not strictly Orthodox, they were steeped in the rituals and lore of traditional Judaism. Though most were broken in body or spirit, they made major contributions to organized Jewish life. They were active in Jewish education and culture, playing key roles as teachers in day schools, as contributors to and readers of Yiddish newspapers, and as volunteers, staffers, and patrons of Jewish cultural and Yiddish organizations. Not surprisingly, the survivors also played a role, hesitantly at first, in raising the communal conscience about the Holocaust.[19]

The impact of Holocaust survivors in Canada was greater than in the United States, where the relative demographic weight of survivors was much less. By 1953 about 140,000 Jewish survivors had emigrated to the

United States.[20] If we estimate about five million Jews in the United States in 1950, and about 204,000 Canadian Jews in 1951, the difference in the relative proportions of post-war survivor migrants is truly striking.[21] They comprised only 3 per cent of the American but 16 per cent of the Canadian Jewish population. In time, the survivors became an active political force and a prod to a timid Jewish establishment, particularly when it came to the militant defence of Israel or of Jewish rights in the face of perceived anti-Semitism. Toronto's Rabbi Gunther Plaut recalls: "Survivors of the *Shoah* have played a great part in Canada and made a stronger impact on our community than in the United States. I remember a 1961 Canadian Jewry that was hesitant to speak out publicly, let alone march in the streets. The survivors helped to change that."[22]

MORE RECENT WAVES

An important wave of immigrants from North Africa began to arrive in the late 1950s, settling mainly in Montreal. These immigrants, most from Morocco, were francophone and Sephardi in cultural orientation. They added a unique dimension of pluralism to Jewish life in Montreal. There remains some confusion as to their precise number, since not all French-speaking Jews are North African or Sephardi, and not all Sephardi Jews are francophone or from North Africa. One estimate of the North African population in 1972 ranged from 10,000 to 13,000. By the late 1990s, other estimates commonly cited for the Montreal francophone and/or Sephardi Jewish community ranged from 25,000 to 30,000.[23] A 1996 survey of Montreal Jews found 18 per cent of respondents to be Sephardi, and 21 per cent claimed they spoke French at home, alone or with English; that suggests a lower total of around 21,000 Sephardi Jews.[24] Data from the 1991 Canadian Census found that of all those claiming the Jewish religion, about 5 per cent claimed French as a mother tongue and the language spoken at home. That would yield a still lower figure of 16,000 – for the entire country – but would exclude those (probably few) francophone Jews who were "ethnic" Jews with no religion.

The North African Jews are, as the Holocaust survivors before them, a "traditional" Jewish group. They are rooted in an Old World conception of Judaism far removed from influences of secularism. At the same time, their preference for French led to delicate processes of integration into the larger, more established anglophone Jewish community of Montreal, not without its frictions.[25] In one sense, these immigrants helped to create valuable bridges for Jews to the Québécois, just as Quebec nationalism was emerging full-blown. But in another, they made concerted pro-federalist action difficult, since some of their leaders were seen as "soft." They were not as viscerally federalist as Montreal's anglophone Jews. I can recall attending a meeting of Jewish communal representatives preparing a tripartite brief for the Bélanger–Campeau Commission on the Future of Quebec in 1990. In exasperation at the seemingly tough pro-federalist stance of most of the anglophone Jewish leaders, one francophone leader yelled, "What are you afraid of? What are you afraid of?" Not surprisingly, data from the same 1996 survey show Ashkenazim were more than twice as likely as Sephardim to feel "pessimistic" about life in Quebec.

All this has not been lost upon sovereignist leaders in Quebec, who favour francophone Jews and their organizations as they try to demonstrate an absence of anti-Semitic bias. This "divide and conquer" approach has yielded only a marginal payoff for Parti Québécois strategists. According to the 1996 survey, only 6 per cent of Sephardim supported either sovereignty-association or independence, compared to just under 1 per cent for Ashkenazim. And surprisingly, Sephardi respondents had a slightly higher inclination to consider leaving Quebec. In fact, the Sephardi community of Toronto grew rapidly in the 1980s and 1990s.

Along with the Sephardi immigrants, and following the first wave of Holocaust survivors, came other European immigrants. Over six thousand Jews arrived in 1957, many from Hungary following the failure of the 1956 Revolution. A few managed to arrive from Poland in 1968–70, following reformist tensions and civil unrest. These wavelets of Jewish migration included large numbers of Holocaust survivors as well.

Soviet Jews – as they were called then – began arriving in the 1970s, their numbers depending on Soviet policy. The Soviet authorities manipulated the numbers of visas granted, depending on their needs of the moment. Jews were pawns in the *Realpolitik* of the Cold War.

These immigrants posed a new challenge for the Canadian Jewish communities. As a group, they were highly educated, perhaps more educated
than any other refugee group. But whereas Jewish immigrants had been
usually steeped in traditional Judaism, the opposite was the case here.
Russian Jews were largely unfamiliar with Judaism and Judaic culture.
They had been subjected to decades of anti-Jewish and anti-Zionist
propaganda by the officially atheistic Soviet state. Rampant anti-
Semitism in Russia added a further incentive to encourage Jews to move
far from any Jewish ties. A study of a small sample of Russian Jews in
Toronto found that two-thirds said they had had "negligible" or "weak"
exposure to things Jewish in the U.S.S.R. Half "never or hardly ever"
attended a synagogue, and only one-quarter were affiliated with a Jewish
organization, usually the Association of Soviet Jews in Canada. Their
friendship patterns also were largely concentrated within the Soviet
Jewish community; 87 per cent said that three or four of their closest
friends in Canada were other Soviet Jewish immigrants. Here, as in the
case of Israeli migrants, there seems to be a case of an emergent "community within a community."[26]

Estimates of the size of new immigrant groups always vary, as we
have seen with the Sephardi community in Montreal. At times, it is
hard to define the group for statistical purposes. Their size is also overstated by leaders of these groups competing for scarce communal
dollars, or to establish influence with their own community or with
government. Consider the case of the Soviet or Russian Jews. Published
estimates of their numbers were at 8,000 in 1983 and 20,000 by 1993.[27]
The 1991 census revealed only 11,280 Canadian Jews who had been
born in the U.S.S.R., but that figure does not include Canadian-born
children of Russian immigrants. The estimates continue to grow. By
the end of the 1990s, some claimed there were 10,000 Jews from the
former Soviet Union in the Montreal area alone. If true, that would
mean a dramatic increase for Canada as a whole – which is actually
plausible given the huge outflow of several hundred thousand Jews
from the former Soviet Union in the 1990s.[28] One recent estimate is
"around 50,000" for Canada, based on 25,000 to 30,000 for Toronto,
10,000 for Montreal, and large numbers in the other Canadian cities.

American scholars claim that 280,000 Soviet Jews emigrated to the United States beginning in the late 1960s through 1993.[29]

Jewish communal leaders were torn during the 1970s and most of the 1980s about how important it was to get Soviet Jews to Israel, as opposed to elsewhere in the democratic West and Canada in particular. Most Soviet Jews were able to leave with exit visas to Israel, but increasingly large numbers changed their plans en route in Vienna and sought refuge in the West. Western Jewish communities did not want to appear to be stealing potential immigrants to Israel; thus the interests of Israel, the Soviet Jews, and Diaspora Jewish leaders did not always coincide. In the post-Soviet 1990s, Russian Jews seeking to leave could no longer qualify as refugees under the 1951 Geneva Convention, though some would continue to stretch the rules. As Russian Jews poured out in the 1990s, there were enough to go around to populate both Israel and to a much lesser extent North American Jewish communities. From 1989 to the end of 1997, over 700,000 of these Jews immigrated to Israel.[30]

Israelis are yet another, and the most problematic, immigrant wave. (The Israelis used to be called *yordim*, a pejorative term from the Hebrew word *yored*, which means "one who goes down." This contrasts with the Hebrew term *oleh* for an immigrant to Israel, meaning "one who goes up as if to a better place.") Here, too, no one knows how many have come. One activist in the Israeli Canadian community estimated the number at about 12,000 to 15,000.[31] The 1991 Census yields a total of 9,480 Canadians born in Israel. Not all of these are Jewish, and this figure excludes Canadian-born children of ex-Israelis. In any event, other estimates are much higher. One study mentions an estimate of 30,000 just for the Toronto Israeli community, but with no direct source. Another asserts a range between 20,000 and 50,000 for Canada as a whole.[32] American estimates range from 100,000 to 200,000, though for a long time unconfirmed estimates of 300,000 to 500,000 were bandied about.[33]

The Israeli immigrants posed a much different set of challenges for the host Jewish communities, laced with a bittersweet irony. In one sense they were ideal Jewish immigrants. They were highly knowledgeable about major elements of Jewish culture. They were fluent in

Hebrew, and knew Jewish history and the Bible, and a fair bit about Jewish holidays. But many, perhaps most, were not at all observant. On the High Holidays in Israel, they were as likely to go to the beach as to go to pray. They had no experience with the variety of North American synagogues. Religion in Israel meant "*dati*" or Orthodox, and was tainted by associations with religious parties. Some Israelis assumed positions as teachers in Jewish schools and as staffers in a variety of Jewish communal organizations – replacing in some cases the earlier generation of Holocaust survivors – but others were resolutely secular and had trouble developing a Diaspora-based Jewish identity.

There was an even more profound problem. The Israelis were travelling in the wrong direction. North American Israelis wrestled with ongoing ambiguities and residual feelings of betrayal of the Jewish state. Their presence in Canada challenged a basic premise of Canadian Jewish life, and the Jewish community was unsure of the proper response. Canadian Jewry had long been highly Zionistic, and committed to building up Israel and espousing the value of *aliyah*, or immigration to Israel. Too much of a welcome to the Israelis raised awkward questions for Canadian Jews and Zionists. If it encouraged even more Israeli migration, it might weaken Israel's demographic base. Yet a tepid reception would do a disservice to a possibly needy immigrant group and violate the tradition of immigrant aid so central to Canadian Jewish life. So the ambivalent Israelis were met with ambivalence on the part of the host Canadian Jewish community. Most had minimal contact with the organized Jewish community, and for some time many Israelis retained a "myth of return," or *chazara*, with which they convinced themselves, and others, that their stay in Canada was temporary.[34] That desire to return, or the need for some such justification, has waned in recent years.

This signals another difference between Canadian Israelis and other immigrant groups. Neither Italians nor Poles nor Jamaicans nor Chinese violate a cardinal national or religious myth in leaving Europe or the Caribbean or Asia and coming to North America. The only immigrant groups where such ambivalence exists are those with a struggling homeland. Palestinians, Kurds, black South Africans, Armenians, Iranians, who keep one eye fixed on the travails of the mother country fighting against external or internal oppression, feel like overseas Israelis. But most of those migrants, despite their ideological commitments, are unlikely to return. Life in Canada is just too good. Those with an opportunity to do so – Eastern Europeans since the collapse of communism, or black South Africans since the end of apartheid – have not flocked back. Israelis are no different. Their question is the same: to sink roots in Canada, or to return. The answer is increasingly to stay.

Migration from Israel soon brought an unexpected policy problem. In the 1990s, to the consternation of Canadian Jews, hundreds of Israelis successfully claimed refugee status.[35] These claimants were Jews – and some non-Jews – from the former Soviet Union who alleged they were victims of religious discrimination in Israel – in jobs, housing, the army, by the rabbinate – and that the Israeli government offered them no protection. To many Canadian Jews, the whole thing seemed Kafkaesque. Israel, a state created as a haven for those who had suffered religious persecution, was now labelled before the world as a violator of the human rights of the very immigrants who sought freedom there. More to the point, few Canadian Jews believed that these Russians had in fact remotely experienced the kind of state-sponsored persecution that was supposed to trigger refugee protection. That these acceptances came disproportionately from Immigration and Refugee Board hearings in Quebec added to the suspicions, since it was feared that some of the IRB decisions in the province were motivated by general anti-Israel sentiments. The numbers were significant. In 1993, 1,894 Israelis laid new claims for refugee status in Canada. In addition, 1,089 previous claims for refugee status were processed to completion, and 157 were actually accepted.[36]

Not surprisingly, the issue led to friction between the Israeli and Canadian governments. The story broke in July 1994, when the Israeli newspaper *Ha'aretz* reported that Canada had accepted about 160 Israeli refugees the previous year. The Israeli deputy foreign minister, Yossi Beilin, was furious, claiming that "the situation in which the Canadian government grants refugee status to Israeli citizens is really ridiculous." Replying to Beilin's comments, Canadian immigration minister, Sergio Marchi, in what one Israeli journalist called the "sharpest riposte ever heard from a Canadian Minister in the 46 years of Israel's existence," responded, "I don't think it is the business of another country to dictate to Canada who can and who cannot be considered a refugee. Israel should deal with her own problems and not try to dictate rules of behaviour to others."[37] Eventually, matters were smoothed out. After strenuous representations on the part of Canadian Jewish organizations, the acceptance rate of these alleged refugees from Israeli persecution declined to just to twenty-four and twenty-nine in 1998 and 1999.[38] Of course, from the staunchly pro-Israel Canadian Jewish perspective, even one is too many.

Jewish migration has not ended with Israelis. Others continue to come, from South Africa, Ethiopia, Latin America, the United States, indeed, the four corners of the earth. The 1991 Census revealed 25,895 foreign-born Jews had immigrated just in the previous ten years. Of these, 24 per cent were born in the Soviet Union; 19 per cent in Israel; 14 per cent in the United States; 11 per cent in Africa, excluding North Africa (this means essentially South Africa and Ethiopia); 9 per cent in non–Eastern Europe; 7 per cent each in North Africa and Eastern Europe; and the remainder in places like Latin America, the Middle East, or Australia. As with Canada as a whole, large, sustained immigration has been a part of the Canadian Jewish experience since the 1880s. Immigration continues to shape the identities of Canada and Canadian Jews.

IMMIGRANT INTEGRATION: AN OXYMORON?

All these Jewish immigrants need to be integrated – a process that transforms Canada just as it transforms the established Jewish community. But what kind of integration? Social scientists speak of economic, social, political, and cultural integration; others talk of adaptation, absorption, settlement, or incorporation. Behind these terms, which all mean similar things, lies a basic question. How much integration is needed for immigration to be considered a success? Some observers perceive failures or even crises of immigrant integration in Canada in the 1990s. Perhaps they have unrealistic expectations.

I take a minimalist approach. An immigrant who supports himself or herself and/or a family and obeys the law is in my view successfully integrated. I do not expect most immigrants to Canada to earn high incomes or to appreciate the novels of Margaret Atwood or the plays of Gratien Gélinas, or even to master quickly English and/or French – though of course all that would be nice.

The first axiom of immigrant integration, which applies to Jews as well as to any group, is that immigrants rarely integrate directly into the host society. The term "immigrant integration" is almost an oxymoron. Integration into what? Into their smaller-sized communities of origin, not into Canada as a whole. These intermediate groups buffer what is a difficult, at times traumatic, process of adjustment in a new environment. Adult immigrants have one foot in the old country, and most *never* fully integrate into Canada. Their children and grandchildren are the ones who do that. Adult immigrants retain ties of language, culture, and kin to the old country. They in fact integrate first into an extended family, if there is one already in Canada. Then into an ethnic subcommunity and often an ethnic church, and then into a larger ethnic community, replete with its own culturally specific institutions. Most remain hyphenated Canadians in a real, sociological sense. This is not a tragedy. Rather, this process of "nested" integration eases traumas associated with immigration into a new society.

This is also the pattern of Jewish immigrant integration. My parents illustrated this process when they arrived in Canada in 1948. They did not integrate into Canadian society, or even Montreal, or even the full Jewish community. Rather, they integrated – quite happily, I might add – into a particular sub-group of Polish Jewish Holocaust survivors. Though they knew English, they spoke Polish or Yiddish with their friends. A similar pattern is true for most Jewish immigrants to Canada, and, indeed, for most immigrants of any kind. I recall a recent conversation in Toronto with a black cab driver who spoke with an African accent. He identified himself not as black, not as an African, not as Nigerian, but as a Yoruba, one of the major tribes of Nigeria. And he congregated with other Yoruba, and belonged to Yoruba associations. For Jews or Africans, these patterns are not tragedies, not "failures" of integration. Just life being lived.

The Jewish community maintains one key organization devoted to the integration of Jewish immigrants: the Jewish Immigrant Aid Services. It offers help of all sorts to Jewish immigrants in the first three years of their arrival. Other immigrant communities have sought to develop comparable immigrant services, though these often rely on governmental as opposed to internal communal funding. But JIAS is not the whole story. All Jewish immigrant groups have set up their own organizations, which add to both the diversity and fragmentation of the local Jewish community. Some are largely autonomous, others are part of mainstream agencies. The YMHA has special programs aimed at specific groups of immigrants, such as Soviet or Ethiopian Jews. Jewish schools and social service agencies are sensitized to the specific cultural needs of immigrants. These various organizations are marked by the distinctive languages these groups speak. The survivors speak Yiddish and other European languages, the North Africans speak French, the Soviet Jews speak Russian, and the Israelis speak Hebrew.[39]

Consider the Israeli case. In the 1990s, Israelis in Toronto had their own literary clubs, a short-lived school, a weekly Hebrew radio broadcast, a Hebrew community newspaper, a Scouts organization, two senior citizen's clubs, Hebrew-speaking chapters in pro-Israel organizations such as Hadassah, Na'amat, the Organization for Education Resources and Technological Training (ORT), and Pioneer Women, and congregations for Israelis organized by Sephardim and Chabad-Lubavitch.[40] In Montreal, an organization named Betzavta, founded in 1986, began to sponsor cultural and Hebrew-language programs. Under the umbrella of the YMHA, Betzavta has about six hundred members, and is well accepted by the Jewish community. Part of this greater acceptance by Canadian Jewry reflects a more accommodating attitude by Israel towards its expatriates.

The Russian Jewish migration also has its own organizations. The Association of Soviet Jewry in Canada, based in Toronto, provides medical, legal, educational, and cultural programs and direct assistance. The Russian Jewish Program at Montreal's YMHA is another example. Founded in 1982, it offers a variety of cultural and service programs to Russian Jews, many of which accentuate Russian as much as Jewish cultural traditions.[41] Children's classes in art, math, ballet, chess,

Russian language, and drama inculcate Russian cultural traditions. One of the traits of the Russian Jewish migration is that many community members are not Jewish according to *halacha*, and indeed many outright non-Jews participate in these programs. This includes attending synagogue services provided for Russian Jews. According to one observer, "Many *Goyim* are there, they like it, they get vodka at the *kiddush*." The Russian and Israeli organizations will likely not be as permanent as those serving Sephardim. The former are devoted to immigrant integration, and they will fade like the earlier *landsman-schaften* as the second and third generations get established. The Sephardim, however, rightly see themselves as preserving a permanent and distinctive Judaic tradition. Their organizations will last well after the passing of the immigrant generation.

These ethno-specific organizations peculiar to the various immigrant sub-groups have various purposes. In one sense they prevent integration into the broader Canadian society and into the mainstream Jewish community. Yet in another sense they facilitate integration into a new society by providing a warm, familiar environment in which the immigrant can feel at home. This Jewish mini-tribalism is an indispensable asset. Moreover, the task of integrating immigrants provides native-born Jews with a unifying mission and sense of purpose.

Because Toronto and Montreal have the largest and oldest Jewish communities, we might assume that they also have exceptionally high proportions of immigrants. Not so. Foreign-born Jews have been moving to and settling in the West. A survey of Calgary's Jewish community found that over 7 per cent spoke Russian at home and that one-quarter of Calgary's Jews were raised outside Canada.[42] Jewish immigrants are found in all regions of Canada. Some examples: The lowest concentrations are in Nova Scotia and New Brunswick, where only one-fifth and one-tenth of Jews are immigrants. We find 36 per cent in Quebec and 32 per cent in Ontario. Perhaps most surprising are the high percentages found further west: 25 percent for Saskatchewan, 31 percent for Alberta, and 32 percent for British Columbia.[43] The welcoming and integrating of Jewish immigrants is a challenge for Canadian Jews throughout the country.

The Jewish community is concerned not only with Jewish immigrants, but with immigration policy in general. Jews as individuals and through the Canadian Jewish Congress or the League for Human Rights of B'nai Brith have been strong advocates of generous immigration and refugee levels. Immigration is for Jews a political litmus test; it is hard to imagine Jews en masse supporting candidates calling for major cutbacks in immigrant numbers. It is not surprising that Jews, like cabinet members Gerry Weiner for the Conservatives and Elinor Caplan for the Liberals, have been ministers responsible for immigration. Canadian Jews are soft on immigration and more likely to give refugee claimants the benefit of the doubt. How could it be otherwise for the "wandering Jews?" The ancestors of many North American Jews probably lied to immigration officers. Some of those claiming to be tailors had never sewn a button. Jewish Immigrant Aid Services has lobbied against measures seen as restrictionist, such as bills C-55 and C-84, passed in the late 1980s. The former bill dealt with the refugee determination process in Canada, the latter provided sanctions to deter illegal immigrants from trying to enter Canada, and smugglers and carriers from transporting them.[44]

The Canadian government has recognized JIAS's expertise in immigration matters, and consults regularly with JIAS senior staff. Provinces also now play direct roles in Jewish immigration. Quebec has since the 1960s assumed greater control of immigration matters. Quebec and JIAS have undertaken several successful projects, dating from the early 1990s, each one recruiting and settling one hundred Russian Jewish families. The government of Manitoba has been pursuing with the Winnipeg Jewish community a similar plan aimed at bringing Argentinian Jewish families to Winnipeg.[45] All this is a far, far cry from the dark days of the 1930s, when government bureaucrats worked to keep Jews out.

Jewish organizations are right to take an interest in immigration, since immigration has been such a defining feature of Canadian Jewish life. Back in 1911, during the period of mass migration, fully two-thirds of Canadian Jews were foreign-born. For the rest of the century the proportion was one-third – still very high.[46] This is almost twice as high as the general Canadian figure of one-sixth foreign-born and three times as high as for American Jews. So while many in Canada think of Jews as an established native-born group, the truth is otherwise.

The picture is dramatically different in the United States. There, immigrants make up only 10 per cent of the Jewish population, and analysts of American Jewish life pay them little heed. A case in point: in the close to one hundred pages of tables and text of the American 1990 NJPS, there is *no* sustained discussion or analysis of foreign-born Jews. In only one parenthetical sentence do we discover that 10 per cent of the adult core Jewish population are foreign-born.[47] For American Jews, immigration is something that affected their grandparents or great-grandparents; for Canadian Jews, it is an ongoing reality.

BITTERSWEET ENCOUNTERS

It is a paradox of Jewish life that a community that has been so dependent on immigration, and has dedicated resources and energy to help Jewish immigrants integrate and to support liberal immigration policies, has a record of a lukewarm personal acceptance of Jewish immigrants. In terms of interpersonal contacts and attitudes, prejudice and tension have been the rule. This is a continuing theme in the history of Jewish immigration to North America. The conventional account stresses the elitism, perhaps prompted by insecurity, of the established affluent and educated Jews, influenced by Germanic, Sephardi, or British cultural elements. The masses of Eastern European immigrants brought with them the culture of the shtetl, the small Jewish towns and villages popularized in the fiction of Sholom Aleichem. These Jews were working-class, spoke Yiddish, worshipped in Orthodox synagogues, and were often socialist and/or Zionist. Many of the established Jews viewed these newcomers with alarm. They feared they would rock the boat and stimulate anti-Semitism. They were, in a word, an embarrassment.

So there was mutual antipathy. The Eastern European immigrants through the 1930s resented their alleged benefactors as inauthentically Jewish and opposed to working-class values. The reaction of the established Canadian-born Jews ranged from ambivalence to condescension to hostility. Rarely did they reflect unbridled enthusiasm. This was also the case much later for the Holocaust survivor migration, or the *green-ers*. This story is one of the great dramatic tales of the Canadian Jewish experience, and it is bittersweet at best.[48] The antipathy was not only cultural, as after all both the old-timers and the newcomers were of European Ashkenazi background. There was another factor: guilt by the native-born at not having done enough to pry open the gates before the war, or to pressure their governments to rescue more during the war. Many realized that by quirks of fate they could have been the survivors, or worse.

My father's story captures this element of historical chance and then distance in contacts with Canadian-born Jews. He was born in Poland in 1902, but his uncle had already struck out for Canada in the late nineteenth century. Part of that uncle's family stayed in Montreal, another part moved out West. My father had two siblings. His older brother left Poland and arrived in the United States in 1922. His sister escaped from Europe in the late 1930s, and arrived in the United States in 1939, one of the few. My father felt he could not leave his parents even as the storm clouds gathered, and was trapped in the whirlwind of the Holocaust. His first cousins and their children were safe in Canada. He survived, married my mother – who had no family left – and immigrated to Canada, settling in Montreal.

The reaction of his now very established and affluent Montreal relatives to his arrival after the war was, to say the least, restrained, and no connections were ever made. No great loss. My parents established a rich social life without them. But the insecurities in that post-war period ran deep. My father was certainly close to his brother and sister, who had settled around Washington, D.C. But he once confided to me that he sensed – it is not clear if he had real proof – that they were pleased he had settled far away in Canada. My uncle had married an American-born Jew and spoke English with no European accent at all. My aunt worked for the Library of Congress and was a profound American patriot. Both were highly Americanized. I doubt they made valiant efforts to sponsor my father into the United States.

It would be easy to harp on the moral failings of my relatives, or of the Canadian-born Jews who received the survivors in the post-war period. But that would miss the point. We tend to overlook the overwhelming social insecurity which those Jews felt. Beneath the facade of acculturation and material success, Jews were threatened, or felt threatened, by a palpable anti-Semitism. A Gallup Poll taken in Canada just after the war found Jews ranked as the second-least desirable – just ahead of the Japanese – of any prospective immigrants to Canada.[49] Major institutions, like top corporations, universities, and the public service, still had their highest ranks closed to Jews. So it is not surprising that the established Jews looked at the newcomers with trepidation. In any event, the survivors managed to rebuild their lives and overcome the physical and psychological horrors they had to endure. They made great contributions to Canadian Jewish life, in the fields of Jewish education and Yiddish culture, as well as to Canadian society in general. While some lived modestly, others prospered. Indeed, in a recent *National Post* list of the fifty wealthiest Canadians, of the approximately ten Jews listed, five – Marcel Adams, David Azrieli, Leslie Dan, Saul Feldberg, and Paul Reichmann – can be identified as Holocaust survivors in one sense or another.[50]

The ambivalence to immigrants did not stop with survivors. North African migrants of the 1950s and 1960s encountered even greater hostility. Here, the issue was less insecurity and more the greater cultural differences between the host English-Ashkenazi Jewish community and the French-speaking Sephardi immigrants. One survey of Montreal North African immigrants in 1972 found they were three times more likely to prefer to work with French Canadians than with Canadian-born Jews. They were also more likely to marry French Canadians than to marry Canadian-born (Ashkenazi) Jews. While these intermarriage rates have come down in subsequent years, the tensions then were real. Ashkenazi Jews had little respect for "the Moroccans," and some in private routinely expressed condescending attitudes. Doubtless, this rejection played a role in the high degree of social interaction the North Africans established with the French Canadian population.[51] Such antipathies are common wherever waves of Jewish immigrants have settled. These Canadian sentiments echoed similar prejudices in Israel and in France against the North Africans. Earlier, established communities in France and Germany looked down on the *Ostjuden* from Eastern Europe who had arrived prior to the Second World War.

By the end of the 1990s, marriages between Ashkenazi and Sephardi Jews were still rare in Canada. One Montreal study released in 2000 estimated that 13 to 14 per cent of married Sephardim had an Ashkenazi spouse, and that a slightly higher percentage was married to people not born Jewish.[52] (Exactly half of those spouses who were not born Jewish had later converted to Judaism, which is extremely high by North American standards.) There are still in Canada educated Ashkenazi Jews who recount their horror stories and negative impressions about "the Moroccans." These individuals would deny strongly that they are creating or perpetuating unfounded stereotypes. They are simply, in their view, recounting their experiences and generalizing about some franco-phone Jews and their behavioural traits. A physician told me stories about such Jews refusing to wait their turn in a waiting room. A social-service worker told me that Moroccan Jewish clients are unreliable, ask for welfare when they do not really need it, and are more likely to be those involved in spousal and child abuse. A retailer claimed "they" are dishonest. This is Jewish racism, pure and simple. These feelings may also reflect the insecurities of anglophone Ashkenazi Jews faced with their ongoing loss of power, and the increasingly key role played by francophone Jews in Quebec. Perhaps worst of all, some Jewish teenagers in Montreal recycle these stereotypes and prejudices. The same survey found that 36 per cent of Sephardim found relations with Ashkenazim to be "not harmonious" compared to 45 per cent who reported "harmonious" relations.

While there is more interaction at the level of community organizations, these tensions are reflected there as well. Most of the major Jewish communal organizations have few Sephardi members on their boards. According to insiders, this is due both to lack of interest by Sephardim, and their reluctance to become a token and perhaps endure subtle prejudice. Sephardi communal leaders associated with the Communauté Sépharade du Québec, even by the end of the 1990s, retained a kind of love-hate relation with their Ashkenazi/anglophone counterparts.

North Africans are not alone. The Russian Jewish immigrants have also had problems. It is true that Canadian Jews, like other Diaspora communities, fought mightily to help pry open the gates of the Soviet

Union. But even that success did not eliminate prejudice. Much as in Israel, there is a tribal shorthand that at times disparages "the Russians." Some are labelled as criminals, tarred by the emergence of organized Russian crime syndicates. Others fight against the doubts that they are authentically Jewish, or adequately committed to Jewish life. Some Canadian-born Jews find them ungrateful, and whiners, or given to inflate their educational credentials. And in response, some Russians decry Canadian Jews – often with reason – as materialistic, uncultured, and cold.

But these resentments are not the whole Jewish immigration story. As important is the high degree of communal help extended to poor immigrants then and even more so now. Whatever its motive, and despite the fact that the help may have been accompanied by patronizing attitudes, and that most immigrants remained socially isolated within their own subcommunities, the immigrants did not and do not stand alone. Support for Jewish immigrants is far, far greater than that by other Canadian ethnic groups for their recent arrivals. It parallels, though lags far behind, the support Israel extends to Jewish immigrants, which exceeds the aid provided to immigrants by any country on the planet.

THE COMMUNAL AND CULTURAL LIFE OF IMMIGRANTS

By many criteria, Jewish life was indeed more "authentic" in the early immigrant era. Yiddish was for most Jews their common language. Contact with non-Jews was minimal. Not being wealthy, the immigrant Jews emphasized spiritual and cultural traits of their families and communities. However, we should not over-romanticize the warmth and idyllic nature of their lives. Mordecai Richler's depictions of the sleazier side of immigrant Jewish life offer a counterpoint, even if exaggerated. Religious observance among the immigrants rapidly gave way to the requirements for economic success, such as working on the Sabbath. Immigrant Jewish neighbourhoods also saw high rates of poverty, family disintegration, and crime. For example, in 1933 the crude (unadjusted) crime rate for Canadian Jews, many of them immigrants, was almost 22 per cent higher than the Canadian average.[53] There were other problems within the Jewish immigrant communities. Cases of desertion and marital discord were not rare, and neither were unwed mothers and Jewish juvenile delinquents. The children of immigrants felt the beckoning tugs of even an anti-Semitic Canada very strongly. The lure of the *shiksa* predated the intermarriage upswing in the 1970s. Some resented parental restrictions, or felt embarrassed at their parents' Yiddish or accented English or old-fashioned, Old World ways. Anti-Semitism also was common in employment, social and educational discrimination, and in street brawls with Gentile toughs.[54]

The impact of immigration remains greater on Canadian than American Jewry. In part this is because immigrant Jews are relatively far more numerous in Canada. But there is also a more nuanced historical reason. The Eastern European Jewish immigrants to Canada differed from their counterparts who went to the United States in an important respect. The bulk of the American Jewish mass migration began in the period 1880 to 1900. In the case of Canada, the migration was more concentrated in the 1900 to 1920 period. This twenty-year gap made a difference. The Yiddish culture established by the Americans was more "assimilationist." The Canadian migration, arriving somewhat later, had more time to be influenced by the more nationalist ideologies of Zionism and Bundism. Both Herzl's Zionist Organization and the Bund were founded in 1897. They flourished in the early twentieth century and competed successfully against purely class-based left-wing ideologies, which leaned towards universalist, non-Jewish identities. From the pure socialist perspective, why be a Jew when you could be a member of the revolutionary working class? In stark contrast, left-wing Zionism offered a way to link progressive politics to Jewish identification and the ancestral homeland of the Jews through the ideal of building a workers' state in Palestine. The ideology of the Bund celebrated Yiddish culture, socialist politics, and a territorial solution to the "Jewish Question" in Eastern Europe. But both these ideological currents, stronger in Canada, reinforced a sense of Jewish peoplehood and were resistant to assimilation.[55]

In one sense, Jewish immigrants in the past had it easier. The large numbers of Jewish immigrants at the turn of the last century meant that the majority of the community was immigrant, and that immigrant Jewish culture steeped in Yiddish was the major Jewish culture in the country. But in another sense they had it harder. Jewish culture back then was branded as second-rate, while today Jews and Jewish themes are at the centre of Canadian cultural discourse. This is new. At the time of the mass migration in the early 1900s, the strongly Anglophilic culture of English Canada had little respect for the culture of new immigrants. All immigrants faced varying combinations of occupational discrimination and social prejudice, and Jews were no different. Nevertheless, Jewish immigrants were able to fashion a dynamic communal life, as were many other immigrant groups.[56] They did this all without government grants or the support of departments of multiculturalism. The later genera-tions of Jews could not resist the drift from the immigrants' Jewish life. Drift they did, but not too fast, nor too far. The experience of centuries of migration, the building of new Diaspora communities, and the multi-dimensional nature of Jewish identity helped point the immi-grant communities toward permanence.

While Jewish immigration remains strong, Jews – like other Canadians – have also been moving from Canada to the United States. There are no precise figures, but beginning in the 1970s my impression is that more and more Jewish Canadians have moved south. I have no idea how that compares with numbers of American Jews who have moved north. But my hunch is that by the late 1990s the tide had turned against Canada. Increasing numbers of Canadian Jews are going to American universities for undergraduate and graduate studies. Fewer are returning. Jewish graduates of leading law, medical, and other professional schools are starting their careers in the United States. The North American Free Trade Agreement makes it easier for them, and a green card follows. In addition, as more Canadian and American Jews marry, the economic lures are now likely to pull the couple south. This is a *Yiddishe kop* drain, which, as it increases, deprives Canadian Jewry of valuable talent. As with the general Canadian brain drain, it bears watching.

SPREADING OUT

Canadian Jews are not spread evenly throughout the country, and they are almost exclusively urban. In 1871, almost all Canadian Jews lived in Central and Eastern Canada, 48 per cent in Ontario and 42 per cent

in Quebec, with about 7 per cent in Western Canada. By 1931, as the mass
migration wave came to an end, 80 per cent of Jews were in Ontario and
Quebec and almost 20 per cent out West. Jews quickly moved to the
cities. The proportions living in rural areas declined from one-third in
1871 to only 4 per cent – about 5,500 people – in 1931. These rural proportions were highest in the West, notably in Saskatchewan, where over
one-fifth of Jews were rural.[57]

Jews are the ultimate urbanites. As far back as 1931, almost four-
fifths of Canadian Jews lived in Canada's three largest cities, a ratio that
has remained almost constant ever since. By comparison, that was the
case for only one-third of Canadians in 1991. If we consider the eleven
cities with the largest populations in 1981 and 1991, they accounted for
roughly 94 per cent of the Canadian Jewish population in both census
years. This metropolitan concentration means that Jews are where the
action is. In every city where Jews and other immigrants have arrived,
they have created a cosmopolitan atmosphere not found in cities dominated almost exclusively by Canadians of British or French stock.
Jews can make their presence felt in the cultural, social, political, and
economic domains of North American life in a way that leverages
their relatively small proportion of the population. This explains why
surveys have found that the American public overestimates the Jewish
percentage of the population. (See Appendix II: Demographic
Predictions and Comparisons.)

Commentators on early Canadian Jewish history are often faced
with a dilemma. On the one hand, most immigrants were urban, and
the centre of gravity of Canadian Jewish migration has always been the
biggest metropolises. On the other hand, emphasizing the urban roots
of Canadian Jewry reinforces negative stereotypes. It weakens the claim
that Jews played an early role in all the rugged varieties of the Canadian
experience. The myth of the land has long been a powerful element of
Canada's national character and pioneering image, and Jews want in.
From this perspective, extolling the contributions of the minority of
Jews who were involved in the fur trade, in farming, in rural peddling,
or even as merchants, shopkeepers, or professionals in small-town
Canada meets a strategic need. It sustains an exotic, heroic and more
"Canadian" version of the Jewish experience.

Thus, there are two themes to the pattern of Jewish settlement. The dominant story is that of heavy concentration in Montreal and Toronto, creating a dense, quintessentially urban Jewish community and culture similar to that found in New York and other American cities. The occupational profile and rhythms of Jewish life were urban and industrial. Jews clustered in clearly identified neighbourhoods. In Montreal, this was defined by streets like St.-Laurent ("the Main"), St.-Urbain, or Park Avenue, stretching from Mount Royal and parts of Outremont down to the waterfront. The greatest Jewish concentrations were found in the wards of St.-Louis and Laurier, in which just over half of the population was Jewish in 1931. This is where the immigrant Jews concentrated in the "downtown" area of Montreal, with the wealthier, Anglicized, Canadian-born Jews in the "uptown" areas, such as Westmount.[58]

In Toronto, the area of Eastern European Jewish concentration was The Ward, bounded by Queen, Yonge, and Gerrard streets and University Avenue. Jews eventually moved to Kensington and Spadina to the west. In the 1930s, these concentrations were somewhat less than in Montreal, with less than a third of the area being Jewish. Winnipeg by 1931 was home to over 17,000 Jews, who were concentrated largely in the West End along Selkirk, though less so than in Montreal or Toronto. Winnipeg's Ward Three was the area of early Jewish concentration, with one-fifth of its population Jewish.[59]

These neighbourhoods symbolize the immigrant Jewish experience. They were in many ways recreated shtetls. Yiddish was heard on the streets and seen on signs in shop windows, and Jewish schools and synagogues were everywhere. Jewish butchers, bakers, and grocers supplied Jewish goods to a largely but not exclusively Jewish clientele. These Jews were mainly working-class, though eager to escape upward through commerce or education as the opportunities arose. Among many older Canadian Jews, the "old neighbourhood" remains a fiercely held element of their Jewish identity, even after they have moved out to the suburbs.

Two Montreal Jews meet in the street. "Hello Rosenberg!" says one. Rosenberg replies, "My name is no longer Rosenberg. I

read that people are changing their names to represent their
roots, so I changed my name to C. D. St.-Urbain." His friend:
"C. D. St.-Urbain? I understand the St.-Urbain, because you
used to live on St.-Urbain Street. But why the C. D.?" Rosenberg:
"Easy. Corner Duluth!"

I periodically hear Canadians today, including senior government officials, complaining about "Chinese malls" in Toronto and Vancouver. Almost all the storeowners, personnel, and customers are of Chinese origin, and Chinese is spoken and seen on store signs. The officials fear that these malls will prevent the Chinese from integrating into Canadian life, and will provoke a major backlash against all recent immigrants. But memories are short. These commercial concentrations are not very different from those that existed on New York's Lower East Side, on the Main, or around Kensington market generations ago. Then, it was Yiddish that was ubiquitous, yet the children and grandchildren of the immigrants integrated. Let's not panic yet.

Today there is a distinctive tribal character to Jewish life in Toronto and Montreal. Toronto Jewry is enormously diverse, made of separate entities. There are the old-time Toronto Jews, Russian Jews, Israeli Jews, Sephardi Jews, South African Jews, religious Jews of various persuasions blended with newer sub-communities of ex-Montrealers and other Jewish migrants from small-town Ontario or elsewhere in Canada. All have created formal and informal sub-communities. In Montreal the two major tribes are the Ashkenazim and Sephardim, with the latter gaining in size and clout, with a host of much smaller groupings that parallel those in Toronto. The notion of one mainstream Canadian Jewish community does not hold.

But the second theme, as mentioned above, is that Jews were never exclusively urban, and never tied only to the East. Jewish electoral politics in Canada has traditionally been linked to heavy concentrations of the "Jewish vote" in key ridings in Montreal and Toronto. But the opposite pattern has also been found. From earliest times Jews spread westward through Canada. In 1860, Selim Franklin was the first Jew to be elected successfully to a seat in any Canadian legislative body, not in Ontario or Quebec but in British Columbia. The first Jew to sit in the House of Commons was Henry Nathan in 1871, representing Victoria. Moreover, for three decades through the end of the 1990s, Herb Gray was re-elected repeatedly from his Windsor riding, with no Jewish vote to speak of. British Columbia's Dave Barrett, the first and only Jewish provincial premier, did not rely on any Jewish bloc.

The early movement of Jews to the West was in large part orchestrated by the established community. Many of the leaders in Montreal, faced with the beginnings of mass migration of Russian Jews in the face of the pogroms of 1881, developed plans to direct the migration past Montreal and Toronto. Several early attempts were made to establish Jewish farm colonies on the prairies. After an initial failure, a Jewish farm colony was established in 1888 in Wapella, Saskatchewan, which was reasonably successful (among the new arrivals to Wapella was one Ekiel Bronfman). In the meantime, Montreal Jewish leaders were able to persuade the Baron de Hirsch, a wealthy Jewish philanthropist, and his Jewish Colonization Association to underwrite some Jewish farm settlements in Western Canada. In 1892, the colony of Hirsch was established. With the change in Canadian immigration policy under Laurier in 1896, even more opportunities were available for Jewish migrants to the West. Winnipeg emerged quickly as the third centre for Canadian Jewry. Over a dozen farm colonies and settlements were established on the prairies from 1882 to 1911. None survived past the mid-1940s. Not all Jews west of Winnipeg were farmers; many were traders and peddlers.[60]

Winnipeg deserves special mention in any discussion of the dispersion of the early immigrant Jewish community. Jews there, of Russian origin, were more rooted in Yiddish culture, more progressive in outlook and politics, and more integrated into mainstream social and political life than in Toronto and Montreal. Certainly, a mythology has emerged about the achievements and strength of character of Winnipeg Jews. According to Abraham Arnold, historian of Western Canadian Jewry, there is indeed a "mystique of western Jewry," and Winnipeg acquired a reputation as a new *Yerushalayim*. This mystique could defy any easy explanation. Allan Gotlieb, Winnipeg native and former Canadian ambassador to Washington, was once asked at a social gathering to account for the singular achievements of Winnipeggers,

Jewish and non-Jewish alike. To the query "Why Winnipeg?" he replied, "Why Athens?" Certainly, the geographic isolation incubated a populist Jewish culture, often in opposition to the power centres farther east, that sought "an equal place in Canadian Jewish leadership."[61] Jews have been prominent in the Liberals, Conservatives, and CCF/NDP in Manitoba. Jewish life in the Prairies, particularly given the large number of Ukrainian and other European immigrant groups, most closely approximated Old World conditions. Western Canada had a weaker Anglocentric tradition and weaker established elites. Indeed, one of the features of the history of the Jewish and all ethnic minority communities in Montreal and Toronto was the struggle to overcome a deep-seated anti-Semitism and general prejudice on the part of the entrenched Anglo ruling elites. And in Montreal, Jews had very little early contact with the francophone elites – a third solitude. In the frontier society of Western Canada, Jewish communities did not face those barriers to the same extent.

Toronto and Montreal are the dominant centres of population, with 162,605 and 101,210 Jews respectively in 1991. But more Jews are moving west. A central element of that move is the exodus from Quebec. One of the newest Jewish sub-communities in Toronto consists of ex-Montrealers. And while many Montrealers stop at Toronto, others travel further west, approximating the general flow of the population. In the face of the exodus, one peculiar source of Jewish immigration to Montreal has been Hasidim from New York and elsewhere. These Jews have been attracted by Quebec's support for religious schools, and by a now-dismantled Quebec baby bonus program worth several thousand dollars per child. That migration has helped stabilize Montreal's declining Jewish school-age population.

In 1991, under 2 per cent of Canada's Jewish population, as defined by ethnic origin, lived in Atlantic Canada; 27 per cent in Quebec; 53 per cent in Ontario; and about 18 per cent in the West, with British Columbia at 8 per cent. In fact, it makes more sense to analyze Canada's Jewish population growth by city than by province. Between 1981 and 1991, the greatest Jewish percentage growth took place in Vancouver, at over 30 per cent. In descending order, Ottawa and Toronto grew just over 25 per cent in the same period, Halifax just over 20 per cent, Calgary and Edmonton 18 and 17 per cent, London just under 15 per cent, and Hamilton just over 10 per cent. The largest population declines took place in Windsor at 15 per cent, Winnipeg at 6 per cent, and Montreal at 2 per cent.[62]

It is also important to look at the differences in the proportions of each city comprised by Jews. Clearly, the greater the absolute and relative numbers of Jews, the greater the potential for Jewish life. There is no Canadian equivalent of New York City, teeming with Jews and called "Jew York" by anti-Semites.[63] But in many ways Jews set the tone in Toronto and in English Montreal, in business, the professions, higher education, the media, and culture. So the Jewish presence "feels" greater than the actual numbers, which are modest. Jews made up 4.2 per cent of the Toronto metropolitan population, 3.3 per cent for Montreal, 2.3 per cent for Winnipeg, 1.3 per cent for Ottawa-Hull, and 1 per cent or less for all other Canadian cities, according to the 1991 Census. These numbers mean that Jewish life in Toronto and Montreal has a different dynamic than that in the other Canadian cities.

For all the general talk of a united Canadian Jewry, there are two regional fault lines that divide the community. One is between Toronto and Montreal, nurtured by a Montreal chauvinism that ranges from bagels and smoked meat to a perception of a warmer, tightly knit community. Part of this may be sour grapes in the face of Toronto's tremendous economic and demographic ascendance, as well as overlap with a general stereotype of Toronto as colder, at least in terms of its pre-war Anglo heritage. "Toronto the Good" is not "Toronto the *heimish.*" A 1998 letter to the *Canadian Jewish News* is a lament by a transplanted Montrealer now living in Toronto.

... Did someone say that Jews take on the attributes of their environment? Perhaps they have to.

My wife and I came to Toronto 20 years ago, after she retired from a successful teaching career at McGill University. ...

Knowing only former Montrealers, we tried to get acquainted with Toronto people. To this end we would from time to time invite people we had met, for dinner and a pleasant evening. ...

The invitees were a mix of Jew and gentile. Over the years we thus entertained probably more than 60 or 70 such couples, separately or in a small group. Everyone said they had a lovely dinner, a most enjoyable evening, and left. We never saw one of them again, although one woman did come back to retrieve an umbrella she had left behind.

Now I may be traducing Torontonians, but during our many years in Montreal, whenever we invited people for an evening, everyone, without exception, would sooner or later invite us back, whether for dinner or otherwise. We thus formed many good and lasting friendships that lasted even after we left Montreal.

Does this mean that Montrealers are different from Torontonians, perhaps more warm blooded, perhaps less shy to get close to strangers? The answer is beyond me. More than once I have heard from recently arrived South Africans of the impossibility for them to break into Toronto circles.

Traits like "warmth" are obviously hard to quantify, and as a Montrealer I should resist the temptation to disparage Toronto. On a per capita basis, Montreal outperforms Toronto in terms of Jewish philanthropy and – in my view – the variety and vibrancy of its Jewish institutions. But there are other subtle differences in the character of the two communities. Montreal Jews seem to have a more comfortable, more confident sense of Jewish identity. In the words of Gershon Hundert, a native Torontonian teaching Jewish history at McGill, "The difference has to do with the 'Orangeness' of Toronto. Toronto Jews seemed to act with a certain discretion about their Jewishness, which is not the case in Montreal. In Montreal, Jews had their place in the social landscape."[64] In Toronto, it is a short hop from insecurity to smugness, to compensate for Jewish underachievement. Montreal's place in the social landscape – a "third solitude" – could lead to greater self-confidence. Whatever the case, the Montreal Jewish community for a long time set the standard for Jewish cultural creativity and communal leadership. In the words of historian Frank Bialystock, Toronto's Jews are chronic underachievers, "180,000 people sitting on their ass."[65]

Toronto Jewry has more people, power, and money, all of recent vintage. For whatever reason, Montreal, a declining community, has more *ta'am* (good taste) and *savoir faire.*

LIFE IN THE OUTLYING REGIONS

The second regional fault line in Canadian Jewish life lies between the Centre – Toronto, Ottawa, and Montreal – and the regions, notably other Ontario cities, the West, and Atlantic Canada. The regions have been neglected by the "national" Jewish community, which should be a familiar plaint to Canadians. The presidency of the Canadian Jewish Congress has generally rotated between Toronto and Montreal. The same applied to the CJC conventions, held every three years, until 1998, when the convention was held for the first time in Winnipeg. Toronto and Montreal have large, deeply rooted Jewish communities. They both support a wide array of Jewish communal and cultural institutions, and Jews from these two cities are by many – but not all – measures more "Jewish" than those in other cities, particularly in Western Canada. Intermarriage is lowest in these two cities, while higher further west and in Halifax. Orthodoxy is more vigorous in Montreal and Toronto.

The special texture of Jewish life in smaller cities and towns has been captured in Canadian fiction.[66] The struggles of smaller Jewish communities nourished their own fierce loyalties and positive experiences. Sheldon Maerov, a senior Jewish community worker in Toronto, is a native Albertan who was raised in Calgary and then worked in Edmonton before moving east. He reflects on his Western experiences:

> Everyone knew everyone. And not just in Calgary. When you grew up in Western Canada, you knew everyone from Vancouver to Winnipeg. Between BBYO [B'nai Brith Youth Organization] and Young Judea, you touched a lot of bases, whether you were involved in Jewish life or just on the periphery. We also knew everyone from Saskatchewan, because twice a year there were conventions. In the West there was not this great range, mainly BBYO and Young Judea.

In my time, every kid in Calgary went to the Talmud Torah.
I didn't know a Jewish kid who didn't go to the Talmud
Torah or the Peretz School. It was expected, and assumed.

But Maerov contends that by the next generation things had
changed. His children growing up in Edmonton attended a Jewish
school, but many Jewish children did not, and his children knew non-
Jews in a way he did not. Are any of these sentiments particular to the
West, or do they just reflect the conditions of life in small Jewish communities anywhere? It is not at all clear how or whether Jewish life
in Alberta, or small-town Ontario, or the Maritimes, is a reflection of
each specific region. Maerov suggests one specific characteristic of the
West is distance. "In the West you're isolated. In London or Kingston,
you're a few hours by car from Toronto. In the West, a few hours by car
and you're still in the middle of nowhere. Your world really is much
smaller, and you have to become more self-sufficient."[67]

Jewish identity in Canada varies by region, but in no consistent
pattern. (See Table 5.) On some measures, Jews in Montreal and
Toronto score higher than those from the other areas, on some lower.
For example, Jews from smaller cities in Ontario and cities in Western
Canada are more likely to belong to a synagogue or to a Jewish organization, though less likely to light Sabbath candles. Even the small
Jewish communities of Atlantic Canada contain more Jewish vitality
than is commonly understood. While some communities have been hit
by population declines, the major centre, Halifax, saw its Jewish community actually increase by one-fifth between 1981 and 1991. In the
words of sociologist Sheva Medjuck, "There are out there in all these
scattered centres, active Jewish communities which despite obstacles
are maintaining their Jewish identity and in many cases thriving." In
her survey of Jewish life in Atlantic Canada in the 1970s, 69 per cent
kept some degree of kashrut – often harder to do without local kosher
butchers, 58 per cent reported some form of Sabbath home ritual
observance, 85 per cent attended Passover Seders, and 75 per cent lit
Hanukkah candles.[68] The point is that for those Jews in Atlantic
Canada and other smaller communities, Jewish life does indeed exist

– for those who remain – though it is weakened by a steady drain of younger generations of Jews to larger centres. There, they look for either professional opportunities, or Jewish husbands and wives.

Despite heroic efforts, the long-term prognosis for Jewish life in the smaller cities and towns is bleak. Can this be changed? Perhaps modern technology can come to the rescue. Computers and the Internet can offer on-line educational and cultural programming, and there is already plenty of software in the area of Jewish education. A home computer can try to replace a Jewish school, and video or audio tapes can try to substitute for a Jewish deli or bakery or a large communal rally. But software is not a substitute for a fresh *challah* or the locker room of a JCC. It would seem that for Jews, "life is with people." Still, a virtual Internet Jewish community is better than no Jewish community at all. Recall our earlier warning about prediction. It may still be premature to write off smaller Jewish cities and towns. In any case, Canadian Jewish Congress has as one element of its mandate the provision of services to smaller communities. They may disappear, but they have not been abandoned.

What will happen to Canadian Jewish life if more of the population moves west of the Ontario–Manitoba border? Intermarriage rates suggest that Jews who move out West are less committed to Jewish tradition and less tied to extended Jewish families. Western Canadian Jewish communities do not yet match the quality of Jewish life found back East. Either new waves of Jewish migrants will invigorate Western Canadian Jewish life, or laid-back, West Coast, New Age attitudes, combined with some rugged individualism will dilute the Jewishness of new arrivals. A more practical issue has to do with philanthropy. There is not yet a comparable set of moneyed and committed Jewish families to bankroll the Jewish institutions needed to sustain a vibrant communal life. Some wealthy Western Canadian Jews, like the Belzbergs and Izzy Asper, have made huge contributions, but they represent older generations. The jury is still out on all these issues.

So Canadian Jews are renewing themselves through continuing waves and wavelets of immigration. And the community is also on the move, to Toronto as well as to points west. These immigrants to

Canada are a microcosm of world Jewry, and enhance the pluralism – and yes, the divisions – within Canadian Jewish life. Like Canada, Canadian Jewry must wrestle with issues of immigrant integration, as well as regional differences. What nourishes the community also presents challenges.

4

EARNING A LIVING

From Work to Wealth

"The more property, the more worry ... the more Torah, the more life."

– Pirkei Avot 2:8

"I have been poor and I have been rich. Believe me, honey, rich is better."

– Sophie Tucker

MAKING IT

To borrow the phrase popularized by writer Norman Podhoretz, Jews have "made it" in Canada. And how. Any doubters are welcome to inspect the cars parked outside any YMHA or JCC. Take your pick: Mercedes, BMW, Jaguar, Lexus, Audi, Volvo, Jeep, SUV, or fully loaded minivan. Canadian Jews have exceptionally high levels of education, occupational status, and income. This is not new. Indeed, it is part of a great paradox of modern Jewish life, in North America as well as most other Diaspora communities. Everywhere, Jews have had to contend with legal discrimination and/or popular prejudice. And yet everywhere, from Montreal to Moscow, from Toronto to Tunis, Jews have done well economically.

The roots of Jewish economic achievement in Canada are old and deep. They go back to the earliest periods of Jewish settlement. Even when the masses of Jews were working-class, in the first years of the twentieth century, Jews were still relatively concentrated among the professions and in business. And those who were workers brought with them a drive to succeed, which they passed on to the next generations. Their commitment to the working class was fleeting; all wanted something better for their children. It is not easy to account for this broad-based success, but I will try. Of course, not all Jews are doing well. A fair percentage among immigrants, the elderly, single mothers, and others are struggling below or near the official poverty line. But the central story is that of success.

And in Canada today there is more. Not only are Jewish incomes high; that is true for other Canadian minority groups, like the Japanese. Jews are now statistically overrepresented among the most affluent, the movers and shakers in Canada's elite economic circles. This *is* new. For a long time, conventional wisdom held that even if Jews as a group were doing well educationally and economically, they were still largely shut out from the bastions of Canadian corporate power by a WASP establishment. In his 1965 classic, *The Vertical Mosaic*, sociologist John Porter found that Jews made up less than 1 per cent of the economic elite, far below their population percentage. (The economic elite was defined as comprising the 985 people holding directorships in 170 dominant Canadian corporations.) Moreover, even the few Jews that made it were a group apart: they did not belong to the same clubs or associations, and their philanthropic activities rarely overlapped.[1]

Things improved slowly. Porter's disciple Wallace Clement published a follow-up analysis of the Canadian corporate elite that addressed Jewish representation. Clement studied the origins of 775 directors and senior executives of Canada's top 113 corporations in 1972 and found 32 Jews, or 4 per cent. This was a dramatic increase over Porter's data from the 1950s. But the social isolation persisted. Clement noted that 25 of the 32 stemmed from only six families, involved in family firms often one generation old. Jews were much less visible as directors of banks or insurance companies, 2.4 per cent and 1.2 per cent respectively. So the historic pattern of exclusion of Jews from centres of financial power continued. Most significantly, only two belonged to one of the six exclusive Canadian men's clubs.[2] Wealthy Jews tended to belong to Jewish clubs, like the Montefiore or the Elmridge Golf Club in Montreal. Like Groucho Marx, perhaps they did not want to belong to any club that would have them as a member. More likely they were, or felt, excluded. Though rich, perhaps the source of their wealth set them apart. Historically, Jewish fortunes were made in areas like retail trade or real estate, not the traditional sources of wealth or power of the Canadian establishment at the time.

Other chroniclers of the sagas of the Canadian wealthy documented slow but steady progress. Of the 171 members of the Canadian business establishment identified by Peter C. Newman in 1975 – mainly men of wealth, CEOs and company presidents, as well others who were well connected – about ten, or 6 per cent, were Jews.[3] Even as Porter, Clement, and Newman were documenting the entrenchment of WASP economic power at the expense of Jews and others, change was underway. Many Jews become uncomfortable at any mention of Jewish economic success, thinking it stirs up resentment and anti-Semitism. Maybe it does. But Jewish economic achievements are so striking, and so important to other social and cultural features of Jewish life, that there is no escaping them. It is the foundation for so much else that is related to Jewish cultural and communal development. This is the communal meaning of the rabbinic passage: "If there is no bread, there is no Torah."

FROM EARLY ELITE TO ROOTS IN THE WORKING CLASS

The early Jewish community in Canada before the mass migration of the 1880s was relatively affluent. Moreover, Jews made disproportionate contributions to the economic development of the new country. Jewish immigrants throughout the 1700s tended to be traders and merchants. In the late 1700s, Jewish entrepreneurs and pioneer traders, such as Ezekiel Solomon and Jacob Franks, helped develop commercial trade along the St. Lawrence and Great Lakes routes. By the mid-nineteenth century, the small Jewish community was overwhelmingly upper-crust, and included bankers, merchants, lawyers, and doctors. The Joseph family of Montreal was a case in point. Abraham Joseph helped found the Banque Nationale; Jacob Henry Joseph was a founding partner of the Union Bank and Bank of British North America; Jesse Joseph served as the head of the Montreal Gas Company.[4] To the extent there was a definable economic or corporate elite in Canada at the time, Jews were certainly well represented. They seemed to face little or none of the discrimination which was soon to colour their experience in Canada.

It began to change with the influx of the Eastern European Jews in the late nineteenth century. These Jews were mainly workers or small traders and peddlers. Many were involved in the early union movements as members or organizers. Certainly, their Eastern European experience had made some of them open to socialism and working-class solidarity. The conditions of these immigrant Jews, many of whom found work in the garment industry's sweatshops or doing piecework at home, were exploitative. None other than Mackenzie King, in a series of newspaper articles on the subject, described the hellish conditions. King found that 60-hour work weeks were the norm; one contractor worked his employees 13 hours a day, seven days a week.[5] Often, the Jewish workers were locked in fierce disputes with Jewish employers, who needed to keep labour costs low to sustain any reasonable profit margin in a fledgling industry. The conflict was exacerbated by the cultural gulfs between the Anglicized owners and their Yiddish-speaking workers.

By 1900, some of the major firms were Jewish-owned and subject to fierce strikes. In Montreal in 1912, Jewish workers struck against the entire clothing industry, and while they did not achieve union recognition, they managed to wring concessions in a compromise resolution. A second fierce strike across the garment trade took place in 1916 and 1917, which involved the organizing efforts of the Amalgamated Clothing Workers of America.[6] A different conflict erupted in 1917, when Jewish bakers in Toronto decided to raise the price of their bread to keep pace with inflation due to wartime shortages. Militant Jewish women organized boycotts and at-times-violent protests against the bakeries, while also baking their own bread. In the post-war slump of 1920–22, bread prices were lowered and the dispute faded away, leaving much bitterness in the community.[7] Conflict between Jewish labour and owners persisted into the 1930s, even as the Depression made most workers wary of striking. The International Ladies Garment Workers Union, a product of socialist and Labour Zionist effort and membership, faced a challenge from the communist-inspired Industrial Union of Needle Trades Workers. To meet the communist threat, the mainstream unions entered a militant phase, successfully raising wages. Organizing also continued, with the Toronto Jewish Bakers' Union succeeding in organizing most of the Jewish bakeries in Toronto.[8]

Why did immigrant Jews at the time take to the garment industry? For many, it was the only area for which they had any training. In addition, there were cultural factors that made the needle trade attractive. Jews could expect not to have to work on the Sabbath or major Jewish holidays when working for Jewish employers. They could also expect not to encounter anti-Semitism from Jewish co-workers. Then, as now, Jewish economic activity could be seen as part of a "Jewish sub-economy" linking employers, employees, consumers, and suppliers in one network. This kind of economic network provided some initial opportunities for Jewish immigrants, in the way that other new immigrants found jobs through contacts in their ethnic communities.[9] The common origins also set limits for the friction among workers, and between workers and bosses. Some of the smaller employers led lives not all that different from their employees; in some cases, they lived near each other, and even frequented the same kosher butcher, synagogue, or cultural or fraternal association. Moreover, anti-Semitism at home and abroad served to unite Jews, cutting across gulfs of wealth and social class. Indeed, it was during the turn-of-the-century migrations that we see the beginning of classical economic anti-Semitism appearing in Canada. In 1898, the Montreal Chamber of Commerce for the first time denied an applicant membership explicitly because of his Jewish origin.[10]

Like many ethnic groups, from their earliest days Jews in Canada had a distinctive occupational and industrial profile. Concentrated in cities, they wanted up and out of the working class, at least for their children. They were in the working class, but for the most part never of it. Indeed, throughout the period between 1880 and 1920, as more recent immigrants replenished the Jewish working class, others assumed the lower rungs of the occupational ladder. And within the working class, whether in New York, Montreal, or Toronto, Jews were concentrated in the ranks of skilled as opposed to unskilled labour. We forget that tailors and most of the workers in the garment industry at the time were considered skilled workers.[11]

Census data reveal the working-class character of Canadian Jewry on the eve of the Depression, but also their footholds in the middle class. While figures for Jewish and non-Jewish men are similar, Jewish women had higher rates of paid employment than other women because they were largely urban and not part of farm families. The major differences lay in the choice of occupations and industrial sectors. Close to a third of all Canadians were in primary industries – farming, mining, or logging – compared to just over 1 per cent for Jews. Other differences in occupations were equally pronounced. Jews were far more likely to work as merchants, clerks, skilled, and semi-skilled workers, non-Jews as unskilled workers. Half of Jewish women worked as clerks or in sales, compared to the Canadian figure of 28 per cent.[12]

If we designate "professionals" and all the categories of "proprietors, managers, and officials" as a "capitalist" class – not strictly kosher according to Marxist *halacha*, but convenient – we arrive at a figure for the 1930s of 30 per cent. Then we can say with some confidence that more than two-thirds of the Canadian Jewish population was working-class. This figure is practically identical with that for Canada as a whole. But it would be woefully misleading to equate the Jewish and general class structures in the thirties. There were two crucial differences. For non-Jews, more than half of this "capitalist" class were farmers and only 1 per cent were wholesale and retail merchants; for Jews, the pattern was essentially reversed. Second, within the working class, Jews were more likely to be clerks, salesmen, skilled, and semi-skilled workers, whereas most Canadians were unskilled workers. So the foundations for the rise into the middle class were set as far back as the 1920s and 1930s.

The relative rarity of Jewish unskilled workers can not be explained entirely by Jewish concentration in cities. If we compare the occupational distribution of Jews to Italians, who were also a relatively urban immigrant group in 1931, we still see a different pattern. Close to one-half of Italians were unskilled workers. In other words, the Jewish occupational traits were clearly brought with them from the old country. Unlike Italians, who were largely of peasant or rural stock and became "urban villagers" in North America, Jewish immigrants included large numbers who had lived in cities or towns in Europe.

Jews, like immigrant groups past and present, developed certain economic niches to call their own. In 1931 one-fifth of Canadian Jews and over two-fifths of Jewish immigrant women were working in the textile industry. Jews were twelve times as likely as all Canadians to work in textiles – and twenty-one times as likely to work in the fur industry.[13] But the peculiar occupational characteristics of Jews did not stop at workers' choice of industry. We find as early as 1931 that Jews were more than twice as likely as non-Jews to be lawyers, notaries, physicians, and surgeons. This advantage was reduced substantially, but still persisted, within Canada's largest cities. Jews were also seven times more likely to be working in recreational services, notably as "owners and managers of theatres and theatrical agencies." So here the census confirms the anecdotes about the role of Jews in the fledgling entertainment industry. These patterns have persisted over the decades. By contrast, Jews in 1931 were less likely to be working as public servants and in finance. Indeed, for every one Jew employed in finance, there were six employed in agriculture.[14] That has changed.

Although immigrant Jews and their children were slowly moving up, there was little room for them at the very top. In the 1930s, systematic overt as well as covert anti-Semitism restricted Jewish economic opportunities in senior positions with dominant Canadian corporations. This type of exclusion of Jews was documented by demographer Louis Rosenberg. Under the pen name Watt Hugh McCollum (say it quickly) in his popular booklet *Who Owns Canada?*[15] Rosenberg compiled a list of fifty corporate "big shots" and found not a single Jew among them. Even as Jews began to penetrate slowly into the economic elite in the 1950s and 1960s, they did so only in a few areas. They were still closed out of old-money firms in banking, insurance, and heavy manufacturing.[16] These wealthy Jews were certainly unwelcome in the elite private clubs catering to the old Anglo money in Canada. In addition, qualified Jews faced restrictions in the senior public service, the judiciary, and in senior positions in universities.[17] Jews were a socially insecure group, afraid to rock the boat or to assert demands for equal rights even as they moved up the economic ladder.

ECONOMIC MOBILITY, JEWISH STYLE

Beginning with the post-Second World War economic expansion, Jews in Canada began to leave the working class in droves. Much of the success of these children and grandchildren of immigrants was fuelled by education. Many became professionals, though among the business classes children often inherited the family firm. In the economic boom, Jewish incomes almost immediately rose above the national average. But these high incomes were surprisingly not related to leaving the Jewish economic enclave. For most minorities in North America, moving up has meant moving out and breaking economic ties. Not so for Jews. In one way or another, Jewish "connections" proved valuable in earning a living. Or at least, they certainly were not a liability.

In 1979 I surveyed a sample of Jewish household heads in Montreal and found that 70 per cent were either self-employed or worked for mainly Jewish-owned firms, and 35 per cent had Jews as most or all of their business associates – all without any negative impact on incomes. Jews whose economic activities were wrapped up in the cocoon of Montreal's Jewish sub-economy did as well as other Jews.[18] Moreover, participation in this Jewish sub-economy was as common among third-generation Jews as among immigrants.[19] This contradicts the conventional wisdom according to which economic concentrations are pronounced for immigrants, but decrease for their children and grand-children. I could not pinpoint the attraction of the sub-economy. It was not the fear of anti-Semitism, or the desire to work in an environment more receptive to religious requirements, as would be suggested by historic explanations for such Jewish concentrations. It was not the prospect of higher incomes; their incomes were no higher or lower than incomes of Jews not part of the Jewish sub-economy. So why they did it is difficult to explain. One possibility is simply inertia. Jews born or raised in Montreal may have inherited from their parents, or from their friends, existing networks which they maintained over the years.

This trait is not unique to Montreal. A study by sociologist Jeffrey Reitz found similar patterns in Toronto in the late 1970s. Unlike other minority groups, successful Jews did not abandon Jewish neighbour-hoods; they recreated middle- and upper-middle-class Jewish neigh-bourhoods in the suburbs.[20] Jews had distinctive occupational patterns, similar to those noted by Rosenberg for Canada in 1931. Reitz found that "Jewish men are ... 8 times more likely than other men to work in textile products. They are also 6 times more likely to be physicians, 7.9 times more likely to be lawyers, and 3.5 times more likely to be university teachers. Jewish women are three or four times more likely than other women to work in sales, particularly real estate. Jewish women are also concentrated as social workers (2.7 times more likely), in commercial and fine art (2.3 times) and as lawyers and social scientists."[21] Reitz also found that Jews in Toronto had higher ethnic economic concentrations compared to other groups, and – as in Montreal – that these levels were just as high for third-generation Jews as for immigrants.[22] In most cases, these proportions were even higher than for immigrant Jews.

All this is rather unexpected. Historically, Jews suffered in ghettos. Concentration in neighbourhoods and in certain occupations or industries stemmed from exclusion. These were not auspicious conditions, and Jews fought for full economic equality. Yet in the modern period as economic restrictions have all but disappeared, these concentrations linger, and with no apparent harmful effects.

What is this Jewish sub-economy? One section consists of all the Jewish communal organizations, which employ staff and provide services. A second consists of businesses which provide special "Jewish" services for Jews. The Montreal and Toronto Jewish business directories for the year 2000 list scores of kosher bakeries, butchers, fish markets, caterers, and supermarkets, as well as Judaica gift stores and bookstores. Toronto has thirty-six kosher restaurants or delis – including two Second Cups! A third is the sector where the business networks are Jewish but the products made or sold are not. The rag trade is the historic example. A Montreal Jewish telephone directory called the "Blue Book" listed in its 1998 edition three thousand companies and organizations. These included, for example, twenty computer consultants, twenty-seven photographers, eighty-seven accountants or accounting firms – and the lists are not exhaustive. But the message is clear. "What's the Blue Book's purpose? To help you find, within our community, companies that can supply you with the products or the services that you need."[23] There is an irony here. By urging Jews to patronize their own they are in effect supporting a boycott of majority-group stores. I leave it to historians and moralists to compare this to the "Achat Chez Nous" boycott in Quebec in the 1930s, which urged French Quebeckers to shop at French-owned stores, often at the expense of Jews.

Though the Jewish sub-economy has persisted past the immigrant generation and into the middle class, we no longer think only of Jewish shops clustered along Bathurst Street in Toronto or in the Snowdon area of Montreal. The phenomenon has become more upscale. Jewish lawyers, physicians, dentists, and accountants are often in partnerships or share offices with other Jewish professionals, and will often have more Jewish clients than would be likely by chance. There is no research on possible differences in the ways Jews in the professions or business conduct themselves, with colleagues, clients or patients. But consider the following anecdotal examples.

A Toronto Jewish businessman involved in a high-tech service industry, who has worked for and had dealings with both Jewish and non-Jewish businesses, distinguishes between his personal comfort and business relations. He admits that he feels more comfortable with Jews. He can relate better to them and they to him, particularly in the social interactions that accompany business meetings. But that does not translate into "dollars and cents. I would not be swayed if a person was a Jew, I want to get the best price no matter." Moreover, he has never experienced any direct anti-Semitism. He actually prefers to deal with non-Jews when it comes to prompt payment of bills. And within the Jewish fold, ethnic stereotypes are alive and well. "The Israelis and Moroccans are the worst, they're slow and will try to kill you." He much prefers to deal with (non-Jewish) Lebanese, who "keep their word." So, whatever comfort level drew him to prefer working with Jews, it does not extend to uniform business judgments in favour of all types of Jews.

A successful Jewish lawyer with a prominent "Jewish" firm feels Jewishness intrudes in several ways. He claims that Jews are drawn to law historically because of the affinity with the legalistic nature of the Talmud. (Easy to assert, harder to prove.) There is a distinctive culture in Jewish law firms. For example, in a "WASP" law firm, he says, there will be a lock on the liquor cabinet; in his law firm they lock the supply of cookies. (Jackie Mason would understand.) WASP firms have more decorum; in Jewish firms there is more outspokenness, "more yelling." But wait, there are subcultural differences by region. He believes that Jewish lawyers in Quebec yell more, while those in Ontario will try to "out-WASP the WASPs." Moreover, he feels that Jewish clients prefer Jewish lawyers. On the one hand, they would feel more comfortable confiding in them; on the other, it would be easier to "give them shit." And what of the substance of the law, rather than its style? His view was that the American liberal tradition was not as strong in Canada, despite the record of outstanding progressive lawyers and judges like Rosalie Abella, Alan Borovoy, Maxwell Cohen, Irwin Cotler, Bora Laskin, Clayton Ruby, to name a few. Among the younger Jewish lawyers he meets, financial rewards are looming larger as a motive to practise law. "They can do well."

A doctor who works in a "Jewish" hospital insists that he chose medicine in no way because he is Jewish. Still he recalls that the Jews in his medical class certainly tended to socialize together. The atmosphere in the Jewish hospital is close-knit and friendly, and "when things happen in Israel, people in the hospital want to fly off." And what of the medicine itself? He observes no obvious difference in the medical practice of Jewish physicians versus non-Jews – though Jewish patients tend to be more demanding.

There is likely an effect of referral networks at work here. Jewish doctors, for example, might be more likely to refer patients to other Jewish doctors, people whom they already know. But despite these various sorts of subjective rationalizations, the objective fact remains. Jews in business and the professions, especially in Toronto and Montreal, interact very disproportionately – and in some cases differently – with other Jews.

INTO THE MIDDLE CLASS

Jews are solidly entrenched in the middle class and higher. A few statistics on education, occupation, and income make the case. Among young Jews aged twenty-five to thirty-four in 1991, 55 per cent of the men and 50 per cent of the women had at least a bachelor's degree;

the relevant national Canadian percentages were only 16 per cent for both men and women. Quite a spread. The Jewish rates were the highest of any ethnic group in Canada.[24] The advantage is even more pronounced for advanced degrees, fourfold or higher.[25] This young cohort of Jews is well placed to succeed in the future.

In North America, broad-based Jewish educational achievement of the sort described here marched along with specific outstanding intellectual accomplishments. For example, Jews made up one-half of a list of the top American intellectuals compiled in 1971.[26] Jews comprised between 30 to 40 per cent of American Nobel Prize winners in science and economics through the 1970s, and 20 per cent of the professors in the leading American universities as early as 1975.[27] Since Jews make up roughly 2 per cent of the American population, these figures are impressive. In Canada, the pace of change was slower. Relying on data from the late 1950s and early 1960s, sociologist John Porter described a dismal picture regarding Jewish representation in Canada's intellectual life. He used as a measure membership in Section II of the Royal Society of Canada, dealing with English literature and civilization. Finding only one Jew out of 104, he concluded, "What is striking is the absence of Jews in the higher levels of the intellectual community."[28] Things have improved. While there are no definitive figures, it seems that Jews are highly represented today among Canada's scientific and intellectual elite. One study of the Royal Society of Canada's Section II membership in 1987 identified about 5 per cent as of Jewish background.[29] This marks a significant increase over the 1 per cent found by Porter, and is well above the Jewish share in the population. Still, the percentage is well below the levels found in the United States. It may be that the Royal Society lags behind the openness of actual educational institutions, which are less elitist and more meritocratic. Only 5 per cent of the Royal Society members in 1987 were female, for instance. These figures "raise concerns about the possibility of ethnic, gender, and religious discrimination in a significant Canadian institution."[30] Regardless of the numbers and significance of the Royal Society, Jews are now found as deans, principals, and chancellors at major Canadian universities.

These large Jewish advantages in education are not simply a result of Jews living in cities, where educational levels are higher. Within the populations of Montreal, Toronto, and Vancouver, we find a similar pattern.[31] The proportion of Jews over fifteen who either are in university or have completed at least a bachelor's degree is roughly 40 per cent for Montreal, 50 per cent for Toronto, and 57 per cent in Vancouver. In each case, this is roughly twice the percentage for non-Jews. The differences among the three cities do not reflect different aspirations for educational success. They result from different demographic profiles, notably the higher proportions of aged Jews in Montreal and the younger, more mobile population in Vancouver.

As a result of this high level of education, and other factors, Jews do very well in terms of all other measures of economic achievement. Jews have significantly lower rates of unemployment than non-Jews.[32] Jews also have higher-status occupations. Jokes about Jewish doctors and lawyers are rooted in reality. Jews have retained and expanded their 1931 statistical overrepresentation in law, medicine, and business, as well as in newer fields like university teaching. There has been a steady movement out of small business, wholesale, and retail, and into professional and service occupations. The 1991 Census shows that in each of Canada's three largest cities, Jews are statistically overrepresented in medicine, law, and accounting, as well as human service professions like teaching and social work. And they are statistically underrepresented in manual labour and clerical positions.[33] But we should not push stereotypes too far. In none of these cases do Jews come close to being a majority of the profession.

Professional occupations translate into higher average incomes for Jews. In 1991, for Canadian Jews (defined by religion), 38 per cent lived in households with incomes over $75,000, precisely double the rate for non-Jews. And 22 per cent of Jews lived in households with over $100,000 income, three times the rate for non-Jews. Looking at individual earnings in Montreal, Toronto, and Vancouver, we find that the proportion of Jews earning over $75,000 is three times that for non-Jews. These high incomes translate into other broad measures of wealth. The value of Jewish homes in these cities is also above average.

INTO THE BOARDROOMS

The economic success of Jews is equally pronounced at the level of the economic elite. Today, Jews are among the richest and economically most powerful North Americans, both in sectors which had hitherto been closed and through their traditional family owned firms. In these days of multinational and global economic networks, the old Anglo-Canadian establishment is no longer dominant. Their monopoly power is over. Families like the Bronfmans and, in their day, the Reichmanns represent just the tip of a growing and extremely affluent segment of Jewish society in Canada. Even as these wealthy Jews – and their money – become accepted in Gentile high society, they often retain strong loyalties to and status within the Jewish community. They remember, or are not allowed to forget, their roots. These commitments – often typified by gala fundraising dinners for Israel Bonds or Israeli universities – are routinely chronicled in Canadian Jewish publications.

In the United States it is easy to monitor the ups and downs of Jewish wealth. *Forbes* magazine produces an annual list of the four hundred richest Americans. Wealth is measured in painstaking fashion. While it is fairly easy to estimate wealth based on publicly traded shares, *Forbes* also estimates assets from privately held companies. A detailed study done on the magazine's 1982 list found that Jews comprised 23 per cent of the total list, and 40 per cent of the top forty. Of course, wealth is not identical to corporate power, as reflected in CEOs who make key business decisions but are not among the very wealthiest themselves. A 1986 study found that Jews comprised only 7.4 per cent of the senior executives in America's largest businesses, much less than the 23 per cent range for wealth.[34] Jews are wealthy, but still far from dominant controllers of the levers of corporate power. A rough rule of thumb is that Jews today are found to represent 20 to 25 per cent of the richest Americans but far fewer are top CEOs. And what of Jewish wealth in Canada?[35]

Jewish wealth and economic power in Canada are now substantial. The growth can be traced in books and magazines. The second volume of Peter Newman's *The Canadian Establishment*, "The Acquisitors," focuses on new movers and shakers at the top of Canadian corporate power. Though published in 1981, just six years after Newman's first volume, this study of the newer generation of wealthy Canadians reports a greater presence of Jews. For example, while families like the Belzbergs and Reichmanns get only passing mention in the first volume, by the second their stories are told over many detailed pages. Diane Francis's *Controlling Interest: Who Owns Canada?*, published in 1986, reveals even further penetration of Jews into the Canadian corporate elite. She lists thirty-two "dynasties" of great Canadian family wealth and concentrated corporate power. Of those, ten – a *minyan* – are identifiably Jewish. (Some wealthy Canadian families may have partial Jewish ancestry. The Bentleys of British Columbia are directly descended from Austrian Jews who escaped in 1938 to Canada and then became Anglicans.)[36] Francis's tally certainly compares well with that in the United States.

Different lists, with different procedures, will come up with slightly different numbers. The *Financial Post* published a list of the fifty richest Canadians in January of 1996, in which I estimate that seven of the families were Jewish, or 14 per cent.[37] But this list does not include personal assets and has to rely on guesstimates for privately held firms. The fiftieth place on the *Financial Post* list is nailed down at $145 million. According to one source familiar with the contours of Jewish wealth, a significant number of Jewish families – another five to seven – ought to have been on the list. That would have yielded a figure of roughly 25 per cent, similar to Francis's list, and to the American ratio. The *National Post* published a list of the wealthiest Canadians as of April 2000, and I estimate that approximately ten of the fifty names are Jewish, again not far from the American percentage.[38] Another list published in August 2000 by *Canadian Business* found at least seventeen Jewish entries in a list of the hundred richest Canadians.[39] These Canadian Jewish percentages are actually more impressive than the American, because Canadian Jews comprise only 1.3 per cent of the Canadian population, compared to over 2 per cent in the United States.

It is not clear how the national pattern varies by province, but one study of wealth in Quebec is revealing. The magazine *Affaires Plus* listed the sixty-six largest Quebec fortunes in 1997, and I estimate about one-quarter were Jewish.[40] Their list is based only on valuations of shareholding in public enterprises, so the basis of the estimate is narrow. There are many wealthy Jewish Quebeckers not on this particular list who definitely should be, according to one insider. As a rule, Jews, compared to the older establishment money, have come later to the process of taking companies public. The lowest-ranked valuation on this Quebec list stands at only $11 million – peanuts for some Jewish families. The same insider speculated that perhaps a hundred Jewish families would likely come in above that, were privately held wealth included. However, many children of these wealthy Montreal families have migrated, which may have already changed the picture in Quebec.

So far we have been discussing wealth – where Jews do very well – not corporate power. For that, we need another list compiled by the *Financial Post* for November 1995. Canada's corporate elite is defined by the newspaper as the top executives of Canada's 125 largest companies, as well as CEOs of the fifteen largest subsidiaries, the fifteen largest financial institutions, the largest life, property, and casualty insurers, the country's most profitable companies, and the CEOs of the largest companies in each of Canada's primary industrial sectors. I estimate that sixteen of the two hundred elite members, or 8 per cent, are Jewish, surprisingly similar to the 7.6 per cent figure for American senior executives in 1986. Again, given that Jews are a smaller proportion of the population in Canada than in the United States, the Canadian Jewish figure is impressive.

As in the United States, Jews are more concentrated among the wealthiest Canadians than among CEOs. Nothing new here. It remains easier for Canadian Jews to amass wealth than to rise to the top of a major public corporation. Is this a result of anti-Semitism, or simply an indirect exclusion resulting from an old boys' network? Perhaps residual anti-Semitism plays a role in the publicly traded corporations, and in the more established banking, insurance, or heavy manufacturing firms. Perhaps Jews with business talent prefer to pursue careers in their own private firms, as investors, or in areas such as real estate. The CEOs counted above are drawn from companies which are traded publicly, and thus many large and powerful private Jewish firms are omitted. True, the 8 per cent of Jews on that CEO list is far greater than the Canadian Jewish population percentage. But it is probably not greater than the Jewish proportion among lawyers or accountants or MBAs, which are the better comparison groups.

By the close of the twentieth century, the issue of Jewish access into the Canadian business establishment has become moot. As described in Peter Newman's *Titans*, the new Canadian establishment includes Jews, francophones, other Europeans, and Asians.[41] The old private clubs that safeguarded the old Anglo establishment have become mausoleums, more likely to be boarded up than used as bastions of privilege. Jews are everywhere, and for the most part comfortable. Jewish wealth and influence are now mobilized to assist in all manner of non-Jewish causes. Newman describes as the epitome of this Jewish arrival the role played by investment advisors Ira Gluskin and Gary Scheff in helping launch the Barnes exhibit of French Impressionists at the Art Gallery of Ontario in 1994. Not only did they donate $1 million to help meet the exhibit costs, they also sponsored an exquisite opening-night dinner – not kosher – for over three thousand guests. The menu itself was four pages long. My favourite item is "Buckwheat Blinis with Red Caviar (with sour cream chive)." Blintzes with caviar? That's a long way from the old country. *Toronto Life* described the event as the most lavish black-tie party in Toronto history. According to critic Robert Fulford, "the evening illustrated one of the most significant changes in the history of the city, the absorption of a remarkable number of Jews by the late twentieth century equivalent of the Family Compact."[42]

Jews today are benefactors and board members of universities, hospitals, and cultural organizations in most Canadian cities. They are pleased to mingle with the scions of English and French elite families, and are generally well received. At times, key individuals play a crucial role. The decision of Sandra Kolber, wife of Senator Leo Kolber, to get involved with the Montreal Symphony Orchestra allegedly coincided with an increase in Jewish financial support for the orchestra. People bring their networks with them. Universities also benefit from Jewish largesse. As reported by Peter Newman, the executive team of the University of Toronto's fundraising campaign in the fall of 1997 included at least six Jews among the twenty-seven movers and shakers.[43] The University of Toronto's National Report for 1997 identified seventy-eight non-corporate donors of $100,000, of whom I estimate sixteen were Jewish, and ninety-nine donors of between $25,000 and $99,999, of whom fifteen were Jewish. The McGill campaign of 1995–96 yielded

246 donations of $5000 or above, at least 12 per cent of them from Jewish donors.[44]

But despite this new interaction, the process through which Jews become involved in some mainstream philanthropic endeavours is not random. In the case of medical charities, there are some causes – diseases or hospitals – which become more identified with Jewish involvement than do others. This reflects key roles of Jewish physicians in certain hospitals or of Jewish fundraisers involved with a disease who call upon their networks in the Jewish community. For some medical charity balls or dinners, there will be a large Jewish presence. These events, according to one insider, become de facto Jewish charities, in terms of ambience and the people organizing and attending, even though the events are non-denominational. The segregation is never complete; there are often prominent Gentiles at such largely Jewish affairs, and prominent Jews at those organized by Gentiles. But there is a tangible difference – and everyone knows it. Often, Jewish organizers use these formally non-Jewish charities later to develop contacts – Jewish and non-Jewish – to solicit funds for specific Jewish charities. Of course, there are other gala balls which are exclusively Jewish, such as Israel Bond evenings or Combined Jewish Appeal dinners. They are an important part of the social scene for the organized Jewish community. Yet even here, a pattern has emerged in which prominent non-Jews are featured as honorees. This cross-fertilization expands the scope of Jewish networks into the affluent Gentile sectors.

Jewish philanthropists shoulder a dual burden. They give generously to Centraide in Montreal, the United Way in Toronto, and to their equivalents in every Canadian city. But these services flow disproportionately to non-Jews, who are more likely to require social assistance. Jews also support a parallel set of Jewish welfare institutions, to which far fewer non-Jews contribute, and where the costs are high. Jewish campaigns, notably the annual Federation Appeals, are almost totally funded by Jews alone. Jewish support for mainstream charities and welfare is part of a general socio-political liberalism, which many Jews share, and is considered a simple civic duty. But there is a clear if unstated strategic consideration at work. Jews are grateful to Canada. No matter how successful, they carry a historical baggage of insecurity and marginality. As a result, this mainstream giving offers Jews benefits apart from the intrinsic rewards of good citizenship. It confirms their social acceptance. It persuades non-Jews reciprocally to value, if not support financially, the Jewish community's own welfare charities. Finally, it is a kind of insurance policy. Perhaps ameliorating the conditions of the worst off Canadians will mitigate feelings of resentment towards Jewish wealth.

This business success and philanthropic prominence entrenches Jews in Canadian "high society." Over the years, there has clearly been a blurring of the Jewish–Gentile boundaries with regard to organizing and attending Canada's major fundraising balls, as guests at private dinner parties, or as good friends. This is happening in large part with wives of wealthy Canadians, who often play a key role in this world. In *The Glitter Girls*, her volume about affluent women, society journalist Rosemary Sexton describes Toronto socialite Catherine Nugent: "Nor is Catherine a bigot. She was perhaps the first to give parties bridging the WASP and Jewish worlds. She mingled the Grafsteins, Kofflers, Kayes, and Cohons with the Scriveners, Irvines, and Kilgours, and still does."[45] Of course, some subtle barriers persist. Social functions covered in the society pages of major Canadian newspapers can still be categorized as being basically Jewish or non-Jewish. No one should assume that the Canadian establishment has become blind to ethnicity, race, and religion. As one inside observer told me, "People still know who is who."

They may know, but the boundaries are now permeable. About one-quarter of the Toronto socialites profiled by Sexton are Jewish. Moreover, the affluent lifestyles which wealthy Canadian Jews and non-Jews enjoy – posh condos in Florida, magnificent homes, the fanciest cars, European vacations – are also converging. Being a Jew just matters less, at least to the non-Jewish elite. If so, there is no longer much point in bean-counting the numbers of Jews in the various new establishment lists that Peter Newman provides – for two reasons. First, as the new establishment becomes more diffuse, it becomes increasingly difficult to derive the best list to measure status: it could be wealth, corporate power, philanthropy, or social clout. And second, whatever list one picks, Jews are likely to be well represented. Game over.

JEWISH POVERTY

But the economic picture is not all rosy. A high average level of Jewish income masks the paradox of Jewish poverty. There are some Jews – they would never admit it – for whom the discovery of Jewish poverty is good news. Many who fear anti-Semitism are made insecure by high average incomes and profiles of Jewish wealth, so poor Jews mean that not all Jews are rich exploiters. For some progressive Canadian Jews, Jewish poverty reconnects Jews to other disadvantaged Canadians and serves an ideological function. Indeed, because of the widespread perceptions among Jews and Gentiles alike that all Jews are well off, poor Jews have been called "invisible." How extensive is Jewish poverty? Using data from 1981, one analyst concluded that almost 16 per cent of Jews were poor or near poor; for Canada as a whole the figure was 25 per cent.[46] By 1991 the gap had narrowed. Sixteen per cent of Canadian Jews were still poor or near poor, but the figure for all Canadians was down to 19 per cent. By 1996 the Jewish and non-Jewish poverty rates were each pegged at 17 per cent.

One possible explanation for the lack of any decline in Jewish poverty is that it has become more concentrated among the ever-increasing elderly population. Incomes of retired Jews would not benefit as much from upswings in the general economy, or dual-earning households. Even more surprising was the finding that the poverty rates among the Jewish elderly were higher than among the non-Jewish elderly, at 21 to 17 per cent.[47] (I find all this hard to believe given what else we know about Jewish average incomes. My hunch is that poor and elderly Jews of whom many are immigrants may be under-reporting their income. Many may also own their own homes or condos and have other assets, and manage to make do on a limited annual income.)

In some ways, the Jewish poor resemble the bulk of the Canadian poor, but in others they differ. Like the general poor population, poor Jews are concentrated among the elderly, immigrants, the working poor, and single-parent families. But there is a difference. More Jews are full-time or part-time graduate students, whose incomes are mis-leadingly low. Along with the elderly, the foreign-born make up a larger proportion of the Jewish poor.[48] This is because Jewish poverty is more likely to be a transient, one-generation phenomenon. There are relatively fewer poor Jews whose poverty results from a multi-generational cycle of poverty intersected with chronic unemployment and underemployment, poor education, single parenthood, out-of-wedlock births, homelessness, criminality, drug and alcohol abuse, and dysfunctional or abusive marriages. In other words, there is no "culture of poverty" that conditions the lives of poor Jews. Jewish poverty, like Canadian poverty, also varies by region. Poverty rates are greater in Montreal than in Toronto, 20 per cent to 13 per cent. This reflects the generally worse economic conditions in Montreal, and the higher proportion of Jewish elderly.

Perhaps the distinguishing characteristic for the Jewish poor in Canada is the shadow cast by the very affluence of the community. It is hard enough to be solidly working-class or in the "struggling" Jewish middle class, given the cost of supporting a Jewish lifestyle (see pages 120–23). Even worse to be poor. But with so many affluent Jews, there is an even greater embarrassment, a sense of self-blame and failure. This translates into a reluctance to admit need or to use available Jewish welfare resources. And at the same time, the image of Jewish affluence has tended to bump poverty off the communal agenda. Hence the term "invisible poor."

Some of the pockets of poverty are linked to specific sub-groups of Jews. In a Montreal study of ultra-Orthodox groups, the Belz and Satmar Hasidim in Outremont, as well as a grouping of Yeshiva-oriented Jews further west, I and my colleagues found that 41 per cent, roughly double the rate for Montreal Jews and Montreal as a whole, fell below the poverty line. For these Jews, poverty was a product of three factors. Many married men were not committed to full-time work, but to religious study. Those who were committed lacked the training needed for high-paying employment. Finally, almost all families had many children, which pushed many below the poverty line despite nominally adequate wages.[49] The Hasidic Jewish population is the fastest-growing segment of Canadian Jewry. Despite the threat of growing poverty, it is still a mystery as to how others in these ultra-Orthodox communities are able to afford what seem to be, from the outside, decent – if crowded – homes, some expensive clothing, and large cars for their large families. In the past, philanthropy from a few wealthy patrons who were members or supporters, like the Reichmanns, kept these communities afloat. (In the case of the Tash community of Boisbriand, Quebec, the so-called "Robin Hood rabbi" convicted in 2000 of fraud in Israel allegedly channelled millions of swindled dollars to the community's coffers.) But all that seems no longer sufficient. If ways are not found to integrate their men into the modern labour force, the economic burden on the mainstream Jewish community will increase. It is a paradox that in this "most Jewish" of sub-communities, there is the greatest danger of deep-seated structural poverty that can persist over many generations.

THE MYSTERY OF JEWISH SUCCESS

How to explain the above-average Jewish incomes? One answer is straightforward. High incomes are obviously related to high levels of education. Jews are more educated, hold better-paying jobs, and earn more. Jewish workers are also middle-aged or older and live in Canada's largest cities, both associated with higher incomes. Perhaps they work more hours per week. These factors are easy to measure, and serve to demystify those high Jewish incomes. And some studies have found that these factors alone can "explain" all of the income advantage. Insecure Jews can breathe easier.

Sociologist Jeffrey Reitz conducted a study that found Jewish men in Toronto were earning their higher incomes based largely on their education and occupation. "The high incomes of Jewish men do not appear so high after adjustment for higher qualifications."[50] On the other hand, the study found incomes of Jewish women to be below average, and I have no idea why. Perhaps some Jewish women had husbands with high incomes and less of an incentive to maximize their own earnings. A highly technical national study based on 1991 Census data found that Jews earned about 34 per cent more than the Canadian average, and Jews with a university degree still earned about 18.5 per cent more than similar Canadians. The analysis then took into account the distributions by gender, age, marital status (marriage tends to boost earnings), province of residence, metropolitan or non-metropolitan residence (incomes are higher in large cities), geographic mobility, period of immigration, knowledge of official languages, occupation, industrial sector, weeks worked and full-time versus part-time work. The earnings of Jews were then compared to British-origin Canadians, for similar levels of education. And lo and behold, the extent of the Jewish income advantage disappeared.[51]

But other studies reach different conclusions. They have found that education, occupation, and other background variables – "the usual suspects" – could not fully explain Jewish income advantages. Sociologist Peter Li's detailed study based on the 1981 Census found Jews earned $3,230 above average – quite a bit in those days – even after controlling for the usual background factors. This was like an unexplained bonus for being Jewish. Not all minority groups fared well. For example, blacks and Chinese earned $1,626 and $821 less than might be expected based on their backgrounds, a net penalty.[52]

Studies using the data from the 1986 Census found similar patterns. One found only 40 per cent of the income advantage of Jewish men could be accounted for by these other socio-demographic factors.[53] Of course that left 60 per cent unexplained. Another found that a gross income advantage of Jewish men of roughly $11,000 was only reduced to about $7,000 or $9,000 when other background variables were considered.[54] Most recently, another study by Peter Li, using 1991 Census data, found that Jewish earnings from employment were almost $5,400 above the average after taking into account Jewish educational, occupational, and other beneficial characteristics. Still a large unexplained income advantage for Jews.[55]

These higher Jewish incomes are actually not that mysterious. Perhaps Jews work "harder" if not longer because of a fear of real or latent anti-Semitism or because of the need to earn more to support a Jewish lifestyle as I shall describe below. Jews drink less, and so their productivity may be higher. Maybe Jews have better interpersonal skills – play golf or squash, tell better jokes – which can translate into higher incomes. Most important, they may work "better," as a result of attending better schools. Li's original study also found that Jewish incomes increased more per extra year of schooling than was the case for other groups.[56] This is another way to explain the apparent "income bonus" for Jews. Jews in Canada have been graduating from higher-quality (at least by reputation) Canadian universities, such as McGill or the University of Toronto, since that is where most Jews live. Their credentials may be worth more on the job market. It is also possible that Jews may have been doing better academically at these presumably demanding universities than other Canadians. If this is true, then they may actually have been learning more, over and above the value – perhaps inflated – of their degree. So simply comparing Jewish and non-Jewish university graduates, as these studies do, might be misleading. Canadian census data treat every degree and every year of schooling at every level as equivalent. They also offer no evidence about grade point averages. If Jews were either learning more or impressing employers, both could translate into better jobs, better career trajectories, and more income. Finally, it may be that Jews are able to mobilize valuable social networks – contacts and connections – which also lead to higher incomes.

Despite their differences, all these studies agree on the important role of higher levels of education in explaining the high Jewish average incomes. So it is logical to focus on Jewish educational levels as a foundation for their general economic success. Consider first the remarkable record of Jewish educational achievement: more years of schooling at more-demanding schools. We know from Chapter One that Jews in North America have above-average IQs, which likely contribute to the academic success of Canadian Jewish children. Intelligence may also affect job performance, which could translate into higher incomes. Innovations by successful entrepreneurs are also a product of intelligence.

CULTURE AND SOCIAL STRUCTURE

Why do Jews do well in school? Leaving aside issues of intelligence, we can identify both cultural and social explanations. One view has it that traditional Judaic culture, with its emphasis on the value of learning and education, somehow – the exact route is not specified – leads to success in secular education.[57] Accordingly, the importance attached to the rabbi – who is a teacher and not a priest – and to the mastery of the Talmud somehow extends to secular subjects in the modern period. There are even deeper cultural explanations. Elements of Jewish theology and religious organization allegedly play a role in leading to independent thinking. The non-hierarchical nature of organized Judaism does not stifle individual creativity. Jews have no Pope. While Orthodox Jews obey a uniform *halacha*, they also know that "Every Jew makes his own Sabbath." This anti-hierarchical tradition is allegedly manifested in Jewish child-rearing patterns which are more child-centred and less authoritarian, and which pave the way for independent thinking, problem solving, and school achievement.

In traditional Jewish communities, learning is the basis for Jewish religious authority and communal status. For a people with no state and no armies, power is intellectual, as befits the "people of the book." In theory at least, the wealthy defer to the rabbis. Every Jewish male can become a Torah scholar and write a commentary of his own. Another argument linking Judaic learning with secular education focuses on the rational-legal basis of Talmudic argumentation. The rabbinic tradition, epitomized by the Talmud, inculcates a reverence and aptitude for logical debate which is conducive to rational thought and planning. All these are important middle-class values with alleged payoffs in the physics or history classroom, and the workplace.

This upbeat and instrumental portrait of Judaic culture is often contrasted with Catholicism, which is perceived as an excessively hierarchical religion. It allows no room for questioning the fallibility of the Pope, of Catholic doctrine, or even the local priest, and as a result does not inculcate the spirit of independent inquiry needed for secular success. Judaism has no single dominant denomination. Even within Orthodoxy, rabbinic schools have routinely clashed over interpretations of the Torah, dating back over two millennia to the polarized camps of Hillel and Shammai, the Perry Mason and Hamilton Berger of Talmudic jurisprudence. These kinds of arguments which link Judaism to independent thinking do not only explain Jewish educational success. They also account for Jewish economic innovation, in the scrap business, the needle trade, show business, retailing of all sorts, or real estate and development. The denigration of the economic value of Catholicism dates back to 1905 and the work of Max Weber. Great Britain and the Netherlands were prominent in the development of modern capitalist economies. The spirit of capitalism was at root nourished by Protestantism, though Weber's fellow German social theorist Werner Sombart suggested that Judaism also played a key role. Sombart noted that Jews were early pioneers in the use of finance, of credit, and of international trade and commerce though their diasporic connections. But no one had a good word for Catholicism, which purportedly stifled individual initiative and was slow to nurture capitalist economies.[58]

Before we return to the Jews, a digression of good cheer for Catholics. For some decades, the average income of American Catholics has exceeded that of white Protestants. Whatever the alleged impediments associated with Catholicism, they are gone. Indeed, those Catholics with more Catholic schooling are even more advantaged, compared to other Catholics and to Protestants.[59] More recent studies have found that students in Catholic private schools in the United States were doing better than comparable students in public schools.[60] Maybe those alleged Catholic values of discipline and respect for authority are not so inimical to success after all. Canadian data from the 1991 Census also confirm the Catholic resurgence. Largely Catholic ethnic groups, like the Italians and the Poles, have 18 or and 19 per cent among their Canadian-born who have some post-secondary education. This is higher than largely Protestant groups, such as the British with 16 per cent, and the Dutch and the Germans each at 13 per cent.[61] And of course, the Quiet Revolution in Quebec also raised Catholic educational attainment.

Now back to the Jews. The cultural arguments for Jewish success are appealing, and they make Jews feel good. If true, they underscore a paradox. They postulate a link between mastering religious texts and mastering scientific studies or doing well in school or in the job market. Jewish material success in the modern world owes much to values and traditions rooted in a pre-modern, pre-Western, pre-industrial, pre-secular, and pre-capitalist world. Historically, the relation between education and religiosity was inverse for Jews. In Europe and North America, Reform Jews were more likely to have more education and higher incomes. At the other end of the spectrum, Hasidic Jews have low levels of secular education and low incomes, as we have noted.[62] To be sure, the relation is becoming more nuanced. Modern Orthodox Jews have clearly begun to succeed in educational and occupational endeavours; there are knitted *yarmulkas* all over Ivy League campuses as well as McGill and the University of Toronto. And the example of the Reichmann family indicates that enormous economic success can be reconciled with devotion to Orthodoxy.

The harsh fact is still that the basis of religious Jewish education differs from that of scientific Western thought. In the traditional Judaic religious system, the truth, or rather the Truth, is known. Knowledge is deductive, created by applying the Torah's truth and basic laws and principles to specific cases. Rabbis and schools of Judaic interpretation can argue about middle-range issues, but generally not about the basics of the faith. Too much independence and questioning can lead to excommunication, as Spinoza discovered. In the Western scientific tradition, by contrast, the truth is never known. Theories are always being overturned. Knowledge is inductive, building from experiment to experiment, getting closer to – but never attaining – a final truth. There is no built-in reverence for the authority of the ancients; the new takes precedence over the old. So, while learning is valued in both traditional Judaism and modern society, the types of learning would seem initially to be diametrically opposed.[63] I am not persuaded by the cultural arguments. The Jews who are most immersed in traditional Judaic texts are not the highest achievers in secular education. In fact, a rabbinic dictum warns Jews not to study religious texts "in order to receive a prize" whether in this world or the next. The rewards are supposedly intrinsic to the act of study.

Another set of arguments for Jewish educational and occupational success is rooted in social structure. This view holds that the success stems from the social experience of Jews, and not from Judaic culture. European Jews were involved in trade and commerce in villages, towns, and cities. This was also comparatively the case for Jews from North Africa and the Middle East. They did this in part due to preference, and in part because they were excluded from owning land, or from certain craft guilds. They were used to money, credit, merchandising. They had a long experience in the Diaspora, often as a "middleman minority" linking other competing national or ethnic groups, holding on to specific trading niches. All this made them well suited for success in urban North America. Perhaps the insecurity of minority status also forced Jews to work harder; they had to be better than the *Goyim*. It also made them used to taking the sorts of risks that entrepreneurs have to take. Features of the early Jewish migrations also played a role. Jewish immigrant families were historically smaller, which permitted a more nurturing environment, and led to more material and emotional resources for each child. The early generations of Jews in Canada mainly immigrated to stay, fleeing second-class status or persecution, so they had to make good in North America and invest in the future success of their children. They also came as families, or sent home for spouses, which created a relatively stable home environment. This, too, led to greater efforts for academic success for the children.[64]

Social structural arguments are also paradoxical. They suggest that out of adversity, out of minority status, out of persecution and migration, have come the elements of contemporary educational and economic success. Being prevented from owning land in parts of Europe or having to study harder to overcome anti-Jewish quotas in the Canadian past would thereby lead to higher achievement today. Pushed to an extreme, this kind of vulgar neo-Darwinism implies that Jews owe a debt of thanks to anti-Semites past and present. Luckily, we do not have to push the argument to that extreme, and can still recognize the kernel of truth in the structural position.

In any case most sophisticated social structural arguments would not claim that Jewish cultural values play no role in Jewish economic achievement. It is just that these alleged Jewish values are not uniquely Judaic. Much has been made about similar so-called Asian values and their link to educational success.[65] The energy and work ethic of Asian immigrants – East Asians, South Asians, and West Asians – indeed remind me of the earlier generation of Jewish immigrants. And for some time Asian students have been bumping Jewish students off the top high school and university honour rolls. Hard-working and supportive parents committed to the welfare of their children, and a long-standing religio-cultural literary tradition which values learning, will yield positive outcomes for Jews – and anyone else.

There is no definitive answer that can account for Jewish educational and occupational success, and certainly no conclusive Canadian research on the question. Wherever Jews happen to be, in Europe, the Americas, as well as North Africa and the Middle East – their education, earnings, and social position on average have been and are far higher than that of their non-Jewish neighbours. Canada is no exception.

CONSEQUENCES OF AFFLUENCE

These high incomes and related wealth support Jewish communal life. They are the basis for funding the rather large network of organizations that make up the Jewish polity – a kind of "public sector" for the Jewish community and sub-economy – which includes the Canadian Jewish Congress, B'nai Brith, and the federations, as well as synagogues, Jewish schools, and specialized social and cultural agencies. These organizations could not thrive to the same extent in a low-income community. It is ironic that the affluence which can seduce individual Jews away from their heritage is also indispensable for its preservation. The foundation of all this is a set of "big givers" who can be tapped to provide the bulk of the funding. But there is more. The public sector of the Jewish sub-economy is a form of income redistribution within the Jewish community. These organizations generate employment for a large variety of Jewish (and non-Jewish) communal workers. Jewish teachers, rabbis, social workers, administrators, youth organizers, librarians, researchers, planners, and clerical staff occupy paid positions. Financial aid is available for help with school or camp fees, and there are grants to the Jewish poor or to Jewish immigrants administered by the various agencies. About 80 to 90 per cent of the total amount contributed to the annual Jewish Appeal comes from 10 to 20 per cent of the donors. This is an effective form of progressive, voluntary taxation and subsequent redistribution.

Jewish affluence also sustains Jewish life in a more personal way. It helps meet the high cost of "living Jewishly." For those Canadian Jews who seek to live a comprehensive Jewish life, the costs can be crushing. A committed middle-class Jewish family often pays for private Jewish schooling, potentially lavish bar or bat mitzvah celebrations for the children, occasional trips to Israel, Jewish summer camps, membership in a synagogue and other Jewish organizations, and an added premium for the cost of kosher food. These expenses are not luxuries, but costs

related to living a complete Jewish family life. Here are some rough estimates for a middle-class Jewish family of four, drawn from my own
experiences and informal conversations. Some items are annual, and
some reflect one-time expenses. Some are eligible for tax deductions as
charitable donations. The amounts reflect annual averages from communities across Canada; the aim is to provide an "order of magnitude"
rather than a precise amount. Brace yourself.

1. Annual synagogue membership and/or purchase of High Holiday
    seats: $750 to $1,500.
2. Jewish schooling for two children of elementary-school age, a blend
    of full day-school tuition and the less expensive afternoon school
    option: $5,000 (day schools can cost between $4,000 and over
    $10,000 per child).
3. Donations to the Combined Jewish Appeal and other Jewish com-
    munal and Israel-related charities: $1,000.
4. Membership in a YMHA or Community Centre: $500 to $750.
5. Premium for keeping kosher, mainly the cost of kosher meat: $600
    to $1,000 (this ignores the cost of purchasing two sets of daily and
    two sets of Passover dishes).
6. Costs when a child becomes a bar or bat mitzvah can be stagger-
    ing. These include paying for lessons, entertaining one hundred to
    three hundred people at a reception. This can mean renting a hall,
    printing and mailing invitations, ordering flowers, hiring a band
    or deejay, and last but not least, providing the food. The food
    usually consists of hors d'oeuvres, a main course, a range of desserts
    or a sweet table, and an open bar (cash bars are unheard of at
    Jewish affairs, because they are tacky and because Jews are moder-
    ate drinkers). Many celebrations include more than one meal or
    party. There is a kiddush after synagogue Saturday morning, a
    Saturday evening party, and sometimes a lavish brunch on Sunday
    morning for the out-of-town guests, close friends, and relatives.
    Such affairs also yield an income of sorts, in that most guests will
    bring generous gifts, usually cheques, to the bar or bat mitzvah. This
    income remains in the family. But the net cost of a modest simcha,
    or celebration, can easily run from $4,000 to $15,000.

7. Trips to Israel for the children and the parents. Such trips are often taken in conjunction with Jewish school or youth programs, or as part of bar and bat mitzvahs, or as family vacations, or special missions to Israel organized by the community. Depending on the length of the trip, they can range between $2,500 and $4,500 per person.

8. Jewish summer camps are part of Jewish life for many families. These camps range from lower-cost "Zionist movement" camps, religious camps, and Jewish community camps, to expensive private camps in Canada or the United States with mainly Jewish campers. Costs for a full summer can range from $2,500 to $7,000 per child.

No point in adding up these numbers. It is too painful. These amounts are often beyond the reach of hard-pressed middle-class Jewish families, burdened with all the other expenses associated with housing, feeding, and raising children. The Jewish communal agencies try to make them affordable for those struggling middle-class families, which often earn too much to qualify for significant financial aid. The costs are certainly beyond the means of Jewish single-parent families and those with low income. Interestingly, almost all of these costs are related in one way or another to raising and socializing the children. This is not selfish spending by adults on their own pastimes and pleasures. Middle-class Jewish parents will routinely cut corners on their own personal spending to help pay for these other "Jewish" expenses.

There is more. Apart from these "necessities" of Jewish life, there are a host of expenditures which reflect Jewish "conspicuous consumption" and add to the struggle to "keep up with the Cohens." There is a crass materialism, perhaps reflecting the nouveau riche syndrome, in some of the opulent homes and lifestyles found in the more affluent Jewish neighbourhoods. There are no definitive studies; what follows are largely impressions. But there is clearly a Jewish upper-middle-class sub-culture. It is marked by upscale cars, designer clothes and jewellery, fancy vacations, luxury condos down south and/or a house in the country, elite health clubs and spas, high-priced summer camps, and *objets d'art*, including works by Israeli or Jewish artists. And when these affluent Jews host family *simchas*, the costs can go through the roof.

These families, whose wealth comes in equal measure from successful businesses or careers in law, medicine, dentistry, and accounting, exert
strong pressures on the less affluent but still middle-class members of
the Jewish community – including professors like me! These are not evil,
or ignorant, people. Many contribute generous amounts of time and
money to worthwhile Jewish and non-Jewish causes. They include many
donors who sustain the organized Jewish community. They care deeply
for their children and families. But they do set a tone which provides
fodder for satirists, as well as angst for those struggling to keep up. The
combination of wealth and a presumed tendency among Jewish families to spoil their children can be a potent mix.

*The son of a wealthy Jewish matron is being carried by the
chauffeur from his mother's mansion into her car. A passerby
sees this and asks worriedly, "I'm sorry, is your son unable to
walk?" The mother replies, "Of course he can, but thank God
he doesn't have to."*

For some nouveau riche Jews, it is easy to blur the lines between
class and crass. There is a perception that Jewish wealth is spent too
lavishly, while old WASP money is the epitome of refined understate-
ment. On the contrary, as several of the high-society families featured
in Rosemary Sexton's *The Glitter Girls* demonstrate, Jewish American
Princes and Princesses need not be Jewish. And yet ... and yet.... The
description of the bar mitzvahs of Dale Lastman in 1970 and his brother
Blayne in 1975, sons of Toronto Mayor Mel Lastman and his wife,
Marilyn, reads like something penned by Mordecai Richler and delivered by Joan Rivers.

For Dale's bar mitzvah, the family rented out the entire convention
floor of the Royal York Hotel – nine large rooms – and one thousand
guests were invited. As Rosemary Sexton describes the event: "Marilyn
made Dale King for a Day. A moonlighting CBC television crew built
a stage fit for a Broadway show. Constructed for King Dale's court was a
throne (a red velvet upholstered throne-like chair that Marilyn borrowed from a relative of a friend who was a monsignor in the Catholic
church)." As for the tablecloths, "Draped over the top of the royal-blue,

floor length tablecloths were shiny Mylar overlays made with fourteen carat gold thread. Mylar was not sold then in Canada, says Marilyn, so she brought it in from New York."[66] The good news here is that Dale managed to grow up reasonably unscathed; he has become a top securities lawyer in Toronto, as well as CEO of the prestigious law firm of Goodman, Phillips, and Vineberg.[67] For the bar mitzvah of son Blayne in 1975, according to Sexton, "$25,000 of orchids were flown in." For Blayne's wedding thirteen years later, which allegedly cost $150,000, seven hundred guests partook of a 230-kilogram cake shaped like a flying saucer, and which contained 59 smaller cakes inside.

Such ultra-lavish affairs may not be typical even of affluent Jews. But a more representative portrait of the "lifestyles of the Jewish rich and famous" can be gleaned from the glossy upscale magazine entitled, appropriately enough, *Lifestyles*. The bimonthly magazine is published out of Toronto in a Canadian and American edition and aimed at affluent Jews in New York, California, South Florida, and Canada. (If you've never seen it, you know where you stand.) A typical issue contains ads for Louis Vuitton, BMW, Mercedes Benz, Porsche, Jaguar, Rolls-Royce, Waterford crystal, Wedgwood china, Cartier watches, Rosenthal tableware, Armani clothes. . . . You get the picture. The magazine is available by subscription only. *Lifestyles* profiles successful Jews in business, the arts, politics, entertainment, or Jewish communal leadership, from Elie Wiesel and (Israeli politician) Avram Burg to Bette Midler and Steven Spielberg. The Canadian issue profiles Canadians as well, like theatre entrepreneur David Mirvish, filmmaker Robert Lantos, or McDonald's Senior Chairman George Cohon and his wife Susan. Apart from the stories, the magazine features society reports and photos of black-tie Jewish fundraising events, often featuring Jewish jet-setters raising funds for indeed very worthwhile causes, as well as weddings and bar or bat mitzvahs.

It is too easy for academic analysts, or satirists, to dismiss this kind of magazine, and the lavish lifestyle it describes and idealizes. The magazine is not simply glitz. It seeks to build a bridge between affluence and Jewish achievement, whether in business, the arts, scholarship, or philanthropy. Perhaps critics are secretly jealous, or resentful. Some people would like to think that this wealthier group of Jews is thoroughly distinct from the more heart-warming Jewish prototypes: the dedicated physician, the civil-rights lawyer, the school teacher or professor, the Nobel-bound scientific researcher, the artist or poet or writer, the rabbi or Judaic scholar, the social worker, the therapist. This is wishful thinking. There are personal, familial, social, and cultural links which bind these various Jewish lifestyle communities to each other. The enemy – if there is one – is us.

5

THE BONDS
OF INTIMACY

Jewish Families and Relationships

"Honour thy father and thy mother.... Thou shall not commit adultery."

— Exodus 20: 12, 14

"Now take my wife ... please!"

— Henny Youngman

COMPETING IMAGES

Family, sex, gender, marriage, and generational issues are the emotional battlegrounds of modern Jewish life. Laughter and tears, joy and heartache, gratification and guilt, respect and resentment are the weapons of choice. These issues frame a fundamental contradiction. As a highly educated, urban, and cosmopolitan group, North American Jews are at the frontier of the newest trends of family life and interpersonal relations. But as a religious community with a deep sense of history, reverence for tradition, and memories of life in the old country, many Jews support traditional, conservative approaches to these issues. Some Jews solve the problem by choosing one or the other. Hasidic families and radical feminist/egalitarian families each chart their own very different Jewish courses. This range of Jewish lifestyles, from the most traditional to the avant-garde, reflects the different cultures of different groups of Jews. It is both a source of conflict and an adaptive strength. Many Jews – like me – try to integrate both competing perspectives into their personal lives and fashion a workable synthesis. It can be fulfilling as well as draining.[1]

The Jewish family is popularly thought to be, in the words of historian Paula Hyman, "warm, supportive, and ever nurturing." Not only Jews hold this somewhat idealized view. Abbé Henri Grégoire, supporter of Jewish emancipation at the time of the French revolution, wrote in a famous 1789 essay: "They [Jews] have placed strong barriers against libertinism. Nothing is more rare among them than adultery; their marital union is truly edifying; they make good spouses and good parents."[2] Linked to such views are popular stereotypes that Jewish men make good husbands, since they do not drink or beat their wives, and that Jewish mothers are devoted to their children.

Why should we expect Jewish family life to differ from that of Italian-Canadian or Chinese-Canadian or Christian families? Surely, every ethnic or religious group cherishes families and so-called family values. No group openly values adultery, promiscuity, child abuse, or the neglect of the elderly. The fact that Jews think their family ties are special is not proof. One difference is the role of the Jewish family in the peculiar struggle for Jewish continuity, which has few parallels among other Canadian groups. The family replenishes the supply of Jews, and socializes children into Jewish life and community. Any weakening in the family, and Jewish survival is threatened. Trends that might stem that generational flow – fewer marriages, more familial abuse, increasing divorce rates, falling fertility rates, increasing homosexuality, and of course, increasing rates of mixed marriage – are not just potentially problematic for those directly involved. They are also viewed with alarm by Jewish survivalists. Indeed, it is hard to find a Jewish communal leader whose family is untouched by mixed marriage.

Imagine an idealized Jewish family: a loving, supportive Jewish husband and Jewish wife, with scant premarital and no extramarital sex, no fighting, with a goodly number of children, and perhaps an aged parent living in the home. The intergenerational bonds among grandparents, parents, and children are warm and supportive, with parents *schepping naches*, or drawing parental satisfaction, from their high achieving, drug-free, soon-to-be-happily-married children, while also doting on their beloved aging *bubbies and zaidies*. Where are such families today?

And where were they in the past? Revisionism has come to Tevye and Goldie. Improved historical research has challenged the saccharine images of the old country and the immigrant generation. Life among the Jewish families in the old country, or among the immigrants in earlier periods, was not always idyllic and harmonious. Even in Eastern Europe, marital breakup through divorce or desertion and generational strife were far more common than assumed.[3] The letters to the editor of New York's Yiddish newspaper *The Forward* were full of tales of family conflict among the early waves of Eastern European immigrants.[4] Jewish family life today – perception and reality – is a blend of myths, stereotypes, and reality that co-exist in an uneasy equilibrium.

The competing images of Jewish women offer one example of this unease. A blend of the *balabusteh*, or efficient homemaker, and the *Yiddishe mameh* suggests a pre-feminist image of a devoted wife, mother, and grandmother. She is prepared to sacrifice her all for the family, cooking gargantuan helpings of food, doling out chicken soup, and demanding nothing for herself. To wit: *How many Jewish grandmothers does it take to change a light bulb? . . . Never mind, I'm fine, I'll sit in the dark.* Notice the manipulative undertone of self-sacrifice – another time-worn stereotype – that lurks beneath the seeming dedication. So the same Jewish mother image can be, and is, transformed into a suffocating and overprotective mother. In contrast, the notorious Jewish American Princess, another current image, is egocentric, spoiled at birth by protective parents. She grows up to be an emasculating, materialistic woman, single or married, whose self-centred preoccupations are mainly her clothing and her looks. This latent misogyny is typified by JAP jokes. *What does a JAP make for dinner? . . . Reservations.*[5]

With the move towards women's equality, new images compete with these earlier ones. Women who combine successful professional careers with family obligations are very different from the JAP stereotype. They make other Jewish women wonder why they, too, cannot be over-achievers. Most Jewish women have to struggle while the new Jewish superwoman seems to be having it all, from professional success to designer homes to designer children, who in turn manage to juggle schoolwork, sports, and music so effortlessly. Sustained by a support staff of maids, babysitters, cleaning ladies, as well as a supportive husband, parents, and in-laws, they rush from rewarding professional work to fitness classes to volunteer board meetings, barely raising a sweat. Feh!

The stereotypes surrounding Jewish men are less pronounced, perhaps because the comics and writers who have developed these images have been mainly men. Accordingly, Jewish men inevitably make good husbands, since they are good providers, do not drink or beat their wives, and do not fool around, or divorce. At the same time, they may also be henpecked or unlucky or plain wimps. While the *yenta*, or gossip, is inevitably feminine, the *schlemiel* and the *schlemazzel* (the former spills soup on the latter) are invariably masculine.

Stereotypes about sexuality also loom large. Accordingly Jewish women, despite the erotic legacy of the Song of Songs and of the myth of the Jewess as an exotic temptress, are generally uninterested in sex. That is, after they are married. Beforehand, if it was ever true that Jewish girls "didn't do it," they do now. Monica Lewinsky has laid that to rest. And indeed, non-Orthodox Jewish women are highly unlikely to be virgins at marriage. Many (I am told) are sexually precocious. On the other hand, Jewish men are known more for intellectual or financial success than for sexual endowment or prowess. Jewish men increas-ingly seek out *shiksas* who will be both sexually exciting – these men clearly need all the help they can get – and materially less demanding after a marriage. Monica Lewinsky apparently subscribed to this wimpish stereotype of Jewish men, as seen in her joke recorded on the Linda Tripp tapes: *What happens to a Jewish man with an erection who walks into a wall? . . . He breaks his nose.*

As we look at intimacy and Canadian Jewish family life, we are not concerned with the stereotypic images that are nurtured by traditional sources or modern writers or entertainers. Jewish family and personal relations at present, particularly for those who are not among the ultra-Orthodox, are caught between two competing forces. Modernity, on the one hand, tugs Jews towards gender equality in all spheres, families that are smaller and decidedly nuclear rather than extended, and greater possibility of marital breakup, of homosexuality, and of mixed marriage. It is a force that seems to threaten the Jewish future. Tradition tugs in the opposite direction. Somehow a balance is struck.

WOMEN AND JUDAISM

To understand Jewish intimacy and family life, we begin with the changing status of women in the religious and economic spheres. The move to equality for Jewish women – like all women – helps to set the context for the other interpersonal challenges. The Jewish religious tradition as inherited from the past is sexist. So what else is new? On this issue, traditional Orthodox Judaism is no different from traditional Christianity – both Catholicism and Protestantism – and Islam. Some examples: The morning prayers recited by Jewish males include the infamous thanks to God that He – and It is definitely a He – did not make the supplicant a woman. During menstruation women are considered unclean. Only men are counted in the *minyan*, and only men can lead prayer services or read from the Torah or serve as rabbis. These are all precepts of Orthodox Judaism, and are not followed rigorously by the other denominations. This deep-rooted gender inequality has spawned a number of hostile reactions among contemporary Jewish women, who have challenged the confining traditional roles of wife, mother, and caregiver. But for the most part the reactions have led not to a rupture, but to a seeking of higher status for women within families and within Judaism and all other aspects of communal life.

Consider first women and organized religion. Reform Judaism, Reconstructionism, and the New Age Jewish Renewal movement have embraced gender equality in all areas. Conservative Judaism is moving in that direction, albeit with some turmoil. The biggest dilemma is faced by the Orthodox, mainly the Modern Orthodox. Many Orthodox women are versed in the doctrines of feminism and embrace principles of equality. Some have sought to soften the harsh legacy of the

Orthodox tradition, or even reinterpret its essence. They have a tough assignment. There are maverick Orthodox egalitarian *minyans* and *chavurot* (small, intimate, informal congregations), like the Narayever Synagogue in Toronto, that buck the rightward drift of Orthodoxy. But this option will not satisfy all Orthodox women seeking change. Another approach, a kind of "separate but equal," involves Talmud study groups or religious services for women alone. Some feminists have noted that in the Bible and the Talmud there are examples of heroic women. The *eshet chayil*, or woman of valour, is seen as the strong equal partner of the man. Much is made of female personalities like the judge Deborah of the Biblical period or the learned Beruryah of the Talmudic period. These feminist leaders and scholars have argued that the exclusion of women from serious Torah study and religious leadership was due more to custom than to clear *halachic* dictates.[6]

But for some Canadian Jews, Orthodoxy and feminism can never be reconciled. My late father, a sweet, gentle man, was raised in Orthodox synagogues in Poland. He could never make his peace with the services in my Reconstructionist synagogue, ranging from the heavy use of English to the complete gender equality. They made him uncomfortable. So "progress" for women has been weakest in Orthodoxy. In Orthodoxy, according to Concordia University's Norma Joseph, "there is a real fear of the feminist challenge, and the lines are drawn."[7] A Toronto woman offers the following poignant account:

> The synagogue I used to attend was the one in which my parents were married, my brothers celebrated their bar mitzvah, and I was named and married. When I was pregnant I told myself that if it were a girl I would find a more progressive synagogue because I wanted to assure my daughter greater equality in her Jewish life. My family was devastated. My grandfather, in an attempt to restore *shalom bayit* [peace in the home], concluded that it was not so terrible. Since I would stay if I had a son, he and my father would still have the pleasure of sitting with him in a synagogue, of seeing him *davening* [praying], of seeing him learn his Bar Mitzvah. I realized that

implicit in this was that they would not really miss much if I had a daughter and left their synagogue because her participation in synagogue life was so minimal. This argument convinced me to change synagogues no matter the sex of my child. I wanted my child to understand equality.[8]

There are at best ten practising female rabbis in Canada, and close to four hundred registered with the Reform and Conservative movements in the United States. Some North American women rabbis have reported episodes of sexual harassment, and others of being paid less than male counterparts. But clearly, the Judaic status of women is in flux. Jewish women have created or reinterpreted religious rituals.[9] A young girl becoming a bat mitzvah is now *de rigueur* among non-Orthodox branches of Judaism and is emerging in modified form within Modern Orthodoxy. A monthly ceremony ties in to *rosh chodesh* (the new moon) and celebrates fertility and renewal. In some feminist circles, there has even been a renewed interest in the *mikveh*, or ritual bath, used by very observant women following menstruation, albeit with a progressive gloss. In both egalitarian Orthodox or all-women *minyans*, women assume all religious functions. More and more women in non-Orthodox synagogues are found wearing a *kippa* and *tallis*, skullcap and prayer shawl. The *havdalah* service, which closes the Sabbath Saturday evenings, requires no *minyan*, and thus more Orthodox girls in synagogues are getting involved in the ceremony. Instead of reading from the Torah as part of a bat-mitzvah ceremony – which they are not permitted to do – Orthodox girls may have a *kiddush* and deliver a *d'var Torah*, a commentary on the Torah, without calling it such. One Orthodox synagogue has a ceremony for girls after Shabbat services, devised by the rabbi, but without any *talleysim*.[10] There has also been progress within the formal organizations of the community, though there is more work to do. The Canadian Jewish Congress has had two women presidents, and women are becoming more visible in both professional and lay positions in Jewish federations. Organizations are scheduling more meetings at lunchtime, rather than at 5:30 p.m., when many professional women morph into mothers and wives. These changes in the status of women in Judaism will spill over into gender relations between Jewish men and women.

The position of Jewish women in the world of work has also been changing. In many ways, it is easier for traditionalists to accept Jewish women as earners as than as religious equals. After all, in many communities in Eastern Europe, it fell to women to assume many of the breadwinning functions if their husbands devoted themselves to study.

Not surprisingly, Jewish women lag behind Jewish men on most measures of educational and occupational success. But as we saw in Chapter 4, they compare very well with other Canadian women, as do Jewish men with other men. One-half of Jewish women aged thirty-five to forty-four have a university degree, compared to one-sixth for all Canadian women.[11] American patterns are almost identical, and in both countries the Jewish advantage is even greater at the level of graduate degrees.[12] In Canada, 6.4 per cent of Jewish women hold a master's or a doctorate, compared to just 1.4 per cent for non-Jewish women. Part of this gap can be explained by the Jewish concentration in large cities, where higher education is common. But even there, the differences remain dramatic. In Toronto, the proportion of Jewish women with at least a university degree is 45 per cent, compared to the city average of 20 per cent. In Montreal, the figures are 38 per cent to 21 per cent, and in Vancouver 41 per cent to 21 per cent. These advantages translate to other economic gains. For example, among Jewish women, 36 per cent are employed as senior managers, middle and other managers, or professionals; the comparable figure of non-Jewish women is 21 per cent.

But along with this greater educational and occupational success have come lower fertility rates. I remember attending Jewish communal meetings where rabbis proposed a "baby bonus" paid by the organized community to get Jewish women to have more children. Traditionalists concerned with Jewish survival blame these low fertility rates on feminist objectives (note women are blamed rather than men).[13] But there is a more optimistic interpretation as well. Educated and working women with fewer children can contribute to Jewish life by increasing family incomes and by getting involved in leadership roles. Even as they have fewer children, Jewish mothers paradoxically seem to be more committed to raising them. American research by economist Barry Chiswick finds that "Jewish women with no young children at home are more likely than other women to be in the labor market, but if they have children at home, particularly if they are preschool children, Jewish women are less likely to work, and if they do work it is for fewer hours per year."[14] An attempt to synthesize tradition and modernity.

Chiswick argues that this pattern of Jewish women working less than other women when they have young children optimizes their "investment" in their children, which allows the offspring to succeed in turn. Chiswick reports on a similar study using Canadian census data, in which married Jewish women worked less than other married women.[15] He contends that this maternal pattern is linked to the high achievement of Jewish children and Jewish adults, as well as to the maintenance of Jewish identity. Of course, among Jewish women there is variation. Generally, religious Jewish women are more likely to stay at home.[16] Few analysts are willing to raise the sensitive question of how increasing career commitments of Jewish women and increasing reliance on child care might affect the educational and economic performance of future generations of Jews. If in fact the nurturing role of the Jewish mother has been part of the explanation for Jewish economic success, the issue has ramifications beyond the change in family roles. Jews may lose their economic advantages if Jewish children receive less nurturing. In theory, paternal care or high-quality daycare – there is no reason to "blame" mothers – can make up any slack. But children are not raised in theory. Chiswick gingerly poses the question: "A challenge facing the Jewish family is the maintenance of high levels of achievement while supporting the evolving role of Jewish women in the labor market. There is a new challenge and a new opportunity for the Jewish community – Jewish child care arrangements and Jewish day schools as a communal response to the evolving role of Jewish women in the labor market."[17]

But these painful dilemmas outlined in neutral scholarly terms take their toll on Jewish women. Jewish men, on the other hand, like all men, have abdicated the primary parenting responsibility to mothers. This is rather ironic. Jewish fathers in the old country actually were involved in child-rearing and concerned about the Jewish dimensions of the home and the child's Jewish education. In North America, this male duty atrophied; the father's role became that of breadwinner.[18]

Suppose Jewish men become more egalitarian in their parenting. That would help a bit. But the real threat to Jewish parenting is not women working; it is the devotion to career of *both* parents. The child-centredness of traditional Jewish families, and the investment of time in raising children, will decline if Jewish women – and men – increase their commitment to work. It is unclear whether non-Jewish nannies, no matter how well-intentioned, or even a Jewish-run daycare centre, can effectively socialize Jewish children and nurture their Jewish identity.

SEX

Equality for women in religious doctrine or the workplace builds on conceptions of women – and men – as more than sexual beings, and as such holds some promise for change. But men and women are also sexual beings. Without sex, there would be no Jewish continuity. Judaism is relatively more affirming about sexual pleasure than Christianity, though never as celebratory of beauty and the body as was Hellenism. The Song of Songs is erotic love poetry, but it is an exception in the body of Jewish religious writing. The Orthodox rabbinic tradition even claims that this erotic text refers to the love of God and the people of Israel rather than that between a man and a woman. (Does anyone ever really believe that?) As sex therapist Dr. Ruth Westheimer has confirmed, in traditional Judaism the sex act is seen as a joyous occasion – within the bounds of marriage – where spouses are required to try to fulfil the sexual needs of their partners.[19] The conventional wisdom, at least among Jews, is that Judaism is less ambivalent about sexual pleasure than is Christianity.

A rabbi and priest are sitting on a train. The priest asks, "Rabbi, I know you are supposed to keep kosher, but haven't you ever eaten pork?" The rabbi replies, "Father, I'll admit once when I was a student in the Yeshiva I was consumed with curiosity, and I did eat some pork." The priest grins. A few minutes later the rabbi asks, "Father, I know you are supposed to be celibate, but didn't you ever have sex with a woman?" The priest replies, "Well, rabbi, when I was a seminary student, I too was curious, so I found a girl and had sex with her." The rabbi smiles, "Beats the hell out of pork, doesn't it!"

Jokes are one thing. But where do Jews rank compared to other groups in terms of sexual attitudes and behaviours? The general liberalism of North American Jews spills over into attitudes about sex and gender issues. American attitude surveys have routinely found Jews to be more liberal on such matters. Jews are more likely to accord civil rights to gays, to be more tolerant of pornography, and to support gender equality, sex education in schools, the right to abortion, and the availability of contraceptives. These liberal views coalesce around the defence of rights of privacy, as well as free speech. And this Jewish liberalism and tolerance is not simply a reflection of Jews being college graduates. Studies have found that at all levels of education, American Jews are more tolerant.[20] We do not have quantitative studies of Canadian Jewish attitudes. But Jewish communal organizations would generally support liberal positions on private behaviour and other policy issues, such as equal rights for homosexuals, access to contraception and abortion, and opposition to most censorship. The only difference is the Canadian restrictions on hate speech, which I shall discuss in Chapter 11.

So let us assume Jews hold more liberal attitudes. But actions speak louder than words. There are few national surveys of sexual behaviour that include enough Jews for statistical analysis. One landmark study of a sample of Americans included only 54 Jews. It found that 33 per cent of them claimed to have had eleven or more sex partners, compared to 17 per cent for Catholics, 21 per cent for liberal Protestants, and 17 per cent for fundamentalist Protestants.[21] While certainly not definitive, the study at least suggests that Jews are sexually curious. A survey of students at the University of Toronto carried out in 1968, and therefore somewhat dated, found that "unmarried Jewish men have frequent sex in more than twice as many cases (31 per cent) as do unmarried Catholic or Protestant men." Interestingly, the same survey found that Jewish girls had a higher virginity rate than others.[22] We can infer from this that some of the Jewish men were, as stereotypes suggest, pursuing non-Jewish women.

In general, we know little about North American Jews and sex. A recent survey of CEGEP (junior college) students in Montreal included anglophone and francophone Jewish students in the sample. Respondents were asked if they had participated in any of nine different sex acts, ranging from kissing to vaginal and anal sex. Here the Jewish scores were moderate. The average scores ranged from 7.2 out of 9 for French Canadians, 6.4 for English Canadians, 6.2 for francophone Jews, 5.8 for Haitians, 5.4 for anglophone Jews, 5.1 for Italians, and 3.5 for Greeks.[23] It is hard to know how to interpret these findings, other than to assume that young Jewish men and women are at least normally adventuresome. Not oversexed, not undersexed. Sex is also there among the unmarried Orthodox, according to one Orthodox rabbi. At least into the 1980s – things may well have tightened up more recently – the concept of the "*tefillin* date" was current among students at Yeshiva University. It referred to the practice among some Orthodox young men out for a date to take along their *tefillin*, or phylacteries, should they not get home in time for the next morning prayer.

Enough titillation. No popular or scientific evidence about adventurous sexuality among Jews can detract from the basic framework, which is still traditional. Sexual pleasure, according to Jewish tradition, is certainly recognized but is unimportant compared to the obligation of marriage and child-rearing. Sex belongs in marriage, and its highest purpose is procreation. Even Monica Lewinsky told interviewers that what she wanted most was to be married and have children. Jews have no choice in the matter. Jews are commanded to marry, bear children (*pru u'rvu*) and instruct them in Jewish tradition (*veshinantem levanecho*). These religious prescriptions also resonate strongly among less religious or even secular Jews. The concern for *naches* is strong among all Jews. Is it uniquely Jewish? There is no immediately apparent equivalent expression in English; the dictionary translations of "pleasure or satisfaction or pride in one's children" are just too tepid. It is the *raison d'être* of family life for many Jews, the *quid pro quo* received in exchange for continual sacrifice for the children. And having children – for Jews – means getting married.

HUSBANDS, WIVES, AND CHILDREN

The Jewish family is generally pictured as a model of caring and harmony, between spouses and between parents and children. This harmony is the guarantor of generational continuity, represented by succeeding generations of well-adjusted, high-achieving, and committed Jews. While this picture is true compared to some other groups, it is not the full story. There has always been marital and generational conflict within Jewish families, to say nothing of normal tension. The 1995 Canadian General Social Survey, a large national sample, included 81 Jewish respondents who were married or living common-law. While 74 per cent of the total sample indicated they had a "very happy" relationship with their spouse, the Jewish respondents averaged 62 per cent, the lowest percentage of any religious group. So much for greater Jewish harmony! Even more interesting is the gender breakdown. Turns out that Jewish women were slightly more likely than other Canadian women to claim a very happy relationship, 77 per cent to 73 per cent. But only 51 per cent of Jewish men did so, well below the Canadian men's average of 75 per cent.[24] The sample is small, so this is not the time for misogynist jokes about henpecked Jewish men.

Relations with children and among siblings have never been entirely smooth. Cain killed Abel, Abraham almost sacrificed Isaac, and Jacob, with his conniving mother, tricked Isaac and stole Esau's birthright. Even Tevye's daughters rebelled against him and his "tradition." Children of Jewish immigrants, whether in the mass-migration period or more recently, would often rebel against their parents. Juvenile crime is a graphic indicator of such family problems. Rates of juvenile delinquency among Jews in the New York of the 1920s and 1930s were as high as among any immigrant group, and Jewish organizations agonized about possible solutions. In Canada in the 1920s, Louis Rosenberg reports that the crude rate for Jewish juvenile delinquents convicted of major offences was more than double the Canadian rate.[25] When adjusted for the largely urban residence of Jews, since crime is higher in cities, the gap narrowed, but Jews were still above the national average. By the 1930s rates of Jewish delinquency had dropped dramatically, and stayed low. But they did not disappear. Today, social-service workers routinely encounter troubled Jewish teens, often from immigrant backgrounds.

But if youth crime is generally less of a problem, other issues now shake the idealized image of the Jewish family. The problems of spouse abuse, child abuse, and elder abuse have emerged. Specialized agencies operate to look after battered Jewish women.[26] It is not at all clear whether there has been an increase in abuse or simply more awareness of and publicity about the issue. But Jewish divorce rates, like all divorce rates, have increased, which may be related indirectly to increases in actual abuse. This is true even in the ultra-Orthodox communities. No hard figures are available, but conversations with social workers reveal a strong consensus that even in these communities, divorce rates are rising – despite the availability of more courses preparing these religious young men and women for marriage. Over the years, these special courses in family purity have changed to include sections on relationships, though men and women attend these courses separately. Traditional matchmaking and courtship patterns remain alive and well in these communities, but expectations of those getting married have changed. The women are becoming more worldly than the men, which adds to the stresses in these marriages. The women take college or post-secondary courses and seek employment while the latter continue to study in yeshivas or in *kollels*, which are adult education institutions for Judaic learning.

As a community with many members trained in the helping professions, Jews are not reluctant to seek help for marital or family problems. There are many options, including Jewish social workers and Jewish agencies. There are also specific agencies aimed at the ultra-Orthodox, that either provide services or act as a conduit linking ultra-Orthodox clients to specific professionals. The issue of Jewish family violence has emerged from the closet. Auberge Shalom in Montreal, founded in 1989, is the first Jewish agency in Canada aimed mainly at abused Jewish women. Besides providing physical shelter, it also runs a support group, offers a twenty-four-hour support hotline, and can send staff into people's homes. The staff includes non-Jews, mainstream Jews, as well as ultra-Orthodox women, who counsel members from their own community. Jewish Women International of

Canada operates safe apartments for abused Jewish women, has access to another in Winnipeg, and is developing one in Vancouver.[27] Some ultra-Orthodox abused women will turn to rabbis, who in turn might consult with mainstream Jewish agencies or with specific social-service agencies geared to the ultra-Orthodox community.[28] In a different vein, members of these communities are even consulting with sex therapists for problems similar to those confronting other Jews; others are seeking out prostitutes as a source of sexual gratification.[29]

But wait: all families have troubles, and revisionism has its limits. Compared to Christian and other ethnic groups, the Jewish family remains strong and cohesive, and less prone to severe dysfunction. Relative Jewish sobriety alone could explain this advantage for Jewish family life, since alcohol often leads to violence and discord. And fewer economic pressures also mean fewer stresses to erode family solidarity. Of course, Jewish families have seen generational confrontation and teenage rebellion. Which families have not? In recent times, the sources of generational clashes have changed. The celebrated red-diaper babies of the 1960s, radical children, confronted their liberal parents on issues ranging from politics to pot. Now, inter-faith dating and intermarriage have emerged as key flashpoints. Most Canadian Jewish parents have heard the shrill teenage complaint: "You tell me not to be racist or prejudiced, yet you don't want me to go out with a non-Jew!"

Traditional Jewish mothers – the *Yiddishe mammeh* – are not as harmfully overprotective as stereotypes suggest. Jewish parents, notably mothers, actually encourage independence on the part of their children – quite different from a smothering overprotectiveness. In the post-war period, suburban Jewish parents may well have shifted towards independence as a better route towards success.[30] But even the presumed earlier overprotectiveness of the Jewish mother has been identified as a key factor in the success of Jewish children and adults.[31] Nagging children to eat properly or dress warmly can in fact lead to better health. Regardless of its impact, this overprotective and guilt-inducing image of Jewish mothers is common. I recently received one of my daily e-mail messages of Jewish jokes, which I promptly forwarded to my own list. The title was "Things a Jewish Mother Would Never Say." Some of the better entries:

– Be good, and for your birthday I'll buy you a motorcycle.

– How can you see the TV sitting so far back?

– Don't bother wearing a jacket – it's quite warm out.

– My meeting won't be over till later tonight. You kids don't mind skipping dinner, do you?

– You don't have to call every week. I know how busy you are.

– Your wife knows best – forget about the advice I gave you.

– Mother's day, shmother's day, you just go to the beach and enjoy yourselves.

Children are central to Jewish religious and family life, which is marked by the rituals of the life cycle. Indeed, the religious practices most commonly observed, even by relatively assimilated Jews, are those associated with birth, puberty, marriage, and death. Much of the religious behaviour of average Jewish families is oriented toward maximizing the Jewish environment of their children – a form of "pediatric Judaism." Jewish holidays, for instance, are observed to the extent they provide meaningful Jewish experiences for children as much as for the intrinsic spiritual nature of the holiday. Hanukkah with presents, dreidels, and latkes; Purim with costumes; Sukkoth with children decorating the Sukkah; and Passover with children asking the four questions and looking for the *afikomen*, a hidden piece of matzo, benefit in ways that the High Holidays and Shavuot do not. This new child-centredness is of course common to Christianity as well. The benefits flow to the cause of continuity. They do not enhance Jewish spirituality, which is after all an adult enterprise.

My guess – I have no hard proof – is that Jewish parents dote on their children more than, say, Canadian-born Anglo-Christian families. They are certainly more expressive. Health is the biggest worry of all, which may tap into other Jewish cultural traits. One time I was an assistant coach at a neighbourhood children's soccer game. One youngster came off the field in great pain, limping severely. I took him over to his mother and her friend, hoping it was not serious. The mother, of Anglo-Protestant origin, and speaking more calmly than I was, commented to her friend, "You know, this has happened several times in the past few days. . . . I think it might be a good idea to take him to the doctor." Imagine Jewish parents in a similar situation. At the first suggestion of a mysterious limp, they would be at the emergency room of their local hospital while on the cellphone to their GP trying to identify the best pediatric orthopaedist in town.

This concern for children does not translate into higher fertility rates for Jewish women. Despite the heroic efforts of the ultra-Orthodox, aggregate Jewish fertility remains below that for non-Jews. Jews were, for better or worse, trailblazers in the race to low, and in the United States below replacement, fertility rates. Jews were early and efficient contraceptors. One American study published in 1959 found that 83 per cent of American Jewish women who employed contraception started such use before their first pregnancy, compared to 52 per cent of Protestant women. (The question was not even posed to Catholics.)[32] The pattern of low fertility dates back to the turn of the century, when Jewish families were smaller than other immigrant families. The first birth-control clinic opened by Margaret Sanger was in the Jewish immigrant section of Brownsville in New York – unlikely a chance event.[33]

In the United States in 1990, the average number of children born to Jewish women in every age group was below that of other white Americans. In Canada today there is a similar pattern, clearly visible in 1981 Census data and beyond.[34] My estimate for 1991 is that for one thousand women over fifteen, Jews (by religion) had given birth to 1,601 children compared to 1,772 for non-Jews. Clearly, Canadian Jewish fertility remains far below that of non-Jews, despite the fact that fewer Jewish women are childless, and a greater proportion of Jewish men and women do get married.[35] But there is significant variation within the Jewish community. One estimate for Hasidic women is that their fertility is a staggering four times higher than the Canadian Jewish average.[36] By contrast, non-Hasidic and non-Orthodox Jewish couples are also having children, but relatively few.

Are Jewish marriages more stable? Judaism does not see marriage as a prison, and the Jewish attitude to divorce is more liberal than the Catholic. But it is doubtful that the rabbinic authorities who legitimated divorce envisioned the high rates which would come to prevail in modern societies, among Jews as well as all others. Divorce was stigmatized within folk Jewish traditions, even if it was not as rare as sometimes assumed. And of course, the Orthodox rules of divorce penalize women routinely. It is the man who must grant a divorce decree, or *get*; a wife cannot issue a *get* to her husband. On the other hand, a wife must consent to a *get* before the divorce becomes final. The potential for abuse is significant, mainly directed against women who cannot really initiate divorce proceedings. These women for whom the decree is withheld, often as blackmail, remain in a kind of limbo, unable to remarry.

The plight of these women, or *agunot*, remains a central issue on the Jewish feminist agenda. A 1987 Canadian study by B'nai Brith identified 311 cases of conflict over a *get*, with 202 arising because of the husband's refusal to grant one, and 92 because of the wife's refusal to accept one. Both the lawyers and rabbis involved in that study confirmed that women suffered more from the proceedings.[37] In a rare example of the state interfering in religious affairs of a community, the Canadian Parliament came to the defence of the *agunot* after lobbying from Jewish women's groups and other communal organizations. In 1990, a federal law, section 21.1 of the Divorce Act, was passed which "allowed divorce courts to require affidavits indicating that barriers to remarriage within the deponent's religion had been removed by the applicant and empowering the courts to dismiss any application for failure to comply with this requirement."[38] So Jews who withhold a *get* or refuse to accept one will be prevented from obtaining a civil divorce. Indeed, under the law, judges would not hear the pleadings regarding the details of a divorce settlement from the party who was impeding or not accepting a *get*.

Marriage does seem in better shape among Jews. The proof is in the numbers. Over the past decades, levels of divorce in North America in general have been on the rise. But according to the 1991 Census data on marital status, Canadian Jews (by religion) are less likely to be divorced and separated than are non-Jews. For men, the difference was 4.5 per cent to 6 per cent; for women, 6.6 per cent to 7.7 per cent. For demographers, these are large differences. Moreover, the Jewish–non-Jewish gap has grown since 1981.[39] So in this sense Canadian Jewish family life is more traditional, and more stable. American divorce rates for both men and women, Jews and non-Jews, are higher than the Canadian rates; no surprise there. America's more liberal culture makes divorce more frequent across the board, for everyone.

Jews are also less likely to have children out of wedlock. This is actually an old story. In the 1920s and 1930s, the Jewish percentage of illegitimate births was only one-fifth the Canadian average.[40] In Canada in 1991, about 2.3 per cent of single or never married women had a child; among Jews the rate was 0.5 per cent. (These exclude women who may have children outside of marriage and then subsequently marry or live common-law.) Fewer Jews are also found in common-law and lone-parent families; 5.4 per cent to 11.1 per cent for women, and 3.4 per cent to 6.9 per cent for men. How much of these gaps reflect the impact of Jewish cultural values and how much higher socio-economic status for Jews, I do not know. Jewish marriage and family patterns vary by city. Vancouver is trendy, Montreal and Toronto are more traditional.[41]

GETTING MARRIED

Most Jews want to get married, and they do. But not all. A few Jews are single by choice. They are a small minority, and they pose a frontal ideological challenge to ideas about Jewish families. For most singles, the problem is finding the right mate. There have always been single-parent families in Jewish communities, usually widows, with a lesser number of divorced women. Jewish singles and single-parent families challenge religious and communal institutions to accommodate their needs through innovative programming.[42] And single-parent families face daunting economic barriers to providing a Jewish life for their children, given the cost of living "Jewishly."

Most Jews seem to want to marry other Jews – at least as an initial preference. We can get a sense of this desire for Jewish partners by taking a somewhat voyeuristic look at personal ads in major Canadian dailies. What you find is that Jews are more likely than any other religious or ethnic group to identify themselves as such in the personals. And Jews are more likely to specify that they are seeking a Jew. There are fewer ads that specify "Anglican seeking Anglican" or "Italian seeking Italian" or "Chinese seeking Chinese." Where non-Jews do self-identify, they generally will take all comers. The most common counterpart to the Jewish pattern, if still less frequent, is "Christian seeking Christian" or "white seeking white." But there is a difference between Jewish men and Jewish women. More Jewish women self-identify, and more of them are seeking Jewish mates. Jewish men, however, are more likely to be looking for anyone, possibly their dream *shiksa*. Indeed, in the odd case Jewish men will specify they are looking for a non-Jewish woman; Asians seem much in vogue.[43] It is tough going for single Jewish women.

The growth of the Jewish singles scene, and accompanying organizations, attests to the drive to get married, and to marry other Jews. The increasing numbers of divorced and single-parent women add a newer, more urgent element to the marriage market. In the Jewish singles scene both joy and despair co-exist, and stereotypes of Jewish and Gentile men and women abound. The impressions below – stereotypes or not – are distilled from several members of Jewish singles organizations. Both Montreal and Toronto have Jewish Singles Registries, which cater to a mainly non-Orthodox clientele. Both have more women than men. Toronto members report their level of Jewish observance on their applications, but there is no actual verification as to whether or not the member is even Jewish. There is also no screening at the door of group events, and it is not uncommon to find non-Jews attending Jewish singles events. Presumably, if things get serious, those details get ironed out.

What is it like out there? The reports I have heard from the field are distressing. One Montreal woman in her forties was thrust into the dating scene following a divorce. She found Jewish men were concerned "totally" with looks, while women tended to overlook the appearance of the men. What matters to the Jewish women, according to a Toronto observer, is whether the man is a "doctor, dentist, or lawyer." The newest buzzword is "calibre," which seems to be a euphemism for affluence. And the men want a "princess" with looks, and who is slim. One single woman reports that many Jewish men find Gentile women attractive because they feel that those women want "me for me, not my car." Moreover, some of the Jewish men want to sow their wild oats, which adds to the attraction of the Gentile women. While many Jewish women are interested in a Jewish partner, some get involved in the non-Jewish singles scene, in part because of the shortage of available

Jewish men, or curiosity about non-Jewish men. Jewish women also have wild oats to sow. The non-Jewish club or party scene is allegedly looser, more relaxed and less inhibited, perhaps because there tends to be more drinking. At a non-Jewish party, women will rarely refuse to dance, while Jewish women will only dance if they are interested in the man. And Jewish men in general "do not like to dance. . . ."

These singles organizations can work. They are not as goal-directed as Orthodox matchmakers, who have a much higher success rate, but they do make modest claims. According to the director of the (for-profit) Toronto Jewish Singles Registry (cost $395 a year, about 850 active files), there had been thirty marriages or engagements that he knew of by 1998.[44] The nonprofit Montreal Jewish Singles Registry (cost $335 a year, about 2,100 files) estimated a rate of one marriage or engagement per month.[45] I have no way of knowing if these reports are accurate. Let's hope.

Matchmaking in the traditional style is still the norm in the ultra-Orthodox community, though couples now also meet through friends or relatives, and then move to the services of the *shadchan*, or match-maker. In the yeshiva world, if the *shadchan* approves, the young couple may meet several times in "dates," where they will sit in public areas and chat, usually about direct practical concerns. Among the Hasidim, there are far fewer boy-girl meetings. But things get talked about to avoid problems during the marriage. In one reported Toronto case, a prospective marriage within the ultra-Orthodox community fell apart because the two families could not agree on the future length of the young boy's sidecurls, or *payess*. I knew a Jewish woman who was a radical, liberated feminist in the late 1960s, but once made a surprising confession only half in jest. She wondered if maybe she should let her mother choose her a husband. After all, nobody knew her or wanted her happiness like her mother . . .

GAYS AND LESBIANS

The sad truth is that for most Canadian Jews, having a gay child is deeply troubling. The same could be said for non-Jews, but there are differences which make this Jewish discomfort surprising. Jews are politically liberal, and certainly support non-discrimination against gays. While there is an

Orthodox stigma against homosexuality, the other denominations are less hostile. But other factors make acceptance more difficult. The major one is the extreme family- and child-centredness of Judaism; parents want grandchildren. Another is communal, and relates to continuity. Gays and lesbians do not reproduce, and rear fewer children than straight Jews, so can be seen as contributing less to the generational struggle for continuity. This shadow hangs over Jewish gays – and those who are voluntarily childless – and adds to the other personal challenges of accepting gay and lesbian family members. But in the future more Jewish gays and lesbians will become parents, posing new challenges to Jewish schools and synagogues.

Jewish liberalism on homosexuality applies mainly to support for tolerance on the part of the state. Jews and national Jewish organizations oppose public discrimination against gays and lesbians, and would extend human rights protections – though not marriage – to them without question. So far so good. But what goes on within Jewish families, and the formal Jewish community, is different. Jewish liberalism may soften the antagonisms, but gay and lesbian Jews have been only grudgingly accepted by mainstream Jewish organizations, Jewish communities, and Jewish families. (In August 2000, an openly gay person was appointed as director of the Philadelphia Jewish Federation.) The conflict is waged mainly within synagogues and denominations, and within Jewish minds and souls. The struggle of gays for equality and dignity within the Jewish community parallels the struggle within Canada as a whole. Homosexuality tests the limits of Jewish pluralism and the adaptability of Jewish family life. And as gay and lesbian Jews defend their interests, they do so in time-honoured Jewish fashion – by organizing.

Naches was the first formal organization representing gays in Montreal, and its history is revealing. It was founded in 1972–73 to provide an unthreatening environment where gay Jews could celebrate Jewish traditions. Before that, gay Jews found themselves having to choose between identifying as gays or as Jews, and more often they would choose the former. By 1978, Naches was registered as a nonprofit organization and had a functioning board. The very early years were tough. Membership grew slowly, from ten to twenty. The organization received hostile and obscene phone messages. The *Canadian Jewish News* would not accept ads, and people held meetings in homes because no community organization would grant them space. By the 1980s, there were over one hundred members, but because so many were still concerned about anonymity, there was only a telephone list – no addresses – and first names only.

Things began to change in the late 1980s. Membership was approaching two hundred. The name was changed to Yachdav, meaning "together." Under the leadership of Harvey Cohen, who was visible in both the gay and Jewish communities, Yachdav approached the YM-YWHA for affiliation. That process took about eighteen months, and was possibly helped by the fact that one of Cohen's relatives was very active in the Y. Cohen recalls that following a meeting after the positive decision was made, the executive director of the Y commented, "They really are nice people."[46] After the breakthrough with the Y, there were other outreach efforts to become more involved with the established Jewish community. One major stride came about over the organized participation of Yachdav in a Combined Jewish Appeal Super Sunday fund-raising effort. At first there was resistance to allowing Yachdav to participate as a group, but eventually that changed. One member who volunteered was a teacher at a local Jewish school, who claimed, "I was so nervous I could lose my job."

By the 1990s, things had changed even further. Yachdav had a newsletter, close to four hundred members, of whom about 60 per cent were men, and charged dues of $54, or $90 for a family membership. They even received a grant from the Jewish Community Foundation, and also started a support group for Jewish parents of gays and lesbians. Only the rabbinate, understandably, was slow to welcome the group. At one point an invitation to meet with Montreal's Rabbinical Council was rescinded due to opposition. Yachdav has not evolved into a "gay shul" as is the case in Toronto, so the direct religious challenge is minimal. It is affiliated with the World Congress of Gay and Lesbian Jewish Organizations, and is seeking affiliation with the World Jewish Congress.

Organized gay life in Toronto dates back at least to the mid-1970s, when a group with the name Ha-Mishpacha emerged. Through the

1980s, the small group encountered a cold reception from the Bloor JCC and the established community. Over time it changed its name (B'nai Kehillah, Chutzpah) and emphasis, and eventually opted to become a congregation, taking the name Keshet Shalom in 1992. In its first years, it went through many acute debates on Jewish ritual, though it never grew to be a full-fledged gay congregation as found in some American cities. Keshet Shalom has recently foundered; all the programs for 2000–2001 have been cancelled. But at the same time, the organized Toronto Jewish community has begun to subsidize – how times have changed – a newer gay Jewish group aimed at university students and young adults called JLGBT, or Jewish Lesbian Gay Bisexual Transgendered students and young adults. This group was formed in March 2000. For a long time, according to gay activist Howard Goldstein, there was not much of a social scene in Toronto outside of Keshet Shalom, no specific clubs or bars where gay Jews might congregate.[47] Still, there are prospects for growth and other signs of acceptance in Toronto. There are AIDS support groups at Holy Blossom and Beth Tzedec congregations, and Holy Blossom has a third seder every year associated with the AIDS program, which is frequented by gay Jews. A congregation aimed at Jewish lesbians holds High Holiday services every year.

Gay and lesbian Jews also confront interfaith relationships, and tend to be more tolerant than straight Jews. According to Cohen, most Jewish lesbians are involved with Jewish women, but the opposite is the case for Jewish gays, where mixed couples are the norm. Yachdav does not allow non-Jews to join directly, but they can be invited to events by a member, or may be part of a family membership. Cohen reports that there are many non-Jews who call Yachdav for information, eager to join. The issue has to be treated with care. Once, a non-Jewish woman joined Yachdav, became active, and was made president. But some members became suspicious during an Oneg Shabbat when she was handed a siddur and began to leaf through it in the wrong direction. She was exposed, and impeached. Still, the door is not completely closed. The group will accept a handful of non-Jews if they prove themselves over a long time.

There is no uniform policy on the part of denominations concerning openly gay members of synagogues. The issue for them is a minefield. Gays in Orthodox shuls are not thrown out, according to Goldstein. There is a growing tolerance among some modern Orthodox synagogues.[48] There is even more openness in Canadian Conservative, Reform, and Reconstructionist congregations, but less than in the United States. The official Reform and Reconstructionist movements have essentially embraced full acceptance. The Jewish religious community across all denominations will have to confront the challenges of openly gay members and gay marriages and gay rabbis. Synagogues seem comfortable with a "don't ask, don't tell" policy, but this will not satisfy gays and lesbians. Even if mainstream congregations become more accepting, there will likely be more gay and lesbian synagogues down the road, in keeping with the spirit of Jewish religious pluralism.

The large majority of gay male couples are mixed. Obviously, if there are no children being raised by the couple, these mixed marriages or partnerships are not a source of assimilationist guilt. As it happens, the non-Jews in these relationships are by all accounts very supportive of their partner's Jewish commitments. This promotes the trend whereby for most gay Jews their major loyalty is to their gay identity, where they do not have to confront a double-barrelled guilt at being both gay and involved with a non-Jew. It is simply easier to live in a gay community, where there is far less stigma for being Jewish than there is for being gay in the Jewish community. AIDS has added to the stigma, further pushing gay Jews into the gay community. In the view of Yachdav's Cohen, the Jewish community's response to AIDS has been much too tepid. Many Jews afflicted with AIDS seek treatment in clinics in East End Montreal, where there are very few Jews, and some have been sent out of town by embarrassed families.

Despite these failures on the part of the mainstream Jewish community, gay Jews are carving out a space in the Jewish cultural landscape. One of the more interesting developments within the North American gay Jewish community has been the attempt to define links between homosexuality and the secular Yiddishist culture of Eastern Europe. That culture is seen as a softer one, where Jewish weakness led to a less macho type of sensibility. Gay themes are identified in or with

Yiddish literature and music, along with a notable blurring of gender boundaries. Barbra Streisand's Yentl, a girl who dressed as a boy in order to study in a Yeshiva, symbolizes the intersection of gay camp and Eastern European culture.

THE ELDERLY

All groups venerate their elderly, at least in theory. But Jews are living longer than in the past, and longer than most groups in North America. We could describe this in positive terms, but throughout the organized Jewish community, aging is viewed as a "problem," responsible for mounting costs for local Jewish welfare and social-service agencies. These include communal support for Golden Age Associations, seniors' residences, geriatric hospitals and chronic-care facilities, as well as a variety of home-care services. Middle-aged Jews are also more likely to be burdened for longer as a "sandwich generation," caring for aged parents and in-laws long after their children have grown up. At parties, Jewish baby boomers compare notes about their growing children, their own health worries, and the more serious health problems of their parents. As in many areas, like lower fertility rates or higher educational levels, Jews have been pioneers at the frontiers of modernity. So too with longevity and its consequences.

The increasing proportion of Jewish elderly is due to a combination of decreasing fertility – fewer children – as well as longer life spans. As educated and middle-class Canadians, Jews are likely to have better health and be better able to utilize existing health care than other groups.

There are other factors causing the increasing proportions of aged Jews. One is the growing rate of mixed marriage. As younger Jews marry out, many of their children are lost to the Jewish fold. They are not part of the community, while their older parents and grandparents are. In the census, some of these children may not list their religion as "Jewish." Another is the Holocaust. The survivors, who represent a fair chunk of Canadian Jews over sixty-five, were particularly likely to have fewer children. My parents had just one. Many survivors lost spouses and children during the war. Others had years of peak fertility pass during wartime, when child-bearing was nearly impossible, or simply didn't have the health or energy necessary to rebuild families after the war.

In 1991, Jews over sixty-five comprised over 17.3 per cent of the Canadian Jewish population, compared to just 10.8 per cent for all of Canada. This sizeable gap is of fairly recent vintage.[49] The aging of the early twentieth-century immigrant cohorts and the later wave of Holocaust survivors and North African immigrants has helped in widening the spread. Aging is found in all Jewish populations, with the exception of Israel. The American situation is similar.[50] In both Canada and the United States, age distributions vary widely by city. Looking at the proportions over sixty-five we find youthful Vancouver at 13.1 per cent, Toronto at 15.4 per cent, Montreal at 22.4 per cent, and Winnipeg at 23.9 per cent. In the United States, not surprisingly, we find Miami leading the way at 44 per cent, New York and Philadelphia between 23 and 25 per cent, and Boston, Washington, and Houston relatively youthful at 10 to 12 per cent.[51]

An aging population is not simply a policy problem for North American Jews. It is a wrenching test of Jewish family values and moral principles. This becomes more acute as the Jewish elderly get even older. Over 49 per cent of Canadian seniors are over seventy-five, called the "old old" or the "frail elderly." The myth of a special closeness between aging Jewish parents and their children is alive and well, in anecdotes and in research. In a study of seniors in Hamilton, one respondent claimed: "Jewish families are closer. Children visit their parents. There's always a holiday or *simcha* to get together for."[52] Most Canadian Jewish seniors live in families, usually with a spouse. Because women live several years longer than men, they are more likely to be living alone; 40 per cent for women and only 20 per cent for men. But for all the mythology of the warm extended Jewish families, and beloved *bubbies* and *zaidies*, when their spouse dies very few seniors live with their children. The case of Montreal is typical, where statistics show for every elderly Jew living with a child there are four to five living alone.[53] This profile of living arrangements for Jews does not differ from those for Canadians as a whole. When a spouse dies, Jewish and non-Jewish seniors are on their own.

If elderly Jews cannot or will not live with their children, many feel that the Jewish community, rather than the government, should pick up the slack. In 1996, exactly one-third of Montreal Jews identified the needs of the Jewish elderly as the second-most important Federation responsibility, behind only the needs of the Jewish poor.[54] Moreover, two-thirds of Montreal Jews, and three-quarters of the seniors, preferred expressly Jewish-sponsored seniors' housing. Jewish seniors in Montreal, and, one suspects, in Toronto, prefer to live with or near other Jews. The first Jewish senior citizens' home in Toronto was established in 1913. Today the Baycrest complex is a model agency meeting the needs of the elderly. In Montreal, the Montreal Hebrew Sheltering Home was established in 1910, and evolved into the Maimonides Home for the Aged. But other Jewish communities differ on the need for such Jewish-sponsored housing or care. Two surveys of Vancouver seniors, taken in 1990 and 1993, found that only 34 and 40 per cent expressed a clear preference for seniors' housing built by the Jewish community.[55] If more were available, those numbers might change.

How close are Jewish parents to their grown children? Even if they do not live together, there is a great deal of contact. In a survey of Montreal Jewish young adults, John Sigal and I found that they spoke to their parents very often; the large majority at least daily.[56] The same pattern was found in the study comparing Jewish and non-Jewish senior women in Hamilton.[57] Regardless of the levels of contact, relations between Jewish generations can be strained. The mobility of Jews, young and old, adds to the stress as parents age. Older Jews are often "abandoned" by mobile, professional children who leave their hometowns. As we have seen, taking in elderly widowed parents is rare – and it is unclear how harmonious these living arrangements are or would be. Many Canadian Jewish elderly in turn "abandon" their children by heading to Florida for all or part of the year. When the seniors are healthy and still with spouses, the problems are not severe. They increase when a spouse dies and health deteriorates. Remarriage among the Jewish elderly is one way around the problem – though there are not enough Jewish men to meet the need. Often, the surviving parent still refuses to move in with the children. What is not clear is how much this craving for independence – this not wanting to "be a burden" – results from a fear that they might not really be welcome, or comfortable, living with their children's families. There is no solution that is ideal for seniors, their children, and the community.

INTERMARRIAGE

Last but not least: The threat of intermarriage outweighs every other concern for Canadian Jewish continuity – including anti-Semitism and even the low Jewish fertility rates. For many, it is the darkest cloud over the Jewish future. The term "intermarriage" has many meanings. I use it broadly to refer to the marriage between a Jew and someone who was born non-Jewish. If the non-Jew converts to Judaism, then we no longer have an intermarriage at all. We have a marriage with two Jews. These are often called "conversionary marriages." A "mixed marriage" refers to a marriage between a Jew and a non-Jew, where no formal conversion to Judaism has taken place, or, even "worse," the Jewish partner has embraced the non-Jewish religion. By the mid-1990s about 30 per cent of Canadian Jews marrying each year were in mixed marriages.

The impact of mixed marriage on the Jewish future can be awesome. Assume one hundred adult Jews, all marry each other and have two children per family. This scenario of no mixed marriage leaves the total population steady, generation after generation, at one hundred, based on fifty couples with two children each. A scenario with a mixed marriage rate of 50 per cent means that the next generation of Jews would be half as large: fifty Jews forming twenty-five Jewish couples having two children each, for a total of fifty in the next generation.[58] But conversion matters. Suppose all the non-Jewish spouses of these 50 outmarriages were to convert, or identify strongly as Jews. Then the total Jewish population would actually increase by 50 per cent, to 150 in the next generation: twenty-five Jewish in-marriages and fifty conversionary marriages, for seventy-five marriages with two children each. So conversion or the embrace of Judaism by the non-Jew is crucial. (For more details about trends in mixed marriages across Canada, see Appendix III.)

Let's imagine two polar extremes of Jews who wind up in mixed marriages. One type is the Jew who is very assimilated, with minimal

Jewish identity and communal ties, raised in a home which was minimally Jewish, where family members and friends are already in mixed marriages. In these cases, the mixed marriage is not hard to understand. It puts a finishing touch on a long-term process. It is a symptom, not a cause. The other type is far more intriguing. Here, we have Jews with a significant Jewish background, who came from identified Jewish homes, attended synagogue regularly, had some Jewish education, yet fell in love with and married a non-Jew. They most likely do not flee from Judaism. They feel the lure of the exotic. Many claim that somehow they will continue to live a Jewish family life to some degree – and, indeed, some do just that. Or at least they try. Ask them, and they will identify confidently as Jews. Usually the non-Jewish partner is not a very devout Christian, so their children may well be "exposed" to some Jewish events or experiences. A central question concerns the future Jewish identity and commitments, if any, of these children.

What kind of Jews marry out? Not surprisingly, Jews who are third- or fourth-generation Canadians are the most likely.[59] Studies have found that those whose family of origin is less religiously observant or non-Orthodox and who have less Jewish education – schools as well as Jewish camps, youth groups, and Israel programs – are more likely to marry out. Each of these factors plays an independent role; they are not simply extensions of varying Jewish family background.[60]

American sociologist Bruce Phillips has moved beyond these major background factors leading to mixed marriage.[61] I suspect his findings apply equally to Canada. Again, no surprises. Phillips has found adolescent dating patterns are key. Jews who dated mainly Jews in high school were more likely to be dating mostly Jews later when they found their spouse, and indeed were more likely to marry a Jew. But the process is very fluid. Only half of those who in high school dated mostly Jews, or Jews and non-Jews equally, were dating mostly Jews when they met their spouse. The importance of marrying a Jew declined significantly between high school and college. Nevertheless, as Phillips pointed out, high-school dating is crucial, since "it was only those respondents who dated Jews in high school who would later be dating Jews as adults." And how do Jewish spouses meet? Out-married

Jews were far more likely to meet their spouse in a neutral setting, like work, school, or a party. In-married Jews were more likely to meet their spouse through a social network, such as friends or a blind date or through a formal Jewish group or setting. Hence the logic in those Jewish singles associations. In fact, an unstated aim of so many Jewish activities, like summer camps, youth groups, Israel programs of all sorts, is to pair up Jewish youngsters.

The danger to continuity is only one issue relating to intermarriage. The other is that even in conversionary marriages, Orthodox Jewry does not accept conversions supervised by non-Orthodox rabbis. So these children are not recognized as Jews according to *halacha*. The problem the Orthodox have is allegedly with the conversion process itself, and the inadequate Judaic learning of the rabbi in charge. Yet conversion – any conversion – makes a difference. American research has routinely found that there are few or no differences in Judaic commitments – synagogue attendance, ritual observance, Jewish communal involvement – between conversionary marriages and Jewish in-marriages. There is no debate on the evidence.[62] Possibly, there is self-selection at work; non-Jews who convert could be more predisposed to being Jewish than non-Jews who do not, and converts to Judaism may well take their new faith more seriously than born Jews. Another possibility is that the formality of the ritual inevitably adds a new dimension of commitment and perhaps eases strains with the extended Jewish family. One woman I interviewed who converted to Judaism after her marriage was astounded to see how much closer her Jewish mother-in-law became to her, even though she had not previously pressured her to convert. The growing acceptance of converts to Judaism is ironic, given the long tradition of Jewish humour which has dismissed the seriousness or even the possibility of real conversion from Judaism.

A ninety-year-old Jew is dying, and asks his wife to summon a priest so he can convert before he passes on. His wife complains, "Why are you doing this? You have been a good Jew your whole life." He replies, "Better one of them should die than one of us."

The quasi-racial approach to Jewish or Gentile identity – once a Gentile always a Gentile – might not last as converts become more numerous. Conversion classes, from whatever denomination, fly in the face of this folk superstition. Orthodox Jews claim that Reform classes, or the rabbis who lead them, are not up to the task. Those converts who become Reform Jews may lead less Jewish lives than converts who become Orthodox Jews. But that is not the point. I observed one Reform-sponsored class in Western Canada where the rabbi was on sabbatical leave and the class was run by a woman, herself a Reform convert. This would give the Orthodox fits. Except in my judgment, she did an excellent job. She was both knowledgeable and very respectful of Orthodoxy. The books that were assigned were very informative. The notion that these converts ought not be considered Jews is sociological nonsense. Orthodox conversions are perhaps more demanding, but the final steps may not be as intellectually focused. A woman who underwent an Orthodox conversion in Montreal in the 1980s recalled the process for me. The classes lasted over a year, and covered a wide range of material. Her final test involved questioning by three rabbis, and the issues ranged widely: from detailed queries about the destruction of the second temple and the fast day of *Tisha Be'Av*, to the steps involved in koshering liver. (I wonder if male converts get asked that question.) A visit to the *mikveh*, or ritual bath, finalized the process.

My experience is that many Jews do not really appreciate the sacrifices that converts make. Most of the Jews who are married to or are friends with converts would find it impossible to imagine themselves converting to Christianity. I know I would. There is a good bit of truth to the old stereotype about the convert who is more devout than the typical Jew. But for many committed Jewish converts there are nevertheless memories of family ties and Christmas holidays and Sunday School classes – how could there not be – that remain alive and at times painful.

And what do we know of the "Jewishness" of mixed marriages without any conversion? Bruce Phillips in the United States found a great variety in these marriages, though for the most part they are minimally Jewish and their offspring will likely remain apart from the

Jewish community. When asked how they were raising their children, only 18 per cent said "Jewish only."[63] Does that mean that all the others will be lost to the tribe? Phillips identified six types of mixed marriages, depending on the degree of Jewishness. Only one-seventh were classified in the most Jewish type of mixed marriage. In that category, the balance of religious observance clearly tilted towards Judaism; 86 per cent lit Hanukkah candles, and 40 per cent attended High Holiday Services. On the other hand, 60 per cent still had a Christmas tree! (Compared to Canadian counterparts, it is more common for identified American Jewish families to have a Christmas tree.)

My estimate is that these types apply to Canada, but that the more Judaic forms are more common. Mixed marriage in Canada is not (yet) the Judaic wasteland it is in the United States. But these numbers or types still do not capture the human variety within each mixed marriage. To most Orthodox Jews, this variation is meaningless, but it is a fact of life among the non-Orthodox. I know of one mixed marriage, dissolved after twenty-five years, where the Jew is a professor of Jewish Studies and the spouse is indifferent to things Jewish. In another, the Jewish partner belongs to two synagogues, attends services on major holidays, associates mainly with his old-time Jewish friends, while the non-Jewish wife observes no religion. In yet another, one child has a very Jewish name, a second a very Anglo-Christian name. My first cousin, an American, is in a mixed marriage. But he started his journey out before the marriage, becoming attracted to Ethical Culture (a form of secular humanism) first. I recall spending Hanukkah with his family, with latkes, dreidels, and candles. Yet when his twenty-year-old son visited us one Rosh Hashanah, he told us it was the first time he had ever attended any synagogue service. Despite the creative efforts of some of the Jews involved in mixed marriages, on balance most of the children – and even more likely the grandchildren – will be lost to the Jewish community. All this presupposes that future processes of Jewish identification will mimic those of the past. Should the community widen the net, the losses would be less pronounced.

One of the looming problems in devising a communal response to mixed marriage, assuming that is even possible, is that almost no non-Orthodox Jewish family – and many Orthodox Jewish families –

remains untouched. Alan Dershowitz in his *The Vanishing American Jew* poignantly refers to the mixed marriage of one of his own children, clearly a child who was raised in a committed Jewish home. The stigma is gone. No one is holier than thou. Committed Jews know that, despite their best efforts, it could happen to their children, too. Jewish parents like Dershowitz no longer sit *shiva* if their children marry out. They keep channels open, and still love their children. I know I would do likewise, even though my children know I have a very strong preference that they live a Jewish family life, which means either marrying a Jew or a convert who would embrace Judaism. At most Jewish communal meetings people have to watch their language on intermarriage so as not to give offence. Jews also have to be careful about telling jokes about non-Jews given the large numbers of converts and Gentiles moving in Jewish circles. Stigmatizing those who marry out just no longer works in non-Orthodox circles.

The challenge facing both Jewish communities and individual Jews is how to respond to the process as it unfolds, and once it becomes a *fait accompli*. How are Jewish parents to react when their son or daughter dates a non-Jew, or brings one home? Attitudes of American Jews on intermarriage are now amazingly liberal. The alarm sounded by American Jewish leadership over the NJPS findings of a 52-per-cent recent mixed-marriage rate does not reflect the feelings of the average Jew. The American Jewish Committee's 2000 survey of American Jewish opinion found that only 12 per cent said they "strongly disapproved" of mixed marriages, and almost 50 per cent thought "it is racist to oppose Jewish–Gentile marriages."[64] Canada remains far more traditional. Despite the increasing rates of mixed marriage, Canadian Jews remain initially firmly opposed to it. If told that their child was considering marrying a non-Jew, almost 60 per cent of Montreal Jews would oppose the marriage, and only 9 per cent would openly support it. If the non-Jewish spouse converted to Judaism, the proportion that would actively oppose the marriage declines dramatically to 16 per cent.[65] But this initial opposition to intermarriage is not unique to Montreal. A Toronto survey found similarly that fully two-thirds of third-generation Canadian Jews were strongly opposed to intermarriage, far more than other groups.[66] In these attitudes against intermarriage, Jews are clearly at odds with the vast majority of Canadian public opinion, which strongly favours marriage among Protestants, Catholics, and Jews, as well as between various ethnic or racial groupings. In 1995, for example, 92 per cent of Canadians approved of marriages between Protestants and Roman Catholics, 90 per cent between Protestants and Jews, and 89 per cent between Roman Catholics and Jews.[67] Christians no longer want to persecute Jews, or convert Jews, they want to marry them. My guess is that Moslems share the Jewish opposition to intermarriage.

There is no consensus on a communal strategy. Most Canadian Jewish parents, despite their opposition, will make their peace with mixed marriage. Less clear is whether the organized community should take a hard line or soft line. Should Jewish schools or Jewish summer camps sponsored by the community discriminate against children who are in one way or another non-Jewish? Should Jewish schools or synagogues refuse to hire Jews in mixed marriages as teachers, as the Conservative movement is considering? In the mid-1990s, the Montreal Jewish Federation sponsored a panel discussion entitled "Living with Intermarriage," which included an Orthodox Rabbi. While he argued against communal or religious acceptance of mixed marriage, the fact that he was willing to appear and share a panel with an American guest who described how mixed marriages might be able to work was remarkable, and somewhat brave! To take a hard line, accepting only Orthodox converts, would prevent the dilution of Jewish identity but cut down on numbers. A soft line would welcome marginal Jews – and non-Jews – keeping numbers up, but weakening the average levels of commitment. My argument for the soft line recognizes that mixed marriage today is usually not a result of deliberate rebellion against parents or Judaism. Nor is it a necessary response to societal discrimination against Jews, as was the case in the past. Usually it is just love tinged with adventure. Encouraging non-Jewish spouses to convert will likely lead to a payoff. Some conversions also take place after the mixed marriage. Keeping the doors open makes tactical sense.

THE COMMUNAL FOUNDATION
OF JEWISH LIFE

People, Neighbourhoods, and Organizations

"Hillel said: Do not cut yourself off from the community."
                                    — Ethics of the Fathers, 2:5

"For every two Jews, three organizations."
                                    — Anonymous

THE CENTRALITY OF COMMUNITY

Some time ago, I attended a gathering of prominent Chinese Canadians. During the conversation, which touched on many multicultural topics, the talk drifted to comparisons between Jews and Chinese. One of the Chinese present asked, "What can I do to make sure that my children retain their Chinese identity?" Oy, did that ever sound familiar! It echoed the oft-repeated Jewish alarm, "Are you sure your grandchildren will be Jewish?" In framing my response, I drew on the Jewish model. "You, yourself, can do little. Any answer will have to come from the organized Chinese community."

It is difficult to overemphasize the communitarian basis of contemporary Jewish life. The informal community is the network of interpersonal social relationships – friends, relatives, neighbours, colleagues. It is often bounded by where we live and whom we befriend. The formal community is defined by a vast array of voluntary associations which help structure the public and private lives of Canadian Jews. Look in the Toronto or Montreal telephone book under "Jewish" for a taste. The *Montreal Jewish Directory* for 2000 lists over one hundred Jewish communal agencies, excluding synagogues and schools. *The Jewish Community Services Directory of Greater Toronto* is a mind-boggling compendium of organized communal life. It is an annotated listing with four pages of Jewish community agencies; sixteen pages of educational services and schools; twelve pages of Israel- or Zionist-related organizations; thirty pages devoted to "Organized Community Life," which includes subheadings for community organizations, camps, choirs, dramatic groups, film clubs, kosher restaurants, newspapers and periodicals, radio and television resources, Scouts and Guides, seniors associations, social, sport, and country clubs, societies (fraternal and cultural groups), and youth groups; and twenty-five pages devoted to synagogues and religious organizations.

A fascinating paradox: as individual Jewish identities are threatened by assimilation and mixed marriage, the organized Jewish community thrives. New buildings are going up, moneys are being raised, new projects are being launched. To be a Jew means to join, to volunteer, to make donations, to go to events, and, yes, to attend meetings. The culture of the "meeting" thrives in the Jewish world. For both community professionals and lay-leaders, meetings and activities are the coin of the realm. Reading the weekly *Canadian Jewish News* is an excellent way to get a sense of the range of events sponsored by Jewish organizations in a typical week. Lectures, fundraisers, gala dinners, dances, raffles, exhibits jostle for attention, along with the routine activities sponsored by the myriad organizations. In fact, the *Canadian Jewish News* itself is a good indicator of the vitality of the organized community. While Jewish academics routinely disparage it as being an establishment organ, it sets the standard for the ethnic press of many other Canadian communities. It really does reflect the community, for better or worse.

Of course, the Jewish community today is divided. But from the 1890s to after the Second World War, the divisions were deeper. It made no sense, in the decades before the 1950s, to speak of a single, unified Jewish community.[1] Certainly, there was substantial division in Montreal, Toronto, and Winnipeg along lines of economic class, birthplace, ideology, and cultural style. A major cleavage was between the anglicized wealthier Jews and the poorer East European immigrants, or, in then-current parlance, the uptown and downtown Jews. These distinctions persisted into the post-war years, with tensions between the old-timers and the newcomers, or *di greeneh*.

Just as fierce were the ideological and cultural divisions within the working-class East European Jews themselves. Within the left, as well as within the more assimilated upper classes, there were also tensions between the Zionists and the non-Zionists. And of course there were sharp divisions between the left-wing and right-wing Zionists.[2] Some of these divisions persist. Attitudes on Israeli politics and the peace process are still polarized. Tensions among the religious denominations have become even more fractious. But we should not overstate the degree of actual friction. In fact, there is sufficient self-segregation within the Jewish world to keep it to a minimum. Secular Jews and the ultra-Orthodox have nothing to do with each other, by mutual choice. So the antagonisms are minimized. And there is even an upside. As sociologist Lewis Coser has argued, one of the positive spin-offs of conflict among social groups is it may reinforce and deepen the identities of each.[3] The differences within the Jewish world, and within Jewish communities, mean that there has been the potential for growth, for finding better options, and for adapting to changing or threatening realities.

Many Jews like to trace the origin of the Jewish communitarian thrust to the Biblical teachings of Judaism itself. Accordingly, it is embedded in the fundamental religious law that requires that prayer can only take place in the presence of a quorum of ten adult men (a *minyan*), which serves indirectly to bind the community together. Moreover, the Bible commands Jews to provide for the needy – widows, orphans, strangers, and the poor – a task best fulfilled communally. There is some truth to this cultural explanation. Unlike Eastern religions, and Catholicism, Judaism is firmly grounded as a "this worldy" religion. Belief in God is not enough to guarantee salvation. The Torah lists a total of 613 commandments, or *mitzvot*, most of which are obligatory acts for the observant Jew. The tradition of the mystic or the monk, while present, is not central to Judaic conceptions of spirituality. The family and the community are the agents through which holiness is expressed. The Talmud is really a compendium of legal decisions and commentary, relating in part to day-to-day problems. Jews are commanded to pursue justice on this earth. The verse "*kol Yisrael arevim zeh la-zeh*" ("all of Israel is bound up one to another") captures this ethos. The German Jewish psychologist Kurt Lewin claimed that Jews shared an "interdependence of fate."

But culture does not tell the whole story. These cultural predispositions were reinforced for Jewish communities in the Diaspora by anti-Semitism, which required Jews to look after their own and, indeed, fostered a tradition of self-governance. In the first instance, Jews would act collectively to meet religious requirements. Jewish Diaspora communities have always administered Jewish cemeteries and set up burial societies. This was important to guarantee burial – even for indigent Jews – according to traditional Jewish law. In addition, Jewish schools, orphanages, and relief organizations were established.

Moreover, Gentile rulers tended to recognize the corporate existence of Jews, and to relate to Jews through designated representatives. Jews have two thousand years of experience in diasporic living and related self-government. Most of this took place not in pluralistic, liberal-democratic environments in which religious or ethnic groups had their own voluntary hierarchical organizations. It happened in pre-modern societies, where membership in the Jewish community determined one's life chances. Jews had no choices. They were faced with many restrictions and exclusions, which in turn reinforced their sense of community. Being a Jew in medieval Europe or the Middle East nurtured the fact and legitimacy of Jewish communal self-government. In Amsterdam, the formal community could excommunicate Spinoza. In Eastern Europe, the *va'ad arba aratzot*, or the Council of the Four Lands – essentially Poland including the Western Ukraine and Lithuania – was a model of Jewish self-government. And Napoleon had no compunction about reconstituting a Sanhedrin – based on the self-governing

Jewish councils in Palestine, which flourished during the Second Temple period – in 1807 to represent French Jews vis-à-vis the state. Communal organization has been second nature to Jews.

The organized Jewish community has always had two functions. One has been internal, a form of self-government reflected in the many Jewish organizations that cater to Jewish needs. This internal function is now recognized as a key weapon – and the military metaphor captures the spirit of the moment – in the battle for Jewish continuity. The second function has been external, representing the interests of Jews to the outside world. In an earlier period, this role often fell to key individuals. From the eleventh century, it was filled by the *shtadlan*, or intercessor, who petitioned the king or the religious authorities on behalf of Jews, seeking to avoid persecution both physical and financial. A most delicate, and often thankless, task. Later, similar tasks were filled by *Hofjude*, or "court Jews," who emerged in the German states in the seventeenth century. Unlike the *shtadlan*, the court Jew usually had a strong personal relation with a ruler, was a person of great wealth, and had wide commercial contacts. Both figures reflected the societies in which they lived, in which notions of equal citizenship for Jews were non-existent. Today, the internal and external organizations are supported through charitable giving, a kind of voluntary taxation, which works rather well.

GHETTOS AND NEIGHBOURHOODS

The formal organizations of Jewish communal life rest on a foundation of informal community life, sustained by Jewish neighbourhoods and friendship patterns. In the Old World and later in Canada, these reflected social divisions based on wealth, Jewish learning, or lineage. Any sense of unity was nurtured by the ever-present danger of anti-Semitism, and made possible by the smaller scale and relative homogeneity of Jewish residential areas.[4]

Though restrictive ghettos have disappeared, where Jews choose to live within cities affects their Jewish lives. In the early periods of mass migration, Montreal, Toronto, and Winnipeg had heavily Jewish neighbourhoods. In this respect, surprisingly little has changed. As Jews have spread throughout the regions of Canada and moved out from the original areas of settlement in large cities, they have retained a high degree of "residential segregation." Jews not only stick together, they live together, or at least, near other Jews. Jews are by far the most residentially concentrated ethnic group in every large Canadian metropolis, and notably Montreal and Toronto.[5] Some Canadians might think that the most residentially concentrated groups in Canada would be blacks or Asians, or perhaps Italians. But they do not come close to Jews. This remarkable concentration is found not only in older communities, but even in the newer cities out West. While Jews there are more dispersed than their counterparts in Montreal and Toronto, they are still far more concentrated than any other group.[6]

This Jewish togetherness is particularly surprising. For most minority groups in Canada, those with higher levels of education or income tend to be less residentially concentrated. They have the money and desire to move out of the ethnic enclave.[7] We associate ghettos, or ethnic neighbourhoods, with poor or working-class immigrants. Not so for Jews. Even as Jews move into the suburbs, and experience greater mixing than in the past, they tend to cluster in disproportionate numbers in middle-class neighbourhoods. Jews have recreated their institutions – schools, synagogues, community centres, butchers, and bakeries – as they moved into the suburbs. This has been the case in Toronto, as Jews moved north along Bathurst and into Thornhill, and in Montreal, as Jews have moved into Côte St.-Luc and Hampstead, and then into the West Island.

Why do Jews continue to live together? When social scientists first began to study residential segregation, the consensus was clear: any observed clustering was due to discrimination. Jews lived near other Jews because housing markets discriminated against them. Some might do it for fear that Gentile neighbours might be anti-Semitic. The bitter legacy of the "ghetto" hung over any ethnic or racial neighbourhood. Researchers who studied this residential clustering initially chose a word which would echo the racist sentiments of the American South: "segregation." They wrongly equated the experience of racial minorities – blacks, Asians, Latinos – with that of European immigrant groups and Jews. Researchers tend today to prefer the term "concentration,"

which is more neutral. It allows for the possibility that minorities –
especially those who speak a different language – might actually prefer
to live in minority neighbourhoods.

In the case of Jews, residential concentrations reflected a historic
legacy from the old country, as well as practical responses to current
realities. In the old country, Jews lived in shtetls or in Jewish streets or areas
in towns and cities. That reflected historic restrictions but also evolved
into a preference. The move to the New World changed little.
Immigration is in general a traumatic experience, and any ethnic community or neighbourhood can provide a "psychic shelter" from an
unfamiliar and perhaps hostile majority group. For the Orthodox,
being within walking distance of synagogues – a necessity, as they
cannot drive on the Sabbath – and Jewish schools added an impetus
to the formation of neighbourhoods, where kosher butchers and bakeries also proliferated. All this is understandable in the case of the
mass-immigration generation of Jews. Poverty also restricted residential options of those Jews who clustered along the Main or near
Kensington Market and Spadina. But again, how to explain the
persisting concentrations in suburbs and among second- and third-
generation Jews?

Suburban Jews in Winnipeg, Toronto, and Montreal, even more
than their counterparts in many American cities, have created "gilded
ghettos" for affluent Jews. Indeed, one of the pioneering works of
Canadian social research dealt with the 1950s suburban community
of "Crestwood Heights," actually Forest Hill in Toronto, which was at the
time almost one-quarter Jewish.[8] Early Jewish residential concentration may have been due to discrimination by landlords or real-estate
agents, and poverty. But today many Jews voluntarily choose, partly for
reasons of convenience, to live near Jewish institutions and other Jews.
When moving to new areas, Jews have been known to check for *mezuzahs*
on doorposts to determine the Jewishness of new surroundings.
Perhaps there is a subliminal fear of recurring anti-Semitism, which
leads some Jews to seek safety by circling the wagons.

A leading Israeli-born American scholar, Amitai Etzioni, argued in
the late 1950s that the need for residential proximity among Jews and

other groups would decline, simply because with telephones and cars there would be less need for ethnic neighbourhoods.[9] In one sense, this is true. A new definition of a Jewish "neighbourhood" is anything within ten or fifteen minutes' driving distance. Many Jewish children are carpooled that long, and longer, to Jewish schools that are not really neighbourhood schools. But technology has obviously not eliminated the need for proximity. New Jewish neighbourhoods are recreated in the suburbs. And this does not mean that ties to the "old neighbourhood" are gone forever. Jewish families in the suburbs routinely visit the older areas of settlement for a more authentic, usually gastronomic, experience. Many suburban Jews in Montreal still trek back to the Main for smoked meat at Schwartz's, a "special" at Wilensky's, or a breakfast at Beauty's. Toronto Jews may return to Kensington and Bathurst – but more for nostalgic reasons than for the food. And the same is true for other minority groups, who move away but still visit the shops and markets they knew from their youth.

Jewish neighbourhoods in Toronto and Montreal, and to a lesser but still apparent extent in other Canadian cities, are alive and well. A Jew visiting any Canadian metropolis will be able to find those areas where Jews have clustered together, even if not as thickly as in Toronto or Montreal. They are not far from synagogues and Jewish schools. There will be a Jewish-style bakery or deli at hand. Find the Jewish Community Centre, and you will find Jewish homes close by. Jewish areas can be identified also by the proportions of homes which do not have Christmas lights glowing, though many, not to be outdone, will now have *chanukiot*, or Hanukkah candelabras, in the windows. These high levels of Jewish residential concentration are no accident. People know where they live, and why.

But Jewish neighbourhoods themselves are not homogeneous. Social class separates different groups. Jews know where their wealthy live, as compared to the broad middle class, the *amcha*, or typical Jew. Moreover, religion also differentiates Jewish areas. Again in Toronto and Montreal, there are well-known areas where ultra-Orthodox Jews live, and even Modern Orthodox tend to live close to Orthodox synagogues and institutions.

FRIENDSHIPS

Jews not only live together, they stick together. Over three-quarters of adult Canadian Jews in 1990 claimed that "most of their friends" were Jewish, compared to one half – still high – for American Jews.[10] This finding is all the more remarkable because in Montreal or Toronto at most only 3 or 4 per cent of the metro population is Jewish. In 1996, 58 per cent of Montreal Jews indicated that "all or almost all" of their closest friends were Jewish, and another 27 per cent said "most" were Jewish. And this was the way they liked it. Over 70 per cent said they felt close to other Jews "to a great extent."[11] Religious Jews were more likely to have all or almost all Jewish friends: 77 per cent for the Orthodox, to 69 per cent for the Conservative, to 36 per cent for Reform or secular Jews.

For first-, second-, and third-generation Toronto Jews in the late 1970s, between 50 and 55 per cent indicated that all of their three closest friends were Jews. This was much higher than for other European immigrant groups, where mixing rose dramatically after the immigrant generation. For the few third-generation Toronto Italians and Ukrainians, the figures were down to 10 and 3 per cent respectively – what you might expect by chance alone.[12] These ties are found even in the smaller Jewish centres. Over 80 per cent of Calgary Jews in 1997 claimed that at least half of their close friends were Jewish. And Jews comprise less than 1 per cent of the Calgary population.[13]

So the classic anti-Semitic stereotype popularly held about Jews, that they are "clannish," is true. Such a clear pattern is just not found for any other European immigrant group. Perhaps for Québécois. Perhaps for some visible minorities in Canada, especially if there is a high immigrant concentration. Perhaps for First Nations, or Hutterites. But among white, middle-class, Canadian-born groups? No. A health professional in Montreal in his late fifties reminisced about the peculiar magic of growing up Jewish in Montreal. "It was a real ghetto," he sighed, approvingly.

This pattern of social self-segregation is perplexing precisely because, on so many levels, Jews and Gentiles are blurring cultural and social differences and crossing boundaries. Why does it persist? Fear

of intermarriage is an obvious explanation. Jews face a religious pro-
scription against intermarriage that is not faced by other comparable
ethnic groups. The social segregation which begins in childhood and
persists into young adulthood helps to minimize interfaith dating
and eventually intermarriage. It is quite common for Canadian Jewish
families from rural areas or smaller cities and towns to send their children to university in Toronto or Montreal largely to meet young Jews.

Anti-Semitism is an unlikely explanation. The evidence of extensive or deep-seated anti-Semitism is just too weak, as we shall see in
Chapter 11. And the Gentiles with whom Jews are likely to come into
sustained contact are mainly educated, urban, and more cosmopolitan. They are more likely to marry Jews than beat them up. Still, the
fear of latent anti-Semitism may play a role. Many Jews feel, correctly,
that few Gentiles share their depth of concern about the security of
Israel, or Jewish assimilation, or anti-Semitism at home or abroad. This
is not anti-Semitism. Gentiles relate very openly and warmly to Jews
as human beings, but less effectively to Jews as Jews. Many committed
Jews therefore compartmentalize their relationships with Gentiles.
They share all sorts of things – working in the office, playing tennis,
going to a movie or dinner party, and even discussing family troubles –
but are unable or unwilling to communicate the depth of concerns
about Jewish issues. The fact that their Gentile friend, or colleague, or
neighbour, may be somewhat indifferent to Israel's security, or more
willing to blame Israel for Middle East conflict, or reluctant to call an
anti-Semite an anti-Semite, is best left unexplored. This sort of insecurity, in different form, was first described among American Jews on
the new suburban frontiers of the 1950s and 1960s. Sociologist Marshall
Sklare claimed that some Jews felt they must play an "ambassadorial
role" in interactions with non-Jews, making a good impression on
behalf of the group.[14] If that is still the case, it militates against the
honest communications generally required for meaningful friendships. Polite small talk is preferable to making a "faux pas."

There is also a seamier side to this communications barrier, a long
and still extant tradition in Jewish folk culture that makes fun of
Gentiles, or the *Goyim*. That undercurrent, to the extent it still exists,

also impedes the formation of true friendships across the Jewish–Gentile boundary. Gentiles are seen as, well, different. It's just easier to socialize with Jews.

Today, we find that Canadian Jews are typically middle-class and well educated. These commonalities extend into recreational activities. Jews – for whatever reason – still tend to drink less than non-Jews in social situations, get drunk less often, and suffer less from alcoholism and related pathologies. This is true even though I assume – based on reports from my teenage children – younger Jews are drinking more than my generation did. Jewish sobriety was once a hot research topic, and various esoteric explanations emerged. These stressed the sacred and ritualistic role of wine in Jewish religious life, which does explain why relatively few Jews are complete abstainers. Other arguments linked Jewish sobriety to the need to be prepared to face anti-Semitic dangers. The contrasting image of the Gentile as a drunkard, often given to acts of violence, is deeply embedded in Jewish folklore, and in the folksong and expression *shikker iz a goy*, or "drunken is a Gentile."[15] The pattern of Jewish sobriety can be confirmed by scientific studies – including data from Israel – and informal observations. Interviews with experienced bartenders confirm it; they will order far less liquor for a Jewish party than for a Gentile affair. If cash bars seem to be less common than open bars at Jewish parties, this is partly because the hosts know they will not go broke. So while Jews today may be drinking more than in the past, the Jackie Mason joke still rings true: After a movie, Gentiles are more likely to go out for a drink, and Jews to go out to eat, preferably for coffee and cake, and preferably for good-sized portions!

At another level, some Jews are reluctant to recount Jewish jokes to Gentiles, either for fear that some of the in-group references might be lost, or worse, they might appear politically incorrect. Again, as Yiddish and Jewish pop culture seep into the mainstream, this may diminish. I have waged a single-handed campaign to break down these barriers. I forward Jewish jokes I get on e-mail to a select group of non-Jewish friends, as well as to a Jewish gang. So far, no complaints. It is not clear how much Jews differ, controlling for class and education, in other lifestyle patterns. Is it still the case that "Jews buy wholesale, and

Gentiles buy retail?" If so, that might make shopping outings difficult. There is greater convergence in eating patterns between Jews and Gentiles than in the past. But even going out for a meal might still pose some problems. Some Jews are strictly kosher. Others will not eat pork, or seafood. The Jewish preference for Chinese food, or for deli, or for a brunch of bagels, cream cheese, and lox, may not be matched by Gentiles. Canadian Jews and Gentiles both winter in Florida, but often on different coasts.

There are differences in sports and recreation. While Jews today are rare among professional athletes in Canada, they participate enthusiastically in the fitness craze, and in all manner of racquet sports, golf, skiing, and cycling. But they are less likely to be gun owners, horseback riders, pet owners, avid gardeners, hunters, and fishers. I may just be a nerd, but I do not own a gun, and neither do my Jewish friends. I have never gone hunting. I have never fired a real gun. Historically, the Jewish presence in elite Canadian sports was more noticeable, because of top sports teams produced by local YMHAS, and outstanding athletes. But nowadays, as Jewish youngsters get into their later teens, they are less likely to try to become champion or professional athletes, compared to Gentiles. Affluence, and alternate routes to economic success, are likely causes.

One final point. As in the case with residential patterns, Jews who socialize together do not do so randomly. Like seeks out like. In particular, ultra-Orthodox, Orthodox, non-Orthodox, and secular Jews are more likely to socialize – and marry – within their respective groups. Most of my close Jewish friends tend to be Jews like me, for better or worse. This voluntary social segregation probably minimizes frictions among Jews.

So the Jewish community is sustained by these subtle affinities. The stage is set for us to explore the formal organizations of the community. These in turn rely on a foundation of social cohesion and interpersonal comfort among the various sub-groups that form Canadian Jewry. The organizations that comprise the Jewish polity are not simply administrative entities set up to get things done. They rest on a network of relationships, shared convictions, and bonds of intimacy.

THE JEWISH POLITY

The degree of specialization and sophistication found within the organized Jewish community is without parallel in any comparable ethnic or religious group. At times it defies explanation. There are formal organizations for everything, and they make up a Jewish polity, a kind of self-governing quasi-state. A polity comprises governing institutions as well as organizations that provide services. It requires a decision-making process that links rank-and-file members to those who are chosen as leaders. An ethnic polity can be more or less "institutionally complete," a term first coined by Canadian sociologist Raymond Breton.[16] The term refers to the degree to which the organizations of a minority community can meet the various needs of its members. Jews are perhaps the most institutionally complete group in Canada, comparable to on-reserve First Nations and Hutterites, both of whom live apart from the general population.

A Jew can live his or her entire life within an institutionally complete Jewish community. He or she can be born in a Jewish hospital; attend a Jewish daycare or nursery, Jewish day schools or supplementary schools, and summer camps; take Jewish Studies on campus and socialize at a Jewish Students' Union; find work within a Jewish organization; pray within a Jewish house of worship; patronize a Jewish library and health club and play in Jewish sports leagues; get help from a Jewish social-service agency; read Jewish papers and magazines, listen to Jewish radio, and watch Jewish TV programs; attend plays, concerts, and lectures of Jewish interest; spend his or her post-retirement years participating in programs at a Jewish Golden Age Centre; move into a Jewish old-age home or seniors' residence or hospital as needed, and be buried in a Jewish cemetery. Orthodox Jews involved in civil disputes can even go to a religious court, or *Beth Din*. The organizations that provide these cradle-to-grave services are funded by internal Jewish sources as well as the government. And to this can be added the private sector – Jewish-owned firms of all sorts and kosher bakeries, restaurants, or butchers – which add to this self-contained environment.

Political scientist Daniel Elazar outlined five spheres of communal activity: religious-congregational, educational-cultural, community relations-defence, communal-welfare, and Israel-overseas.[17] But the internal boundaries of the Jewish polity are fuzzy. Some organizations belong clearly in certain spheres: synagogues for the religious-congregational sphere, or Jewish schools for educational-cultural. But some organizations are active in more than one of these spheres. This possibility of overlap, and resultant turf battles, is a constant feature of Jewish life. While many complain, in fact it is a source of strength. It reinforces the underlying pluralism of Canadian Jewish life, and means that, despite formal agreements and jurisdictions, no one organization has a monopoly on a given area. For example, synagogues hold programs relating to Israel. Educational programming is found not only in Jewish schools, or university Jewish Studies courses, but in synagogues, Jewish community centres, arts centres like the Koffler Centre of the Arts in Toronto or the Saidye Bronfman Centre in Montreal. Some organizations, like the Canadian Jewish Congress or the Jewish federations, directly or indirectly act in all spheres.

From the outside, and often from the inside, the Jewish polity can seem a jumble of similar or competing organizations. Here is a brief, simplified overview. The major national Jewish organization is the Canadian Jewish Congress. For all its weaknesses, it is seen as a model for other Canadian minority groups. It was founded in 1919, lay moribund through the early 1930s, and then revived in 1933–34 to deal with the rising tide of anti-Semitism overseas and in Canada. In its early days the CJC was a force for democratic change and equality within the Jewish community, and a threat to the entrenched power and authority of the establishment, notably in Montreal. The CJC was seen as a "Parliament of Canadian Jewry." The Eastern European immigrants used it to challenge the authority of elite-run institutions such as the Baron de Hirsch Institute. The Labour Zionists were staunch advocates of the CJC, and were opposed initially by the establishment Federation of Zionist Societies. But by 1917, with large numbers of Jews in Europe needing aid, and with the Jewish *yishuv*, or settlement, in Palestine growing, the community edged closer together. In March 1917, an estimated 25,000 Jews went to the polling booths, and selected 209 delegates to the CJC, perhaps the greatest exercise of democratic governance in the history of Canadian Jewry.

The second convention brought 3,800 delegates to Toronto in 1934. It was a feisty affair with all segments of the community contesting elections.[18] It is ironic that today the CJC is seen as the establishment, and is at times challenged as being too timid in defending Jewish interests, or as being out of touch with ordinary Jews.

The CJC has a loose regional structure representing Canadian Jews nationwide. There are triennial conventions and elections, in which all organizations can participate and candidates run for office. Its mandate is to represent Jewish communal interests to government, usually at the federal or provincial levels. But the CJC does not reign unchallenged. The B'nai Brith, a national fraternal organization made up of individual lodges, has remained outside the CJC umbrella, and often bickers with it over jurisdiction. B'nai Brith usually petitions government on matters relating to anti-Semitism and human rights through the League for Human Rights, which it sponsors. Thus both the CJC and B'nai Brith had standing before the Deschênes Commission on war criminals in the 1980s, and each presented separate briefs.[19]

National Zionist and Israeli-linked organizations also play a role in the polity, though Zionist organizations have lost much of their importance in recent years. Zionist ideologies, like all ideologies, have lost their appeal, and all of Canadian Jewry more or less supports Israel. The Zionist message is no longer that all Jews ought to move to Israel. It is that Israel is the focal point of the Jewish world. So these organizations continue to run advocacy and educational-cultural programs. The umbrella organization is the Canadian Zionist Federation (CZF). Zionist organizations include Mizrachi, the organization of religious Zionists; the Labour Zionists on the left; the Revisionists, supporters of the Likud party, on the right; and the Zionist Organization of Canada, a centrist group. Standing apart from these is Hadassah, the women's pro-Israel organization, which has more members than any other Jewish organization in Canada. It was founded in Canada in 1917 and today boasts tens of thousands of members. The CJC, the CZF, and the B'nai Brith have jointly established the Canada–Israel Committee, the main lobby for Israel in Canada, which functions somewhat comparably to the American Israel Political Affairs Committee in the United States. In general, the CIC, as well as the mainstream national organizations cited above, supports the Israeli government's positions regardless of the party in power, and regardless of the specific issue. The official community position is that only Israelis should criticize their own government. But that has been changing. Public criticism by Jews of Israeli policies increased in the 1980s, though the levels were lower in the more deferential Canada than in the United States.[20] With the peace process of the 1990s, dovish Jewish groups such as the Canadian Friends of Peace Now became less marginal.

Other active organizations represent Israeli institutions for fund-raising purposes. These are "Canadian Friends of" universities, yeshivot, and hospitals in Israel, or organizations like ORT (Organization for Education Resources and Technological Training), which runs vocational and training school programs in Israel. The Jewish National Fund is active in promoting agricultural settlement and forestation in Israel, while Israel Bonds raises funds from private and institutional investors. Other national organizations do not have an Israeli focus. Some are affiliated with the CJC, like Second Generation, an organization originally comprised of children of Holocaust survivors but now generally oriented to Holocaust awareness and education. The work of JIAS (Jewish Immigrant Aid Services) in the area of immigrant integration has been described earlier. The Simon Wiesenthal Centre is active in combating anti-Semitism.

It is at the local level, however, that the bulk of Jewish communal organization takes place, and that the power concentrations within organized Jewish life are found. In Canada, as in the United States, the welfare federations are the units responsible for collecting general communal funds and then disbursing them to a variety of welfare, social, cultural, and recreational agencies. All these agencies are run by volunteer lay boards and paid professional staff. Occasionally, there is tension between the two, with power relations varying by agency and specific personalities.[21] Quite often, seasoned professionals wield more power than do elected or selected lay leaders from the community – not unlike the power wielded by senior public servants in Ottawa.

There are also organizations indirectly affiliated with the Jewish community, such as Mount Sinai Hospital in Toronto and the Sir

Mortimer B. Davis Jewish General Hospital in Montreal. These hospitals were founded initially because of the difficulties faced by Jewish doctors in securing positions, and in providing kosher food and a supportive environment for Jewish patients. But today they are funded basically by the provincial governments, and their staff and patient profile is decidedly mixed, though Jews are probably well represented. In theory, the state provides medical care and Jews can go anywhere. In practice, Jews are fiercely loyal to their hospitals. A community survey in Montreal found that most Jews listed health care as the number-one priority for the Jewish community.[22] Other organizations were founded as alternatives to non-Jewish counterparts, such as the YM-YWHA, and continue to enjoy communal funding. Finally, private "Jewish" golf clubs and dining clubs were created when Jews faced exclusion from Gentile clubs. Even as access to these "Gentile" clubs is now generally open to affluent Jews, some Jewish clubs continue to exist.

A final element of the local community is the network of Jewish schools. Large cities have networks of private Jewish day and afternoon schools, which span the ideological range from ultra-Orthodox to liberal/secular. Historically, Jewish schools jealously guarded their autonomy, and in general were funded by fees and private donations. In recent years, federations have recognized a communal responsibility for Jewish education. They have established agencies to assist the schools, directly through educational services and indirectly by helping schools provide financial aid to needy students. I explore the issue of Jewish education in Chapter 8.

Anti-Semites accuse Jews of constituting a "state within a state," and of having dual – and conflicting – loyalties to their host countries. On the first part of the allegation, the anti-Semites are right, with one important caveat. The Jewish polity is only *like* a state within a state (so is most every minority polity). Jewish organizations have no power of compulsory membership or taxation and cannot use force. Jews can construct a meaningful, private Jewish identity while remaining detached from the Jewish polity. On the other hand, participation in the Jewish polity does not mean disloyalty or treason to Canada. There is no evidence that this high level of Jewish institutional completeness in fact poses any conflict. Jews remain among the most loyal, patriotic Canadians. They cherish freedom more than other Canadians who have suffered less from its absence. That was the case for my parents. And many Canadian Jews are as active in the general Canadian community as they are in the Jewish community.

Canada and Israel have never been at war. But that does not mean that interests of Jews, or any minority group, are always identical to Canada's presumed national interest. Japanese Canadians know all too well the dangers that can arise when Canadians seek to question the loyalty of a group of citizens *in extremis*. Far short of war, Israel provides litmus tests for Canadian Jewish loyalties. These questions allow of no easy answer; I will pick up the thread in Chapter 9, on Jews and politics.

CULTURAL SENSITIVITY

Jews are not forced to seek services, or live their lives, within the Jewish polity and its organizations. Since so many do, we have to assume that is what they prefer. Even if aspects of this participation come close to a kind of ghettoization – especially for the ultra-Orthodox – there is in general no coercion involved. So we wonder what Jews get out of it. The concern for "cultural sensitivity" in the provision of all manner of services in Canada has become a mantra among policy-makers in the human service area as well as for advocates of minority groups.[23] And effective ethnic polities are one way to ensure culturally sensitive – and presumably more effective – services.

There are historical roots to all of this. The expansion of the welfare state in the post-war period meant that governments began to fund or regulate the services that had sprung up to meet the needs of minority and immigrant communities. Canadians forget that most immigrant communities had thriving networks of organizations – political, recreational, social, cultural, fraternal – long before official multicultural grants appeared on the scene. As the public sector expanded, however, so did the legitimate concerns for equal rights and equal treatment. Discriminatory, second-class treatment by mainstream institutions of the state, by design or by default, was no longer acceptable. The new assumption in the field of social services is that minority groups have specific cultures which must be considered.[24] Otherwise, they may be victimized by overt or covert racism or attacks on their self-esteem. For this reason, policies in areas like health, social service, education, law and policing, and media recognize that a diverse population requires diverse modes of service. Recognizing diversity is both fair and effective, better than offering homogeneous, one-size-fits-all services. Of course there are limits. A liberal-democratic society like Canada does not tolerate every type of ethno-specific cultural practice; the debate on female genital operations is perhaps the most dramatic case in point.[25]

The root of the concern for what we now call cultural sensitivity in North America can be found in the experience of Jews and Catholics at the end of the 1800s and earlier. Jewish and Catholic social service agencies and hospitals provided culturally sensitive services to the masses of Jewish and Catholic immigrants. Jewish agencies multiplied. In Montreal, the Young Men's Hebrew Benevolent Society was formed in 1863, later renamed the Baron de Hirsch Institute after a substantial donation in 1890 by the baron. The aim was to care for the needy and elderly. The Federation of Jewish Philanthropies was set up in 1916 with twelve constituent agencies, including a Yiddish library founded in 1905 and the precursor of the Jewish Public Library, the Herzl Health Clinic founded in 1907, and Mount Sinai, a tuberculosis hospital, which opened in 1912 in the mountains of Ste.-Agathe. In 1934 the Jewish General Hospital was created. In Toronto, the roots of the Jewish polity and the establishment of specific Jewish institutions date back to the same period. The Ladies Montefiore Benevolent Society was formed in 1878, the Jewish Mutual Benefit Society in 1896, a Jewish Old Folks Home in 1914, and the Mount Sinai Hospital in 1922. Toronto's Federation of Jewish Philanthropies was established in 1916 and became the United Jewish Welfare Fund in 1937.[26]

Well before contemporary scholars tried to analyze the meaning of culturally sensitive services for ethnic and racial minorities, Jewish social workers were wrestling with similar questions. (And not only Jews. In journals such as *Catholic Charities Review*, practitioners would seek to clarify what was essentially "Catholic" about the service in a Catholic welfare agency or hospital. Often, these debates revolved around out-of-wedlock pregnancy and adoption – issues still with us.) In publications like the *Journal of Jewish Communal Service*, professionals tried to define the "Jewish" values and principles which should inform a community centre or any other Jewish social-service agency. In recent years, Jewish federations throughout North America have renewed this concern with a vengeance. They seek to infuse more and more of the general social services with a heightened Jewish consciousness, linked to the continuity agenda. It is now common to begin board meetings of Jewish agencies with a *d'var Torah*, an analysis of a religious text. Another indication is the steady increase among the ranks of professional Jewish communal servants of observant, *yarmulka*-wearing Jews. Up until the early 1970s, Jewish social-service agencies were run by secular, progressive Jewish professionals, whose agenda was often concerned more with social justice than with Jewish survival.

The question remains: What is Jewish about these Jewish social service agencies? Do ethno-specific Jewish agencies by definition yield culturally sensitive services? Imagine a Jewish family in acute crisis, where a child wants to marry a non-Jew against the wishes of one or both parents and one or more grandparent. All hell is breaking loose, and they need counselling desperately. A secular state-run agency that employed non-Jewish professionals, and whose practice took no account of Jewish cultural sensibilities, would not be delivering Jewishly sensitive service. A situation of maximal cultural sensitivity would likely be one in which a Jewish client received help in a Jewish agency from a Jewish professional, and whose manner and content reflected knowledge of and sensitivity to Jewish cultural constraints. But even employing Jewish professionals need not guarantee culturally sensitive service. A secular Jew might not empathize with the concerns of an ultra-Orthodox Jew. A third-generation Canadian middle-class Ashkenazi Jew might not understand the culture of a struggling, immigrant Russian Jew or North African Jew or Israeli.[27]

The Jewish community is diverse. My parents' world was that of Polish Jewish survivors. Their Montreal world barely connected with that of the largely Canadian-born, acculturated, and affluent Jews of Westmount. Today, within the Montreal or Toronto Jewish communities, there are formal organizations representing Sephardi, Israeli,

Ethiopian, and Russian Jews. These organizations are seen as best able to meet certain needs of the sub-community members, not only by speaking the language, but by empathizing with their problems. As noted in Chapter 5, Hasidic or ultra-Orthodox Jews need even more specialized services. In providing them, is the Canadian Jewish community acting responsibly, or risking further fragmentation? This is precisely the same question that Canada must ponder, regarding the limits of multiculturalism and the balance between diversity and social cohesion.

GIVING

If the range of Jewish organizations is hard to believe, so, too, is the extent of Jewish fundraising. Jews give until it hurts. The Jewish concept of *tzedakah* (this Hebrew term has the same root as the word for "justice") differs dramatically from the Christian concept of charity. The Jewish approach sees giving as an obligation, a commandment. The Christian view sees giving as an act of loving-kindness. Jews should rejoice when approached by a beggar, since they now have a chance to fulfil a commandment. For that reason, my father never left the house without some change for panhandlers. It is a Jewish custom to give travellers a bit of money when they are about to leave on a trip, to give to the first poor person they see when they arrive. The practice is supposed to guarantee a safe journey, since the traveller is now going not for his or her own pleasure but as a *shaliach mitzvah*, a messenger sent to commit a good deed.

The annual Jewish Appeals raise money not only for the communal agencies, but for Israel as well. This fundraising is separate from the national and Israel-related agencies mentioned above, and from synagogues and schools, which all raise their own funds. Historically, more than half the funds collected in the annual Appeal in Canadian communities were earmarked for Israel. But that percentage has been declining steadily over recent years, as Israel's economy strengthens and as Israelis recognize that supporting Jewish identity in the Diaspora is in the long run the best support for Israel. Jewish philanthropy is prodigious, and Canadian Jews are perhaps the most generous givers in the Jewish world, rivalled only by South Africans. Jews give more than most comparable religious and ethnic groups. (There are exceptions.

Mormons continue to tithe, for the most part, which is a much higher rate of giving than among Jews.) But there is nevertheless a deep-seated gloom within the world of Jewish philanthropy. Annual federation campaigns have become flat. Fundraisers are worried about the declining loyalties of the next generation of Jews, especially the children of big givers, and the fact that Israel will lose its lustre as a target for philanthropy. One analysis of Jewish fundraising in the United States found a 25-per-cent reduction in the number of gifts from 1974 to 1987, and that "relative to the growth of U.S. philanthropy, giving to Jewish causes has fallen since the early 1970s."[28]

In general, as Jews become more accepted in mainstream North American circles, Jewish philanthropic dollars are flowing to non-Jewish charities, notably universities and medical research. In fact, Jews have historically been large givers to both Jewish and non-Jewish charities. But there is a shift underway. As one Jewish communal leader put it, involvement in charities such as Centraide/United Way simply means "less money for Jewish causes."[29]

Jewish giving can be understood as in part fee-for-service, and in part straight philanthropy. As indicated earlier, fee-for-service includes the purchase of memberships in synagogues or the JCC or YS, or paying for Jewish schooling or camping. These fees usually are supplemented by fundraising to meet the total cost of the service; the more affluent users help support the needy. Similarly, the purchase of Israeli Bonds can be understood as an investment, though an emotional one. Philanthropy, in contrast, is writing a cheque while receiving nothing tangible in return.

In recent years, Jewish giving has been marked by three major innovations. First is the habit of directed giving to specific agencies or causes, and away from federations and appeals. An example is the New Israel Fund, which receives donations aimed at progressive causes in Israel. Giving to specific institutions like Israeli universities or hospitals, or Jewish studies programs, or yeshivot in Israel or North America, has become more popular. Another example is giving to Holocaust museums, memorials, or educational centres. Yet another is the "continuity" binge of the past decade, with its crisis atmosphere. Even here, there have been competing thrusts, notably between inreach and out-reach programs. The former want to strengthen the identity of Jews who are already involved, the latter want to reach out to the unaffiliated or marginal. In both cases, funds are set aside for new continuity projects. (My own bias tilts slightly towards inreach efforts, based on the business adage that "the best customer is the one who is already in the store." It is arrogant for Jewish communal planners to assume that unaffiliated Jews are poor misguided souls who need information or special prodding. Most are people who have deliberately chosen a life in which Judaism plays little or no role, and most are reasonably content. If they are not, most have access to Jewish friends and are bright enough to find out how to integrate back into the community. If they so decide, wonderful. But the return on the investment may not be great.)

The second innovation is the development of Jewish community foundations in the major cities. These foundations, in conjunction with federations, collect donations or bequests. The interest from these endowments supplements the money collected through the annual appeals. In this approach, the organized community retains a large degree of control through consulting with donors, though ultimately the donor can decide to target the gift. Historically, Jews have been much more comfortable with annual giving than with giving through foundations. They preferred to leave capital untouched. This is changing. Bequests to foundations are a way of assuring that Jewish causes receive support long after the family patriarch has passed away, without leaving things up to children and grandchildren whose Jewish commitments may be diluted.

The third innovation is the thousands of private Jewish family foundations which have been created over the years in the United States and Canada. Many of these give only in part to Jewish charities. One study of twenty-one American Jewish family foundations, each with over five million dollars in annual giving, found that nearly all gave two-thirds of their grants to non-Jewish causes.[30] Some of the family foundations are set up through community foundations; others are truly independent. The effect is to "privatize" the process of giving, and to allow individuals to set priorities which can affect the Jewish future. If Steven Spielberg values Holocaust remembrance and survivor testimony, if Charles Bronfman values trips to Israel for every North American teen or young adult, if Ronald Lauder values the rebuilding of Eastern European Jewish communities, and if Leslie Wexner values training Jewish lay leaders and communal professionals, then that is what they and their foundations do. The explosion of activity in the entire area of Holocaust commemoration – from academic chairs to conferences to museums and monuments – has been driven more by committed donors than by Jewish communal planners. To label this as incipient anarchy in the world of major Jewish philanthropy would be an overstatement – for the time being. While these activities are all commendable, some more than others, there is certainly no master plan.

Canadian Jews give more than Americans. According to 1990 survey data, 41 per cent of Canadian Jews gave one hundred dollars or more to the Appeal, compared to only 21 per cent in the United States. Moreover, for those households who do give one hundred dollars or more, the average gift in Canada is $1,700, compared to $1,300 in the United States.[31] But an emphasis on average or median gifts is misleading. It is a rule of thumb in Jewish fundraising that about 5 to 10 per cent of the gifts yield 80 to 90 per cent of the dollars. An American study in 1987 found that of the $710 million raised by American federations, 60 per cent was raised from just over 1 per cent of the givers.[32] Wealthy families usually set the tone for each annual campaign by their gifts, and others follow suit. This pattern has distinguished Montreal from Toronto. In Montreal, the Bronfman family was long the mainstay of the campaign, and established wealthy families took their cue. Toronto has not had a Bronfman, nor a cadre of old-moneyed families, which explains why per capita the UJA still yields more funds in Montreal than in Toronto.

The role of key givers has yielded its share of anecdotes. Sam Bronfman summoned wealthy Montreal Jews to an urgent parlour meeting just before the Six Day War in 1967. According to the story, he asked those attending to take out their chequebooks and start writing. One person handed him a cheque, allegedly for $250,000 – real money in those days. Mr. Sam tore it up, and waited for more. What is interesting about this story is that while it may be apocryphal, no one doubts it could be true. Jews are not shy about asking other Jews to give. And in Jewish folklore, the Jewish needy are never reluctant to press their moral claim.

> *A beggar stops Lord Rothschild on a drive through his village, asking for charity. Rothschild gives the man ten zlotys. The beggar says, "But last year you gave me twenty zlotys." Rothschild replies, "But this year was bad for my investments." The beggar, "So just because you had a bad year, I should suffer?"*

Jewish fundraisers, like beggars, are also not known for timidity.

> *A Protestant, Catholic, and Jew are shipwrecked on a desert island. The Protestant builds a big fire. The Catholic writes a huge "HELP" in the sand with a log. The Jew is lounging on the beach. They go over and ask, "Don't you want to be rescued?" He answers, "Look, before we left I made my pledge to the United Jewish Appeal but didn't pay up. Don't worry, they'll find me."*

In any event, the Appeal in Montreal, with a Jewish community of less than one hundred thousand, raised roughly $32 million per year through the mid-1990s.[33] The figure for Toronto, with a population two-thirds greater, was $35 million. These figures have been increasing moderately at best, though community foundations and family foundations have become far more popular. The Montreal "flat" trend is actually commendable, given the steady exodus – to Toronto – of potential givers, and the generally weaker economic conditions in the city. By the end of the 1990s, the Jewish Community Foundation in Montreal had collected an endowment of $104 million. The figures for Toronto were an estimated $84 million, for Winnipeg $29 million, and Vancouver $12 million.[34] The interest on these amounts is still far less than the annual campaign, but the endowments are increasing significantly, and these amounts should be seen as relative orders of magnitude. The stock market run-up of the 1990s and the aging of Canadian Jewry fuelled the increase in bequests. No other ethnic or religious group has set up foundations which are as well developed. Not even close.

Jewish family foundations play an even larger role than community foundations. Jews are highly represented among such foundations, to put it mildly. According to Canada's *Directory of Foundations* for 1997, there were 990 family foundations in Canada, with assets of $4.6 billion and total grants of $367.6 million (from 1993 to 1995). About 29 per cent of them made grants to Jewish causes, including Israel. These would overwhelmingly – but not entirely – be Jewish family foundations. Of these foundations, their total grants were $50.4 million (based on most recent reporting years), and of this amount $27.2 million, or almost 55 per cent, went to Jewish recipients. In other words, over 7 per cent of the actual amounts granted from all foundations went to Jewish causes. How many foundations gave to other ethnic or religious groups? Very few indeed. Nine made donations to Ukrainian organizations, three to Chinese, two to Italian, thirty-six to Catholic churches and organizations, twenty-three to general Christian schools and education, forty to Christian organizations in general. (There would be double counting here.) Far below the 287 which gave to Jewish causes.[35] How does this compare with the American case? The 55 per cent Canadian figure is far higher. A recent estimate for large Jewish foundations is that only one-third of their giving went to Jewish causes.[36]

So we have established that rich Jews give to Jewish causes. They do so more than any comparable group, and more in Canada than in the United States. What of the broader range of giving? It is difficult to make comparisons with Christian churches, since the closest analogue would be giving simply to synagogues and direct religious organizations. According to a 1987 Decima survey, the proportion of Canadians who contributed to religious organizations ranged from 35 per cent for those under thirty-five to 60 per cent for those over sixty. The median donation was $160 for thirty-five to fifty-four year olds, and $170 from those over fifty-five. Very nice, but well below the average donations to the Jewish Appeal.[37] Part of the extent of Jewish giving reflects the group's above-average incomes. But not all. Sociologist Reginald Bibby, a leading student of Canadian churches, has bemoaned the coming financial crisis facing churches in the wake of declining observance and memberships. This lament should not mask the profound differences between Christian and Jewish traditions of fundraising. As mentioned,

Jewish fundraisers can be rough, but they are effective. Bibby described the emergence of typical "planned giving" programs in Canadian churches, and then writes, "Crass though all this might sound to some, especially those already wary of religious groups appeals' for money, it has become an extremely common practice in Canada."[38] Jewish fundraisers are less concerned about appearing crass when appealing for money. In their view, the end does justify the means.

PARTICIPATION AND DEMOCRACY

Jewish organizational life is full of duplication and turf battles.[39] Even the scheduling of events in the crowded Jewish communal calendar leads to days on which lectures, fundraising dinners, and graduations conflict. This means there are enough leadership positions to go around, and organizations to suit everyone. To be sure, some organizations have few ordinary community members. Their leaders are generals without troops, and they have inflated memberships, are poorly funded, and mainly for immigrants. This can be found among many minority groups, though less so for Jewish than for non-Jewish organizations.

Minority organizations fill a psychic and social need. Participating in them is a form of cultural identification, particularly for the leaders, who are often Canadian-born and middle-class. North America has traditionally valued joiners. Organizational involvement replaces religious observance or immersion in an ethnic culture as a way of expressing an identity. Many Jewish leaders run from meeting to meeting, but are not highly religious. This kind of voluntary involvement persists long after knowledge of Yiddish is gone and keeping kosher is a distant memory. Even Jews in mixed marriages use this organizational route as a link to a Jewish identity. (As a result American Conservative Judaism has recently moved to prohibit Jews involved in mixed marriages from assuming leadership roles in the movement.)

For whatever reason, Jews are joiners par excellence. In 1990, 47 per cent of Canadian Jews claimed to belong to a Jewish organization, 31 per cent to actually do volunteer work, and 25 per cent to belong to a board or committee. These figures are even higher than those for American Jews, which were 37 per cent, 24 per cent, and 24 per cent.[40] My hunch is that when Canadian Jews join a Jewish organization, they are more likely to do so as Jews; when American Jews join, they are more likely to do so as Americans or volunteers. We know a fair bit about the kinds of Canadians who are involved with Jewish organizations. They are more likely to be fifty-five to sixty-four, with children who have already grown up. They are more likely to be Orthodox, and to be wealthy. (In Toronto 51 per cent of Jews with incomes over $150,000 volunteered. Money matters.) Volunteering is also higher for those born in their city of residence or for those who have lived there longer.[41] In Montreal and Toronto about 38 per cent of Jews are members of Jewish organizations, and 26 to 28 per cent are volunteers. Even though Americans are great joiners, Canadian Jews match or beat American Jews in the organizational sweepstakes.[42]

And no group in Canada joins like Jews. A Toronto study found that Jews are more likely than other ethnic groups to know of communal organizations, to belong to an organization, and to express views about community affairs. And with the exception of Ukrainians – a group with long roots in Canada and which was invigorated with a post-war wave of migration – the gaps between Jews and the other groups are large. Jews have contradictory attitudes about their communal organizations. Most of those same Toronto Jews did not feel they were "close to the centre of community activities" despite their high levels of participation. Perhaps they felt that there is a core group of *machers*, or big shots, which is the real, establishment centre of the community. In any case this perception contradicts others from the survey. Jews were most likely to claim that they knew communal leaders personally, had frequent contact with leaders, and were informed about their activities.[43] Yet they did not feel close.

There is a reason for this ambivalence. Jewish communal leaders carry a special burden, a legacy of the Holocaust. Jewish leaders in Germany, and Jewish leaders in the ghettos – members of the Jewish Councils – have had to wrestle with accusations that they were not sufficiently aggressive in resisting the rise of Nazism or the actual implementation of the Final Solution. Others have wondered whether Jewish leaders in North America really did all they could to pry open the gates for desperate German Jewish refugees, or, later in the war, to encourage the Allies to make the rescue of Jews a top priority. Many answers have been offered. But regardless of the explanations of the past, one thing is clear. Jewish communal leaders by the 1980s and 1990s had taken heed of the tragic lessons of the past.

The survivors were decisive in this move to greater militancy. An early case involved the response to a small neo-Nazi movement growing in Ontario in the 1960s. The established organizations were monitoring the group, but avoided public and violent confrontations. Many survivors felt that militant action was needed. On May 30, 1965, several hundred Jews and anti-Nazis protested violently against an attempted Nazi rally at Allan Gardens in Toronto, and several were arrested. The aftermath of the riot exposed the fault line between the militants and the more conventional communal leaders.[44]

So-called establishment leaders no longer reflexively hold back; one thinks of Edgar Bronfman's campaigns against Kurt Waldheim and to restore looted Jewish assets from European banks. Few leaders wish to appear timid in the defence of Jewish communal interests and security, even when they take cautionary positions.

Despite the obvious fact that communal leaders are not demographically representative of the range of the community, and despite the folkloric populist resentments toward the "establishment," rank-and-file members of the community are reasonably satisfied.[45] In fact, Canadian Jewish leaders are as responsive and representative as the Canadian government. Communal leadership is not a closed shop. At one level, the wealthy Jewish families who comprise the "big givers" exercise power either through direct holding of office in the federations or though behind-the-scenes contacts with communal agencies. Top community professionals are in regular communication with these donors. However, through the 1970s and 1980s, positions of lay leadership slowly became more representative and meritocratic.[46] While earlier, power was concentrated among elderly businessmen, this group has been broadened with the infusion of other professionals (lawyers, doctors, academics, rabbis), women, the Orthodox, and younger people. In Montreal, francophone Jews have both established their own organizations, notably the Communauté Sépharade du Québec, and begun to involve themselves as leaders in the general community. It is certainly true that the less well-off, the very old, and recent immigrants, remain underrepresented in leadership positions. (The same is true of Parliament.) But by and large, positions of power on lay boards are open to those who have the time and talent to contribute. Those who do well are generally rewarded with more responsibilities, as the demand for leaders exceeds the supply. The bias here favours the middle-class, rather than an elite group of Jews.

The big givers who play leadership roles are responsive to constituents, and on many issues actually reflect popular sentiment. If Jewish leaders are not socio-economically representative of their community, neither are members of the Canadian cabinet. There is probably a much better chance for a Jew to be active in Jewish communal affairs than for a typical citizen to play a meaningful role in federal, provincial, or municipal politics. It used to be said that Jewish communities were run according to the Golden Rule: whoever has the gold, rules. That is less and less the case.

None of this means that all is rosy and light. If most Jews feel the leaders are representative, some remain disgruntled and marginalized. There is a venerable tradition within Jewish folklore that pokes fun at Jewish communal leaders, and tries to keep them humble. The Talmudic sage Rabbi Gamliel, in the Ethics of the Fathers II: 2, warns: "Let those who occupy themselves with the [affairs of the] community do so only for the sake of Heaven." The message is that some leaders do line their pockets. An old joke, attributed perhaps apocryphally to Israeli Prime Minister David Ben Gurion, describes a conversation with President Eisenhower in which each leader claims he has the tougher job. Ike says, "I am the president of two hundred million people." Ben Gurion replies, "But I am the prime minister of two million presidents." And then there is the classic joke below.

A Jewish traveller arrives in town looking for a meeting with a Mr. Goldberg, the head of the local Jewish community. The traveller asks for directions to his house. "Goldberg, that thief! Two rights, then a left." Getting lost again, he asks another person for directions. "Goldberg, that pig! Turn left for two blocks, and then a right." So it goes with more insults until the traveller finds Goldberg's house. As they sit down for their meeting, the traveller asks, "Mr. Goldberg, being the head of the local community must take up so much of your time, meeting upon meeting. Why do you do it?" Goldberg sighs, "I know it's not easy, but I do it for the honour."

The history of all minority politics in Canada, and Jews are no exception, is a history of internal battles and divisions, of shifting coalitions and power blocs, and of changing political and communal agendas.[47] Even as most Jews recognize the efficacy of their leaders and communal institutions, they also recognize major cleavages. In one study, two-thirds of Toronto Jews felt their group is divided "very much or somewhat" between rich and poor; 29 per cent between political groups, 63 per cent between religious groups, and 43 per cent between regional groups. Moreover, 61 per cent of Jews perceived two or more divisions, far more than any other group.[48] Remember, the ancient Israelites were torn by division while wandering in the desert. This is nothing new.

Most of the perceived divisions are no longer dangerous. Apart from religious tensions, the community is far more united than it has been in the past. For example, the organized Jewish left declined even before the end of the Cold War. The Workmen's Circle, long a mainstay of the immigrant progressive community, has shrunk in size and influence. The more radical United Jewish People's Order has all but disappeared. The community is united in support of Israel and the basic principles of the welfare state. The problems of immigrant integration and concern for the poor remain, but without the earlier class and ethnic conflict. Still, there have been policy issues which have challenged the organized community in the post-war period. By and large, after initial periods of resistance, the established organizations have co-opted the new groups and broadened the communal agenda to include their concerns. This has been the recurring pattern of conflict resolution in the Jewish community. There are only two litmus tests for inclusion today: support for Israel's right to exist, and for basic liberal democratic values. Thus, groups like the right-wing Jewish Defence League, which has advocated violence, and radical left-wing or ultra-Orthodox groups who are actively opposed to the very existence of a Jewish state of Israel, are outside the broad consensus. They are not represented in the Canadian Jewish Congress.

The Jewish agenda has never been cast in stone, and has been surprisingly responsive to pressure from below. Among those Jews who are less conventional, or who are less deeply committed, mainstream Jewish organizations will have less impact.[49] Marginal or creative Jews have an aversion to formal, organizational life of any sort, whether in terms of large suburban synagogues or large-membership organizations. Smaller, grassroots, and more informal organizations will meet their needs. But if successful, these will eventually become incorporated into the Jewish mainstream.

The movements for Soviet Jewry, for Ethiopian Jewry, and for communal funding for Jewish education are examples of successful populist movements from the 1960s through the 1980s. The younger militants were eventually brought into the fold, and their agenda became the community's. Another struggle had to do with the Canadian Friends of Peace Now. For a long time, their internal criticism of Israeli policy, of both Likud and Labour governments, was considered too left-wing. As Montreal Peace Now activist Dr. Frank Guttman recalls, in the early days the group had trouble finding a platform in the Jewish community, particularly during the Begin and Shamir years. They were unwelcome in most synagogues and communal agencies. But in recent years, as the peace process emerged in the Middle East, the group has found open doors, including in Orthodox synagogues. Guttman himself has been a member of the Canada–Israel Committee, Quebec Region. The group today claims about six hundred members in Toronto, two hundred in Montreal, and smaller chapters in a few other cities. One difference between Peace Now in Canada and in the United States was the policy not to take out paid ads (letters to the editor and articles were acceptable) critical of the Israeli government in the mainstream Canadian press. American

Peace Now routinely sponsored ads in the *New York Times*. All the Canadian ads have been "in-house," in the *Canadian Jewish News*. The more reserved Canadian Jews keep disputes in the family. Guttman explains the difference: "We're Canadian."[50] Some may see all this as a form of clever co-optation. Perhaps. But the Jewish polity today is an inclusive "big tent," with most disagreements kept inside.

7

BETWEEN HIGH CULTURE
AND DAILY LIFE

From Literature and Art to Klezmer and Kugel

"To get away from Judaism is what most of those who began
to write in German wanted, usually with the vague approval
of their fathers ... this is what they wanted; but with their little
back legs they were glued to the Judaism of their fathers, and
their little front legs could find no new footing. Their despair
over this was their inspiration."
— Franz Kafka, in Letters to Max Brod,
Letters from 1902 to 1924

"Julie, I told him, Julie, don't go!"
— Wayne and Shuster, "Rinse the Blood Off My Toga,"
skit about Julius Caesar and the Ides of March

THE ELEMENTS OF JEWISH CULTURE

My adolescent son is into what he calls "the Jewish *schvung*." This is not
religious. Rather, it is Jewishness expressed as tribal kitsch, group habits
or stereotypes, and in popular culture as television sitcoms and Jackie
Mason tapes. He follows the exploits, for better or worse, of Jews in the

news, with a hopeful eye out for the triumphs of (the too few) Jewish athletes. The ex-Blue Jay Shawn Green is a solid ballplayer, but he is no Hank Greenberg. Still, my son will take what he can get, and wonders – his litmus test – if Green would play on Yom Kippur . . .

The proof that Jews are a multicultural group par excellence in Canada is most obvious in the domain of culture. Yet this success comes with its own paradoxes. Compared to that of most other ethno-cultural groups, Jewish culture is thriving, but this coincides with agonizing fears of assimilation and cultural dilution. And the contribution of Jews and Jewish styles and themes to the broader Canadian culture is large, despite – or maybe because of – a perceived cultural distinctiveness. Jews remain cultural insiders and outsiders at the same time.

What is Jewish culture? What isn't? It includes Jewish foods, rituals and customs (both religious and secular), Jewish objects displayed in Jewish homes, Jewish mannerisms, habits, and values, and Jewish music, art, and literature, ranging from Wayne and Shuster to Montreal's Yiddish Theatre and Toronto's Ashkenaz festival, from the novels of Mordecai Richler to the works of expat philosopher Emil Fackenheim. Culture exists on different levels. It is, in the anthropological sense, the stuff of everyday life. It is folk or popular culture. It is the high culture of an artistic elite. Religion is for some the bedrock of Jewish culture and will be explored in Chapter 10. Because of the diversity of the Canadian Jewish community, there are several distinctive Jewish sub-cultures, some reflecting ethnic differences, others differences of ideology or lifestyle.

The interaction between any minority culture and the so-called majority-group culture is a two-way street. This has certainly been the case for Jews. Consider first that Jewish culture has been influenced by the Canadian context. Some see this influence leading to decline, others to transformation. Some see true Jewish culture only as "Judaic" culture, a unique set of religious values and traditions. Others see it as the product of social circumstances common to many European immigrant groups, or groups with a history of persecution.

Moreover, is there anything distinctively Canadian about Canadian Jewish culture, or is Canadian Jewish culture the same as that originating in the United States? The insecurities of Canadian cultural nationalism have few resonances among mainstream Canadian Jews. Canadian Jews, certainly those involved in communal organizations, are not generally America-bashers. American Jews are comrades in arms. The American tie has often been a lifeline in the struggle to remain Jewish, even though as a whole Jewish culture by any measure remains more vibrant in Canada. By force of numbers, America remains for Canadian Jewry a welcome source of creativity, personnel for Jewish institutions, and training for Jewish communal workers. In this sense, Canadian cultural nationalists and Jewish survivalists in Canada have diametrically opposed attitudes toward the United States.

Consider as well the impact of Judaism and Canadian Jewry on Canadian art and culture. Canadian culture, both popular and in its high form, has been enriched, and indeed transformed, by contributions of Jews and other non-English and non-French immigrant groups.[1] Think of a bagel, preferably warm and fresh with some cream cheese and lox. Is a bagel simply Jewish food, or is it part of a general Canadian food scene? This chapter looks at both Jewish culture in Canada, and the role of Jews in Canadian culture. Let us begin with the former.

JEWISH LANGUAGES

Language is the foundation of culture. The two major Jewish languages in Canada are Hebrew and Yiddish.[2] In pre-war Eastern Europe, nearly every adult Jew could speak Yiddish. It was the daily language of most Jews, the exceptions being the urbanized and educated, though even those Polish- or Russian-speakers knew some Yiddish. Most Jewish men and some Jewish women could also read Hebrew, the language of the Bible and daily prayer. Very few could speak modern Hebrew, with the exception of some Zionists.

Yiddish has lost ground. In Canada, as in the United States, it has declined over the decades as a language of daily use, and as a mother tongue.[3] Only among certain Hasidic sects do we find Yiddish used daily, and given their large family size, there is some growth potential for Yiddish in this group. Hebrew is faring better. With the proliferation of organized Jewish school systems, and the effects of travel and links to Israel, knowledge of Hebrew has been increasing steadily. Not only do most Jews know how to read the Hebrew of the Bible and prayers, but many can now speak conversational Hebrew. Hasidim prefer not to use Hebrew, a Holy language, for mundane secular purposes.

Here are the numbers. Yiddish has declined as a mother tongue in Canada, from 32,800 speakers in 1981 to 26,250 in 1991.[4] It has also dropped as the language spoken at home, from 10,650 in 1981 to 8,000 in 1996. The increasing Hasidic population, and some recent elderly immigrants from the former Soviet Union, has helped offset the loss as old-timers and older Holocaust survivors die off. More Canadians – 46,650 in 1996, down from 53,420 in 1991 – can speak some Yiddish than claim it as mother tongue or home language. Hebrew is on the upswing. In the 1991 Census, 13,850 claimed Hebrew as their mother tongue, up from 8,300 in 1981. Moreover, 8,250 in 1996 claimed Hebrew as their home language, up from 3,850 in 1981. These are mainly ex-Israelis. But a surprising 60,750 Canadians in 1996 claim they can hold a conversation in Hebrew, up from 52,455 in 1991. Here we see the influence of increasing levels of Jewish education and travel to Israel.[5]

Hebrew is sustained mainly through Jewish education, both day schools and supplementary schools. Hebrew is also taught in Ontario and Quebec within the public schools system as part of heritage language programs.[6] And the language is promoted through the presence of Israeli immigrants in Canada. Israeli artists, singers, and dance troupes perform regularly in Canada, drawing both ex-Israelis and Canadian-born Jews to their concerts. Hebrew songs, both religious and secular, are sung at Jewish bar and bat mitzvah celebrations, and at wedding parties.

Survey data confirm these census findings and interpretations. They report 37 per cent of Canadian Jews can converse in Yiddish (higher than the rate estimated by the census) and 25 per cent in Hebrew. Older Jews tend to speak Yiddish, and younger Jews to speak Hebrew.[7] The future is brighter for Hebrew, with one exception. A recent study of adult Hasidim in the city of Outremont, Quebec, found 75 per cent claimed they were totally fluent in Yiddish, and another 12 per cent who could speak it, but not fluently.[8] And unlike other Jews, Hasidic fluency in Yiddish is not a function of age; 91 per cent of those aged seventeen to twenty-four claimed to be fluent! (A study of Sephardim in Montreal reported that one-sixth could speak "Spanish" fluently and about one-quarter somewhat. About 13 per cent – primarily elderly – said it was the language they spoke in their homes.[9] Many likely meant Ladino or Judeo-Spanish.)

One of the great unknowns is whether the use of Yiddish in the Hasidic world – where it is spoken everywhere, is taught in schools, and where it is the language of newspapers, magazines, and religious literature – can help revive Yiddish more generally. Could we conceive of a Hasidic/Yiddish theatre or poetry dealing with religious themes? It sounds far-fetched (is that word English or Yiddish?) since their current cultural orientations are starkly different from those of the immigrant, secular Yiddish culture. In any case, the Hasidic milieu is the only hope for a serious Yiddish language revival.

Both Yiddish and Hebrew are important in the symbolic sense, used not for communication but to mark specific rituals or occasions, as songs, prayers, names of food items, curses. They are often used as code words or signals among Jews, and to add flavour to conversation. Most Canadian Jews – and some non-Jews – probably know some Yiddish words, like *schlep*, *schlemiel*, *goniff*, and *nebbish*; they can be found in reputable English dictionaries. It is hard to measure this symbolic significance, but I sense it is very real. Jews will twig to the use of Yiddish by a Jewish or non-Jewish speaker, like Wayne and Shuster, former Prime Minister Kim Campbell, or U.S. Secretary of State Colin Powell. Some years ago I was listening to a radio show dealing with auto repair, with a car mechanic as the host. She had mentioned that she was non-Jewish but married to a Jew. You can imagine my surprise when she told one caller, "Look, I don't want to *hack* you a *tchainick* [remind you repeatedly]." This external acceptance of Yiddish enhances Jewish self-esteem. The power of a language as a means to strengthen identity can persist well after fluency in the language is lost and it stops being a language of daily communication. Television and movies have helped the spread of these Yiddishisms; from Johnny Carson's routines about the accountants H. and R. Gonniff to Mike Myers's impression of Linda Richman, the Coffee Talk *yenta* on *Saturday Night Live*. Knowledge of Yiddish can be used to measure "real" Jewishness. Most Jews know what *kvetch* (complain) means, but how many know the meaning of *kvell* (take pride in)?

But all this fun does not foretell a Yiddish revival. Many ethnic languages become important as symbols and validating codes for members of minority groups. Used as symbols and for rituals, as well as in speech patterns and accents, ethnic languages blend with English and create "ethnolects." Italian and Caribbean Canadians perhaps come closest to Jewish Canadians in this sense.[10] These languages affect so-called standard English. American author Gore Vidal would routinely complain about the way in which the "Yinglish" of American Jewish writers would corrupt the English he wanted to preserve and defend.[11] In any case, Yiddish is in much better shape in Canada than in the United States. I recall the American Jewish leader Rabbi Arthur Hertzberg cheerfully beginning a lecture at Montreal's Jewish Public Library speaking in Yiddish, knowing that it would be appreciated by most of his audience. And he was right. For many observers this greater tenacity of Yiddish – and Hebrew – could be construed as a uniquely "Canadian" aspect of Canadian Jewish culture. But, alas, it is largely a result of Canada's more recent immigration sequence. Eventually the gaps will narrow.

As for secular Yiddish culture, it is down but not out. Some years ago, during a visit to Montreal, Isaac Bashevis Singer recalled that when he arrived in New York just before the war, Jewish journalists had asked him to comment on the immanent death of Yiddish. With his trademark impish grin he told his Montreal audience, "Fifty years later, Yiddish is still alive but those journalists are all dead." Yiddish is taught to Jewish school children in some Jewish schools in Canada, which trace their origins to the Yiddishist *folkshule* tradition. Yiddish is also taught in university courses. The Yiddish Theatre in Montreal, pioneered by Dora Wasserman and continued by her daughter Bryna Wasserman, has continued to sponsor several Yiddish-language musical productions a year, with thousands in attendance. In 1998 the Quebec Theatre Guild extended a prestigious lifetime achievement award to Dora Wasserman and recognized her Yiddish theatre as an important element of Quebec's cultural scene. The highly emotional event took place at the historic Monument Theatre and was broadcast live on Radio-Canada. In Toronto, a Friends of Yiddish group promotes Yiddish language and culture, as does the formally quadrilingual Jewish Public Library in Montreal.

The surprising revival of klezmer music in the late 1980s and 1990s was, like most new cultural movements, unpredicted. Klezmer (the term derives from the Hebrew words for musical instruments) is lively Eastern European Jewish music, traditionally played at weddings and Jewish festivals. Klezmer tapes and CDs sell well. In Montreal, an annual Klez Canada summer retreat, modeled on "Klez camp" in the Catskills, has proved a huge success. These events are devoted to the study and enjoyment of klezmer music and Eastern European Jewish culture, and draw several hundred participants yearly. According to Dr. Hy Goldman, initiator and organizer of Klez Canada, there may be fifteen to twenty klezmer bands in Canada. The attraction of klezmer in Montreal has spread beyond the Jewish community. One of the more popular bands is named Raoul, and consists entirely of Québécois musicians who have embraced the music, and perform at Jewish weddings and bar mitzvahs as well as for Quebec French audiences. Toronto's Ashkenaz festival brings thousands of Toronto Jews and non-Jews down to Harbourfront to take part in an array of concerts and other artistic productions. The emphasis at Ashkenaz extends far beyond klezmer music, and includes displays of Jewish fine arts as well as literary events, all celebrating Jewish culture in general and Eastern European Yiddish culture in particular. One of the high points is a spirited parade with many costumed participants that begins in Kensington Market, the old Jewish immigrant area, and wends its way down to Harbourfront.

But klezmer cannot sustain a real Yiddish revival. The days of a totalistic Yiddish culture à la "Days of our Fathers" are gone. Yiddish is certainly being kept alive. But it will never again be the *mameh loshen*, or mother tongue, of Canadian Jews. Secular Yiddish culture is on life support. There are a very few non-elderly secular Jews for whom Yiddish and Yiddish culture remain central. These are Jews associated with theatre groups, or cultural groups, or klezmer music, or Yiddish as part of Jewish Studies programs. But that is all. There is no longer a stream of vibrant scholars, polemicists, writers, and poets working in Yiddish with a substantial audience for their efforts. English has become the new

Yiddish, a language seized by energetic Jews and made their own, mobilized on behalf of causes and ideologies. For many years, Canada, and particularly Montreal, was home to major Yiddish poets such as Sholem Shtern, Melech Ravitch, Rachel Korn and to a thriving Yiddish culture.[12] Even A. M. Klein, whose poetry was written in English, knew Yiddish and was deeply influenced by the immigrant Yiddish tradition. The influence of Yiddish now operates by osmosis, through sensibilities rather than language. Similarly, the Yiddish press has disappeared, though in its heyday Canada boasted three major Yiddish dailies: *Der Kenader Adler* (Canadian Eagle) in Montreal, *Der Yiddisher Zhurnal* (Jewish Journal) in Toronto, and *Der Kenader Yid* (Canadian Jew) in Winnipeg. The *Eagle*, which began publishing in 1907, gave Canadian Jews an alternative to the New York Yiddish press and, like The *Forward*, served as an agent of subtle, gentle Canadianization and acculturation.

Writers can explore Jewish or Judaic themes in languages other than Hebrew or Yiddish or Ladino; they did so in earlier periods in Aramaic, Arabic, Spanish, German, Polish, and other languages. In Canada they use English and French. A. M. Klein's and Naïm Kattan's poetry and Mordecai Richler's prose are dripping in Judaic and Jewish references. Does this mean there has been a seamless transition from, say, Yiddish to English? No. At some point, any ethnic culture in North America is inevitably diluted as fluency in the mother tongue is lost. For now the symbolic uses of Yiddish and Yinglish count for much, indeed more than most other immigrant languages. Hebrew is still sustained by its religious role and the tie with Israel. Let Jews be thankful for that.

JEWISH LITERATURE AND ART

Jewish literary culture in Canada today is largely produced in English and, to a lesser degree, French. Authors such as Leonard Cohen, Matt Cohen, Naïm Kattan, A. M. Klein, Irving Layton, Anne Michaels, Mordecai Richler, Victor Teboul, Miriam Waddington, Adele Wiseman, among others, are well-regarded Canadian writers whose work has been influenced by Jewish history, the Jewish immigrant experience, and eternal Judaic themes. But they do not speak with one voice, or one Jewish sensibility. The Canadian group is really a grouping. Moreover, the degree of Jewishness in their writings and its significance remain a matter for debate. But these writers are, at the same time, producing Jewish culture and, as we shall see below, Canadian culture.

What, in fact, is Jewish about these writers? Canadian Yiddish scholar and Harvard professor Ruth Wisse has argued that we should not confuse the culture of Judaism – ideas and values – with the sociology of Jews, or what Jews happen to be doing. For her, Jewish culture must be clearly "Judaic" in its preoccupation.[13] Or at least it must be a totally enveloping entity, as was found among the pre-war Yiddish communities in Montreal, Toronto, Winnipeg, and of course New York. According to Wisse, going to the Yiddish theatre would have been one small part of a total Jewish environment. Not so for a Canadian Jew watching Wayne and Shuster, Jerry Seinfeld, or Fran Drescher in *The Nanny*. From her perspective, there is little today that could be construed as authentic Jewish culture in Canada. Jews writing about the daily life of Jews is not enough. Jewish art is not simply anything produced by a Jewish artist, be it a poem, a painting, or a song. The purist position argues that if it does not have authentic Judaic content, it does not qualify as Jewish culture.

My own position is less demanding. We can recognize that in North America there is no longer a holistic Judaic experience, and still find cultural significance, if not profound meaning, in the habits of everyday Jewish life. A work of Jewish art can be "about" Jews. This is a more sociological approach to the Jewish basis of Jewish art, to which I plead guilty. The difference is that between A. M. Klein's *The Second Scroll* or much of the poetry of Seymour Mayne, and the work of Mordecai Richler. The first two are steeped in informed Judaic tradition and lore. Publisher Malcolm Lester describes Klein's work as "Jewish universalism as particularized in the Canadian experience."[14] Richler, in contrast, plays off various Jewish experiences, uses Jewishness as a backdrop and even as a source of images or phrases. His fiction is an artistic rendering of the anthropological meaning of Jewish culture.

In a sense the debate is moot. Jewish cultural expression outside Israel, with the exception of some Orthodox Biblical commentaries, will no longer be produced in a Jewish language or reflect a total commitment to Judaic traditional values. Even the writing about Jewish life and the Jewish experience has changed. Something has been lost in the transition from the alternately heroic and conflictual immigrant experience to that of the unfocused suburban second and third generation. The new Jewish themes are the neurotic introspective dilemmas of the affluent middle class. Writers of Asian and Caribbean background in Canada today are the producers of the new "Jewish" fiction that deals with the older themes. They are the ones grappling with the travails of migration, racism, poverty, generational tensions, and raw identity conflicts.

Jewish high culture in Canada also includes music and other art forms. Cantorial music, religious songs, or *zmirot*, classic Israeli folk music, and the newly revived klezmer music are authentic examples. Israeli popular music, of which there is plenty, is perhaps more difficult to categorize, but has an audience among Canadian Jews. Well-crafted Judaic ritual objects, such as Torah covers, seder plates, skullcaps, candlesticks, Hanukkah candelabras, or prayer shawls, also constitute clearly Jewish art forms. But secular Jewish painters and sculptors abound in Canada. What, if anything, about their work qualifies as Jewish art, or Canadian Jewish art? Consider a Canadian Jewish painter like Sam Borenstein, himself a product of a European Jewish background. He most often painted powerful Laurentian landscapes. But he also produced a portrait of the Montreal Jewish poet Esther Segal. And in his development as an artist, Borenstein was highly influenced by the French-Jewish painter Chaïm Soutine. There is something going on here that is not simply Jewish, not simply Canadian, but in ways that are subtle but real both Jewish and Canadian.[15]

OTHER FORMS OF JEWISH CULTURE

Jewish popular or folk culture can be found in Canada in many forms. My favourite is food. Jewish food is available both in strictly kosher form – under rabbinical supervision – and as "kosher style." Over the years, kosher food has gone notably upscale in all large cities in North America. Kosher caterers have branched out into the exotic, offering mock shrimp and kosher Chinese food to discerning consumers. Sales of kosher food in North America reached U.S.$3.25 billion in 1998, reportedly increasing 12 per cent from 1996.[16] The many ways Jews keep kosher is itself a cultural phenomenon.

It is too easy to poke fun at the gastronomic Judaism of "bagel and lox" Jews, who may be ignorant of the philosophy of Maimonides or the fiction of Agnon. A Jewish deli, with or without kashrut, has a certain distinctiveness, as does the way Jews eat, or at times overeat. Every Jewish holiday has some special food associated with it. There is matzo and horseradish on Passover, *hamantashen* (triangular shaped pastry with prune or poppy-seed filling) on Purim, potato latkes on Hanukkah, apples and honey on the Jewish New Year, and no food on Yom Kippur. In fact, some of these foods mirror the process of embourgeoisement of the Jews. Used to be that matzo was matzo. No longer. Now Jewish food sections in supermarkets are awash with matzo for every taste and lifestyle: egg matzo, whole-wheat matzo, onion matzo, garlic matzo, and chocolate matzo. There are even rolls, cakes, and cookies made from matzo meal. All this is a long way from "the bread of affliction" and the true meaning of Passover.

Jews love to eat, and then to complain about how they "overate" at the most recent holiday, wedding, or bat mitzvah. No festival at an Ashkenazi home, including Friday night Sabbath meals, is complete without a fresh *challah*, gefilte fish, chicken soup, a nice *kugel* (there are two types of Ashkenazi Jews, some pronounce it *kugel*, some pronounce it *kigel*), chicken or roast beef, knishes, carrot *tzimmes*. Jews believe they have a special relationship with food, in much the same way that non-Jews have with alcohol. My students routinely downgrade the importance of food as a component of ethnic culture or identity. They think it is superficial. They want ethnicity, identity, and multicultural-ism to be something deeper. What do they know? Pass the brisket.

Material culture – ethnic artifacts of all sorts – is another form of popular culture. Many of these artifacts are works of art; others are kitsch or Jewish bric-à-brac that is scattered throughout Jewish homes. A *mezuzah* on a Jewish doorpost, a Jewish calendar on the wall, a set of candlesticks, some Israeli or Jewish sculpture or artwork – Chagall prints are common – or *tchotchkes* (knickknacks), some skullcaps lying around, all signify that this is a Jewish home. Many Jews wear around their neck a Star of David or a *chai* (the Hebrew letters that spell "alive," a symbol of good luck). In my more cynical moments, I suspect there is an unsettling correlation such that the bigger and gaudier the *chai*, the more ignorant the Jew. But these symbols can also have a material payoff. My son wears a chain with a Star of David around his neck (as do I). On his part-time job delivering pizzas, he often had customers with a *mezuzah* on their doorpost. He would flip the chain over his shirt so the Jewish customer could see it, fishing for a bigger tip. It seemed to work.

Obviously, at one level food and material culture are less significant than ideas and values of traditional Judaic culture or the total cultural immersion of the immigrant Jewish milieu.[17] But eating ethnic foods at holidays and other times, observing ethnic customs, and possessing ethnic artifacts are still important. In a perverse way, the fact that Jews now eat so many non-Jewish foods adds weight to those occasions where Jewish foods are central. Canadian Jews are more involved with their own popular and material culture than are other groups. A Toronto survey asked Jews whether they consumed ethnic food at holidays or at other times, whether they practised ethnic customs, and possessed ethnic articles. Those who observed these "every time, often or sometimes" scored around 90 per cent on all questions, with no decline between immigrant and third-generation Jews.[18] We underestimate the symbolic force of these seemingly minimal forms of Jewish identification.

THE POPULAR AND INTELLECTUAL JEWISH PRESS

Jewish culture in Canada is both reflected and shaped by a robust Jewish media. Most prominent is the weekly newspaper, the *Canadian Jewish News*. (Conflict-of-interest declaration: I write a monthly column for the CJN.) It is sent to tens of thousands of households, usually those who make a minimal contribution to the Combined Jewish Appeal, and also distributed free in Jewish communal buildings. There are separate Toronto and Montreal editions, which add local items to a central core of national news material. In this way, the CJN strives to create a national Jewish consciousness and is a model for other ethnic community newspapers. I am amazed to discover how wide the readership is, and that many Jews read it from cover to cover. Canadian Jewish intellectuals routinely dump on the CJN for being

insufficiently intellectual or critical of Israel or the Jewish establishment. Their criticism is misplaced. There are plenty of other Jewish or
non-Jewish periodicals that play those important roles. The CJN reflects
the mainstream Jewish community. I am actually struck by the breadth
of the paper. Its news and commentary on Israel do not toe the prevailing Israeli government line; it presents opposition views. It covers
a wide range of communal activities and reflects a diverse portrait of
Judaism.[19] There are other Jewish community newspapers from coast
to coast, and they too are read. About 60 per cent of Canadian Jews
report reading a "Jewish" newspaper regularly, compared to only 33 per
cent in the United States.[20] Of course, the Jewish ethnic press today
in Canada is now in English or French (*La Tribune Juive* is a Jewish
periodical in Quebec), and not in Yiddish. This explains in part why
readership does not decline following the immigrant generation, as it
does dramatically for all other ethnic groups.[21]

As successful as the Canadian Jewish press is in a communal sense,
it does not, it cannot, nourish a cohesive sub-community of Jewish
intellectuals, with their own institutions and publications. In the United
States, with a much larger Jewish population base, the "New York Jewish
intellectuals," such as Irving Howe, Irving Kristol, Nathan Glazer,
Norman Podhoretz, were active throughout the post-war period, talking
to and arguing with each other. Today, younger American intellectuals
use Jewish journals like *Commentary, Moment, Tikkun,* the *Jerusalem
Report,* the *Forward,* and non-Jewish periodicals like the *New York
Times,* the *New Republic,* the *Nation,* and the *New York Review of
Books* to create a virtual community of American Jewish intellectuals.
The debates can turn nasty, as in any family feud, but they can also
invigorate. Nothing comparable exists in Canada. There is simply
an insufficient critical mass of engaged Canadian Jewish writers.[22]
According to critic Robert Fulford, the Canadian Jewish writers repre-
sent "separate dots of light," while in the United States, they were busy
"hating each other and loving each other."[23]

Despite this failure, there has been an interesting trend within the
non-Jewish press. No Canadian newspaper matches the *New York
Times* as a "Jewish" paper of record. Again, issues of critical mass. But

it seems to me that over the years mainstream Canadian papers, including the *Globe and Mail* and later the *National Post* have been increasing news coverage and opinion pieces on Jewish issues. They in fact complement the Jewish press. The bittersweet maxim "Jews are news" is at work. During a hectic week in February 2000, after right-wing Austrian politician Jörg Haider's surprise visit to Canada, after saturation coverage in all Canadian newspapers, the *Globe and Mail* published a lengthy op-ed piece on the Haider visit by former CJC president Irving Abella. Four days later, the paper published an article focusing on efforts of a Vancouver Holocaust Centre to acquire Holocaust-era artifacts. The article made reference to a column by Rabbi Gunther Plaut in the CJN. The point here is not the substance of the debate. It is that an internal Jewish community dialogue was being held in the pages of both the CJN *and* the *Globe and Mail*.[24]

The intellectual conversation about the future of Jewish life is rooted in the United States and Israel. All other Jewish diaspora communities are bystanders. In the Canadian case, it may also be that too much civility is not conducive to tough-minded polemics. Canadian Jewish intellectuals have to piggyback onto American debates, both reading them and participating in them. Canadian nationalism is not a dominant concern in the discourse of Canadian Jewish intellectuals on the Jewish future. As mentioned earlier, in these Jewish debates there is no reflexive anti-Americanism. The ideological debates revolving around religion and secularism, socialism or capitalism, liberalism or conservatism, Zionism and non-Zionism, debated in Jewish and general intellectual journals have been generic or American. There has been nothing uniquely Canadian about them, and American Jewish life sets the terms of reference for the engaged Canadian Jewish intellectual. General Canadian intellectual debates differ; they routinely seek to distance themselves from American models, and have sufficient Canadian literary outlets to do so. Jewish Studies programs or departments in several Canadian universities nourish a significant number of academics who focus on Jewish subject matter in their teaching and research. Many are prominent. But in an institutional sense, Canadian Jewish intellectual life remains a branch-plant operation.

ISRAEL AND THE HOLOCAUST

Any discussion of the content of contemporary Canadian Jewish culture must recognize the thematic roles played by Israel and the Holocaust. Most Jews think about these two issues far more than they think about God.

Israel is far more than just a political concern for Canadian Jews. It is a central part of day-to-day Jewish culture. Two-thirds of Canadian Jews have visited Israel, 85 per cent feel if Israel were destroyed it would be a "personal" tragedy, over 20 per cent claim to have considered emigration to Israel, and 42 per cent would consider themselves to be Zionist. Fully 79 per cent can identify the year of Israel's independence, and 72 per cent can identify the year of the Six Day War.[25] These numbers are much higher than for American Jews; for example, only 40 per cent of American Jews according to the NJPS know the Six Day War was in 1967. More than one-sixth of Canadian Jews can converse in Hebrew, which enhances the tie to Israel. Israel has an important place in the curriculum of Jewish schools, and many of the teachers are of Israeli origin. Most Jewish high schools sponsor summer-long tour programs in Israel for their students, and other organizations have similar summer and yearlong programs.

Many Canadian ethnic groups retain ties with an ancestral homeland, particularly within the immigrant generation. But by later generations these links have dramatically weakened. No Canadian minority group has developed the extensive networks of travel, philanthropy, and cultural exchanges with a homeland that Jews have with Israel. *Yom Ha'Atzma'ut*, Israel's Independence Day, has become a major date on the Jewish communal and indeed religious calendar. For some Jews, Israel has become the very essence of their identity. This is reinforced because Israel, as part of the still-troubled Middle East, is always in the news. Jews ride the emotional roller coaster of hope for peace and despair at the renewed violence of the intifada which erupted in 2000. The ties are also strengthened in more conventional ways, as thousands of Canadian Jews have gone on *aliyah* (emigrated to Israel) and many Israelis now live in Canada. No avenue is left unexplored as a vehicle to expand links with Israel. The Maccabiah Games serve to enhance the Canadian–Israeli tie through sport. Canadian philanthropy helped build the Olympic-size ice-skating rink in Metulla. Summer programs in Israel now include hockey camps for Canadian and Israeli youngsters run by Canadian hockey coaches and players. A newspaper story about Canadian Jews in Israel described ex-Montrealers Ruby and Linda Wolbromsky, and emphasized their collection of NHL hockey sticks: Jean Beliveau, Ralph Backstrom, and Terry Harper's, to be exact.[26] I can relate. During a year I spent studying in Jerusalem, when the Stanley Cup play-offs came around a group of us hockey-starved Montreal Canadiens fans would gather eagerly to listen to cassette tapes of play-off games.

Can anything weaken the tie to Israel? Possibly. Contrary to many Jews, I think both Israel and the Diaspora could survive an estrangement. I certainly do not advocate it, and I think nothing could alienate me personally from Israel. But for my not-yet-born great-grandchildren? Israel is a strong industrial or post-industrial country, developing its own cultural style. As the generation of the Holocaust in the Diaspora dies off, their children and grandchildren may not share the visceral tie to Israel. If some form of peace comes to the Middle East, some wonder if the bonds would be sustained as Israel became less threatened. The next generation of Jews will not be raised with an image of Israel as a fragile, weak state at the mercy of hostile Arab neighbours. As Israel has become relatively affluent, the need for financial support has decreased. This is reflected in the allocation of the funds collected by Jewish Appeals throughout North America. In earlier years, most of the funds went to Israel. By 2000, the allocations had shifted dramatically with less going to Israel.[27]

The cycles of euphoria and angry despair regarding the "peace process" can have unpredictable, and contradictory, consequences. The latest round of Palestinian terrorism, in the wake of bold Israeli concessions in the pursuit of peace, might cause some Jews to lose heart. Jewish students on North American campuses report energized anti-Israel campaigns by the growing number of Arab and/or Islamic students. Jewish supporters of Israel feel under siege, undermined by the media's misplaced evenhandedness, or clear anti-Israel bias (with the exception of the *National Post*). By 2001, Jewish travel to Israel fell to negligible proportions for security reasons, and after agonizing soul-searching several Canadian Jewish high-school summer tours were cancelled. I recall a summer visit to Israel during the first intifada in the late 1980s. My Jerusalem hotel was nearly empty. One day, two buses pulled up to the hotel, but they were not full of North American Jewish tourists. One was a German tour, the other was Japanese. As the visitors spilled out of their buses, I offered an ironic prayer of thanks to the former Axis powers . . .

For a very few Jews, the new demoralization might lead to a rejection of Israel. The far broader impact of the renewed violence is a tightening of the bond with Israel, and a shift to the political right – along with the Israeli electorate. Liberal Jews who in the past were critical of Israel for both internal and foreign policy reasons restrain themselves when Israel is under threat. Before the recent hostilities, the well-known tensions between the Orthodox and the non-Orthodox in Israel had actually eroded some liberal Diaspora support. This was expressed as feeling a growing "discomfort" in Jerusalem, where these progressive Jews were surrounded by the increasingly belligerent Orthodox. They did not embrace Israel to feel like a minority. Israeli Judaism was not their Judaism. A diasporic survivalist perspective argues that Jewish life in North America, for those who want to revel in it, can be just as rich as Jewish life in Israel. Israeli Judaism is a polarizing force separating a minority of Orthodox and a majority who are either indifferent or hostile. I recall spending a Passover in Jerusalem as a student in a Hebrew University dormitory with ten Israelis in our unit. As Passover approached, the major concern for most of my roommates was establishing a rotation for trips to the bakeries of Arab East Jerusalem to guarantee a steady supply of fresh bread.

Let's push this a little further. Right now there are strong ties of family, perhaps distant family, that bind North American Jews to Israel. There are distant cousins to visit. But over time, many scenarios are plausible. In one, the generations will die off and the cousins will become more distant. As the Sephardi population of Israel increases, family ties to the largely Ashkenazi population in North America will weaken. Israel may develop an even more indigenous Israeli culture, more removed from North American Jews. If, in this scenario, Orthodoxy and ultra-Orthodoxy continue to grow with their political power unchecked, more and more non-Orthodox Jews (and perhaps some Modern Orthodox) will be disenchanted with Israel.

Most Jews reflexively feel that a widening of the gulf between Israel and the Diaspora would be disastrous. But this cannot be proved. Remember that the Jewish future is unpredictable. The fact is, for most of the past two millennia, the ties between Diaspora Jews and Israel were extremely weak, far weaker than they are now. This was true even for the first part of this century. If the ties were to weaken, then non-Orthodox North American Jews might in the distant future regard Israel as Italians in North America regard Italy. Italy still means a great deal to many Italian Canadians. Israel would still be important for Jews, but it would not be central to their Jewishness. Israel would have a symbolic rather than concrete role, as an older type of Zion common throughout the pre-state centuries.

At present the ties remain strong. On balance, the renewed threats to Israel's security will strengthen them dramatically. Visits to Israel have emerged as a key element in the strategy for Jewish continuity. In the early 1990s, Charles Bronfman's CRB Foundation commissioned a study to understand how "the Israel experience" affected Canadian Jews.[28] It is hard to distinguish cause from effect in estimating the link between Israel trips and Jewish identification. But adults who have been to Israel score higher on measures of Israel or Jewish involvement. The study asked them directly about experiences which had a "strong positive impact on Jewish life." The most cited response was "a trip to Israel." Similarly, for those who indicated when their commitment to Judaism crystallized, the highest response was a trip to Israel again – even higher than a birth of a child, or marriage. As a result of these findings, Bronfman helped create Birthright Israel, a program begun in 2000 that aimed to send young North American Jewish adults on free ten-day educational tours to Israel.

Not surprisingly, the motivations of Jewish youth going to Israel differed from those of adults in the CRB survey. About 50 per cent of the youth sample had visited Israel, and two-fifths of these on an organized group trip. About 80 per cent listed as their main motive for

going the desire to "have fun." Only 46 per cent went to "see the homeland of the Jewish people." The emphasis on fun may well frustrate
Jewish educators, but it reflects the life of most teens. It is still too early
to know the long-term impact of the Birthright Israel trips. In any case,
committed Jewish families include a trip to Israel, if they can, as part
of the Jewish socialization of their children.

In recent years, the Holocaust has also emerged as a central cultural
theme of Diaspora Jewish life. This has been entirely unexpected.
In the immediate aftermath of the war, North American Jews responded
with silence and guilt to the horrors of the *Shoah*. Only among the sub-
communities of Holocaust survivors did the memory endure. I recall
going to annual Holocaust memorial events in the early 1960s with my
parents which were attended only by survivors themselves. Yiddish and
perhaps Polish would be spoken at these events.

The Eichmann trial, and in 1967 the Six Day War, cracked the silence.
Slowly but surely, the Holocaust emerged on the Jewish community's
cultural and political agenda. The NBC miniseries *Holocaust*, in 1978,
brought the Holocaust to a popular and non-Jewish audience in a way
that previous films had not, paving the way for *Schindler's List* two
decades later. No longer is the Holocaust seen as the province of Jews
alone. Canadian universities offer courses in the subject, which are
taken by non-Jews as well as Jews. Innovative movies, dramas, or even
comedies, are now produced. The hunt for Nazi war criminals emerged
tentatively as a Jewish policy concern, and culminated in the exposure
of the Nazi past of Austria's Kurt Waldheim. (In Canada, little action
has been taken. Trials in Canada and efforts at denaturalization have
generally not been successful.) And the fallout from the war continues.
It seems as if every week or month a new issue of some controversy or
public fascination arises. European banks are discovered to have held on
to dormant Jewish bank accounts. Museums are accused of reaping the
benefits of holding and displaying art looted from European Jews. Crosses
are erected near the gates of Auschwitz by militant Polish Catholics, to
the consternation of Jews. Canadians debate whether to include a
Holocaust exhibit as part of a revamped Canadian War Museum.
Prosecutions are launched against proponents of Holocaust denial like
Ernst Zündel, Jim Keegstra, and Doug Collins. Holocaust denier David

Irving launches, and loses, a libel trial in England. Jörg Haider's party is invited into the Austrian government, and he makes a quick trip to Montreal. And so it goes, on and on.

These Holocaust-related events revive old memories and animosities, at least among ethnic groups where there is a history of anti-Semitism. A Jewish delegation accompanied Prime Minister Jean Chrétien on a visit to Auschwitz in January 1999, part of his state visit to Poland. Polish Canadians, angered by their exclusion from this part of the delegation, threatened the prime minister with political repercussions. As they reminded all who would listen, they, too, suffered during the war, and tens of thousands of non-Jewish Poles worked and died at Auschwitz. For Jews, it seems like Poles are eager to muddy the waters of Jewish tragedy with their own, and also deflect attention away from consideration of possible complicity. Poles comprise the largest group of nationals among the "Righteous Gentiles" who risked their lives to save Jews during the war. But Winnipeg historian Allan Levine reminded *Globe and Mail* readers of a study by Israeli historians which concluded that "the overwhelming majority of Jews who approached Poles for help fell prey to the Nazi police or the gendarmerie, to rabid anti-Semites in Polish society and the Polish underground." Bernard Wisniewski of the Canadian Polish Congress responded to Levine's "accusatory musings" in his own op-ed article. His article is a defence of the record of Polish resistance against the Nazis replete with exculpatory quotations from Jewish scholars. Clearly, Poles want nothing (like a blanket charge of collaboration) to detract from their status as victim. In this they resemble Jews.[29]

The Holocaust shapes Jewish culture and identity in many ways. Even as the survivor generation dies off, for many of their children and other Canadian Jews it is too soon for the terms German, Polish, or Ukrainian to evoke a neutral response. More time has to pass. And the response is not monolithic. Survivors and students of the Holocaust often engage in a grisly debate to see which European nation was the "worst" in its treatment of Jews and complicity with the Final Solution. Surprisingly, Germany is not always the first choice. My parents, both survivors, refused to visit Poland or Ukraine after the war – the memories were too bitter. But my father visited Germany and Austria, with few qualms. (For other survivors, the reverse was the case.) After my father moved to Israel, he decided to vacation one summer in the German Alps near Munich, where I visited him. The scene was Kafkaesque, and given that Kafka's sisters were liquidated by the Nazis, the term is doubly apt. His hotel was packed with aging Israelis of European extraction, many Holocaust survivors. They all chose to be there, and politeness reigned supreme.

In any case, living in Canada dulls the edge of potential confrontations, and old wounds are never fully reopened. This was true for Ukrainian–Jewish relations in the wake of the Deschênes Commission on war criminals and the Demjanjuk trial in Israel. The temperature rose, but never boiled.[30] The same is true for Polish–Jewish relations. Indeed, despite the odd flare-up, several organizations dedicated to Polish–Jewish rapprochement operate in Canada.

The Holocaust fills an ideological vacuum for contemporary Jewry, apart from its specific impacts on survivors and sensitive Jews. It continually recertifies the Jewish communal claim to victimhood, which for some Jews is part of their identity. This is a valuable counterweight to the image of Jews as oppressors of Palestinians, or as rich supporters of the status quo. It also is a main mobilizing force for Jewish survival, and for the aggressive defence of Jewish interests. After Auschwitz, according to philosopher Emil Fackenheim, the eleventh commandment for Jews is simply to survive. "Never again" has become a rallying cry with deep resonance for modern Jews, of any persuasion. It is also a warning to North American Jews to be vigilant, to act decisively for their brothers and sisters.

Indeed, over the decades, the agents of Holocaust villainy have grown and diversified. Early on, the guilty were the Nazis, or, if one preferred, the Germans. Later, guilt extended to active collaborators, including many later prosecuted for war crimes. Later still, guilt extended to the Allies, who might have done more to admit Jewish refugees, or to stop the Nazi threat early on, or at least to bomb the camps and railway links so as to stop the slaughter, and, after the war, to hunt down Nazi war criminals. Corporations, banks, insurance companies, museums, government agencies – German, other European, even American or British, and, who knows, maybe Canadian – are guilty. Finally, some guilt remains for North American Jewish leaders, who were not adequately militant, and even European Jews, in the persons of those who worked as *Kapos* in the camp or as members of Jewish Councils. The point here is not to ascertain the accuracy or motivation behind these new stages in the evolving discourse on Holocaust guilt. Rather, the expanding universe of Holocaust guilt helps explain the staying power of the Holocaust in Jewish consciousness. There are always surprises.

The Holocaust also has also invaded Canadian Jewish school curricula with a vengeance. I was a student in Jewish day schools from 1955 to 1966, and I can barely recall any intensive discussion or focus on the Holocaust. Almost nothing. And in my personal view, that was not too bad. My children's experience in Jewish day schools has been quite different. Every year, the Holocaust played a role, in books they read – in Hebrew, English, and French – and in special projects. How much is enough? The March of the Living is an annual pilgrimage in which Jewish teens are taken for a gut-wrenching tour of European death-camp sites followed by a visit to Israel. The effort is well-meaning, and my son took part. For him, it was a deeply moving Jewish experience. But I have no illusions. The trip may be many things, but one of them is heavy-handed shock treatment. It socializes Jewish children into a fearsome commitment to survival. Children in Jewish day schools, as well as increasing numbers of children, Jewish and non-Jewish, from other schools, are also taken for tours of Holocaust centres or museums. Holocaust survivors are routinely invited into Jewish and non-Jewish schools to tell their stories, both to sensitize the students and undermine the Holocaust denial movement.

This new centrality of the *Shoah* in Jewish education, and in the discourse of Jewish public life, is a mixed blessing.[31] It risks reducing a complex rich Jewish heritage into a vale of tears, or what historian Salo Baron used to call "the lachrymose" interpretation of Jewish history. Jewish identities ought to be built on a positive foundation. Even Holocaust educators have twigged to the danger, and have begun to emphasize the rich legacy of Eastern European culture as part of their program and of the March of the Living itinerary. Imparting the "lessons" of the Holocaust is also an ambiguous exercise. For some, the lessons are the importance of tolerance to all minorities, and vigilant defence of human rights and freedoms. For others, the lessons are those of an ethnocentric self-reliance and a rejection of the non-Jewish world.

Holocaust survivors have emerged as an interest group in Jewish political life. Moreover, they and their children, the "second genera- tion," have become the object of special curiosity and compassion by Jewish health care and social service workers. The "survivor syndrome" emerged from clinical reports and studies, and described a pattern of psychological disorders including depression and psychosomatic symptoms which allegedly did not spare their children as well. Self-help groups aimed at children of Holocaust survivors proliferated in large cities, which inadvertently perpetuated the stigma for survivors and their children. Yet my own research with Dr. John Sigal calls those stereotypes into question. Looking at non-clinical (that is, more rep- resentative) samples of survivors and their children, we were struck by the resilience of survivors, despite ongoing torments, and by the high level of socio-economic achievement and psychological adjustment of the second generation.[32]

The Jewish passion for erecting communal buildings to foster identification has been called an "edifice" complex. The Holocaust is no exception. Holocaust centres or museums have been established in Canadian cities to commemorate the tragedy. Montreal's Holocaust Centre launched a multi-million dollar campaign in 2000 for a massive renovation. But there will be nothing on the scale of the Holocaust Museum in Washington or the Wiesenthal Museum of Tolerance in Los Angeles. The Washington Holocaust Museum reflects through its location in the U.S. capital and proximity to the Smithsonian an inte- gration of the Holocaust message with the core values and images of the American experience. The *Shoah* has become Americanized.

But not yet Canadianized. Indeed, in 1977 the Canadian War Museum in Ottawa announced it would include as part of an expan- sion plan a section devoted to commemorating the Holocaust. Some Canadian veterans' organizations opposed the idea, saying that Holocaust commemoration did not belong in a museum dedicated to the role of Canadian veterans and warfare itself. Defenders of the idea countered that the human toll of genocidal warfare was part of any modern account of war, and would also offer a perspective on the reasons for Canadian involvement in the struggle against Nazism. A cynic might add that Jewish donors might also be more easily recruited to help finance the War Museum's expansion. But just as the Holocaust Museum has thrust itself, or been thrust, into the centre of American historical consciousness in Washington, so, too, albeit in much lesser scale, has it begun in Canada with the debate on the War Museum. Jewish communal opinion is actually divided. Some want a specific Holocaust Museum. Some favour including the Holocaust as a part of a separate museum of intolerance. The idea of a Holocaust section in the Canadian War Museum has since been abandoned, though the British War Museum in 2000 opened a permanent Holocaust exhibit. If plans do go ahead for a separate Holocaust Museum in Ottawa, look for a clamour from all other minority groups to have their travails so memorialized, and for the European groups to make certain they are not maligned by a Holocaust Museum.

Canadian artists and intellectuals have been wrestling with the Holocaust. Anne Michaels' award-winning 1996 novel *Fugitive Pieces* had the Holocaust as a thematic backdrop. Earlier, the poetry of Irving Layton and Leonard Cohen grappled with the *Shoah*. Layton's 1968 poem "For My Sons, Max and David," a meditation on Jewish victimhood, ends with the hard-nosed charge to his children, "Be gunners in the Israeli Air Force."[33] The Holocaust is now a trendy, low-cost way for some largely secular Jewish intellectuals to identify publicly as Jews, and to reconnect with a heritage which has been dormant for some time. It is, for writers and artists, like reading a book or attending a lecture about Hasidism, or Kabbalah. This "Holocaust chic" is the ultimate in political correctness for Jews who do not want to be too Jewish. Its universal message of suffering appeals to Jews estranged from the Jewish community and mainstream Judaism. It is a route back without the need for synagogue attendance or ritual observance or Jewish schooling for the kids or defending or worrying about Israel or donating to Jewish charities or volunteering to help run Jewish agencies.

A case in point is the well-meaning 1995 volume *Beyond Imagination: Canadians Write About the Holocaust*. The essays are poignant and well-written. A few contributors are known scholars or writers about the Holocaust. For at least one, the legacy of the Holocaust has been a central, personal theme of her life. Alti Rodal, a historian of modern Jewry and a child of survivors, has charged her children with a demanding legacy: "You are the grandchildren of people endowed with a powerful instinct for survival. To my mother's blessing, 'May life be good to you,' I add: May the strength of all your grandparents give you strength to withstand life's trials – we owe it to them. And may the perseverance and values of their heritage be expressed through you, within and beyond our community, so that we survive."[34]

But some contributors to the book (almost all are Jews) have a tenuous connection to Canadian Jewish life, and to Jewish identity. Some are married to non-Jews. While the Holocaust troubles them, it is not a core experience which has added Jewish dimensions to their lives. Peter C. Newman writes: "I could claim neither the exultation of actively practising the Jewish religion, nor was I a victim of the Holocaust.[35] David Lewis Stein has started to attend an Orthodox shul in his neighbourhood, even though "I am not observant and my wife is not Jewish."[36] And Barbara Kingstone writes, "I was not a very good Jew in the traditional sense. Still am not. I don't feel threatened by some greater power if on the high holidays I don't attend synagogue."[37] In fact, the volume is as useful as a description of the many minimalist forms of contemporary Jewish identity as it is a study of the Holocaust. The essays also demonstrate how the Holocaust has an ability to rally Jews of very different backgrounds to demonstrate a transcendant identification with some sort of Jewish experience.

JEWS AND CANADIAN CULTURE

The Jewish cultural impact on Canada has been mainly through individual artists who have at times incorporated a Jewish sensibility. But the Jewish community has also made a collective contribution to the Canadian cultural and artistic scene. The Saidye Bronfman Centre of Montreal and the Koffler Centre of the Arts in Toronto are known for their high-quality work. Both institutions are sponsored by the Jewish community, but their artistic and cultural programming – in education and in performance – is available to the wider public. At times, they can be torn between filling a mandate as a Jewish institution and as a part of the broader artistic and cultural community. They blur the lines between Jewish culture in Canada and Canadian Jewish culture.[38]

Just as in the American case, Canadian Jews have been prominent as authors, poets, painters, sculptors, comedians, musicians, actors, directors, producers, journalists, and broadcasters. Jewish writers served as an opening wedge in the penetration of a largely anglophilic cultural establishment. They were among the first to sensitize Canadians to styles and themes different from those of the more established Anglo-Canadian writers. Jews helped introduce the immigrant experience and the urban experience into the corpus of Canadian writing. The success of poet A. M. Klein beginning in the 1930s helped launch a Jewish Canadian tradition in both poetry and prose.

There is little dispute that these Jewish and other immigrant writings – the best of them – have become accepted into the evolving Canadian literary canon.[39] This has not been easy, given the elitist tradition in much of Canadian high culture. It happened later in Canada than in the United States, in part because the American Jewish mass migration arrived ten to twenty years before the Canadian. As Concordia University English professor Mervin Butovsky has suggested, the American Jewish literary breakthrough began in the pre-war period, with writers like Ludwig Lewissohn, Ben Hecht, Henry Roth, and Daniel Fuchs. "When we speak of Canadian culture at the time of large scale Jewish settlement, we are not speaking of a situation with free cultural interplay, one in which all kinds of contributions were valid. . . . Our Canadian culture was much more akin to Anglo-Saxon culture. Our public schools were much narrower in their definition of what it meant to be a Canadian – it usually meant British style, British speech and mannerisms, and so on."[40] For Canadian Jews, the breakthrough came in the 1950s and 1960s. Howard Roiter, professor of English at Université de Montréal, does not mince words when describing the period before the 1950s. "The problem facing the country then was that English Canadian culture was a second or third rate imitative culture. . . . A culture that has been following in the footsteps of a much greater culture has an inferiority complex. It is much less open to innovation and creativity. Can you imagine Irving Layton at the Canadian Poetry Society of the 1930s? It would have been catastrophic!"[41]

Happily, there is little evidence in Canada of any resentment of this penetration by Jewish authors and a resulting "debasement" of the language. It is also harder to make a claim that Canadian publishing and literary criticism has been controlled by a cabal of Jewish writers and publishers as was expressed by American authors such as Truman Capote or Gore Vidal. Canadian publisher Malcolm Lester recalls the interview which landed him his first job with Holt, Rhinehart and Winston in 1964. The person who hired him did so because he felt that Jews "would get the better of him." In Lester's view, the man did not think he was being anti-Semitic, but stating what he saw as a simple fact – that Jews would be better at business.[42] According to Butovsky, Adele Wiseman used to complain about the anti-Semitism of the Canadian literary establishment. But that is a minority view. Lester recalled the early role played by critic Nathan Cohen in Canadian letters, in print and on television. No one doubted that Cohen was a Jew, and indeed he had written early on for a Yiddish paper. But his style as a Canadian critic was "high mandarin, very erudite and intellectual." Robert Fulford argues that in the 1950s and 1960s, Canadian literature "did not even have a club to keep people out of, there was no door to bang at." Butovsky also recalls that literary critic Northrop Frye wrote very positively of the poetry of Irving Layton.[43] And according to critic and poet Eli Mandel, Canadian critics have welcomed themes of marginality, alienation, and a psychological or cultural doubleness.[44] Finally, the role of Jews in Canadian publishing – Avie Bennet, owner of McClelland & Stewart from 1986 to 2000, is perhaps the prime example – militates against public expressions of literary anti-Semitism.

Canadian Jewish writers fit right in. They have been able to remain more authentically Jewish because at the time they entered the scene, there was not a well-entrenched, indigenous Canadian literary culture. And there was also no ideological pressure for rapid assimilation as in the United States. Certainly a preoccupation with "survival," described by Margaret Atwood as typifying English Canadian literature, also resonates well with the historic Jewish experience, though in much different circumstances. Canadian survival meant defying the weather, terrain, and, later, the force of American power. Jewish survival referred to the dual threats of persecution and assimilation. But this parallelism on the issue of survival led some critics to integrate the scruffy Jewish experience into the centre of the traditional Anglo-Canadian world. George Woodcock said of Jewish writers, "They have revealed with a particular force and sensitivity the tensions that are characteristic of Canadian life and particularly Canadian urban life. This, it seems evident, is because the themes of which they treat with such a complex heritage of experience, the themes of isolation and division, are also the themes from which it is difficult for any writer in Canada to escape."[45]

I recognize similar patterns of cultural insecurity among Jews and Canadians. But not everyone agrees. For Harvard critic Ruth Wisse, Atwood's pessimistic paradigm of "survival" does not resonate with Jewish sensibilities. And certainly not when lamenting the impediments of Canada's geography and climate. "Margaret Atwood's theory of Canadian literature as a mythology of survival leaves out the Jew entirely. Although she does bring in some examples from Irving Layton and Adele Wiseman, she reflects nothing of the true Jewish experience. Do you know what the term 'Canada' signified in Auschwitz? Canada was the detail that collected the possessions of incoming prisoners, it was a synonym for 'plenty.' From a Jewish point of view how can one interpret Canada as a deprived and barren country, when it is the land of all possibilities?"[46]

For some, the notion that Jewish writing deserves or has a central place in the contemporary Canadian canon reflects the status of Jews not as marginals, but as an essentially white and European group in a position of domination *vis-à-vis* non-whites. Jews are now acceptable. But not non-whites, according to some critics. And even where they seem open to racial minorities, the cultural industries that sustain the canon are engaging in cultural appropriation or misrepresentation.[47] From this perspective, to say that Jews have made it into the canon is to say that Jews have shed their historic labels as victims, and are now automatically ranged with the exploiters of non-white immigrants. This would make liberal Jewish artists uncomfortable, if it were not so wrong-headed. My own reading of the cultural scene is different. Jews and non-whites are both making it. The gates to the Canadian literary pantheon are more open today to visible minorities and recent immigrants than was the case, say, for Jewish and other European ethnics in the 1930s. In literature, the acceptance seems unlimited. Think of Neil Bissoondath, Austin Clarke, Rohinton Mistry, Bharati Mukherjee, Michael Ondaatje, Marlene Nourbese Philip, or M. G. Vassanji, to name a few. In other areas, like music, it is far less.[48]

But the status of Jews and Jewish cultural contributions can still seem more entrenched than that of some groups. The 1993 production of *Showboat* rubbed salt in open wounds. In the eyes of some Toronto blacks, Jews specifically were actively involved in fostering both negative stereotypes of blacks and contributing to the cultural appropriation of the black experience.[49] The play depicted the lives of both blacks and whites on a gambling riverboat sailing on the Mississippi. The "Jewish" link was based on many things. The author of the original 1926 play, Edna Ferber, was Jewish, as were Jerome Kern and Oscar Hammerstein, who turned it into a musical. So was musical impresario Garth Drabinsky, who produced the show. The play was the opening production of the Municipal Arts Centre of North York, where the Jewish Mel Lastman then served as mayor. One trustee of the North York Board of Education argued that whites, and especially Jews, would routinely write or produce plays casting blacks in a negative light.[50] This case was perhaps the first Canadian episode which combined the culture wars and black–Jewish tensions, old hat for Americans. For a while, observers might have confused North York with New York.

Some liberal Jews shared reservations about the choice of *Showboat* as an opening production. The Canadian Council for Reform Judaism supported the effort to boycott the show, as did Reform rabbis Gunther Plaut and Dow Marmur. The Canadian Friends of the Hebrew University decided to cancel a fundraising evening at the play. At the same time, Jews were upset by what they perceived as direct or indirect anti-Semitism from the black community, typified by articles by Arnold Auguste, publisher of the black community newspaper *Share*. For blacks and other non-whites in Toronto, the controversy solidified the perception of Jews not as an oppressed minority, but as part of the city's power structure.

Canadian Jews have been instrumental in the development of Canadian films, theatre, and television. Names like Izzy Asper of CanWest Global, Garth Drabinsky, formerly of Livent, Harold Greenberg of Astral, Robert Lantos of Alliance Atlantis, entertainment lawyer Michael Levine, Moses Znaimer of CITY-TV, among others, have made innovative contributions to popular culture in Canada. The effect is noticeable, but the total impact seems less than that found in the United States. The Jewish influence both in New York and Hollywood is extensive, and often feeds into anti-Semitic stereotypes about Jewish domination of the media. Canada does not have the same critical mass of talented Jewish writers, actors, and directors; indeed, many of the best, like other talented Canadians, move south.

All this relates to English Canada. Language barriers explain the cultural gaps that persist between Jews and francophones in Quebec. With very few exceptions, like the popular television hostess Sonia Benezra, Jews do not play a role in French popular culture. There is no – for the time being – francophone Jewish counterpart to the English Jewish poets and writers discussed above. When English Canadians watch American television shows or movies or plays, they receive a dose of culture filtered through the lens of New York or Los Angeles Jewish sensibilities. The viewers, through osmosis, become receptive to Jewish cultural styles. Think of Jerry Seinfeld, Woody Allen, or Neil Simon. This is not there for the Québécois. Jews and Jewish themes are absent from popular French cultural production. While the general image of the Jew has been that of the outsider, there have been sympathetic treatments of Jews, such as in Yves Thériault's novel *Aaron*. Things may improve. Many Québécois have taken to Jewish-style smoked meat with gusto – check out the crowd at Schwartz's on the Main. But there is nothing like the infiltration of Yiddish words into English. At the same time, even here there are openings. When Guy Bouthillier, head of the nationalist Société St.-Jean-Baptiste de Montréal, recites a Yiddish poem at a kosher ssjb launch of three French-language books on Jewish themes in Montreal in June 2000, even if done for political considerations, something has changed.[51]

What, if anything, is Jewish about this Jewish contribution to popular culture? Specifically, in what way do these efforts actually shape Canadian culture in a "Jewish" manner? Anti-Semites can claim that Jewish control of Hollywood is part of a Jewish conspiracy to promote Jewish interests, such as a preoccupation with the Holocaust.

(See Chapter 11, on anti-Semitism, for a Canadian case in point.) In the United States, however, the conventional wisdom is that the Jewish influence, mainly through the writers and creators of movies and TV shows, has been liberalizing, in the broadest sense of the term. Sitcoms like *All in the Family*, developed by Norman Lear, preached the tolerance and urban cosmopolitanism valued by Jewish liberals by poking fun at the conservative Archie Bunker. A similar sensibility pervaded the Canadian sitcom *The King of Kensington*, with Al Waxman portraying a good-hearted liberal Jewish character. Wayne and Shuster did for Canada what scores of American Jewish entertainers based in vaudeville, burlesque, and the Borscht Belt did a generation earlier for the United States. Few can forget Wayne's Einsteinian portrayal of Professor Weingartner, the absent-minded Jewish genius. And most Canadian Jews of at least middle age recall the Sunday-night family ritual of watching the Ed Sullivan show and *kvelling*, as Jews and Canadians, whenever Wayne and Shuster were featured.

Like food, humour remains a staple of popular Jewish culture. It unites Jews, whatever their denomination or politics, and reinforces their Jewish identity with minimal obligations. In the words of (ex-Canadian) William Novak and Moshe Waldoks, editors of *The Big Book of Jewish Humor*: "It is even possible to argue that Jewish humor, which once represented a secular corner of many otherwise religious Jewish lives, has now come full circle to fulfill a kind of religious need in the lives of many non-practising Jews."[52] The Internet helps. Intersecting international e-mail networks – I am on several – circulate Jewish jokes with as much enthusiasm and interest as major rabbinic responsa in an earlier age. Jewish humour is distinctive. First, there is a lot of it. I think Jews value humour more than other groups, perhaps as an antidote to a history dotted with persecution. My shelves contain several thick anthologies of Jewish humour. I suspect there are more of those around than, say, anthologies of Methodist or Islamic or Swiss or First Nations humour. Jewish jokes also reinforce Jewish identity, with or without Yiddish in the punchlines. And based on the jokes my children bring home, new generations are embracing this tradition of humour that is both self-deprecatory as well as life-affirming. Freud's 1905 quip that "A new joke is passed from one person to another like the news of the latest victory" applies to Jews.[53]

But is there a specific Jewish comedic style? I cannot identify a common thread linking Woody Allen, Sandra Bernhard, Lenny Bruce, Jerry Lewis, Rich Little, the Marx Brothers, Jackie Mason, Mordecai Richler, Don Rickles, Joan Rivers, Mort Sahl, Jerry Seinfeld, Neil Simon, David Steinberg, Wayne and Shuster, and Henny Youngman – except that they were and are funny. As is the case with Jewish writers, for some the Jewish content is direct, for others it is oblique. But it is there, and Jews know it. All in all, the texture of Canadian Jewish culture is not deeper, but wider. To use assimilation as the dominant metaphor for the Jewish cultural reality is inadequate. Too much is going on.

8

THE PEOPLE
OF THE BOOK

Jewish Education and Jewish Survival

"A man lacking instruction cannot be pious."
                    — "Ethics of the Fathers," II: 6

In high school I occasionally posed impertinent questions. I once asked my Hebrew school teacher the following: Suppose there was only one vacancy in heaven and two applicants showed up at the same time. One was Theodore Herzl, who founded modern Zionism but who was thoroughly unreligious. The other was Rabbi Akiva, the wise and devout sage of antiquity. How would God decide who got in? My teacher pointed toward the door and shouted, "Weinfeld, get out!"

THE SCOPE OF JEWISH EDUCATION[1]

Jewish education is not sexy. I can sense yawns coming. But it is a crucial element of the Jewish experience, and linked intimately to Jewish survival. Jews are called the People of the Book, and for good reason. They were the first group to advocate and achieve universal male literacy, a requisite to being able to read the Bible and to pray. (The

Scots, under the influence of John Knox, followed suit.) Rabbis, who are learned teachers rather than priests, are the dominant figures of modern Judaic life. The study of Torah is considered the highest calling for Jews, who are commanded to ponder the text "day and night." Indeed, the sages have written that the requirement to study the Torah stands *keneged kulam*, as equivalent to all the rest of the commandments.

The practical foundation upon which the study of Torah rests is a system of Jewish education. And Jewish education today is not only religious; it includes the study of Hebrew, Jewish history, and Jewish literature and philosophy. Books about other Canadian ethnic groups do not include separate chapters devoted to ethno-cultural education, and in some cases they do not discuss the issue at all.[2] In other words, looking at Jewish education is perhaps the best way to see just how different Jews are from Canadians of other ethnic and religious backgrounds.

In North America, Jewish education is available to boys and girls, and in a variety of formats: day schools, sponsored by all denominations, including yeshivot for the very Orthodox; afternoon and Sunday schools, usually sponsored by congregations but also by communities; and private tutors. In Canada in recent years, day schools have become popular. As well, more attention is being paid to the "informal" sector of Jewish education. This includes Jewish summer camps and trips to Israel, both of which are heavily subsidized by North American Jewish communities.

A word about Jewish summer camps is in order. The impact of these camps on generations of North American Jews has never been fully researched, but it is impressive. The camps are as diverse as North American Jewry itself. There are camps associated with specific Zionist movements, general Jewish community camps, camps associated with specific religious denominations, and privately owned camps with Jewish owners, predominantly Jewish campers and staff, and some form of Jewish atmosphere. Some camps are basic, others very posh, where the Jewish American Prince or Princess reigns supreme. In some camps, Jewish content is front and centre, in others, it is offered in smaller doses. But from coast to coast in Canada, Jewish identities are being forged in these camps, helped by hormones and sustained by memories.

I spent ten years, eight as a camper, in Camp Massad, a Hebrew-speaking summer camp in the Laurentian Mountains north of Montreal. The camp took Hebrew language and culture as seriously as any camp anywhere. I can still recite the Hebrew terms, coined by staffers at the camp and unknown to Israelis, for every baseball position and eventuality. (Actually, this is another affinity between Jews and Québécois, who also had to invent baseball terms in a new language!) I have no doubt that my camp experience contributed to my Jewish education and socialization as strongly as did my eleven years of Jewish day school. It helped shape me as a Jew. And I am positive most former Massadniks would agree. No Canadian minority group has a comparable system of summer camps.

And similarly, no minority group has an educational system as extensively developed, as multi-dimensional, as do Jews. Most of the one-morning-a-week "Saturday" schools for ethnic minorities have catered to immigrant families, and their enrolments decline dramatically after the immigrant generation. Ethno-cultural education also takes place in special heritage or multicultural programs in public schools, sparing ethnic groups the bill.[3] Jews also benefit from these programs, and for some parents they are an acceptable alternative to Jewish schools. These programs are minimal – in Quebec, for example, the Jewish program available through the Protestant School Board of Greater Montreal offered just two hours of Jewish studies per week, a bit of Hebrew, some history and traditions – but they are probably better than nothing.

Even the religious aspects of Jewish education set Jews apart. Christian religious education does not loom large as a subject for analysts of religion in Canada. Reginald Bibby's 1993 study *Unknown Gods: The Ongoing Story of Religion in Canada*, has no chapter on religious education, and just five brief references to Sunday schools. Bibby's national surveys show that the proportion of Canadians with school-age children who were exposing them to religious instruction, such as Sunday school, declined from only 35 per cent in 1975 to 28 per cent in 1990. The 1990 figure for Catholics was 36 per cent and for Protestants 23 per cent.[4] It is not clear what these parents thought was meant by instruction, but it was not likely to be a day school education lasting many years. In any case, these rates are far lower than for North American Jews. In the words of a respected Baptist minister, "Sunday School, which for two hundred years has been the major recruitment, teaching, and evangelistic arm of church life, is almost gone in Canada."[5]

Some non-Jewish ethnic and/or religious schools are all-day private schools with similarities to Jewish day schools. Catholic schools are the best-known case in point, though the degree of actual Catholic instruction varies by school system and by province, and is quite limited. Fundamentalist and evangelical Protestant private schools take their religion very seriously. So do the Muslim schools slowly taking root. Some European ethnic groups also sponsor day schools, such as the Greek Socrates school in Montreal or Ukrainian schools in Western Canada. Schools catering to First Nations students, with a significant Aboriginal curriculum, have also been set up. In 1998 Ontario had over six hundred private schools, with over two-thirds having some kind of religious affiliation. These included thirty-five Jewish schools, seventeen Islamic Schools, twenty-eight First Nations schools, and almost one hundred Amish or Mennonite.[6] There might be more such schools in Ontario if the province would extend funding to these non-Catholic schools, as is done in other Canadian provinces. The Ontario Jewish Association for Equity in Education, along with the Alliance of Christian Schools, fought the case for funding as far ask the Supreme Court of Canada. In 1996 the Court ruled against them, citing the fact that Ontario Catholic Schools were constitutionally protected and the others were not, even though there was an inequity in the situation. That fight is not over. In a budget statement in the spring of 2001, the Ontario government proposed extending tax credits to parents with children in all private schools. Public-school supporters launched a counterattack. Whatever emerges, it is likely to be far from equal treatment with the Catholic schools.

Providing Jewish education is both a familial and communal obligation; there is no choice in the matter. The Torah stresses the responsibility of parents to educate their children Jewishly. The biblical commandment "*veshinantem levanecho*" instructs Jewish fathers to teach their (male) children the basics of the Torah. But eventually parental teaching and private tutors gave way to schools. Like the creation of Jewish cemeteries and the provision of kosher slaughter for meat, the setting up of Jewish schools is now a requirement of every Jewish *kehilla*, or organized community. In the old country, the ideal marriage partner for a young Jewish woman, especially if her father had money, was the brilliant rabbinical student, or *talmid chacham*. Indeed, every Jewish male child was expected to become literate in Hebrew, and poverty, in theory, was no excuse.

Jewish education is widespread among Canadian Jews. In Toronto in 1990, an estimated 90 per cent of Jewish children at one time or another had received some form of Jewish education, and 58 per cent were currently enrolled. Some 86 per cent of parents of pre-school children expect them to receive some form of Jewish education.[7] A 1996 survey of Montreal Jewry found that 73 per cent of adults (82 per cent of those under 35) had at one point in time received some Jewish education, down from 81 per cent in 1991.[8] These figures are far higher than the national Canadian figures for Christian education cited above. Much of this Jewish education in Canada is focused on all-day schools.[9] The level of formal Jewish education of Canadian Jewish children today is on the whole much greater than that of their Canadian-born parents or grandparents, whose education consisted mainly of tutors or Sunday schools or a few years of afternoon schools. This flies in the face of the assimilationist perspective that assumes each generation has less Judaic knowledge. These gains are most pronounced for women. The disappearance of the huge gender gaps in formal Jewish schooling is the most striking feature of post-war North American Jewish education.

The Jewish education system in Canada is extensive and intensive.[10] Canada's first Talmud Torah was started in Montreal in 1896. Toronto's first Talmud Torah was founded in 1907, and grew into the multi-branch Associated Hebrew Schools. A more Orthodox school, the Eitz Chaim, was founded in Toronto in 1915. During the First World War, Montreal's Yiddish Peretz School and the bilingual Yiddish and Hebrew Jewish People's School were founded; they have since merged. In both Toronto and Montreal, there are many educational options. Both cities boast a number of ultra-Orthodox and Hasidic schools, strictly segregated by gender, and yeshivot for the older male students.

Other day schools span the spectrum from Modern Orthodox to Conservative to more liberal.[11] This incredible variety is difficult to appreciate, but it is a microcosm of modern Jewish life.

Montreal boasts twenty-six Jewish elementary schools, of which nineteen are day schools (some are multi-branch schools). In addition, there are twenty-five "Jewish" daycare centres (some of these are private operations). There are, moreover, six full-day high schools – none of which is ultra-Orthodox – and seven rabbinical schools, all of which are ultra-Orthodox. The variety includes Sephardi/francophone as well as Ashkenazi/anglophone. In Toronto, there is also a wide array of Jewish schools. The tilt in Toronto is toward Orthodox or traditional schools, particularly at the high-school level. There is nothing in Toronto like the Bialik high school in Montreal, with its Yiddishist cultural orientation. However, Toronto boasts a Leo Baeck Day School (elementary) affiliated with Reform. There are twenty-seven day schools in Toronto – some with multiple branches – and another forty-one supplementary schools. Of Toronto's thirteen high-school options, the large majority are very traditional. There is a wider range of Jewish high-school options in Montreal. Toronto's relative strength is in Orthodox and supplementary education.[12] Day schools have sprung up throughout the country. One or more elementary schools are found in Ottawa, London, Hamilton, Kitchener, Winnipeg, Calgary, Edmonton, and Vancouver. Jewish high schools, whether yeshiva-type or general schools, are found in Ottawa, Hamilton, Winnipeg, and Vancouver.

Jewish education is big business. Consider the case of Montreal. The estimated total budget for all Jewish day schools affiliated with the Jewish Education Council is forty-two million dollars. This money comes from school fees ($17 million), provincial grants ($18 million), community grants ($2 million), and the balance from other fund-raising campaigns. About 40 per cent of students receive some form of tuition assistance.[13] Jewish education in Toronto is comparably costly. Montreal's BJEC (Bronfman Jewish Education Council), and its counterpart in Toronto, the BJE (Board of Jewish Education), co-ordinate communal activities in Jewish education (like the National Bible Contest). They also assist with teacher training, in-service professional development, audio-visual and library services for Jewish teachers and students, lobbying for Jewish education with Federations, channelling of financial aid to students, and even curricular innovation. The commitment to Jewish education, and day-school education, is not limited to the major centres of Toronto and Montreal. In Calgary, for example, there are over seven thousand Jews and two day schools. A survey based on a sample derived from various Jewish communal lists – thus excluding assimilated Jews – found 71 per cent claimed their children did or would attend a Jewish day school.[14]

These levels are all much higher than those found on the U.S. scene as reported in the 1990 National Jewish Population Study.[15] But Jewish education is not as central in the United States. Consider that Jewish education was not analyzed at all in the first hundred-page report on the 1990 NJPS.[16] Such an omission would be inconceivable in a comparable Canadian document. And of the Jewish children who were enrolled in American Jewish schools, only 27 per cent were in day schools.[17] Part of these American and Canadian differences can be traced back to the constitutional context in the two countries regarding church and state. The Canadian tradition of public support for religious education is a key factor making religious schooling popular and affordable. In contrast, American Jews have embraced the mythic image of the public school as the avenue of economic mobility and Americanization.

It is paradoxical that despite this importance of Jewish education, the vast majority of Canadian Jews are only barely literate as Jews. They may be doing better than Christians or other ethnic groups, but that is cold comfort. To say that Jews value education is not to say that they value Jewish education, at least not to the same degree. The irony is that Jewish achievement at the level of secular education is formidable, extending into graduate and post-graduate work. But when it comes to an understanding of Jewish civilization in all its dimensions, Jews just scratch the surface. If Jews are the People of the Book, for too many that book is not the Torah. And when most Jewish children do study Torah, it is at the most superficial level. Another paradox is that the function of Jewish education today is not education in the sense of imparting knowledge. Its major task is creating and nurturing the Jewish identity of students. What the home, neighbourhood, and synagogue did in the past falls now to Jewish schools. It is doubtful that Jewish schools can maximize both the creating of Jewish identity and the transmission of Jewish knowledge. But they try. They have no choice.

THE EFFECTS OF JEWISH EDUCATION

For some time, Jewish education has been dominated by the "vaccination" approach. Assimilation and intermarriage are the disease, and Jewish education is the vaccine. So the case for Jewish education as a sound individual and communal investment is made in terms of strengthening Jewish identity. But this instrumental model is an odd way to understand Jewish education. For almost all of Jewish history, Jewish identity was a given, and there was little danger that it would be lost or diluted. It was nurtured both by a hostile society and a seamless pattern linking family to synagogue to community. Identity had little or nothing to do with education. Jewish education did not create Jewish identity, it taught students how to be more fulfilled, more complete, and, most important, more knowledgeable Jews. It was undertaken *li'shma*, for its own sake. Jewish education was important because knowledge was important. Studying the classic Judaic texts would make one a better human being and a better Jew. It didn't make you want to be a Jew, or feel good about being a Jew.

In traditional Judaic thought, the study of Torah was something that adults (males of course) were to do. The admonitions concerning Torah study in *Pirkei Avot*, or The Ethics of the Fathers, are directed to adults and advocate what we might today call lifelong learning. For example, Jews are instructed to set aside a fixed time for regular study, or to reflect on the optimal relation between work and study. The norm common to many non-Orthodox Jews in North America, that Jewish education and Torah study would stop after a child's bar or bat mitzvah, was inconceivable for the pre-modern period.

Parents and the Jewish community have faith that Jewish education will lead to stronger Jewish identification. Are they right? A Toronto study asked students who were receiving some form of Jewish education about its likely impact on their participation in Jewish communal life, intermarriage, and religiosity. In the view of the students, the positive impacts were minimal indeed. Only one-third felt it would have an impact on their avoiding intermarriage and 28 per cent on their becoming more religious. "On no issue," concluded the study, is the impact of the school very high, and on all aspects combined, it is very small indeed."[18] Ironically, most of these students still believed it was important that they receive a Jewish education. Perhaps the students felt that other factors, like their family background, are more decisive in determining their Jewish future. (Or more likely, like most Jewish adolescents, they did not really think through these sorts of issues; they were too busy being teenagers.)

Despite the views of these students, we have to assume that Jewish education has a positive impact on Judaic knowledge. Jewish students are taught facts and, if they are lucky, Jewish skills and ideas. But we know very little of what Jewish students retain from their Jewish education. How good is their Hebrew, what do they know of Jewish history, or the Bible, or Talmud, or Jewish philosophy? There are almost no studies of these long-term effects. The logic is overwhelming, though. Learning about something leads to knowing more than not learning about it. This is supported by the finding in 1990 that Canadians under thirty-five – those most likely to have benefited from the increase in Jewish day-school attendance – were able to converse in Hebrew better than older Jews.[19]

Research on Jewish adults clearly does show an effect of Jewish education on subsequent Jewish identity. But the link is mysterious. Most Jews know at least one other Jew who can barely distinguish an *aleph* from a *bet* but is still a highly committed Jew. And many Jews know the opposite, the *apikoros*, a Jew learned in Judaica yet who remains an unbeliever and disengaged from the Jewish community. There are no guarantees. But these cases, while fascinating, are, as we shall see, minor chords. Judaic learning and Jewish identity usually reinforce each other.

There is actually a third possible effect of Jewish education, which is omitted from most discussions of the topic. Jewish education can affect the type of human being Jews become. We are not certain that students with more Jewish education are more compassionate, tolerant, honest, or law-abiding, but we would like to think that Jews with a deeper Jewish education, with more exposure to Jewish moral teachings, would also be better human beings, have more *menschlichkeit*, or decency. Within the Jewish tradition, there has always been a presumed link between Jewish study and ethical behaviour – note the quotation at the beginning of this chapter. While this has generally not been a major research question, it would be worth knowing. Is there less stealing, or cheating, or gossip, or jealousy, or rudeness, or selfishness, or fighting, in Jewish day schools compared to public schools which have many Jewish students? I have no idea. A roundabout approach to the question might be to compare Orthodox and non-Orthodox Jews – the former would also have more Jewish education – on measures of ethical behaviour.

The main thing scholars have studied is the net impact of Jewish education on the various attitudes and behaviours associated with living a Jewish life – with being a committed Jew. Ironically, most Jews can tell horror stories about some aspect of their Jewish schooling, and many recount how Jewish school turned them off Judaism. And recent research suggests there is something there. In their recent qualitative study of "moderately affiliated" American Jews, Steven Cohen and Arnold Eisen interviewed about sixty representative middle-of-the-road Jews, and identified several "obstacles to involvement." They concluded that Jewish education was one such obstacle. "Hebrew school was consistently named, even by strongly identified Jews, as a negative feature of their childhood experience of Judaism. Jabs at Hebrew school seemed to come routinely in our interviews, almost as if they were expected and a marker of someone in the know."[20] The Toronto study cited earlier also reported cases in which students were critical of their Jewish schooling.

But this is not the last word on the matter. There are many quantitative scientific research studies of Jewish adults, usually with much larger samples. These studies uniformly find that there does seem to be an impact of Jewish education on positive Jewish outcomes. Jewish education either causes, or reinforces, Jewish identity.[21] (For details see Appendix IV: The Effects of Jewish Education.)

This contradiction between the qualitative and quantitative research traditions is more apparent than real. They are both right. It is not surprising that American adults, when asked to think back to their (mainly supplementary) Jewish schooling, would not have fond memories.

Sunday school or afternoon school took up time from socializing or other extracurricular activities. And no doubt many teachers, and the subject matter, were boring. I taught teenagers at Hebrew School from nine until noon on Sunday mornings when I was a graduate student. No matter how enthusiastic I was, I just knew they did not want to be there. They had partied late the night before and wanted to sleep in. I couldn't blame them. So those negative feelings, or recollections, are real. But the quantitative studies take a different approach. They ask not if it was fun, but if it had a positive effect years later. It may be that there is an impact of Jewish education that adults may not even realize. How many people whose parents forced them to eat vegetables and fruit instead of sweets and junk food look back fondly at the experience? Very few. But chances are those children are healthier as adults now. For many Jews, their Jewish education was like spinach. So both the qualitative anecdotes and the quantitative findings are correct. One newer problem is that Jewish parents, like all middle-class parents, have become more reluctant to force their children to do things they do not enjoy. The challenge for Jewish educators is to come up with a tasty, low-calorie, spinach ice cream . . .

There is no doubt there have been routes to Jewish identity outside formal Jewish education. Jewish youth movements, Israel experiences, as well as summer camps play a role. My wife is a good example. She never had one minute of formal Jewish education. As a child she went to synagogue on the High Holidays, perhaps. But at age thirteen, she joined Hashomer Hatzair, a socialist-Zionist youth movement, and at age seventeen, she left with her *garin*, or group, to settle on a kibbutz. Her years with Hashomer, summers at Camp Shomria, and her three years in Israel, one on a kibbutz and two in Israeli universities, were her "Jewish education." Today, we keep a kosher home, are shul-goers, and have sent our children to Jewish day schools. But there are two other factors which can explain my wife's evolution, and which may limit its relevance for the future. First, her background. She is the daughter of Holocaust survivors and her mother tongue was Yiddish. Those facts no doubt shaped her early years in countless, if subtle, ways. Second, while she did not attend a Jewish school, her Montreal public high school, Wagar, was over 90 per cent Jewish. It was a school full of Jews. Her peer group was totally Jewish. On major Jewish holidays, the school was empty. Her experience raises the question of the relative importance of peers compared to the formal and informal curriculum in a Jewish school. What makes Jewish education in general effective in reaching its goals? In terms of Jewish identity, it may well be the inter- action with other Jewish kids – playing sports, doing a lab, dating – that is decisive, not the Judaic curriculum.

Jewish day schools have become more popular over the past two or three decades among those who are not Orthodox. One reason is they are considered good schools. They seem to prepare students well in secular subjects and for future success in university. Graduation rates and cumulative student averages for private and public high schools in Montreal, including Jewish day schools, are published yearly in the Montreal *Gazette*. With the exception of schools catering to ultra- Orthodox students, which do not emphasize secular studies, the Jewish day schools compare well with other private or public schools. I suspect the same is true of Jewish day schools in other cities. But the reason may not be the "Jewishness" of the schools. Researchers have found that a bright and motivated peer group promotes academic achieve- ment, even more so than lavish new buildings or facilities, or well-paid teachers. In other words, a school climate is key. Catholic and other private schools in the United States are more effective than public schools in teaching students from all income levels. Those schools are more disciplined (I am not saying Jewish schools have more discipline), devote more class time to actual work, and assign more homework.[22] It is not because of any distinctly "Catholic" teaching. There is nothing "Catholic," or "Jewish," about doing well in a math test. Or is there?

For a long time Jewish day schools were stigmatized as being aca- demically inferior, associated with images of ultra-Orthodox Jews uninterested in university studies. While that view has changed, there are still some Jews – I have met them – who are unconvinced. They fear that a time-consuming Jewish education, particularly the study of a second language like Hebrew, might lead to a weaker mastery of English and other subjects. They worry that Jewish studies take time away from the more important secular subjects. In fact, the research on bilingual education offers no support for this view. A Montreal evaluation of Jewish day-school students further refutes it. These students were involved in trilingual education – English, French, and Hebrew – and their academic achievements in English and secular studies were in no way impaired.[23] Many of these students also do well at the postsecondary level. Perhaps a more demanding multilingual curriculum, with both secular and Judaic studies, in Darwinian fashion equips Jewish students for subsequent success at university. It is also possible that students going to private schools are just brighter. Jewish day schools, like Catholic and private schools, draw a self-selected sample of students, from families that value education and are able and prepared to spend more for a private school. Most of the students may well come from middle-class homes, where high educational aspirations are nurtured. So their doing well is not really caused by the school; they are just better students. For whatever reason, Jewish day-school graduates are now found in the best Canadian and American universities. One sees knitted *yarmulkas* everywhere.

Another reason for the increase in popularity of day schools is that they are the new incubators of future Jews. More and more Jewish parents who are not themselves religious have been sending their children to Jewish day schools. Many see them as providing a better alternative to public schools, with a better peer group, less sex and drugs – which may be wishful thinking – and as a way to prevent intermarriage. Many parents want these schools to inculcate Judaism in a way they are unwilling or unable to. Other parents choose a Jewish school because they want their children to be in school with other Jews. Their own commitment to Judaic Studies is minimal; often the children wind up socializing their parents into Judaism and Jewish life.

But these schools are not perfect. Because many of these schools draw upon a homogeneous middle- or upper-class clientele, there is a danger they will foster a school culture which is narrow, shallow, ethnocentric, and materialistic.[24] My oldest daughter came home after her first day in a Jewish kindergarten following the winter vacation. I asked her what she had learned in school that day. She answered, "Daddy, what's Barbados?" In at least two of the leading Jewish high schools in

Montreal, the highlight event of the school year for students is the annual fashion show. At some daytime school functions, there may be more nannies than parents. I have met Jewish day-school graduates whose universe is confined to a narrow corridor running from Montreal or Toronto down to Boca Raton. Jewish day schools are aware of these dangers and try to counteract them with programs of exchanges and dialogues with other schools. It is not easy.

BARRIERS TO DAY-SCHOOL EDUCATION

There are three reasons why Jewish parents do not opt for Jewish day schools for their children. One is the financial burden, which penalizes working-class and lower-middle-class parents. While financial aid is often available, many Jews don't like asking for it. Moreover, in some cases middle-class parents earn too much to qualify for significant aid, and are unprepared or unable to spend less in other areas. Tuition ranges from about four thousand dollars a year in Montreal to ten thousand in Toronto and elsewhere.

This leads into the second reason: Jewishness is important, but not that important. A Jewish day school may be seen by some parents as providing too much Jewish education, with the risk of making their children too narrow and ill-prepared to function in a non-Jewish world. And for wealthier families, the alternative of an elite non-Jewish private school is appealing because of the perceived quality of the schools. Parents like the uniforms, the discipline, the extra-curricular options, from drama to sports, and what seems like a tough, no-nonsense academic environment. Across Canada, there are elite private schools with growing proportions of Jewish children. These schools used to have a distinct odour of anti-Semitism, and were also unaffordable. Now Jewish parents can afford them, their children (as well as visible minorities) are welcome, and there are enough Jewish students already in many of them to ease the adjustment. In fact these schools are now the major competition for Jewish day schools. The parents who enroll their children in them should not be considered un-Jewish, or uncommitted to the Jewish future. Not at all. Many are leaders in the community. They simply feel that other Jewish alternatives beyond school exist for their children, and, obviously, Jewish education is not the very highest priority. A 1996 survey of Montreal Jews asked parents to explain why they were not sending their children to Jewish day schools. The most common reason (53 per cent) was that they wanted them to socialize in a wider milieu.[25] These parents want their children to be Jews – to be different – but not too different.

A third reason is that a Jewish day-school education is too demanding for some students, as it usually results in a longer day and a dual English–Hebrew curriculum. In Montreal, a French–English–Hebrew curriculum means even greater demands. In one school system, Yiddish adds a fourth language. My youngest daughter recently attended a Montreal Jewish elementary school in which the day began at eight and ended at four, with just a half-hour for lunch. That is a very long day, and it started in Grade One. Some students find it too much, and with homework on top, there is little time for music, ballet, sports, and just plain relaxation. This has led to calls – generally unsuccessful – for forms of Judaic streaming in day schools, and to calls for cutting back on the hours of Judaic instruction.

THE FORM AND CONTENT OF JEWISH EDUCATION

There is an ongoing debate about what makes for success in education, and Jewish education is no exception. Good charismatic teachers and administrators are important. Curricular innovations also play a role, at the level of more effective pedagogy, so that graduates will actually retain more Judaic knowledge. Common sense also suggests that having fun, or a meaningful, enjoyable experience, is crucial, since in many cases – Sunday school and afternoon school in particular – the students do not want to be there.

In the old country, Jewish education traditionally took place in *cheders*, small schools for elementary-age male children, and in yeshivot, academies of higher learning aimed at teenagers whose curriculum comprised mainly the study of Talmud. The pedagogy was not progressive, and the education was far from child-centred. Indeed, the emphasis was clearly on rote learning, on mastering the texts and the commentaries. Depending on the specific yeshiva, these commentaries might include traditional sources like Rashi, Maimonides, Nachmanides, Saadia Gaon, the Vilna Gaon, as well as more recent

Hasidic *rebbes* and yeshiva scholars specific to various sects. There was little interest in what the young students thought about the texts, or about any novel interpretations they might develop. In some cases, yeshiva students would also be exposed to minimal amounts of *musar*, a form of moral education aimed at applying Judaic principles to the real world. Originality and creativity in textual interpretation would have to wait until the end of their studies, where only the best among them would be encouraged to think independently. But we should not stereotype the yeshiva world. Boys will be boys. Yeshiva students, then and now, are not devoid of mundane concerns, jealousies, passions, and ambitions.[26]

Jewish education has not been static. Many schools use modern technology such as computer programs aimed at the study of Bible or Talmud. Judaic studies can be found on the Internet and CD-ROMs. There has been change in content as well as in form. By the end of the nineteenth century, the influence of the *Haskalah*, or Enlightenment, extended the traditional curriculum to include elements of Jewish history and Hebrew language and literature in the Talmud Torah network of schools. In addition, a network of secular Yiddishist schools was established in Eastern Europe, and transplanted to North America. In these schools, often called people's schools, or *folkshuls*, Yiddish language and literature replaced the emphasis on Hebrew, secular ethics and social justice were stressed, and the Bible was included as literature rather than as the word of God.

Modern Jewish day schools (except for the ultra-Orthodox) seek to accomplish a dual task. They must provide their students both with a first-rate secular education and a meaningful Jewish education. The former is instrumental in getting a job and earning a living; the latter is a form of enrichment or values education. This sets many parents and Jewish educators at loggerheads. For many parents, particularly the non-Orthodox, the secular education is more important. They want top computer training, as well as sports, art, and all the main curricular subjects. But most Jewish educators are tenacious in defending the priority of the Jewish portion of the curriculum. One increasingly popular solution is to integrate the two streams where possible, in areas such as literature or history. Thus, while in their general history students are learning about the French Revolution and Napoleon, in Jewish history they might be studying the impact of the Revolution and Napoleon on Jewish life in Western Europe. Another ongoing curricular debate in Jewish education concerns "*Ivrit be'Ivrit*" ("Hebrew in Hebrew"). The issue is whether all the Judaic curriculum should be taught in Hebrew, or just the Hebrew language courses. My own day-school experience involved learning all Jewish studies subjects in Hebrew. In retrospect, I think I would have been better served by studying subjects like Jewish history, religion, philosophy, and perhaps Hebrew/Jewish literature, in English, as they do in introductory Jewish Studies courses in university.

Over the years, Jewish schools have come to emphasize the "informal" curriculum as seriously as the formal elements described above. As Jewish schools are expected to socialize children into Jewish adulthood, the informal, experiential dimensions of Jewish schools become more important. As already suggested, simply having an all-Jewish peer group may be as important for subsequent Jewish identity as anything learned in the formal curriculum. For students in Jewish schools, plays, Holocaust memorials, sports meets, field trips, dances all get drafted into the cause. If they do anything, Jewish day schools facilitate Jewish dating. So do summer camps, youth groups, or Israel experiences. The object of the exercise – stated or unstated – is to channel those teenage hormones.

THE COMMUNAL POLITICS OF JEWISH EDUCATION

Although formally private, Jewish day schools in North America have become a de facto public-school system of the Jewish community. Jewish communities have taken to proclaiming in heroic fashion that no child will be denied a Jewish day-school education because of inability to pay. The emergence of Jewish education, especially day schools, as perhaps the key – and most costly – element of a Canadian Jewish public agenda poses interesting problems of school independence versus communal control. Most Jewish schools zealously guard their autonomy, and resist any interference in decisions made by their boards, parents, or administrators. This is a result of their histories, in which they arose as private institutions, founded by dedicated visionaries with a clear ideological focus. But as costs have risen, and more schools seek assistance from the organized community, the question arises as to what influence the community at large can or should have on educational matters. It is useful to think of Jewish schools not as private schools, but as the public-school system of the Jewish polity. If so, they must be accountable to some broad communal consensus to receive funding.

The growing concern for Jewish unity offers the best example. Imagine a "Jewish" school which promoted the transformation of Israel into a democratic secular state under Palestinian control. Such a school might well fall under either extreme left-wing or certain ultra-Orthodox auspices. Or imagine a school dedicated to promoting Jewish assimilation and mixed marriage. Or a school which preached a philosophy based on the views of the Jewish Defense League's Meir Kahane or Dr. Baruch Goldstein, who shot dozens of Arabs praying at Hebron. Or one which claimed that certain Jews, be they "black hats" or Reform, should be excluded from the Jewish community. While these are extreme examples, they raise the question of whether a core set of principles could be imposed on specific schools.[27] Or put it another way: could a Jewish federation ask schools seeking its financial assistance for a commitment to inculcate the pluralistic principles of *ahavat Yisrael* or *klal Yisrael* – a love of Israel – in some ways in their curriculum? The sparks would fly.

These are not theoretical debates. The Jewish Education Council of Montreal already has a series of requirements which must be fulfilled by schools seeking affiliation. Among these requirements are items directly related to curriculum. For example, Requirement Number 9 reads:

Affiliated schools shall strive to imbue their pupils with a desire for identification with and knowledge of:
a) their Jewish heritage
b) Jewish moral and religious values
c) the Jewish people and its continued survival
d) the Jewish community of Montreal
e) Canada and Quebec
f) the State of Israel.

This list wisely does not specify the specific values of Point b. Yet Point f excludes anti-Zionist schools, whether of the left or the right. And in Montreal, there are some Hasidic groups whose schools are affiliated with the JEC – those run by Lubavitch, Belz, and Skver – and others that are not – Satmar and Tash. How actively the first set of schools actually promotes "identification" with the State of Israel is, of course, another matter. I suspect the effort is minimal.

Jewish day schools are not like stereotypical elite private schools. Many of the day-school families are not part of a religious Jewish elite. The schools are not as well-equipped as the elite private schools. And Jewish day-school parents are not all wealthy. They include the full range of economic classes. It is time to think about Jewish schools and their links to the Jewish community the way we analyze public schools and their link to the broader society which supports them. Educational reformers have long debated whether public schools change society or simply reflect existing arrangements. Jewish educators must wrestle with the same questions. If there is a problem of Jewish unity, can it be solved using the Jewish school system? (Anti-racist programs in public schools are an analogy. Here, the school is being used to solve the social problem of racism.) In fact, there are many programs in which Orthodox and non-Orthodox schools participate and interact socially, such as sports tournaments, song festivals, rallies, Holocaust and Israeli Independence Day events. No one knows the impact of such efforts. They certainly do no harm. But they are not very meaningful encounters or structured dialogues about pluralism and tolerance. And ultra-Orthodox schools are often not involved.

The education of Jewish children has been an item on the public-policy agenda in Canada for generations, particularly in Quebec. Under the British North America Act of 1867, only Catholics and Protestants are granted public education rights. In Quebec, the place of Jewish children, teachers, and parents in the Protestant and Catholic school systems was a matter of heated debate. As the Jewish population of Montreal grew, the proportion of Jewish children in the Protestant (English) school system increased. Eventually, in 1903, an act of the Quebec legislature established this access in law. Yet Jews were still not permitted to work as teachers or to be active on the Protestant School

Board, even though they paid taxes. The wealthier uptown Jews argued for equality within the Protestant School system. But among some of the immigrant community, a preferred option was to create an independent Jewish School Board. This would not only enhance Jewish cultural survival, but eliminate the practice by which Jewish children in "Christian" schools were forced to participate in Christian rituals and prayer. Compromise solutions began to evolve in the 1930s, despite opposition from nationalist forces in Quebec. Eventually Jewish parents and teachers were admitted into Protestant schools, and the religious character of those schools began to decline.[28] In 1970, private Jewish day schools in Quebec received recognition as Associated Schools in the public interest and were thus entitled to receive government grants for the secular portion of their school funding, as is the case with schools serving other religious and ethnic minorities. These grants have continued, as long as these schools continue to meet minimal government requirements regarding the hours of French instruction. Jewish day schools in Ontario, like other non-Catholic private schools in the province, remain out of luck.

This issue highlights an important difference between Canadian and American Jews, and indeed between the two countries. American Jews, at least as represented by official organizations, have been fierce supporters of the separation of church and state. They regularly oppose any curricular or extracurricular intrusion of religious symbolism in the public schools or on school grounds. No crosses, no nativity scenes, no Hanukkah lights. They usually oppose public funding of private religious schooling, seeing Jewish schools as potentially ghettoizing. American Jews and Jewish organizations are staunch defenders of the American public-school system, since many immigrant Jewish children made their way up the occupational ladder via the public schools, and many American Jews entered the white-collar ranks as teachers and then administrators. Canada never developed an American mythology about the egalitarian nature of the public-school system, and does not have the same separation of church and state.[29]

The BNA Act of 1867 recognized and legitimated differences. It gave rights to speakers of English and French, and to Protestants and Catholics. This constitutional tradition has continued right through the 1982 Charter of Rights and Freedoms, with Section 27 recognizing multicultural rights. It was not unreasonable that Canadian schools should reflect, not eradicate, those cultural characteristics. By contrast, the Americans' fear of separateness is linked to their constitutional separation of church and state, which affected American immigrant Jews and their descendants. American Jews have always wanted desperately to become American, to fit in. Canadian Jews do not mind having a large network of private day schools, and having governments foot some of the bill where possible. But, obviously, many Canadian parents remain reluctant to send their children to those schools.

Jewish communal leaders now recognize the importance of Jewish education in the fight for continuity. It was not always thus. I recall a meeting of some wealthy Montreal Jews, around 1969 or 1970, where the aim was to sell the importance of Jewish education in general and a new program of Jewish Studies for McGill University. One of the philanthropists commented (I am paraphrasing), "I don't understand all this fuss about Jewish education. I never had a single day of Jewish education and that never did me any harm." Whatever their reservations, the philanthropists came through. But all the talk about the importance of Jewish education masks some painful realities. Few Jewish parents, no matter how committed to Jewish continuity, would dance for joy if their daughter – and certainly their son – told them they wanted to become a Hebrew-school teacher. Even as salaries and job security have increased, there is still a sense that Jewish teachers do not enjoy the esteem – or the income – that Jewish physicians, lawyers, and accountants do.

Actually, Jewish education is a growth area, and there is a shortage of teachers, administrators, and principals. In the past, Israelis comprised a large percentage of the Jewish teachers in Canada. Some came on special limited-term contracts; others were immigrants. Other teachers were Holocaust survivors. Some had little training in modern pedagogic techniques, to say the least. In my eleven years of day school in the 1950s and 1960s, I can recall only one or two Canadian-born teachers in Judaic subjects. Let me be clear. I think my Hebrew-school teachers did a fine job. I remember most of them clearly and with affection, even after thirty-five or forty years. At times we were rude and misbehaved, which I regret, and I spent my fair share of time getting thrown out of class. (My school was diabolically clever; when you were thrown out, at least in elementary school, rather than stand in the hall you had to go to the library.) Like most of my classmates, I did not always take my Judaic studies seriously, and we tended to make more trouble for the Hebrew teachers than for those teaching secular subjects. This was generally known throughout the day-school system. As the years passed, concerns were expressed that Israeli teachers, particularly those who came for just a few years, lacked the familiarity with the local Canadian scene to enable them to understand their students. Who knows? In any case, the trend has been towards recruiting and training Canadian Jews, through teacher-training programs available at McGill and York universities.

BEYOND JEWISH SCHOOLS

Jewish education begins before elementary school and continues after high school. Jewish nurseries, playgroups, and daycare centres are now common in every Jewish community, and cater to every Jewish orientation. The segregation and socialization of Jewish children starts when they are barely toddlers. A similar explosion has taken place at the post-secondary level and beyond. Ultra-Orthodox Jewish men are able to continue studying, even after they get married, in *kollels*. For more secular types, the campus has become an increasingly important venue. The growth of Jewish Studies courses, chairs, programs, and departments has augmented what was available from formal Jewish schools. Bible, Jewish History, Rabbinics, Jewish Philosophy, Hebrew and Yiddish Language and Literature are the traditional core of Jewish Studies. More recently, areas dealing with the social scientific study of modern Jewish life, the Holocaust, Israel studies, or English-language Jewish literature have opened up. Jewish Studies courses are taught on 40 Canadian campuses. The first Canadian program was launched at McGill in 1969, under the leadership of Professor Harry Bracken and Rabbi David Hartman of the Philosophy Department, and Professor Ruth Wisse of English. McGill has the only actual department of Jewish Studies in Canada. The University of Toronto has developed a major Jewish Studies program, and York University and Montreal's Concordia University operate a joint Centre for Canadian Jewish Studies. Many other campuses have programs or at least courses in Judaica – quite distinct from divinity-school courses in the Old Testament. This latter type of courses can have a Christian spin and are often taught by Christian theologians and scholars.

University-based Jewish Studies can also run into problems of bias and objectivity, albeit different from the biases of teaching Judaica in Christian seminaries. The problem is similar to that found in programs of Black or any Ethnic Studies, which have proliferated on North American campuses. They all run the risk of becoming hagiographic, of aiming to venerate group traditions rather than study them, as academics love to do, with a critical eye. They can become sites for communal cheerleading, for promoting group interests rather than the academy's goals of dispassionate teaching and research. Some Fredonians might want the professor of Fredonian Studies to be a Fredonian and of a certain type. If so, how critical could the Fredonian professor be about certain received wisdoms of Fredonian history, or philosophy, or communal politics, especially if the Fredonian community helped fund the program? (Don't panic. Fredonia is a fictitious country in a Marx Brothers movie.)

The first academic breaks with Jewish communal solidarity and a religious perspective took place in the nineteenth century. A scientific, non-theological Jewish Studies emerged in Germany as *Wissenschaft des Judentums*, or the Science of Judaism. This new field challenged the conventions of traditional Jewish learning. Texts were studied as literary or historical documents, not as the word of God. Indeed, the study of these texts became an exercise in scholarship, not in the affirmation of piety or religious commandments. Even non-Jews could pursue the scientific study of Judaism. Orthodox rabbis of the period frowned upon university-based Jewish Studies for that reason. In the modern period, rabbis of the major denominations have all made their peace, more or less, with the academic approach to Jewish Studies. Yeshiva University and the Jewish Theological Seminary, both in New York, the Hebrew Union College in Cincinnati, and the Reconstructionist College in Philadelphia are examples of how the major denominations have integrated the Western scholarly perspective into the education of young Jews and rabbis. Only the ultra-Orthodox continue to resist. It is becoming increasingly common to find rabbis with one or more graduate degree in Jewish Studies to go along with their ordination. There is no Canadian institution serving Modern Orthodoxy and the other denominations which ordain rabbis. Canadian Jews rely on Americans or on Canadians who go south for their training.

For Jewish Studies, issues of objectivity and detachment remain crucial, though the fault line is both religious and communal. After all, classical Jewish learning, as in the model of the yeshiva, made no pretence of detachment or objectivity. Critical thinking was not encouraged. These issues appear differently in rabbinical seminaries, compared to Jewish Studies programs in secular universities. In Modern Orthodox, Conservative, Reform, or Reconstructionist seminaries, there are obvious limits to the degree of critical inquiry that Judaic scholars can pursue. (These limits will differ for each denomination.) Rabbis or professors of Rabbinics who advocate doing away with *kashrut* or integrating the Virgin Mary into Judaic belief while teaching at such institutions will find the going very rough.

These limits cannot, in theory, apply to the mainstream academy, where most Jewish Studies teaching takes place. Here one can imagine the full gamut of "heretical" academics: anti-circumcision zealots, anti-Zionist professors, professors who scathingly criticize mainstream Jewish communal organizations and philanthropists. In some cases, they might be welcome as debunkers of conventional wisdoms and tweakers of authority. In others, they might become pariahs, like flat-earthers in a department of astronomy. Some professors of Jewish Studies do not like to see themselves as public Judaic role models for their students, and tend to distance themselves from the local Jewish community lest their "integrity" be compromised. Do Jewish Studies professors have to be observant, or marry another Jew, or support Israel, or value Jewish continuity, or even be Jewish? (My answer is "no" to all these questions – but it wouldn't hurt.) Some recoil from Jewish identity politics; others embrace it. These tensions between academic Jewish Studies and mainstream Jewish communities remain unresolved. There are thousands of students in American and Canadian universities, mostly Jewish, who take university-level courses in Jewish studies.[30] We know little about the impact of these courses on Jewish identity.

I began teaching a course on the Sociology of North American Jewry at McGill in 1977, the first of its kind in Canada. I estimate that about one-fifth of my students over the years have been non-Jews (many dating Jews), and I would guess that the grades of the non-Jews have been higher than those for the Jewish students. Why? Perhaps some of the Jews figured that since they already had some formal Jewish schooling, they would somehow coast through. Perhaps non-Jews have to be deeply interested to take such a course. Among my best students ever were two non-Jews, an exchange student from Munich and a Canadian of Pakistani origin. But every year I get several Jewish students for whom my course serves as a kind of last-chance exposure to some kind of Jewish experience and knowledge, having missed out in their earlier years. I have no idea how my course has affected this sort of Jewish student. Deep down, I would like to think that it did more than impart some information. Though I should not admit it, I hope it brought some of them back into the fold.

Jewish schools and universities are not the only arenas of Jewish education. Other agencies have embraced Jewish family education and adult education. Family education refers to experiential or learning activities that involve the entire family. Such programs are often based in synagogues, centred around holiday celebrations, and involve families learning together. Adult education has long been a feature of Jewish life. Among the Orthodox and ultra-Orthodox, it is part of a long tradition in which Jews try to find time for a *shiur*, or Talmud lesson, at a local yeshiva or *beis medrash*, a house of learning. Ultra-Orthodox Jewish males pursue advanced Talmudic studies at *kollels* either on a full-time or a part-time basis, even after they are married. All synagogues offer lectures, courses, or study groups on various topics, and a variety of alternative adult institutions do so as well. Toronto boasts a *kollel* for liberal Jewish learning, affiliated with the Reform movement; the Research Centre of Kabbalah, which sponsors courses on the Zohar, reincarnation, meditation, astrology, along with general principles of Kabbalah; and the Women's Institute of Advanced Torah Study, which offers classes especially for women, from an Orthodox point of view.

One of the more original innovations in adult Jewish education is the *Daf Yomi*, or Daily Page. It takes seven and a half years to read the entire Talmud, at one page a day. All over the world, groups of Jewish men (there may be some women) have undertaken to do just that, studying the very same page on a specific day. A Jew who is travelling therefore never has to miss a day. In Montreal, there are about ten such groups, meeting in the mornings at Orthodox synagogues either just before or after morning prayers. A typical group numbers between eight and twenty participants, and each session lasts about forty-five minutes. It is not only simple piety that makes the *Daf Yomi* popular. The organizer of the project in Montreal explained the attraction. He emphasized that many members in their youth had studied at yeshiva, only to leave it for decades as they grew up. For older or retired Jews, it is a way for some to recapture their youth.[31]

For those who cannot make it to a class, there are other options. "Dial-a-Daf" or "Torah phone" offers a complete *shiur* on the phone. There are other telephone options, most of which seem to be engineered by the Lubavitcher Hasidim. One number gives you "Torah on Line," for those who only have a few minutes to spare. The phone menu includes a weekly portion, a Maimonides message, a selection from the Book of Commandments, a selection from Tanya, Hasidic philosophy, festivals, and a *Moshiach* (Messiah) message. There is also a children's Torah line, which includes a Torah mystery minute, a Jewish thought, a *Moshiach* message, and a Jewish story. (The one I heard was the story of David hiding in a cave from an angry King Saul, where he encountered an ugly spider. David lamented that he had to fear for his life while God tolerated the existence of this apparently useless, ugly spider. Of course the spider eventually saved his life.)[32]

These activities should surprise no one. Traditionally, Jewish learning was the obligation and duty of adults. It is mainly among the Orthodox that this admonition has been heeded. In *The Vanishing American Jew*, Alan Dershowitz concludes that an energized new commitment to a liberal, accessible Jewish education for adults holds the key to a meaningful Jewish survival. He writes: "There must be classes, discussion groups, study groups, lectures, videotapes, computer programs, books, book clubs, newsletters, and other mechanisms of Jewish learning."[33] (I might add that I have my own form of *Daf Yomi*. I refer here to the near-daily messages I receive on the Internet from my

Jewish Studies network. Each daily communication consists of several queries and responses in all areas of Jewish Studies, from scholars all over the world. Topics range from the last words of Jesus to rabbinic views on smoking to cowboy songs in Yiddish. I suspect these modern-day responsa do for me what the *Daf Yomi* does for pious Jews.) The problem with the Dershowitz solution is that all these already exist, in synagogues and Jewish community centres, and those who partake are already among the committed, whatever their denomination. The challenge is how to lead those who are uninterested to the neglected wonders of Jewish learning. There are reports from Israel about a growing number of secular Jews involved in text-based study groups. Some claim a renaissance is underway. Contrary to conventional thinking, there will be Jewish continuity, or even renewal, but higher levels of Jewish study will likely be a consequence as much as a cause.

Jewish education is still not sexy. But it illustrates again how Jews are like all other groups, except very different. Most ethnic and religious groups in Canada make some efforts at socializing and teaching their children. But none come close to the quality and range of the Jewish educational system. The further irony is that as Jewish education increases its profile, its success is measured less by educational criteria and more by the ability to socialize Jewish children. And all things considered, that record is impressive.

9

JEWS, JUDAISM, AND THE PUBLIC SQUARE

The Political Behaviour of Canadian Jews

"The law of the country is binding."
 — Talmud (Nedarim 28a)

"American Jews in the 1930s and 1940s, it is said, believed in three worlds, or, in Yiddish, *drei velt: die velt,* this world, *yenne velt,* the world to come, and – *Roosevelt.*"
 — Anonymous

The selection of Senator Joe Lieberman as Al Gore's running mate in the 2000 U.S. presidential election brought Jewishness to the centre of the North American political debate as never before. Most Jews were elated, some were apprehensive. Lurking behind that nomination were the issues of Jews in politics and Jews and politics – the use of the political system to defend Jewish interests. This chapter delves into both. While the focus is Canadian, the dilemmas are generic. We explore sensitive topics like the Jewish vote, the role of Jewish elected officials, and the informal exercise of political power and influence, through lobbying and public relations, on various public-policy issues.

Herein lies yet another paradox. The more Jews participate in the mainstream of Canadian politics, the better able they are to defend their own specific interests. Sometimes, these interests seem to clash with Canada's national interest, or with the interests of other groups.

JEWS AND THE LEFT

Jews are liberal, or to be more technical, found mainly on the centre-left half of the political spectrum. Given their relative affluence, Jews should long ago have abandoned liberal politics. Yet, they continue to support politicians and policies dedicated to reform, to equality, and to social justice for the less fortunate. It is fascinating to trace out the influence on Jewish politics of this progressive commitment. More difficult is trying to *account* for this leftward tilt. Is there something about Jewish culture that propels people to the left, or is it simply a fear of anti-Semitism or some other strategic calculations based on the Jewish position in Canadian society?

This tie dates from the Old Left rooted in Europe to the New Left and countercultural movements of the 1960s – from Leon Trotsky to Abbie Hoffman. American evidence is far more extensive than Canadian. It consistently reveals that American Jews hold more liberal positions than non-Jews on all manner of policy issues, and are more likely to label themselves as liberals. They are far more likely to think well of the American Civil Liberties Union and poorly of the National Rifle Association than are American non-Jews. More important, they are the most loyal to the Democratic Party – well before Joe Lieberman – even after controlling for education and income.[1]

There have been fewer studies in Canada documenting the link between Jews and progressive politics. Electoral politics offers some evidence. J. B. Salsberg and Fred Rose were both elected in 1943 in largely Jewish ridings, the former to the Ontario Legislature and the latter to the federal Parliament from Montreal, as Communists.[2] Rose in fact was arrested in 1945, convicted of espionage, and sentenced to six years. Released in 1951, he lived out his days in Poland. Jews were active throughout the 1930s and 1940s, along with Ukrainians and Finns, in the Communist Party as organizers and workers.[3] The Jewish labour movement in the 1930s and 1940s supported various left-wing political candidates. Jews like David and Stephen Lewis, Dave Barrett, Cy Gonick, and Gerald Caplan were prominent leaders in the New Democratic Party. In general, Jewish votes in Canada have gone to the centre/left mainstream parties. The one relevant voting study shows Jews have been more likely than other Canadians to vote for the CCF/NDP or the Liberals, even taking into account factors like trade-union status, education, and economic status.[4]

Jews did not shift en masse to the Conservatives during the Mulroney years. One 1987 study of a non-random sample of rabbis, Jewish academics, and communal leaders aged twenty-five to forty from Montreal and Toronto found 41 per cent called themselves Liberal, 21 per cent Conservative, and 15 per cent NDP.[5] There is little research about recent voting preferences of Canadian Jews. But it seems that any flirtation with the Conservatives under Mulroney was not motivated by deliberate ideological shifts to the right. We do not know what role Jewish voters in Ontario, concentrated in Toronto, have played in the Mike Harris revolution, but it is likely small, given the Harris Conservative government's fundamental challenge to basic premises of the welfare state, and that Harris drew minimal support from Toronto itself. But individual wealthy Jews, according to one well-placed observer, have benefited from lower taxes and rising property values and changed their politics accordingly; some are prominent donors to the Ontario Progressive Conservatives.

Why this attachment to the political left by Jews?[6] One explanation is cultural. The historical experience of Jews as underdogs sets the foundation in some subliminal fashion. Embedded within religious Judaism are certain tenets linked to progressive politics: the emphasis on seeking justice in this world; the Prophetic yearning for peace and preference for decent behaviour over simple sacrifices; the respect imparted from the Talmud for the use of reason and the rule of law as a basis for settling disputes.[7] This logic explains part of the Jewish support for Franklin Roosevelt's New Deal, as a way to apply intelligence to solve a social problem. The idea of Jewish rationalism as typified by the Talmud can even be extended (all this is subconscious) to greater support for planning by governments. In addition, Jews are reminded every year at Passover that they were slaves in Egypt. Classic texts exhort Jews to act righteously. This nurtures a push to support liberal politics. In other words, something about being a Jew, about understanding the Jewish experience, leads to a sympathy with the underdog. In one of his films, Woody Allen's character recalls a scene from his youth in which his mother complained that their maid was stealing from them. His father, more understanding, made less of a fuss, claiming, "From who else should she steal if not from us?"

But there are also social structural forces that push Jews to the left. One argument is that Jews are liberal because their socio-demographic profile fits liberals generally. Because they are highly educated and live in large cosmopolitan cities, they tend naturally to liberal positions. Another argument claims Jews are on the left because their enemies, especially anti-Semites, are on the right. It was from the liberal left that opposition to the anti-Semitism of the right was most pronounced. The left supported civil rights for Jews dating back to the French Revolution. Jews also tend to support progressive positions for defensive reasons. Often, discrimination against any group leads to discrimination against Jews. Racism, nativism, and anti-Semitism are expressed by the same right-wing extremist groups. This explains why Jews and Jewish organizations have been strong supporters of equal rights for all minorities in Canada, and staunch defenders of Canadian multiculturalism. There is a dose of self-interest here.

Jews also support policies which reduce income differentials. This means support for the basic principles underlying the welfare state: progressive taxation, a significant package of welfare benefits, and, of course, medicare. Why? The cultural argument sees these as an extension of Judaic values. Jews are commanded in the Torah to help the less fortunate, the poor, the orphan, the widow, and the stranger, for they, too, were strangers in the land of Egypt. The social structural argument says too much inequality will lead to social instability, which has often been harmful to Jews. And when inequalities are coupled with ethnic grievances, Jews get it in the neck. So when Jews support elements of the welfare state, including progressive taxation or new welfare programs, they are supporting higher taxes on themselves to pay for benefits which would flow largely to non-Jews. A kind of insurance policy.

Despite the prominent roles of individual Jews in the Progressive Conservative Party and the NDP, the major consequence of these views has been support for the Liberal Party. As one analyst has concluded, "Jews are much more likely than Protestants to vote Liberal; Jews are much more likely than Catholics to vote Liberal in Quebec, but not in English Canada, and Jews in general are overwhelmingly Liberal, particularly in Quebec."[8] The historic Jewish support for the Liberal Party is not hard to explain. It begins with the fact that the highest periods of mass Jewish migration took place under Liberal governments, first under Wilfrid Laurier, and later under Louis St. Laurent and Lester Pearson. (The restrictive policies of Mackenzie King's Liberals are either unknown, forgotten, or forgiven.) In the post-war period, Jews – and many other immigrants – were moving from a European experience marked by extremism of the left and right: communism and fascism and their attendant brutalities. They wanted no part of that in Canada. Seeking the relative safety of the ideological centre, immigrants, including Jews, found their home in the Liberal Party. They felt – incorrectly – that possible dangers of European-style extremism were associated with the CCF/NDP and Conservative parties. This was certainly my parents' view; it was inconceivable for them to vote for any party other than the Liberals. But by the time they realized that the European analogies did not hold, Canadian Jews had grown comfortable with the Liberal centrist welfare-state policies.

JEWISH POLITICS

Many non-Jews feel that Jews wield enormous political influence, far greater than their numbers in the electorate would warrant. Some feel that Jewish lobbies in particular are too powerful (see Chapter 11, on anti-Semitism). Jewish communal leaders and elected officials try to avoid the charge of dual loyalty when they defend Jewish interests. When I was a child I loved to ask my father the following two questions. If there was a war between Canada and Israel, who would win? (I now know the answer to that one.) And which country would we support? (That remains a tough question.)

Jews have always played significant roles in Canadian political and civic life. Even when there were only handfuls of Jews in Canada, they were contesting and winning legislative office from Quebec through to the West Coast. The saga of the Hart family is well known, though it still leaves a bittersweet taste in Jewish mouths. In 1807 Ezekiel Hart won election to the Assembly in Lower Canada for Trois-Rivières, collecting 59 of 116 votes cast in a field of three candidates. He was denied his seat because he would not take the oath "as a Christian." He was elected again in 1809, and again was denied a seat, simply because he was a Jew. He did not run a third time.

The good news is that the non-Jewish electors of his riding were prepared to vote at least twice for a Jew. (This pattern continues. Jewish politicians like Liberal Herb Gray from Ontario, and NDP Premier Dave Barrett from British Columbia enjoyed success in ridings with very few Jews.) The bad news is that the controversy about the oath brought forth hoary canards of immorality and dual loyalty against Hart, and Jews. An anonymous writer to *Le Canadien* asked, "By what right can a Jew who is only worried about himself and his sect expect to look after the interests of the whole nation?"[9] The fear of dual loyalty eventually became dormant, not visibly affecting the political or governmental careers of Canadian Jews.

Dormant, but not dead. Canadian Jews have never had to wrestle with the stark dilemma of a Jonathan Pollard affair, in which an American Jew working at the Pentagon was convicted of spying for Israel in 1985 and sentenced to life imprisonment. American Jews who felt the sentence was excessive – and from a comparative perspective it was – were deeply conflicted. But short of such drama, there have been cases in which Canadian Jews were caught in similar dilemmas. They have all dealt with Canadian policy towards Israel and the Middle East. Canada has in general been a solid supporter of Israel. But the position of the Canadian government on specific issues of Middle East policy has routinely differed from that of Israel and the major Jewish organizations. The early reluctance of the Canadian government in the 1970s to enforce action to oppose the Arab economic boycott of Israel and of Canadians doing business with Israel directly and indirectly is a case in point.[10]

The promise by Joe Clark's short-lived Conservative government to move the Israeli embassy from Tel Aviv to Jerusalem in 1979 was a major challenge. The idea raised opposition from many pro-Arab circles, and also led to conjecture that somehow Clark's policy shift was a response to concerted pressure by Canadian Jews and their organizations, which was not the case. In 1988, as minister of external affairs, Joe Clark was involved in a second episode. He criticized Israeli human-rights violations during the intifada at a gathering of the Canada–Israel Committee, and was greeted by a hostile reaction from his Jewish Canadian audience. That event led some commentators to raise the issue of dual loyalty and a powerful Jewish lobby. Ottawa's *Citizen* published an editorial on March 12, 1988, entitled "The Nerve of Him: Clark Speaks the Truth." An editorial in the *Toronto Star* on the same day put the matter bluntly when referring to Clark's message: "It was also a necessary reminder to members of the Jewish community of Canada that they are citizens of Canada, not Israel." The response from Charles Zaionz and Rose Wolfe of the Ontario Region of the Canadian Jewish Congress, in a letter to the *Star* of March 15, was unusually tough: "The *Star* by questioning the loyalty of Jewish Canadians to Canada, has crossed the line from unrelenting criticism of Israeli government policy into anti-Semitism."

The issue was revived again in the 1990s in the case of Norman Spector. When Spector was appointed ambassador to Israel in 1992 by Brian Mulroney's government, the idea of a Jewish ambassador to Israel seemed troubling to some Canadians. Spector was the first Jewish diplomat, let alone ambassador, who was posted to Israel.[11] Some objected to the appointment because Spector had not been a career diplomat and the appointment to a sensitive post had the appearance of a classic patronage appointment. But Spector's Jewishness was also a factor. Following his appointment, an Arab group condemned the appointment of, in Spector's words, "a Zionist, who was close to the Bronfmans." Spector recalls that at his committee hearing examining the appointment, "Christine Stewart looked at my CV and asked whether in light of the fact that I spoke Hebrew, I would undertake to learn Arabic. I expected she or someone would note that I was the first ambassador sent to Israel who could speak the language of the country and was shocked at the tone of her question. I committed on the spot to learn Arabic, which I did, thus becoming the first ambassador to speak either of the country's official languages."[12]

Veteran foreign affairs analyst and insider Peyton Lyon addressed these issues in an unpublished letter to the *Globe and Mail*, a copy of which he sent to me. His letter was a response to a June 23, 1998, article I wrote dealing with Hugh Segal's race for the Progressive Conservative leadership, Jewishness, and the issue of dual loyalty.[13] My article also referred positively to Spector's tenure. Lyon disagreed with my assessment of Spector. In an accompanying letter he claimed that his views reflected "a large majority view among our professional foreign service officers." Referring to these officers, he claimed that they believed that Canadian interests and policies differed widely from those of Israel. And they resented "the lobbying that has distorted what they believe best for Canada, the States, and even Israel."

According to Lyon, the first person suggested by Ottawa as ambassador to the new state of Israel was David Croll. He claims the Israelis discouraged the appointment. "They feared that a Jewish-Canadian ambassador would be excessively concerned to demonstrate his loyalty to doubting Canadian countrymen." Regarding Spector's appointment, Lyon claims that there "never had been a Canadian policy to flatter any ethnic group by sending one of their number to the land of their heritage." In his view it was not surprising that Jews with only 1 per cent of the population had not yet produced an ambassador to Israel. With regards to Spector's record, Lyon disagrees with my assessment that "by all accounts Spector's tenure was a model of fairness and defence of the Canadian interest" and claims it "evoked laughter and scorn at the weekly meeting of ex-ambassadors that I usually attend." I stand by my assessment, and can indeed recall instances when prominent members of the Canadian Jewish community objected to some of Spector's actions, feeling they tilted towards the Palestinian or Arab side. In Lyon's view, Spector's achievement "was to perpetuate doubts about Canadians who seem more responsive to the interests of their ancestral homelands than to those of Canada."[14] In other words, dual loyalty.

Another major conflict of interest for Canadian Jews took place in the fall of 1997. It concerned the use of false Canadian passports by Mossad agents in a botched assassination attempt in Jordan. The Canadian government angrily recalled David Berger, then ambassador (another Jew) to Israel. Norman Spector argued publicly that the use of

Canadian passports by Israeli security was not news to CSIS, though it may have been to Foreign Affairs Minister Lloyd Axworthy, and that co-operation between Israeli and Canadian intelligence "goes well beyond information sharing to include some operations worthy of a James Bond thriller." As the story unfolded, a number of Jewish Canadians reported being approached by Israeli officials seeking to "borrow" their passports. At any rate, Israel issued a formal apology to Canada about the affair, and undertook measures to see it would not be repeated.[15]

How should a Canadian Jew respond to a seemingly serious conflict between Canadian government policy and the welfare of Israel? The Pollard case in the States involved the sale of information to Israel concerning the military assets of several hostile Arab countries, which Pollard felt was crucial to Israel's strategic needs. Pollard felt that sharing the information would not harm the United States (he was wrong, since it risked compromising the network of American electronic espionage as well as blowing the cover of American agents) and that the United States should have shared it with Israel in any case. I can understand that logic, even though it defends a clearly treasonous act. Before the screams begin, consider the following hypothetical case.

Imagine the year is 1940 or early 1941. An American of British origin working for American intelligence discovers some crucial information bearing on major plans for German air strikes into Britain. The United States is officially neutral at the time and the information is not given to the British. How would we judge, legally and morally, the intelligence officer if he or she decided to violate American law, endanger American intelligence operations, and, à la Pollard, pass on this vital information to the British?

Jews have not been the only ones charged with dual loyalty or special pleading. We all know of the travails of the Japanese in North America during the Second World War. But Catholics were also not immune. People now forget how novel – and narrow – John Kennedy's election victory was in 1960. There has still been only one Catholic president. And even in the early 1990s, New York Governor Mario Cuomo, a serious, believing Catholic, was treated with suspicion by pro-choice activists. In Canada anti-Catholicism has been linked to anti-French prejudice, but given the proliferation of Catholic prime ministers that issue is moot. Or is it? In recent decades in Ontario there have been fewer Catholic than Jewish leaders of Ontario political parties or mayors of Toronto. Ironically, it is Moslems and Arabs in Canada who are most likely to have their loyalties questioned by Canadians these days. Canada's participation in the Gulf War against Iraq was tough for many Canadian Arabs and Moslems. While they were exposed to prejudice and false allegations of terrorism, many were deeply conflicted by Canada's role in that war. These issues are less acute in Canada than in the United States. Canada's weight in international affairs, and certainly in the Middle East, is far less, and so the stakes are not as high. But it is premature to say that Canadian Jews whose public actions defend Jewish interests will always escape the dual loyalty accusation. They will not.

THE EVOLUTION OF JEWISH POLITICAL INVOLVEMENT

Canadian Jews have moved steadily into the mainstream of Canadian political life and power. Throughout most of the period of Canadian Jewish settlement before the mass migration around 1900, the politics of Canadian Jews reflected their positions as merchants and professionals. In a sense, all politics in the pre-democratic period was elite politics, and Jews were no exception. By no means were all Jews well-off, and many worked as peddlers or craftsmen.[16] But few worked as unskilled labourers, and fewer still were indigent. Nevertheless, their position as a religious minority tended to make Jewish elected representatives predisposed to tolerance and sensitive to discrimination generally.

In the second half of the nineteenth century, the Eastern Europeans brought with them a tradition of left-wing politics. Among the immigrant Jews there were socialists, anarchists, leftists of various persuasions as well as supporters of liberal and centrist parties. In the United States, the tie with the left is better known. German Jews in the United States supported Lincoln and the Republicans, the liberal and anti-slavery party. But by the 1930s, American Jews had begun their unbroken attachment to the Democratic Party and liberal politics. Jewish liberal support surpasses that of any white ethnic or religious group in the United States. And despite their economic mobility, Jews remain loyal. As neo-conservative Irving Kristol tells it, "Jews earn like Episcopalians and vote like Puerto Ricans." Moreover, this Jewish electoral liberalism continues to defy predictions and the hope of some Jewish neo-conservatives that Jews will find their natural home on the right. In any event, Jews soon held high executive office. Judah Benjamin was the secretary of state in the Confederacy. In 1906, Theodore Roosevelt appointed Oscar Straus as secretary of commerce and labour, the first Jew in the American cabinet. "I want to show Russia and some other countries what we think of the Jews in this country," Roosevelt said to Straus when explaining his choice.[17]

In Canada, by the beginning of the First World War, several Jews had been elected as aldermen from Quebec to British Columbia. S. Hart Green was elected to sit in the Manitoba Legislature, and Peter Bercovitch was elected to the National Assembly in Quebec. By the 1930s, there were three Jewish MPs: Sam Jacobs from Montreal, A. A. Heaps from Winnipeg, and Sam Factor from Toronto. David Croll won election to the Ontario Legislature in 1934, and as minister of labour and welfare was Canada's first Jewish cabinet minister. Later on, after entering federal politics and being denied a federal cabinet position, he became Canada's first Jewish senator. In the post-war period, an increasing number of Jews have held elective office, in all parties, even though they have been clustered in the centre-left part of the political spectrum.

Herb Gray became Canada's first Jewish federal cabinet minister in 1969 – six decades after Straus was appointed in the United States – in the Liberal government of Prime Minister Trudeau. The NDP has had strong representation of Jews among its leaders. Dave Barrett of British Columbia served as the first Jewish provincial premier in 1972. David Lewis was the leader of the national NDP. His son Stephen was NDP leader in Ontario and later ambassador to the United Nations. Larry Grossman was leader of the Ontario Progressive Conservatives. Three mayors of Toronto – Nathan Phillips, Phil Givens, and Mel Lastman – have been Jews. For federal Conservatives, Gerry Weiner served as cabinet minister in areas of immigration and multiculturalism in the government of Brian Mulroney. Hugh Segal, a red Tory, has long been an insider among mainstream Conservatives, and contested the party leadership in 1998. Had Segal been successful, he would have been the first Jewish leader of one of Canada's two governing parties. What is fascinating is that, in the news reports and commentary about that leadership race, the fact that he was Jewish was not mentioned. The silence was rather deafening, and contrasts with the extensive public discussion of Senator Joe Lieberman's Orthodox Jewishness in the American media. Segal's first ballot showing of less than 20 per cent was disappointing, and I would not rule out either deliberate or unconscious anti-Semitism among some right-wing Conservatives as one possible factor. Conservatives wanting to "unite the right" may have assumed that Segal would be a tougher sell to some Reformers.

It is only with federal parties to the right of the Conservatives, specifically Social Credit and later Reform and the Canadian Alliance, that Jewish support and candidates are minimal. Minimal, but not non-existent. Journalist David Frum has been a prominent influence in right-wing Canadian (and American) politics, and young Ezra Levant, from Edmonton, was a special assistant to Reform leader Preston Manning. But there is not much of a Jewish constituency for their views, in part because of lingering suspicions of anti-Semitism, similar to those that dog American Republicans in their pursuit of Jewish voters. The Reform Party and its successor, the Alliance, have not shown the same degree of extreme populism or militant Christianity reflected by people like Pat Buchanan or Pat Robertson. But its image remains problematic for many Jews. In the battle for the Alliance leadership between Preston Manning and Stockwell Day, rumours about possible anti-Semitism in Day's background swirled around the candidate.[18] Whereas Manning's relations with Jews in Alberta were positive, Day, whose own political future is uncertain, is still an unknown quantity.

In trying to break through in Ontario, the Canadian Alliance will have to find a way to appeal to Jews and other minorities. The challenge will come as they try to broaden their demographic base of support. Talk about strange bedfellows. The Jewish community, in fact, is not united in opposition to Day and the Alliance. During his leadership race against Preston Manning, Day and certain segments of the ultra-Orthodox community found common ground. Though it was not reported in the media, some among the ultra-Orthodox were prepared to mobilize in support of Day, in appreciation of his support for government funding of Jewish day schools. (The fact that the federal government does not have jurisdiction over provincial educational policy did not derail the bargain.) But that kind of partisan politicking would have jeopardized the schools' tax-exempt status. The mainstream organizations of the Ontario Jewish community were alarmed, and furious. They prevailed on the ultra-Orthodox Alliance supporters to keep their support informal – personal, not organizational – and they complied. Those ultra-Orthodox Ontario Jews who were prepared to support Day were not concerned about his conservative social agenda, or whether somehow Christianity would be injected into the public schools. Their priority was, first and foremost, funding for Jewish schools.

Apart from their role in party politics, Canadian Jews have also served as senior public servants. Chief Justice Bora Laskin has been the only Jewish member of the Supreme Court to date, compared to seven in the United States.[19] There is no tradition of a "Jewish" seat on the court as in the U.S. In part, this reflects the prior allocations to three Quebec judges, usually francophones of Catholic background. During the run-up to the appointment of Ian Binnie in 1997, there was speculation in Jewish circles that Ontario Judge Rosalie Abella might be selected. She was not. There is no evidence that latent anti-Semitism played a role.

Jews have moved rapidly through the ranks of the federal public service, as well as attaining influence as political advisors. Bernard and Sylvia Ostry have held senior cultural and economic positions respectively. Louis Rasminsky was governor of the Bank of Canada from 1961 to 1972. Many other Jews have been prominent as provincial civil servants. Three principal secretaries to Prime Minister Mulroney were Jews: Stanley Hartt, Norman Spector, Hugh Segal. And so have been several of the closest advisors to Prime Minister Jean Chrétien: Eddie Goldenberg, Chaviva Hosek, and David Zussman. Another Jew, Mel Cappe, was named in late 1998 as the new clerk of the Privy Council.

This is a far cry from the 1930s, when unsympathetic public servants such as F. C. Blair could play a major role in preventing the immigration of German Jewish refugees. The increasing role of Jewish elected politicians and public servants reflects the increasing sophistication and self-confidence of the Canadian Jewish community. In the words of Irving Abella, former president of the Canadian Jewish Congress, "We have clout that we never had before."[20]

What is unclear is whether the Jewishness of these politicians and public servants played any role in shaping their political thinking or their careers. My guess is that in most cases it has. Hugh Segal believes his origins as the son of a working-class Jewish immigrant in Montreal helped to develop his outlook as a red Tory. Former cabinet minister Gerry Weiner cites his Jewish background as helping him identify with all minority groups and take a hard line against discrimination. Liberal MP Irwin Cotler's commitment to human rights and social justice has been in part nourished by his understanding of the Jewish experience. Here, Jewishness becomes a springboard for concern for the general good, or the welfare of others.

JEWISH POLITICAL INFLUENCE

Jews try to use politics to defend their (liberal) values and Jewish interests. This is what any ethnic polity does.[21] The mobilization of ethnic votes, whether in elections or even nomination meetings, is emerging as an important new element in Canadian politics.[22] But political influence is channelled in many other ways. Jews in Canada are influential in political parties and causes, and they are prominent as donors and fundraisers (though less than in the United States), but they rarely act as part of any co-ordinated campaign led by formal communal organizations. Other avenues of political influence are the informal networks linking Jewish politicians and Jewish communal leaders. The best example is former CJC president Irwin Cotler, who became an MP from Quebec in 1999.

Jewish political clout is greater in the United States than in Canada. It is ironic that the separation of church and state has made it more important for American Jews to mobilize to defend their interests than it is for Jews in Canada, where religions have legal status and ethnic diversity is enshrined in the Constitution. Moreover, the American political system, with its distinction between the legislative and executive branch, gives American Jews more points of leverage to influence policy. There is little in Canada – so far – to warrant a book ominously titled *Jewish Power*, written by American journalist J. J. Goldberg.[23] That volume chronicles the links between Jews, the organized Jewish community, and the American political system, and at times reads like a political whodunit. American Jews are major contributors to political campaigns. The magazine *Mother Jones* listed the top four hundred political donors for 1998, and Jews are very well represented.[24]

Compared to American Jews, Canadian Jews are more likely to be foreign-born and thus less acculturated into politics. They are also a smaller proportion of the population. Moreover, the international stakes are just not as great in Canada on any issue on the Jewish political agenda, from the Middle East to repayment of Nazi-era financial claims. So Jewish political mobilization and participation in Canada is less important, and less effective. One 1993 study reported that just over 7 per cent of members of the U.S. Congress were Jewish, compared to fewer than 2 per cent of Federal MPs.[25] As of 2000, there were eleven Jewish members of the U.S. Senate. The Jewish vote in the United States has historically been key in certain northeastern districts, as well as some in Florida and California. This, plus the fact that Jews are more likely to vote and donate to both parties, gives American Jews seemingly greater influence than numbers alone warrant. There are no studies of the electoral consequences of the Canadian Jewish vote. But there are ridings in Montreal and Toronto which are heavily Jewish, and which have traditionally elected Jewish representatives or those sympathetic to the political concerns of the community. None of this is a secret, at least not to Jews.

Jews and other minority groups are acting more and more like interest groups. Canadian Jews are certainly concerned with Canadian policy in the Middle East, and through the Canada–Israel Committee promote Israel's interests in a non-partisan way.[26] Traditionally, policymakers in External Affairs have not welcomed input from any ethnic group on a homeland issue, as the correspondence from Peyton Lyon suggests.[27] Ethnic groups are seen as promoting a special interest which may clash with so-called national interests. Ottawa mandarins like to think that the national interest is best determined through their expertise, and in a rational, detached manner. Involving interested parties would, in this view, distort the process. But, of course, a democratic perspective on the question differs dramatically. It suggests that elites and experts should heed the voice of citizens, particularly those who are most concerned with an issue. Minorities mobilizing to defend their interest politically are not a distortion of the democratic process. They *are* the democratic process.

LA SURVIVANCE: JEWS IN QUEBEC

The Jews of Quebec are the one Jewish group in North America whose future is clouded by the danger of basic political instability. Indeed, since the rise of the Parti Québécois to power in 1976, and even before, Quebec Jewry has been in "continual caucus." In Quebec, it is an open secret that Jews, the organized Jewish community, and community leaders opposed Quebec independence, and thereby the Parti Québécois, from the very start of the 1970s' round of constitutional debates.[28] Jews cast almost all their votes for the Liberal Party of Quebec.

The threat of Quebec sovereignty and the reality of French nationalism has had a draining effect on Montreal Jewish life. The demographics do not look good, as many of the younger generation have left to points west or to the United States. The High Holidays and Passover are particularly poignant times. The streets of Montreal's Jewish neighbourhoods are filled with Ontario licence plates, as children visit parents and grandparents. Yet at the same time, Montreal retains an amazingly rich Jewish communal and cultural life. In my view – and I hope I am not being a Montreal chauvinist here – on a relative basis, it is richer than in Toronto. I refer here to more than the difference in the per capita donations to the Federation annual appeals. The Montreal community with all its challenges has also just invested millions in an expanded new community campus for the Federation as well as renovations to the Jewish Community Centre. By 2000, informal estimates had the Toronto Jewish community at almost double the size of that in Montreal. Yet you could not tell this by comparing the Toronto and Montreal Jewish Directories. The Montreal Directory, at 128 pages to Toronto's 120 pages, more than holds its own. This high quality of Jewish life in Montreal remains all the more remarkable given the uncertainty that dates back to the 1960s.

The leaders of Quebec's Jewish community, notably the Canadian Jewish Congress and Fédération CJA, face difficult choices when defending Jewish interests. Members of the Montreal Jewish communal leadership often differ with what they call "deep Côte St.-Luc," the heavily Jewish and middle-class suburb in Montreal.[29] The latter favour a more aggressive, populist opposition to the Parti Québécois government, and in particular its restrictions in matters of language. They consider the Jewish establishment too timid, the Jewish equivalent of the meek "lamb lobby" of anglophones. (Jewish leaders conversely see these populists as unrealistic or unsophisticated.) Some Jews supported the Equality Party, some the militant radio personality Howard Galganov. Others have played leading roles in the "softer" Alliance Québec. Jews are arrayed right across the English/federalist political spectrum in Quebec. In contrast to the hard-liners, there are other Jewish intellectuals who continue to promote dialogue with French Quebec, including its nationalist elements.[30] In recent years Jews and other allophones have begun to play a more central role in English-speaking Quebec, crowding the old dominant Anglo-Saxon and Celtic elites. Many of the major anglophone cultural institutions, like McGill and Concordia universities and the *Gazette*, have had Jewish leadership.

In Chapter 11 we explore the issue of anti-Semitism in Quebec. There is no doubt that Quebec nationalists are wary about the charges of anti-Semitism that are levelled, with his inimitable wit, by Mordecai Richler. They recoil at the writings of Esther Delisle, who has exposed the anti-Semitic and fascist leanings of Lionel Groulx, *Le Devoir*, and the Quebec intelligentsia generally from the 1930s to the 1960s.[31] But despite the tensions, the general political climate in Quebec is not directly hostile to Jews. In the 1960s among politically aware university students, it was common to find sympathy among Jews to the French struggle for *la survivance*. Parallels were drawn, and to some extent are still drawn, between the struggle for Hebrew in Israel and for French in Quebec. Most Jews, even as they remain strong federalists, understand the desire of a minority to resist assimilation. Even the Parti Québécois government has kept open contacts with Jews, particularly with francophone Jews.

In September of 1998 – perhaps in anticipation of a fall election – the Parti Québécois government announced an $820,000 grant to establish a French-language Chabad-Lubavitch Centre in Côte St.-Luc.[32] In the late 1990s the Société St.-Jean-Baptiste began to take out newspaper ads promoting rapprochement. The Parti Québécois would welcome political participation by Jews, and indeed electoral candidates – in much the same way that the Reform party would. For some Péquistes it would be genuine, for others a clever tactic. But it is also impossible to imagine a Jewish leader of any major Quebec political party – like a Stephen Lewis or Larry Grossman in Ontario, or a Dave Barrett in British Columbia. At least not soon. Despite this political marginality, Jewish institutions, notably schools, have not suffered unduly in Quebec.

Neither Jews nor Quebec politicians have any illusions about the convictions of Jews on constitutional issues. In a 1996 study, about 45 per cent of Montreal Jews preferred the federalist status quo, about 38 per cent a revised federalism with more provincial power, with the rest sprinkled among other options including sovereignty-association, and complete independence.[33] It is thus not difficult to estimate how Jews vote in provincial elections and how they voted in the 1995 referendum. But even within this monolith there are internal divisions. The Sephardi community, notably some leaders of the Communauté Sépharade du Québec, are less strident in their federalism. Sephardim are much less likely, at under 32 per cent, to prefer the constitutional status quo. Almost 6 per cent, three times the general communal proportion, are inclined to support either sovereignty-association or independence for Quebec. It is very unlikely, therefore, though certainly possible, that an estimated 10 per cent of Sephardi Jews voted PQ in the 1998 provincial election, as claimed in a French-language CBC TV report.[34] The point here is still that the overwhelming majority of francophone/Sephardi Jews oppose the PQ and sovereignty. It is widely known that Parti Québécois officials have long hoped to attract francophone Jews to their camp, as they have tried with other French-speaking immigrant groups. So far, the success of this version of "divide and conquer" has been minimal.

THE JEWISH POLITICAL AGENDA

What do Canadian Jews want out of Canadian politics? They want stability, prosperity, and decency. The political agenda of Canadian Jews reflects these concerns through support for specific policies. First, is support for a united Canada. While Jewish communities nationally share this commitment, there has not yet emerged a concerted and effective national Canadian strategy for mobilizing Jews and other citizens, and lobbying federal and provincial governments, on the federalist cause. Many Jews in Ontario and in the West are ex-Montrealers and share a visceral sympathy with family and friends in Montreal. Many desire Canadian unity while appreciating the efforts in Quebec to preserve a French identity. But at the same time there are Canadian Jews, few in number, who share the "let them go" attitude regarding Quebec. What remains unclear is what steps, if any, Jews outside Quebec would take to help Quebec Jews in the event of a rapid deterioration of the social climate there, perhaps after a "Yes" vote in yet another plebiscite. It would certainly put the sense of communal solidarity to the test. Most Jews prefer not to contemplate the possibility.

A second plank in the Jewish political agenda is support for immigration in general and Jewish immigration in particular. It is hard to find many Jews who would rally around a political party or movement which was, or was perceived to be, anti-immigrant. Jews seem genetically programmed to welcome all immigrants and especially refugees. The memories of the Holocaust, and of Canadian borders closed to desperate European Jews, are too fresh. Many Jews are, moreover, either immigrants or children of immigrants. This does not mean Jewish organizations advocate an open-door policy, but JIAS and the Jewish community have been supportive of generous policies towards *bona fide* refugees and immigrants. And Jewish immigrants in particular are welcome, despite the costs they impose on local Jewish communities.

The defence of Israel's right to live in peace and security is a third item. This does not mean that Canadian Jewish organizations, to say nothing of all Jews, inevitably support every policy of the Israel government. They do not. But the bedrock principles are pretty near inviolate. Should Israel be in unambiguous danger, almost all Canadian Jewry will defend her ferociously. Jewish organizations close ranks when the Canadian government levels serious criticism at Israel. Criticism from the outside continues to make Jews defensive. But over the years, and within the "family," some Canadian Jews have accepted the legitimacy of dissent from specific Israeli policies, even if this may seem to endorse Canadian government policy shifts. A 1987 Canada-wide survey of Jewish communal leaders, professors, and rabbis aged between twenty-five and forty found fully 56 per cent felt they had the right to criticize Israeli policies and actions publicly.[35] In fact, Jewish communal and intellectual elites, in Canada and the United States, have generally been more willing to dissent from Israeli policies than the Jewish rank and file.

On the whole, Canadian Jews have been less likely to criticize Israeli policy in public than have American Jews, where petitions, counterpetitions, and op-eds in the *New York Times* are common.[36] Like many Jews, I wrestle with the limits or obligations of my visceral solidarity with Israel. I would never put my name to an ad directed uniquely at Israel's shortcomings in any mainstream newspaper. It is only with three or four of my non-Jewish friends that I am comfortable enough to express completely the depth of my passion for Israel. On rare occasions, I will tailor my views to fit my audience. If there is some dishonesty here – and there is – so be it. I at times make a point of defending Israel or shading any criticism as best I can in certain social settings – like sitting around a friendly table at the McGill Faculty Club – where Middle East politics comes up. This will depend on the tenor of the particular conversation and the roster of participants. At other times I will voice serious criticism. I play a tactical version of Marshall Sklare's "ambassadorial role," but this time defending Israel rather than Diaspora Jews. Though I am no Likud supporter – far from it – I can and have made their case at times.

Where dissent has been expressed in Canada, it has usually been in the pages of the *Canadian Jewish News*; that is, within the tribe. Moreover, ads that have appeared have tended to be evenhanded in tone and criticism, combining a critique of Israeli policy with one of Palestinian or Arab actions. A case in point is a full-page ad sponsored by Canadian Friends of Peace Now, which appeared in the *Canadian Jewish News* of October 1, 1997. The ad began with the following non-threatening quote by Israeli author Amos Oz: "There is a simple truth. Israel will not choose the path of peace if their blood continues to be shed. Palestinians will not choose the path of peace if their land continues to be occupied." This milder, less abrasive critique is so quintessentially Canadian.

Another item on the Jewish policy agenda is opposition to racism, xenophobia, and anti-Semitism, and a general support for human rights and the principles of multiculturalism. In Canada as elsewhere in the West, this encompasses two sorts of problems. The first is the response to mercifully rare overt anti-Semitism. But when it surfaces, as in actions of neo-Nazi groups, acts of vandalism, public expressions of contempt, or hate messages on the Internet, the Jewish position is generally clear. Canadian Jewish organizations support laws against hate literature and hate speech, laws promoting employment equity, and anti-discrimination legislation.

The second involves the many grey areas of public policy. They may or may not denote anti-Semitism, and may lead to action by the public authorities. There are many cases, for example, where "reasonable accommodation" to Jewish religious concerns or sensibilities – in jobs, schools, or elsewhere – must be determined. The discourse of anti-Semitism is no longer really applicable to many of these kinds of issues, even though they harm Jewish interests, and certainly offend Jewish sensibilities. Recently, Le Sanctuaire, a posh high-rise condo in Montreal, sought a permanent court injunction from the Quebec Superior Court against those residents who might build a sukkah, a makeshift wood hut covered with branches, used by Jews during the holiday of Sukkoth, on their balconies. The issue of religious freedom was at stake, at least on the part of the religious condo owners. To adjudicate the case, the court heard conflicting expert testimony from two rabbis. Eventually, the court sided with Le Sanctuaire, citing the testimony of their expert witness, Rabbi Barry Levy. In his view, residents could use sukkahs at local synagogues. It was not religiously crucial for Jewish residents at the condo complex to have their own sukkah on their balconies. So no sukkahs at Le Sanctuaire.[37]

We can imagine other examples. Schools, other government services, and businesses must accommodate the religious requirements of Jewish workers or employees. How far, say, should the Canadian Armed Forces go to accommodate religious requirements of an Orthodox Jewish recruit? Where do you draw the line between legitimate debate over aspects of the Holocaust and Holocaust denial and hate speech? What of possible challenges to kosher ritual slaughter on the grounds that it is perceived by some animal rights advocates as inhumane? Suppose activists decide, as an extension of the opposition to female genital operations, that male circumcision is a form of criminal assault. Indeed, this is precisely the point that has been made recently by Professor Margaret Somerville, of the McGill University Centre for Medicine, Ethics, and Law. Dr. Somerville believes that in almost all cases, male circumcision is therapeutically unnecessary and therefore criminal assault. She recognizes that circumcisions done for religious reasons might deserve a different approach. Rather than prosecute Jews, it may be possible to engage in dialogue with rabbis to lead them to modify their views, in the light of new medical evidence. Presumably, laws would be drafted, and then Jews could be persuaded through dialogue to abandon the practice. Though this is all well-meaning, it would bring us to a new form of medieval disputation in which Jews had to defend their faith against non-Jews.

While I am not a physician, I have reviewed the relevant studies and am not overwhelmed by the harm caused by *milah*, or circumcision. True, there may be no clear medical benefits, but there are no clear harms. The associated risks of removing or retaining the foreskin seem to break even. Recent studies have found a correlation – though not a causal connection – between male circumcision and low rates of HIV.[38] There is not a shred of evidence that Jewish boys or men have historically suffered higher rates of disease or death or any adverse long-term outcomes associated with the procedure. The major problem for opponents seems to be pain and possible harmful aftereffects for the infant. Painkilling ointments can alleviate the discomfort. There should be no religious objection to such a modification. As for post-circumcision traumas, there is no evidence that Jewish boys become undernourished, or develop a weaker bond with the mother. Quite the opposite, to judge by the classic routine of Mike Nichols and Elaine May. In any case, it would be a political nightmare for Jews if this budding movement grew to the point where legislation criminalizing circumcision were anticipated. Some Jews do indeed refuse to circumcise their children, and they have that legal right; prohibiting all Jews from doing so would be quite something else. The level of civil disobedience would be staggering.[39]

Opposition to anti-Semitism blends in with support for multiculturalism, which legitimates the Jewish concern with cultural survival. The ideology of multiculturalism also blends with Jewish liberalism. They both reach out to underdogs and victims; Jews love it. Jews, like other minorities, see in the public rhetoric around multiculturalism symbolic recognition of their valued place in Canada. Indeed, as I have been arguing throughout this book, Jews are the multicultural group *par excellence*. Jews do what they can to preserve multiculturalism, in fact and as a symbol.

A final item on the Canadian Jewish political agenda is support for the welfare state. While no one will publicly defend budgetary deficits these days, Jews more than most see value in an activist government. Of course, part of this support reflects Jews' predominant belief that it is right to help the unfortunate. Case closed. But there is another reason, again likely subconscious, for the support of the public sector. Jews are overrepresented in the health, social service, and educational professions, all of which rely in one way or another on government spending. Thus there is also clear self-interest, intentional or unintentional, in Jewish support for a strong public sector. While state services may flow to the poor or general population, who are less likely to be Jews, the salaries of the deliverers of service are more likely to flow to Jews, as middle-class professionals. Jewish organizations in general steer clear of positions on economic policy. But one exception to this has been the opposition of Jewish welfare organizations both in Canada – at the federal and provincial levels – and the United States to the budget cuts in the 1990s in the areas of health and social services.[40] Those cuts have downloaded many of the welfare burdens to private agencies in general and Jewish agencies in particular.

COALITION POLITICS AND PARTISAN POSITIONS

There is strength in numbers, especially for minorities. Jewish politicians, public servants, advisors, voters, and, of course, donors can do only so much.[41] Wherever possible, Canadian Jewish organizations have also used a coalition approach. Jews have deliberately played a key role within the human rights and anti-racist community in Canada, as they have historically in the United States. Jews have joined with other minority ethnic, racial, or religious organizations, human-rights groups, and labour unions on matters of common interest.

In the United States, these coalitions have historically been linked to the Democratic Party. In Canada, the coalitions have tended to be more non-partisan and ad hoc. A recent exception was the coalition among the organized Jewish, Italian, and Greek communities in Quebec to support the Charlottetown accord, extending into the 1995 referendum debate in Quebec. The collaboration continued despite differences in the social, political, and cultural characteristics of the three communities.[42] The three groups were largely federalist and hoped that constitutional reform would defuse the separatist threat. The accord represented an effort to amend the Constitution with the consent of Quebec. The Canadian Jewish Congress entered the Tripartite Coalition with the National Congress of Italian Canadians and the Hellenic Canadian Congress, and together the group played a visible role. In the autumn of 1991 they toured several Canadian cities. They presented a brief to the Beaudoin–Dobbie Special Committee in February 1992, and while there were some reservations, they agreed in August 1992 to support the accord. So did B'nai Brith. So did Pioneer Women–Na'amat Canada, which suspended its membership in the National Action Committee on the Status of Women when the latter came out against the accord. There is no way of knowing to what extent these political representations by the Jewish community (and other ethnic groups) affected sentiment either among Canadian Jews or in the country as a whole. There was strong support for the accord in those areas of Montreal and Toronto with large Jewish concentrations. In Quebec, 57 per cent of the population voted no, but in the largely Jewish provincial riding of D'Arcy-McGee, the yes vote came in at 92 per cent! In Toronto, the yes vote in areas with large Jewish concentrations – Willowdale, St. Paul's, Don Valley East, Eglinton–Lawrence – came in around 60 per cent.

On the other hand, Jews in the West were less committed to Charlottetown than were Eastern Jews, who saw the issue as much as a Jewish issue as one dealing with constitutional change. Calgary's *Jewish Free Press* published the results of a non-scientific hotline poll in its October 30, 1992, issue. Of those who responded, a full 87.5 per cent reported they had voted no! (That probably overstated Jewish opposition.) Clearly, regional sentiments played a role in how Jews viewed the accord, and perhaps even the importance of national unity. In the West, the Jewish grassroots may have felt less obliged to support the directives of the national Jewish elite organizations, catching the very populist spirit that sunk both the Meech Lake and Charlottetown accords. The tripartite coalition predictably raised the ire of Quebec sovereignists. In an interview with the *Canadian Jewish News* on June 24, 1993, Quebec Premier Jacques Parizeau described the role of Jewish leaders as "extremely dangerous." This view foreshadowed his harsher comment that "money and ethnic votes" had cost the Parti Québécois the 1995 referendum.

The future of Canadian ethno-racial coalition politics is dicey. The multicultural community includes a range of groups that can be divided into two rough categories. One comprises older, European groups, largely Canadian-born, who are doing well economically. Their concerns are cultural retention and status politics. The second comprises groups that are more recent, mainly non-white, immigrant, and low-income. Their concerns are mainly the fight against racism and discrimination. Canadian Jews have shared the concerns of both groups and have managed to ally themselves with both, a tough balancing act. But these two groups really have different interests. If the multicultural coalition comes apart due to racial polarization, the

Jewish community will find itself in a delicate situation. The Jewish self-perception as a vulnerable group will clash with the facts of Jewish success in Canada, particularly in the eyes of other groups.[43]

Black–Jewish relations in Canada are still good, at least compared to the United States, where the historic liberal alliance involving blacks, Jews, and labour has been fractured over issues like affirmative action. There is an uneasy coexistence which persists in the U.S. Democratic Party. My impression is also that black–Jewish relations are better in Montreal than in Toronto. In Toronto, Jews are more easily identified with the white majority. They are true insiders, where blacks are not. In Montreal, both blacks and Jews are identified more as non-francophone and federalist groups. They are both outside the conception of "*un vrai Québécois.*" The bonds are tighter.

How long can this Canadian inter-group honeymoon last? The political demography for Canadian Jews is changing for the worse as the proportion of visible minority immigrants increases. This is not because of overt anti-Semitism on the part of visible-minority immigrants. In advocating its interests, the Jewish community has been able to draw upon common experiences with other European immigrant groups, for whom the Holocaust and support for Israel are part of a shared historical discourse. The rituals like Remembrance Day on November 11, and the symbols like the swastika or the camps, still resonate for the European groups and sustain the image of the Jew as a victim. Many visible-minority Canadians do not share the same frame of reference. This is certainly true for the increasing numbers of Arabic and/or Islamic immigrants. These groups bring their own historical legacies of slavery and colonialism, of economic exploitation, of warfare, and even genocides. For them, Jews and Israel are allied with the wealthy, and with Western powers and colonial exploiters. There were numerous reports in the United States of defections from the Democratic Party by Arab and Moslem Americans in the wake of the Lieberman nomination.

Canadian Jews have so far been able to retain their moral standing as a victim community in alliance with visible minority groups when dealing with issues of racism. This is due to an extreme racist right that targets both Jews and non-whites. And employment equity in Canada has yet to engender the conflict and tensions it has between Jews and blacks in the United States. There is also no parallel in Canada – yet – to the influence of Louis Farrakhan and the Black Muslims within the Canadian black community. But in both Canada and the United States, the growth of Moslem and/or Arab origin groups through immigration will pose specific problems for Jews seeking to defend Israel's interests. If the Canadian scene is a generation behind the United States, then Canadians can soon expect to experience the same type of fierce identity politics, cultural wars, and inter-group confrontations. A harbinger of such tensions is the flap over the Toronto production of *Showboat* in the fall of 1993, described in Chapter 7.[44]

But if Jews, or the Jewish lobby, are perceived as powerful, the truth is more nuanced. The Jewish lobby is far from omnipotent. Look at the track record. As is the case with most pressure groups, it is hard to win on every issue. The Canadian Jewish community tried to mobilize action against Nazi war criminals in Canada; it took close to forty years for any progress to be made. A crystallizing event in the campaign was the Deschênes Commission of Inquiry on War Criminals, established in 1985, in which the Canadian Jewish Congress and the League for Human Rights of B'nai Brith found themselves opposed at Commission hearings by two Ukrainian groups. So much for ethnic coalitions. The ultimate recommendations by the Commission, and actions taken since by the War Crimes Unit in the Department of Justice, have generally fallen short of the hopes of the Jewish community.[45] There have been no successful prosecutions in Canada, and just a handful of early deportations. More recently, there have been acquittals or dismissals of proceedings, and the future looks bleak for any large number of convictions or deportations of Nazi war criminals who might be in Canada. Indeed, allegations of anti-Semitism were levelled against key personnel in the unit involved in the prosecution of war criminals in the late 1990s. While an independent inquiry exonerated the targets of the accusations, others are not that certain. Bill Hobson, the first director of the War Crimes Unit, who made the allegations, called it a "whitewash," and Canadian Jewish Congress President Goldie Hershon expressed "preliminary disagreement" with the findings of the report.[46] Similar allegations were made about personnel at the Immigration and Refugee

Board.[47] As described earlier, for some years members of the Immigration and Refugee Board would routinely and to great embarrassment for Canadian Jews grant refugee status to "Jewish" refugee claimants from Israel. There have been other policy failures. The decision of Joe Clark's government in 1979 to move the Canadian embassy in Israel to Jerusalem from Tel Aviv proved a fiasco. Efforts of Jews in Ontario to obtain equitable government financial support for Jewish day schools, via court rulings or new legislation, have been unsuccessful.

On the other hand, even if the track record is not perfect, Jews have a strong sense of their own political strength and the linkages between the Jewish community and the government. The setbacks described above are not really major. True, a recent Toronto survey found that 55 per cent of Jews who had heard of the Toronto Jewish Congress did not know what it did.[48] But generally Jewish organizations are, or seem to be, more effective than those of other minority groups. Jews tend to be more aware of the existence of their communal organizations compared to other Toronto ethnic groups.[49] Jews perceive a higher degree of political efficacy on the part of their communal leaders, in terms of influencing politicians, even if they are fuzzy on the organizational details.

This relative confidence in the political acumen of Jewish communal leadership will be tested in the near future. The ongoing tensions around Canadian unity will likewise pose challenges of statecraft and leadership to these leaders. And the issue of conflicts of interest – dual loyalty – for Jewish public servants or politicians will resurface periodically. Canadian Jews may witness the fraying of their coalition strategies with visible minority groups. And yet Jews are likely to remain both liberals and Liberals. The paradoxical Jewish love affair with the centre-left will continue.

A HOLY NATION

Canadian Judaism between Tradition and Modernity

"Hear, O Israel: the Lord our God, the Lord is One."
— Deuteronomy 6:4

A joke making the rounds on the Internet claims that most Jewish holidays can be described in nine words: "They tried to kill us. They failed. Let's eat."

UNDERSTANDING JUDAISM: GOD AND SPIRITUALITY

To understand Canadian Jews, even secular Jews, we must understand Judaism. The Jewish religion affects all spheres of Jewish life, directly or indirectly. In its current diversity, Judaism incarnates the paradox of the Jewish experience – the blending of the traditional and the modern. The roots of Judaism run deep. But contemporary Judaism is a mix of constancy and change, well adapted to uncertain times. For Jews as a whole, the tensions created by these opposites – even when they result in conflict – are ultimately beneficial. All religions are still struggling to find their place in Western societies which are formally secular and rational. Judaism is doing rather well.

For most Christians, Jews and Judaism are one and the same. Jews are defined in religious terms. For many believers, Jews are those cantankerous people who at one point refused to accept the divinity of Jesus. But Judaism and Christianity have much in common, beginning with the fact that Jesus was a Jew. Both revere the Old Testament, both are basically monotheistic and more or less believe in the same God, both subscribe to common codes of human conduct and values. These commonalities are often labelled as "Judeo-Christian" for convenience, though that term bothers some traditional Jews and, for all I know, some fundamentalist Christians. Moreover, Canadian Jews and Christians by and large draw upon a European heritage, despite the origins of both religions in the deserts of the Middle East and the hills of Judea. This is true also for Sephardi Jews from North Africa or the Middle East, where French, British, and Spanish influences loomed large. The elements of both Judaism and Christianity have evolved in tandem – though not without conflict – with the basic tenets of liberal democracy.

But there are differences. The conventional wisdom, which I think is right, is that Judaism as a religion is more concerned with actions, while Christianity is more concerned with faith. What Jews believe is not that important. The Jewish religion is a faith built on commandments, often onerous, which is why Judaism is at times compared in scripture to a yoke. At the risk of oversimplifying, salvation in Christianity is ultimately a result of belief in Jesus Christ. A strict embrace of any Jesus-centred Christianity would yield the following: Hitler on his deathbed, should he sincerely give himself to Christ, is saved. Good works are desirable but not mandatory for Christian access to the afterlife. For traditional Judaism, believing in God is not enough. Salvation also requires good deeds.

As a result, social scientific studies of Judaism in the post-war period are invariably behavioural. Researchers measure actions and ritual observances. I confess that I, too, share this bias. Feeling very spiritual is nice, but for me it must be accompanied by a series of actions. From one perspective, the essence of Judaism is the fulfilling of the *mitzvot*, or commandments, which number some 613, according to the Biblical record. At an interfaith dialogue I attended some years ago, the late American Jewish intellectual Milton Himmelfarb turned to one of the panelists and asked in all sincerity: "Tell me, what do Presbyterians *do*?" He brought down the house. Most of the studies of Jewish religiosity focus on easily measurable behaviours: denominational affiliation, synagogue membership and attendance, and observance of domestic religious rituals. The assumption is that people who carry out more of these behaviours more frequently are more "religious." There are limits to this approach, recognized by the Judaic tradition itself. Counting these kinds of behaviours does not measure the intensity of such acts, or their spiritual meaning to individuals.

A Hasidic tale describes a barely literate young Jew at Yom Kippur services. Instead of reciting the prayers, which he cannot do, but wanting to participate, he emits a loud whistle. God is so moved by the boy's sincere whistle that He answers the prayers of the entire congregation.

Conventional social research on Judaic observance will miss the importance of that whistle. As a result, relatively little is known about what Judaism as a faith really means to most Canadian and American Jews.[1] Most religious Jews do not get mushy about finding God or salvation. They do not ponder the nature of heaven or hell, of saints or Satan. But they do feel a strong identification with the Jewish people, and an appreciation of Jewish culture, religious rituals, and religious texts. To what extent are God and spirituality part of the lives of Canadian Jews? Is prayer a meaningful part of Jewish religious life, or is prayer mainly ritual and rote? The answer will vary by denomination.

Anyone who has seen committed Orthodox and ultra-Orthodox Jews praying in synagogue will have witnessed clear expressions of spiritual devotion, or *kavanah*. Such Jews will periodically immerse themselves into a trancelike condition, eyes closed, rocking back and forth, in a kind of religious rapture. This is a moment of unambiguous transcendence, mixed in with some inevitable element of showing off, or what sociologists call "the presentation of self." Public displays of such religious fervour are expected and encouraged. Most non-Orthodox Jews and some nominally Orthodox will rarely, if ever, attain that degree of ecstasy. This is not to suppose that for Orthodox Jews every minute spent in synagogue is deeply spiritual. On the contrary. In Orthodox congregations a loud buzz of conversation often drowns out the cantor. Many Orthodox Jews feel knowledgeable enough about what is going on to pay little attention to the service. Many feel they know more than the rabbi himself, and maybe some do. Congregants are either schmoozing, to the despair of the rabbi and cantor, or trying to outdo their neighbour in a loud display of piety. In Conservative and Reform congregations, the services are more decorous and deferential. Congregants are less confident in their Judaic and ritual knowledge, so they follow the service.

For those who are not formally Orthodox, there can still be spiritual moments, and unscripted paths to religious experience. My wife is an interesting example. As a child she almost never went to synagogue. As we raised a family, we joined a Reconstructionist congregation and began to go more often, for all the major Jewish holidays. But then, after losing both her parents within the space of a year and saying *kaddish*, she found that going every Shabbat brought her tremendous comfort and peace. She continued going almost weekly even after the mourning period. My case is different. I attend services less often, and when I do I usually find prayer itself tedious. (But I remember an exception. It was Friday night, not in Jerusalem, but in the tiny synagogue in New Delhi, India, in the mid-1980s. As a visitor, I was given the honour of leading the service. At that time, the official Jewish population of New Delhi was listed as only nine families, yet they persevered to hold services over Shabbat, and even published a quarterly newsletter. I asked the community leader whom they counted when trying to make a *minyan*, given the small population. I will never forget his response, a model for Jewish inclusiveness: "We can't be choosy." Singing the Friday night prayer *Lecha Dodi* in such a forsaken, remnant Jewish community, filled me with a sense of awe and mystery. In retrospect, I realize the spirituality I felt during those services was more appreciation of the tenacity of the people than a spiritual encounter with God or the Sabbath. No matter.)

When I go, I enjoy congregational singing. Other Jews prefer the operatic voices of cantors, or the near-professional quality of some synagogue choirs. Instead of praying, I review the weekly Torah portion. I read some Biblical commentaries or some other Judaic text I take from my synagogue library and sneak into my pew. I enjoy a good sermon. My synagogue encourages questions and comments from the congregation after the sermon. I like the democratic angle of that custom, though the odd time you have to suffer through some long-winded inanity. What probably draws me, and most people, to synagogue – and to most churches – is the social interaction with friends and fellow congregants: schmoozing during the prayers or during the *kiddush* served after services. I know of Jews for whom the food at the *kiddush* is by far the major incentive for attending services. One Jewish academic routinely rates the food on a ten-point scale. For some Jews, their congregation is like an extended family. As French sociologist Émile Durkheim (himself a son of a rabbi) understood, religion is a social rather than spiritual activity; and this is true even for Orthodox Jews.[2] All this emphasis on communal bonding may be an overly Durkheimian approach to religion, but it works for me and for many others, Jew and Gentile alike.

American evidence confirms that Jews downplay the general importance of religion and God. Gallup polls of Americans in general and New Yorkers in particular taken in 1989 and 1991 found that Jews are the least likely Americans to answer that their religion was "very important." The 1989 survey found that 90 per cent agreed or agreed strongly that a Jew can be religious even if he or she isn't particularly observant, a clear inroad of New Age spirituality. But attitude questions alone often yield inconsistent findings. For example, keeping with the de-emphasis on belief, another study found that among Reform Jewish leaders, 44 per cent said a person could be a good Jew without believing in God at all![3] This should surprise no one. There is a venerable tradition of Jewish folklore about Jewish atheists who nevertheless act as pious Jews.

When our children asked us if there really was a God, we were actually stuck for an answer. We finally came up with the following: "While we are not sure if there is a God or not, it is better to act as if there is." In rabbinic Judaism, spirituality is something obtained through obeying the commandments and living ethically in the real world – working, raising a family, dealing fairly with friends and community, and, of course, studying Torah. No one is encouraged to live on a mountaintop and meditate. Judaism does not venerate monks and mystics. Being a good religious Jew does not require separation from the material world.

Still, it would be wrong to assume that God and spirituality are totally removed from the lives of average Canadian Jews. In moments of crisis, God reappears; there are no atheists in a foxhole. And certainly, Jews who have had a traditional Jewish education have a religious sensibility which while dormant can reawaken as needed. Years ago, a friend of mine who had just become a quadriplegic was fighting off an infection in hospital. His grieving father – an educated, sophisticated, albeit traditional, European Jew was at his side. I remember vividly how the father passed his days wrapped in his *tallis* and *tefillin*, pacing the corridors and reading *tehillim*, psalms. The infection passed, and his son survived. Another story: When my wife was expecting our third child, she decided to include a midwife in the birthing experience. Don't ask me why. Anyway, I felt a bit marginalized, with a deep need to do something. So I sat in the hospital room and read my favourite Judaic text, the *Pirkei Avot*, or Ethics of the Fathers. Here, too, the prayers must have worked, as our daughter was born healthy and whole. Whenever I find myself with an ethical or moral problem, I invariably turn to Judaic ethical teachings, summoning snippets of texts to help light the way. I would not call myself very religious, though I suppose this qualifies as religious behaviour.

THE EVOLUTION OF JUDAISM

Judaism has never been static. Priestly Judaism, which included sacrificial ritual at Solomon's Temple in Jerusalem, was dominant during the pre-exilic period. Following the exile and the destruction of the temple in 70 A.D., rabbinic Judaism emerged as the dominant form. Even here, doctrinal disputes between the more liberal school of Hillel and the more conservative school of Shammai were typical of debates and disputes around the interpretation of text. The rabbi's role is that of teacher and scholar, rather than priest or holy man. He would be called upon to issue authoritative interpretations of the Torah, and to solve disputes of a legal or quasi-legal nature. Rabbis, like scholars and judges, could and did disagree. The Torah, and the corpus of Jewish law which evolved from it, deals both with the laws covering the relation between humans and God and the relations of humans to each other.

After the destruction of the Temple, rabbinic academies proliferated, and a body of commentary known as Oral Law developed. Eventually, these commentaries were recorded and codified, first into the Mishnah, written in Hebrew in approximately 200 A.D. Then a commentary on the Mishnah written in Aramaic, known as the Gemara, was compiled and codified around 500 A.D. The Mishnah and Gemara together constitute the Talmud. The Talmud is a huge, multi-volume work which might best be compared to a contemporary collection of Supreme Court decisions, with accompanying explanatory notes, amicus briefs, and expert testimony. Eventually, a consensus emerged, distilled from the Talmud and other commentary, as to the proper form of ritual and observance. These laws and guidelines are described as *halacha*, or "the way," and some were codified in the Middle Ages in a text called the "*Shulchan Aruch*," or the "Set Table."

Until the twentieth century, most religious Jews could be classified as Orthodox; even if they occasionally deviated from strict Orthodox observance, there was no question as to the normative standard, the *halacha*. Yet religious Judaism, then and now, never had a single hierarchical structure like that of the Catholic Church. The Jews have never had a pope. A variety of distinguished Orthodox rabbinic scholars in various countries claim spiritual authority by dint of their intellectual reputation, charisma, and organizational power. Today, pluralism is rampant both within religious movements and among them. Reform Judaism emerged in Germany in the nineteenth century and espoused a liberal, rational, and universalist philosophy. The original objective was to eliminate the nationalistic as well as supernatural elements within Judaism, thus little use of Hebrew, no Zionism, no concept of a chosen people, no miracles. Conservative Judaism was developed later in the United States at the end of the nineteenth and in the early twentieth century, by scholars associated with the Jewish Theological Seminary in New York. Conservative Judaism sought to synthesize elements of Reform and Orthodoxy, to become an authentic Americanized version of Judaism. It created a more traditional form of religious expression, which took *halacha* as a guide but which countenanced deviations where appropriate, like driving to Sabbath services.[4] In recent decades, the progressive Reconstructionist and Jewish Renewal movements have emerged as even more modern and egalitarian Jewish religious options.

Canadian Jewish denominations are usually affiliated with American umbrella organizations. In the United States, Reform Judaism was the first branch to institutionalize, but German Jewish Reform made a negligible impression in Canada, and has never caught up. The early anti-Zionism of classical Reform did not sit well with the Eastern European Jewish community in Canada. Reform temples in Canada are affiliated with the Union of American Hebrew Congregations. Conservative congregations are affiliated with the United Synagogue of America. Orthodox congregations include much greater diversity, and a looser organizational framework. They range from small, informal synagogues, or *shtibels*, to Modern Orthodox congregations in large new facilities. Many Orthodox synagogues are affiliated with the American Union of Orthodox Congregations, but by no means all.

THE CONTEMPORARY SCENE

In Canada today, the boundaries between Judaism and Christianity, and religious and secular Judaism, have become more permeable. As described earlier there are thousands of Jews who are no longer "religious" Jews, and their numbers are growing. For example, in the 1981 Census, just over 6 per cent of Jews who claimed to be Jewish by ethnic origin also claimed either no religion (Jewish agnostics or atheists) or a non-Jewish religion (usually Christians with Jewish ancestry).[5] By 1991, of those who claimed a Jewish ethnic origin – alone or with another origin – over 10 per cent claimed to have no religion. But some of those self-declared Jewish atheists or agnostics still engage in some religious practices and observances. For example, in Toronto, 20 per cent of Jews who *never* attend services still fast on Yom Kippur, and one-third attend or host a Passover seder.[6] In addition, there are now more Jews with Christian ancestry (converts to Judaism) as well as Christians of Jewish ancestry. So more and more Jews have some familial connection to Christianity. At bar and bat mitzvah celebrations which involve a convert, Jewish parents have to be careful when delivering a charge to their child. "You are now following in the footsteps of your ancestors – or at least some of your ancestors."

Efforts to convert the Jews have not ceased, though they are now less coercive. A full page ad in the *Globe and Mail* before Christmas 1998 asked this jarring question, in the boldest of print: "Is it reasonable to be Jewish and believe in Jesus?" (By the way, the answer to this question is no.) The ad featured fifteen smiling adults and one baby, who claim, "Maybe the most reasonable thing – the most Jewish thing – we have ever done is to believe in the Messiah." *Oy!* This is not the first time that such Jews for Jesus ads have appeared, though this one was sponsored by the Chosen People Ministries. While I am sure such ads upset many Jews, there is no way to prevent newspapers from accepting them. The ad violates no law. But note, this ad is not one that promotes the glories of Christianity. It singles out a specific minority group, and implies in subtle fashion that Jews who reject Jesus are irrational. Of course, newspapers are not obliged to accept such ads, which is quite a different story . . .

Consider the following. Is there a point at which such ads, were they to proliferate in newspapers, on television and radio, on buses and subways, on lawns and balconies, would begin to encroach upon the constitutional guarantee of freedom of religion? There is no doubt the Constitution prohibits forced conversions and discrimination on the basis of religion. But is that all? Imagine a barrage of such ads and posters assaulting Jews as they went about their daily life. They may or may not be successful in attracting converts away from Judaism. I have not seen any reliable estimates of the numbers of such "Jewish Christians," though these conversion efforts are allegedly making inroads among recent Russian Jewish immigrants. But even if the ads were not persuasive, they could well make the practice of Judaism increasingly burdensome, like the annoying Jehovah's Witnesses – and they all recognize a *mezuzah* – ringing your doorbell. At some point, free speech becomes harassment.

Of course Jews can fight back. Historically, Jews have never been very active proselytizers, at least not since the days of the Roman Empire. Perhaps this is because the playing field has never been level, and Jews like other minorities would never want to risk a backlash by an angry majority. (Imagine if Moslems in North America or Europe were to embark on an aggressive public campaign to recruit and convert Christians. It would certainly fan the flames of racism.) The closest thing to in-your-face conversion efforts have been those of the Lubavitcher Hasidim, aimed at wayward fellow Jews. I know Jews who find the Lubavitchers' efforts almost as annoying as those of the Jews for Jesus. But some Jews have begun to suggest that the time is right for some gentle persuasion directed at willing or curious Christians. A synagogue in Los Angeles has begun the process. And lo and behold, a Conservative synagogue in Montreal has very gingerly followed suit, with an ad not in the mainstream press but in the *Canadian Jewish News*. Addressed to Jews, the ad asks: "Are you dating someone who is not Jewish? Do you know a non-Jew who is interested in Judaism? Conversion to Judaism is an option." The ad then offers information about conversion classes. What if such ads, blown up to full-page size, were to proliferate in the major Canadian dailies? In fact, a discussion with the rabbi responsible revealed that the motivation behind the ad was not really to convert gentiles. The motives were more parochial. One was that Orthodox conversions were apparently becoming more lengthy and onerous. The other was a desire to present the Conservative option as an alternative to the more "suspect" Reform conversions.[7] So the motive was more market share than a mission to the Gentiles. Had the Conservative movement been really serious about converting gentiles, they would have taken out the ad in the mainstream press. Not yet . . .

The synagogue is the centre of contemporary Judaism. The Hebrew term for synagogue is *beit knesset*, which means house of assembly. So it should not anger purists that synagogues have become *de facto* mini Jewish community centres. Apart from the holding of services, synagogues run study groups, sponsor lectures, and organize bridge clubs, youth groups, bazaars, drama productions, and sports events. They hold communal activities celebrating the various holidays, and they organize trips to Israel, casino nights and other fundraisers, and so on. Of course, there is also prayer.

There is a spectrum of religiosity among Jews. For those Canadian Jews who identify religiously, about 19 per cent are Orthodox (9 per cent in the United States), 37 per cent are Conservative (38 per cent in the United States), 11 per cent are Reform (43 per cent in the United States), and 32 per cent "other Jewish" (9 per cent in the United States), which would include terms like "traditional." In 1990, two-thirds of Canadian Jewish adults were members of a synagogue, and the pattern of memberships followed roughly the pattern of identification.[8] This confirms the relative strength of Reform in the United States and Orthodoxy in Canada. Part of the large Canadian percentage claiming "other Jewish" reflects the large Sephardi proportion, in which the denominational categories of Conservative and Reform do not apply. Sephardi synagogues are in fact "Orthodox," but Sephardi respondents do not choose the designation. A 2000 survey of Montreal Sephardim found that one-half identified themselves as "traditional" Jews.[9] Canadian Jews who are lapsed Orthodox or even Conservatives also might choose the term "traditional" more than Americans. It evokes ties to a more recent immigrant past, to Yiddish, to a strong cultural sense of communal Jewishness, which is one generation further removed for American Jews.

Jews are not avid synagogue-goers. A 1996 Montreal survey found 20 per cent claimed they attended only on special occasions (for example, bar mitzvahs), which means they otherwise never attended. A 1990 Toronto study found a bit more attendance, because the city in general is more observant. Only 10 per cent never attended. At the other pole, 10 per cent of Jews went to synagogue once or several times a week, and about 13 per cent once or several times a month. In every North American study of synagogue involvement, attendance is more likely for those who are Orthodox, moderate for those who are Conservative, and least for those who are Reform or other. But there is still incongruence in the denominational patterns. For example, 56 per cent and 67 per cent of Orthodox Jews in Montreal and Toronto attend synagogue at least once a month, far more than the other denominations. But where are the other 44 or 33 per cent? So a large minority of the nominally "Orthodox" are playing hooky from synagogue. Many of

those absent are older Orthodox women, where the custom of attending services is less common.[10] In fact, these Jews call themselves
Orthodox, and belong to Orthodox congregations, but are likely not
fully observant in their private lives. On the other hand, about 20 per
cent of Toronto's Reform Jews attend at least once a month! One of the
perplexing challenges in understanding Judaism is how to compare
the religiosity of, say, a self-defined "Orthodox" Jew who attends
monthly and a Reform Jew who attends weekly. If I were forced to rank,
and happily I am not, I would tilt towards the Reform Jew, in keeping
with my behaviourist bias.

Canadian Christians generally attend services more frequently than
Jews, even though their rates are in a sort of free fall. If the drop continues, Christian rates will soon fall below those for Jews. Weekly
service attendance declined from 53 per cent in 1957 to 23 per cent in
1990.[11] There has been nothing like this steep decline for Judaism
in Canada, or the United States for that matter. So the attendance
outlook is brighter for Judaism in Canada than it is for Christianity,
despite Jewish fears of assimilation. I'll go a step further. In my view,
Christianity, at least in its non-fundamentalist or non-evangelical
variant, is in close to full retreat. In part because of the new multicultural political correctness, in part because of natural processes of
erosion, Christianity has lost its self-confidence. I see this starkly during
the Christmas season. I can recall radio stations beginning to play
Christmas carols weeks before Christmas. Now they are barely heard
by Christmas Eve. Christians have become afraid to wish people "Merry
Christmas" lest they catch a non-Christian or atheist and give offence.
A colleague who was involved in anti-racist efforts in Canada used to
bristle when Air Canada personnel, some years back, would wish him
"Merry Christmas" as he disembarked. In any event, almost everywhere
the wimpy "Happy Holidays" and "Season's Greetings" reign tri-
umphant. Hanukkah, Kwanzaa, Ramadan, and Passover have crowded
out Christmas and Easter in daycares, schools, and radio morning
shows. For members of religious minority groups, all this is delightful. And perhaps it is. But I never felt offended when non-Jews who
did not know I was Jewish wished me a Merry Christmas. Nowadays,

more non-Jews wish me Happy Hanukkah, which is fine. Still, I make a point of wishing my Christian friends a Merry Christmas.

Perhaps I am too harsh on Christianity and its future. Perhaps a decline in church attendance or in adherence to formal organized churches is not the same thing as a decline in Christian spirituality or a belief in God or a reverence for Jesus Christ.[12] Anecdotal reports come in about corporate spirituality seminars, and people studying the Bible. And according to some poll evidence, more Canadians are interested in spirituality than in religion, and only 8 per cent in 1995 declared firmly they did not believe in God.[13] I am a stubborn sort, and have little faith in this sort of distinction – my behaviourist bias wants to see action. Most of us would doubt someone who claimed to be very athletic but never exercised and played no sports. In the future, more spiritual forms of Christianity may become institutionalized. But until that happens, if Christians increasingly refrain from going to church, I maintain Christianity is in trouble, more trouble than Judaism.

Many Jews belong to congregations which do not correspond to their own identification, and some affluent Jews belong to more than one. A few Jews belong to synagogues up North and in Florida. When it comes to congregational membership, Canadian Jews and Christians differ. Christian congregational membership has declined dramatically, even more than their attendance, from 82 per cent in 1957 to 29 per cent in 1990.[14] Jews are far more likely, at 67 per cent, to belong to congregations than are Christians, but so far they are less likely to attend weekly services (23 per cent to about 10 to 15 per cent). So are Jews hypocrites? Not really. Being an official member of a congregation clearly has more symbolic and communal meaning for Jews. Judaism, unlike Christianity, is expressed religiously in many ways other than weekly attendance at services, mainly through major annual holidays and life-cycle rituals.

DENOMINATIONAL CHALLENGES

In both Canada and the United States, each of the three major denominations has been undergoing dramatic changes, at times involving painful soul-searching. Before looking at the denominations themselves, we should note that all of them are marked by tensions between the left and the right, and between elite and folk religion. The left-right split means simply that every denomination can be understood as having a liberal and conservative wing. These factions will at times conflict with each other while finding common ground with adjacent wings of other denominations. So the conservative wing of the Conservative movement shares some affinities with the liberal (Modern Orthodox) wing of Orthodoxy. At times, tensions within denominations can be as intense as those between them, in the same way that civil wars are unusually ferocious. Some years ago, members of the Satmar and Belz Hasidim waged a pitched battle on the streets of New York. In the case of Orthodoxy, it may be more useful to speak of a wide continuum of possible Orthodox options, from Modern Orthodox to ever-more-pious ultra-Orthodox groups. In this type of Orthodox one-upmanship, the Orthodox compete to see who can be most scrupulous in terms of *halachic* observance. Charles Silberman described this move to hyper-stringent observance as belonging to the "*chumrah*-of-the-month club."[15]

Often, the left-right distinction among the Orthodox is expressed in where one eats, or where one can trust the quality of the observance of the dietary laws. For the most pious, a label of "kosher" on a food product does not really suffice. Most Hasidic Jews, for example, would probably not eat a full meal containing meat in the home of a Modern Orthodox Jew, and certainly not in my home, even though it is nominally "kosher." They are making the right decision. In my home, we keep two sets of regular dishes, and two sets of Passover dishes. But we do bring non-kosher food in and eat it on paper plates. So, like many Canadian Jews, our dishes are reasonably kosher, but our stomachs are *treif*, or unclean. This is part of the spectrum of kosher *mishigas*, or craziness. And, of course, we eat in non-kosher restaurants, like many others who keep a kosher home. Some Orthodox and/or kosher Jews will eat fish or salads in a non-kosher restaurant, others will not. One of the more frequent topics of debate in strictly Orthodox circles concerns which products are revealed to be unkosher, and which kosher, and according to which groups' supervision, and why.

The second distinction is between elite and folk religion. According to social scientist Charles Liebman, every one of the denominations, and perhaps every religion, includes a doctrinal set of prescriptions mandated by the elite; that is, rabbis and religious scholars. These are combined with a populist set of practices and attitudes which emanate from the religious folk themselves.[16] These are the things people do, as opposed to what they ought to do. Elite religion flows from the top down, while folk religion flows from the bottom up. Most of the members of Orthodox, Reform, Conservative, and Reconstructionist congregations have not studied the theological writings of their respective rabbinic authorities or gurus, from David Hartman to Abraham Joshua Heschel to Eugene Borowitz to Mordecai Kaplan. Many, perhaps most, do not know the "official" denominational position on various issues, from dietary laws to the status of women to Sabbath observance. They just evolve their own approach, their own compromise based on their daily efforts to make sense out of their Jewish lives. At times a dialectical relation between elite and folk Judaism can lead to cross-denominational creativity. For some people, Conservative Judaism represents the incarnation and institutionalization of elements of folk Orthodoxy. For the majority of Jews who are "moderately affiliated," a new form of folk religion is a liberal individualism, a pick-and-choose approach to belief and sentiment which downplays the role of any religious elites or organization. Indeed, in their recent study of such Jews, Steven Cohen and Arnold Eisen identified "rabbis and congregations" encountered by young adults or newlyweds as obstacles to adult Jewish involvement or participation.[17] In matters of religion, Jews, and many Christians, like to do their own thing.

How are the denominations doing?[18] By all indicators, Orthodoxy is the most vibrant. It is losing the fewest adherents, and its large families are adding to the population base. Ultra-Orthodoxy, whether Hasidic or yeshiva-based, epitomizes this vitality; their communities, synagogues, and schools are bursting with children. The Orthodox see themselves, and with some justification, as the guarantors of the Jewish future in the face of assimilation. Indeed, all indicators of assimilation, notably mixed marriage, are lower for the Orthodox.[19]

It is hard to overemphasize how unexpected this Orthodox resurgence has been. No social scientist who studied North American Jewish life prior to the 1970s anticipated it. On the contrary, it was felt as axiomatic by observers, like pioneer sociologist Louis Wirth, that Orthodoxy in North America was doomed. It was too much at odds with the prevailing culture, too Old World, too opposed to modernity.[20] Of course, Wirth was an assimilated German Jew, so perhaps some of that was a personal prejudice. These views were part of the general social scientific infatuation with modernization. Accordingly, ethnic cultures and religion, and certainly religious fundamentalism, would fade as societies became more educated, urbanized, industrialized, and cosmopolitan, and as the immigrants to the new world gave way to native-born generations. This, too, was wrong. Indeed, right-wing or fundamentalist Christians, Moslems, and Jews have shown themselves adept at utilizing elements of modernity, like computers or faxes or videos or music CDs, to help propagate their conservative message. The Lubavitch Hasidim were among the first to pioneer the use of worldwide live TV when they began broadcasting the *farbrengen* and commentaries of the late *Rebbe*. In addition, a form of "Modern Orthodoxy" developed in the post-war period which sought to integrate faith with active participation in the external world. One study of Orthodox life in Toronto's suburbia has found a remarkable degree of adaptability. The expansion of Orthodox day schools as well as the development of a sophisticated "religious consumerism" allow these Jews to enjoy their lives with a degree of material sophistication.[21]

In the later twentieth century, Orthodoxy moved to the right. Triumphalism caused strains between the newly militant Orthodox and the Modern Orthodox, on issues like ties with non-Orthodox Jews. Some of the Modern Orthodox are embarrassed by the exclusiveness of the militant Orthodox, in the same way that some supporters of the Lubavitch Hasidim are embarrassed by the efforts of certain Lubavitchers to argue that the late *Rebbe* remains alive in some Elvis-like way and is "continuing his work," as one follower told me. The left wing of Orthodoxy, or the Modern Orthodox, have some elements in common with the right-wing Conservatives, though less so recently. And the right wing of Orthodoxy embraces increasing degrees of piety and religiosity, typified by the tendency among the youngest generation to become more devout than the parents. An example of the strength of Orthodoxy are the *baalei teshuva* – adherents of a kind of

Jewish born-again movement – who move from limited or moderate levels of Judaism to very pious Orthodoxy and ultra-Orthodoxy.[22] Specific yeshivot in Israel cater to these new seekers, though some in the Orthodox community remain skeptical about their commitment. Today Hasidism, tomorrow Buddhism, then who knows? A program of deliberate outreach – some might say intra-Jewish proselytizing – has been developed by the Aish HaTorah organization, which claims that its intense Discovery Seminars, a kind of crash course in Jewish identity and piety, have reached seventy thousand participants in North America.[23] There is no denying cultlike elements have seeped into the new Orthodox fervour.

Reform Judaism in Canada has never been as stridently doctrinaire as American Reform. It has been more ethnic, more open to Israel, more open to particularism, all without losing the traditional Reform concern with social justice, universalism, and integration into host societies. In a sense, Reform in Canada has anticipated the evolution of American Reform in the post-war period, which now embraces Hebrew and Israel and other elements of tradition. At the same time, Reform has, paradoxically, had to embrace increasingly marginal Jews and innovations to accommodate mixed-marriage families.[24] It is common for many Orthodox and Conservative Jews to condemn Reform for its seeming association with assimilation. And, indeed, most studies find that Reform Jews are most assimilated and most likely to be in a mixed marriage. But it would be foolish to assume that Reform in any sense "causes" assimilation. None of the studies can solve the problem of self-selection. Jews who are already more prone to assimilation or more predisposed to greater contact with the non-Jewish world, are also more likely to choose or to have been raised in Reform (and like-minded) families. Reform Jews are simply articulating a specific, liberal version of Jewish identification that works for them.

A far more sympathetic interpretation of Reform Judaism would be to see it as occupying the front lines in the desperate struggle *against* assimilation. Liberal Reform congregations are the most likely to include non-Jews as members or associate members, usually through mixed marriages. And Reform congregations thereby wrestle regularly with the boundaries to be set between Jewish and non-Jewish members. Reform is most involved with outreach to those on the margins, seeking, often against great odds, to bring them back to the fold. Their congregations wrestle with issues like how or whether non-Jewish spouses of temple members can participate in the services or congregational life. To the Orthodox, this is lunacy, as well as heresy. But from a different perspective, this is rescue. A pro-continuity case can be made for both a hard and soft line on such questions. Of course, for Reform rabbis, conversion remains preferable, but Reform has no choice but to try to navigate the uncharted waters of mixed marriage, in which Jews with non-Jewish spouses and children try to find a workable approach that will not alienate the family from Judaism.

All denominations have conversion classes. These cater to some individuals, but mainly serve couples where there is a prospect of a conversion and true Jewish marriage. They get the job done, though the Orthodox will not recognize non-Orthodox conversions. More provocative are outreach programs aimed at married couples where the non-Jewish partner is not planning to convert but the couple wishes to retain some familial tie to Jewish life – the proverbial "We will raise the children with both religions, and when they are older they can choose." Consider the following rather courageous "Living Intermarried" workshops sponsored by Montreal's Reform Temple Emanu-El–Beth-Sholom:

1. I'm not religious but (Ethnicity and Identity)
2. December Dilemma (Holiday Celebrations)
3. Briss or Baptism (Lifestyle Choices)
4. If I'm Jewish and you're Christian, what are the children (Choices in Child Rearing).[25]

The fact is that Reform and all liberal congregations are doing the community's dirty work without receiving much thanks. They are providing a last-ditch option for linkage with the Jewish community and tradition for those dangerously close to the way out. In doing so, they are also inadvertently perpetuating the Orthodox stereotype of Reform as being very weak on authentic Judaic content.

A Jew goes to an Orthodox rabbi and asks, "Rabbi, can you give
me a bracha (blessing) on my Jaguar?" The rabbi answers,
"What's a Jaguar?" The Jew then asks the same question of a
Reform rabbi, who answers, "What's a bracha?"

Conservative Judaism has had a checkered history. The denomination has been seen as the ideal model for North American Judaism, and as the one most consumed with conflict and dissension. The strength of Conservatism is in its origins in North America, as an indigenous response out of New York's Jewish Theological Seminary designed to create an alternative for the problem children of East European immigrants straying from Orthodox Judaism. It was homegrown, pragmatic in the best American sense, and tailored to the dilemmas of North American life. It strove for compromise with *halacha* and created institutions like the Jewish community centre. At one point, one could predict it would outstrip all rivals, drawing left-wing Orthodox and right-wing Reform Jews into the fold, producing a consensual North American Judaism.

But Conservative Judaism has been beset with its own left-right conflicts. Moreover, the tensions between the elite rabbis and the folk have been severe.[26] Canadian Conservative Judaism is generally more traditional than American Conservatism. In the United States, it has been a battleground on issues of the status of women. Rather than offering a happy medium, Conservatism has appeared inadequate compared to the absolute gender egalitarianism of Reform and Reconstructionism and the self-confident traditionalism of Orthodoxy. Orthodoxy retains its zealous and often unyielding commitment to Jewish law and its own self-described purity. Indeed, because of the hostile Orthodox stance on Reform and Conservative conversion, Conservatism has often found itself in an uneasy alliance against Orthodox exclusivism. Conservative Judaism has never lost its affinity with the turbulent Jewish student movements of the 1960s, which spawned the Jewish countercultural movements like the Havurot and other innovations. A recent example of Conservative innovation is the new *Rabbi's Manual* published by the Conservative Rabbinical

Assembly. It includes new blessings for sending children away to college or to camp, and like the new Conservative prayer book *Sim Shalom*, does away with masculine names for God such as "Lord" or "King." In the words of sociologist Samuel Heilman, "It's *The Jewish Catalogue*, 30 years later."[27]

DILEMMAS OF CANADIAN JUDAISM

Judaism in Canada is a branch-plant operation. Reform, Conservative, and Reconstructionist Judaism in Canada are all completely dependent on their American counterparts for infrastructural support, and, more importantly, for the major rabbinic seminaries. These rabbis in Canada must be trained in the United States. There are some ultra-Orthodox rabbinic seminaries in Canada, but the larger, Modern Orthodox institutions such as Yeshiva University are south of the border.[28] The majority of pulpit rabbis in Canada have historically been American. Only recently has there been an increase in Canadians who receive ordination in the United States and then return to Canada. The situation is less pronounced in Jewish communal service, though leadership positions in many federations have been filled by American-born professionals. Sound familiar? All this is reminiscent of the 1960s plaint about the preponderance of American professors in Canadian universities. Canadian universities solved the dependency problem either by hiring Canadians trained in the United States, or beginning to recognize the value of Canadian-made Ph.D.'s. But unlike the resulting expansion of Canadian universities and a shift in hiring, Rabbinical seminaries have not emerged in Canada. Canadian Jews still do not have the necessary critical mass, and so the American institutions – Orthodox, Conservative, Reform, and Reconstructionist – continue to serve the Canadian market.

Is this a problem? Of course, American rabbis are unfamiliar with the general Canadian scene. Many in Montreal have never learned French or become familiar with the history of French–English relations. But most eventually realize that the Canadian and American Jewish communities differ and that the separation of church and state does not exist in Canada as in the United States. This American dominance of Canadian Jewish institutions is not as tragic as Canadian nationalists might fear. There may – or may not – be an authentic Canadian culture which deserves protection from American domination, but there is no such authentic Canadian Judaism, no movement indigenous to Canada, no Judaic philosophers who have produced a distinctly Canadian Jewish voice. The two leading "Canadian" Judaic thinkers have been Dr. Emil Fackenheim of Toronto and Rabbi David Hartman of Montreal. Both these philosophers were immigrants to Canada, born and raised in Berlin and New York respectively. And both moved to Israel to continue their scholarly writing. With its ties to the United States and to Israel, Canada has not yet been able to generate or sustain new creative movements of Jewish theology and philosophy.

Even Canadian Jewish contributions to religious custom, or *minhag*, have been few. The best known are the unique customs which used to occur in Montreal and Toronto – and I presume other Canadian Jewish communities – during the first or second Passover Seder, which used to conflict with the Stanley Cup playoffs. In the 1950s, 1960s, and 1970s Canadian Jews were passionate hockey fans, like all Canadians, before expansion and inflated salaries changed everything. Many Seders were routinely punctuated by kids and some adults excusing themselves, finding a TV, and then updating everyone on the score. I remember how a close game in the third period, or worse, overtime – and those were the days before VCRs – would be a real test of commitment for Montreal and Toronto Jews, and further incentive to finish the Seder quickly. I remember how a loss by the Canadiens would take the punch out of our *chad gadya*. The whole thing is parodied in "A Montrealer Seder," a fictional ethnographic study in *The Big Book of Jewish Humor* which we now read as a regular feature of my Seders. Let me commend it to everyone:

> Another unique Montrealer custom concerns the afikomen. The father sends the youngest child to search for it, and upon finding it, the child runs back to the table and whispers in his father's ear. The father then jumps to his feet, raises his hands skyward, and shouts "Agol, Agol!" the rest of the males then rise with their arms raised and respond, "Hahllo Habs, Ahwei-Ahwei."[29]

FAITH AND PEOPLEHOOD

The Jewish religion, Jewish people, and the land of Israel are intimately linked, making it easy to be religious without much theology. Passover is a holiday celebrating the national liberation of the Jewish people, contrasting the value of freedom with the horror of slavery. Even the Sabbath, arguably the paradigmatic religious event in the Jewish calendar, has a national/ethnic subtext. The requirements of Sabbath observance, like the prohibitions of kashrut, do more than separate the sacred from the profane. They separate Jews from non-Jews. As essayist Ahad Ha'am once put it, "It is not that the Jews keep the Sabbath, it is that the Sabbath keeps the Jews." In sociological terms, all of Judaism is a thoroughly ethnic religion. (There are some similarities with German Mennonites and with the various Orthodox churches. Most Greek Orthodox are also Greek.) Converts not only embrace the Jewish faith but, as we are taught in the story of Ruth in the Bible, join the Jewish people. The Reform movement tried to create a purer form of intellectualized religion, based on universal principles and ideals, and failed. Ritual and peoplehood have crept back in.

Judaic observance relates to ethnicity and community in a number of ways. First, while some Jewish holidays emphasize normative ethical issues – such as the need for repentance on Yom Kippur – many others commemorate specific national-historical events such as the exodus from Egypt (Passover), wandering through the desert (Sukkoth), and receipt of the Torah (Shavuot). The Passover Seder includes the unsubtle hint, "Next year in Jerusalem." Holidays which emerged later, like Hanukkah and Purim, celebrate historic confrontations with external oppressors in ancient Israel or in the Diaspora. So Judaism is tied to the Jewish people, and both are tied to Israel.

Second, in all branches of Judaism, though less in Reform and Reconstructionism, Hebrew predominates as the language of prayer and reading of the Torah. There is no movement afoot to parallel the Catholics' unfortunate rejection of Latin. Even Reform Judaism has increased the use of Hebrew in the service, and now requires Hebrew language as an element of a Reform education. Hebrew is the language of the Jewish people, and links all Jews together in time and space. The Biblical Hebrew used in prayer also serves to demarcate the sacred and

the profane, which is, after all, one of the central purposes of organized religion. Third, prayer is a social activity, requiring a quorum of
ten. Jews cannot recite the prayer for the dead, *kaddish*, without a
quorum. Jews must pray with other Jews, not as isolated mystics.

Finally, two new holidays have emerged in the twentieth century,
and both tap into the national/communal dimension of the Jewish
experience. These are *Yom Ha'Shoah*, which commemorates the
Holocaust, and Israel's *Yom Ha'Atzma'ut*, or Independence Day. Both
of these have no historical/theological significance as related to the
Torah and the Biblical experience. But modern philosophers wrestle
with their meaning, and try to ascribe a *post hoc* religious significance
to them, around the motif of redemption. They are routinely com-
memorated in one form or another in synagogues of all branches of
Judaism. Prayers for Israel are part of the Sabbath service. Most congregations give as a bar- or bat-mitzvah present a certificate for trees
planted in Israel.

In short, the Jewish religion embraces both universal and particular elements functional for Jewish survival. Conversion to Judaism is
thus more difficult than acceptance of Christianity. It entails casting
one's lot with the Jewish people, linking one's fate with horrors of the
Holocaust – and with anti-Semitism today – as well as developing a
deep empathy with Israel and her travails. It also involves adopting
a repertoire of religious rituals, Hebrew prayers and songs, customs,
and foods that play a role in specific holidays.

THE NUTS AND BOLTS OF RELIGIOUS OBSERVANCE

Some years ago, for reasons that are unclear – it may have had something to do with the death of my father – I decided to build a sukkah,
and have done so every year since. I enjoy the physical work of erecting it, the exotic nature of it, the involvement of family in putting it
up. I am proud to say it is an authentic Canadian sukkah – I use wooden
skis and hockey sticks for the roof, on which I lay the covering of
branches. I buy a *lulav* (a bundle of green plants) and *etrog* (a citron:
a lemon-like fruit). We say the blessings a few times, but don't even
make a point of eating a full meal in the sukkah. Just having it around
for seven days is enough.

For Jews, religion means doing, and they do a lot more than Methodists. First and foremost, Canadian and American Jews observe Jewish life-cycle rituals.[30] Even largely assimilated Jews, if they marry Jews, have a Jewish wedding. If they later have a boy, they will almost certainly have a circumcision. Increasingly for baby girls, parallel ceremonies have evolved among Jews of all denominations, though without any cutting. These range from the *simchat ha'bat*, which features remarks from the parents, to a *brit banot*, which can include immersing the girl in water.[31] They will likely offer their children a bar- or bat-mitzvah ceremony. (The terms "bar mitzvah" and "bat mitzvah" are perhaps the most misused in Jewish life, and I too am often guilty. It may be picky, but a *bar mitzvah*, translated from Hebrew, is *not* a noun referring to a party or ritual. It is the designation of the boy who at thirteen becomes someone who must obey the commandments. So to say "I went to a bar mitzvah" is like saying "I went to a thirteen-year-old boy." The correct form would be to say "I went to a party celebrating David's becoming a bar mitzvah," or, more loosely, "I went to a bar-mitzvah party.") And last but not least, Jews will choose to be buried according to Jewish ritual, and in a Jewish cemetery. They will observe some form of *shiva* for their dead parents. These cut across all denominations.

Since life-cycle rituals are infrequent, they are therefore more likely to be observed. But they certainly can be onerous. A bar or bat mitzvah can monopolize a family's psychic energy for six months or more.[32] And the cost is a real burden. Some families have taken to combining the celebration with a family trip to Israel. The emotional impact of coming of age at the Wailing Wall or on Masada is great, but for parents it may be just one more event to plan, and to pay for. It is really a rite of passage for the whole family, and is probably more stressful for the parents preparing the festivities than for the boy or girl. I speak from experience.

Is it worth it? No one knows if having a bar or bat mitzvah celebration contributes significantly to the future Jewish commitments of the young boy or girl. A bar- or bat-mitzvah celebration, however, honours not just the young adolescent, but the family, and by extension the community. Like a Jewish wedding, these occasions reflect on the family and the community by being a public statement about commitment to Jewish continuity. I cry at Jewish *simchas* not so much for the joy of the bride and groom or the bar or bat mitzvah, but because of the public display of solidarity with a Jewish community still burdened with memories of the Holocaust. A Jewish wedding, with the promise of Jewish children, is a slap in the face of anti-Semites. These celebrations are an affirmation of Jewish life by the family and friends, who are representatives of the entire community.

For this reason, the presence of grandparents at these celebrations – or their saddening absence – is a big deal. They symbolize the generational chain of Jewish continuity. At the celebrations for our children, my wife and I included a slide show with photos of recently deceased grandparents as well as other European relatives who died before or during the Holocaust, an idea we copied from some friends. I suspect our decision stemmed from the fact that as children of Holocaust survivors, we felt a special obligation to Jewish memory. It is also a ritual during such festivities to thank all the out-of-town relatives and friends who have travelled a great distance to attend. (It would be interesting to look at the distances guests travel to attend Jewish affairs, and the fuss made over them, compared to the family get-togethers of other groups. My hunch is that some immigrant groups, say Italians, approximate this Jewish obsession. Many ethnic/immigrant weddings boast the same warmth and communal spirit, with dancing and singing in the mother tongue, and all sorts of ethnic foods and customs to mark the occasion.) The farther flung the guest list, the better. These are tribal sentiments. They blur the line between the personal, the familial, and the communal, which is a strength of religious ritual generally and Judaism in particular. The deliberate melding of these three domains should not obscure the coming-of-age value of the bar and bat mitzvah. For some youngsters, the event, especially the preparation of the Torah portion and the increasingly common *d'var torah*, or sermon-like speech, may be traumatic or exhilarating, or both.

The rituals concerning death are quite unique. Perhaps the most onerous life-cycle ritual is the saying of *kaddish*, the prayer for the dead.

It requires those Jews who accept the burden in the Orthodox tradition to attend the morning, afternoon, and evening service every day for eleven months, in order to find a minyan to recite the *kaddish*. Reform and Reconstructionist Jews say it every Sabbath for a year. Jews saying *kaddish* will often go to elaborate lengths to try to catch a minyan during the day, or find out about faraway synagogues if they happen to be travelling. When my mother died in the early 1970s, I was a single graduate student at Harvard. The local small Cambridge synagogue heroically tried to offer twice-daily services, even though the Jewish population base was very tiny, consisting of a few "townies" and a collection of university students who lived in the area. I became a regular, and my commitment was strong, because I felt I just could not let the side down. I originally feared that getting up that early – and half past six is early for students – to make a minyan would cramp my limited social life. But it was not too bad. For their understanding, I thank again some of the women I dated.

Observing a period of *shiva*, a week of intense mourning after the burial, is another powerful ritual observed in some degree by almost all Jews. I recall seeing Christian friends showing up for work a couple of days after the death of a loved one, looking haggard, lost, and forlorn. Jews who sit *shiva* basically stay home for the duration, and are visited by friends of the deceased, both close and distant, who console them. In many cases, daily services will take place in the home, transforming it into a sort of synagogue, and light food is served after the morning services. Often, family friends will supply food for the week. Jewish mourners do not have to think about what they should do, or about what is proper. The automatic pilot of the *shiva* ritual kicks in. At times, the thick crowd of visitors becomes a kind of social gathering, where old acquaintances see each other – though it will generally not reach the level of festivities found in Christian wakes. The blurring of the personal, the familial, and the communal is again obvious.

Apart from life-cycle events, Jews also observe key yearly holidays. As sociologist Marshall Sklare noted about American Jews, Canadian Jews tend to observe holidays which are infrequent, which can be invested in universal or modern themes, which do not demand social isolation, which have a counterpart in the Christian calendar, and which are child-centred.[33] This could explain why more Jews in both Canada and the United States light Hanukkah candles than fast on Yom Kippur, though the latter is arguably the most important Jewish religious holiday. Hanukkah comes once a year, while lasting eight days. It parallels Christmas in timing and in the practice of gift-giving. It celebrates the struggle for freedom by Jews against colonial invaders, a universal message. And it is profoundly child-centred, given the gift-giving, the lighting of candles, and the spinning of the dreidel. These traits also explain the popularity of Passover. The feast celebrates the universal holiday of freedom, parallels Easter, and the Seder is often child-centred. These themes also explain why complete Sabbath observance is rare, except for the strictly Orthodox.

The most faithfully observed rituals of Canadian Jews are Passover Seders (92 per cent), lighting Hanukkah candles (87 per cent), and fasting on Yom Kippur (77 per cent), all higher than in the United States. Sabbath observance is marked by a range of rituals and practices; 54 per cent of Canadian Jews light Sabbath candles compared to only 26 per cent in the United States. However, strict Sabbath observance – for example, not handling any money – is observed by only about 15 per cent in both countries. One of the key elements of kashrut is keeping two sets of dishes, one for dairy foods and one for meat; 46 per cent claim to do so in Canada, compared to only 18 per cent in the United States.[34] But as already described, keeping kosher involves a mish-mash of competing definitions and practices, from "kosher style" to the ultra "glatt kosher." This populist variation confirms the centrality of Jewish folk religion as well as the old Jewish proverb "Every Jew makes his own Sabbath." Every Jew makes his or her own kashrut.

Food intersects with Judaism in other ways. Jews have become infatuated with Chinese food in North America.

A Jew and a Chinese are arguing. The Chinese says his people have been around for four thousand years. The Jew says his people have been around for five thousand years. Asks the Chinese, "Well, what did you people eat for the first thousand years?"

There are kosher Chinese foods and restaurants, and no kosher caterer is without a strong Chinese menu, including "mock shrimp." Kosher restaurants incur onerous costs. They pay more for kosher meat, they must pay for the services of a recognized *mashgiach*, or food inspector, and they close on the Sabbath and Jewish holidays. Jewish delis feature the less expensive "kosher style" option. Passover is another interesting case. Here, Orthodox resourcefulness has led to a variety of products, referred to in Chapter 7, which remain kosher for Passover, but which thoroughly undercut the spirit of the holiday.

RELIGIOUS VARIATION

Levels of religious observance in Canada vary by region and by social characteristics. They are higher in Montreal and Toronto, lower in Western communities. This is not surprising. Interestingly, there is no evidence of decline in religious observance among younger Jews. Perhaps due to the higher fertility rates of religious Jews, there are more younger Jews who are observant. Observant Jews also tend to be those with a more Jewish social network, and who live in Jewish neighbourhoods.[35] Levels of observance are, of course, highest among Orthodox Jews, followed by Conservative and Reform. An Orthodox Jew must in theory recite prayers three times a day, and many Orthodox men do so. Most Conservative synagogues also feature daily services. By contrast, daily prayers are not required for Reform or Reconstructionist Jews.

Religious expression is no longer easily described by the conventional denominations. In cities throughout Canada, as in the United States, alternatives have been emerging. New Age synagogues affiliated with the Jewish Renewal Movement try to create a level of spirituality that is absent from the mainstream. New forms of "secular" Jewish associations have developed in Toronto and Montreal, seeking to celebrate holidays without the overlay of belief, perhaps the best proof of the non-theological nature of Jewish religiosity. Havurot, or small independent congregations, stressing informality, innovation, and community, have sprung up. So have egalitarian Orthodox *minyans*, congregations which follow Orthodox traditions but have complete gender equality, like the Narayever in Toronto. Both respond to perceived needs that were not met by established denominations.

Much of the experimentation in new Jewish forms is based on the West Coast. The boundaries of the major denominations no longer hold in a frontier society where traditions are weak. An ad for an assistant rabbi by a self-described liberal congregation in Vancouver captured these new developments.[36] The ad described the 525-family congregation as "completely egalitarian, yet also has two days of Rosh Hashana. Conversions are ke'dat halacha, and Jewish identity is established through matrilineal descent or conversion." This unnamed congregation clearly does not conform to the accepted doctrines of the major denominations. New Age Judaism is alive and well. Vancouver's 220-family Or Shalom Spiritual Community and their rabbi, David Mivasair, have embraced the environmental movement with "religious" zeal. In the rabbi's view, "Eating food grown or produced in a way that is destructive to the earth is not kosher. We are not allowed to participate in things that destroy the earth." That means no foam plates or plastic cutlery, and a preference for locally grown foods. The Pacific region of the Canadian Jewish Congress is even debating a position paper on the environment, with the involvement of Rabbi Mivasair.[37]

Jews in Vancouver have had to be resourceful. One informal "mini-Havurah" of five or six couples, with children, gets together once a month for potluck Friday night Shabbat dinners and also meets around holidays. They attend each other's life-cycle celebrations. The group is drawn from different synagogues, and at least three individuals are converts to Judaism. Almost all the members have no Jewish family roots in Vancouver, so what they have created – quite deliberately, it seems to me – is a surrogate extended family, with a warm, *heimish* atmosphere. One Friday night, the children decided to entertain the adults with their unique rendition of the prayer *Adon Olam* sung to the tune of the *Grease* hit "Summer Love." For all this experimentation, it is paradoxical that the glue that holds this surrogate family together is Shabbat and the accompanying ritual, which imposes an inevitable commitment. The link between the Jewish family and Jewish religious ritual operates in both traditional and experimental Judaism.

There is a relation between these experiments and the established denominations. Many of the innovators are themselves products of mainstream denominations. Mordecai Kaplan, founder of

Reconstructionism, as well as leaders of Camp Ramah or the Havurah movement, emerged out of Conservative Judaism. Many of the innovations – those that stand the test of time – are slowly accepted by synagogues. Eco-Judaism has been prefigured by forms of Judaic social consciousness and the concern shared by the Jewish Renewal movement and other progressive Jews for *tikkun olam*, or the healing of the world. The progressive positions of Reform rabbis Abraham Feinberg, Harry Stern, and Gunther Plaut in Canada appealed to many Jews. The organization Mazon has encouraged Jewish families to set aside 3 per cent of the cost of their bar mitzvah or wedding celebrations to feed the hungry.

A major challenge faces Jewish religious life in Canada as well as the United States. Judaism, as I have argued, has been a largely communal religion. Even more than other faiths, religious observance is rooted in the collectivity. Yet a new individualist ethic has spread throughout religious life in recent decades, particularly among the more liberal religious movements. In the words of sociologists Wade Clark Roof and William McKinney, "Of all the recent religious changes in America, few are more significant or more subtle than the enhanced religious individualism of our time. Americans generally hold a respectful attitude toward religion, but also they increasingly regard it as a matter of personal choice or preference."[38] Individuals are charting their own journey, by themselves or with like-minded groups. For "moderately affiliated" Jews, religion is becoming a cafeteria, and prescriptive texts more like a menu from which individuals can pick and choose.[39] It also accounts for the emergence of small-scale alternatives like Havurot, feminist *minyans*, or Jewish Renewal congregations. This trend is all the more pronounced in the United States. But it has begun in Canada.

For most Canadian Jews, religious life goes on in the mainstream synagogues. Synagogue politics can be nasty, even if based on seeming trivialities. The same might be said for political fights within other religious congregations as well. Congregations can break apart on clashes of personality, doctrine, or combinations of the two. Rabbis are often targets, with supporters and the disgruntled in opposing camps. One such case occurred in an Orthodox synagogue. A clash between supporters and opponents of the incumbent rabbi blended into an earlier clash about the *mechitza*, or partition, separating men from women. The two factions were split over whether it was several inches too high or too low. I am not making this up. Much later, the rabbi left the congregation. The punchline "and that's the shul I wouldn't set foot in" is grounded in the occasional sad truth. There are more tensions within Orthodoxy – between and within ultra-Orthodox and Modern Orthodox – than within any of the other movements. But the major fault line is now between the Orthodox and the non-Orthodox. Witness the pending marriage within ultra-Orthodox circles, referred to in Chapter 5, that broke up because the two families could not agree on the length and style of the *payess*, or sidelocks, to be worn by any boy the couple would produce.

RELIGIOUS PLURALISM, RELIGIOUS CONFLICT

Religion has in recent years taken over from differences in ethnicity, class, and political ideology as the major basis of conflict within the Jewish community. With the rise in intermarriage, tensions have mounted over the issue of "who is a Jew?" and "who is a rabbi?" This is the Jewish version of religious wars found in most other faiths. None is immune: Shia versus Sunni Moslems, Catholics versus Protestants, fundamentalist Protestants versus liberal Protestants. To an outsider, the grievances can seem picky. The Sikh community in Canada has been split between fundamentalists and moderates over whether tables and chairs should be removed from Sikh temples. Reform Judaism has broken explicitly with Orthodoxy and Conservatism by accepting patrilineal descent as equal to matrilineal descent as a basis for being a Jew. Moreover, Orthodox rabbis do not accept as "legitimate" marriages and conversions carried out under Reform, and often Conservative, auspices. (No Reform or Conservative rabbi would dare challenge the Jewish status of an Orthodox convert – at least not yet.) Because of intermarriage, non-Orthodox conversion, and the large numbers of mixed marriages and "Jews by choice," there are now in Canada tens of thousands of Jews who are not recognized by the Orthodox.

The Orthodox position derives support from Israel, where issues of marriage and family status for Jews are administered by the official rabbinate, which is resolutely Orthodox. (Christians and Moslems in

Israel are also governed by their respective religious bodies.) Reform and Conservative rabbis, while often devoted to Israel, are second-class clerics. Given that 80 per cent of the population of Canada – and Israel – is non-Orthodox, the possibilities for friction are large. One rabbi argued to me that the rising intermarriage rates were decisive in increasing the tensions. Another pointed out that some of the tensions have always been there, but have been exacerbated by polarization in Israeli politics. Most Orthodox rabbis tend to be pro-Likud, while more of the non-Orthodox tend towards Labour. The assassination of Israeli prime minister Yitzhak Rabin in 1995 was a flashpoint in several Canadian Jewish communities. Harsh accusations were directed by both the right and the left, Orthodox and non-Orthodox. For example, Montreal Reconstructionist Rabbi Ron Aigen was quoted in the *Gazette* as claiming that the Orthodox rabbinate in Israel had "blood on their hands." Many in the Orthodox community were outraged. But the anger did not erupt. Orthodox and militant Zionist Rabbi Reuben Poupko defended Aigen and did not isolate him.[40]

The United States has had it much worse. The kind of invective common in New York or Jerusalem is not really prevalent in Canada. As Toronto Rabbi Moshe Shulman explains, the non-Orthodox in Canada are more traditional than in the United States, so there is more crossover and less tension.[41] Tensions are lower, but still present. A liberal rabbi recounted how in the early 1980s, two Orthodox rabbis, including one with whom he had been very friendly, refused to join him to sit on a conversion Beth Din. He was also dismayed to find that Orthodox *mohels* refused to circumcise children of some of his converts.

It is crucial to realize that the dangers of Jewish disunity are overblown. For the vast majority of Jews, the doctrinal differences that define these conflicts do not intrude on their daily lives. Most Jews voluntarily and happily self-segregate. They are not forced to interact with Jews with whom they disagree. Jews go to synagogue, educate and raise their children, and socialize with Jews who are like them or with whom they get along. In the view of Reform Rabbi John Moscowitz, the segregation is not complete, and socially, friendships exist between the Orthodox and the non-Orthodox. Conservative Rabbi Baruch Frydman-Kohl notes that while some Jews do live separately in terms of public religiosity, that is not the whole story. At the personal level, people discover commonalities when meeting in business or at social gatherings. He senses that many in Toronto's Modern Orthodox community are open to more public relationships with the non-Orthodox.[42] Nevertheless, it is unpleasant when Reform or Orthodox Jewish leaders in North America or Israel are quoted in the *Canadian Jewish News* making nasty remarks about each other. But these displays of intolerance really have little impact. Orthodox Jews marry, for the most part, other Orthodox Jews. This is even truer for the ultra-Orthodox. And what if an Orthodox and non-Orthodox Jew fall in love? The thing resolves itself one way or another. If the family of the Orthodox Jew is not satisfied, then perhaps, to keep the peace, the other partner will embrace Orthodoxy with an Orthodox conversion if needed. If not, maybe the Orthodox family will grudgingly accommodate themselves to the marriage, which may produce a blended religious lifestyle sometimes called Conservadox. Or the lovers will decide not to marry. Or they may marry and break, at least temporarily, with one or both sets of parents. Sad, but not the end of the world. This happens often, for all sorts of reasons, to all sorts of couples. I see absolutely no evidence that cross-boundary marriages are a major social problem for North American Jews.

Anyway, the news is not all grim. Annual Simchat Torah celebrations beginning in the fall of 1998 in Montreal have been marked by a massive interdenominational communal celebration of the Torah. Modelled after a similar event in New York, several synagogues – Orthodox, Conservative, Reconstructionist, Sephardi – are invited by the Orthodox Tifereth Beth David Jerusalem to converge in the street before the shul, marching from their own *hakafot* ceremonies. Joyous circles of men and of women holding the Torah dance in front of the synagogue, and rabbis speak to the crowd on the theme of Jewish unity. At a recent *Yom Ha'Shoah* community memorial held at an Orthodox synagogue, the opening remarks were delivered by Reconstructionist rabbi Ron Aigen. He also served at one point as the president of the Board of Jewish Ministers.

But that is Montreal. To risk an unfair generalization, it seems tensions among the denominations are greater in Toronto. One Toronto scholar reported that a multidenominational Simchat Torah rally could not take place there: "The Orthodox would not play ball, the Reform would find it unseemly to dance in the street, the Conservatives would worry that the insurance on the Torahs would not permit them being in the street. And whoever was planning the event would forget to invite the Reconstructionists." In Toronto, critics tend to lump the Orthodox into the same camp as the ultra-Orthodox. I have found it common to hear non-Orthodox Jews in Toronto lament the increasing power of the "black hats" with a venom not found in Montreal. (Montreal also never had the precise counterpart of the Reichmann family. Their giving was directed mainly at the ultra-Orthodox.) Why the difference? In part, it is because of the differing natures of Orthodoxy in the two communities. One Orthodox rabbi claims that in Toronto the Orthodox congregations are more homogeneous, with more members who are personally very observant. In Montreal, Orthodox congregations are more eclectic; they are at best institutionally Orthodox. Members join for traditional familial reasons, because their parents were members, rather than for any deep personal Orthodox convictions. The Montreal Orthodox rabbinate has no choice but to act accordingly, and thus more tolerantly. In the words of another rabbi, Toronto's dynamics are like those of Baltimore and Cleveland, while Montreal's are like those of Boston and more liberal parts of New York Orthodoxy. In Montreal, the Orthodox rabbis are more focused on community and communal solidarity, while in Toronto it has fallen to Conservative and Reform rabbis to play larger roles. Yet even in polarized Toronto, boundaries are crossed. In late January 2001, thousands of Jews rallied on behalf of a united Jerusalem, addressed by an Orthodox, Conservative, and Reform rabbi.

None of the denominations is homogeneous, and the same applies to their rabbis. For example, in Montreal the Orthodox rabbis established a new Orthodox *Beth Din*, but two of the more liberal Orthodox rabbis are not part of it, and do not perform conversions. Another Canadian Orthodox rabbi describes a nuanced approach to his faith. He endorses an "uncompromising" commitment to *halacha*. Yet he laments the frequent description of Orthodoxy as "right-wing." His view of Orthodoxy entails no ghetto walls, no closure from the outside world. He concedes that when a Jew attends a Reform or Conservative service, it is a "positive Jewish experience." It is hard to imagine ultra-Orthodox rabbis and even many Orthodox rabbis, whether in North America or in Israel, agreeing. There are also internal divisions within liberal ranks, such as Reform and Reconstructionism. Some rabbis will perform mixed marriages, others will not. Some will refuse to officiate at a bar mitzvah ceremony, regardless of which parent is Jewish, if told by a mixed married couple that their child "is being raised in both religions." Some liberal rabbis across Canada do not mind.

A major area of controversy has been the status of women and, to a lesser extent, gays and lesbians. The Reform and Reconstructionist denominations have achieved complete gender equality, and some liberal Conservative congregations are edging closer. In these congregations, seating is mixed, women are counted in the minyan and are becoming rabbis, cantors, and synagogue presidents. The text of prayers has also been amended to avoid sexist language and to omit certain phrases or prayers which might offend women. An example is the deletion of an offending morning benediction in which men bless God for His not creating them women. Another is the inclusion of Sarah, Rebecca, Rachel, and Leah, along with Abraham, Isaac, and Jacob, in the major prayer, the *shmoneh esrei*.

Some Orthodox Jewish women are engaged in struggles, too, though the parameters are far different. Orthodox inequalities are pronounced. We have already discussed the problem of granting a *get*, or divorce decree. There is no Orthodox constituency for the ordination of women, or for mixed seating, or indeed for full gender equality as usually understood. Men and women occupy different spheres, separate but equal. A few Orthodox women have experimented with all-women services in which they fulfil the various functions, including the chanting the Torah portion, permissible if no men are around. The tensions within Orthodoxy will increase as more and more Jewish women pursue higher-level Jewish studies, including Talmud. For the moment, however, gender conflict is greatest in the Conservative movement, with its intermediate position. There, the debate is not yet settled. Some Conservative congregations have mixed seating; others do not. In this area, the Canadian Jewish response is usually influenced by developments in

American rabbinical seminaries, but with a time lag.[43] I suspect that the Conservative movement will eventually adopt the Reform model of complete equality.

The religious community has avoided confronting homosexuality. The first gay synagogue was organized in Los Angeles in 1972, and since then an estimated twenty gay congregations have been established in North America.[44] There is at least one such congregation active in Toronto. Individual gay and lesbian Jews belong to all types of congregations, but it is only among Reform or Reconstructionist Jews that issues like the status of gay Jews, gay couples, or gay rabbis are discussed. The legitimacy of ordaining homosexual rabbis was established by the Reform's Central Conference of Reform Rabbis in 1990. Predictably, more traditional Reform leaders felt the movement had gone too far, while more militant gay and lesbian rabbis felt it had not gone far enough.[45] In March 2000, the Reform movement declared that Reform rabbis, if they desired, could officiate at homosexual unions.

As these examples indicate, nowhere are Jewish pluralism and conflict more evident than in the religious arena. But the impact of these tensions on daily life is minimal. Moreover, they are signs of adaptation, vitality, and creativity.

STICKS, STONES, AND SOCIAL RELATIONS

The Evolving Forms of Anti-Semitism

"Come, let us deal wisely with them; lest they multiply, and it come to pass, that, when there befalleth us any war, they also join themselves unto our enemies, and fight against us, and get them up out of the land."

– Exodus 1:10

"An anti-Semite is someone who hates Jews more than is really necessary."

– Anonymous

In my McGill University course on the Sociology of North American Jewry, I routinely ask my Jewish students how many of them have been victimized by anti-Semitism. Most say they have. I then ask for details. Most often they report anti-Semitic graffiti in the bathrooms, or hearing upsetting JAP jokes. A student once told of a grade-school teacher who had made an explicitly anti-Semitic remark. When I asked what happened, the student replied that she told her parents, who then told the school administration, who then reprimanded the teacher. End of story. Almost none of the students had been beaten up, and none had been given a lower grade in school, been denied a job or paid lower wages, been denied accommodation or service, or had their property vandalized or defaced. But most of them felt sincerely that they had been victimized. And who could argue?

I personally have never experienced serious anti-Semitism, any episode in which I was directly victimized. I was never assaulted by anti-Semites on the street, even as a kid, though there I was lucky. As a teenager I took a summer job in a hardware store in the French East End of Montreal. I was the only Jewish or English worker in the place. After a few days, I noticed another employee was yelling in my direction across the store, "Hey, rabbi, rabbi!" This was the first time I had encountered racial taunting. For days I wondered how to respond – the fellow was older and bigger than I was. Luckily, a few days later, I realized he had been calling out to his friend at the other end of the store. The friend's name was Robert, which in French slang or *joual* came close to "rabbi" . . .

Almost every adult non-Jew I have encountered professionally and socially has been, in my view, either neutral – often curious – or philo-Semitic. Most older Canadian Jews will tell a far different story, usually about past slights, the Jewish equivalent of the rude Anglo saleslady in Eaton's forty years ago telling francophones to "speak white." Obviously, I, like most Jews, do not hang out with anti-Semites. University faculties today are not crawling with bigots, despite the fears of some activists in the antiracist movement. Perhaps my view is distorted by my exposure, through my family and my academic studies, to the issues of the Holocaust. My bar may be set too high. I know the real thing. Understanding anti-Semitism in Canada means understanding the paradoxical relation between two divergent trends. On the one hand, compared with earlier periods of Canadian history (and certainly by comparison with most Western societies), anti-Semitism in Canada today is not a major problem. By conventional measures it is in decline. On the other hand, the anti-Semitism which does remain, and the new forms which have emerged, are all the more disturbing and difficult to overcome.

If this book were written in the 1950s, this chapter would be as large as several others combined, and would be at the front of the book. Simply put, anti-Semitism was the dominant issue of Canadian Jewish life. Jews in Canada, and indeed in the United States, were part of a still profoundly marginal and insecure community. Intermarriage and assimilation were not recognized, by Jews and Jewish institutions, as threats; non-Jews were just not eager to marry Jews. The key issue facing Jews in their private and public lives was discrimination, in its many forms. Quotas, formal and informal, still operated in universities and corporate boardrooms. An effective legal structure dealing with human rights, non-discrimination, and expressions of hate did not exist. Negative and demeaning stereotypes about Jews were widespread in all segments of the Canadian public. Jews faced discrimination in employment, in accommodation, and in housing. Jewish children in public schools were usually expected to take part in all manner of Christian rituals and prayer. There were no human rights acts or human rights commissions, no hate literature laws, no constitutional protections. Jewish Holocaust survivors still had to overcome resistance to enter Canada after the war.[1]

Up to the 1950s, Jews lived in a profoundly Jewish solitude, for reasons of choice and reasons of exclusion. There was still an unease in informal social interactions, quite apart from anti-Semitism. Jews were relatively uncomfortable with non-Jews, and vice versa. Yet during the very period when anti-Semitism was a real force in Canadian society, Jews were breaking out of the poverty and marginality of the immigrant generations. Today, while anti-Semitism is objectively in decline in Canada by most measures, it still remains alive and even thrives in the sensibilities of Canadian Jews and Canadian Jewish organizations.

Throughout most of the twentieth century, the fledgling social scientific study of Jews in North America focused on anti-Semitism and inter-group relations. This paralleled the preoccupation of postwar scholars working in the more general area of prejudice and racism. It was anti-Semitism that made Jews interesting. The landmark study *The Authoritarian Personality*, published in 1950, looked at causes of anti-Semitism and fascism. Other general American studies of prejudice in the 1950s dealt equally with anti-black racism and anti-Semitism within a broader framework.[2] In addition, several major studies focusing directly on anti-Semitism were published in the 1960s and 1970s.[3] The first major research projects on American Jewish life in general included studies of social relations, exclusion, and by extension subtle forms of anti-Semitism. There was no concern with Jewish identity or culture. This dates back to the pioneering sociological study of Chicago Jews by Louis Wirth, *The Ghetto*, first published in 1926. Later research in the 1950s and 1960s focused on Jewish life on the new post-war suburban frontier or in the "gilded ghetto" far from immigrant Jewish neighbourhoods. These American studies did not focus on glaring or violent anti-Semitism, but on day-to-day interactions between Jews and their non-Jewish neighbours.[4] In Canada, the pioneering study of Forest Hill in Toronto, *Crestwood Heights* by John Seeley and associates, included sections describing Jewish interactions with the then-majority non-Jewish populations. Canadian Jews in the 1950s played down their Jewish identity, still insecure in their new-found middle-class suburban status. Even in the 1970s, discussions of Canadian Jewish life would stress the role of group boundaries, separating Jews from non-Jews.[5] Despite the general improvement in social conditions for Canadian Jews in recent decades, anti-Semitism remains a defining feature of the Canadian Jewish consciousness. The most successful book ever written on a Canadian Jewish topic was *None Is Too Many*, exploring the anti-Semitism which provided the context of Canada's closed-door policy toward Jewish refugees before and during the Second World War.[6]

In many ways, perceptions of anti-Semitism today are determined by memories and received wisdoms of the past. Things were indeed much worse for Jews two generations ago, and earlier. But how bad were they? The Canadian experience, both past and present, has been relatively benign for Jews. Some see the glass as half full, others as half empty. But by any comparative and historical yardstick, Canadian Jews have historically *not* suffered an enormous degree of anti-Semitism. There have been no forced conversions, no expulsions, no pogroms, no crematoria, no Nuremberg Laws, not even a Dreyfus affair and related organized anti-Semitism. No political party or movement of any consequence has had Jewish issues as a central plank. There was no historic legacy of a "Jewish problem" crying out for a political solution, final or otherwise, in North America. The anti-Semitism of Social Credit in Alberta, like that of American populism, remained on the fringe geographically and politically. In Quebec and Ontario, both elite and populist anti-Semitism were the norm, in attitudes if not behaviours. But Jews were never the absolute pariahs as they were in Europe and occasionally in Arab countries. French–English polarization and the victimization of First Nations and non-white minorities assured Jews a margin of acceptability and buffered the hatred. It is not even clear that individual Canadian Jews have been murdered by anti-Semites, as happened in the United States in celebrated cases like the 1915 lynching of Leo Frank.

After the 1950s, the American appetite for traditional public and private expressions of anti-Semitism shrank even further, though they may now be taking new forms, as we shall see.[7] There has been a similar slow but steady improvement in Canada. Not only is discrimination in the public sphere now against the law, but the prevalence of stereotypes and prejudice has declined as well. Declined, but certainly not disappeared. It is important to recognize the distance travelled by Canadian Jews in their struggles against anti-Semitism and discrimination. But it is also important to recognize that anti-Semitism persists among certain fringe elements of the far right, notably those involved in Holocaust denial. In addition, it remains present as background contextual noise, as prejudice, the holding and asserting of negative stereotypes, and residual discomfort in social interactions. And as we observed in Chapter 9, on politics, it may be manifested as insensitivity to Jewish interests, which leads to policies that can be harmful to Jews, notably regarding Israel.

There are different ways of defining and measuring anti-Semitism. It is important to get a sense of the spectrum of meanings. Some anti-Semitism is explicitly mandated in, or permitted by, legislation, or so interpreted by courts. The Canadian Constitution, which includes the British North America Act, itself contains a form of legal discrimination against Jews, in the area of educational rights. Protestants and Catholics enjoy educational rights unavailable to Jews and other religious minorities. For a long time anti-Semitism was not even illegal in

Canada. It was not uncommon in the 1930s for resorts, employers, and landlords to discriminate openly against Jews. Universities and hospitals were more subtle, but as effective. A CJC study in 1934 uncovered such extensive anti-Semitism, most of it relatively legal, that the report was never released lest it prove demoralizing to Canadian Jews and help legitimate anti-Semitic expressions.[8]

But by and large, the force of law in Canada today protects Jews and other minorities from discrimination.[9] The role of government has shifted away from one of oppression of Jews and other minorities – think of the 1930s immigration restrictions or the Chinese head tax. The shift took place in stages. From the post-war period to the 1960s, government adopted a neutral posture, not actively discriminating but also not rigorously proscribing discrimination. By the 1960s, we see a move toward a new role of government, as protector of minorities. This is typified by the adoption of the non-discriminatory immigration points system and the enactment of human rights legislation at provincial and federal levels. Nevertheless, as we have already seen, there remain clear cases where law, or the interpretation of law, can harm Jewish interests. These often deal with "reasonable accommodation." Should universities cancel classes or tests on Jewish holidays? Well-meaning court decisions may accidentally become anti-Semitic state actions.

Everyday anti-Semitism consists of acts by individual Canadians or institutions which may or may not be illegal but which do harm Jews. Some of these acts are motivated by anti-Jewish feeling, like an employer choosing not to hire a Jew. Others may simply have harmful consequences, like scheduling examinations on Passover. (Note the inadvertent scheduling of exams on Passover, for example, or a refusal to reschedule for Jewish students, could be described as systemic anti-Semitism; a subsequent court challenge that failed might be considered legal or state-sponsored anti-Semitism.)

Overt expressions of anti-Semitism come in many forms. One type are acts of serious violence, which are rare, or the more common defacement of property or general vandalism. Another type is overt discrimination in employment or in any other public domain. This, too, is rare, or at least ineffectual, given that Canadian Jews are doing well economically. This form of discrimination can be discovered by documenting socio-economic inequalities in official income statistics, as well as in field studies of discrimination, or by looking at cases reported to human rights commissions. These cases include harassment as well as explicit acts such as firing, denying a promotion, or paying unequal salaries. All this evidence, while it demonstrates significant discrimination against non-whites, reveals essentially no anti-Semitism.

Another type of anti-Semitism is attitudinal. This is often hidden. Most anti-Semites do not act out their prejudices, or even express them in public (although they may express them to selected friends and neighbours), because that is politically incorrect or because they risk some sort of sanction. We know from surveys that many Canadians hold negative attitudes about Jews. Some of these attitudes are clearly vicious, while others are stereotypes ranging from benign to misinformed. These prejudices do not translate into real discrimination and real inequality except in rare and isolated cases. The effects of these attitudes are sometimes seen in what social scientists call social distance, which measures the propensity of non-Jews to interact socially with Jews. But social distance is not necessarily what it seems. Often it is Jews who choose to keep their distance, reflecting simple preferences or a fear that too much intimate socializing will lead to assimilation or intermarriage.

And there is more. Studies of racism in Canada or elsewhere almost never focus on the attitudes of minorities toward majorities. This is certainly true regarding Jews. Many Jews hold negative stereotypes about non-Jews, and they are just as demeaning. The same is true for blacks and Asians, who may hold negative views about whites or Europeans. And many of these border on racism. The belief that only the powerful can be racist is semantic hocus-pocus. Though minority groups lack the power to implement their racist views, intergroup relations have increasingly become a two-way street. It is not clear how many Jews believe, for example, that every non-Jew is a potential anti-Semite. Or that non-Jews drink too much, or have different cultural styles. But some do. As a result, they may be happy to socialize just with other Jews.

Finally, anti-Semitism can permeate high culture and popular culture. Historically, this began as anti-Judaism, and would include the theological conviction that Jews were Christ-killers, or that Judaism posed a threat to Christianity. Today it is more subtle, like the use of terms such as "Christian morality" rather than "Judeo-Christian." Beyond that, it includes demeaning images of Jews in literature or intellectual discourse or daily language, or the absence of Jews or Jewish themes in Canadian cultural production. The images of Shylock, or of rapacious Jewish businessmen, or the use of "Jew" as a verb, are well-known examples. This type of cultural anti-Semitism was far more prevalent in the past, in both English and French Canada. If it exists today, it must contend with the unexpected spread of a general tolerance and even with philo-Semitism, in which others find Jews and Jewish culture exotic and interesting. Consider the increasing fascination with the Holocaust on the part of many sympathetic non-Jews. In general, curiosity and admiration are replacing fear and dislike. Which is just fine.

THE HISTORICAL BACKGROUND

Anti-Semitism in Canada dates back to before Confederation. It was found among both the French and English communities, and was largely religious in character. The conflict over the election in 1807 of Ezekiel Hart to the Legislative Assembly of Lower Canada included elements of anti-Semitism, though scholars debate whether it was his Jewishness or his affinity with the English which was decisive. Indeed, a theological anti-Semitism existed throughout the pre-Confederation era, even in the near absence of Jews.[10] In French Canada, a steady stream of anti-Semitic thought was present, some homegrown and some imported from France. The Dreyfus case galvanized French and Catholic anti-Semitism in Canada around the turn of the century. Many French Catholic publications and personalities supported anti-Dreyfusard sentiments. Some newspapers published the anti-Semitic tracts of Edouard Drumont. A persistent drumbeat of anti-Semitism in Quebec to 1914, which would eventually grow louder, included not only theological prejudice, but acts of street vandalism as well.[11]

In English Canada, an example of the prevailing anti-Semitism can be gleaned from the credit-rating reports of R. G. Dun and Company in the mid-1800s, which are replete with derogatory comments and stereotypes about Jews and Jewish businessmen.[12] Theological anti-Semitism was expressed in evangelical and missionary activity aimed at converting Jews in Canada, and supporting such efforts elsewhere.[13] English Canada also developed a brand of "intellectual" anti-Semitism, typified by the writings of Goldwin Smith in the late nineteenth century. Smith, a scholar and writer with wide-ranging interests, was a classic liberal on issues such as separation of church and state. Yet his writings, beginning in the 1870s, contain many anti-Semitic thoughts and references. He criticized Judaism as a tribal religion, condemned the alleged Jewish materialism, and raised the canard of Jewish dual loyalty. Smith, who influenced Vincent Massey and Mackenzie King among others, helped set the stage for twentieth-century anti-Semitic prejudice while giving such views a gloss of respectability.[14] Anglo anti-Semitism of this type helped feed into discrimination at Canadian universities. Jewish enrollment at McGill declined between 1925 and 1935 from 25 to 12 per cent of the student population.[15] Anti-Semitism was less prevalent in the Canadian West at the turn of the century, due in part to the absence of entrenched upper-class Anglo elites in an essentially polyglot and immigrant pioneering society. Yet anti-Semitism did exist, often finding expression in newspaper treatments of Jewish issues. Even though the Western Canadian press was, for example, supportive of the Dreyfusards in France, some papers would occasionally publish latently anti-Semitic articles and did not attack anti-Semitic ideas per se.[16]

Canadian anti-Semitism reached its peak in the 1930s. Explicit fascist organizations existed in both English and French Canada. In English Canada, anti-Semitism fed on a base of Anglo-Saxon nativism and unemployment. The 1930s saw the development of swastika clubs and associations. Indeed, the swastika figured in the largest Jewish–Gentile riot in Canadian history, which broke out in 1933 in Toronto's Christie Pits after a baseball game between a largely Jewish team and an Anglo-Saxon club.[17] The formation of a Swastika Club at Balmy Beach that year had been followed by sporadic clashes between supporters and young Jews.[18] In Christie Pits, thousands of combatants were involved. The event traumatized Toronto Jews at the time, and old-timers still recall the riot in most dramatic, perhaps embellished, terms. But there was no loss of life and few serious injuries. As race riots go, it was, thankfully, not a big deal.

Movements such as the Canadian Union of Fascists took root in Ontario and Western Canada, inspired by Oswald Mosely's British Union of Fascists. Adrien Arcand, a Quebec fascist and anti-Semite, also extended his activities into Ontario. A national fascist convention in 1938 attracted an estimated 1,500–2,500 participants, but their ulti-mate success was limited.[19] Indeed, among English Protestants in Canada, there was consistent opposition to the various anti-Semitic policies of the Third Reich. This opposition on the part of the Protestant clergy was welcome to Jews, though perhaps not as vocif-erous as it could have been.[20]

In Quebec, the situation was more serious. Opposition to con-scription helped fuel traditional anti-Semitic currents, and vice versa. Moreover, in the inter-war period, French nationalism embraced three themes, all of which fed anti-Semitism: re-francization, with Jews being identified with the English; promoting French entrepreneurs through the "achat chez nous" movement, which involved boycotting Jewish firms; and anti-immigration sentiment.[21] The conservative Catholic Church in Quebec opposed liberal and radical tendencies, identified with Jews, at home and abroad.[22] Father Lionel Groulx expressed sympathies with certain anti-Semitic currents as well as fascist governments, though there is debate among scholars as to the degree and influence of his anti-Semitism. Even more pronounced was the steady anti-Semitism in articles, letters, and columns published in the influential *Le Devoir*.[23] In comparison to the English press, or to the Protestant churches, the silence from mainstream Quebec circles about the defence of European Jews or anti-Semitism generally was marked.[24] In 1934, Dr. Samuel Rabinovitch, a top graduate from the Université de Montréal's medical school, was awarded an internship at Montreal's Notre Dame Hospital. In protest, all of his fellow non-Jewish interns walked out, soon joined by interns in other Catholic hospitals. Eventually, the doctor resigned his appointment. More telling, the interns' strike enjoyed support from all sectors of Quebec society, including *Le Devoir*.[25]

Adrien Arcand formed his National Social Christian Party on a Nazi model in 1934. His brand of anti-Semitism influenced popular French-language newspapers like *Le Patriote* and *Le Goglu*. Moreover, the conservative and nationalist Quebec government of Maurice Duplessis offered an environment in which more extreme forms of anti-Semitism could thrive. For example, the unopposed passage of the Padlock Law in 1937 enabled the government to close any establishment used to propagate communism but ignored fascist and anti-Semitic organizations.[26] To be sure, Arcand's movement numbered only in the hundreds, not the thousands. It petered out during the course of the war, though elements of anti-Semitism animated the Bloc Populaire and the anti-conscription movements. But the bald fact that over 80 per cent of Quebec voters, and more among francophones, rejected the possibility of conscription in the referendum in the spring of 1942 is revealing. Quebec intellectuals have yet to have an honest confrontation with that vote, and indeed with that period. Esther Delisle's second book (published in 1998) dealing with the anti-Semitism and Nazi sympathizers in the post-war period, was, like her first, greeted with a blend of silence and contempt.[27] The contrast with the eager *mea culpa*s and enthusiastic reception in English Canada of Irving Abella and Harold Troper's *None Is Too Many* is stark.

While organized anti-Semitism was weaker in Western Canada, there was some among immigrant German communities, most notably Mennonites.[28] Anti-Semitism in the West also drew some strength from Social Credit and Prairie populism, which attacked the influence of Eastern bankers, presumably Jewish, whose high interest rates penalized Western farmers. Social Credit premier William Aberhart of Alberta did not openly espouse anti-Semitic views, unlike the British founder of Social Credit, Major Douglas. But Norman Jacques, Social Credit MP from 1935 to 1949, would routinely rail in the Commons against "the international financial conspiracy." Ernest Manning, father of Reform Party founder Preston, fought the Douglasite anti-Semitic tendencies in the party in the 1940s.[29]

After the war, organized political anti-Semitism was largely discredited. But there remained a strong residue of popular anti-Semitic sentiment. A national survey at the end of the war found that most

Canadians ranked Jews as among the least desirable of possible immigrants to the country. But slowly, over the decades, as educational levels rose and as the notion of human rights took root in the culture, anti-Semitism became less acceptable as both private attitude and public expression.

THE CONTENT OF EXTREME ANTI-SEMITISM

There is a myriad of extreme right-wing groups in Canada who espouse elements of fundamentalist Christianity, anti-Semitism, anti-communism, and racism. Among the better known are the Western Guard, the Ku Klux Klan, the Heritage Front, and various skinhead movements.[30] Most of the organizations are small and unimportant. But some are not. Anti-Semitism, as described below, is purveyed regularly by extremist fringe groups through magazines and books, which are read devotedly by followers. When police seize arms caches from these groups, they usually find white supremacist and anti-Semitic literature close by.

The content of explicit anti-Semitism has always been of four types. Religious anti-Semitism feeds on the hoary Christ-killer theme. The Jewish refusal to accept Christ stands as a permanent challenge to Christianity. Evangelical Christians continue to call routinely for the conversion of the Jews, as in the *Globe and Mail* ad described earlier. The modern version of religious anti-Semitism is a far cry from the gross religious calumnies common in the past, like blood libels or linkage of Jews with the devil or Antichrist. Jews for Jesus, active in several Canadian cities, would be horrified to be accused of any ill will towards Jews. They speak fondly of Jews, of Judaism, and of Israel; they simply want Jews to accept a better, a more complete alternative. But they are a serious problem, and have targeted Russian Jews whose Jewish learning and identity are weak. The Jewish community has been lobbying Bell Canada to exclude the institutions of Jews for Jesus from the telephone directory's listing of synagogues. Some years ago, I decided to explore the movement. I wrote a letter to a Canadian representative, claiming I was a Jew who was having doubts about my faith. I received back some pamphlets and a detailed, personalized three-page, single-spaced letter urging me to make contact. I was impressed with their apparent sincerity –

which makes their efforts all the more dangerous – and a genuine concern. But make no mistake, the attempt to get Jews to abandon their "misguided" religious beliefs is religious anti-Semitism.

A second type is racist anti-Semitism, rooted in biology, not belief. According to this racism, Jews are either non-human or sub-human, or at the very least biologically distinct, a different race from Aryans or other Caucasians. Racist anti-Semitism reached its zenith in Nazi films, writings, and propaganda, in which Jews were described as parasites and depicted as mice. Accordingly, the supposedly innate Jewish inclination toward usury or crime was a biological trait. Neither political emancipation nor religious conversion would solve the biological problem. Only extermination, or genocide, would suffice. The medieval myth of the Jews as the non-human Devil, with horns, linked both themes.

There are also two types of political or economic anti-Semitism. Right-wing anti-Semitism opposes Jews because they are either liberal or socialist or communist. Jews are the ultimate modernizers and urbanites, challengers of the old order, opposed to monarchs and aristocrats and even to liberal capitalists. The image of the Jew as Bolshevik subversive epitomizes the fears of right-wing anti-Semites. More recently, Jews tend to be identified with detested liberal or progressive positions – pro-choice, pro-sex education, pro-gay rights, earning the enmity of the religious right. Left-wing anti-Semitism naturally takes the opposite tack. It opposes Jews because they are seen as the arch-capitalists, greedy exploiters of the working class, devoted to moneymaking and material pursuits. The image of Rothschild, of Jewish bankers and financiers, captures its essence. This strain goes back again to the Middle Ages, when the image of the Jew as usurer or moneylender gained currency. It had a populist variant found in anti-Semitism of Ukrainian peasants in the seventeenth century and among American inner-city blacks as well as French Canadians in the twentieth century. In all these cases, Jews were assumed to hold the levers of power, when in fact they did not, compared to dominant Anglo-Protestant corporate elites. It has another variant which sees Judaism, like other religions, as socially conservative on a host of issues. And yet another attacks Zionism as reactionary nationalism, and Israel and her Jewish supporters as an extension of Western imperialism aimed at oppressing Arabs. Marx himself used satire and invective to establish the link between Jews and capitalism.

How could Jews be, at the same time, a religious group and a racial group, communists and capitalists, freethinkers and ultra-Orthodox? How do all these contradictory representations of Jews hang together in the minds of serious anti-Semites? The answer is conspiracy theory. The myth of a Jewish conspiracy resolves all contradictions. All types of Jews are thus part of one overarching conspiracy – aided by Jewish control of the media – aimed at world domination and the further-ance of Jewish power.[31] Hitler's *Mein Kampf*, in its section dealing with the Jews, contains elements of all four types of anti-Semitism, as well as a section on the international Jewish conspiracy. A sampling:

Religious anti-Semitism: "His [Jewish] spirit is inwardly as alien to true Christianity as his nature two thousand years previous was to the great founder of the new doctrine. . . . Christ was nailed to the cross while our present day party Christians debase themselves to begging for Jewish votes."[32]

Racial anti-Semitism: "The mightiest counterpart to the Aryan is represented by the Jew." Jews are a "typical parasite" and a "noxious bacillus." "The Jew has always been a people with def-inite racial characteristics and never a religion."[33]

Right-wing anti-Semitism: "All at once the Jew becomes liberal and begins to rave about the necessary progress of mankind. . . . From now on the worker has no other task but to fight for the future of the Jewish people."[34]

Left-wing anti-Semitism: "He [the Jew] begins to lend money as always at usurious interest. . . . Finance and commerce have become his complete monopoly."[35]

The role of the press in concealing the international Jewish conspiracy: "Freemasonry is joined by a second weapon in the service of the Jews: the press. . . . To what extent the whole exis-tence of this people is based on a continuous lie is shown

incomparably by the Protocols of the Elders of Zion so infii-
nitely hated by the Jews. They are based on a forgery, the
Frankfurter Zeitung moans and screams once every week;
the best proof they are authentic."[36]

Such vicious expressions of hate did not die with Hitler. Extremist
anti-Semitism in Canada today downplays (but does not ignore) the
religious and racial theme, but emphasizes elements of the left- and
right-wing positions, and, of course, the linchpin, conspiracy theory.
The reason is that anti-Semites seek some degree of plausibility, and
political and economic arguments seem more likely to be supported
by "facts" and half-truths than debates about religious doctrine or
Jews as a race. Conspiracy theories in general have gained a certain
degree of acceptance, particularly after the John F. Kennedy assassination, and as historical revisionism has come into fashion. Thus, John
Ross Taylor, a leader of the Western Guard, believed that in the 1970s
Canada had been embroiled in a secret civil war between Anglo
Freemasons and Jewish Freemasons. The latter were supported by
Pierre Trudeau, René Lévesque, France, and Russia. To take another
example, veteran Canadian right-wing extremist Ron Gostick argued
he was not anti-Semitic but just opposed to political Zionism.
Nevertheless he has written that the U.S. Supreme Court's 1954 school
desegregation decision was a Jewish plot, that the Anti-Defamation
League promotes hate and bigotry, that Anne Frank's diary is a fraud,
and that Jews themselves and communists are behind increases in
anti-Semitic incidents.[37] An essay written by one of Jim Keegstra's students (see below) brings the message home clearly: "The Jews since 1976
have financed and supported the spread of Communism because it is
a step toward what they must feel is heaven. Their heaven would be a
New World Order under a One World Government. This government,
of course, would be led by these cutthroats themselves."[38]

HATE SPEECH, FREE SPEECH

The expression of direct or indirect anti-Semitism is often defended
by claims of freedom of speech. The case of British Columbia colum-
nist Doug Collins is revealing. For years, Collins' column in the *North*

Shore News had infuriated Jews, among others. A column he wrote on March 9, 1994, went too far for one irate Jewish reader, who took action against Collins under the British Columbia Human Rights Act. The relevant section of the act prohibits publication of material which is "likely to expose a person or a group or class of persons to hatred or contempt because of the race, colour, ancestry, place of origin, religion, marital status, family status, physical or mental disability, sex, sexual orientation, or age" of that person or group or class.

The column in question dealt with the movie *Schindler's List*, and was entitled "Hollywood Propaganda." The column is well-written, full of sarcasm and invective, designed to push Jewish buttons while promoting a cynical distrust of Jews. It is also an unambiguous piece of Holocaust denial. Both the tone and thrust of the column are captured by Collins's use of the term "Swindler's List" to describe the movie. The column cleverly compares movies like *Schindler's List* to the work of Goebbels. It calls the figure of six million Jews who died "nonsense." It focuses on Jewish producers wanting to "cash in" on the Holocaust, reviving the image of the money-crazed Jewish capitalist. Most of all, the column develops the idea of a conspiratorial Jewish-controlled Hollywood that deliberately disseminates Holocaust-related films that defame Germans while serving the needs of Jews and Israel.

I served as an expert witness in this case for the Attorney General of British Columbia, to make the point that hate speech can harm its targets and indeed society as a whole. Let me be clear. I am not one of those anti-racists who advocates much-greater use of hate speech laws. I take seriously the concerns of civil libertarians and supporters of free speech. The laws should be used sparingly; if everything is racism or genocide or hate speech, then nothing is. Luckily, there is no evidence in Canada that such laws at the provincial level or in the Canadian Criminal Code have been abused and overused, leading to a chilling of speech. The thought police do not reign supreme. But the Collins column was a clear example of Holocaust denial and hate speech. If this column was not hate speech, then nothing would be hate speech.

The Collins column is best understood in its socio-cultural context. The content of most overt anti-Semitism in Canada today relies on the recurring myth of an international Jewish or Zionist conspiracy, dating back to the Protocols of the Elders of Zion. A potent new element in the arsenal of anti-Semites is Holocaust denial in its many forms. This is promulgated under the guise of free speech or academic freedom or the value of a relativistic approach to the search for truth.[39] In fact, one Canadian survey in 1985 found that only 50 per cent of Canadians agreed that about six million Jews were killed in the Holocaust. Moreover, about 16 per cent claimed that the Holocaust was "partly" the fault of Jews themselves.[40] Such views do not always represent direct expressions of anti-Semitism; they can flow from simple ignorance. But they do illustrate that the onslaught of Holocaust revisionism has caused some skepticism and can find fertile ground in which to grow. Indeed, attitudes about the Holocaust, notably expressing doubt about received wisdoms, are often correlated with anti-Semitic views. Canadians who felt that Jews were "too powerful" were more likely to blame the Holocaust on its victims and to say the estimate of six million was too high.[41] This despite the fact that the staunchest of Holocaust deniers would deny being in any way anti-Semitic; they are simply researchers pursuing the truth.

Three Holocaust denial cases in the 1980s led to a great deal of media attention, and were precursors of the Collins case. Ernst Zündel is a German-born publisher of materials denying the Holocaust and preaching a Jewish international conspiracy for world domination. He was prosecuted under an obscure Criminal Code provision against the spreading of false news. After an original conviction, he was eventually acquitted by the Supreme Court, which found the original statute unconstitutional. During his trial, expert witnesses testified that the concentration camps were really resorts, which was duly reported in the media. But there is no evidence that such media coverage led to an increase in anti-Semitic belief.[42] As of 2001, Zündel had left Canada for the United States. But he continues to produce hate literature for distribution throughout the world, and an Ontario Human Rights Tribunal is investigating his Web site.

Jim Keegstra was a social studies teacher in Eckville, Alberta. He was initially prosecuted in 1985 under the hate literature laws in the Criminal Code for "wilfully promoting hatred" against the Jewish people. He taught his high-school students that the events of Western history were largely the result of a deliberate international Jewish conspiracy.[43] The case eventually wound up in the Supreme Court, which upheld the constitutionality of the hate literature laws as a legitimate restriction of free speech under Section One of the Charter of Rights and Freedoms. Another recent case involved New Brunswick school teacher Malcolm Ross. Ross did not mix his views on Holocaust revisionism into his classroom work as a mathematics teacher. But his students knew about those views, which he expressed in public outside of class. Ross was prevented from returning to the classroom in a decision by a Human Rights Tribunal which was upheld by the Supreme Court.

Is there a danger in prosecuting Holocaust deniers, such that the coverage of the trials might spread their message? The answer is no. Ernst Zündel himself had welcomed his trial and the free publicity it brought him. But Canadians who followed media coverage of the Zündel trial did not have higher levels of anti-Semitism or increasing doubt about the Holocaust. My guess is that people who were clear in their views on Zündel – pro or con – were more likely to follow the issue in the media. If so, press coverage of these issues would simply reinforce pre-existing views. Moreover, journalistic reports of the contents of hate speech are very different from hate speech itself.

The tensions between the rights of free speech and hate speech laws will never be resolved; there are dangers inherent in restricting the scope of either. New cases with slightly different twists, in new jurisdictions, will arise. Hate messages on the unregulated Internet are a troubling new version. If you are curious, you can find the Zündel Web site and spend a few minutes reading the kind of semi-sophisticated Holocaust revisionism that he peddles. I've done it with my children.

As an academic, I have a reflexive appreciation of free speech, and a visceral admiration for its staunch defenders, such as Canada's Alan Borovoy, or Alan Dershowitz in the United States. The American defence of the First Amendment is clearly more eloquent and more consistent. However, there is a role for carefully crafted and judiciously applied restrictions on hate speech. There are two clashing visions of a dangerous slippery slope in the debate on free speech and hate speech.

From the civil libertarian perspective, restricting hate speech leads to greater restrictions on any controversial or provocative speech, and any speech that anyone might find offensive. Political correctness would reign supreme. But there is another slippery slope. Here, one racist column might become ten or a thousand, legitimating and exacerbating latent bigotry in the population, until it is too late. In my testimony in the Collins case, it was fairly easy to demonstrate that the material in the column conformed to classic Holocaust denial and anti-Semitism, and that such material can, and has in the past, caused harm to targeted minorities. In Canada, these are not hypothetical issues. Some anti-Asian writings in mainstream British Columbia newspapers in the first decades of the twentieth century would be classified as hate speech by current standards. They prepared the public for the wartime internment of Japanese Canadians.[44] Another grotesque example was the fixation on Jewish noses and circumcision found in *Le Devoir* in the 1930s.[45]

The initial decision in the Collins case went in support of Collins and his newspaper. It raises questions about what we consider serious anti-Semitism. The reasoning of tribunal member Nitya Iyer seemed highly complex, and to me incomprehensible. On the one hand, she found that the relevant section of the British Columbia legislation, prohibiting public speech "likely to expose" minorities to hatred, was indeed constitutional. And she found the Collins column "obviously anti-Semitic" and that it reinforced "negative stereotypes" of Jews, with a meaning that was "offensive and harmful." She found the tone of article to be "nasty" and "mean-spirited." She also agreed that Jews were "extremely vulnerable to persecution and discrimination." But despite all this, she found that the content and tone of the column, taken together, did not capture the "degree of calumny, detestation, and vilification" signified by "hatred and contempt."[46] She reasoned that the relevant statute did not restrict all anti-Semitic expression, even "all offensive and injurious anti-Semitic expression," only those that she claimed signified "extreme emotions of ill-will towards their targets." In effect her reasoning would protect clever, witty, sophisticated hate speech, while penalizing gross and grotesque hate speech which could be considered as extreme. "Jews are evil hateful scheming bastards" might violate the statute, but "Swindler's list" does not. The problem is that the witty and sophisticated Collins column is far more effective in spreading hatred of Jews.

Collins and the newspaper were ably defended by attorney David Sutherland. One of the tough questions he posed to me was about the differences between the free-speech environment in America and in Canada, where federal and provincial statutes place clear limits on free speech. If such laws protect minorities vulnerable to hate speech, like Jews, then it would stand to reason that Jews in the United States, denied those protections, would be much worse off. He wondered if that, in fact, was the case. The basic fact – and he likely knew it – is that in general American Jews do not feel threatened or worse off. I had to scramble, like a graduate student at an oral examination.

I knew that the objective comparative evidence was not conclusive. The only relevant study found no difference in levels of day-to-day anti-Semitism when it compared anti-Semitic incidents collected by B'nai Brith in the two countries from 1982 to 1992. There was a roughly ten-to-one ratio in favour of the United States, and the authors compared that to the similar ten-to-one advantage in general population by the United States.[47]

At the Collins hearing, the best I could do on this point was find different arguments to show that the position of American Jews was more precarious than their level of integration might suggest. After all, Jews in the Weimar Republic were doing very well on socio-economic measures before Hitler's rise to power. But economics is not everything. The socio-political environment affects the actual, perceived, and potential well-being of Jews. I argued that American white supremacist, racist, and extremist groups, often armed and militaristic, with links to militias and right wing organizations, are more prolific than in Canada, and more dangerous, as seen in the Oklahoma City bombing. And there was no ready analogue in Canada to Pat Buchanan and Pat Robertson as major, seemingly mainstream political forces. American Jews were apprehensive about their perceived anti-Jewish positions and ties to the Christian right. The Reform Party or Canadian Alliance did not come close.

Collins' victory was short-lived. A second Tribunal investigation of him was decided in early 1999 with a different outcome. This time, four columns were at issue, including the one from the 1997 case. And this time tribunal member Tom Patch found that while individually the columns might not rise to the level of hatred envisioned by the legislation, taken together the columns did cross the line. Collins and the *North Shore News* had to pay the complainant, Harry Abrams, two thousand dollars. This ruling stressed the concept of the quantity of the expression as much as the quality of the expression as determining whether some expression is hate speech. The ruling is well-meaning, but it actually muddies the waters, since there may not be a consistent formula blending the quality and quantity of speech to yield a measure of hate.

A key benefit of hate speech legislation is symbolic. It makes minorities feel better about themselves, and more secure. It also sends a signal to Canadians that public expressions of bigotry are unacceptable. Striking down such laws runs the risk of sending out the opposite message. The same could be said about the periodic debate about doing away with multicultural policy in Canada. The paltry amount now spent by the federal government on multicultural programming in the Department of Canadian Heritage – far less than twenty million dollars – are not significant, and by themselves do not lead to either cultural retention or the end of racism. The value of official multiculturalism is symbolic, like the value of laws against hate speech. And in my view, symbols are very important. They define who we are.

Canada's various hate speech laws in the Criminal Code and in provincial statutes recognize that absolutes are rare in the world, and that more often principles will jostle against one another. When that happens, we have a court system to sort things out. Prosecutions should be rare, to avoid the stifling effect of self-censorship on debate and ultimately freedom. The laws should not be used capriciously. They are a kind of societal insurance policy. The ideas of free speech were nurtured to protect political reform and new ideas. In fact, in almost all court cases challenging these laws as restricting speech, the defendants are racists or pornographers – a far cry from Galileo and Voltaire. So far, speech remains vigorous in Canada and in the many European countries which have comparable, or even tougher, legislation.

EXAMPLES OF CANADIAN ANTI-SEMITISM

Canadian episodes of overt anti-Semitism are rare. Most cases that get publicity deal with grey areas of public policy where Jewish interests or sensibilities are at stake, like the sukkah on the condo balcony discussed earlier. That proceeding was one where both parties were private citizens. In other instances, Jews find themselves confronting state agencies directly. The infamous "Matzogate" flap in Quebec during Passover in 1997 is a case in point. Kosher-for-Passover products, coming in limited supply from the United States, were suddenly barred from Quebec because they had English-only labels. One hopes that was the result of a too-rigid obedience to language policy, rather than anti-Semitism. But it is a fair bet that new cases will come along regularly to pit Jewish rights against some other legitimate government policy. Andrew Liebmann was a Jewish officer in the Canadian Armed Forces who was not allowed to serve with Canadian forces during the Gulf War. He was told he could not take part because he was Jewish. The basis for the military's action was DCDS 9/83, later redrawn as CFAO 20-53, the policy on peacekeeping missions, which was used in Liebmann's case even though the Gulf War was not a peacekeeping operation. The policy states that persons could be disqualified for duty if dangers to the "health and safety of individuals was heightened because of the cultural, religious and other sensitivities" of the parties to the conflict. An associate defence minister apologized to Liebmann, admitting in a letter that some officials had raised concern "as to whether your religion would create problems with respect to your personal safety and your interaction with the local authorities who are Islamic."[48] The reasoning here is similar to the Canadian adherence to the Arab boycott of Israel in the 1970s, which was eventually rejected. But the difference is that the ostensible excuse given for the discriminatory behaviour is the welfare of the soldier rather than the success of the mission.

The most acute example of policy-based anti-Semitism concerns Israel. In its most extreme form we have anti-Zionism. Opposing the right of Jews to a state of their own, given the fact that millions of Israeli Jews already live in such a state and would defend its existence, is unambiguous anti-Semitism. To be blunt, it is a call for a de facto genocide against Israeli Jews. But what of opposition to one or more

Israeli policies? This is obviously more complex. After all, much of the Israeli electorate at any time, from left to right, opposes some Israeli policy, and they are not anti-Semitic. However, that is not the point. As overt anti-Semitism has become unfashionable, anti-Zionism and, yes, opposition to aggressive Israeli security policies have become, for some critics, convenient substitutes. Policies that would weaken Israel in the face of real threats are anti-Semitic in their effect if not – always – in their motivation. In Canada, the pursuit of a more "even-handed" position on the Middle East has become a code for tilting away from strong support for Israel. Canada's voting record on UN resolutions has included routine condemnations of Israeli policy, often at odds with the United States. For many Canadian Jews, this betrays a naive or ignorant attempt to be the helpful fixer in a cut-throat neighbourhood where compromise is still seen as weakness, all at Israel's expense.

The Canadian government – the same government which slammed the door shut on Jewish refugees in the 1930s – evinces little overt anti-Semitism, and universities and hospitals boast many Jewish students, professors, doctors, and deans. Still, anti-Semitic outbursts occur regularly. Perhaps the best source of data on such acts is the annual report on anti-Semitic incidents of the League for Human Rights of B'nai Brith. The report counts incidents of both vandalism and harassment clearly motivated by anti-Semitism.

The number of incidents reported for 2000 was 280, down from the all-time high of 331 in 1995 but higher than the 240 reported for 1998. Since 1982, when the report was first issued, the number of incidents documented increased about four- to fivefold. The count remained in two digits up until 1988. But we must be cautious here. Much of the increase comes from more effective collection procedures. No Canadian Jew should conclude that anti-Semitism has increased five times over the past fifteen years. But the general increase does correspond to the increase in certain forms of Holocaust denial and hate speech in Canada. The regional breakdown of incidents follows the regional pattern of Jewish population distribution. In recent years, numbers in Toronto and Montreal reflect roughly their weight in the Canadian Jewish population. In contrast, incidents in the rest of Ontario, Atlantic Canada, and the West were proportionally more numerous.

What sorts of incidents are these? The following descriptions from the League's 1999 annual report gives us a sense of the range.

January – In Toronto, a Jewish student was assaulted in the laundry room of his residence at the University of Toronto.

March – A reporter in P.E.I. received hate propaganda from a white supremacist group known as the Celtic Sons and Daughters. He used that information to gain an interview with the members of the group and later wrote an article exposing hate-group activity in Charlottetown.

May – A swastika was spray-painted on a car parked in front of a Toronto synagogue on Friday evening. More anti-Semitic graffiti was found on the sidewalk and bus shelter near the building.

August – In two separate incidents, a Jewish cemetery in Winnipeg was severely vandalized. In the worst of the two incidents, vandals toppled 219 headstones, causing $100,000 damage and untold emotional distress.

November – A man harassed a rabbi speaking at a public Remembrance Day service in Halifax when he shouted "Save the world. Kill a Jew."

December – A messianic group took Toronto by surprise when they mass-delivered their propagandist newspaper to many different neighbourhoods by targeted postal delivery. Wrapped in a blue plastic bag with a Star of David on it, the group engineered the drop-offs to appear as Hanukkah presents.

But is this a "great deal" of anti-Semitism? Obviously, perceptions are shaped by media reporting of individual incidents, so that the extent of bigotry is inevitably exaggerated. Both the League and police services claim that reported incidents represent 10 per cent of all cases. If so, in 2000 there may actually have been 2,800 episodes. Each one can hurt dozens or thousands of Jews, depending on the degree of publicity.

ANTI-SEMITIC PREJUDICE AND JEWISH–NON-JEWISH INTERACTIONS

Prejudice is not illegal. People have a right to their negative stereotypes, and to socialize with those who are like them. Some Jews themselves hold negative stereotypes of non-Jews and are uncomfortable in mixed social settings. None of these manifestations, on its own, is illegal, and it is important to stress the long-term trend of increasing acceptance. Ironically, the rising rate of intermarriage, while of concern to many Jews, is also an indicator of social acceptance by non-Jews.

But how extensive is anti-Semitic prejudice, and where is it concentrated? One national survey in 1984 found that one in seven Canadians held negative attitudes toward Jews; the rest were either positive or neutral. The provinces with the highest levels of anti-Semitism were Newfoundland, New Brunswick, and Quebec, while, perhaps surprisingly, Alberta, Keegstra notwithstanding, had the lowest. This study, like others, found Catholics and French speakers to be more anti-Semitic. In Quebec, people who labelled themselves on the left and on the right were more anti-Semitic than those who labelled themselves in the centre. In other words, in Quebec anti-Semitism is of two sorts: a traditional church-based anti-Semitism, and a more modern secular anti-Semitism in which Jews are distrusted for being anti-nationalist, and perhaps wealthy or exploiters of Québécois. For Canadians as a whole, anti-Semitism is also concentrated among the less-educated. One-quarter of those with less than high-school education were anti-Semitic, but only 7 per cent of those with at least some university.[49] Another study found that religiosity is no longer a source of anti-Semitism; those who believed that a "Christian commitment was needed for salvation" were not more apt to be anti-Jewish.[50] Contact with Jews also plays a role. Canadians who had met at least one Jew were apt to be less prejudiced.[51]

Distrusting Jews in positions of political power is another common indicator of anti-Semitism. In the 1980s, the percentage of Canadians who claimed they would not vote for a Jew hovered in the single digits.[52] (American surveys also find about 8 per cent would not vote for a Jew.) Surveys every five years directed by sociologist Reginald Bibby are particularly valuable in describing trends in anti-Semitism. When asked if Jews had "too much, too little or the right amount" of power in national affairs, 14 per cent of Canadians in 1995 answered "too much."[53] Asians were identified by 16 per cent, East Indians/Pakistanis by 18 per cent, and blacks by 9 per cent. Most surprising, whites were identified as too powerful by 9 per cent![54] As always, it is hard to interpret such survey questions. Jews over the years have had a substantial profile in Canadian politics, in many cases due to non-Jewish votes. The Bibby surveys also shed light on the social acceptability of intermarriage. From 1975 to 1995, there was a clear increase in the approval of Jewish–non-Jewish marriages. For marriages between Protestants and Jews, the increase went from 80 to 90 per cent; and for Catholics and Jews, from 78 to 89 per cent. So about one-tenth of Canadians disapprove. By comparison, the approval rate for marriages between whites and blacks was only 81 per cent (also up from 57 per cent in 1975). As we have seen, the actual rates of Jewish intermarriage increased as well.

Manuel Prutschi of the Toronto Jewish Congress fears that simple survey data may underestimate the nature and extent of anti-Semitism. He feels that public confrontations, like the Michaud affair, can have deeper significance. He also notes that anti-Semitism can be found in other minority communities. The Eastern European press in Canada will occasionally run anti-Semitic commentary. The renewed intifada in 2000 unleashed a wave of anti-Jewish incidents, many emanating from Arab and/or Moslem communities.[55]

Anti-Semitic stereotypes still abound among a minority of Canadians. One 1987 study found that about 19 per cent of Canadians agreed that "most Jews don't care what happens to people who aren't Jews." About 34 per cent agreed that "most Jews are pushy." About 21 per cent disagreed that "Jews have made an important contribution to the cultural life of Canada." And 23 per cent agreed that "Jews are more willing than others to use shady practices to get ahead." My guess is that Canadians know they are not supposed to hold these views so they understate them. In any case, these numbers are higher than the percentages who would not vote for Jews, or who disapprove of Jewish–Gentile intermarriage.[56] For some reason, these negative stereotypes do not spill over into other assessments of Jews.

Survey researchers have learned the trick of asking respondents how "others" view minority groups. This can avoid the problem of people understating their own negative opinions. A study of the perceived "social standing" of various groups found that English Canadians ranked Jews behind the French and other Western and Central European groups, but just ahead of Southern and Eastern Europeans, and non-whites.[57] These assessments of "social standing" have been matched by later studies which have looked at the degree of comfort which Canadians feel around Jews, and other groups. A 1991 national survey found that 64 per cent of Canadians felt "very comfortable" around Jews. That figure was higher than for a set of visible minorities, who ranged from 43 per cent for Sikhs to 61 per cent for West Indian blacks. But it was below other European origin groups, and even the Chinese, who scored 69 per cent. (It is always hard to figure out what these number mean. Only 83 per cent of Canadians felt very comfortable around British-origin Canadians.) British-origin Canadians were by far the most comfortable with Jews. Italian, French, Ukrainian, and German Canadians, all with similar rankings, followed them. Jews, for their part, felt reasonably comfortable around British, French, and Italian Canadians, and least comfortable with Germans, no doubt a residue of The Second World War.[58] Is the fact that 36 per cent did not feel very comfortable with Jews cause for alarm? Of course not. There is a difference between not feeling "very comfortable" around Jews and feeling unease and of course active dislike. The Bibby national surveys for 1995 found only 6 per cent claiming to be "uneasy" around Jews. This was lower than for four comparable visible minority groups, with East Indians and Pakistanis leading at 15 per cent.[59]

So far I have focused mainly on majority attitudes towards Jews. But remember there are likely many Jews who are "not very comfortable" around non-Jews.

*An Orthodox Jew goes to university and for the first time tries
to sustain a conversation with a non-Jew. At a loss for subject
matter and feeling increasingly uncomfortable, the Jew finally
asks, "So tell me, does Christmas come early or late this year?"*

Jews tend to establish their friendships with other Jews. This is
probably a result of their comfort levels, not any exclusion on the part
of non-Jews. Moreover, younger Canadian Jews are as likely as seniors
to have a mainly Jewish circle of friends. The 1990 Canadian national
survey found 76 per cent of those 34 and under, and 79 per cent of those
65 and over had mainly Jewish friends.[60]

We can push this far beyond issues of friendship and social comfort
levels. To what extent would non-Jews take serious risks to defend or
protect Jews? Failed lessons of the Holocaust, of non-Jewish bystanders
who did not help Jews, hang heavy in the shadows. How many
Canadians in British Columbia opened up their homes and hid
Japanese neighbours who sought to avoid relocation? There are no
known cases. And Jews should not be self-righteous. How many Jews
would have been prepared to do so? I don't know how far I would have
gone. Our commitments to "others" are best understood when put to
the most extreme tests, when there is a real inconvenience, even a
danger, to our well-being. Better none of us should have to take that
test; most would fail.

The good news is that contact with Jews is associated with lower
levels of anti-Semitism. The bad news is that many Canadians, particularly those who do not live in major cities, have minimal contact
with Jews. In one survey, only 17 per cent of Canadians said they "often"
had contact with Jews; 34 per cent of English-speaking Canadians and
fully 68 per cent of francophone Canadians reported no contact at all
with Jews.[61] These levels were comparable to those for Asians and
blacks. Given the finding that knowing at least one Jew reduces prejudice, it seems that much of the greater anti-Semitism among
francophones in Quebec reflects a lack of contact.

Anti-Semitism in Quebec, past and present, has a distinctive edge
to it. There has never been a collective reckoning in Quebec with the
depth and breadth of anti-Semitism of the 1930s and 1940s.[62] In

Quebec today anti-Semitism is more than the residue of staunch Catholicism. Jews in Quebec are federalists and are perceived as such by Quebec nationalists and independentists. Jacques Parizeau's attack against "money and the ethnic vote" after the 1995 referendum jarred many Jews, as did Yves Michaud's provocative comments about the Holocaust, and the support for him in some nationalist circles. While Parti Québécois leaders have generally opposed anti-Semitism, Jews fear French nationalism like they fear all ethnic nationalistic movements. No minority – like the Québécois – with a sense of ongoing victimization and grievance likes to be depicted as an oppressor of other minorities. Certainly not Jews, when the issue of Israeli treatment of Palestinians or Israeli Arabs comes up. On the other hand . . . higher levels of attitudinal anti-Semitism in Quebec today have *not* been associated with any increases in overt anti-Semitic acts by people or the government. The picture is blurred. In 1999, Toronto reported 119 incidents of anti-Semitism compared to 37 in Montreal.[63] In 2000 there were 100 incidents reported in Toronto compared to 71 in Montreal. These numbers vary in no consistent pattern, but Toronto's higher total reflects its greater Jewish population. And Quebec has long supported government aid to Jewish schools where Ontario has not.

Regardless of the evidence, North American Jews themselves perceive a significant amount of anti-Semitism. Among American Jews surveyed in the 1980s, "two thirds to three quarters agreed that anti-Semitism might become a serious problem in the future."[64] The best Canadian data is from a 1996 survey of the Montreal Jewish community, but the basic patterns apply anywhere. Fifteen per cent felt there was a "great deal" of anti-Semitism in Quebec; 62 per cent said "some"; 20 per cent said "little." About 40 per cent said anti-Semitism in Quebec had remained the same, 33 per cent said it had increased; and 8 per cent said it had decreased. Yet only 15 per cent said they had personally experienced anti-Semitism in the past two years, and another 37 per cent said they had experienced some anti-Semitism in their lives.[65] These experiential figures are clearly lower than for the perception of anti-Semitism. So, many Quebec Jews, like Jews anywhere in North America, like most minorities, like Québécois who remember the Plains of Abraham, like women, believe themselves to be potential victims, without having actually been victimized. The idea of "systemic" discrimination does not require specific episodes of victimization. There is an ideology of omnipresent anti-Semitism which is quite clearly part of modern Jewish identity. It explains the potency of the Holocaust as an image for Jews far removed from the death camps in Europe, and why Jews who are affluent, indeed powerful, will still feel insecure. Of course Jews know from their history that danger can always lurk. Surveys may not pick up resentments which are no longer expressed even confidentially to pollsters. But the basic facts remain. Things have been, and could be, a lot worse, yet Jews are, and must be, on guard.

A CANADIAN
JEWISH MODEL?

Jewish life in Canada is a success story. I do not make that assessment in order to gloat, and I also hope it does not seem naive. Like most social scientists, I am programmed to think about societies in a "critical" fashion. In fact there are many tensions, conflicts, and dilemmas facing Canadian Jewry. This book has outlined them in unsparing detail. But Canadian Jews, through their diversity, possess the resources to meet all these challenges and make sense of the multiple paradoxes of the Canadian Jewish experience. The pieces of the Jewish mosaic fit together well. A Canadian Jewish equilibrium balances the forces of tradition and change.

The Jewish community in Canada is on its way to becoming the second-most important Diaspora community, after the United States. But the quality of Jewish life in Canada is higher. Canada is a post-Biblical Garden of Eden, for those seeking both participation in the general society and a vibrant Jewish culture. Canadian Jews rank with Americans in terms of freedom and affluence, but they enjoy a deeper Jewish cultural and communal life. This ability to participate fully in Canadian life while retaining a rich multidimensional heritage is the mysterious essence of the Jewish experience.

But Canadian Jewish life is not static and may yet approximate the American model. The advantages of a more recent and relatively larger Jewish immigration will likely fade. The much-vaunted Canadian rhetoric and policies of multiculturalism will not stem the tide of assimilation, or at least transformation. The North–South links between the two Jewish communities are formidable. Jewish cross-border marriages will likely increase. As the Old World influence recedes, a new variant of Jewish civilization will emerge in Canada, likely along American lines.

Note that I do not equate this future convergence with any likely disappearance of Judaism in Canada, or indeed, in the United States. Jewish life will survive. Even high levels of mixed marriages will be mitigated by new forms of voluntary affiliation, and demographic replenishment – more babies – from the thriving ultra-Orthodox communities. I remain an optimist about the Jewish future in Canada, even without the frenetic efforts of "continuity" committees aimed at cultural engineering. The innovation found at present in Jewish life flows both from the bottom up, reflecting real concerns felt by a range of Jews, and from the top down, as in Birthright Israel.

Jews are an extremely diverse group, and that diversity is a strength. Pluralism is becoming more and more pronounced, and seems to be more abrasive. But I am also optimistic about the so-called "unity" issue. This fractious pluralism has paradoxically always been, and remains, a source of strength, innovation and vitality. And as I have argued, the actual daily frictions are minimized through the voluntary segregation that accompanies Jewish pluralism. Jews live near, marry, socialize, pray, and join organizations with Jews who are like them. Moreover, from these frictions can emerge creative solutions. Conflict and debate are signs of life. Jews care about their future.

I cannot predict if the fault line between the Orthodox and non-Orthodox, in Israel and in the Diaspora, will become an unbridgeable chasm. I likewise cannot predict if these "who is a Jew" tensions will lead to an irreparable gulf between non-Orthodox Diaspora Jews, even the highly Zionistic Canadian community, and Israel. But even if, Heaven forbid, such splits would emerge, Jews and Jewish life would continue, and thrive. Jewish unity is in the main a myth, save for anti-Semites. (Hitler never fussed about ideological differences and pedigrees.) Moreover, the dominant metaphors for the Jewish experience, back to the Bible, have been those of loss and schism. Think of the list. Expulsion from the Garden of Eden, the genocide of the Flood, the destruction of Sodom and Gomorrah, the break between Ishmael and Esau, the attraction of the Golden Calf, the mysterious disappearance of the ten lost tribes, the split of the post-Solomonic Kingdom of Israel, the destruction of the two temples, the expulsions, and the debilitating civil war among the Jews of ancient Palestine. . . . Need I go on? Indeed, when have Jews been united? Antagonisms within and between Jewish groups were the norm, even in the idealized Eastern European "world of our fathers" and in the early decades of this century in North America. Jewish life in the Diaspora has survived for centuries without unity, and indeed, without close ties to Israel. And if need be – and I hope not – it will again. Not only Judaism has survived sharp division. So have Christianity and Islam.

But these apocalyptic scenarios are far off for Canadian Jewry. The more likely disruptions would be homegrown. It is still impossible to predict the denouement of the Quebec independence movement and the long-term future of Quebec Jews. It is also possible – though not probable – that an energized right-wing Canadian Alliance would isolate Jews politically. But at present, life remains good for Canadian Jews, faced with a range of rich cultural and communal options, from the traditional to the trendy. Anti-Semitism is not gone, and nothing should be ruled out. But anti-Semitism remains increasingly irrelevant to the daily lives and opportunities of Canadian Jews. Jews are less an object of disdain, and more an object of admiration or at least curiosity. Even non-Orthodox Jews seem able to live a life with a spiritual and cultural content that exceeds that of nominal Christians. Indeed, the variety of Jewish lifestyle options is increasing to match the non-denominational idiosyncrasies of modern Jews.

But I do reach one conclusion which bothers me. As a sociologist, I have long espoused a comparative approach to the study of all minority groups, including Jews. I have done that in this volume and I routinely encourage my students to do comparative research papers, arguing the best way to understand group X is by comparison with group Y. My mentor, Seymour Martin Lipset, argued that such comparative study would inevitably confirm the old adage attributed to the German poet Heinrich Heine that "the Jews are like everyone else, except more so." By this is meant that Jewish social patterns such as low fertility, universal post-secondary education, urbanization, and liberalism are simply precursors of general societal trends.

I now have serious doubts. The comparative approach has a built-in bias towards assuming basic commonalities – differences in degree but not in kind. I have come to question the utility of routine comparisons between Jews and other groups. As I have argued, Jews are like everyone else, but different. Not better, but different. There are too many paradoxes which confound normal theories and expectations of other minority groups. More and more, Jews strike me as being one of a kind, rather than as usefully comparable to other groups. While Jews are a multicultural group par excellence, I am not convinced that Jews can be the poster group for multicultural policy in Canada. The successful Jewish model may not be replicable by other groups, because in fact a unique set of circumstances work in the Jewish favour. This Jewish uniqueness is a combination, as we have seen, of particular social contexts and of a unique cultural heritage, and owes little or nothing to government policies.

The official rhetoric of multiculturalism certainly nourishes a tolerant environment for Jews. But the roots of Jewish success long predate official multiculturalism. This is not a criticism of Canadian multicultural policy. I have no doubt that multiculturalism taps into a core Canadian value, and its message is important for Canadian minorities. But it is not clear if the policy is easily exportable. A policy may work in one society, for example, but will it work in others? One day a Japanese social scientist came to my office. He was part of a delegation of seven Japanese scholars spending the summer in Canada, on a mission to study Canadian multiculturalism. Each scholar was assigned one ethnic group; my visitor was studying Jews. Why the mission? Japan, though over 99 per cent ethnic Japanese, was worried about increasing diversity, from other Asian source countries. In order to be prepared, what better model to study than Canada, which enjoyed and still enjoys a worldwide reputation of inter-group harmony and tolerance? These scholars assumed that studying the experience of Jews or Italians or other minorities in Canada might help Japan cope with social strains caused by increases in its Filipino or Thai community. Well, perhaps, but I have doubts. I am not sure what lessons the fate of Canadian Jews can or should have for Filipinos in Japan.

It is also not clear if all or most Canadian minority groups will be able to emulate the multicultural success of Canadian Jews. All Canadian minority groups are unique. But with apologies to Lipset and George Orwell, Jews are more unique than others. They have several strengths which help them realize multicultural objectives. These strengths derive ultimately from Jewish culture, from the social characteristics of Jews, and from the interaction between the two. First, as mentioned throughout this volume, Jews are both a religious and ethno-cultural group. This gives Jews an unusually large repertoire of cultural traits: languages, literature, a homeland, festivals, beliefs, art, music, rituals, customs, and foods that comprise Jewish identity. Moreover, Jewish religious requirements – whether for kosher food or the need to care for less fortunate Jews – reinforce the need for developing a Jewish polity. No minority group is better equipped for survival.

Second, Jews have a two-thousand-year experience as a Diaspora community, with the majority of the group outside the homeland. Being a minority is second nature to Jews, as are forms of voluntary self-governance. Jews were practicing multiculturalism long before the concept became fashionable. No group – not Italians, not Ukrainians, not Chinese – has such a dense network of self-governing organizations. Jewish skill at being a successful minority has been honed over centuries.

Third, Canadian Jews are overwhelmingly white. They are not trapped at the bottom of a racist stratification system based on skin colour. That honour in Canada falls to First Nations groups, to blacks, and to some Asian groups. There is no tradition of a festering "Jewish Question" in Canada. Moreover, those Jews who so desire can pass easily into the mainstream, unlike visible minorities. Jews in North America have never been the most oppressed group, the eternal outsider, as was the case in Europe. They could belong.

Fourth, the peculiarities of Jewish history, as well as some cultural legacies, have led to high socio-economic achievements of Canadian Jews in what is now a relatively open, non-discriminatory society. This success is unmatched by most other groups. This Jewish affluence, and Jewish philanthropy – rooted in both cultural traditions and social circumstances – is the foundation for the proliferation of communal organizations and thereby for Jewish survival. The will to survive is not enough. Jews also have the means.

And lastly, more than specific multicultural policies, the non-separation of church and state in Canada has enabled Jews and Jewish schools to benefit from government support in some provinces. As a result, Jewish schools have thrived in Canada. No other ethnic group, with the possible exception of First Nations, has such a comprehensive and diverse school system. This system gives Jews survival advantages that other minority groups cannot match.

If we put this together, it is not clear how much other Canadian groups can borrow easily from the Jewish experience. The Canadian ideology of multiculturalism legitimates and reinforces traits which have long been part of the Jewish experience. A series of coincidences have created the situation where Jewish communities in Canada can make the best of their immediate options. And they do. There will be challenges ahead, no doubt. But for the present and near future, this paradoxical people survives, and thrives.

BIBLIOGRAPHIC ESSAY

The following is a selection of books and sources, by no means exhaustive, that have been written on aspects of contemporary Canadian Jewish life.

A brief yet informative overview of the Canadian Jewish experience, with an engaging collection of photographs, is Irving Abella's *A Coat of Many Colours*, Toronto: Lester and Orpen Dennys, 1990. The pioneering history of Canadian Jewry was written by the journalist B. G. Sack in Yiddish in 1948, and then translated into English as *History of the Jews in Canada*, Montreal: Harvest House, 1965. Gerald Tulchinsky's two-volume study of Canadian Jewry is the definitive history. Volume One, *Taking Root: The Origins of the Canadian Jewish Community*, Toronto: Lester Publishing, 1992, ends at about 1920. Volume Two, *Branching Out: The Transformation of the Canadian Jewish Community*, Toronto: Stoddart, 1998, continues into the 1990s. Louis Rosenberg's *Canada's Jews: A Social and Economic Study of the Jews of Canada*, Montreal: Canadian Jewish Congress, 1939, republished by McGill–Queen's Press, 1993, is a detailed socio-demographic study of Canadian Jewish life in the 1920s and 1930s, relying on extensive analysis of census data and other statistics.

There are a number of regional works, many on Quebec. Michael Brown's *Jew or Juif? Jews, French Canadians and Anglo-Canadians, 1759–1914*, Philadelphia: Jewish Publication Society, 1987, is a historical account of the Jewish experience in Quebec. A French-language overview of the condition of Quebec Jewry can be found in *Juifs et réalités juifs au Québec*, edited by Pierre Anctil, Quebec: Institut québécois de recherche sur la culture, 1984. Joe King's *From the Ghetto to the Main: The Story of the Jews in Montreal*, Montreal: Montreal Jewish Publication Society, 2000, and Mackay Smith's *Jews of Montreal and Their Judaisms*, Aaron Communications, 1998, are readable overviews of Jewish life in Montreal. Two collections of essays on Montreal Jewish culture and society edited by Pierre Anctil, Mervin Butovsky, and Ira Robinson, published by Véhicule Press, are *An Everyday Miracle: Yiddish Culture in Montreal*, 1990, and *Renewing Our Days: Montreal Jews in the Twentieth Century*, 1995. Stephen Speisman's *The Jews of Toronto: A History to 1937*, Toronto: McClelland & Stewart, 1979, is an account of the development of the communal and organizational structure of Toronto Jewry. Arthur Chiel's *The Jews in Manitoba*, Toronto: University of Toronto Press, 1961, Cyril Leonoff's *Pioneers, Pedlars, and Prayer Shawls*, Victoria: Sono Nis Press, 1978, and Sheva Medjuck's *Jews of Atlantic Canada*, St. John's: Breakwater Press, 1986, describe the history of the Jews in Manitoba, British Columbia, and Atlantic Canada, respectively.

Several studies focus on specific issues. Joseph Kage's *With Faith and Thanksgiving*, Montreal: Eagle Publishing, 1962, is a pioneering review of Jewish immigration to Canada, and the role of JIAS in particular. Lita Rose Betcherman's *The Swastika and the Maple Leaf*, Toronto: Fitzhenry & Whiteside, 1975 is a detailed review of the development of fascist anti-Semitism during the 1930s. A broader review of anti-Semitism in Canada from a variety of perspectives and covering the early colonial period to the present can be found in *Anti-Semitism in Canada: History and Interpretation*, ed. Alan Davies, Waterloo: Wilfrid Laurier University Press, 1992. Esther Delisle's two historical volumes on Quebec anti-Semitism, *The Traitor and the Jew*, Montreal: R. Davies Publishing, 1992, and *Myths, Memory, and Lies: Quebec's Intelligentsia and the Fascist Temptation, 1939–1960*, Westmount: R. Davies Multimedia, 1998, have stirred opposition among French nationalist circles in Quebec.

A number of studies have focused on specific cases of anti-Semitism, public policy, and inter-group relations. Irving Abella and Harold Troper, *None Is Too Many*, Toronto: Lester and Orpen Dennys, 1982, is a study of Canada's restrictive immigration policy toward Jews before, during, and after the Second World War. Harold Troper and Morton Weinfeld, *Old Wounds: Jews, Ukrainians, and the Hunt for Nazi War Criminals in Canada*, Toronto: Viking, 1988 is a study of the inter-relationship among Jews, Ukrainians, and the Canadian government in the face of the Deschênes Commission of Inquiry on War Criminals in Canada. Howard Margolian's *Unauthorized Entry: The Truth about Nazi War Criminals in Canada, 1945–56*, Toronto: University of Toronto Press, 1999, explores the interaction of the Canadian government and

Jewish community concerning the issue at the time. Cyril Levitt and William Shaffir, *The Riot at Christie Pits*, Toronto: Lester and Orpen Dennys, 1987, is a retrospective study of a major riot between Jews and Gentiles in Toronto in the early 1930s.

Etan Diamond's, *And I Dwell in Their Midst: Orthodox Jews in Suburbia*, Chapel Hill: University of North Carolina Press, 2000, is a study of Orthodox Jewish life in Toronto. *The Jews in Canada*, ed. Robert Brym, William Shaffir, and Morton Weinfeld, Toronto: Oxford University Press, 1993, is a collection of social scientific articles dealing with various aspects of contemporary Jewish life. An earlier collection of such research can be found in *The Canadian Jewish Mosaic*, ed. Morton Weinfeld, William Shaffir, and Irwin Cotler, Rexdale: John Wiley of Canada, 1981. An early study of changes in Canadian Jewish identity can be found in Evelyn Kallen, *Spanning the Generations*, Toronto: Longmans, 1973. A collection of essays as well as biographical information on individual Canadian Jews can be found in *Canadian Jewry Today: Who's Who in Canadian Jewry*, ed. Edmond Y. Lipsitz, Toronto: J.E.S.L. Education Products, 1989 and the third edition in 2000. Daniel Elazar and Harold Waller's *Maintaining Consensus: The Canadian Jewish Polity in the Post-War World*, Lanham, Maryland: University Press of America, 1990, is an analysis of the internal political organization of the Jewish community in Canada. An interesting collection of essays on socio-political aspects of Canadian Jewish life can be found in *Multiculturalism, Jews, and Identities in Canada*, ed. Howard Adelman and John H. Simpson, Jerusalem: The Magnes Press, Hebrew University of Jerusalem, 1996.

Archival material on Canadian Jewry can be found in the Canadian Jewish Congress National Archives in Montreal, in the Ontario Region CJC Archives in Toronto, and in various collections at the National Archives of Canada in Ottawa. Much of the CJC archival material has been published by David Rome in a series Canadian Jewish Archives. Other archival sources include the Jewish Public Library in Montreal, and the Jewish Historical Societies of British Columbia and of Western Canada. Bibliographies include David Rome, Judith Nefsky, and Paule Obermeir, *Les Juifs du Québec: Bibliographie retrospective annotée*, Montreal: Institut québécois de recherche sur la culture, 1981; Susan

Vadnay, *A Selected Bibliography of Research on Canadian Jewry, 1900–1980*, Ottawa: mimeo, 1991; Stuart Schoenfeld and Dwight Daigneault, *Contemporary Jewish Life in Canada; A Bibliography*, Toronto: Centre for Jewish Studies, York University, May 1992.

Several social scientific journals have featured articles dealing with Canadian Jewish life. These include *Canadian Jewish Studies, Canadian Ethnic Studies, Canadian Journal of Sociology, Canadian Review of Sociology and Anthropology*, and the *Jewish Journal of Sociology*.

TABLES

TABLE 1
U.S. and Canadian Jewish Populations
by Identity Constructs

POPULATION GROUP (Definition*)	U.S. 1990 NJPS N	%	CANADA 1991 CENSUS N	%
JEWS BY RELIGION				
Jewish Ethnic Origin				
BJR (U.S.)	4,210,000	76		
JRJE (Canada)			281,680	79
Other Ethnic Origin				
JBC (U.S.)	185,000	3		
JROE (Canada)			36,390	10
Total	4,395,000	80	318,070	89
JEWISH BY ETHNIC ORIGIN				
No Religion				
JNR (U.S.)	1,120,000	20		
NRJE (Canada)			38,245	11
Total CJP (U.S.)	5,515,000	100		
JSD (Canada)			356,315	100
JEWISH ETHNIC AND RELIGIOUS PREFERENCE POPULATION				
Jewish Ethnic Origin/with Other Religion				
JCO/JOR/JCOR (U.S.)	1,325,000	19		
ORJE (Canada)			49,640	12
Core/Standard Jewish Population				
CJP (U.S.)	5,515,000	81		
JSD (Canada)			356,315	88
Total	6,840,000	100	405,955	100

*Abbreviations, in the order in which they appear, are as follows:

BJR: Born Jewish;
JRJE: Jewish by religion and Jewish by ethnic origin;
JBC: Jewish by choice;
JROE: Jewish by religion and other than Jewish ethnic origin;

continued on next page

continued from previous page

JBR: Jewish by religion;

JNR: Secular Jews, no religion;

NRJE: No religion, Jewish by ethnicity only;

CJP: Core Jewish population;

JSD: Jewish by religion, or Jewish by religion and Jewish by ethnic origin, or no religion and Jewish by ethnic origin;

JCO: Adult born/raised in Judaism, converted to another religion;

JOR: Adult of Jewish ancestry, born/raised and currently of another religion;

JCOR: Child under 18 being raised in another religion;

ORJE: Other religion and Jewish by ethnic origin.

From Barry Kosmin, "The Demographics and Economics of the Jewish Market in North America," in *Creating the Jewish Future*, ed. M. Brown and B. Lightman, Walnut Creek: Altamira (Sage), 1998, pp.216–33. Reproduced with permission.

TABLE 2

Measures of Religious Involvement in Canada and the U.S.
(Entries are percentages; data weighted by number of Jews
in the household)

	CANADA	UNITED STATES
Attends Passover Seder	92	76
Lights Hanukkah candles	87	78
Fasts Yom Kippur	77	64
Lights Sabbath candles	54	26
Has meat and dairy dishes	46	18
Handles no money on the Sabbath	15	14
Observes Fast of Esther	11	6
DENOMINATION		
Orthodox	19	9
Conservative	37	38
Reconstructionist	1	1
Reform	11	43
Other Jewish	32	9
Synagogue member	67	50
SYNAGOGUE MEMBERS' DENOMINATION		
Orthodox	25	12
Conservative	43	45
Reconstructionist	1	1
Reform	14	38
Other Jewish	19	5

*Source of U.S. data: The 1990 National Jewish Population Study. Source of Canadian data: The 1990 CRB Foundation survey of Canadian Jews.

TABLE 3
Measures of Jewish Communal Involvement in Canada and the U.S.
(Entries are percentages; data weighted by number of
Jewish adults in the household)

	CANADA	UNITED STATES
Reads a Jewish newspaper	60	33
YMHA or JCC member	38	23
Jewish organization member	47	37
Volunteers for Jewish organization	31	24
Serves on a board or committee	25	24
Donates $100 or more to UJA	41	21
Mean UJA/Federation gift		
All households	$ 700	$ 300
Donors of $100+ only	$1700	$1300
Most close friends are Jewish	78	51
Can converse in Yiddish	37	–
Can converse in Hebrew	25	–

*Source of U.S. data: The 1990 National Jewish Population Study. Source of Canadian data: The 1990 CRB Foundation survey of Canadian Jews. Though dollar amounts are in their countries' respective currencies, they are an accurate reflection of the different rates of gift-giving, as the U.S. average income is correspondingly higher than in Canada.

TABLE 4
Measures of Israel Involvement in Canada and the U.S.
(Entries are percentages; data weighted by number of Jewish adults in the household)

	CANADA	UNITED STATES*
VISITED ISRAEL		
Twice or more	39	17
Just once	27	18
Never	34	65
Corresponded with Israeli	44	23
Spoken by telephone to Israeli	37	10
Israel important to being a Jew	87	73
If Israel destroyed, personal tragedy	85	66
Often talk about Israel	70	62
Feel very close to Israel	42	22
Will visit in three years	44	24
Consider self Zionist	42	25
Fuller Jewish life in Israel	35	10
Considered *aliyah*	21	13
Know year of Independence	79	66
Know year of Six-Day War	72	40
Israel should recognize only Orthodox conversions	14	6
Very upset if Israel recognizes only Orthodox conversions	47	57
FAVOURABLE IMPRESSIONS		
Ultra-Orthodox Israelis	14	8
Modern Orthodox Israelis	53	41
Secular Jewish Israelis	53	49
Israeli doves	35	36
Israeli hawks	23	28

*Source of U.S. data: For visiting Israel, the 1990 National Jewish Population Study; for corresponded with Israelis and spoken by telephone with Israelis, the 1988 National Survey of American Jews; for all other variables, the 1989 National Survey of American Jews. Source of Canadian data: The 1990 CRB Foundation survey of Canadian Jews.

TABLE 5
Religious, Communal, and Israel Involvement by Region in Canada*

	TORONTO	MONTREAL	WINNIPEG	BRITISH COLUMBIA	OTHER
Attends Passover Seder	90	95	92	83	91
Lights Hanukkah candles	84	90	90	77	88
Fasts Yom Kippur	69	88	77	58	75
Lights Sabbath candles	54	59	46	42	42
Has meat and dairy dishes	42	54	39	34	36
Handles no money on the Sabbath	13	22	2	5	2
Observes Fast of Esther	9	17	1	5	1
DENOMINATION					
Orthodox	14	28	7	10	14
Conservative	39	31	59	32	47
Reconstructionist	1	2	–	2	–
Reform	15	3	11	16	16
Other Jewish	31	37	21	40	22
Synagogue member	61	69	79	54	82
SYNAGOGUE MEMBERS' DENOMINATION					
Orthodox	22	36	8	5	18
Conservative	45	33	62	49	54
Reconstructionist	–	–	–	–	–
Reform	20	5	17	21	18
Other Jewish	14	26	13	25	10
Reads a Jewish newspaper	62	72	41	20	44
YMHA or JCC member	28	48	44	38	40
Jewish organization member	41	47	60	49	60
Donates $100 or more to UJA	42	35	43	36	56
Most close friends are Jewish	81	83	77	48	64
Can converse in Yiddish	38	40	48	28	25
Can converse in Hebrew	24	31	14	16	21
Visited Israel	65	73	47	59	60
Feel very close to Israel	39	51	35	40	31
Often talk about Israel	67	75	72	63	66
Will visit Israel in three years	40	56	20	37	33
Considered *aliyah*	21	26	8	15	18
Considered self Zionist	40	43	45	49	41
Israel important to being a Jew	86	90	90	85	83

*Source of data: The 1990 CRB Foundation survey of Canadian Jews.

TABLE 6

Religious, Communal, and Israel Involvement by Age in Canada*

	UNDER 34	35-49	50-64	65+
Attends Passover Seder	96	91	92	87
Lights Hanukkah candles	86	89	88	80
Fasts Yom Kippur	82	76	76	70
Lights Sabbath candles	50	54	52	58
Has meat and dairy dishes	49	43	44	49
Handles no money on the Sabbath	21	15	8	13
Observes Fast of Esther	15	12	5	9
DENOMINATION				
Orthodox	22	19	13	16
Conservative	35	35	47	36
Reconstructionist	–	2	–	–
Reform	10	13	9	9
Other Jewish	34	31	31	36
Synagogue member	54	70	66	75
SYNAGOGUE MEMBERS' DENOMINATION				
Orthodox	37	25	18	22
Conservative	34	42	54	40
Reconstructionist	–	2	–	–
Reform	13	16	13	10
Other Jewish	18	16	15	28
Reads a Jewish newspaper	52	56	67	70
YMHA or JCC member	41	36	40	37
Jewish organization member	43	39	49	64
Donates $100 or more to UJA	32	42	46	42
Most close friends are Jewish	76	74	84	79
Can converse in Yiddish	14	27	51	64
Can converse in Hebrew	35	25	21	20
Visited Israel	70	64	66	65
Feel very close to Israel	33	37	47	56
Often talk about Israel	58	66	75	81
Will visit Israel in three years	42	43	50	39
Considered *aliyah*	29	22	22	10
Considered self Zionist	40	35	48	51
Israel important to being a Jew	87	85	90	88

*Source of data: The 1990 CRB Foundation survey of Canadian Jews.

SOURCES OF EVIDENCE

My arguments in this book rest mainly on three major sources of evidence. The first is the scholarly research and writing that deals with various aspects of Jewish life in Canada and the United States. Where few or no Canadian studies exist, I rely on American research where it applies. I include here the use of newspapers and popular magazines both Jewish and non-Jewish, as well as articles in academic journals and monographs. I have not tried to be absolutely exhaustive, to integrate every thesis ever written on a Canadian Jewish topic, or to provide an exhaustive review of media portrayals of Jews or Jewish issues. There is no need, and that would be another book.

The second source is a set of interviews with a cross-section of "typical" Jews and my own observations of Jewish settings across Canada. These interviews and observations are designed mainly to tap into the sentiments of Canadian Jews from the ground up. In general I have avoided speaking to the many celebrities and *machers*, or big-shots, in the Canadian Jewish scene – the Canadian Jewish "rich and famous" – and the official heads of the major Jewish communal organizations. Though some names are named, there is little gossip and few personality profiles. That would be another, albeit interesting, book. I did not find my informants by using any high-powered sampling procedure. I used contacts, friends of friends, names I was given by others, and tried to reflect the diversity which is so much a facet of Canadian Jewish life. At times I have kept the identity of the informants confidential.

The third source is statistical, surveys of Canadian and American Jews and Canadian census data, mainly from 1991. (The 1991 Canadian Census is more reliable, since it identifies Jews by ethnicity and religion; the 1996 Census asks only about ethnicity.) The main American source is the 1990 National Jewish Population Survey, a survey of over 2,000 American Jews, which is cited in many publications.[1] The main Canadian surveys, and the ones which are most recent, are one taken of 516 Jewish households in Montreal in 1996[2]; one taken of 1,400 Jewish households in Toronto in 1990[3]; one taken of 972 households from the entire Canadian Jewish community in 1990 and financed by the CRB foundation[4]; one taken of 680 households in the Calgary Jewish community in 1997[5]; a survey of seven ethnic groups in Toronto directed by sociologist Raymond Breton and his colleagues, which included 168 Jews of a total of 2,338 respondents, taken in 1979.[6] How reliable are these surveys? Finding a truly random and representative sample of Jews is a daunting task, given that Jews are a small minority of the population. It is easier in Canada than in the United States, since the Canadian census, which collects data on Jews, offers a basis for verifying the accuracy of any survey. There are different ways to draw a Jewish sample. While all the surveys I have used have limitations, they meet accepted standards when used appropriately.[7]

Finally, I will on occasion use personal and familial anecdotes to make a point. Why not? What are we, chopped liver? In some ways – not all – we are typical Canadian Jews. And in any case the sources – me and my family – are exceptionally reliable. I will also not shrink from using jokes, some of the classic genre. To try to explain Jewish life without recourse to the vast storehouse of Jewish humour – greater than for other groups in my view – makes no sense, like coffee without cake. Jokes do not come from nowhere. They are a vital folkloric counterpoint to the stodgy tools of social science. They are a distillation of a wide-ranging social experience, and a source of essential truths. Besides, since when does a Jew need an excuse to tell a joke?

APPENDIX II

DEMOGRAPHIC PREDICTIONS AND COMPARISONS

Predicting the future size of Canadian Jewry is a difficult task and will depend on several factors. One is the difference between Jewish fertility and mortality rates. The Jews are an aged group. In 1991 over 17 per cent of Jews were aged 65 and over, compared to under 11 per cent for the Canadian population. So this age structure suggests there is little demographic momentum likely to fuel natural increase in the immediate future. A second factor is the net result of moves into and out of the Jewish community due to conversion or assimilation. A third is the relative rates of Jewish immigration to and emigration from Canada. These factors in turn depend on historical events and changing social norms, most of which are simply unpredictable.

Nevertheless, recent demographic predictions have been pessimistic. Leo Davids, a sociologist at York University, estimated in a paper published in 1989 that the Canadian Jewish population, measured by religion, would be down to 310,000 in the year 2001. As we have seen, that figure was already surpassed even by 1991 – though of course the numbers for 2001 are not yet in. In an apprehensive look at the Jewish demographic future, Davids also was not optimistic about the role of migration:

". . . we are talking about fairly small numbers today, and the total net effect of Jews settling in vs. leaving Canada is likely to remain insignificant as a factor of total population in the country."[1]

Even more pessimistic was the analysis of University of Toronto sociologist Robert Brym, entitled ominously "The Rise and Decline of Canadian Jewry?" and also first published in 1989.[2] Brym's pessimism was based on a comparison of the 1981 and 1986 Census questions on ethnicity (the 1986 Census had no question on religion). Between 1981 and 1986 there was a decline of 7 per cent in the number of Jews claiming Jewish as a single ethnic origin. In part this is because in 1981 the Canadian Census for the first time allowed respondents to choose more than one ethnic origin, a practice that became more common in 1986. That decline led Brym to warn: "if that trend continues – and I emphasize this is an extrapolation, not a forecast – Canada's total Jewish population will be about 100,000 and Canada's [single] ethnic Jewish population will be under 100,000 in the year 2050, just 57 years from now."[3] *Oy vey 'zmir.* Like Davids, Brym is also not optimistic about the impact of immigration in forestalling population decline. "Few Jews have immigrated to Canada in recent years and in any case many of the immigrants are highly assimilated and/or want little to do with organized Jewish life. The Jewish community's panacea will not be found among the Russian, Israeli, and American Jews who come to Canada."[4]

Both these pessimistic analyses may well turn out to be accurate. As we have seen, there have been steady rises in the Canadian mixed-marriage rate, though the levels and the rate of increase remain far below those for American Jews. And indeed the Census of 1996 indicates a decline in the number of Canadians claiming Jewish as their ethnic origin, in whole or in part, from 369,565 in 1991 to 351,705 in 1996. There was a substantial decline in those who claimed "Jewish only" as their ethnic origin category, from 245,840 to 195,810, and an increase in those who claimed a multiple ethnic origin which included Jewish, from 123,725 to 155,900, or 26 per cent.

The release of these 1996 data on Jewish ethnicity prompted conflicting interpretations. Brym cites these latest figures as further proof of Jewish assimilation. Moreover, the provincial variations in this pattern are telling. In Quebec and Ontario, there are far more people claiming to be "Jewish only" than there are those claiming Jewish and other ethnic origins. The pattern reverses out West; in Alberta and British Columbia there are almost twice as many Jews who are Jewish along with other ethnic origins as there are those who claim Jewish alone. McGill professor of social work Jim Torczyner is less apprehensive than Brym, arguing that data from the religion question, to be asked in 2001, are needed to be certain about any trends. "If these figures are anywhere near correct, it's a fluke." Brym maintains that regardless of the religion figures, the ethnicity pattern is real and troubling. "You can compare numbers on ethnicity from 1991 to the numbers on ethnicity in 1996. Why doubt them?"[5] Brym is in any case correct about the systematic decline in the proportions of Canadians claiming a single Jewish ethnic origin.

As we have seen there remains a significant impact of immigration on the Canadian Jewish community. The early analyses by Brym and Davids may not have anticipated the demographic gains through immigration, and thus they could not foresee the increase in population found between 1981 and 1991. But we do not know whether those gains have been replicated for the period 1991 to 2001 or will be in the future.

With data from the United States' National Jewish Population Survey of 1990, we can compare roughly the basic identity profile of the Canadian and American Jewish communities. (We should recall that the American data are estimates based on a national survey, and are less reliable than the Canadian census figures. See again Table One.) The so-called "core Jewish population" in the United States combines those who are Jews by both religion and ancestry, secular Jews who are of Jewish ethnic origin but with no religion, and "Jews by choice." The latter are people of non-Jewish origin who embrace Judaism, with or without formal conversion. The first National Jewish Population Survey sampled the American Jewish population in 1970 and estimated a core Jewish population of 5,420,000. The second NJPS in 1990 estimated 5,515,000. So the total American Jewish population was nearly stagnant for twenty years![6] The modest increase of 2 per cent is a far cry from the much higher rate found in Canada.

In a recent paper, demographers Sergio DellaPergola and Uzi Rebhun extrapolated Jewish populations from 2000 into the future. They projected a Canadian figure growing to 381,000 by 2020, then declining to 348,000 by 2050. The American Jewish population is projected to decline continuously from 5,697,000 in 2000 to 4,688,000 in 2050.[7]

Census data and population estimates can also shed some light on the qualitative aspects of Jewish population, as these relate to survival prospects for the Jewish future. While most people reflexively assume that American Jews have experienced more assimilation than Canadian Jews, it is difficult to find estimates of that difference. The 1991 Canadian Census and the NJPS of 1990 can help. Using the three Jewish categories above, as well as a fourth category of those of Jewish origin who have embraced another religion, helps us frame a comparison. See again Table One in the Appendix. (There are in the American national survey data an estimated 700,000 children under 18 who are being raised in a non-Jewish religion, but who have a "qualified Jew" as a parent. A qualified Jew is a parent who is either Jewish or of Jewish descent. These non-Jewish children are not counted in the American "core" Jewish population, but can tell us something about historic patterns of assimilation.)

For every 100 born (ethnic) Jews who also currently claim the Jewish religion, note the following in 1990/1991:

In Canada, we have 13.5 secular Jews, 17.6 non-Jews of Jewish ancestry, and 12.9 Jews by choice, or Canadians with Jewish religion but non-Jewish ethnic origin. In the United States, we have 26.6 secular Jews, and 14.8 non-Jews of Jewish ancestry, excluding the 700,000 children under 18 from the calculation. Including them – which is more comparable with the Canadian procedure – yields a whopping 31.4! In addition, there are 4.4 Jews by choice.

What do these comparisons tell us? First, there seems to be a much higher level – almost double – of secular Jewishness in the United States (26.6 to 13.5). Whatever these people may or may not do regarding Jewish practice, the proportion of American Jews who refuse to label their religion as Jewish is almost double that found in Canada. This is our first indicator of the more religiously diluted nature of American Jewish life.

The other two comparisons must be made with a bit more caution. The proportions of those of Jewish ancestry who claim another religion – who themselves or whose families have left the Jewish fold – are somewhat similar if we exclude the 700,000 American Gentile children mentioned above. If we include them all – and there is no compelling reason not to – then the American proportion is close to double that for Canada (31.4 to 17.6), another strong indicator of greater historic and ongoing assimilation in the United States.

We have to be most careful about the issue of Jews by choice. At first glance there seem to be almost three times the proportion of Jews by choice in Canada (12.9 to 4.4). But here we are less confident of the meaning of the Canadian data. As we noted, it is possible that these Canadian Jews did in fact have Jewish ethnic ancestry, but simply chose to select another option, such as Canadian or Polish or British or Moroccan, when responding to the census question on ethnic origin. So they would not be converts into Judaism. On the other hand, I have no doubt that formal conversions to and informal affiliations with Judaism are relatively more common in Canada. My best guess is that the Canadian rate of conversion – or the prevalence of true Jews by choice – would be double, not triple, the American rate: still a substantial difference.

The basic conclusions of this arithmetic exercise – that Canada has proportionally fewer secular Jews, more Jews by choice, and fewer non-Jews of Jewish ethnic origin, are not in dispute. But two observers can look at the same set of data and can be struck by, or choose to emphasize, different findings. I stress the current cultural and demographic disparities between the two countries, including rates of mixed marriage. Barry Kosmin, a noted Anglo-American scholar, finds these Canadian–American differences less remarkable:

"This statistical data suggests that the societal processes affecting Jews in both nations are similar and that the resulting Jewish identity constructs run along similar lines. Canadian Jewry is indeed more traditionally Jewish at present, but the gap is not as wide as some expected."[8]

One final digression. Canadian Jews represent just above 1 per cent of the Canadian population, and American Jews about 2 per cent. What do non-Jews think is the proportion of Jews? While there is no Canadian evidence, a 1998 survey by the American Anti-Defamation League of B'nai Brith is valuable. American non-Jews have an unbelievably inflated view of the size of the Jewish community, and I suspect similar patterns would be found in Canada. About 23 per cent of the American population felt that Jews comprised over one-quarter of the United States population; another 43 per cent felt that Jews represented between one-tenth and one-quarter! And those who held anti-Semitic views were also more likely to believe Jews were more numerous.[9] This is a double-edged sword. Some Jews would be pleased to have their numbers – and perhaps their power – so over-estimated, others might be worried. But it is interesting to juxtapose Jewish concerns about their population decline with the inflated perceptions of their neighbours.

MIXED MARRIAGE
IN CANADA

While some Jews yell *gevalt*, by comparison with other ethnic and religious groups, Jewish mixed-marriage rates are low. Indeed, they have always been relatively low in Canada, though rising of late.[1] Researcher Leo Davids estimates the 1991 stock of Jews in mixed unions (marriages and cohabiting couples) at 21 per cent.[2] But this figure hides the recent increase.

The annual mixed-marriage rate in Canada has risen steadily from 1961, as seen in Table Two.[3] For men, the rate increased from 10.3 per cent in 1961 to 29.1 per cent in 1997. (Beginning in 1974, the province of Quebec no longer compiled religious data on marriage, and the Canadian rate increased to 24.2 per cent. This reflected the fact that rates were lower in Quebec. At times the rates published also excluded data for Alberta and B.C., and some of the Atlantic provinces.) For women, the 1961 rate was 4.4 per cent, rising to 24.9 per cent by 1997. The greatest increases were in the 1960s and 1970s; by the 1980s and 1990s the rates increased very slowly, if at all. If we assume that the Quebec rate would still be lower than in the rest of Canada – which seems clear – we can guesstimate that in Canada in 1997, about 28 per cent of Jewish men and 24 per cent of Jewish women, married someone who was not Jewish. Note that these rates are also well below those for other endogamous religions. The overall 1997 Canadian mixed-marriage rates were 28 per cent for Mennonites, 42 per cent for Catholics, and 50 per cent for Eastern Orthodox. The Canadian Jewish numbers are also far below those for the United States, estimated at between 41 to 52 per cent for people marrying between 1985 and 1990, depending on the definitions and calculations.[4]

Mixed-marriage rates in Canada vary by region. Looking at the six major Canadian Jewish cities, we see great differences in the proportions of mixed couples among all Jewish couples. For Montreal, Toronto, and Winnipeg, the levels are lowest at 18, 22, and 24 per cent. Ottawa and Calgary are intermediate at 52 and 54 per cent. Vancouver is the least traditional at 75 per cent. In general, mixed marriage is highest in the West and in the Maritimes, while being much lower in Ontario and lower still in Quebec.[5] This corresponds to American patterns which find much higher rates of intermarriage outside older Jewish population centres in the Northeast.[6] Part of the reason lies in the demographic concentrations; intermarriage rates for Jews will be higher in those places with fewer Jews. On the other hand, there is some self-selection at work. Jews who move to outlying or frontier regions are likely less attached to Jewish tradition and community.[7]

My own sense is that eventually – decades rather than years – West Coast and East Coast intermarriage rates will converge, as will those of Canada and the United States. As seen in the table, the rates increased most dramatically in Canada from the early 1960s to the mid-1970s. From the mid-1970s to the mid-1990s the rates continued to increase, but at a much slower pace. There are two opposing trends. Natural processes of assimilation push rates higher. But the steady outmarriage of the more assimilated Jews means that those who remain may be more committed. In any event, intermarriage, as both mixed marriage and conversionary marriage, will always be a fact of life in Canada.

Canadian Jews, Mixed Marriages

YEAR	MALES			FEMALES			MALES AND FEMALES		
	Number Married	Number Entering Mixed Marriages	Percentage Entering Mixed Marriages	Number Married	Number Entering Mixed Marriages	Percentage Entering Mixed Marriages	Number Married	Number Entering Mixed Marriages	Percentage Entering Mixed Marriages
1926–30	.....	.....	.....	.....	.....	.....	.....	.....	2.5
1961	1562	161	10.3	1465	64	4.4	3027	225	7.4
1962	1440	174	12.1	1343	77	5.7	2783	251	9.0
1963	1485	182	12.3	1416	113	8.0	2901	295	10.2
1964	1547	185	12.0	1463	101	7.1	3010	286	9.5
1965	1655	205	12.4	1560	110	7.1	3215	315	9.8
1966	1812	201	12.0	1733	122	7.0	3545	323	9.1
1967	1999	247	12.4	1917	165	8.6	3916	412	10.5
1968	2253	312	13.8	2141	200	9.3	4397	512	11.6
1969	2353	366	15.6	2224	237	10.7	4577	603	13.2
1970	2429	394	16.2	2311	276	11.9	4740	670	14.1
1971	2462	435	17.7	2298	271	11.8	4760	706	14.8
1972	2521	456	18.1	2361	296	12.5	4882	752	15.4
1973	2316	449	19.4	2225	358	16.1	4541	807	17.8
1974*	1410	341	24.2	1329	260	19.6	2739	601	23.0
1975	1496	377	25.2	1409	209	20.6	2905	667	23.0
1976	1483	400	26.9	1370	307	22.4	2853	707	24.7
1977	1329	334	25.1	1274	279	21.8	2603	613	23.5
1978	1453	446	30.6	1357	300	22.1	2810	746	26.5
1979	1422	376	26.4	1339	293	21.9	2761	669	24.2
1980	1411	363	25.8	1500	452	30.1	2911	815	28.0
1981	1590	454	28.6	1523	387	25.4	3113	841	27.0

NOTE: *Excludes province of Quebec, from 1974, where about 30–40 per cent of Jewish marriages in Canada occur.

Table continued on next page

Canadian Jews, Mixed Marriages Cont'd

YEAR	MALES			FEMALES			MALES AND FEMALES		
	Number Married	Number Entering Mixed Marriages	Percentage Entering Mixed Marriages	Number Married	Number Entering Mixed Marriages	Percentage Entering Mixed Marriages	Number Married	Number Entering Mixed Marriages	Percentage Entering Mixed Marriages
1982	1466	413	28.2	1444	391	27.3	2910	804	27.6
1983	1417	424	29.9	1346	353	26.2	2763	777	28.1
1984	1397	432	30.9	1305	340	26.1	2702	772	28.6
1985**	1289	356	27.6	1183	250	21.1	2472	606	24.5
1986**	1257	353	28.3	1147	243	21.2	2404	596	24.8
1987	1346	359	26.7	1281	294	22.9	2627	653	24.9
1988	1373	383	27.9	1282	292	22.8	2655	675	25.4
1989	1393	408	28.3	1303	318	24.4	2696	726	26.9
1990	1464	429	29.3	1402	367	27.2	2866	796	27.8
1991	1446	430	29.7	1375	359	26.1	2821	789	28.0
1992	1358	413	30.4	3307	362	27.7	2665	775	29.1
1993**	1322	431	32.6	1222	331	27.1	2544	662	30.0
1994**	1242	374	30.1	1176	308	26.2	2418	682	28.2
1995**	1263	403	31.9	1186	326	27.5	2449	729	29.8
1996**	1157	372	32.1	1069	284	26.6	2226	656	29.5
1997**	1194	348	29.1	1127	281	24.9	2321	629	27.1

Source: Data from 1926 to 1930 from Louis Rosenberg, "Intermarriage in Canada 1921–1960," in *Intermarriage and Jewish Life: A Symposium,* ed. W. J. Cahnman, New York: Herzl Press, 1963; for 1961 to 1978, from Statistics Canada, Census Division, Vital Statistics Annual Reports. NOTE: **No data or poor response rates from British Columbia, Alberta, Quebec, New Brunswick, and Nova Scotia in various years.

APPENDIX IV

THE EFFECTS OF JEWISH EDUCATION

Quantitative research tries to disentangle the effect of Jewish education from that of family background, for various Jewish outcomes. Children who get more Jewish education are usually raised in more-Jewish families. What seems to be an effect of Jewish education may really be the impact of the family. So researchers try to compare Jews from similar family backgrounds, to see if variations in Jewish education alone lead to variations in Jewish identity. But even this approach is not foolproof. Even two Jewish families with identical family background characteristics, such as income, home observance, or synagogue attendance, may be qualitatively different if one family opts for a day school education for their children and one does not. So what seems to be an effect of Jewish education may still be the result of a more committedly Jewish family which chooses more Jewish education for their children. This type of self-selection can never be fully "controlled" in any experimental study or statistical exercise. Despite these problems, researchers have for some time tried to pinpoint the precise impact of Jewish schooling. The research is American but in general lines would apply to Canada.

An early study concluded that a minimum threshold of three thousand hours of Jewish education was required in order to have an impact. The three thousand hours could be obtained from any combination of day or supplementary schools. But Jewish schooling seemed to have a greater impact on adult religiosity compared to alternative experiences like attending a Jewish summer camp.[1] Some studies have focused on mixed marriage as an outcome. Two researchers concluded that "the great majority of day schoolers are married within the faith. . . . versus less than half of those who studied in the other types of Jewish schools."[2] Another study with 1990 NJPS data concluded that "compared to those with no Jewish education, therefore, persons who have six or more years of a Day School education are 17.5 per cent less likely to intermarry, all other characteristics being held constant."[3] Yet another study found that those with more Jewish education, notably day school education, had more memberships in Jewish organizations and synagogues, and lower rates of intermarriage.[4]

Researcher Bruce Phillips has added a level of complexity to these findings, in his study of the link between Jewish education and mixed marriage. In the United States he found that much of the effect of day schools is likely a result of being an immigrant or a child of immigrants. In his view "most of the day school graduates in the NJPS were first- and second-generation Jews who rarely married non-Jews regardless of the Jewish education they received. Thus, after controlling for gen- eration, Jewish day-school education has no more impact on mixed marriage than does a 2–3 day a week Jewish education." He concluded further that it is the duration of a Jewish education, notably past the age of thirteen, that is more important than the intensity of the type of Jewish education in determining the future probability of mixed mar- riage.[5] If Phillips is right, a good afternoon-school experience lasting into high school can be as effective as a day-school experience that ends at thirteen.

Canada has not yet produced the same extent of research on the consequences of Jewish education. One preliminary study in Montreal compared recent Jewish graduates from four Jewish and five "non- Jewish" high schools. On every measure, from ritual observance to actual intermarriage to Israel attachment, those who attended Jewish high schools scored higher. But the study could not definitively control for the probable differences in the respective family backgrounds of the two sets of students.[6]

ENDNOTES

INTRODUCTION: A PARADOXICAL PEOPLE

1. Charles Silberman, *A Certain People*. New York: Summit Books, 1985.
2. Calvin Goldscheider, *Jewish Continuity and Change*. Bloomington, Indiana: Indiana University Press, 1986.
3. Alan M. Dershowitz, *The Vanishing American Jew*. New York: Little, Brown and Company, 1997; Elliott Abrams, *Faith or Fear: How Jews Can Survive in a Christian America*. New York: The Free Press, 1997; Jack Wertheimer, *A People Divided: Judaism in Contemporary America*. New York: Basic Books, 1993; Samuel G. Freedman, *Jew Versus Jew: The Struggle for the Soul of American Jewry*. New York: Simon & Schuster, 2000.
4. Simon Rawidowicz, "Israel, The Ever-Dying People," in *Israel: The Ever-Dying People, and Other Essays*. Cranbury, N.J.: Associated University Presses, 1986, pp.53–54.
5. See David Vital, *The Future of the Jews*. Cambridge, Mass.: Harvard University Press, 1990; and Bernard Wasserstein, *Vanishing Diaspora: The Jews in Europe since 1945*. Cambridge, Mass.: Harvard University Press, 1996.
6. Edmond Y. Lipsitz, *World Jewish Directory*, 1996 Edition. Toronto: J.E.S.L. Educational Products, 1996, pp.308–310.
7. Cited in Milton Gordon, *Assimilation in American Life: The Role of Race, Religion, and National Origins*. New York: Oxford University Press, 1964, p.147. Kallen developed the idea of cultural pluralism in articles written in *The New Republic*, and apparently was first to use the term itself, in 1924.
8. Cited in Paul Yuzyk, *Ukrainian Canadians: Their Place and Role in Canadian Life*. Toronto: Ukrainian Canadian Business and Professional Federation, 1967, p.74.
9. Louis Rosenberg, *Canada's Jews: A Social and Economic Study of Jews in Canada in the 1930s*, ed. Morton Weinfeld (First pub.

Montreal: Canadian Jewish Congress, 1939). Montreal: McGill–
Queen's University Press, 1993. Rosenberg was an interesting
character. He was a lifelong Zionist and socialist. While working
for the Jewish Colonization Association in Western Canada, he
was active in the CCF. And while doing his research on Canadian
Jewish life he published, under the pseudonym of Watt Hugh
McCollum, the popular anti-capitalist tract *Who Owns Canada?
An Examination of the Facts Concerning the Concentration of
the Ownership and Control of the Means of Production,
Distribution and Exchange in Canada* (Regina: CCF Research
Bureau, 1935).

10. Ernest van den Haag, *The Jewish Mystique*. New York: Stein and
Day, 1969.

11. Raphael Patai, *The Jewish Mind*. New York: Charles Scribner's
Sons, 1977, p.8.

12. See my Introduction in *Who Speaks for Canada? Words That Shape
a Country*, ed. Desmond Morton and Morton Weinfeld. Toronto:
McClelland & Stewart, 1998, pp.xvi–xx.

13. Historian Jonathan Sarna, in stressing the particular Canadian
immigration sequence, emphasizes the recent influx of North
African Jews to Montreal and their unique influence on strengthening tradition. Gunther Plaut, Biblical scholar and rabbi emeri-
tus of Holy Blossom in Toronto, focuses on the greater proportion
of Holocaust survivors in Canada. He recalls that at Canadian
Jewish Congress meetings during the 1960s, "speakers could talk
Yiddish in a debate and no translation was deemed necessary. In
those days, too, half my Temple Board could speak or understand
it." Sociologist Robert Brym also does not feel that the differences
stem from innate social and political features of Canada and the
United States: "I feel that too much is often made of Canadian
multicultural policies as a force perpetuating ethnic culture, including Jewish culture; we're no more of an ethnic mosaic, and no less
an ethnic melting pot, than the U.S.A."

Sociologist William Shaffir recognizes the role of immigration,
but "is not entirely convinced that the two communities will, over
time, display common features." Political scientist Daniel Elazar

and sociologist Stuart Schoenfeld stress that Canada does not share the American rigorous separation of church and state, which works to strengthen Canadian Jewish communal life and Jewish education compared to the American case. These views were sent to me in personal communication. Sociologists Jeffrey Reitz and Raymond Breton have questioned whether this celebrated melting pot versus mosaic distinction really makes a difference in the lives of minorities in Canada and the United States. See their *The Illusion of Difference: Realities of Ethnicity in Canada and the United States*. Toronto: C.D. Howe Institute, 1994.

14. For an exception see Harold Troper and Morton Weinfeld, *Old Wounds: Jews, Ukrainians, and the Hunt for Nazi War Criminals in Canada*. Markham, Ont.: Viking, 1988.

15. Seymour Martin Lipset, "The Study of Jewish Communities in a Comparative Context," *The Jewish Journal of Sociology* 5:2, 1963, pp.157–66.

16. Weber argued that certain tenets of Protestantism were more conducive than Catholicism for the kind of innovative and risk-taking behaviours needed for capitalist entrepreneurs. Max Weber, *The Protestant Ethic and the Spirit of Capitalism*, trans. Talcott Parsons. New York: Charles Scribner and Sons, 1958.

1. WHO ARE THE JEWS?:
The Elements of Jewish Diversity

1. Irving Abella, *A Coat of Many Colours: Two Centuries of Jewish Life in Canada*. Toronto: Lester and Orpen Dennys, 1990; Gerald J. J. Tulchinsky, *Taking Root: The Origins of the Canadian Jewish Community*. Toronto: Lester Publishing Co., 1990; and Tulchinsky, *Branching Out: The Transformation of the Canadian Jewish Community*. Toronto: Stoddart, 1998.

2. Raphael Patai, *Tents of Jacob: The Diaspora, Yesterday and Today*. Englewood Cliffs, N.J.: Prentice Hall, 1971.

3. Louis Rosenberg, *Canada's Jews*, ed. Weinfeld.

4. Some of this is captured in the letters to the editor of *The Forward*, the Yiddish daily in New York. See *A Bintel Brief*, ed. Isaac Metzker. New York: Doubleday, 1971.

5. Jean-Claude Lasry, "A Francophone Diaspora in Quebec," in *The Canadian Jewish Mosaic*, ed. Morton Weinfeld, William Shaffir, and Irwin Cotler. Toronto: John Wiley and Sons, 1981, pp.221–40.

6. Nicholas Wade, "Africans Exhibit Jewish Ancestry," *The Gazette*, May 9, 1999.

7. An example is the cephalic index, which measures the ratio of the distance from the top of one ear to the other, divided by the distance from the forehead to the back of the head.

8. Patai, *Tents of Jacob*; Patai, *The Myth of the Jewish Race* (rev. ed.). Detroit: Wayne State University Press, 1989.

9. Quoted in Richard M. Goodman, *Genetic Disorders among the Jewish People*. Baltimore: Johns Hopkins University Press, 1979, p.29.

10. For a review of these and other cases, see Hillel Halkin, "Wandering Jews – and Their Genes," *Commentary*, September 2000, pp.54–61.

11. For a review see Richard M. Goodman, *Genetic Disorders among the Jewish People*, and *Genetic Diseases Among Ashkenazi Jews*, ed. Richard M. Goodman and Arno G. Motulsky. New York: Raven Press, 1979.

12. Ivan Oransky, "Studies of Mental Illness Train Spotlight on Genes," *The Forward*, August 20, 1999.

13. Rosenberg, *Canada's Jews*, ed. Weinfeld, ch.9. In fact, the Jewish death rate was 5.5 per 1,000 compared to 10.3, and the Jewish infant mortality rate was 39.8 per 1,000 compared to 82.4.

14. Odin Anderson, "Infant Mortality and Social and Cultural Factors: Historical Trends and Current Problems," in *Patients, Physicians and Illness Sourcebook in Behavioral Science and Medicine*, ed. Egbert Gartly Jaco. Glencoe, Ill.: The Free Press, 1958, pp.21–22.

15. David Mechanic, "Religion, Religiosity, and Illness Behavior: The Special Case of the Jews," *Human Organization*, 22:3, 1963, p.206.

16. Sheryl Gay Stolberg, "Concern among Jews is Heightened as Scientists Deepen Gene Studies," *New York Times*, 22 April, 1998, p.A24.

17. van den Haag, *The Jewish Mystique*, ch.1; Arno G. Motulsky, "Possible Selection Effects of Urbanization on Ashkenazi Jews," in *Genetic Diseases among Ashkenazi Jews*, ed. Goodman and Motulsky, pp.301–315.

18. Thorstein Veblen, "The Intellectual Pre-eminence of Jews in Modern Europe," *Political Science Quarterly* vol.34, 1919, pp.3–42.

19. Patai, *The Jewish Mind*, pp.318, 339–41.

20. L. D. Cranberg and M. L. Albert, "The Chess Mind," in *The Exceptional Brain: Neuropsychology of Talent and Special Abilities*, ed. L. Kobler and D. Fein. New York: Guilford Press, 1988.

21. Bertha Brody, *A Psychological Study of Immigrant Children at Ellis Island*. Baltimore: Williams and Wilkins, 1926; Thomas Sowell, "Race and IQ Reconsidered," in *Essays and Data on American Ethnic Groups*, ed. Sowell and Lynn Collins. Washington, D.C.: The Urban Institute, 1978; Sowell, *Race and Culture: A World View*. New York: Basic Books, 1994, ch.6.

22. M. E. Backman, "Patterns of Mental Abilities: Ethnic, Socio-economic, and Sex Differences," *American Educational Research Journal* vol.9, 1972, pp.1–12. The advantage in the math and verbal tests ranged from one-half to a full standard deviation.

23. Christopher Jencks, "What Color Is IQ: Intelligence and Race," in *The Fallacy of IQ*, ed. Carl Senna. New York: The Third Press (Joseph Okpaku), 1973, p.39.

24. For a review of all these studies see Miles D. Storfer, *Intelligence and Giftedness: The Contributions of Heredity and Early Environment*. San Francisco: Jossey-Bass Publishers, 1990, pp.316-17.

25. Kevin Marjoribanks, "Ethnic and Environmental Influences on Mental Abilities," *American Journal of Sociology* 78, 1972, pp.323–37. The Jewish advantages in the verbal and number tests were almost one-and-a-half standard deviations.

26. See Storfer, *Intelligence and Giftedness*, pp.324–29 for a review.

27. Arthur Koestler, *The Thirteenth Tribe: The Khazar Empire and Its Heritage*. New York: Random House, 1976.

28. See Joshua Trachtenberg. *The Devil and the Jews: The Medieval Conception of the Jews and Its Relation to Modern Antisemitism* (second paperback edition). Philadelphia: Jewish Publication Society, 1983.

29. See Rich Cohen, *Tough Jews*. New York: Simon & Schuster, 1998.

30. Robert Slater, *Great Jews in Sports*. New York: Jonathan David Publishers, 1983.

31. Peter Levine, *Ellis Island to Ebbets Field: Sport and the American Jewish Experience*. New York: Oxford University Press, 1992.

32. Stanley R. Barrett, *Is God a Racist? The Right Wing in Canada.* Toronto: University of Toronto Press, 1987.

33. "Project Targets Visit to Israel," *The Globe and Mail*, November 17, 1998. The Birthright Israel project is a new initiative which eventually aims to send thousands of young Jews, aged 18–26, to Israel each year at little or no cost. Initial estimates of the cost of this and related Israel youth projects are $300 million over five years.

34. Marcel Danesi, "Ethnic Language and Acculturation: The Case of Italo-Canadians," *Canadian Ethnic Studies* 17:1, 1985, pp.88–103.

35. Raymond Breton, "Institutional Completeness of Ethnic Communities and the Personal Relations of Immigrants," *American Journal of Sociology* 70, 1955, pp.193–205.

2. QUALITY, QUANTITY, AND CONFLICT:
The Social and Demographic Context of Jewish Survival

1. In this section I rely heavily on my "Between Quality and Quantity: Demographic Trends and Jewish Continuity," in *Creating the Jewish Future*, ed. Michael Brown and Bernard Lightman. Walnut Creek, Calif.: Altamira Press (Sage), 1998, pp.216–33.

2. *The Jerusalem Report*, Letters, October 31, 1996.

3. S. Liberman and M. Weinfeld, "Demographic Trends and Jewish Survival," *Midstream* vol.24, November 1978, pp.9–19.

4. David Singer, "Living with Intermarriage," in *American Jews: A Reader*, ed. M. Sklare. New York: Behrman House, 1983, pp.395–412.

5. Steven M. Cohen, "Cohen Defends his Views," *Moment* vol.20, April 1995, pp.68–69.

6. Milton Himmelfarb and Victor Baras, *Zero Population Growth – For Whom? Differential Fertility and Minority Group Survival.* Westport, Conn.: Greenwood Press, 1978.

7. John A. Hostetler and Gertrude Enders Huntington, *The Hutterites in North America.* New York: Holt, Rhinehart and Winston, 1980.

8. Rosenberg, *Canada's Jews*, ed. Weinfeld, ch.9.

9. There are exceptions to every rule. High intermarriage rates in Weimar Germany did not prevent the rise of Hitler to power. And in the former Yugoslavia, high rates did not prevent wholesale atrocities by Serbs, Croats, Kosovar Albanians, and Bosnians against each other.

10. Readers will discern a strand of socio-biological reasoning in this argument.

11. Lewis A. Coser, *The Functions of Social Conflict*. Glencoe, Ill.: The Free Press, 1956.

12. Joanna Stark Glassman, "The Relationship between Jewish Ethnic and Religious Identity" (M.A. thesis, Department of Counselling Psychology, University of British Columbia, August 1992), quoted from *Focus for the Future*. Vancouver: Jewish Federation of Greater Vancouver, November 1993, report no.5.

13. These figures are taken from J. L. Torczyner, S. Brotman, K. Viragh, and G. Goldmann, "Demographic Challenges facing Canadian Jewry: Initial Findings from the 1991 Census." Montreal: Council of Jewish Federations and McGill University, 1993.

14. To be sure, the fairly impressive Canadian gain of 14.2 per cent is deceptive. Most of the increase comes from the category of secular/ethnic Jews. If we look at just those Jews who claim to be Jewish by religion, the increase is from 296,000 to 318,070, an increase of (only) 7.5 per cent. This is the category likely to contain fewer secular or assimilated Jews. Still, this is an increase.

3. BUILDING A COMMUNITY:
Migration and Regional Settlement

1. Abella, *A Coat of Many Colours*, pp.6–7.

2. Joseph Kage, *With Faith and Thanksgiving: The Story of Two Hundred Years of Jewish Immigration*. Montreal: Eagle Publishing, 1962.

3. Stephen Birmingham, *The Grandees: America's Sephardic Elite*. New York: Harper and Row, 1971.

4. Lloyd Gartner, "Immigration in the Formation of American Jewry, 1840–1925" in *The Jew in American Society*, ed. Marshall Sklare. New York: Behrman House, pp.31–50.

5. Kage, *With Faith and Thanksgiving*, p.263.

6. Gerald Tulchinsky, *Taking Root*, pp.57–58.

7. Stephen Birmingham, *Our Crowd: The Great Jewish Families of New York*. New York: Harper and Row, 1967.

8. In 1851, Jews were found in nine towns, and by 1871, in 29. Kage, *With Faith and Thanksgiving*, p.27.

9. H. H. Ben-Sasson, *A History of the Jewish People*. Cambridge, Mass.: Harvard University Press, 1976, p.757.

10. Rosenberg, *Canada's Jews*, ed. Weinfeld, pp.135–36.

11. Kage, *With Faith and Thanksgiving*, p.24.

12. Gartner, "Immigration in the Formation of American Jewry," in *The Jew in American Society*, ed. Sklare.

13. Abella, *A Coat of Many Colours*, pp.87, 112; Stephen Speisman, *The Jews of Toronto: A History to 1937*. Toronto: McClelland & Stewart, 1979, p.57.

14. Kage, *With Faith and Thanksgiving*, pp.30–31.

15. See Erna Paris, *Jews: An Account of Their Experience in Canada*. Toronto: Macmillan, 1980; and Abella, *A Coat of Many Colours*.

16. Thomas Kessner, *The Golden Door: Italian and Jewish Immigrant Mobility in New York City, 1880–1915*. New York: Oxford University Press, 1977; Rosenberg, *Canada's Jews*, ed. Weinfeld, p.162.

17. Irving Abella and Harold Troper, *None is Too Many: Canada and the Jews of Europe, 1933–1948*. Toronto: Lester & Orpen Dennys, 1982.

18. Kage, *With Faith and Thanksgiving*, p.129.

19. M. Giberovitch, "The Contribution of Holocaust Survivors to Montreal Jewish Community Life," *Canadian Ethnic Studies* 26:1, 1994, pp.74–85. Franklin Bialystok, *Delayed Impact: The Holocaust and the Canadian Jewish Community*. Montreal: McGill–Queen's University Press, 2000.

20. William B. Helmreich, *Against All Odds: Holocaust Survivors and the Successful Lives They Made in America*. New York: Simon & Schuster, 1992, p.264.

21. The American population estimate is from S. Goldstein, "American Jewry: A Demographic Profile," in *The Jew in American Society*, ed. Sklare, p.101. The Canadian figure is from Kage, *With Faith and Thanksgiving*, p.261.

22. Rabbi Gunther Plaut, personal communication, December 31, 1997.

23. Jean-Claude Lasry, "Sephardim and Ashkenazim in Montreal," in *The Jews in Canada*, ed. Robert J. Brym, William Shaffir, and Morton Weinfeld. Toronto: Oxford University Press, 1993, pp.395–401; personal communication with Lasry, Aug. 18, 1998.

24. Charles Shahar and Randal Schnoor, "A Survey of Jewish Life in Montreal," Part II. Montreal: Federation of Jewish Community Services of Montreal, 1997, p.3; Charles Shahar, personal communication, Nov. 24, 1998.

25. See Jean-Claude Lasry, "A Francophone Diaspora in Quebec," in *The Canadian Jewish Mosaic*, ed. M. Weinfeld, W. Shaffir, and I. Cotler, pp.221–40; Lasry, "Sephardim and Ashkenazim in Montreal," in *The Jews in Canada*, ed. Brym, Shaffir, and Weinfeld; Weinfeld, "The Jews of Quebec: An Overview," in *The Jews in Canada*, ed. Brym, Shaffir, and Weinfeld, pp.171–92.

26. Yaacov Glickman, "Russian Jews in Canada: Threat to Identity or Promise of Renewal?" in *Multiculturalism, Jews, and Identities in Canada*, ed. Howard Adelman and John H. Simpson. Jerusalem: Magnes Press, 1996, pp.192–218. The Russian Jewish migration has also raised the spectre of a new Jewish association with organized crime with international dimensions, in Canada as well as the United States, Israel, Russia and elsewhere in Europe. It fits models of crime associated with earlier waves of Jewish immigrants.

27. Roberta L. Markus and Donald V. Schwartz, "Soviet Jewish Émigrés in Toronto: Ethnic Self-identity and Issues of Integration," in *The Jews in Canada*, ed. Brym, Shaffir, and Weinfeld. Toronto: Oxford University Press, 1993, p.402.

28. See Rina Cohen, "The New Immigrants: A Contemporary Profile," in *From Immigration to Integration: The Canadian Jewish Experience: A Millennium Edition*, ed. Ruth Klein and Frank Dimant. Toronto: B'nai Brith and Malcolm Lester, 2001, pp.216–17.

29. Steven J. Gold, "Soviet Jews in the United States," in *The American Jewish Yearbook*, vol.94, ed. David Singer. New York: The American Jewish Committee, 1994, pp.3–59. Recall that the American Jewish population is about fifteen times that of Canada.

30. Ministry of Immigration and Absorption, *1998 Annual Report on Immigration and Absorption in Israel* (Jerusalem, 1998.)

31. Tzila Baum, personal communication, January 20, 1998.

32. Gerald Gold and Rina Cohen, "The Myth of Return and Israeli Ethnicity in Toronto," in *Multiculturalism, Jews, and Identities in Canada*, ed. Adelman and Simpson, pp.179–91. Rina Cohen, "The

New Immigrants," in *From Immigration to Integration*, ed. Klein and Dimant, p.221.

33. Steven J. Gold and Bruce A. Philips, "Israelis in the United States," in *The American Jewish Yearbook*, vol.96, ed. David Singer. New York: The American Jewish Committee, 1996, pp.51–104.

34. Gold and Cohen, "The Myth of Return," in *Multiculturalism, Jews, and Identities in Canada*, ed. Adelman and Simpson, 179–91.

35. See Robert F. Barsky, "Refugees from Israel: A Threat to Canadian Jewish Identity?" in *Multiculturalism, Jews, and Identities in Canada*, ed. Adelman and Simpson, pp.219–62; Irwin Cotler, "Refugees, Human Rights, and the Making of Israeli Foreign Policy," in *Still Moving: Recent Jewish Migration in Comparative Perspective*, ed. Daniel Elazar and Morton Weinfeld. New Brunswick, N.J.: Transaction Publishers, 2000, pp.265–84.

36. In addition, 303 claims were abandoned and 629 were refused.

37. Cotler, p.271. "Refugees, Human Rights, and the Making of Israeli Foreign Policy," in *Still Moving*, ed. Elazar and Weinfeld.

38. Ron Csillag, "Canada Continues to Accept 'Refugees' from Israel," *The Canadian Jewish News*, August 17, 2000, p.22.

39. For a discussion of the integration of Jews and the role of JIAS and other agencies, see Morton Weinfeld, "The Integration of Jewish Immigrants in Montreal: Models and Dilemmas of Ethnic Match," in *Still Moving*, ed. Elazar and Weinfeld, pp.285–98.

40. Gold and Cohen, "The Myth of Return," in *Multiculturalism, Jews, and Identities in Canada*," ed. Adelman and Simpson.

41. Anna Rubalsky, personal communication, January 28, 1998.

42. Daphne Gottlieb Taras and Gerry Beitel, *Preliminary Analysis, Jewish Community Council Survey As at January 30, 1997*. Calgary: Jewish Community Council, 1997.

43. These data are from Statistics Canada, *Religions in Canada*, 1991 Census, Census Catalogue no. 93-319-XPB.

44. Anne Kilpatrick, "The Jewish Immigrant Aid Services: An Ethnic Lobby in the Canadian Political System." (M.A. thesis, Department of Sociology, McGill University, 1993.)

45. Bob Luck of JIAS, Montreal, personal communication, August 24, 1998.

LIKE EVERYONE ELSE . . . BUT DIFFERENT

46. Torczyner et al., *Demographic Challenges Facing Canadian Jewry*, p.24. About 28 per cent were foreign-born in 1991. This figure is based on those claim Jewish religion and those who are Jewish by ethnic origin with "no religion," or secular Jews. The proportion is even higher, roughly one-third, for those who are Jewish by religion, excluding secular Jews, who are more likely to be Canadian-born.

47. Goldstein, "American Jewry," in *The Jew in American Society*, ed. Sklare, p.102. Of far greater interest to American Jewish researchers are internal United States migration and the southern and western drift of American Jews. See Sidney Goldstein and Alice Goldstein, *Jews on the Move: Implications for Jewish Identity*. Albany: State University of New York Press, 1996.

48. Franklin Bialystok, *Delayed Impact: The Holocaust and the Canadian Jewish Community*. Montreal: McGill–Queen's University Press, 2000.

49. Nancy Tienhaara, *Canadian Views on Immigration and Population: An Analysis of Post-War Gallup Polls*. Ottawa: Department of Manpower and Immigration, 1974, p.59.

50. Rod McQueen, "Special Report: The Rich List," *National Post*, April 22, 2000, p.E2.

51. Lasry, "A Francophone Diaspora in Quebec," in *The Canadian Jewish Mosaic*, ed. Weinfeld, Shaffir, and Cotler, p.232.

52. Charles Shahar, "Sépharade 2000: Challenges and Perspectives for the Sephardic Community of Montreal." Fédération CJA Montreal, 2000. The study is based on a survey of 441 Sephardi Jewish adults in Montreal, drawn from a sample built from Sephardi-sounding names in the Montreal telephone directory, the Combined Jewish Appeal list, and the *Voix Sépharade* mailing list. So the sample is not random, and might tend to undercount Sephardi women married to non-Sephardi and indeed non-Jewish men.

53. When adjusted for urban-rural difference – Jews were heavily urbanized and crime rates are always higher in cities – the Jewish rate fell to 226. Rosenberg, *Canada's Jews*, ed. Weinfeld, p.289.

54. Isaac Metzker, *A Bintel Brief*: Tulchinsky, *Branching Out*, ch.7; Cyril H. Levitt and William Shaffir, *The Riot at Christie Pits*. Toronto: Lester & Orpen Dennys, 1987.

55. Eugene Orenstein, "Yiddish Culture in Canada: Yesterday and Today," in *The Canadian Jewish Mosaic*, ed. Weinfeld, Shaffir, and Cotler, pp.293–315.

56. Jean R. Burnet and Howard Palmer, *Coming Canadians: An Introduction to a History of Canada's Peoples*. Toronto: McClelland & Stewart, 1988.

57. Rosenberg, *Canada's Jews*, ed. Weinfeld, pp.19, 23.

58. Ibid., pp.31–36.

59. Speisman, *The Jews of Toronto*, pp.82–93; Rosenberg, *Canada's Jews*, ed. Weinfeld, pp.31–36.

60. Rosenberg, ibid., ch.23; Abella, *A Coat of Many Colours*, p.91; Arthur A. Chiel, *The Jews in Manitoba: A Social History*. Toronto: University of Toronto Press, 1961.

61. Abraham Arnold, "The Mystique of Western Jewry," in *The Canadian Jewish Mosaic*, ed. Weinfeld, Shaffir, and Cotler, p.260.

62. Torczyner et al., "Demographic Challenges," p.6.

63. In 1991, Jews comprised about 14 per cent of the population of the city of New York, and 11 per cent of the suburbs, both down slightly from earlier years, as the American Jewish population spreads south and west. Goldstein and Goldstein, *Jews on the Move*, p.291.

64. Gershon Hundert, personal communication, August 21, 1998.

65. Interview with Franklin Bialystok, March 30, 2001.

66. As examples see Morley Torgov, *A Good Place to Come From*. Toronto: Lester & Orpen, 1974; and Fredelle Bruser Maynard, *Raisins and Almonds*. Toronto: General Publishing, 1972.

67. Sheldon Maerov, personal communication, December 12, 1997.

68. Sheva Medjuck, "Jewish Survival in Small Communities," in *The Jews in Canada*, ed., Brym, Shaffir, and Weinfeld, pp.363–78 (quotation from p.363).

4. EARNING A LIVING
From Work to Wealth

1. John A. Porter, *The Vertical Mosaic: An Analysis of Social Class and Power in Toronto*. Toronto: University of Toronto Press, 1965, p.287.

2. Wallace Clement, *The Canadian Corporate Elite: An Analysis of Economic Power*. Toronto: McClelland & Stewart, 1975, pp.237–38.

3. Peter C. Newman, *The Canadian Establishment*, vol.1. Toronto: McClelland & Stewart, 1975.

4. Abella, *A Coat of Many Colours*, pp.12, 38.

5. See Tulchinsky, *Taking Root*, pp.133–34.

6. Abella, *A Coat of Many Colours*, pp.135–43; Tulchinsky, *Taking Root*, pp.214–23.

7. Speisman, *The Jews of Toronto*, pp.195–97.

8. Abella, *A Coat of Many Colours*, pp.194–95.

9. Morton Weinfeld, "The Ethnic Sub-economy: Explication and Analysis of the Jews of Montreal," in *The Jews in Canada*, ed. Brym, Shaffir, and Weinfeld, pp.218–37.

10. Abella, *A Coat of Many Colours*, pp.143, 109.

11. Kessner, *The Golden Door*; Rosenberg, *Canada's Jews*, ed. Weinfeld, ch.16, 17.

12. Ibid., p.162. The actual percentages reveal the dramatic differences. We find that 18 per cent of Jews were merchants compared to three per cent for all Canadians; 30 per cent were clerks compared to 13 per cent, while only 6 per cent were unskilled workers compared to 33 per cent.

13. Ibid., pp.169, 176.

14. Ibid., pp.191, 214.

15. McCollum [Rosenberg], *Who Owns Canada?*

16. See Clement, *The Canadian Corporate Elite*; Newman, *The Canadian Establishment*; Porter, *The Vertical Mosaic*.

17. Ibid.

18. Weinfeld, "The Ethnic Sub-Economy," in *The Jews in Canada*, ed. Brym, Shaffir, and Weinfeld.

19. About 28 per cent of the third generation said most of their clients were Jewish, 61 per cent said they were either self-employed of worked for Jewish firms, and 28 per cent said most of their business associates were Jews.

20. Jeffrey Reitz, "Ethnic Concentrations in Labour Markets and Their Implications for Ethnic Inequality," in Raymond Breton et al., *Ethnic Identity and Equality: Varieties of Experience in a Canadian City*. Toronto: University of Toronto Press, 1990, p.192. The survey

included 168 Jewish respondents: 64 immigrants, 64 second-generation, and 40 third-generation.

21. Ibid., p.165.

22. Ibid., p.186. Reitz found that among third-generation Jews, 33 per cent were employed in occupations of Jewish concentration, 43 per cent were self-employed, 26 per cent worked in a Jewish-run business, and 54 per cent had "more than a few" Jewish customers or clients. The Jewish proportion of the Toronto population was between 3 and 4 per cent.

23. The directory is a project of The Jewish Business Network, directed by Rabbi Ronnie Fine of Lubavitch, and founded in 1992. It has as its main activity a series of monthly luncheons, each of which can draw up to 200 people.

24. Scott Davies and Neil Guppy, "Race and Canadian Education," in *Racism and Social Inequality in Canada: Concepts, Controversies and Strategies of Resistance*, ed. Vic Satzewich. Toronto: Thompson Educational Publishing, 1998, pp.131–56. The Jewish statistics refer to Jews by religion.

25. Statistics cited refer to my own analysis of the Statistics Canada 1991 Census Public Use Microdata file, unless otherwise cited. Of Jewish men, 8 per cent had a master's and 2.3 per cent had doctorates, compared to 2.3 per cent and 0.8 per cent for non-Jews. For Jewish women the proportions are 5.6 per cent and 0.8 per cent, compared to 1.3 per cent and 0.1 per cent for non-Jews.

26. Charles Kadushin, *The American Intellectual Elite*. Boston: Little, Brown, 1974.

27. Seymour Martin Lipset and Everett Carl Ladd, Jr., "The Changing Social Origins of American Academics," in *Qualitative and Quantitative Social Research, Papers in Honor of Paul F. Lazarsfeld*, ed. Robert K. Merton, James S. Coleman, and Peter H. Rossi. New York: The Free Press, 1979, p.326.

28. Porter, *The Vertical Mosaic*, p.501.

29. R. Ogmundson and J. McLaughlin, "Changes in an Intellectual Elite 1960–1990: The Royal Society Revisited," *Canadian Review of Sociology and Anthropology*, 31:1, 1994, pp.1–13.

30. Ibid., p.7.

31. The data for the three cities are taken from the following three studies, all based on 1991 Census data: James Torczyner and Shari Brotman, *Diversity and Continuity: The Demographic Challenges Facing Montreal Jewry*. Toronto 1994; James Torczyner, Shari Brotman, and Jay Brodbar, *Rapid Growth and Transformation: Demographic Challenges Facing the Jewish Community of Greater Toronto*. Montreal, 1995; James Torczyner, Shari Brotman, and Jean Gerber, *Diversity, Identity and Rapid Growth: Critical Issues Facing the Greater Vancouver Jewish Community*. Toronto, 1995. All these studies were produced by the McGill Consortium for Ethnicity and Strategic Social Planning, in conjunction with the Council of Jewish Federations (Canada).

32. In 1991, Jewish men had a 5.7 per cent rate and Jewish women were at 8.6 per cent. This compares with 10.1 per cent and 10.2 per cent nationally.

33. In 1991 Jews made up 3.3 per cent of Montreal's population, yet they comprised 10.1 per cent of the doctors and dentists and 5.4 per cent of the accountants, lawyers, and notaries. (These percentages are kept down because anglophone Jews do not service francophone populations to the same extent. Moreover, the French middle class in Quebec has historically pursued careers in law and medicine, rather than business.) In Toronto, where they made up 4.1 per cent, Jews comprised one-quarter of the doctors and dentists and 9.1 per cent of the accountants, lawyers, and notaries. In Vancouver, where Jews comprised 1.2 per cent of the population, they were 6.7 per cent of all doctors and 1.9 per cent of accountants, lawyers, and notaries.

34. Quoted in Seymour Martin Lipset and Earl Rabb, *Jews and the New American Scene*, Cambridge, Mass.: Harvard University Press, 1995, p.26.

35. The sources for this information are published lists of wealthy Canadians, taken from books which update the analyses of John Porter, Wallace Clement, and Peter C. Newman discussed earlier, and from magazine and newspaper articles. By examining first and second names, consulting with informants, and checking with basic references like *Canadian Who's Who*, I count those who "seem"

Jewish. Some errors creep in; people who are Jewish may be omitted, and some who are not may be mistakenly so identified and counted. My apologies to those mislabelled, assuming they take offence. But these few cases will not detract from the general patterns of Jewish representation, and the two types of errors may well cancel each other out. In any case, they do not affect the orders of magnitude.

36. Peter C. Newman, *The Acquisitors: The Canadian Establishment*, vol.2. Toronto: McClelland & Stewart, 1983; Diane Francis, *Controlling Interest: Who Owns Canada?* Toronto: Macmillan, 1986. The ten families are: Bronfman (Charles and Edgar), Ivanier, Steinberg, Posluns, Bronfman (Edward and Peter), Reichmann, Mann, Wolfe, Singer, and Belzberg.

37. *Financial Post Magazine*, January 1996, p.14.

38. *National Post*, April 22, 2000, section E.

39. *Canadian Business*, August 7, 2000, 72:14, pp.60–107. This list included both public and privately held corporations, as well as real estate and other assets.

40. *Affaires Plus*, July/August 1997, pp.34–35.

41. Peter C. Newman, *Titans: How the New Canadian Establishment Seized Power*. Toronto: Viking, 1998.

42. Quoted in ibid., pp.121–22.

43. Ibid., p.583.

44. University of Toronto, "National Report," published by the Division of Development and University Relations, 1998; McGill Fund Council, "Report on Private Giving, 1995–96," McGill University Development Office, 1996.

45. Rosemary Sexton, *The Glitter Girls*. Toronto: Macmillan, 1993, p.58.

46. James Torczyner, "The Persistence of Invisible Poverty Among Jews in Canada," in *The Jews in Canada*, ed. Brym, Shaffir, and Weinfeld, pp.379–94.

47. The 1996 findings are taken from a study by social work Professor Allan Moscovitch of Carleton University, as reported in the *Canadian Jewish News*, August 31, 2000.

48. Torczyner, Brotman, and Brodbar, *Rapid Growth and Transformation*, p.148. For example, in Toronto they represented one-third of the Jewish poor but only one-sixth of the overall poor population.

49. Charles Shahar, Morton Weinfeld, and Randal Schnoor, *Survey of the Hassidic and Ultra-Orthodox Communities in Outremont and Surrounding Areas.* Outremont: Coalition of Outremont Hassidic Organizations, 1997.

50. Reitz, "Ethnic Concentrations in Labour Markets," in *Ethnic Identity and Equality*, ed. Breton et al., p.161.

51. Jason Z. Lian and David R. Mathews, "Does the Vertical Mosaic Still Exist? Ethnicity and Income in Canada, 1991," in *Canadian Review of Sociology and Anthropology*, 35:4, 1998, pp.461–82.

52. Peter S. Li, *Ethnic Inequality in a Class Society.* Toronto: Wall & Thompson Press, 1988, p.116.

53. Monica Boyd, "Gender, Visible Minority and Immigrant Earnings Inequality: Reassessing an Employment Equity Premise," in *Deconstructing a Nation*, ed. Vic Satzewich. Halifax: Fernwood Publishing, 1992, p.305.

54. James Geschwender and Neil Guppy, "Ethnicity, Educational Attainment, and Earned Income," *Canadian Ethnic Studies* 27:1, 1995, pp.67–84.

55. Peter S. Li, "The Market Value and Social Value of Race," in *Racism and Social Inequality in Canada*, ed. Satzewich, pp.115–30.

56. Li, *Ethnic Inequality in a Class Society*, p.102. Jews averaged an extra $1,300 for each year of schooling compared to the average Canadian figure of $800.

57. Nathan Hurvitz, "Sources of Motivation and Achievement of American Jews," *Jewish Social Studies*, Oct. 1961, pp.217–23.

58. Weber, *The Protestant Ethic and the Spirit of Capitalism*, tr. Parsons; Werner Sombart, *The Jews and Modern Capitalism.* London: Collier, 1962.

59. Andrew Greeley and Peter Rossi, *The Education of Catholic Americans.* Chicago: Aldine Publishing Company, 1966; Greeley, *Ethnicity in the United States: A Preliminary Reconnaissance.* New York: John Wiley, 1974.

60. James Coleman, Thomas Hoffer, and Sally Kilgore, *High School Achievement: Public, Catholic, and Private Schools Compared.* New York: Basic Books, 1982.

61. Lian and Mathews, "Does the Vertical Mosaic Still Exist?" p.467.

62. See Shahar, Weinfeld, and Schnoor, "Survey of the Hassidic and Ultra-Orthodox Communities."

63. Miriam Slater, "My Son the Doctor: Aspects of Mobility among American Jews," *American Sociological Review* 34, 1969, pp.359–73.

64. Nathan Glazer, "American Jews and the Attainment of Middle-Class Rank," in *The Jews: Social Patterns of an American Group*, ed. Marshall Sklare. Glencoe, Ill.: The Free Press, 1958, pp.138–46.

65. Harold Stevenson and Shin-Ying Lee, *Contexts of Achievement: A Study of American, Chinese, and Japanese Children*. Chicago: Society for Research on Child Development, 1990.

66. Sexton, *The Glitter Girls*, pp.150–51.

67. Newman, *Titans*, p.333.

5. THE BONDS OF INTIMACY:
Jewish Families and Relationships

1. See Sylvia B. Fishman, "The Changing American Jewish Family Faces the 1990s," in *Jews in America: A Contemporary Reader*, ed. Roberta Rosenberg Farber and Chaim I. Waxman. Hanover, N.H. and London: Brandeis University Press and University Press of New England, 1999, pp.51–88. For a Canadian perspective, see Norma Joseph, "Jewish Women in Canada: An Evolving Role," in *From Immigration to Integration*, ed. Klein and Dimant, pp.182–95.

2. Cited in Paula Hyman, "Introduction: Perspectives on the Evolving Jewish Family," in *The Jewish Family, Myths and Reality*, ed. Steven M. Cohen and Paula Hyman. New York: Holmes & Meier, 1986, pp.2–3. From his *Essai sur la régénération physique, morale, et politique des juifs*, Metz: 1789, p.36.

3. ChaeRan Freeze, "The Litigious Gerusha: Jewish Women and Divorce in Imperial Russia," *Nationalities Papers*, 25:1, 1997, pp.89–101.

4. Isaac Metzker, *A Bintel Brief*.

5. See Gladys Rothbell, "The Jewish Mother: Social Construction of a Popular Image," in Steven M. Cohen and Paul Hyman eds., *The Jewish Family*, pp.118–30.

6. Norma Joseph, "Personal Reflections on Jewish Feminism," in *The Canadian Jewish Mosaic*, ed. Weinfeld, Shaffir, and Cotler, pp.205–21.

7. Norma Joseph, personal communication, January 28, 1998.

8. Quoted in Sheva Medjuck, "If I Cannot Dance to It, It Is Not My Revolution: Jewish Feminism in Canada Today," in *The Jews in Canada*, ed. Brym, Shaffir, and Weinfeld, p.338.

9. For a discussion of feminism and Judaism, including new rituals, see Sylvia B. Fishman, "Negotiating Egalitarianism and Judaism: American Jewish Feminisms and Their Implication for Jewish Life," in *Jews in America*, ed. Farber and Waxman, pp.163–90.

10. Norma Joseph, personal communication, January 28, 1998.

11. Davies and Guppy, "Race and Canadian Education," in *Racism and Social Inequality in Canada*, ed. Satzewich, pp.131–57.

12. Moshe Hartman and Harriet Hartman, *Gender Equality and American Jews*. Albany: State University of New York Press, 1996, p.33.

13. Medjuck, "If I Cannot Dance to It," in *The Jews in Canada*, ed. Brym, Shaffir, and Weinfeld.

14. Barry Chiswick, "Working and Family Life: The Experiences of Jewish Women in America," in *Papers in Jewish Demography*, ed. Sergio DellaPergola and Judith Even, Jerusalem: Hebrew University of Jerusalem, 1997, p.283.

15. Byron G. Spencer, "Labor Supply and Investment in Child Quality: A Study of Jewish and Non-Jewish Women: A Comment," *Review of Economics and Statistics*, 1992, pp.721–25.

16. Paul Ritterband, "Jewish Women in the Labor Force," New York: Center for Jewish Studies, Graduate Center, City University of New York, 1990.

17. Chiswick, "Working and Family Life," in *Papers in Jewish Demography*, ed. DellaPergola and Even, pp.285–86.

18. Medjuck, "If I Cannot Dance to It," in *The Jews in Canada*, ed. Brym, Shaffir, and Weinfeld.

19. Ruth K. Westheimer and Jonathan Mark, *Heavenly Sex: Sexuality in the Jewish Tradition*. New York: New York University Press, 1995. Also see Shmuley Boteach, *Kosher Sex: A Recipe for Passion and Intimacy*, New York: Doubleday, 1999.

20. See Alan Fisher, "The Jewish Electorate: California, 1980–86," in Seymour Martin Lipset and Earl Raab, *Jews and the New American Scene*. Cambridge: Harvard University Press, 1995, pp.131–50; Herbert McClosky and Alida Brill, *Dimensions of Tolerance: What Americans Believe about Civil Liberties*. New York: Russell Sage, 1983, pp.404–406; Steven M. Cohen, "Religion and the Public Square: Attitudes of American Jews in Comparative Perspective, Part Two," *Jerusalem Letter*. Jerusalem: Jerusalem Center for Public Affairs, August 1, 2000.

21. Edward Laumann, John H. Gagnon, Robert T. Michael, and Stuart Michaels, *The Social Organization of Sexuality*. Chicago: University of Chicago Press, 1994, Table 5.1C.

22. *The Globe and Mail*, November 14, 1968. cited in *The Underside of Toronto*, ed. W. E. Mann. Toronto: McClelland & Stewart, 1970, pp.160–61.

23. Joseph J. Levy and Eleanor Maticka-Tyndale, *Sexualité, contraception, et SIDA chez les jeunes adultes*. Montreal: Méridien, 1992.

24. Special communication from Warren Clark, Statistics Canada, September 20, 1998.

25. Rosenberg, *Canada's Jews*, ed. Weinfeld, p.298.

26. Bob Gluck, "Jewish Men and Violence in the Home," in *A Mensch among Men*, ed. Harry Brod. Freedom, Calif.: The Crossing Press, 1988, pp.84–91.

27. Diane Sasson, personal communication, October 28, 1997; Tzipie Freedman, personal communication, June 13, 2001; Penny Krowitz, personal communication, June 13, 2001.

28. Personal communications with Linda Glustein, December 3, 1997; Carol Polter, November 3, 1997; and Harriet Tobman, November 4, 1997. All are professionals dealing in social services and the Jewish community.

29. Irv Binik (psychologist and sex therapist), personal communication, September 11, 1998.

30. Nathan Hurvitz, "Sources of Motivation and Achievement of American Jews," *Jewish Social Studies*, October 1961, pp.217–33; Fred Strodtbeck, "Family Interaction, Values, and Achievement," in *The Jews*, ed. Sklare, pp.147–68.

31. Zena Smith Blau, "The Strategy of the Jewish Mother," in *The Jew in American Society*, ed. Sklare, pp.165–88.

32. Ronald Freeman, Pascal Whelpton, and Arthur Campbell, *Family Planning, Sterility, and Population Growth*. New York: McGraw-Hill, 1959, p.110.

33. Bernard Farber, Charles Mindel, and Bernard Lazerwitz, "The Jewish American Family," in *Ethnic Families in America*, ed. Charles Mindel and Robert Habenstein. Amsterdam: Elsevier North Holland, 1976, p.359.

34. According to the 1981 Census, the number of children born per 1,000 Jewish women aged 15–44 was 1,596; for women over 45, it was 2,236. The comparable Canadian averages were far higher, 1,781 and 3,304. Robert Brym, "The Rise and Decline of Canadian Jewry?" in *The Jews in Canada*, ed. Brym, Shaffir, and Weinfeld.

35. The actual percentages are 31.8 per cent of Jewish women with no children compared to 33.5 per cent. In addition, 37.2 per cent of Jewish women and 42.2 per cent of Jewish men were "never married" in 1991, compared to 43.6 per cent and 48.2 per cent for non-Jews.

36. Leo Davids, "Marital Status and Fertility among Sub-groups of Canadian Jews," in *The Jews in Canada*, ed. Brym, Shaffir, and Weinfeld, p.320. Davids used those who spoke Yiddish at home as a proxy for Hasidim. He looked at the number of children aged 0 to 4 per 1,000 women aged 15 to 44. The figure for all Canadian Jews was 279, while that for Yiddish-speakers was 1,122.

37. Medjuck, "If I Cannot Dance to It," pp.336–37.

38. Ibid, p.337; Rabbi Howard Joseph, personal communication, March 1, 1999.

39. Davids, "Montreal Status and Fertility," in *The Jews in Canada*, ed. Brym, Shaffir, and Weinfeld. pp.315–27. They were 4 per cent for all Canada and 4.2 per cent for Jews. In the United States, 1990 male Jewish divorce rates were also below those of U.S. white men, 6.1 per cent to 7.2 per cent. However, divorce was more common for Jewish compared to non-Jewish women, 9.6 per cent to 9 per cent. I cannot explain this different pattern for American Jewish women. See Sidney Goldstein, "Profile of American Jews: Insights from the

1990 NJPS," in *The American Jewish Yearbook,* vol. 92, ed. David
Singer. New York: The American Jewish Committee, 1992, p.164.

40. Rosenberg, *Canada's Jews,* ed. Weinfeld, p.93.

41. The percentage of divorced or separated Jews was 4.4 per cent in
Montreal, 5 per cent in Toronto, and 6.1 per cent in Vancouver. The
percentage in common-law relationships was 2.2 per cent in
Montreal, 2 per cent in Toronto, and 5.4 per cent in Vancouver. The
percentage of Jews living in single-parent families was 7.4 per cent
in Montreal, 6.6 per cent in Toronto, and 9.5 per cent in Vancouver.

42. Medjuck, "If I Cannot Dance to It"; Rachel Schlesinger, "Changing
Roles of Jewish Women," in *Canadian Jewry Today,* ed. E. Lipsitz.
Toronto: J.E.S.L. Publications, 1989, pp.60–70.

43. This is not simply an impression. Take a typical page of such ads
in the late 1990s, from Montreal's *The Gazette* of November 8,
1997. On that day, 25 of the total of 128 of the "women seeking men"
ads, or 20 per cent, identified a Jew as a seeker. This is much higher
than the Jewish per cent of English-speaking Montreal. Even more
revealing, of the 25 women, 17 (or 68 per cent) specified that they
were looking for a Jewish man. Of the 103 non-Jewish women, only
2 specified any religious category, and they both wanted a similar
partner. While 22 identified their own ethnic or racial background,
only 2 stressed they wanted a similar partner. Of the "men seeking
women" there were only 10 identified Jews out of 70 men, and of
those 10 only 4 specified they were seeking Jewish women, and 2
in fact specified Asians! These lower ratios of like seeking like were
still higher than those for non-Jewish men. But the sad fact is that
17 Jewish women would be competing for only 4 interested Jewish
men. It is important to stress that these numbers will not be typical
of all Canadian cities, and all times of year. But the pattern would
likely hold.

44. Rob Singer, personal communication, December 11, 1997.

45. Heidi Stober, personal communication, October 29, 1997.

46. Harvey Cohen, personal communication, October 27, 1997.

47. Howard Goldstein, personal communication, April 15, 1998. I
thank researcher Randal Schnoor for much of the information and
insights into gay Jewish life in Toronto.

48. While there are individual gays and lesbians in Canadian Orthodox synagogues, there is not as yet an underground movement of Orthodox gays as in the United States. See Naomi Grossman, "The Gay Orthodox Underground," *Moment* 28:2, April 2000, pp.54–61.

49. As recently as 1961, the Jewish proportion was 8.2 per cent, just slightly larger than the 7.6-per-cent national Canadian figure of that time. "Jewish Seniors in Montreal," Part V of 1991 Census Series. Montreal: Federation of Jewish Community Services in Montreal, n.d. In the U.S., 17.2 per cent of American Jews are over sixty-five, compared to 13.3 per cent of the white population.

50. Goldstein, "Profile of American Jews," p.155.

51. "Jewish Seniors in Montreal," p.4.

52. Carolyn Rosenthal, "Aging in the Family Context: Are Jewish Families Different?" in *The Jews in Canada*, ed. Brym, Shaffir, and Weinfeld.

53. Sixty-four per cent of Montreal Jewish seniors live with their spouse; 29 per cent live alone; 2 per cent live with non-relatives; 6 per cent live with children. "Jewish Seniors in Montreal," p.8.

54. Charles Shahar, *A Survey of Jewish Life in Montreal*, Part I. Montreal: The Federation of Jewish Community Services of Montreal, December 1996, p.25.

55. Michael Goldberg, *Jewish Seniors in Greater Vancouver: A Survey of Needs*. Vancouver: Jewish Federation of Greater Vancouver, August 1991; Wendy Menghi, *Jewish Seniors Housing Survey*. Vancouver: Jewish Federation of Vancouver, December 1993.

56. Evelyn Kallen, *Spanning the Generations: A Study of Jewish Identity*. Toronto: Longmans, 1977; John Sigal and Morton Weinfeld, *Trauma and Rebirth: Intergenerational Effects of the Holocaust*. New York: Praeger, 1989, p.95.

57. Rosenthal, op. cit, p.351.

58. We exclude the technical *halachic* point that the children of inter-married Jewish women are Jewish. Actually, a mixed marriage need not be the end of the road. A recent American study by Bruce Phillips reported below found – the good news – that 12 per cent of the children of mixed-married Jews went on to marry Jews, a kind of return in-marriage. The bad news is that 88 per cent did not.

59. Intermarriage among Toronto Jews is more prevalent among fourth-generation Canadian Jews than among first or second; 43 per cent to under 10 per cent. Jay Brodbar-Nemzer et. al., "An Overview of the Canadian Jewish Community" in *The Jews in Canada*, ed. Brym, Shaffir, and Weinfeld, pp.60–61.

60. Ibid.; Shahar and Schnoor, *A Survey of Jewish Life in Montreal*, Part II.

61. Bruce A. Phillips, *Re-examining Intermarriage: Trends, Textures, Strategies*. New York: The American Jewish Committee and the Susan and David Wilstein Institute of Jewish Policy Studies, n.d. For this study Phillips in 1993 contacted 1,123 respondents of the 1990 NJPS who were currently or previously married and under 50 years old, and interviewed 580. In 1995 he also interviewed 256 non-Jewish spouses.

62. Peter Y. Medding, Gary A. Tobin, Sylvia Barack Fishman, and Mordechai Rimor, "Jewish Identity in Conversionary and Mixed Marriages," in *Jews in America*, ed. Farber and Waxman, pp.226–60.

63. One-third said "Christian only," and one-quarter each for "no religion" and "both."

64. Francine Klagsbrun, "Survey Says Intermarriage Is OK." *Moment* 28:2, April, 2001, p.32.

65. Shahar and Schnoor, "Summary of Jewish Life in Montreal," Part II, p.34.

66. W. W. Isajiw, "Ethnic Identity Retention," in *Ethnic Identity and Equality*, ed. Breton et al., 1990, p.78.

67. Reginald W. Bibby, *The Bibby Report: Social Trends, Canadian Style*. Toronto: Stoddart, 1995, p.54.

6. THE COMMUNAL FOUNDATION OF JEWISH LIFE
People, Neighbourhoods, and Organizations

1. Abella, *A Coat of Many Colours*; Tulchinsky, *Taking Root*; Tulchinsky, *Branching Out*; Speisman, *The Jews of Toronto*. The argument that the Jewish "community" remained essentially fragmented is mine, not theirs.

2. Tulchinsky, *Taking Root*, ch.13.

3. Coser, *The Functions of Social Conflict*.

4. Mark Zborowski and Elizabeth Herzog, *Life is with People*. New York: Schocken, 1962.

5. John Kralt, *Atlas of Residential Concentration for the Census Metropolitan Area of Montreal; and Atlas of Residential Concentration for the Census Metropolitan Area of Toronto*. Ottawa, Multiculturalism Canada, 1986; Warren E. Kalbach, "Ethnic Residential Segregation in an Urban Setting," in Breton et al., *Ethnic Identity and Equality*, pp.92–134.

6. There are several ways social scientists measure this concentration. One way is simply to compute the proportion of a group living in the fewest numbers of census tracts, for a given city. For example, how many census tracts might it take to tally up 90 per cent of the Jews in a given city? If Jews were randomly distributed throughout a city, it would require about 90 per cent of the tracts. For Montreal the answer is only 9 per cent of the tracts, for Toronto only 14.5 per cent! For blacks, Chinese, or Italians, the corresponding proportions in both cities range from the mid-30s to 50 per cent. Jews are therefore far more concentrated than other minority groups. Another technical measure is an "index of dissimilarity" for Jews and other groups. This is a measure that ranges from zero to one, with zero meaning no concentration and one meaning complete segregation. (The index measures the proportion of a group that would have to be reshuffled in a city to approximate the distribution of the key comparison group, British-origin or French in Montreal. A score of zero denotes a distribution that was exactly the same as that of the majority group, so very little residential concentration.) The Jewish index is a whopping .907 in Montreal and .787 in Toronto. For blacks, the corresponding indices are .618 and .517, for Chinese .674 and .573, and for Italians .594 and .562. Jewish segregation as measured by these indices is greater in every Canadian city (except Victoria) and compared to every major Canadian ethnic or racial group. T. R. Balakrishnan and Feng Hou, "Residential Patterns in Cities," in *Immigrant Canada: Demographic, Economic, and Social Challenges*, ed. Shiva Halli and Leo Driedger, Toronto: University of Toronto Press, 1999.

7. Kalbach, "Ethnic Residential Segregation," in Breton et al., *Ethnic Identity and Equality*.

8. Judith R. Kramer and Seymour Leventman, *Children of the Gilded Ghetto*. New Haven: Yale University Press, 1961; John Seeley et al., *Crestwood Heights*. Toronto: University of Toronto Press, 1956.

9. Amitai Etzioni, "The Ghetto – a Re-evaluation," in *Social Forces*, March, 1959, pp.255–62.

10. Brodbar-Nemzer et al., "An Overview of the Canadian Jewish Community," in *The Jews in Canada*, ed. Brym, Shaffir, and Weinfeld, p.46.

11. A survey of Montreal Jews in 1991 found about 48 per cent claimed "all or most" of their neighbours were Jews, and another 39 per cent that "some" were Jews. Even more revealing, in a 1996 Montreal survey 44 per cent said it was "very important" and 38 per cent that it was "somewhat important" that they live in a neighbourhood with a sizeable Jewish population. Shahar and Schnoor, *A Survey of Jewish Life in Montreal*, Part II, pp.38–39.

12. Isajiw, "Ethnic Identity Retention," in *Ethnic Identity and Equality*, ed. Breton et al., p.57.

13. Taras and Beitel, "Preliminary Analysis, Jewish Community Council Survey As at Jan. 30, 1997." The study surveyed 680 Jews, in 1996. The Montreal, Toronto, and Calgary surveys used different sampling techniques; Jewish community lists, Jewish-sounding names, or a more random procedure. They all came up with similar results.

14. Marshall Sklare and Joseph Greenblum, *Jewish Identity on the Suburban Frontier*. New York: Basic Books, 1967, pp.287–88.

15. Charles R. Snyder, "Culture and Jewish Sobriety: The Ingroup-Outgroup Factor," in *The Jews*, ed. Sklare, pp.560–94; Patai, *The Jewish Mind*, pp.433–46; personal communication with Montreal bartender Michael Goldman, October 28, 1977. This was also confirmed in an interview with a hotel banquet-hall manager. On the basic fact that Jews drink to excess less often than non-Jews – though some claim they are drinking more than they used to – there is no debate.

16. Raymond Breton, "Institutional Completeness of Ethnic Communities and the Personal Relations of Immigrants," *American Journal of Sociology* 70, 1964, pp.193-205.

17. Daniel Elazar, *Community and Polity: The Organizational Dynamics of American Jewry*. Philadelphia: Jewish Publication

Society, 1976; with political scientist Harold Waller, Elazar has also written the major study of the Canadian Jewish polity: Elazar and Waller, *Maintaining Consensus: The Canadian Jewish Polity in the Postwar World*. Lanham and Jerusalem: University Press of America and the Jerusalem Center for Public Affairs, 1990.

18. Abella, *A Coat of Many Colours*, pp.154–64, 189–90.
19. Troper and Weinfeld, *Old Wounds*.
20. David Taras and Morton Weinfeld, "Continuity and Criticism: North American Jews and Israel" in *The Jews in Canada*, ed. Brym, Shaffir and Weinfeld, pp.293–310.
21. Elazar and Waller, *Maintaining Consensus*.
22. Morton Weinfeld and William Eaton, *A Survey of the Jewish Community of Montreal*. Montreal: Jewish Community Research Institute, 1979.
23. Carl E. James, *Perspectives on Racism and the Human Services Sector*. Toronto: University of Toronto Press, 1996.
24. Harold Troper and Morton Weinfeld, "Diversity in Canada," in *Ethnicity, Politics, and Public Policy: Case Studies in Canadian Diversity*, ed. Harold Troper and Morton Weinfeld. Toronto: University of Toronto Press, 1999, pp.3–25; Morton Weinfeld, "The Challenge of Ethnic Match: Minority Origin Professionals in Health and Social Services," in ibid., pp.117–41.
25. See Alissa Levine, "Female Genital Operations: Canadian Realities, Concerns, and Policy Recommendations," in Troper and Weinfeld, ibid., pp.26–53.
26. See fn.1. in this chapter.
27. These issues are explored in *Ethnicity and Public Policy in Canada*, ed. Harold Troper and Morton Weinfeld. Toronto: University of Toronto Press, 1999.
28. Barry Kosmin, "The Dimensions of Contemporary American Jewish Philanthropy," in *Jewish Philanthropy in Contemporary America. Information Series* no. 2. New York: North American Jewish Data Bank, Council of Jewish Federations, June 15–16, 1988, pp.1–21.
29. Bobby Kleinman, personal communication, October 6, 1997.
30. Richard Greenberg, "I'll Give It My Way," *Moment* 23:6, December 1998, pp.50–56.

31. Though the dollar amounts referred to here are given in their countries' respective currencies, they are an accurate reflection of the different rates of gift-giving, as the U.S. average income is correspondingly higher than in Canada. Brodbar-Nemzer et al., "An Overview of the Canadian Jewish Community," in *The Jews in Canada*, ed. Brym, Shaffir, and Weinfeld.

32. Norbert Fruehauf, "The Bottom Line: Major Gifts to Federation Campaigns," in *Jewish Philanthropy in Contemporary America*, pp.22–43 (ref. on p.22).

33. Sid Gotfrid, personal communication, June 12, 1997.

34. Bobby Kleinman, personal communication, July 5, 2000.

35. *Directory of Foundations and Grants*. Toronto: Canadian Centre for Philanthropy, 1997.

36. Greenberg, "I'll Give It My Way." Another study of data from the *American Foundation Directory* for 1987, ten years earlier than the Canadian data cited above, provides details of 5,148 American private foundations with either assets greater than one million dollars or giving greater than U.S.$100,000. There were 355 foundations which specified Jewish giving, or 7 per cent of the total – much less than the Canadian 29 per cent cited above – though still above the 2 per cent of Jews in the population. Religious causes were popular. There were 437 that specified Protestant giving and 155 for Catholic giving. There were 75 entries targeting Israel compared to only 4 for Italy and 3 for Poland (Kosmin, "Dimensions of Contemporary American Jewish Philanthropy").

37. Reginald Bibby, *Unknown Gods: The Ongoing Story of Religion in Canada*. Toronto: Stoddart, 1993, pp.106–7.

38. Ibid., p.107.

39. Elazar and Waller, *Maintaining Consensus*.

40. Brodbar-Nemzer et al., "An Overview of the Canadian Jewish Community," in *The Jews in Canada*, ed. Brym, Shaffir, and Weinfeld, p.46.

41. Shahar, *A Survey of Jewish Life in Montreal*, Part I, p.12.

42. With regard to membership in Jewish organizations, the 38 per cent for Montreal and Toronto are higher than New York (26 per cent), Los Angeles (27 per cent), Boston (28 per cent), and Philadelphia (31

per cent), but lower than Dallas (46 per cent), Detroit (47 per cent), Cleveland (53 per cent), and Atlanta (57 per cent). With regard to volunteerism, the figures of 28 per cent for Montreal and 26 per cent for Toronto can be compared with 32 per cent in Dallas, 30 per cent in St. Louis, 27 per cent in New York, 24 per cent in San Francisco, and 22 per cent in Baltimore. The New York figure for membership is low, which brings down overall American percentages. Shahar, ibid., p.9.

43. Raymond Breton, "The Ethnic Group as a Political Resource in Relation to Problems of Incorporation: Perceptions and Attitudes," in *Ethnic Identity and Equality*, ed. Breton et al., pp.196–255.

44. Franklin Bialystok, "Neo-Nazis in Toronto: The Allan Gardens Riot," *Canadian Jewish Studies*, special edition, "New Perspectives on Canada, the Holocaust, and Survivors," vols.4,5, 1996–97, pp.1–38.

45. In Montreal, as far back as 1979, only 16 per cent claimed that the "leadership of the Jewish community" represented the interests of "a few Jews" (Weinfeld and Eaton, *A Survey of the Jewish Community of Montreal.*) Most felt that leaders were in touch with the majority. In 1996, only 4 per cent claimed they were unsatisfied with the level of services provided by the Jewish federation (Shahar, *A Survey of Jewish Life in Montreal*, p.26). The situation was very similar in Toronto. Jewish Torontonians, compared to other groups, by and large are most likely to feel ordinary community members have much to say about how things are run, that their leaders are concerned with community problems and interests, and that leaders seek to get community approval. In addition, Jews are the most likely group to feel their leaders are taken seriously by politicians, and have enough connections to do their job (Breton et al., *Ethnic Identity and Equality*). And they are right.

46. Harold Waller, "The Canadian Jewish Polity: Power and Leadership in the Jewish Community" in *The Jews in Canada*, ed. Brym, Shaffir, and Weinfeld, pp.254–69.

47. Burnet and Palmer, *Coming Canadians*.

48. Breton, "The Ethnic Group as a Political Resource."

49. See Steven Cohen and Arnold Eisen, *The Jew Within: Self, Community, and Commitment among the Variety of Moderately*

Affiliated. Boston: The Susan and David Wilstein Institute, 1998.
50. Dr. Frank Guttman, personal communication, February 4, 1998.

7. BETWEEN HIGH CULTURE AND DAILY LIFE
From Literature and Art to Klezmer and Kugel

1. Enoch Padolsky, "Canadian Ethnic Minority Literature in English," in *Ethnicity and Culture in Canada: The Research Landscape*, ed. John Berry and Jean Laponce, Toronto: University of Toronto Press, 1994, pp.361–86.
2. Ladino (Judeo-Spanish), Arabic, and Judeo-Arabic, have been spoken by Sephardi immigrants to Canada. For some Sephardi Jews elements of these languages continue to fulfil many of the symbolic and ritualistic functions of Yiddish for Ashkenazi Jews. But they are not used as instruments of communication, and did not establish themselves in an institutional sense as did Yiddish.
3. Leo Davids, "Yiddish in Canada: Picture and Prospects," in *The Jews in Canada*, ed. Brym, Shaffir, and Weinfeld, pp.153–66.
4. In 1981, the Canadian Census asked respondents to select one mother tongue or home language; in 1991 they could select more than one.
5. Leo Davids, "Yiddish and Hebrew in Canada: The Current Situation," *Canadian Ethnic Studies*, 32:2, 2000, 95–104. Yiddish is relatively stronger in Montreal than Toronto.
6. As far back as the mid-1980s, about 5,000 children were receiving such Hebrew instruction in Ontario schools. Leo Davids, "Knowledge of Yiddish and Hebrew in Canada: The Current Picture," in *Papers in Jewish Demography 1989*, ed. U. O. Schmelz and Sergio DellaPergola. Jerusalem: Hebrew University of Jerusalem, Institute of Contemporary Jewry, Jewish Population Studies 25, 1993, p.22.
7. Brodbar-Nemzer et al., "An Overview of the Canadian Jewish Community," in *The Jews in Canada*, ed. Brym, Shaffir, and Weinfeld, pp.46, 54. Among those aged 65 and over, 64 per cent and 20 per cent can speak Yiddish and Hebrew, respectively. Among those under 34, the figures are 14 per cent and 35 per cent.
8. Shahar, Weinfeld, and Schnoor, "Survey of the Hassidic and Ultra-Orthodox Communities in Outremont and Surrounding Areas."

9. Shahar, "Sépharade 2000; *Challenges and Perspectives for the Sephardic Community of Montreal.*" 2000, draft. p.12.

10. Danesi, "Ethnic Language and Acculturation," 88–103.

11. See Irving Howe, *World of Our Fathers*. New York: Simon and Schuster, 1976, p.588.

12. See *An Everyday Miracle: Yiddish Culture in Montreal*, ed. Ira Robinson, Pierre Anctil, and Mervin Butovsky. Montreal: Véhicule Press, 1990; and Orenstein, "Yiddish Culture in Canada: Yesterday and Today," in *The Canadian Jewish Mosaic*, ed. Weinfeld, Shaffir, and Cotler, pp.293–314.

13. See "Jewish Culture and Canadian Culture," in *The Canadian Jewish Mosaic*, ed. Weinfeld, Shaffir, and Cotler, pp.315–42.

14. Malcolm Lester, personal communication, September 10, 1998.

15. For a review of the work of Sam Borenstein, see William Kuhns and Leo Rosshandler, *Sam Borenstein*. Toronto: McClelland & Stewart, 1978.

16. Craig Smith, "Keeping It Strictly Kosher in China," *The Gazette*, December 5, 1998, p.B1.

17. Butovsky, "Jewish Culture and Canadian Culture," in *The Canadian Jewish Mosaic*, ed. Weinfeld, Shaffir, and Cotler.

18. Isajiw, "Ethnic Identity Retention," in *Ethnic Identity and Equality*, ed. Breton et al., pp.68–69.

19. See Pierre Anctil, "Aspects de la thématique juive dans le *CJN*, édition de Montréal, 1977–1982," *Canadian Ethnic Studies*, 16:1, 1984, pp.29–57.

20. Brodbar-Nemzer et al., "An Overview of the Canadian Jewish Community," in *The Jews in Canada*, ed. Brym, Shaffir, and Weinfeld, pp.39–72.

21. "Ethnic Identity Retention," in *Ethnic Identity and Equality*, ed. Breton et al., p.84.

22. From the late 1970s through the 1980s there was an eventually unsuccessful attempt to transform the periodical *Viewpoints* into a Canadian Jewish intellectual journal, led heroically by William Abrams and his wife Jeannette in Montreal. (I was involved in the effort.) For a time it was included as a supplement to the *CJN*,

which solved its distribution problem. It never really established a significant, independent constituency.

23. Robert Fulford, personal communication, April 28, 1998.

24. The Abella article appeared in *The Globe and Mail*, February 18, 2000. The same issue included a review of a new Holocaust film, *Train of Life*, and a lengthy profile of the film's Romanian-Jewish director. The article on Holocaust artifacts appeared in the issue of February 22, 2000. The extensive coverage of the Haider visit included the Jewish communal reaction, as well as the decision by the Montreal Holocaust Centre not to extend him an official invitation. For that week, the distinction between the Jewish press and the mainstream press was blurred.

25. Brodbar-Nemzer, et al. 1990, p.48. See the Tables in the Appendix to this volume.

26. Leora Frucht, "Israel's Canadian Content," *The Gazette*, April 26, 1998. This article is also the source for the 8,000 figure.

27. In 1998–99, the allocations by Montreal's Fédération CJA were as follows: only 36 per cent to Israel, the rest to local, national and other overseas needs.

28. "The Israel Experience: Summaries of Research Papers Prepared for the CRB Foundation," March, 1992.

29. Jeff Sallot, "Polish Canadians Vent Anger at PM," *The Globe and Mail*, January 23, 1999, p.A5; Allan Levine, "The Prime Minister, Auschwitz, and the Battle for Memory," *The Globe and Mail*, January 26, 1999, p.A17. Bernard Wisniewski, "What the Polish Christian Stake Is in Auschwitz," *The Globe and Mail*, February 8, 1999 p.A13. The recent controversy over the alleged role of Poles in the massacre of the Jews of the town of Jedwabne in 1941 is a new flashpoint. See Jan T. Gross, "Annals of War," *The New Yorker*, March 12, 2001, pp.64–71.

30. Troper and Weinfeld, *Old Wounds*.

31. For a provocative review of the topic see Peter Novick, *The Holocaust in American Life*. Boston: Houghton Mifflin, 1999.

32. John J. Sigal and Morton Weinfeld, *Trauma and Rebirth: Intergenerational Consequences of the Holocaust*. New York: Praeger,

1989. Dr. Sigal is a psychologist and psychoanalyst associated with the Institute of Community and Family Psychiatry of the Sir Mortimer B. Davis Jewish General Hospital in Montreal.

33. Reprinted in *Beyond Imagination: Canadians Write About the Holocaust*, ed. Jerry S. Grafstein. Toronto: McClelland & Stewart, 1995, p.78.

34. Alti Rodal, "Legacies: A Second Generation Reflects," in ibid., pp.74–75.

35. Peter C. Newman, "The Guns of Biarritz," in Grafstein, ibid., p.1.

36. David Lewis Stein, "Dress British, Think Yiddish," in ibid., p.121.

37. Barbara Kingstone, "A Journey into the Holocaust," in ibid., p.127.

38. A classic case took place in the early 1970s when the Montreal Saidye Bronfman Centre was scheduled to produce the play *The Man in the Glass Booth* by Robert Shaw. The play deals with the Holocaust, loosely based on the Eichmann trial, and blurs the clear distinctions between the guilty and the victims. Organizations of Holocaust survivors were deeply offended and demanded that the Saidye Bronfman Centre cancel the play. They did, to charges that artistic freedom was compromised – it was – and this led to the departure of the Centre's artistic director.

39. Enoch Padolsky, "Canadian Ethnic Minority Literature in English," in *Ethnicity and Culture in Canada: The Research Landscape*, ed. J. W. Berry and Jean Laponce. Toronto: University of Toronto Press, 1994, pp.361–86.

40. Mervin Butovsky, "Jewish Culture and Canadian Culture," in *The Canadian Jewish Mosaic*, ed. Weinfeld, Shaffir, and Cotler, p.319.

41. Howard Roiter, in "Jewish Culture and Canadian Culture," in ibid., p.320.

42. Malcolm Lester, personal communication, September 10, 1998.

43. Mervin Butovsky, personal communication, October 10, 1997; Malcolm Lester, personal communication, September 10, 1998; Robert Fulford, personal communication, April 28, 1998.

44. Eli Mandel, "The Ethnic Voice in Canadian Writing," in *Identities: The Impact of Ethnicity on Canadian Society*, ed. W. W. Isajiw. Toronto: Peter Martin, 1977, pp.57–68.

45. George Woodcock, *Mordecai Richler*. Toronto: McClelland & Stewart, 1971, pp.20–21.

46. Ruth Wisse in "Jewish Culture and Canadian Culture," in *The Canadian Jewish Mosaic*, ed. Weinfeld, Shaffir, and Cotler, p.330.

47. Peter S. Li, "The Multicultural World of Visible Minorities and the Art World in Canada," *Canadian Review of Sociology and Anthropology*, 31:4, pp.365–91.

48. For a discussion of the difficulties facing hip-hop and rap music in Canada, see Rebecca J. Haines, "Break North: Rap Music and Hip Hop Culture in Canada," in *Ethnicity, Politics, and Public Policy: Case Studies in Canadian Diversity*, ed. Harold Troper and Morton Weinfeld. Toronto: University of Toronto Press, 1999, pp.54–88.

49. Howard Adelman, "Blacks and Jews: Racism, Anti-Semitism, and *Showboat*," in *Multiculturalism, Jews, and Identities in Canada*, ed. Howard Adelman and John Simpson. Jerusalem: Magnes Press, 1996, pp.128–78: Frances Henry, Carol Tator, Winston Mattis, and Tim Rees, *The Colour of Democracy*. Toronto: Harcourt Brace, 1995, 218–23.

50. Ibid., p.222.

51. Of course, there are likely political and strategic considerations at work here. Still, in the 1930s the same SSJB lobbied the Canadian government to keep Jews out.

52. *The Big Book of Jewish Humor*, ed. William Novak and Moshe Waldoks. New York: Harper & Row, 1981, pp.xviii–xix.

53. Quoted ibid., p.xviii.

8. THE PEOPLE OF THE BOOK
Jewish Education and Jewish Survival

1. This chapter, while revised and expanded, draws from my "The Educational Continuum: A Community Priority," in *From Immigration to Integration: The Canadian Jewish Experience*, ed. Ruth Klein and Frank Dimant. Toronto: B'nai Brith Canada and Malcolm Lester Publishing, 2001, 197–213.

2. See Peter Li, *The Chinese in Canada* (second ed.). Toronto: Oxford University Press, 1998. This does not mean that such books are

flawed, but rather that this issue is not a central one on the group's collective agenda.

3. Jim Cummins, "Heritage Language Learning and Teaching," in Berry and Laponce, *Ethnicity and Culture in Canada*, pp.435–56.

4. Bibby, *Unknown Gods*, p.100.

5. Ibid., p.99.

6. Stuart Schoenfeld, "Transnational Religion, Religious Schools, and the Dilemma of Public Funding for Jewish Education: The Case of Ontario." Downsview: York University, mimeo, 1998, p.19.

7. Jay Brodbar-Nemzer, *A First Look*. Toronto: Toronto Jewish Congress, 1991, p.18.

8. Charles Shahar and Randal F. Schnoor, *A Survey of Jewish Life in Montreal*, Part II. Montreal: Federation of Jewish Community Services, May 1997, pp.26–33.

9. Over half of Jewish Montrealers say their children have received a Jewish elementary day-school education; 28 per cent attended a Jewish high school. The drop-off in day-school education after elementary school, and after bar or bat mitzvah, is common; what is surprising is that the retention rate is as high as it is. About 61 per cent of Montreal parents said their school-age children are currently attending a Jewish day school. (These rates may be high because of provincial funding to help meet the needs of Jewish schools in Quebec.) Levels in Toronto would be slightly less.

10. The system in Canada is more comprehensive than that in the United States or in Europe. Only Jewish communities in South Africa, Australia, and in some Latin American countries compare with Canada in the degree to which children are given a day-school education.

11. For a review see Yaacov Glickman, "Jewish Education: Success or Failure," in *The Canadian Jewish Mosaic*, ed. Weinfeld, Shaffir, and Cotler, pp.113–28.

12. The Montreal data are taken from *The Montreal Jewish Directory of Spring/Summer 1998*. The Toronto data are from the *Jewish Community Services Directory of Greater Toronto*, for 1997. The proliferation of supplementary schools in Toronto reflects the greater costs of Jewish day-schooling in Ontario.

13. In 1997–1998 there were 775 children enrolled in Montreal's Jewish pre-kindergarten schools, and another 7,700 in Jewish full-day elementary and high schools. These figures exclude several ultra-Orthodox Chassidic schools, notably Satmar and Tash, which have chosen not to affiliate with Montreal's Jewish Education Council. They also exclude enrolments of children in supplementary schools, which are usually under 1,000. Between 1985 and 1997, enrolment in mainstream Jewish schools fell from 4,331 to 3,310, a result mainly of young Jewish families leaving the city; this loss has been matched by gains in the ultra-Orthodox sector fuelled by high fertility and in-migration to Montreal. The data are taken from a report on the Montreal Jewish education system described in the *Canadian Jewish News*, April 9, 1998, p.6.

14. Taras and Beitel, "Preliminary Analysis."

15. Of American Jews who claimed to be Jewish by religion, 78 per cent of the men and 62 per cent of the women had received some Jewish education. As in Canada, younger Jews have more extensive Jewish educations, a result of recent increases in day-school enrolments. The median years of Jewish education for the core Jewish population was 4.6 for Jewish men over 45, 4.7 for Jewish women over 45, 6.2 for Jewish men 18–44 and 5.5 for Jewish women 18–44. "Highlights of the CJF 1990 National Jewish Population Survey," New York: Council of Jewish Federation, 1991, p.31.

16. Sidney Goldstein, "Profile of American Jews: Insights from the 1990 NJPS," *American Jewish Yearbook*, New York: American Jewish Committee, 1992, pp.77–173. Subsequent analysis of that data found that for Jewish children 13–15, about 75 per cent had received "some" Jewish education, implying that 25 per cent had none.

17. Alice Goldstein, "Jewish Education and Jewish Identity: Findings from the National Jewish Population Survey of 1990," in *Papers in Jewish Demography 1993*, ed. DellaPergola and Even, pp.289–302. Actually, day-school enrollment in the United States has been increasing. One recent report estimates 200,000 students enrolled in the American day-school system, up 20,000–25,000 children over the 1990s. Marvin Schick, "A Census of Jewish Day Schools in the United States." New York: Avi Chai, 2000.

18. Glickman, "Jewish Education," pp.120–21.

19. Brodbar-Nemzer, A First Look, p.54.

20. Steven M. Cohen and Arnold M. Eisen, "The Jew Within: Self, Community and Commitment among the Variety of Moderately Affiliated." Boston: Susan and David Wilstein Institute, 1998, p.37.

21. Glickman, "Jewish Education."

22. Coleman, Hoffer, and Kilgore, High School Achievement.

23. F. Genesee and W. E. Lambert, "Trilingual Education for Majority Language Children," Child Development, vol.54, 1983, pp.105–114.

24. This theme emerged in my study of Jewish schooling in Montreal, and similar concerns apply to the situation in Toronto. Morton Weinfeld, "The System of Jewish Education in Montreal: An Overview of Current Conflicts and Challenges." Montreal: Jewish Education Council, 1985.

25. Shahar and Schnoor, A Survey of Jewish Life in Montreal, Part II, p.32.

26. William Helmreich, The World of the Yeshiva: An Intimate Portrait of Orthodox Jewry. New Haven: Yale University Press, 1986.

27. Morton Weinfeld and Phyllis Zelkowitz, "Reflections on the Jewish Polity and Jewish Education," in The Jews in Canada, ed. Brym et al., pp.142–52.

28. Tulchinsky, Branching Out, ch.2; Abella, A Coat of Many Colours, pp.130–33; Stewart Rosenberg, The Jewish Community in Canada, vol.2. Toronto: McClelland & Stewart, 1971, pp.265–70.

29. There is some evidence that American Jewish support for public schools may be slipping. A recent poll found that 52 per cent of American Jews supported educational vouchers. The Forward, June 16, 2000.

30. Jewish studies courses are found on over 35 Canadian campuses. For a review of the various programs available, and a summary of the evolution of the field in Canada, see A Guide to the Study of Jewish Civilization in Canadian Universities, ed. Michael Brown. Toronto and Jerusalem: Centre for Jewish Studies at York University and the International Center for University Teaching of Jewish Civilization, 1998. (The Guide is not without omissions. For example, I began teaching a course on the Sociology of Jews in North America at

McGill in 1977, the first such course in Canada, which is not mentioned. While not formally a Jewish Studies course, it is de facto very
much in the field.)

31. Yechiel Glustein, personal communication, October 15, 1998.

32. These were available in Montreal; I presume comparable options
are found in Toronto, and perhaps other Canadian cities as well.

33. Alan Dershowitz, *The Vanishing American Jew*, p.333.

9. JEWS, JUDAISM, AND THE PUBLIC SQUARE
The Political Behaviour of Canadian Jews

1. One recent study aggregated American national survey data from
1972 to 1994, to yield a sufficient sample of Jews for comparative
analysis. Jews were consistently more liberal on all issues, like support
for welfare policies, civil liberties, racial attitudes, abortion and
women's rights, etc. After introducing controls for education, income,
place of residence, etc., the Jewish–non-Jewish gaps narrowed
significantly on most but not all of the measures of liberalism.
(Support for the Democratic party remained unaffected!) This led
the authors to conclude that Jewish liberalism was mainly a result of
socio-demographic traits of American Jews, not the transmission
of specific Jewish cultural values. The authors reached that particular conclusion by comparing *all* Jews with only those Christians who
called themselves secular or were members of liberal Protestant
denominations. Had they looked only at secular or Reform Jews I
suspect the gaps would re-emerge. See Steven M. Cohen and Charles
S. Liebman, "American Jewish Liberalism: Unraveling the Strands,"
in *Public Opinion Quarterly*, 61:3, Fall 1997, pp.405–430: and Steven
M. Cohen, "Religion and the Public Square: Attitudes of American
Jews in Comparative Perspective," Parts One and Two, *Jerusalem
Letter*, Jerusalem Center for Public Affairs, July 16 and August 1, 2000.

2. Abella, *A Coat of Many Colours*, p.221.

3. Donald Avery, *Dangerous Foreigners*. Toronto: McClelland &
Stewart, 1979; Merrily Weisbord, *The Strangest Dream: Canadian
Communism, the Spy Trials, and the Cold War*. Toronto: Lester &
Orpen Dennys, 1983.

4. Jean Laponce, "Left or Centre: the Canadian Jewish Electorate, 1953–1983," in *The Jews in Canada*, ed. Brym et al., pp.270–92. This study is based on evidence from 235 national surveys from 1953 to 1983, which included questions about religion and party preference.

5. Harold Waller and Morton Weinfeld, "A *Viewpoints* Survey of Canadian Jewish Leadership Opinion," *Viewpoints* 15:4, October 8, 1987.

6. For a review of this issue see Arthur Liebman, *Jews and the Left*. New York: J. Wiley, 1979.

7. Lawrence Fuchs, *The Political Behavior of American Jews*. Glencoe, Ill.: The Free Press, 1956.

8. Laponce, "Left or Centre," p.284.

9. Tulchinsky, *Taking Root*, p.25.

10. Howard Stanislawski, "Canadian Jewry and Foreign Policy in the Middle East," in *The Canadian Jewish Mosaic*, ed. Weinfeld, Shaffir, and Cotler, pp.397–414.

11. Norman Spector, personal communication, April 23, 1998.

12. Ibid.

13. Morton Weinfeld, "Hugh Segal and the Ethnic Factor," *The Globe and Mail*, June 23, 1998.

14. Peyton Lyon, personal communication, June 23, 1998.

15. "Passport Problem Solved: Axworthy," *The Gazette*, October 11, 1997. Two years later, reports began to circulate that Israel was using Canadian passports to help their Lebanese Christian allies escape from Lebanon as Israel withdrew its forces from South Lebanon.

16. Tulchinsky, *Taking Root*, p.60.

17. Rufus Learsi, *The Jews in America: A History*. Cleveland: World Publishing Company, 1954, p.202.

18. John Ibbitson, "Leadership Candidates Muddied in the Gutter," *The Globe and Mail*, July 6, 2000.

19. Louis Brandeis, Stephen Breyer, Benjamin Cardozo, Abe Fortas, Felix Frankfurter, Ruth Bader Ginsberg, and Arthur Goldberg.

20. Henry Srebrnik, "Multiculturalism and the Politics of Ethnicity: Jews and the Charlottetown Accord," in *Multiculturalism, Jews, and Identities in Canada*, ed. Adelman and Simpson, p.102. But as mentioned earlier, the Jewish political clout in the post-war period does

not mean that Jewish interests will prevail in every policy dispute.

21. Raymond Breton, *The Governance of Ethnic Communities.* New York: Greenwood Press, 1991.

22. *Ethno-cultural Groups and Visible Minorities in Canadian Politics: the Question of Access,* ed. Kathy Megyery. Ottawa: Royal Commission on Electoral Reform and Supply and Services, and Dundern Press, 1991. The mobilization of Sikhs to swell the membership rolls of the B.C. NDP and elect Premier Dosanjh in early 2000 is a dramatic case.

23. J. J. Goldberg, *Jewish Power: Inside the American Jewish Establishment.* Reading, Mass.: Addison-Wesley, 1996. See also Stephen D. Isaacs, *Jews and American Politics.* Garden City, N.Y.: Doubleday, 1974.

24. "The *Mother Jones* 400," in *Mother Jones,* November/December 1998, pp.48–67. Using name-recognition techniques, I estimate conservatively that at least one-quarter of the major donors are Jewish. By a large margin, these Jewish donors support the Democratic Party.

25. David Taras and Morton Weinfeld, "Continuity and Criticism: North American Jews and Israel," in *The Jews in Canada,* ed. Brym et. al., p.295.

26. *The Domestic Battleground: Canada and the Arab–Israeli Conflict,* ed. David Taras and David Goldberg. Montreal: McGill–Queen's University Press, 1989; Taras and Weinfeld, "Continuity and Criticism," in *The Jews in Canada,* ed. Brym et al.

27. See Stanislawski, "Canadian Jewry and Foreign Policy in the Middle East."

28. Morton Weinfeld and William W. Eaton, *A Survey of the Jewish Community of Montreal.* Montreal: Jewish Community Research Institute, 1979.

29. I attended one such meeting in the mid-1990s, where I first heard the term "deep Côte St.-Luc."

30. One such prominent group is Dialogue St.-Urbain, which has involved Gerard Bouchard, brother of Lucien. Papers on French–Jewish relations in Quebec have been published in Pierre Anctil, Ira Robinson, and Gerard Bouchard, *Juifs et canadiens français dans la société québécoise.* Sillery, Quebec: Septentrion, 2000.

31. Mordecai Richler, *Oh Canada! Oh Quebec!* New York: A. A. Knopf, 1992; Esther Delisle, *The Traitor and the Jews.* Montreal: Robert

Davies Publishing, 1993; and *Myth, Memories and Lies: Quebec's Intelligentsia and the Fascist Temptation, 1939–1960*. Westmount, Quebec: R. Davies Multimedia, 1998.

32. *The Canadian Jewish News*, October 29, 1998. The project became mired in Jewish communal infighting, as some Jewish residents of the area objected to the initiative, claiming it would disturb the area's quality of life.

33. Shahar, *A Survey of Jewish Life in Montreal*, Part I, pp.32–33.

34. Janice Arnold, "Caution, Relief Greet Vote," *Canadian Jewish News*, December 10, 1998.

35. Taras and Weinfeld, "Continuity and Criticism," in *The Jews in Canada*, ed. Brym et al., p.297.

36. Ibid.

37. David Lazarus, "Condo Seeks Injunction," *Canadian Jewish News*, November 6, 1997.

38. These studies were discussed in an international AIDS conference in South Africa in 2000. *The Forward*, July 21, 2000, p.4.

39. Margaret Somerville, "Routine Circumcision of Baby Boys Is Wrong," *The Gazette*, August 7, 1998, p.B6; Margaret Somerville, "Respect in the Context of Infant Male Circumcision: Can Ethics and Law Provide Insights?" Paper presented at the fifth International Symposium on Sexual Mutilations, Oxford University, August 5–7, 1998. In any case, Canadian media reports of the controversy proliferate. See Barbara Kay, "So This Is What Passes for Abuse," *National Post*, February 13, 2001, p.A18; Anne Marie Owens, "Tradition under the Knife," *National Post*, February 20, 2001, p.A13.

40. Linda Kislowicz, personal communication, January 20, 1998.

41. There are no studies of the size and impact of current Jewish giving to Canadian political parties and campaigns. Wealthy Jews have long been supporters of political parties, mainly the Liberals. While they do so as individuals, their involvement helps directly or indirectly in furthering the Jewish policy agenda described above.

42. M. Rosenberg and J. Jedwab, "Institutional Completeness, Ethnic Organizational Style, and the Role of the State: The Jewish, Italian, and Greek Communities of Montreal," *Canadian Review of Sociology and Anthropology*, 29:3, 1992, pp.266–87; Henry Srebrnik,

"Multiculturalism and the Politics of Ethnicity," in *Multiculturalism, Jews, and Identities in Canada*, ed. Adelman and Simpson, pp.128–78.

43. This section relies on my "The Political–Demographic Environment of Canadian Jewry," in *Papers in Jewish Demography, 1989*, ed. U.O. Schmelz and Sergio DellaPergola. Jewish Population Studies 25. Jerusalem: Hebrew University of Jerusalem, Institute of Contemporary Jewry, 1993, pp.204–217.

44. Howard Adelman, "Blacks and Jews: Racism, Anti-Semitism, and *Showboat*," in ed. Adelman and Simpson, pp.128–78; Frances Henry et al., *The Colour of Democracy*. Toronto: Harcourt Brace, 1995.

45. Troper and Weinfeld, *Old Wounds*. See also Howard Margolian, *Unauthorized Entry: The Truth about Nazi War Criminals in Canada, 1946–56*. Toronto: University of Toronto Press, 1999.

46. "No Anti-Jewish Bias in War Crimes Unit," *The Gazette*, March 28, 1998.

47. Ron Csillag, "Complaints against Refugee Board Dismissed," *Canadian Jewish News*, December 10, 1998, p.40. In September 1998 a former IRB member filed complaints about unprofessional conduct against three board members, one of which referred to a member making anti-Semitic and homophobic remarks. A report on the matter by Professor Ed Ratushny exonerated the first two and did not address the third allegation which involved anti-Semitism, since the member was not reappointed to the board.

48. Brodbar-Nemzer et al., "An Overview of the Canadian Jewish Community," in *The Jews in Canada*, ed. Brym, Shaffir, and Weinfeld, p.63.

49. Raymond Breton, "The Ethnic Group as a Political Resource in Relation to Problems of Incorporation: Perceptions and Attitudes," in *Ethnic Identity and Equality*, ed. Breton et al., pp.196–255.

10. A HOLY NATION
Canadian Judaism between Tradition and Modernity

1. For an overview of the meaning of religion to Canadians, and the challenges facing organized religion, see Ronald Graham, *God's Dominion*. Toronto: McClelland & Stewart, 1990. For a more quantitative analysis, see Bibby, *Unknown Gods*.

2. Samuel Heilman, *Synagogue Life: A Study in Symbolic Interaction*. Chicago: University of Chicago Press, 1976.

3. Elliott Abrams, *Faith or Fear*. New York: The Free Press, 1997, pp.127–28.

4. For a contemporary overview of the strengths and weaknesses of the denominations, see Jack Wertheimer, *A People Divided: Judaism in Contemporary America*. New York: Basic Books, 1993.

5. Robert Brym, "The Rise and Decline of Canadian Jewry?" in *The Jews in Canada*, ed. Brym et al., p.24.

6. Brodbar-Nemzer et al., "An Overview of the Canadian Jewish Community."

7. Rabbi Lionel Moses, personal communication, December 30, 1998. The ad appeared in the December 17, 1998 issue of the *Canadian Jewish News*. Rabbi Harold Shulweis in Los Angeles has actively encouraged the "unchurched" to consider Judaism as an option.

8. Of these 25 per cent belonged to Orthodox congregations (9 per cent in the United States), 43 per cent to Conservative (45 per cent in the United States), 14 per cent to Reform (38 per cent in the United States), 1 per cent to Reconstructionist in both countries, and 19 per cent to "other Jewish," compared to 5 per cent in the United States. "Overview of the Canadian Jewish Community," p.43.

9. Charles Shahar, "Sépharade 2000." Draft. Montreal: Fédération CJA, 2000, p.17.

10. Brodbar-Nemzer, *A First Look*; Shahar and Schnoor, *A Survey of Jewish Life in Montreal*, Part II.

11. Bibby, *Unknown Gods*, p.6.

12. Stephanie Nolen, "Give Them Jesus but Hold the Theology," *The Globe and Mail*, January 2, 1999, pp.A1, A5.

13. Bibby, *The Bibby Report*, p.130.

14. Bibby, *Unknown Gods*, p.8.

15. Charles Silberman, *A Certain People: American Jews and their Lives Today*. New York: Summit Books, 1985, p.260.

16. Charles Liebman, *The Ambivalent American Jew*. Philadelphia: The Jewish Publication Society, 1973.

17. Steven M. Cohen and Arnold M. Eisen, *The Jew Within: Self, Family and Community in America*. Boston: Susan and David Wilstein Institute, 1998, p.38.

18. See *The Jewish Community in America*, ed. Sklare; Wertheimer, *A People Divided*.

19. Data from the Jewish day-school system in Montreal illustrate this Orthodox resurgence, even in the face of the exodus of Jews from Montreal beginning in the 1970s. Enrolments at the first-grade level between 1985 and 1997 in Orthodox schools increased from 135 to 230, a significant 70 per cent rise. These numbers include only those schools affiliated with the Jewish Education Council, and exclude some of the ultra-Orthodox schools (see *Canadian Jewish News*, Montreal Ed., April 9, 1998, p.6). With them included the increase would have been greater.

20. Louis Wirth, *The Ghetto*. Chicago: University of Chicago Press, 1928.

21. For an overview of the strengths and dangers of fundamentalism among the three monotheistic faiths, see Karen Armstrong, *The Battle for God*. New York: A. A. Knopf, 2000. For an understanding of the life of Orthodox Jews in Toronto suburbia, see Etan Diamond, *And I Will Dwell in Their Midst: Orthodox Jews in Suburbia*. Chapel Hill: University of North Carolina Press, 2000.

22. M. Herbert Danzger, *Returning to Tradition: The Contemporary Revival of Orthodox Judaism*. New Haven: Yale University Press, 1989.

23. Arthur Magida, "The Aish Phenomenon," *Moment*, June, 1998.

24. Michael Meyer, *Response to Modernity: A History of the Reform Movement in Judaism*. New York: Oxford University Press, 1988.

25. The workshops were held in the spring of 1998, supported by a rather daring (given Orthodox distaste) grant from the Jewish Community Foundation/Fédération CJA of Montreal.

26. Marshall Sklare, *Conservative Judaism: An American Religious Movement* (rev. ed.). New York: Schocken, 1972.

27. "New Rabbi's Manual," *The Forward*, October 23, 1998, p.3.

28. Stuart Schoenfeld, "Canadian Judaism Today," in *The Canadian Jewish Mosaic*, ed. Weinfeld, Shaffir, and Cotler, pp.129–50.

29. Elan Dresher, Norbert Hornstein, and Lipa Roth, "A Montrealer Seder," in *The Big Book of Jewish Humor*, ed. Novak and Waldoks, pp.114–16.

30. Rela M. Geffen, *Elaboration and Renewal: Rites of Passage in Judaism*. Philadelphia: Jewish Publication Society, 1993.

31. Susan Weidman Schneider, *Jewish and Female*. New York: Simon & Schuster, 1984.

32. For a discussion of bar mitzvah, see Stuart Schoenfeld, "Some Aspects of the Social Significance of the Bar/Bat Mitzvah Celebration," in *Essays in the Social Scientific Study of Judaism and Jewish Society*, ed. S. Fishbane and J. Lightstone. Montreal: Department of Religion, Concordia University, pp.277–304. Reprinted in *The Bar/Bat Mitzvah Handbook*, ed. Helen Lenneman, Denver: Alternatives in Religious Education, 1993.

33. Sklare, *America's Jews*, pp.114–17.

34. Brodbar-Nemzer et al., "An Overview of the Canadian Jewish Community," p.43.

35. Ibid., pp.54, 62.

36. *The Canadian Jewish News*, January 9, 1999.

37. Alana Mitchell, "Mother Nature's Holy Alliance," *The Globe and Mail*, January 5, 1999, pp.A1, A8.

38. Wade Clark Roof and William McKinney, *American Mainline Religion: Its Changing Shape and Future*. New Brunswick, N.J.: Rutgers University Press, 1987, p.40.

39. This is the kind of Judaism which Steven Cohen and Arnold Eisen found in their interviews with "moderately affiliated" Jews. Cohen and Eisen, "The Jew Within."

40. Rabbi Ron Aigen, personal communication, January 26, 1998; Rabbi Reuben Poupko, personal communication, January 27, 1998.

41. Rabbi Moshe Shulman, personal communication, January 31, 2001.

42. Rabbi Baruch Frydman-Kohl, personal communication, February 9, 2001; Rabbi John Moscowitz, personal communication, February 2, 2001.

43. Norma Baumel Joseph, "Personal Reflections on Jewish Feminism," in *The Canadian Jewish Mosaic*, ed. Weinfeld, Shaffir,

and Cotler, pp.205–220; Medjuck, "If I Cannot Dance to It," *The Jews in Canada*, ed. Brym, Shaffir, and Weinfeld, pp.328–43.

44. Wertheimer, *A People Divided*, p.76.

45. Ibid., pp.106–7.

11. STICKS, STONES, AND SOCIAL RELATIONS
The Evolving Forms of Anti-Semitism

1. Abella and Troper, *None Is Too Many*.

2. Gordon Allport, *The Nature of Prejudice*. New York: Addison-Wesley, 1954; Bruno Bettelheim and Morris Janowitz, *The Dynamics of Prejudice*. New York: Harper & Row, 1950.

3. For a review of these studies see William Helmreich, "The Sociological Study of Anti-Semitism in the United States," in *Approaches to Anti-Semitism: Context and Curriculum*, ed. Michael Brown. New York: The American Jewish Committee, 1994, pp.134–141.

4. As examples see Herbert Gans, "The Origins of a Jewish Community in the Suburbs," in *The Jews*, ed. Sklare, pp.204–248; Kramer and Levantman, *Children of the Gilded Ghetto*; Marshall Sklare and Joseph Greenblum, *Jewish Identity on the Suburban Frontier: A Study of Group Survival in an Open Society*. New York: Basic Books, 1967.

5. Seeley et al., *Crestwood Heights*; and Evelyn Kallen, *Spanning the Generations: A Study of Jewish Identity*. Don Mills: Longman Canada, 1977.

6. Abella and Troper, *None Is Too Many*.

7. Charles Stember, *Jews in the Mind of America*. New York: Basic Books, 1966.

8. Abella, *A Coat of Many Colours*, p.181.

9. Many in the anti-racist community would disagree with this assessment. They would argue that our legal system, including laws and their implementation, serves to perpetuate racial inequalities and systemic racism in many ways, With the exception of First Nations in Canada, I disagree. There certainly is racism and anti-Semitism in Canada. But Canadian law and governance today – as opposed to the past – work to oppose those evils.

10. Richard Menkis, "Anti-Semitism and Anti-Judaism in Pre-Confederation Canada," in *Anti-Semitism in Canada: History and Interpretation*, ed. Alan Davies. Waterloo: Wilfrid Laurier University Press, 1992, pp.11–38.
11. Michael Brown, "From Stereotype to Scapegoat: Anti-Jewish Sentiment in French Canada from Confederation to World War One," in ibid., pp.39–66.
12. Tulchinsky, *Taking Root*, pp.61–80.
13. Menkis, "Anti-Semitism and Anti-Judaism in Pre-Confederation Canada," in *Anti-Semitism in Canada*, ed. Davies, pp.26–27.
14. Gerald Tulchinsky, "Goldwin Smith: Victorian-Canadian Anti-Semite," in ibid., pp.67–92.
15. Pierre Anctil, "Interlude of Hostility: Judeo–Christian Relations in Quebec in the Inter-war Period, 1919–1939" in ibid., pp.135–66.
16. Phyllis Senese, "Anti-Semitic Dreyfusards: The Confused Western-Canadian Press" in ibid., pp.93–112.
17. Levitt and Shaffir, *The Riot at Christie Pits*.
18. Lita-Rose Betcherman, *The Swastika and the Maple Leaf*. Toronto: Fitzhenry & Whiteside, 1975.
19. Ibid., p.123.
20. Marilyn Nefsky, "The Shadow of Evil: Nazism and Canadian Protestantism," in *Anti-Semitism in Canada*, ed. Davies, pp.197–226.
21. Anctil, "Interlude of Hostility," in ibid., p.156.
22. Henry Milner and Sheilagh H. Milner, *The Decolonization of Quebec*. Toronto: McClelland & Stewart, 1973.
23. See Esther Delisle, *The Traitor and the Jews*. Anctil offers a more nuanced perspective, "Interlude of Hostility," in *Anti-Semitism in Canada*, ed. Davies.
24. Nefsky, "The Shadow of Evil," in ibid., pp.197–226.
25. Abella, *A Coat of Many Colours*, p.180; Anctil, "Interlude of Hostility," in *Anti-Semitism in Canada*, ed. Davies, p.148.
26. Betcherman, *The Swastika and the Maple Leaf*, pp.85–98.
27. Esther Delisle, *Myth, Memory, and Lies*.
28. See Betcherman, *The Swastika and the Maple Leaf*.
29. Howard Palmer, "Politics, Religion, and Anti-Semitism in Alberta, 1880–1959," in *Anti-Semitism in Canada*, ed. Davies, pp.167–96. See

also Janine Stingel, *Social Discredit: Anti-Semitism, Social Credit, and the Jewish Response*. Montreal: McGill–Queen's University Press, 2000.

30. Warren Kinsella, *Web of Hate*. Toronto: HarperCollins, 1994; One study in the 1980s identified 130 such organizations and 586 individual members of these organizations. See Stanley Barrett, *Is God a Racist?* Toronto: University of Toronto Press, 1987.

31. Adolf Hitler, *Mein Kampf*. Boston: Houghton Mifflin, 1943.

32. Ibid., p.307.

33. Ibid., pp.305–306.

34. Ibid., pp.314, 319.

35. Ibid., p.309.

36. Ibid., p.307.

37. Barrett, *Is God a Racist?* pp.94, 209–210.

38. Quoted in Steve Mertl and John Ward, *Keegstra*. Saskatoon: Western Producer Prairie Books, 1985, p.5.

39. Deborah Lipstadt, *Denying the Holocaust: The Growing Assault on Truth and Memory*. New York: The Free Press, 1993.

40. Gabriel Weimann and Conrad Winn, *Hate on Trial: The Zündel Affair, the Media, and Public Opinion in Canada*. Oakville, Ont.: Mosaic Press, 1986, p.105.

41. Ibid., p.124.

42. Ibid.

43. David Bercuson and Doug Wertheimer, *A Trust Betrayed: The Keegstra Affair*. Toronto: Doubleday, 1985; Mertl and Ward, *Keegstra*.

44. Peter Ward, *White Canada Forever*. Montreal: McGill–Queen's University Press, 1978.

45. Delisle, *The Traitor and the Jews*, pp.124-133.

46. Reasons for Decision, in the matter of the Human Rights Code RSBC 1996, c.210, tribunal member Nitya Iyer, November 4, 1997, p.109.

47. Reitz and Breton, *The Illusion of Difference*, p.73. But that comparison could yield a very different conclusion if the authors had used the Jewish – not general – populations in the respective countries. There are close to sixteen times more American than Canadian Jews. Therefore, there should be a sixteen-to-one ratio. To find a ratio of ten-to-one meant that the per-capita number of

anti-Semitic incidents in Canada was much higher than in the United States.

So, Canadian Jews would in fact seem *more* likely to be victimized than American Jews. In relation to hate speech, there are two ways to interpret this. One is that Canadian Jews need more protection by hate speech legislation since they are more vulnerable. The other is that American Jews have prospered without such protections, so Canadians do not need them either. Either makes sense. Whether the lower-than-expected frequencies of anti-Semitic incidents in the United States is due to a regime of free speech or other factors is unclear.

48. *The Gazette*, April 27, 1998.
49. Robert Brym and Rhonda Lenton "The Distribution of Anti-Semitism in Canada in 1984," in *The Jews in Canada*, ed. Brym et al., pp.112–20.
50. Weimann and Winn, *Hate on Trial*, p.144.
51. Paul Sniderman, David Northrup, Joseph Fletcher, Peter Russell, and Philip Tetlock, "Psychological and Cultural Foundations of Prejudice: The Case of Anti-Semitism in Quebec," *Canadian Review of Sociology and Anthropology*, 30:2, 1993, pp.242–70.
52. Taylor Buckner, "Attitudes Toward Minorities: Seven Year Results and Analysis," Montreal: League for Human Rights of B'nai Brith, 1991.
53. The figures for the five-year periods starting in 1975 were 28, 13, 13, and 13 per cent. In other words, a large decrease between 1975 and 1980, followed by stability.
54. Bibby, *Social Trends, Canadian Style*, p.55.
55. Manuel Prutschi, personal communication, January 30, 2001.
56. Reitz and Breton, *The Illusion of Difference*, p.72.
57. Peter Pineo, "The Social Standing of Ethnic and Racial Groupings," *Canadian Review of Sociology and Anthropology* 14, (May) 1977, pp.147–57.
58. J. W. Berry and R. Kalin, "Multicultural and Ethnic Attitudes in Canada: An Overview of the 1991 National Survey," *Canadian Journal of Behavioural Science* 27, 1995, pp.301–320.
59. Bibby, *The Bibby Report*, pp.57–58.

60. Brodbar-Nemzer et al., "An Overview of the Canadian Jewish Community," in *The Jews in Canada*, ed. Brym, Shaffir, and Weinfeld, p.54.

61. Weimann and Winn, *Hate on Trial*, pp.115, 152.

62. This is true even for outspoken condemnations of Quebec anti-Semitism. A recent essay by Gerard Bouchard is a case in point. The essay describes and condemns major incidents of anti-Semitism in Quebec history. But it focuses more on the 1920s than on the more significant 1930s. It ignores the conscription referendum, and includes the ritualistic denunciation of Richler and Delisle. Gerard Bouchard, "Les Rapports avec la communauté juive: un test pour la nation québécoise," in *Juifs et canadiens français dans la société québécoise*, ed. Anctil, Robinson, and Bouchard, pp.13–32.

63. "1999 Audit of Anti-Semitic Incidents," Toronto: B'nai Brith, 2000, p.15.

64. Charles Liebman and Steven M. Cohen, *Two Worlds of Judaism*. New Haven: Yale University Press, 1990, p.42.

65. Shahar, *A Survey of Jewish Life in Montreal* Part I, pp.34–35.

APPENDIX I:
SOURCES OF EVIDENCE

1. The main source for NJPS will be Sidney Goldstein, *Profile of American Jewry: Insights from the 1990 NJPS*. New York: American Jewish Yearbook, 1992, pp.77–173.

2. The results of that 1996 survey are found in two reports, both titled "A Survey of Jewish Life in Montreal" and published by the Federation of Jewish Community Services of Montreal. Part One, by Charles Shahar, was released in December 1996; Part Two, by Shahar and Randal F. Schnoor, was released in May 1997.

3. The results of this survey are summarized in Jay Brodbar-Nemzer, *A First Look: Greater Toronto Jewish Community Study*. Toronto: Toronto Jewish Congress and the Jewish Federation of Greater Toronto, June 1991.

4. The data from this survey are analyzed, and also compared to the NJPS data, in Jay Brodbar-Nemzer et al., "An Overview of the

Canadian Jewish Community," in *The Jews in Canada*, ed. Brym, Shaffir, and Weinfeld, pp.39–72.

5. The data are drawn from Taras and Beitel, "Preliminary Analysis: Jewish Community Council Survey as at January 30, 1997."

6. See Breton, Isajiw, Kalbach, and Reitz, *Ethnic Identity and Equality: Varieties of Experience in a Canadian City*.

7. The Calgary survey relied on a sample selected from a master list of Jews derived from Jewish communal lists. That technique has been used in other communal studies, though it likely underrepresents the more assimilated Jews. The Montreal survey relied on Jewish-sounding names selected from the telephone directory; though this approach has been used in Jewish research it too could miss assimilated Jews and converts. The Toronto survey sampled randomly in census enumeration areas where ten per cent of the population, according to the census, was Jewish, and supplemented this with respondents selected because of distinctive Jewish names and some from a Federation list. The CRB national survey conducted by Goldfarb Consultants of Toronto, used census data to compute weights for the raw sample, which included too many married couples to reflect accurately the Canadian Jewish community. It is the only Canadian counterpart to the American NJPS.

APPENDIX II:
DEMOGRAPHIC PREDICTIONS AND COMPARISONS

1. Leo Davids, "The Canadian Jewish Population Picture: Today and Tomorrow" in *Canadian Jewry Today: Who's Who in Canadian Jewry*, ed. E. Lipsitz. Downsview, Ont.: J.E.S.L. Educational Products, 1989, p.55.

2. Robert Brym, "The Rise and Decline of Canadian Jewry?" in *The Jews in Canada*, ed. Brym, Shaffir, and Weinfeld, pp.22–38. The article was first published in *Canadian Jewry Today*, ed. Lipsitz

3. Ibid., p.23.

4. Ibid., p.34.

5. See the *Canadian Jewish News*, March 26, 1998, pp.1, 4.

6. Sidney Goldstein, "Profile of American Jews: Insights from the 1990 NJPS," New York: *The American Jewish Yearbook*, 1992, pp.77–173.

7. Sergio DellaPergola and Uzi Rebhun, "Projecting a Rare Population: World Jews 2000–2080." Population Association of America. Washington D.C. March 29–31, 2001.

8. Kosmin, "The Demographics and Economics of the Jewish Market in North America," in *Creating the Jewish Future*, ed. Brown and Lightman, p.218.

9. Anti-Defamation League Survey, November 1998, "Anti-Semitism and Prejudice in America." http//www.adl.org/frames/front_survey.html

APPENDIX III:
MIXED MARRIAGE IN CANADA

1. Rosenberg, *Canadian Jews*, ed. Weinfeld, p.108.

2. Leo Davids, "Tracking Demographic Assimilation: Evidence from Canada's major cities," in *Who's Who in Canadian Jewry*, third ed., ed. Edmond Y. Lipsitz.Toronto: J.E.S.L. Educational Products, 2000, pp.3–27.

3. Annual Canadian data on mixed marriage can be taken from Vital Statistics of Statistics Canada, which compile information on religious origins of brides and grooms received from the provinces. Since men have traditionally had higher rates than women, we examine the nature of the increase for both genders. Note that some of the non-Jews involved in these mixed marriages will formally convert to Judaism after the marriages. Nor is there any estimate here of the extent to which the non-Jewish partner in the mixed marriage might accept Jewishness, short of a formal conversion. So these numbers would tend to overstate the degree of Jewish attrition as a result of these mixed marriages.

4. Barry Kosmin, Sidney Goldstein, Joseph Waksberg, Nava Lerer, Ariella Keysar, and Jeffrey Scheckner, *Highlights of the CJF 1990 National Jewish Population Survey*. New York: Council of Jewish Federations, 1991.

5. Davids, "Tracking Demographic Assimilation," in *Who's Who in Canadian Jewry*, third ed., ed. Lipsitz, p.16; Robert J. Brym, Michael Gillespie, and A. R. Gillis, "Anomie, Opportunity, and the Density of Ethnic Ties: Another View of Jewish Outmarriage in Canada," in Brym et al., *The Jews in Canada*, pp.238–48.

6. Goldstein, "Profiles of American Jews."
7. Brym, Gillespie, and Gillis, "Anomie, Opportunity, and Density," in Brym et al., *The Jews in Canada*; and Werner Cohn, "Jewish Outmarriage and Anomie: A Study in the Canadian Syndrome of Polarities," in *Canadian Review of Sociology and Anthropology* 13, pp.90–105.

APPENDIX IV:
THE EFFECTS OF JEWISH EDUCATION

1. Harold Himmelfarb, "Agents of Religious Socialization," *The Sociological Quarterly* 20, 1979, pp.477–94. This early study was based on data from the 1971 NJPS.
2. M. Rimor and E. Katz, "Jewish Involvement of the Baby Boom Generation," cited in Bruce Phillips, "Re-examining Intermarriage: Trends, Textures and Strategies." Boston: Susan and David Wilstein Institute, 1997, p.15.
3. Sylvia Barack Fishman and Alice Goldstein, "When They Are Grown They Will Not Depart: Jewish Education and the Jewish Behavior of American Adults." Waltham: Center for Modern Jewish Studies, Research Report 8. Brandeis University, 1993, p.11.
4. Alice Goldstein, "Jewish Education and Jewish Identity: Findings from the National Jewish Population Survey of 1990" in *Papers in Jewish Demography 1993*, ed. DellaPergola and Even, pp.289–302.
5. Phillips, "Re-examining Intermarriage," pp.16–17. The latter study used a sample of mixed married Jews taken in 1993.
6. Charles Shahar, "The Jewish High-School Experience: Its Implications for the Evolution of Jewish Identity in Young Adults." Montreal: Fédération CJA and Jewish Education Council of Montreal, 1998.

INDEX

Aaron (novel), 223
Aaron, brother of Moses, 22
Abella, Irving, 207, 266, 327
Abella, Rosalie, 102, 265
Aberhart, William, 327
Abraham, 29
Abrams, Elliott, 4
Abrams, Harry, 337
Adams, Marcel, 76
Adult education, 250
Affaires Plus, 106
Affluence, Jewish, 113-15, 117-19,
    120-25
Aging of the Jewish population, *see*
    Senior citizens
AIDS, 149-50
Aigen, Rabbi Ron, 312-13
Aish HaTorah organization, 297
Albright, Madeleine, 54
Alcohol consumption, 121, 140, 171
Aleichem, Sholom, 74
All in the Family, 224
Allen, Woody, 30, 223, 225, 256
Alliance Atlantis, 223
Alliance for Christian Schools, 229
Alliance Québec, 269
Amalgamated Clothing Workers of
    America, 95
American Civil Liberties Union, 254
American Jewish Committee, 159
American Judaism, 207, 300-301,
    347-48
American Union of Orthodox
    Congregations, 288
Anarchism, 262

Anglo-Jewish Association, 60
Anti-Defamation League, 331, 370
Anti-Nazis, 189
Anti-Semitism, 32, 79, 107, 170, 317-46,
    349; after the Second World War,
    327-28; attitudinal, 323; before
    1930, 96, 324-25; Canadian Jewish
    Congress and, 174; cultural, 324;
    examples of Canadian, 338-41; hate
    speech, 331-37; immigration and,
    61-62, 65, 76; in the 1930s, 325-27;
    in the 1950s, 319; institutional, 322;
    Jewish attitudes towards non-Jews,
    323; Jewish institutions and, 177;
    origins of, 29-30; Quebec, 344-46;
    reinforcement of Jewish identify,
    40, 164; Social Credit Party, 321,
    327; surveys of, 341-45; types of,
    328-31
Aramaic, 37, 201
Arcand, Adrien, 326-27
Argentina, 6
Armed Forces, Canadian, 274, 338
Arnold, Abraham, 84
Art Gallery of Ontario, 108
Arts, Jewish support for, 108
Ashkenaz Festival, Toronto, 195, 200
Ashkenazi Jews, 17-20, 22-23, 26-28,
    36, 64, 204, 210; relations with
    Sephardim, 77
Asper, Izzy, 90, 222
Assimilation, 11, 42, 79, 233, 295, 297
Associated Hebrew Schools, 230
Association of Soviet Jewry, 71
Association of Soviet Jews in Canada, 65